DARK PALACE

FRANK MOORHOUSE

DARK
PALACE

The companion novel to *Grand Days*

PICADOR

First published 2000 by Random House Australia Pty Limited

This edition published 2002 by Picador
an imprint of Pan Macmillan Ltd
Pan Macmillan, 20 New Wharf Road, London N1 9RR
Basingstoke and Oxford
Associated companies throughout the world
www.panmacmillan.com

ISBN 0 330 48546 6

Cover painting John Collier, Great Britain 1850–1934
Priestess of Delphi 1891 London
Oil on canvas, 160.0 x 80.0 cm
Art Gallery of South Australia, Adelaide
Gift of the Rt. Honourable, the Earl of Kintore 1893
Cover and internal design by Greendot Design
Typeset by Midland Typesetters, Maryborough, Victoria

1 3 5 7 9 8 6 4 2

A CIP catalogue record for this book is available from
the British Library.

Printed and bound in Great Britain by
Mackays of Chatham plc, Chatham, Kent

TO JEAN-PAUL AND MONIQUE DELAMOTTE,
FRIENDS AND PATRONS

'The League of Nations (1920–1946) . . . mankind's
first effort at permanent, organised world-wide international
cooperation to prevent war and promote human well-being.'

DR HANS AUFRICHT

'Do you know the Abbé Morio? He is a most interesting man . . .'

'Yes, I have heard of his scheme for permanent peace and it is
interesting but hardly practical . . .'

'You think not?' said Anna Pavlovna for the sake of saying something
and in order to get back to her duties as hostess.

LEO TOLSTOY, *War and Peace*

Contents

This book is, in part, based on the dramatic reconstruction of real people, identified by their actual names, and on fictional characters, who sometimes embody features of people who existed at the time, but who are essentially fictional (see Who is Who in the Book). Where people who actually existed say anything substantial, their words are taken from documentary sources or are constructed within the context of existing evidence.

All the substantial events depicted (and quite a few of the insubstantial events) are inspired by documentary sources.

But the book is, above all, a work of the imagination.

Two Young Ladies Laughing Together
Like Maids: The Nature of Wives

G eneva, on the night of October 15, in the year of
1931 ...

Edith and her friend, Jeanne, found themselves in the dining room of the Hôtel des Bergues—Geneva's best—wining and dining in a grand, exuberant, and stately manner.

Not, perhaps, so *stately* a manner.

More two young ladies indulging themselves.

Two young ladies laughing together like maids, actually.

Laugh thy girlish laughter:
Then, the moment after,
Weep thy girlish tears!

Too old now for girlish tears, Edith thought, but there was still some girlish laughter left, even though she was in her thirties.

There they were, two young ladies laughing like maids, in the dining room of the Hôtel des Bergues surrounded by men going about the business of war.

The League's first very serious war.

As well as celebrating the renewal of her contract Edith was there as an Agent. Under Secretary Bartou had put her there to garner unofficial information about the Japanese invasion of

Manchuria. To charm from important men the secrets of the war.

Despite the frightfulness of this Japanese war, it was an exquisite task they had been given, folded, as it were, in the fine lace of paradox, the paradox of enjoying the highly strung business of war while at the same time serving the mission of peace.

And, folded in on that again, the permission to indulge their personal pleasures.

And more. Within their bodies, so elegantly clad, coiffed and made-up, resided their public identity as officers of the League, and Edith relished the aura of that identity.

But while outwardly assuming their proper self-deprecation as international civil servants, and by seeming to keep to their proper female station, they were, in fact, both adopting poses of a delicious, consummate falseness.

For truth be told, they both felt immensely superior. Their immaculate, silk-clad bodies and their charming vivacity veiled a haughty femininity.

Edith was dressed in a new, pale pink silk-satin Parisian evening dress, with a low scooped front, Egyptian emerald bracelet, necklace and ring, and with her short hair set into waves and parted on the side. Tonight, everything about her appearance was right. From hair to toenails, although no one, apart from her husband Robert, would be granted the privilege of seeing her varnished toenails, something she had got perfectly right for once. Others could, however, admire her silken legs and new black satin shoes.

The hotel was one of the brightly lit venues of comings and goings about the war. Despite the international acceptance of the idea of open diplomacy, old habits died hard and many delegates still preferred the corridor whisper and private dining rooms for their diplomacy.

Cigar smoke diplomacy. The discreet squeeze of a hand on an elbow to seal agreement.

Maybe diplomacy would always, in part, be sequestered.

The world was not changing in quite the way she had planned, but she did, she hoped, change the world a little as she passed through.

She laughed to herself. Yes, Edith A. Campbell Berry was definitely still in the business of teaching the world good manners.

Most of the tables in the dining room and the coffee room and the lobby were taken by delegates, military attachés, and those others who had a say in the business of war—many of whom they knew from League business—and she and Jeanne were well positioned to see into the lobby and note who was talking to whom. From time to time, between courses, she took a stroll through the public areas to keep an eye on things, to stop and lean into a table with a familiar hand on a shoulder, pleased by her manicured and varnished fingernails and the exquisite emerald ring on the finger, and her smooth arm and hand displayed to the men at the table, sometimes sitting briefly to give the men some diverting company while she discreetly listened. They liked to impress a young woman with their secrets.

Perhaps she was becoming a married flirt?

Her experience was that men liked married flirts. She had come to realise that in the international circles of Geneva, married women were assumed to be *experienced* and not likely to make a fuss.

Not that she had explored these curious assumptions.

From time to time, delegates and others, knowing one or both of them, also stopped at their table as they passed and exchanged gossip about the crisis.

And to all inquiries about their presence there in the hotel restaurant without male companions, Jeanne would reply, 'We are here to celebrate Edith's promotion, as two professional ladies.'

Laughing together like maids at the ambiguity of the remark.

Although Edith had known that the renewal of her contract

had not been in any doubt, it was still something of a confirmation of herself, and she was basking in that. It helped to charge up her aplomb, the aplomb which allowed her to lean into tables and exchange flirtatious greetings with important men and to place her manicured hand on their shoulders.

The contract renewal also gave her, at least for the moment, a feeling of being impregnable, even if her little inner voice said that something would happen eventually to contest that feeling. Until then, she would lap up her contractual security like warm milk.

She looked at Jeanne again and exclaimed, 'Jeanne, just think, I have another five years with the League!'

'You are still merry about *le contrat*?' Jeanne asked, sipping her glass of wine. 'Oh, Edith dear—you are the very spirit of the League. They could never let you go.'

Edith laughed from within the stronghold of her contract. 'Ah, the sanctity of the contract. A contract with the League of Nations. What else is there to life?'

'The contract of your marriage? Perhaps?'

'Ah—my marriage is a contract with one man: my contract with the League is a contract with the whole world.'

'You cannot sleep with the General Assembly, Edith.'

'We know who has tried.'

They laughed about a female colleague who had a 'reputation'.

Jeanne said, giggling, 'A young lady, who instead of spending her days saying, "Yes, sir" and her nights saying, "No, sir" ...'

Edith joined in, and they said in chorus '... spent her nights saying, "Thank you, kind sir"!'

They giggled.

Edith, dropping her voice, then asked Jeanne seriously, 'What would it be like—to be *loose*?'

Jeanne opened her eyes theatrically as if offended, 'You ask me as if I am a specialist?!'

She smiled, shaking her head, 'Imagine. It must be, well, demanding?'

Jeanne thought for a second or two. 'The word would be passed from man to man—after a time, *very* demanding. Every man would expect it.'

Edith chuckled. 'At least one's social calendar would be full.'

'I could not bear knowing that men talked of me in that way.'

'Perhaps men don't tell tales?'

'I am sure they do.'

'Would they compare notes, do you think?'

'I think.'

'In some detail?'

'I know nothing of the smoking room talk of men, but I suspect that they would compare notes in some detail.'

'Not very gentlemanly.' Edith tried to imagine the details about which they might talk.

'At some point, I would assume they place such women in another category—a category which permits them to talk so.'

'But it is not the category of the *cocotte*?'

'No. Perhaps these women see themselves as a sort of courtesan.'

'Or perhaps they just like it—like that way of life?'

'Perhaps.'

'What if one was loose and not very good at it? So to speak.'

She looked at Jeanne. She was good fun and single but still a respectable young woman from a very good French family. She was not a thank-you-kind-sir woman.

'Experienced men must have some scales of judgment in these matters,' Edith mused.

'Perhaps that it is why it is best that all of us—men and women—marry as virgins,' Jeanne said. 'No expectations. No comparisons.'

Jeanne said she thought it would require such careful management of one's body, to be so available. 'As in the opera where Violetta places a bowl of red roses in the entrance to her apartment when it is that time of the month.'

'And birth control, of course.'

'Matters such as that.'

'There would after a time be some degree of, well, debauchment? Of the body? Do you think? And a risk of venereal problems?'

'Maybe this is not a subject for the dinner table,' Jeanne said, laughing.

'Imagine—different men in your bed, say two a week? Do you think they would have two, maybe more? Do the men then call again? At any time of the night?'

'Edith, your mind runs riot. Do you think of the laundry?'

'Not only the laundry. Expensive underwear. Of course, street women have far more men in a week. What must they feel when they are with their lovers and what must their lovers feel?'

'Edith, stop.' But Jeanne herself went on. 'They must talk of the day's work with their lover perhaps.'

'I suppose they must.' Edith tried to imagine herself doing that sort of work and found it salaciously intriguing.

And what of the married flirt? Tonight they were both parading their feminine attractions in exchange for something. Not that any of the men present who knew them would be under any illusion as to their propriety.

Or were they?

She didn't say anything, but Edith played briefly in her mind with the idea of it all. Of being such a woman. Coming from a slightly bohemian background, she had known free-love women in her parents' circle. And at university. She had never looked down on them. She had, for a time, rather admired them for their audacity in the face of convention.

At the League she found she liked the naughty girls.

Her mind went back to her contract. Although in the renewal she'd been promoted to A group, it looked as if they were soon going to abolish the distinction between A and B, so it meant nothing much.

She'd hoped for more. But for what she'd hoped she couldn't precisely say.

She still had times of not being sure that she was any good. She still kept a file of congratulations and thankyou notes on her desk, so that she could run through them at times of feeling low.

'We are always in self-doubt,' she said to Jeanne. 'And Edith A. Campbell Berry wants a proper title.'

Jeanne reminded Edith yet again that the important thing in life was to savour the moment. 'Enjoy your contract. Take life as with a meal—savour it mouthful by mouthful.'

'Every second mouthful? Is that enough?'

They laughed.

Her contract and promotion still left her in a vague position in the hierarchy of it all. She was still really a private secretary to Under Secretary Bartou but, in effect, she ran his office of four and was therefore *Chef de Section*—almost. But not actually. She was a planner of policy as well. She did write out proposals on matters of substance which went into the cauldron of discussion at Directors' Meetings.

Again she was given much protocol work to do, especially from Sir Eric's office, which meant she was also something of a *Chef du Protocole*.

She no longer took dictation or did typing for Bartou. A woman typed *her* letters now. And she had an assistant, Gerty.

And she was training new people. Only yesterday she had to send a memo to one of their new legal people pointing out the distinction between an 'appointed ambassador', representing a nation and usually resident, and an 'ambassador extraordinary or plenipotentiary or envoy', who was a personal representative of a head of state on a particular mission.

But the only way she could sign the memo was 'Yours Ever, EACB'. No title.

Bartou had once told her that ill-defined positions carried a secret power and could be expanded by an ambitious person. Those around such a person could never be sure where that person's authority ended.

But nor was authority always granted.

She'd tried to upgrade her signature by changing it to Edith A. Campbell Berry, hoping that an impressive signature would make her balloon rise higher, but she was even uncertain of the aptness of that move.

To be such a rickety inner-person could not be good for one.

Oh well.

She took a deep drink of her wine, finishing it too greedily and earning a disapproving look from Jeanne.

As long as one didn't look too rickety from the outside.

'Sometimes I wish I was working for Health Section in an African village, helping to sink a well, having the pump draw the first water, tasting the first pure water, seeing the black children drink it and smile,' she said. 'Making the water flow.'

They all had that yearning from time to time, to flee their desks and the paperwork.

Finding water was what her father did back in Australia. How appreciable his work was. He could actually drink and taste his work. She realised that she had never talked with him much about it.

'You make ideas flow, Edith,' Jeanne said.

'Oh, yes,' she said without conviction. 'Oh, yes.'

'At organising a conference you are a witch. And, as you say, the international conference is the diplomacy of tomorrow.'

'Witch?'

'A female wizard?'

'Wizard, I think, Jeanne, for men *and* women in this case. Or perhaps I am a Good Witch. Or trying to be. Mr Nicolson tells me that our international conferences are make-believe diplomacy.'

'Mr Nicolson is a witty snob. Snobbery is a mind *déformé*.'

She did have access to the Secretary-General which was more than most could say. But she tried not to use that access.

She laughed to herself. What a great diplomatic device—the granting of a privilege which the person could not use: 'Call on me at any time—no need for an appointment.' It rewarded the person thus privileged and, at the same time, held them in a state of hesitation from fear that they might abuse that privilege. Yet it placed the person who had been given the privilege in a position of eternal allegiance.

She wondered whether Sir Eric consciously used it that way.

Did people ever use these stratagems consciously? And if they did, what did it do to their soul and their spontaneity?

If everything they did had to be plotted, wouldn't they then lose the power of improvisation and the impromptu move?

And the special power of sincerity?

'Edith! Hello! Edith!' Jeanne was waving a hand in front of her face.

Jeanne leaned forward. 'To change the subject from your dear self, Edith—I heard the strangest thing today. I heard that in Tokyo, the wife of a Japanese army officer sent to fight in Manchuria committed suicide.'

'In protest at the invasion?'

'Ah. You think as I do—no. Of course, no protest such as that would be reported from Japan. No, she committed suicide so that her husband's bravery would not be compromised. She wanted him not to be weakened by thoughts of her back home waiting for his return.'

'Incroyable!' The *chic* word among their crowd at present.

'Can you imagine it?'

'I don't know the Japanese. The only Japanese I've met are those in the Secretariat.'

Jeanne said she'd met a secretary from one of their delegations. 'A flawless woman.' Jeanne's eyes lit up, 'She was less than five feet high, with full red lips, tight waistband, mincing step, a real *houri*.'

Jeanne said she'd had difficulty taking her eyes off the exotic Japanese woman and had become almost obsessed by her.

'I remember her,' Edith said.

Jeanne went on, 'This woman who suicided said in a note that with her death, her husband would fight more bravely, would not fear death or wounding. Would it ever pass your mind to suicide in this way? Are they so different from us?'

If they began to think that some parts of the human race were inherently different from other parts then there might not be a basis for world organisation. What if some peoples were at a different point in the human chain of evolution?

But she reminded herself of the teachings of Karl Pearson—to improve all, not some, was the only way to ensure the survival of the species.

Edith said, 'I have never heard of any woman of whatever nationality doing that.' She thought about dying for Robert— not in this Japanese way, but in the way that wives were supposed to be ready to sacrifice themselves. Perhaps. Or were they? Had she got that wrong? Not in a Modern Marriage, surely?

Sacrificing oneself for a child would be imaginable.

There was movement now in the hotel lobby with people up from their tables and standing in ever-changing groups, spilling into the entrance to the dining room. Edith and Jeanne paid attention.

'Something happens?' Jeanne said.

'Yes.'

'There goes Briand,' Jeanne said, pretending to fan herself, her voice filled with exaggerated admiration for the French Foreign Minister, President of the League Council. 'And that wonderful Léger.' Her voice became melodramatically concerned. 'They look *très sérieux* but not perturbed.'

Edith glanced at Briand's face but could not read it. She too admired him. She had once seen him eat a whole bowl of caviar. He deserved it for his work for the League. She looked over at Jeanne and made the braying noise of a donkey.

Jeanne brayed back and quoted Briand's famous speech, '"My critics say I bray for peace: then I bray for peace."'

Briand had brayed at the Assembly.

Jeanne waved to him coquettishly. He looked towards them, his craggy face smiling, and waved back affectionately but did not come over. They'd both taken drinks with him at the Bavaria over the years.

She also admired Léger, Briand's *Chef de Cabinet*, who was known in diplomatic circles to be the poet 'St-John Perse'. He remained reserved and did not wave.

'Something is going well,' Jeanne said.

'How do you know?'

'I know how to read the lines of Briand's face.'

Jeanne had been reading faces all night.

'We will discreetly inquire in a moment,' Edith said.

Edith was trying to make her thoughts backtrack to something about her feelings for Robert which she'd skipped over quickly when discussing the suicide of the Japanese woman. Not only would she not suicide in connection with anything about her marriage that she could imagine, there was something else which had crossed her mind and which she had not taken in. She sensed that it was perhaps a shady thought about her and Robert's year-old marriage. It had to do with sacrifice and the marriage contract but she couldn't find the thought.

A uniformed League messenger, wearing an official armband and black puttees, entered the dining room with his cap under his arm, looked around, and then approached their table and handed Edith an envelope stamped: 'Very Confidential'.

Edith signed for the delivery. The messenger said he would wait in case of an answer.

Edith was chuffed at receiving a messenger in the midst of the buzzing atmosphere of tension in the hotel.

She opened the message and read it.

As she did, she heard Jeanne say to the young messenger, in French, 'Would you like to sit?'

The messenger said, '*Merci*,' and sat stiffly on one of the vacant chairs, turning it slightly away from the table as if to indicate that he was not a guest at the table.

The message was from Bartou asking her to 'prepare an additional place' at the League Council table tomorrow. There was a personal hand-written message also, wishing them both a pleasant night.

Bartou was working late. The lights were burning at the Palais Woodrow Wilson.

An extra place at the Council table? Why the cryptic wording?

'You are so important, Edith,' Jeanne said with drollery. 'And the message?'

'Oh, nothing much. Bartou wants something done tomorrow. And he wishes us a good night. I think the sending of a messenger was just a compliment to us.' She realised that she was speaking about the messenger when he was there at the table. She smiled at him in a comradely way.

Edith took out her personal message pad and scrawled a note to Bartou saying she would return to the Palais within the hour. She tore the page out and folded it, placing it in the envelope in which Bartou's message had arrived, tied the string around the envelope button, and held it out to the messenger.

She said to Jeanne, 'I think I should call in to the Palais tonight. After a while.'

The messenger stood, bowed to them, and left.

Jeanne returned to the conversation, 'I would perhaps die to save my child,' she said, watching the messenger go. 'But so that a man could fight better? What sort of *mentalité* is that?'

'One might think he would lose his stomach for war after his wife did that. It's war fever, Jeanne.'

Edith's mind then drifted into mess. It was disordered by the elusive thought about Robert, by the stupid suiciding Japanese woman, the war, and by the enigmatic message from Bartou.

She tried to concentrate on the additional place at the Council table. The additional place must be for the US. They were coming to the League. After all these years of staying apart from the world, they were at last joining the world.

Well.

She wanted to tell Jeanne but thought that she probably shouldn't. 'Sorry Jeanne—I am suddenly besieged from all sides by all sorts of thoughts. Where are we?'

'The Japanese woman must have been *très, très patriotique*. You and I, we do not have such strong love of country. Being, as we are, internationalists. Where should love of country come in the order of things? Not before one's lover obviously.' Jeanne then smiled mischievously, 'Or *lovers* as the case may be ...'

'Be careful *how* you love your country,' Edith said, absently. One of her father's sayings.

She couldn't hold the news in. 'Jeanne, I think the Americans are going to come to Council. I think they're joining the League.'

'You think so? Is that what was in the Very Important Message just delivered?'

'That's what's implied, I think, yes. America is joining in to save the situation.'

'Bravo—then that is that. With the US in the League we can do anything—all is now possible?! Yes?'

To Edith's bemusement, Jeanne then decided discreetly to

examine her make-up in her handbag mirror. From momentous world affairs to the details of her personal vanity, just like that. Edith thought about her own face but restrained herself.

Her attention then did focus. This was extraordinary. She probably knew more than anyone in the Hôtel des Bergues. They should be seeking information from *her*. Or had the slight eruption of activity earlier been about this?

Arthur Sweetser was suddenly standing before them, pulling off his gloves, still in his overcoat. 'Excuse me, Jeanne, I need to speak to Edith.' He used his urgent oh-so-important American voice.

Ha.

Sweetser was the member of section in charge of liaison with the US, although his official position was as Information Officer. There'd been precious little liaison with America to worry about—until now.

His sudden presence confirmed her guess about the Americans.

'Proceed, *Artur*,' Jeanne said, waving at Edith, 'I pass Edith over to your care. I will take a stroll to the balcony. In this heady place with its messengers and urgency, I feel I need oxygen.'

'You don't have to go, Jeanne,' Edith said. Turning to Sweetser, she said, 'For God's sake, Arthur, Jeanne is one of the gang.'

'For your ears only, I'm afraid.' He looked to Jeanne and said, 'Sorry, Jeanne.'

Edith and Jeanne exchanged a glance of amusement as Jeanne got herself together to leave the table.

'A drink, Arthur?' Edith asked.

He nodded and sat.

Edith called the waiter and Sweetser ordered a cognac.

He waited until Jeanne had gone and then leaned over to her and said *sotto voce*, 'We're in, Edith. The US is coming to Council.'

'I just this minute received a memo by messenger from

Bartou,' she said, enjoying the mention of the messenger.

Sweetser was obviously peeved that she knew.

Why did Sweetser say 'we' identifying himself with his country instead of saying 'they', which would identify him with the League?

'Surely, Arthur, it is "they and us"?' she teased.

He said impatiently, 'Yes, Edith, "they"—the US—are joining the League. Protocol will be important,' he said feverishly. 'The whole thing must be done right. After all these years of work I don't want the US to bolt because of some horrendous breach of protocol.'

'When have I ever brought about a horrendous breach of protocol?' She challenged, changing into a bristling professional animal there in her fabulous silk evening dress.

'You haven't. But we have had blunders, as you know only too well. This time we mustn't.'

Her mind went into action. 'For a start, America cannot sit next to China. They will look like conspirators—and Japan will be offended. They can't sit next to Japan, China would be offended. And, as a diplomatically junior and new Council member pro tem, they can't really sit between senior permanent Council members—Britain or France or Italy. Perhaps a side table?'

'Sssshh,' said Sweetser, as someone passed their table. Leaning forward, looking about the busy dining room with its constant movement, he said, 'This is the worst place to be discussing this—can we go?'

She looked about the hotel. 'Can't go just yet. I am Bartou's ears and eyes. He authorised this dinner for Jeanne and myself which we enjoyed immensely. A spy's dinner. And we haven't had coffee and *petits four*.'

Sweetser drew his chair closer, and lowered his voice even more, 'Edith, this is the turning point. This is as important as President Wilson signing the Covenant in 1920. This is another beginning for the League.'

The waiter came with the crumb-tray, swept the table, and placed the cognac before Sweetser. To fill the time while the waiter tidied the table, he asked, in a spirit of forced *bonhomie*, 'What did you order for dinner?'

'We had the *menu gastronomique* and finished with *crepe suzette* with the *sauce caramélisée*. It has to be the best in Geneva.'

'It is.'

The waiter left.

Sweetser leaned back in. 'Japan opposed the Americans being there but late today a secret session cleared that up. The Japs have been silenced. They will accept the US at the Council table.'

Sweetser began to make a diagram of the Council table on the napkin with his capped fountain pen. 'This is how it should be.' She looked at Sweetser's face shining with perspiration. 'I think they should come in the official door for delegates,' he said.

'That is not really diplomatically correct,' she pointed out. 'The status of the US at the Council meeting is not clear. They may be there simply as observers. For them to enter through the delegates' door would mean that they had been in the delegates' lounge. Where they are technically not permitted. Yet.'

'Point taken,' he said, reluctantly.

Edith was trying not to show fuss, trying to be imperturbable. She was trying to allow the news to reach her gradually and composedly.

It *was* probably the most important thing that had happened since she joined the League. Or perhaps in the history of the human polity. Sweetser was right—it was a new beginning.

If the US joined the League then collective world security was truly feasible. All war could be stopped in its tracks.

No nation could take the risk of collective action against it: it would be a threat of unknown consequence.

She looked at her wristwatch. It was not past Robert's newspaper's deadline. She could slip out and telephone him from the lobby. No.

Her mind leapt back to the matter of the US, through the official entrance or not?

She changed her mind. 'They could be invited to the delegates' lounge as *guests*. To hell with strict protocol. Flatter them. Make them immediately members of the club. Let us, as Secretariat, throw them into an allegiance with the League. The allegiance of the delegates' lounge.'

'Perhaps,' he nodded. 'Or is it likely to cause some protest or other?'

Across the lobby she saw Robert come in with 'Potato' Gray, his journalist mate. She waved.

'Here's Robert and Potato,' she warned Sweetser.

They saw Robert say goodnight to Gray—thank God, she detested Gray—and then make his way across to their table.

She watched her husband approach. He was terribly good looking in a bohemian-journalist way although he still didn't respond to her coaching on dress. He wore the same clothes for days. And she could see a spot on his hat even from this distance.

Robert leaned over and kissed her cheek and almost in the breath which came with the kiss, he spoke to Sweetser. 'You don't have to look evasive, Arthur. I've heard about the American diplomatic note.'

She hadn't. She glanced at Sweetser. She could tell that he hadn't either.

'Robert, no business talk. Not just yet,' she said.

Robert sat down and drank from her glass of wine. To her pleasure, he looked at her, taking in her appearance, showing in his look that he found her unusually appealing.

She had caught even her husband's eye.

'What's happening, Arthur?' Robert said, turning his gaze away from her. 'You have news written all over your face.'

Edith spoke to Sweetser, 'Arthur, I think we should wait until all this is cleared.' Sweetser was known to have the Urge to Tell.

'I can say this,' Sweetser said, in a faux-ambassadorial tone. 'There is talk of the Kellogg-Briand Pact of Peace being invoked. That is all I can say.'

Sweetser was hopeless. Robert knew that if this were true it meant that as a signatory of the Pact, the US would become involved with the League.

The Pact to renounce war had been negotiated outside the League, but ultimately the nations which signed the Pact and the members of the League would be entangled now.

'So.' Robert was obviously bowled over by this news. He glanced at Sweetser and at her again. He narrowed his eyes and stared at Sweetser, 'The US is coming to the League? That's it, isn't it?' Even Robert's voice had quickened.

He turned his inquiring look to her, demanding an answer from her.

As his wife?

Edith cut across. 'What's the American note?'

'I've heard that the Secretary of State has written to the League pledging US support for any League action against the Japanese. But I hadn't heard they were joining the League as such.' Uncharacteristically, Robert let his astonishment show. 'Is that confirmed?'

He looked at his watch.

'Can we leave this matter now? It's very late.' She was frightened of jinxing the matter.

At the same time, she found herself taking petty pleasure by withholding something from Robert.

In their marriage, they had an understood tension about her work and its diplomatic secrets and his newspaperman's need to find out. But they had managed it well, she thought.

For whatever reason, Robert did not pursue the matter.

He began a perverse bar-room line of talk, defending Japan, and at the same time searching around for a waiter to order more drinks. 'Japan's just looking after business.'

He went on, 'They built Manchuria: now they want to run it. You're just ganging up on them. And look at the Americans—they seized the Philippines and Hawaii. Why shouldn't the Japanese grab something for themselves?'

'Oh come off it, Robert, the world is done with aggressive expansion,' she said. 'That may have been fine in the last century.'

His surly perverseness no longer threw the fear of God into her, although she could sometimes detect in herself the young bride's fear of being offside with him. But generally, the pugnacious arrogance of Robert The Knowing Journalist had become simply a husband's bombast. And tonight a somewhat crocked husband, as well, she suspected.

' "Outlawing war," ' he said. 'War is itself already "outside the law" ... you can't outlaw lawlessness. You can't outlaw crime.'

This was a tired old line.

In this mood, Robert always moved to explosive positions. And to inversion. He was a person who always said of a bold or idealistic statement, 'What we see as helpful may be harmful.' His mind simply holidayed there in the limbo of inversion. He never thought it through. Which, then, was the harmful way? Was the opposite true or not true?

He cheated himself into thinking that one could never know the truth.

Coffee was served together with more cognacs.

'And anyhow,' Robert rambled on, 'why is China a member state of the League? It's barely a nation. It's an antiquated civilisation. Barbaric. At least Japan's a modernising nation state. China needs uplifting. Needs to be awakened from a sleep of twenty centuries. Who better than Japan to do it?'

Jeanne reappeared. She did not care for Robert. She and Robert coolly nodded at each other. 'Am I permitted back now, *Artur*?'

Robert glanced at Jeanne and Sweetser, realising probably

that Jeanne had left the table so that something could be discussed between Sweetser and her.

It was close to his deadline.

He again looked at her, 'Something is happening—is the US coming?'

She could have gestured to him that her lips were sealed. That in turn, would have tipped him off. Instead, she said, 'Nothing that you don't already know.'

He searched her face and then let the matter go.

Robert could very well be the only person in the hotel who didn't know about the US coming to Council.

Sweetser was in Jeanne's chair. He surrendered it back and beckoned to a waiter for another chair to be brought to the table.

Robert glanced at him standing there. 'Arthur, aren't you rather hot in that overcoat?'

Sweetser looked down as if discovering it. He at last took off the overcoat which he handed to a waiter.

Robert carried on. 'The League has this World Disarmament Conference about to happen and now you have a war which has blown up in your face. Doesn't that tell you anything about the hopelessness of disarmament?'

'This war between Japan and China is the best thing that could have happened for disarmament,' Edith said.

'How!?'

'The war will either be a bloody reminder to the world of the need for disarmament or if the war is stopped it will show that collective security works and that therefore there is no need for a build-up of armaments.'

Before Robert could respond, Edith said, 'Come on, Robert, let's go. I have to call at the Palais. And you should go home to bed. You'll have a big day tomorrow. I can promise you that much.'

There, saying that was *wifely*.

As he stood, Robert tried again with Sweetser. 'Are you

trying to get the US into the League on the back of the Kellogg-Briand Pact?'

'I would think they're going to support the League,' Sweetser said. 'That's as far as I'm prepared to go.'

After saying her goodbyes, Edith took Robert's arm and urged him towards the door.

'You're a dreamer, Arthur,' Robert said.

Sweetser couldn't resist a further superior retort to Robert. 'Wait and you shall see.'

Robert doffed his hat sardonically at Sweetser, placed it back on his head, and smiled.

After calling in at the Palais and finding that Bartou had left, she rejoined Robert in the waiting taxi.

He continued in his difficult mood. 'How do you bear to be around Sweetser?'

She squeezed his arm to indicate that she didn't wish to talk about League matters in front of the taxi driver.

Robert leaned across to the open communication panel, and said to the driver in his coarse French, 'Driver, this passenger beside me is an important person in the *Société des Nations*. Put your hands over your ears.'

The driver ignored Robert.

She pulled him back. 'Robert, be good.'

He slumped in the seat. She always had to jolly Robert out of these waves of surliness. She defended his moods as some sort of frustrated, fretful reaction by him to the derangement of the world. Something he suffered but could never find ways of handling. Journalism was an occupation without solutions. Every certainty of today unravelled tomorrow.

She then whispered to him. 'The Americans are coming to Council tomorrow.'

She braced herself for a storm.

'So,' he said.

She could almost feel him struggling to hold back his anger. 'I wish you'd rung me at the office. Even if you'd told me back there I could have tried to get it through.' He compulsively looked at his watch. 'Damn. There would've been time.'

His voice was a brewing storm.

'You know I couldn't do that.'

'You should've told me.'

'It's confidential League business.'

'You should've told me.'

'How could I?'

'You know why, damnit.'

That was the first time he'd put it that way. They drove in silence. He again looked at the luminous dial of his watch. 'Damn, damn.'

'You'll have the news tomorrow.'

'Everyone will have the news tomorrow. If they haven't got it already. How could you let me sit there and not tell me?'

'It's great news for the world—regardless of when it's published. Publishing it today or tomorrow won't change anything.'

He didn't answer.

'I didn't want to jinx it,' she said quietly.

'Jinx it!'

He pulled away from her. 'I thought Rationalists didn't believe in jinxs?'

'We're allowed to believe in one jinx a year,' she said in her playful voice.

She moved over to him, undid her overcoat and then nestled her breast on to Robert's arm, wondering if a wife's breast had the same effect after marriage as before, sensing that her stylish femininity tonight was stimulating him.

'I intend to teach you the Theory of Diplomatic *Esprit*,' she said softly.

'What is the Theory of Diplomatic *Esprit*?' he said, still miffed.

'It is a way of working against jinxs. If you're a player in world events, even a minor player, then *spirit* is a factor in the outcome. If you behave as if something will succeed, it helps it succeed.'

'How so?'

'All the attitudes of the players on the diplomatic stage have an impact on the psychology of those at the discussions—especially the Secretariat.'

'Does *pretending* to be optimistic still work? Like pretending not to be afraid of a dog? Does that work?'

'Precisely, it's like pretending not to be afraid of a dog. It's the role of the Secretariat to engender an affirmative temperature in international negotiations. Fervour is a diplomatic tool. The Secretariat are engineers of *mentalité.*'

She wondered why a dog would not know if a person was pretending.

He grunted but it was a grunt she knew, the grunt before giving up and becoming pliable, becoming her pet.

'What will you write about it?'

'About the US and the League?'

'Yes.'

Robert adopted the voice of a radio announcer and said, ' "President Woodrow Wilson helped establish the League after the War but the United States Senate voted to stay out. Now it looks as if the United States is joining the world community and that the vacant chair kept for the United States will at last be filled etc, etc, etc." '

She'd got him to be playful. Her breast pressing against his arm through the lace of her brassiere and the silk of her gown was working its magic.

She took his hand and amorously put both their hands on her knee.

His fingers closed on her leg and the silk stocking.

'Talking of Manchuria, I heard a strange story today,' she said. She told him of the suicide of the Japanese woman.

'Have you ever heard of a woman doing such a thing?'

'The Japanese have higher levels of devotion to the state.'

'Do wives have these higher levels of devotion—to their husbands and the state?'

'I suspect so.' Then he added, 'On another scale, isn't that what's supposed to happen in marriage? Devotion.'

'I suppose so.'

She waited for him to press home this point against her behaviour tonight but he veered.

'I once talked with a Japanese general who said that from a military point of view earthquakes were good for the national character and useful for military training,' he laughed. 'He welcomed a good earthquake.'

She decided that he really was a bit crocked.

'Potato wants to leave for Manchuria,' he said.

Good, she thought. Geneva would be a happier place without him. 'Good,' she said.

They sat there silently. Was she, perhaps, in her heart, not properly devoted? And therefore not properly *married*?

That was the point which had been niggling at her all night and it broke through the clouds like a star—she was perhaps *not a proper wife*.

That was the point.

She felt a panic about this thought.

She had a vocation and, as yet, she had no burning desire to have a family, she did not run the household except in the smallest ways, she earned more than her husband, and she had private income, as well, which had survived the Depression. And, for no good reason, after a year of marriage she still hadn't told him everything about the extent of her private income.

And if she were a proper wife, perhaps she would've told him about the United States before his deadline.

How much of the wedding contract had she discounted?

Were they then, just lovers pretending to be man and wife?

Or worse, was he a proper husband and was she just a lover?

What was really *in* her marriage contract?

The Japanese wife was a marker at the far side of the field of marriage. And she was perhaps on the other boundary, if she were, in fact, inside the boundary at all.

She was, perhaps, a Special Companion.

She warmed to that idea but it was a little late perhaps for her to be redefining her bond to Robert.

She nestled her breast against Robert, who moved his hand a little up the silk stocking of her leg. He was responding to her body, her perfume—now a little faded—to the smell of her hair, the feel of her body.

She thought that would be the best way to go now, into the misty world of bodies.

And despite everything, they *were* fine companions.

'We are fine companions,' she whispered to him.

'Companions?'

'Yes, fine companions.'

'I suppose we are that. Odd way of putting it.' He was silent and then said, 'You should've told me about the Americans.' But it wasn't a grumpy voice.

That was what she wanted for her marriage—fine companionship. She would work towards that.

She could have a marriage of an artful and unique design.

Robert had no design, he most likely thought that marriage was something already all set out by the conventions.

She turned into him, putting her head on his shoulder, lightly kissing his neck. She laughed silently at having withheld the news from him, laughed with a mild devilry, a delicious petty devilry.

Or was it more a petty cruelty?

Laugh thy girlish laughter:
Then, the moment after,
Weep thy girlish tears!

The Secret Apartments of Marriage, Their Locks and Their Keys

S he nearly always left for the office before Robert because
he didn't begin his work until early afternoon or at best,
late morning.

It would be earlier today because of the Japanese crisis, but
he was still in bed when she rose.

She often had to fight her resentment at his sleeping in
late, that she had to be the one who rose and faced the apartment alone, and then faced the world. She faced the newspapers alone.

It was as if she'd expected marriage would at least mean
that two people rose together and that, consequently, you
never had to face the world alone.

Perhaps what she wanted was for the Man to rise first and
to inspect the boundaries of life and to see that the world was
safe, as her brother and father had done in Jasper's Brush.

It was also somehow unnatural for her to see a man sleeping late. When she had been growing up, her father and
brother had been the first to rise, although her mother had
usually not been far behind them. Except for Those Days
when her mother slept late and was not present at breakfast.

She would then visit her mother before school, entering

into that oh-so-determined-womanliness which her mother had created around her in the bedroom. The billowing tulle, the lace, the satin bed cover on the canopy bed. The abundance of freshly cut flowers always placed outside the bedroom at night and brought in first thing by her father so that her mother could rise surrounded by the fragrance and sight of flowers. The much loved volumes in the cedar bookcase, the gramophone in the corner.

Her mother's bedroom was a room such as no other in the house and Edith was always enfolded by it, was always reluctant to leave it, yet feared her urge to linger, because to linger so would suggest that she hide there. Forever.

For her mother, the bedroom had been a refuge from and a resistance to the harshness of the country town and the hot bush, the torment of insects both of nature and those within the mind. Her mother was also setting a standard of intimacy, the *grace* of intimacy.

And on some days, her mother could not leave the room.

Edith, having kissed her mother goodbye there in the bedroom, would herself feel the urge to linger, to hang on there, to lie down with her mother and remain in the lavishness of the imported lingerie and rich scents, and the mirrors both normal and magnifying which seemed to invite the nervous delight of self-scrutiny, which gave out the permission to admire oneself, to lavish on oneself the attention which was deserved. Which those around perhaps did not give.

But the mirrors had returned an unreliable reply to her own self-scrutiny, some days saying: I am a thing of beauty in this life; I am charged with high destiny. On other days, giving back an unanswering blankness.

She wondered now if the mirrors had given succouring answers to her mother. Or whether she had daily to live with the absence of answers. Or with fearful answers.

Her own bedroom here in Geneva was an attempt at such

a haven and an expression of all those womanly essences which her mother had celebrated.

In some contradictory way, Edith also felt that true physical passion could only express itself amid such feminine order even though that passion came as a gasping, grunting disruption of that bedroom refinement, as if the order had to be there for it to be violated and then restored, awaiting the next disarraying visit.

Although they slept together, Robert was always a *visitor* to the bedroom. But then, so had been her father. Neither of them 'visited' the bedroom until bedtime.

Both saw it as a female domain, at least during the daylight hours.

And Robert did indeed frequently, and mostly to her pleasure, carnally violate her feminine domain with his carnal noises and thrustings.

She was not like her mother in that she ever locked herself away for days on end. She was generally pleased to rise and to go out into the world.

As today, she was pleased to rise. She'd woken early and had lain in bed briefly, thinking of the challenges of her day, how the presence of the US should be handled at the Council meeting. The management of history's stage. Without that management nothing would happen. Or it would happen badly.

She had a feeling of restive pleasure about the day.

She looked at Robert asleep in bed in his regimental pyjamas, a garment she detested and which he would not give up, something he retained from his life as an officer in the War and insisted on reordering from London Naval and Military Store against her wishes.

She had tried to joke him out of wearing them. She had brought fine, black silk pyjamas from Paris as a gift. He would not touch them.

She had come to abhor not only the dull regimentals, but

also, let it be said, his woollen combination vest and drawers.

She herself also abhorred women's pyjamas, silk or not, despite the fashion.

Some nights she felt her satin, shantung, and voile night-dresses—any of the many which she wore in a considered rotation—were not really friends to his brusque pyjamas. There was a discordance there. And she also chose her night-gowns to glamorise the carnality of the bed. Indeed. Most definitely.

She had tried to tell herself that his pyjamas were virile, but that hadn't altered things much and he hardly needed to proclaim his rather active virility. The virility was there too in the rank, sweaty smell of his leather watchband and its cover when it came near to her face. A virility which had been active last night in response to her *soignée* appearance, or dare she say it, her *glamorous* appearance. He had energetically violated that as well. Rather pleasurably, even if the subtlety of it had been lost through drink.

Of course, he never removed the pyjamas during his virile activities.

Oh no.

Leaving aside these physical matters—about which she had little complaint—her feelings were that one had to sleep in what made one feel sumptuous. One should leave the exhausting waking world for sleep and then return to it the next morning, well turned out, but most of all, feeling sumptuous.

Still, her bedroom did not really reach her mother's standard.

She did not quite have the time to get it right.

One day she would.

He, on the other hand, wanted to preserve the quality of being able to 'sleep rough'. Whatever the quality of 'sleeping rough' was and why it should be pursued in life. 'Sleeping rough' was, she would have thought, more an unfortunate scrape than a virtue or worthwhile life-practice. Robert seemed to be still rehearsing for some crisis in life for which he would then, unlike the rest of the world, be prepared and able to cope. Some nights he slept on the floor of the sitting room or in the second bedroom with a pillow and a blanket. Usually when crocked. But sometimes, she noticed, for no reason at all.

He believed in the hard truths—maybe his regimentals were some sort of philosophical 'exercise' in hard truths for the sleeping mind.

It wouldn't surprise her if he thought that way. Marriage, she'd discovered, was an unravelling of the other person's mind and personality there before one's very eyes. She had once propounded the idea that one should get to know the other before marriage. That idea now made her laugh. She would now argue the opposite. One should avoid ever knowing the other in too much dingy domestic detail. The hairs in the bath of married life should be avoided. She was relieved that they had two bathrooms and that she never had reason to enter his.

She had consciously recoiled from this form of knowing in marriage as soon as she saw it gathering like dust on furniture. Jeanne correctly said that a woman should aim not to be honest but to be beguiling, to be Unknown. But then, Jeanne had never been married. Perhaps she had an expert committee to which she could refer such matters.

And what was Master Robert aiming for in *his* domestic demeanour? To beguile? For mystery? Hardly. His rough-cut self-resilience made him seem like an out-of-place bear as he moved about the apartment.

To be frank, she would like separate bedrooms. He left books open face down on the floor. He left unfinished drinks on the bedside table which, in the morning, filled the room with the odour of a bar-room. Still, part of her resisted the idea of separate bedrooms also, because it seemed to admit to a failure of something in marriage, in her vision of the consolation of marriage.

Leaving the bed, she held the satin nightdress against her body, a sensation which never ceased to affirm her, and which felt cool against her newly waxed legs—the work of the dreaded Mme Lélu and her depilation at the *Institut de Beauté*.

Oh, she was so pleasured by her full body, by her womanhood, by the emollients of womanhood, even if on some days she fell short of the ideals of that womanhood. Too often fell short because of her life of rush.

She had not fallen short last night at the Hôtel des Bergues.

She bathed, dried herself and dusted herself with powder. After all this diplomatic uproar was over, she would give more time to the pampering of her body.

She went from her bathroom back to the dressing room.

She had a sore head. She went back to the bathroom and took out a headache powder from the cabinet, mixed it in the water glass, drank it, grimaced, and returned to her dressing room.

She would wear a soft beret. *Trés chic*. A stiff tie-neck blouse. The dark grey suit with the buttoned cuffs and mid-calf skirt with its off-centre pleat. Yes. Perfect.

One thing she did not suffer was clothing indecision. Mrs Swanwick, the great British feminist delegate to Assembly, would certainly approve of that—no time wasted on trivialities of appearance. But, *Mrs Swanwick*, it didn't mean that she did not consider her daily appearance. She considered it before going to sleep and her mind simply resolved the matter during the night.

Having dressed, she ducked down for the newspapers from the *kiosque*, opening them there in the street and scanning the headlines for the American story.

She felt sick. Most had it.

She'd denied Robert a story which the others had from one source or other. It looked as if the news had come from Washington.

She was guilty and sick both from her action and her sore head.

She got her rolls from the *boulangerie* and went back up to the apartment.

She wrote a note for Robert, something she'd once done every morning when they had first married, but which had faded out of the morning rituals.

In her note, she apologised for withholding the information about the US presence at the Council table until after his deadline, although she pleaded 'diplomatic confidentiality'.

It'd been a little more than diplomatic confidentiality and she was now rather nonplussed by her motive. And failed to find it. Motives were rarely coherent or visible, as Bartou would say.

She gave him, as a gift, the detail that the Japanese had opposed the US being invited to Council but had been defeated at the secret meeting of Council. That wasn't in the other papers. But she swore to herself that it would be the first and last time she breached confidence.

She put the note with his rolls.

Her guilt faded somewhat.

She left the rest of the news unread and had her coffee, cream, and hot rolls and jam with good appetite while she worked out on a sheet of paper the speaking order for the day and the dining protocol.

As she did her face, she smiled to herself about something Mrs Swanwick had once said to her about cosmetics. 'Can you really follow a scientific demonstration or a piece of music when a good part of your thoughts are concerned with the question "Is it time to powder my face?".' Such a grump. Such a prude. And, Mrs Swanwick, the answer is, 'Yes, I can sometimes think of my nails and attend to a complex piece of music at the same time.' And furthermore, myself and the other young lady students in our science course at university could present ourselves smartly *and* follow scientific experiments.

She knew what Swanwick meant, though, about being reminded so much of one's womanly nature when working alongside men, and about how much the *feminine* did intrude. A certain type of scrutiny by men, their glance, their stare, always gave her a renewed sense of her body and its shapes and made her fleetingly curious about what it was that her body silently suggested and stimulated in male eyes. She perhaps knew more than Swanwick about all that.

She *certainly* knew more than Swanwick *about all that.*

It wasn't the powdering of the face that caused the problem. It was the need to appropriately manage these stares and glances of men, caught, but not acknowledged, and to get on with the work. Once the men she was working with and she were caught up in the work, she found no problem. She had dispensed however with sleeveless dresses. They were not fair to men. She worried too about any emphasis to the breasts, the separating and uplifting of them, a question which arose now that such ways of dressing the breasts were fashionable. She made a note to warn Gerty about this. But what of gloves? Were bare hands more stimulating to men than gloves? She felt that long gloves were rather alluring.

She wondered again about the girl from the Japanese delegation, how the Japanese girl felt in her kimono and tight gait. How she felt about the men who watched her. And the women who observed her. As a woman, one had to deal with both inspection by men and by women. She doubted that a man felt perused at all by other men or by women.

Passing out of the apartment, she re-read her morning note to Robert again and frowned at its tone, the asking for forgiveness.

Something else. She had not, in fact, written a note *to Robert*—it was a note to some other *imagined* Robert.

Did she need to recreate Robert in her mind so that she could feel happy about him? It was not that she recreated him as an ideal man but more as the man he *could be*, the man he concealed within himself. Or so she believed. It was as if the Robert with whom she lived and who went about in the world was an unfair presentation of the real Robert. Perhaps that real Robert just couldn't exist at all. Perhaps circumstances and pressures caused this unreal Robert to exist in his place.

Oh dear. All too hard.

She left the note unchanged.

She wanted to be there before Sweetser, who had been temporarily seconded to Bartou's office from Information during the emergency.

Getting there first, no matter how hard she had played up the night before, was an office game for her, although she doubted that Sweetser, or anyone, was aware of it.

She still had a head.

Suffer it through. Have a nap in the nurse's room later in the day. Nurse Hollander was always indulgent of her morning-after condition. Nurse Hollander might give her one of her special sniffing capsules for such conditions, to clear the head.

She loved to see Sweetser's face when he came in and saw that she was already at work. She suspected that he had, on a few mornings, tried to outdo her but had since given up before he looked ridiculous—before he began arriving before daylight. Not that he didn't work as hard as she. His life was all work for the League, his lunches were work, and so were his dinners, his golf, his tennis. He was dedicated. There was no doubt of that.

She reached her office and had her papers out and was working when the telephone rang on Sweetser's desk. She went across and answered it.

It was the American Consul, Prentiss Gilbert. He too was up early.

'Good morning, Consul.'

'Good morning, Berry. Is Sweetser in?'

'Not yet. May I be of assistance?'

There was a pause while Consul Gilbert considered the competence, perhaps, of her offer. 'I think that you could well be. I am never sure to whom I should speak about some matters. I did not wish to bother Sir Eric. It's a matter of procedure. What will be the order of business today? Who speaks and when?'

She was ready with these details.

'The invitation to your Secretary of State will be confirmed by Council this morning. There will be no debate—that was established yesterday at a private meeting of Council.'

Consul Gilbert queried the invitation formalities.

'Sweetser or I will bring the invitation to you by hand and you can telegraph it to Washington. We will wait with you until confirmation of acceptance is telegraphed back from Washington. You will then accompany us to the Council with your advisers.'

She was privately amused by this conversation. She knew that Gilbert already had the authority from Washington to accept the invitation and that the talk of telegraphing was a necessary fiction and, further, that Sweetser had drafted both the invitation and the American acceptance.

'And seating?'

'I have placed you at the left end of the inner table, opposite the Chinese, with seats for two advisers. Three seats have been reserved in the diplomatic section of the gallery. You will be seated in these until your acceptance is formalised. You will then be invited to come down and join the Council table.'

Edith had decided overnight that placing them in the delegates' lounge would risk a protest. Sweetser had been right about that. It was not a time for playing Secretariat games.

Sweetser came in puffing, arms bulging with papers. He stood listening to her conversation. He mouthed urgently the question, 'Gilbert?' and pointed at the 'phone. She nodded to him.

He gestured to her to pass the telephone handpiece to him.

With a delicious exercise of command, she held up a restraining finger at him, a finger which asked him to wait, and she went on to tell the Consul, 'I think it best that we include the complete text of the Council's proposal to you and your government—to avoid the dangers of summary.' Edith loved hearing herself say, 'I think it best . . .'

Sweetser jigged about. She held his impatience at bay with an outstretched hand, nails still painted from last night— perhaps wrong for the office—as he continued to gesture to her to hand the telephone to him.

She'd silently ruled that this was a matter of protocol, which was her business. 'Consul Gilbert, Mr Sweetser is here now and would like to speak with you. Thank you. I will put him on the line—handing over now.'

She was about to hand the telephone to Sweetser but heard Gilbert's voice still talking to her and took it back from Sweetser's eager hand, 'Yes, Consul, I agree entirely. It will be truly an historic day.'

Sweetser slid into his chair as she left it, taking the telephone handpiece from her, arranging his body in a self-important way, taking off his hat, throwing it towards the hat rack, which it missed. He put his hand to his tie. 'Good morning, Consul,' he said, in his diplomatic voice. 'My apologies for not being here when you called. Yes, it is early, but we all have a momentous day ahead of us. Let me run through the procedure.' There was a pause, 'Oh, she has? Good. Oh yes. No. She is in some ways our *Chef du Protocole*. Yes. I am sure that she was correct in everything she said. But I would like to run through it to be sure.'

Another pause.

She went over, picked up his hat, and put it on the hat stand.

'No? If you are satisfied. We will leave it as it stands.'

And then it was obvious that Gilbert had rung off.

Sweetser looked at her balefully. 'I wish I'd been in earlier. Bad practice to not be here to take his call. Damn and blast it.'

'Don't fret, Arthur, I handled it.' She relished rubbing it in. 'I've put them in the diplomatic gallery.'

'That's best,' he said grudgingly.

He looked over at her. 'Stop gloating, Edith.'

She made a face at him.

He screwed up a sheet of paper and threw it at her.

When Sweetser and she went down to the Council room, the place was already filling.

Mary McGeachy from Information told them that around two hundred journalists had asked for tickets. 'They are arriving from all over Europe as fast as transport will carry them.'

'They can't have all known about the Americans so quickly?' she said to McGeachy.

'Oh, they'd sensed something. And regardless of the Americans, they know that the League has to do something about stopping the Japanese.'

In the Council room, the chairs had been placed by the *huissiers* according to her directions, which she'd passed down to them through Gerty. Gerty was putting out the nameplates of the member states.

Sweetser went over to check the American placecard. She called over to him, 'I told Gerty not to put the name "United States", but to use the word "Reserved". I reasoned that it was premature to put up the name of the United States—it not being a member of Council.'

'Yet.'

She'd been inclined to put out the name of the United States as a way of nudging history along, but had resisted. Those sorts of Secretariat manoeuvres had their time and place. Today was not such a time nor place.

She then noticed that one chair had been taken from behind the Japanese to make up the two behind the US. 'The Japanese are a chair short,' she called to Gerty.

Sweetser said, 'I took one from them to give to the Americans.'

'Arthur! That isn't correct.' Her reprimand came out in a motherly way.

He winked at her.

'No, Arthur. That's not correct. We'll have them feeling slighted and then walking out.'

Gerty came over. Edith instructed her to find another chair. 'If it isn't a matching chair, then find two matching chairs,' she told her.

Sir Eric came in to look at the arrangements. He came over to her, said good morning to them and then said, 'Berry—a word?'

He placed an arm behind her and took her to the side of the chamber, leaving Sweetser standing, as lonely as a cloud. 'Who should speak first? After the formalities, that is?' he said.

She said without hesitation that the US should speak first. 'Gilbert should have an opportunity to state the terms on which he represents his country, so that everyone knows what the situation is. Where the Americans stand.'

Sir Eric said, 'My thinking entirely.'

'And furthermore, as a newcomer, Gilbert'll be nervous. Let him get it over with. Put him out of his misery.'

'Exactly.' Sir Eric left her, saying, 'Well done, Berry.'

She went over to Sweetser who wanted to know what Sir Eric'd wanted. She told him. They then circled about, pausing to chat with the gathering journalists. Robert arrived. He looked rumpled.

She prepared herself for his displeasure but he gave a small smile.

He said, 'Thank you for your note. Understood.'

She smiled at him. 'Thank you. I'm sorry.'

McGeachy handed out information papers to the reporters and Robert was taken away into his newspaper world.

The buzzer sounded for the start of Council and she glanced at her watch. It looked as if this would perhaps be the first League Council meeting to begin on time.

The delegates came in from their lounge through the delegates' door.

Sweetser and she took their seats off to the side of President Briand.

Briand declared the Council meeting open.

At the very beginning, in direct contradiction of yesterday's agreement, the Japanese delegate Yoshizawa, rose on a point of order and began, in painfully slow English, to reargue the case against allowing the US into the Council meeting.

'This was all settled yesterday,' Sweetser said to her in a fierce whisper.

Damn. She'd told Gilbert that there'd be no debate about this. Damn them.

The Japanese went on with their public objections to the presence of the Americans.

She sat there bemoaning the diplomatic breach. Things could always go wrong beyond all the expectations of the most experienced diplomats. Or as Bartou once said, nothing ever happened the same way twice which, he said, made 'experience' of limited value. Experience was useful as a lesson in one way only: you were not then immobilised by surprise when a situation went contrary to expectation. She'd been through this with Germany's admission to the League back in '26. Brazil had vetoed it at the last minute, creating international consternation.

She was, therefore, disappointed but not thrown off balance that the Japanese had taken the opportunity of putting their position in front of two hundred of the world's journalists.

Who could blame them?

She could.

Yoshizawa argued that allowing a nation such as the US into the Council deliberations who was not formally a member of Council, who was not even a member of the League, was a dangerous precedent, and an illegal act.

He was, of course, correct. Damn him all the same.

He said that the admission of a non-member state into deliberations was such an important matter that he wished for it to be referred to the International Court at The Hague for a ruling.

Failing this, he felt that, given that it was a matter of substance, League practice required the admission of the US to deliberations to be not just a majority decision, but a unanimous vote.

Which would give the Japanese a right of veto.

She whispered to Sweetser, 'This is a disaster—there'll be a walk-out by Japan if they are not given their way. Or the Americans will walk out. I'll talk to Harada.'

She spotted the Japanese Under-Secretary Harada listening to the debate in the crowded diplomatic gallery and she left the Council room, found a *huissier* and sent him to bring Harada to her in the delegates' lounge.

In the empty delegates' lounge, she told Harada of her fears and he agreed. He would go in to the Japanese delegation, find out their intentions, and curb them if necessary.

She watched while Harada scribbled a note in Japanese and then through the peephole she watched him make his way to the Japanese delegation where he discreetly handed them his note. The note was handed to Yoshizawa who paused in his speech, asked President Briand for his indulgence and read the note. He turned, shook his head, and whispered to Harada.

She saw Harada bow and then make his way back to the lounge. 'There will be no diplomatic incident,' he said. 'I have the assurances of the Japanese delegation.'

She thanked him and he left her. She still did not trust the situation.

She locked the door from the Council room to the delegates' lounge. Their route of departure would be through the lounge and that was now blocked. What would be their reaction if they did walk out and found they couldn't? Would they return to their table? She reasoned that they would retire to the diplomatic section of the gallery. At least they would then still be in the Council room, could be appealed to. They might calm down and perhaps return to the table. It made for more possibility. She decided to stay at the delegates' door and watch the proceedings through the peephole.

Yoshizawa finished speaking, and slowly resumed his place.

All eyes turned to President Aristide Briand.

He stood like a great lion.

Her palms were sweating.

Edith could almost see Briand's French diplomatic mind sharpening away at the solution. She was becoming as bad as Jeanne with her mind reading.

He called for silence and then said in plain French, 'It would be deeply wrong for the future of this League of Nations, the first international organisation, and deeply wrong for the greater future of a civilised world, for us to now be seen to be worrying about matters of procedure when bombs are dropping and armies advancing.'

He paused and it seemed that he looked into the eyes of everyone in the room.

'We would be seen by history as a body without soul, without a humane sense of *urgence*. Without the imagination to overlook simple forms and to see the larger crying demands of our office.'

He rested his hands, knuckles down on the table, leaning forward, and his eyes went from delegate to delegate, challenging them to make their decision.

'At the end of all our diplomatic proceedings, all our

tedious speeches, and of all our communiqués to the world,'
he said, 'there are people in anguish.'

He paused and then spoke with vehemence, 'It would be
une obscénité.' The word gained immense gravity from the
stature of Briand and it reverberated around the room. '*Une
obscénité.*'

There was no demur, no rustling, no coughing, no
movement.

'As President, and as President alone, I therefore refuse the
Japanese request for further legal opinion. We ourselves are a
legal body. We appoint the Court. We are the final judges of
the human predicament. We have an authority beyond that of
any court. We have the authority of the only Council on this
planet which speaks for the world. And on matters of procedure,
I, as President of this court, overrule the Japanese request.'

He lifted the gavel and gave it a light but resounding tap
and then sat down.

It was for Briand an act of personal will.

Edith struggled to assess his decision according to the
League's Rules of Procedure but she found that her emotional
allegiance to Briand had closed her mind. She did not care if
it breached the Rules of Procedure.

Then there was a slight applause from the crowd in the
gallery.

She frowned—applause was not permitted.

Well, maybe today. Maybe for Briand.

All eyes were watching for the reaction of the Japanese
delegation.

They sat silently, motionless, but did not rise to leave.

There was no challenge to his ruling from any Council
member.

The Council then voted to invite the United States to join
the discussion with the Japanese abstaining.

The Council adjourned briefly to allow for the formalities
to be carried out.

She unlocked the door, and went in to rejoin Sweetser. 'I'll go now to the American Consulate,' said Sweetser, who had the invitation pre-typed in an envelope.

'I'm coming too.'

'We don't both have to go.'

She ignored him and went with him from the Council room as he walked urgently out to his car.

'Australia has to be there,' she said.

'Why?!'

'We're closer to Japan than the US—geographically.'

He laughed. 'I don't think that's true. And you are not "Australia"—you are an international civil servant. You corrected me yesterday on the same matter.'

She stayed beside him as they ran for the car. 'Arthur, you've forgotten your hat.'

He stopped.

'Oh, never mind,' she said. 'Let's go.'

'I can't very well turn up at the Consulate without a hat.'

'Arthur, affairs of state may proceed without a hat.'

He still hesitated. 'Come on, Arthur—empty time invites mischief.'

He let her get into the car.

At the Consulate they were shown straight through. The place was jammed with people and with excitement as if it were a consular party. Mr and Mrs Green from Berne were there as well. They seemed to be everywhere. Diplomatic socialites.

Gilbert was almost out of control from nervousness.

In the signals room of the Consulate, the formalities proceeded: the handing of the invitation to the US government, represented in Geneva by the office of the Consul-General, the telegraphing of this immediately to the American State Department whose officers were standing by at the other end, the acceptance by the American end, and then Gilbert handing Sweetser the acceptance of the invitation, already pre-typed by Sweetser and sent around earlier to Gilbert.

That afternoon she heard Briand speak the historic words, 'I invite the representative of the United States of America to come to the table of the Council of the League of Nations.'

Gilbert went in confidently, followed by Everett and Riddelberger, his advisers.

Gilbert spoke first.

The afternoon was taken up with formalities but at least the US was there, seated at last at the great horseshoe table of the world, even if only as a visitor.

When she arrived at the Bavaria that evening, there was an incredibly boisterous atmosphere among the press corps and junior diplomats. There was much congratulating of Sweetser for having got the US to the table, a generous fiction by his journalist mates.

She heard Sweetser say pompously, 'The mood has changed. The US sees that there is only one world and they are now in it. And the Americans will, I assure you, guarantee the national integrity of China.'

'Can we quote you, Arthur?' someone joked.

'Feel free, feel free.'

She laughed. It was Sweetser's finest hour. All he had worked for and dreamed of—the United States symbolically seated at the League.

She went over to Robert.

They touched hands. Robert said, 'I was interested to see that the League would dispense with legal niceties when it wants to.'

'Oh, come on, Robert, we know that legalities are the weapon of last resort in the negotiating room,' she said. 'I would like a drink. Vermouth and soda.'

Robert said, 'Briand's performance was outrageous.'

'These are the days of *machtpolitik*, Robert.'

She heard her voice and realised how throaty and worldly it sounded from the strain of the day and from trying to be heard in the noise of the Club. As usual, there were only about half a dozen women—McGeachy, a couple of woman journalists from Scandinavia, and a few overscented and over-dressed secretaries looking for fun.

An inexplicable thought crossed her mind—she wouldn't mind being at the Molly Club, one of the more unconventional and rather *risqué* nightclubs of Geneva. She wanted to be out of this crowd for a night. She had not been there since the days before her marriage, in the old days with her unusual friend, Ambrose. Well, former lover. Unusual former lover.

But she couldn't see Robert relaxing at the Molly Club. Robert and she had never been there. She doubted if Robert had ever been there. And, anyhow, her bohemian days were over.

And, it had to be said, the Molly Club was *more* than bohemian. It was positively *decadent.*

Her decadent days were over, also. And, looking back, she marvelled that she had ever involved herself in that almost unbelievable part of her life.

The wish to be there now was probably a passing urge to be out of all this for a while. And maybe also the less admirable urge to hear the more salacious Molly Club gossip behind the night's excitement.

Sweetser came over to them and without any discretion at all nearly shouted at Robert, 'Stimson's been talking with Sir Eric on the Trans-Atlantic telephone— Stimson wants the Kellogg-Briand Pact invoked so the US can come into the dispute fully. And that means with the Marines.'

'The Kellogg-Briand Pact has no procedures for military engagement. It is a sail without wind,' Robert said, but without confidence.

'Ah,' said Sweetser, waggling a finger at him. 'Link the Kellogg-Briand Pact with Article XVI—". . . Members of the League shall contribute to the armed forces to be used to protect the Covenant of the League", then you have a military power the like of which the world has never seen.'

Robert ushered both of them over away from the other journalists at the bar. 'When did this happen? This call from Stimson?'

'Just now—twenty minutes ago. I was there. Sir Eric took the call—the first call ever directly from the United States government to the League—first ever.'

Sweetser had an eye for Historic Firsts.

Sweetser went on, 'I can remember—and so can you, Robert—when the American officials came to the League through the basement to avoid unintentional "recognition" of the League.'

As Sweetser elaborated on the remarkable telephone call, Edith wondered precisely on what political grounds the Secretary of State of the United States and the Secretary-General could communicate. Was it communication of information or was it joint negotiation? Was all passing of information a negotiation?'

'It's all *theoretical*,' Robert said. 'No one has enough ships and men over there to reach Japan in any strength.'

'There's the American Pacific Fleet, the British Far East Fleet. They could blockade. They could bombard Tokyo,' Sweetser said.

She'd always argued for the deterring effect simply of the *threat* of collective security. The hard facts of the military side of it were another question.

'It won't happen,' Robert said. 'It just won't happen. A place too far. The modernised Japanese army will go ahead and rout the Chinese. It will be a bloodbath.'

She had a creeping, chilling realisation, as she stood there listening to Robert.

He did not *want* collective security to work—the idea of all League members gathering their military power together to intimidate any warlike nation was not to his taste.

He wanted to wish it away for some deeper reason of his nature, and it was not just curiosity and analysis which drove Robert as a reporter.

His nature was blindingly clear to her now—it was because he itched for chaos and human horror. He was a connoisseur of calamity.

He had no appetite for an ordered world. He was in love with the earthquakes and the uprisings and marching armies, and with the sinister.

Maybe most of the world loved calamity.

She listened with dread to his intransigent scepticism. 'The British want to share China with the Japanese. And—this will interest you, Edith ...' Robert turned his sardonic, intransigent face to her, but it no longer agitated her, '—the British also think that it's better that the Japanese satisfy themselves with Manchuria and China than for them to look further south—to, say, Australia. Ah, but they won't stop!'

His sceptical analysis was always really a yearning for the disintegration of order. A disintegration he could watch from a safe distance.

He had *never believed in the League.* She supposed that he had never really pretended to.

She was the one who had pretended that he believed.

She had needed to pretend this.

Over the last couple of years, she had *willed* that he would be committed to the League. Maybe she'd caused him to make false noises of commitment but they were, she sensed in retrospect, to placate her. To placate her as a *wife*.

Or false noises he'd made in the courting days, to win her.

Why? What sort of prize had she been to 'win'?

She contemplated herself in the mirror behind the bar. Am I a prize? A comely girl from Australia? No, more than comely but not really glamorous either. Somewhere in between. If she made an effort. And with a veneer of Europe, perhaps. Had he thought of her as a carnal prize? She did not think of herself as, say, *voluptuous*. Or more precisely, she tried at times to think of herself as *voluptuous* but was never sure she ever was. Did she *do enough* in bed, for instance? Did French women like Jeanne really know more of the arts of the bed? Yet, arts or no, he certainly still desired her. She'd been somewhat adventurous in these matters, she supposed, when she first arrived in Europe, although she'd never been really *bad* and she'd pulled back from all that by the time Robert had begun to court her. And all that had been during the time with Ambrose whom she'd fancied as being decadent and suave. And she'd been rather eager to learn. As odd as it seemed, if she had any bedroom arts, she'd learned them from Ambrose. Ambrose and his strange nature. For instance, she'd learned that, in bed, curiously, the right small unexpected actions and surprising words could mean and achieve a lot.

What, then, had Robert seen in her and desired?

He had not known of her money, it couldn't have been that.

She was now prepared to sacrifice Robert, in some sense. She would, if necessary, sacrifice him for her vocation. There, she'd said it. Her vocation was her very nature. And, she supposed, in some small details, she had already sacrificed him.

But because of her sense of integrity, she would not sacrifice the marriage. She would stick with that.

The admission of these extraordinary thoughts did not flood her with consternation but more with a sense of exemption. She was exempting herself from most of the demands of marriage but not from the marriage itself.

Her commitment to the League, now seemingly revitalised, once again placed everything in a moral order for her. The League was going to win and to prevail: that which served the League had priority in her life again and that which did not serve the League, well, she would treat *as she chose.*

Yet her sense of exemption was a very solitary possession, it was a truth that could not be shared with Robert. It left her standing alone.

It was a line drawn between them—by her—unknown to him.

Curiously, there was nothing to be discussed with Robert. There was nothing to be said about it.

She would need to love him in a different way, perhaps as a formal social partner, to enter silently and imperceptibly into a love-free marriage, something she had heard discussed among her friends, none of whom had ever known it. Perhaps a love-free marriage was a more suave form of relationship.

To harbour such a private exemption could mean that she would be living forthwith in a lonely apartment within their shared daily life called home.

She watched Robert gesturing with his drink, his face full of the night's bombast, and she thought: it is not because he has an appetite for calamity. It is more: I do not love him because of his style as a man.

He was a brusque man. He had abrasive tastes. If there was snobbery in her attitude, then so be it.

And, make note of this: he had been always thus. It was she who had misled herself.

She made herself take another note: she herself was not free from the cross fascination with upheaval and with the macabre. She knew that this mania lived and prowled in all humans. The difference was that she was not driven by that mania, that craving. She took her deepest pleasure in human *intricacy*, not in human destructiveness. She did not live with a wish to pull the house down. Or in Robert's case, to have someone else pull the house down so that he could watch.

'Edith?' Robert was speaking to her. 'Are we dining out tonight? The Lyrique?'

'I'd like that.'

'Another vermouth, dear?'

'You do not say "another", you say "Would you like a vermouth?" To say "another" draws attention to the count. Thank you, Robert, dear. This time, I would like a gin, a large gin. A very large gin.'

'Gin?'

'Yes, gin.'

He seemed oblivious to her rebuke of his manners and pushed off through the thronging bar to get the drinks.

'I put out a supplementary international press statement,' Sweetser told her.

'Good, Arthur.'

'I thought it all went very well, today.'

'It did go very well.'

She marvelled that, despite the personal revelations and shifts which had just struck like lightning through her very being, her voice remained its own throaty, hearty, public self.

Their marriage was not at all as she had perceived it as recently as yesterday—a marriage of her own designing. It was a marriage that had *befallen* her, it was not of her making, it was something which had unfolded beyond her prediction, and beyond her fervent wish.

She struggled to control a welling sense of panic. She must remember that marriage was a play of many acts: more unpredictability must therefore lie ahead.

And there was nothing in the scheme of things which said that the outcome of that unpredictability ahead had always to be bad.

It could come out *good* as well as *bad.*

Say it's true! Say it's true.

She wanted then to crawl back into her mother's boudoir and to rest there in the tulle and the warmth and the scents. One of those childhood smells from her mother's room had been the sweet smell of the juniper berry, from the dear, sweet smell of what she knew now only too well as the dear, sweet smell of gin, and she took the glass which Robert handed her, and put it to her nose and inhaled that dear sweet smell from childhood.

She would get on with the creation of her own separate bedroom domain. Robert would no longer be any more than an occasional visitor there, as was his right.

'Darling, let's go after this drink,' she said.

She drank some of her gin, soothingly, back, momentarily, in her mother's bedroom, and then it was gone and she was crashingly back in the noise of the bar.

Robert drank deeply from his drink. 'Yes, let's go now. I am fagged. And famished.'

She kissed Sweetser on both cheeks. 'Well done, dear Arthur. This must be your grandest hour.'

'It is, it is. And, well done, Edith,' he said, saluting her.

She finished off her drink and she took Robert's arm and they left the boisterous bar, the very picture of a young, debonair, thoroughly modern couple.

The Doctrine of Non-recognition

I t was a Genevan winter evening before dinner. Snow fell silently against the window panes of her 'parlour' as Edith now called the third bedroom, and she was reading the minutes of the latest meeting of the World Disarmament Preparatory Commission, a glass of sherry beside her. And the bottle. It was more a nervous exhilaration which made her feel that a second sherry would be needed at the end of this day.

The age-old dream of world disarmament was to become a living reality.

The Preparatory Commission had worked for seven years to get ready for it and she'd been in and out of various sub-committees during that time. The aim had been to make sure that much of the hard thinking had been done before the conference.

Towards this end, a Draft Convention for World Disarmament had been prepared before the conference began. The nations had only to make their obligatory minor changes, to leave their mark as a matter of national pride, and then sign their names.

Despite its flirtation during the Japanese invasion of

Manchuria, America had not joined the League but it was coming to the Disarmament Conference.

Edith and Arthur had drunk some long, sorrowful drinks of deep disappointment over the failure of America to join the League, with Arthur at times near tears.

America had, however, joined the Commission of Inquiry into the Japanese invasion and the report was also due soon. She knew the contents—Japan had been condemned—which she was keeping from Robert. Sir Eric had placed armed guards at the printery where the report was being run off.

Maybe she owed it to Robert.

No. No, that was not true. She had to protect the integrity of her position even when it went against his interests.

But despite the condemnation of Japan, she knew there would be no military attempt to stop the Japanese aggression.

Personally, she wanted the League to try the new idea of 'sanctions' against Japan but knew that there were not enough warships to impose the naval blockade which would be needed to impose the sanctions, although sanctions were supposed to be imposed in the marketplace, not on the high seas.

Deep in her heart, she also knew that Manchuria was, for Europe and the Americans, a problem too far. Robert had been right. All too far away from the busy life of the world's capitals.

Because it was militarily impossible, she did not really consider Manchuria a fair test of the League.

And America had also taken a stand against Japan with its new Doctrine of Non-recognition by which it withdrew diplomatic recognition of Japan—the first time any country had done such a thing.

She was interested in the Doctrine of Non-recognition as a diplomatic punishment and the Council had taken it up and endorsed it. Although in the case of the US she feared that it was more a doctrine of pretending a problem did not exist so it would go away.

Nothing serious seemed to flow from the Doctrine which would hurt Japan.

Robert was in his room. She was comfortably conscious of his rustlings and occasional typing.

The gramophone was playing 'The Arrival of the Queen of Sheba'—her choice.

As the sherry relaxed her, she had to admit that she felt a certain repose. It was a repose which in part came from her acceptance now of the settled, rather mundane workings of their marriage.

Which was not to be sniffed at. The marriage did offer these times of repose. Nothing had arisen in their lives together since that Night of Devastating Insight to change her mind. That she did not love Robert no longer panicked her. A sense of *descent* remained—she refused to use the word failure—a descent from the lofty heights of a vision of marriage, but it was encased more and more in what she saw as a best-face acceptance, a stoical reading of her life.

The reading was that she'd made a less than perfect marriage.

Or had she found some new form of marriage—something with its own perfection?

She supposed that was yet to be determined.

She was rather tickled by the idea.

She had ceased to declare that she 'loved' him and he did not seem to notice, or if he did, he did not comment on it. He, likewise, had at some time—she couldn't recall when— let go making the intimate declaration, except for the perfunctory endearments.

She still found other minor endearments to say to him which had a sincerity to them. She still gave herself to him when he required but rarely now did she ever approach him. Paradoxically, this distancing of herself from him sexually had enlivened him.

'You do not give yourself as a woman should,' he said to her one night after finishing.

'I am here for you. You can have my body whenever you need it. You do not have to ask. Isn't that enough?'

As she said these words she was surprised to find that he'd become aroused and took her again.

But there was nothing really passionate in it for her. It was for her a minor pleasure. She had such needs, but she knew they could not be met fully by him now that the intimacy wasn't there, although she'd noticed there was a certain pleasure—even if an incomplete pleasure—in even these mostly routine acts. She would have to let those stronger needs subside, although she prayed that her self-pleasuring would keep the flame alive. Alive for whom?

There was an austerity to this. She could not deny it. Especially when she looked in the mirror and was able still to see the vigour of youth in her body, her attractiveness as a physical woman.

The austerity threatened her at times, so much so that she found herself looking away from her body in the mirror, its wasting allurements, unable to bear the thought of the waste. She did not want to consign this carnal vitality to 'good works' as some sort of secular nun.

A lover? She hardly had the time in her life.

It was imperative that she not permit this renunciation, or descent, to be bitter.

Robert now almost always took the second bedroom but this had been arranged on the basis of his working late and her working early. Their lives sometimes barely crossed paths for days on end.

But tonight she appreciated the marriage and the repose it gave her. She was nearly at peace. She liked Robert being in the other room. She liked their sharing of the music.

She liked that he, too, had a sherry beside him. She had at least got him to change to sherry before dinner instead of his usual ales—about the only thing he had yielded.

She still read things out to him from her reports and he still loved to share with her gossip from his daily rounds.

She loved their large apartment. They had a non-live-in housekeeper and they ate out often either through work or through the tiredness of their day ends. They did not need a cook. The café downstairs in the Place du Bourg-de-Four was very adequate and they sometimes had meals sent up.

She did not know if he loved her still. She would not ask. He was a deeply preoccupied man. He was a rough and ready man.

Her acceptance of the lower-order love—or whatever it was they now had—left the rest of her life with him yawning ahead. She could not face the question of divorce because she did not want to be a quitter and nor did she wish to admit her failure of judgement to the whole world. She did not fancy being a divorced woman with its overtones of rather salacious availability, of being a sexually experienced woman no longer bound by marriage.

She could not quite look at all *that* now in her life. She buried herself in her day-to-day life at the League.

And she religiously cared for her body without objective.

Another thing: she was aspiring and he was not. At the time of their marriage, she had thought that Robert did aspire. His detective book set at the League was funny and middlingly successful, although nowhere as fine as her friend Caroline's book. She had hoped that he might write serious literature. He was writing his second book but she sensed it would never be finished. He was respected at his paper and among the newspaper crowd and that was all he seemed to want now from aspiration.

She stumbled then across another realisation which had been hiding there like a fox in the underbrush. She felt superior to Robert. It didn't seem to have to do with class, especially since being an Australian she was supposed to be above that sort of thing. Class was, after all, rather *passé*, somewhat comical. Even the films made fun of it. She did not wish to feel socially superior and derived no joy from the feeling.

Professionally, being an *important subordinate* was her natural disposition and within it she could flourish. At least at this point in her life. To be the younger person with the wiser older person, as she was with Bartou, was an association she relished. Although as Bartou aged and became increasingly inattentive to things, she felt more his equal. And she had enjoyed the role of important subordinate for some time in the old days with Ambrose.

She would be happy, she felt, to be junior partner in a marriage with a fine and superior man.

She'd married Robert believing him stronger than he subsequently turned out, and she married him because she believed he would eventually be distinguished. It was not going to happen.

She supposed that Robert and she would see each other through life, each pretty much alone within the marriage. It could be worse. They did not scrap with each other as such. They still disagreed strongly on some great issues, but they were not a bickering couple. But nor did they intellectually engage each other the way they had in the beginning.

She supposed that she needed to turn now more to her friends for emotional sustenance. She wished Caroline were living in Geneva.

Ambrose still wrote now and then. He seemed perfectly well again, living some independent existence in the clublands of London. He wrote to say that he'd even practised a little medicine again but that it wasn't really his game.

It was a different League now from the one he'd known in the old days. So much bigger.

No mascot dogs now in the Sections.

Robert came to the door and she jumped as if her thoughts

were spread out before her on the table like playing cards. She was conscious too, that the music had finished.

He stood with a copy of *People* in his hand.

She looked at him questioningly, seeing in his way of standing something unsettling which she could not quite identify. He wanted, she could tell, to read to her from *People*. Not her favourite publication.

When he was further into the light, she could see that he was both edgy and perversely pleased by something.

'Your book is mentioned?' she asked, making a stab at it, trying to forestall surprise.

He held the newspaper before her, the reading lamp caught it in its glare.

'What is it?' She leaned over to read from the newspaper, and saw the headline: 'Society Shaken by Terrible Scandal'.

The article went on '. . . It concerns one of the leading host-esses in the country, a woman highly connected and immensely rich. Association with a coloured man became so marked that they were the talk of the West End. Then one day the couple were caught in compromising circumstances . . .'

She kept staring at the newspaper long after she had finished reading it, blushing and queasy. For a peculiar moment, she even thought it referred to *her*.

She took the newspaper from his hand to read again. The West End Society Scandal resonated with an incident from her earlier life, an incident she'd confided to Robert before they married.

Before their marriage she had told Robert of her exotic, unrepeated, out-of-character encounter with the Negro musician, Jerome, in a nightclub in Paris. She had involved herself, just that one night, for brief moments in time, in what *People* would call a 'compromising circumstance' with the Negro.

Robert and she had tried to be honest with each other on that night of 'telling', but she'd felt, even back then, that she had overwhelmed him with the outlandish nature of her confession and it had never again been mentioned. She'd thought that they'd tacitly agreed to allow some things such as this to be shoved into the attic of their marriage.

'Have you heard who it is?' she asked, her voice falsely steady. Her repose now dissipated, his obvious edginess breaking into her mood.

'There's been talk. Some time back, I heard talk in the *Club de la Presse* about Edwina Mountbatten. I never thought Odhams would permit it to be published—even in *People*. I think I can guess who wrote it.' His voice was unnaturally neutral, constrained.

She had, she realised when asking the question, been interested in who the black man was, not the woman. She wondered if it were Jerome. It couldn't be. She said, 'Edwina Mountbatten!? And who is the coloured man? Do we know that?' She shouldn't have asked—it led the conversation the wrong way.

'I hear that it is either Paul Robeson the actor, or a musician called Leslie Hutchinson.'

Was Jerome one of that crowd? Where was he?

She wondered what Robert's next move would be.

He gave a small sour laugh.

Her confession from before their marriage must be in his mind. She prepared herself.

She could tell that he was in pain from whatever it was that men felt about their women and other men—however far back in life the other men might be—but this tender masculine pride in Robert had always seemed cemented over with a hardiness.

He wasn't saying anything but nor was he leaving.

She wanted once again to reassure him that it was not something for him to tear himself apart about after all this time, but she also felt from the report some strange backhanded endorsement of her own peccadillo.

She did not want to raise the matter again either. Surely, he didn't?

She cherished her peccadillo in the bosom of her memories—well, 'scandal' might be a more honest word than peccadillo—cherished it as one of her early attempts to be intrepid—and for the special, flamboyant, exciting nature of it. It was a pressed flower in her life diary. A rare pressed flower from a high mountain. A black blossom. Whatever stigma she felt surrounded the incident with the Negro, she was more than willing to endure it—at least, as long as it wasn't in the newspapers—in return for the oodles of other enchantments which remained vividly associated with that night and which returned to her again and again, and physically excited her.

Now, queerly, it was somehow endorsed by the conduct of Edwina and her High Society friends. If not *endorsed*, identified as an exotic pleasure which other women pursued. She was not bizarrely alone.

She kept her silence. She read the piece again.

'Well?' he asked, curtly.

'What will happen to her? Will she really have to leave England as the paper suggests? Will the Palace make her do that?'

'I suppose so. Can't have the Palace crowd gallivanting about with coloured folk.'

Robert's tone of speaking about this was wrong and it irked her.

She handed the paper back to him and acted as if she intended to go on reading her reports, indicating that the matter was closed.

As if she had any concentration left for reports.

She pretended to read, head down, a hand shielding her hot face.

He continued to stand there in the semi-darkness outside the light cast by the reading lamp, watching her.

She knew her breathing was broken and heavy and that her breasts were heaving and that he could see this.

After a minute or so, he said, without tenderness or affection, 'Remind you of anything?'

She did not reply.

'Well, Edith,' he said, in a derisive voice, 'your moral deportment has been taken up by High Society. You've set a fashion, it would seem.'

He laughed again his horrible sour laugh, but within the derision, she heard masculine pain. 'You've always hankered for the life of that set.'

Robert had put it rudely, but it was a little true. She did have a silly, fascinated interest in that world, the world of the Mountbattens. For a Jasper's Brush girl it had been a fairy tale world. She almost laughed. That world certainly had not been in her mind back then in Paris. In fact, she'd felt that her action had been some straying from the track of all proper life, an escapade which had to be forgiven by the circumstance of champagne and Paris and jazz and The Times.

He made a noise of contempt, whether for her or High Society she did not know. It carried with it the man's pain she'd sensed in him earlier. She was sorry then that he'd carried that pain buried within him since their marriage.

She could not help that now.

She continued to pretend to read, staring blindly at the documents on her table.

He stood there in the semi-darkness. 'I suppose you still have perverted dreams of your Nigger Prince. Your Othello.' That it had happened with a Negro was part of his pain.

He seemed to want to delve into it.

She did not reply. Robert was perhaps close to rage. She could tell that he wasn't affected by drink.

She felt desperately protective of her difficult, passionate, well-meant young confession from back then in their courtship. She did not want it brutalised.

'You must be pleased to know your morals are the morals of High Society.'

He wanted to goad her.

She prepared an answer and then spoke it, trying to be calm and to be careful of his feelings. 'I've no problem living with my morality.' She said it without looking to him. 'I shared that secret of myself with you back then as a gesture of my love for you. That's all there is to say.'

'I suppose you look at the flies of all men and think about possibilities. Or is it only for black men that you lust?'

She now burned tearfully from the unfairness of his words. She wished she were not in the glare of the reading lamp.

She looked up at him, at his eyes, there in the outer rim of light. 'Please leave me now, Robert. That's all in our past.'

She had no confidence that this would extinguish the matter.

He came back, 'Such a thing can never be buried. What you did with the Black was an outrageous, unwomanly act. You never apologised for it.'

Apologised? To whom? For what? For her youthful zest? She may owe an apology to Ambrose, who'd been her companion on that particular night, and who may or may not have been hurt by it.

'Apologise? Back then, when I told you, I thought I was making a clean breast so that we could begin our life together. I didn't tell you about it so that you could raise it at your perverse convenience.'

Not 'clean breast'—in the telling of it there had been a muffled pride in what she'd done, pride in her Jazz Age intrepidness.

'Did you really believe that I could forget such a thing!?'

Robert had always claimed to be progressive in his views, and something of a bohemian. That pose had fallen away. He was a wretched little prig.

She maintained her position. 'Why did you marry me then, if you saw my character as *besmirched*?'

'I now suspect that you used it to entice me in some per-verted way.'

'What utter rubbish. Please go.'

Was it a *seductive* thing for a woman to talk of such things to another man? Oh God, it probably was salaciously enticing to men.

Without having to look, she became aware then that he was unbuttoning his flies.

Before she could properly come to terms with his actions, she heard him say, 'A husband's *perquisite*?'

She had never heard such an expression. And she had never been so confronted.

Her breathing was now so heavy and erratic as to be discomforting.

'Please leave the room,' she said. She felt queasy.

She couldn't look directly at him, but was vividly aware of his posture from the edge of her vision.

He moved closer to her, standing nearer, so that she could not avoid seeing his flies gaping open, his hand holding himself.

She could smell the male odour of his groin.

'Please get control of yourself, Robert, and leave.'

He stood there in his provocative pose.

'Robert!'

She was disconcerted by his action. She raised her voice. 'Leave me alone.'

He remained there, his hand holding himself, presenting himself to her mouth. It seemed enormous. She had always considered it *long* in comparison with the three others that she'd seen in an excited state—leaving aside Ambrose's German magazines and her mother's copy of the *Kama Sutra*.

The dreadful thing of it was that she was ever so slightly drawn to it, while not being in any way aroused, as if there were a natural call which she was obliged, as a woman, to answer—something in the pit of her being. She would not permit herself to answer.

She felt dizzy from the grossness of his approach and her primitive responsiveness to it.

She dismayed herself by her confusions.

Oh God.

Another thought shot across her mind—that if she succumbed to this gross advance it would in some strange way re-excite their marriage, cause some animal fire to ignite, and would cause her to fall down some other trapdoor of marriage.

Everything would revolve. She would stand in a different way to him. There would be a heavy, bizarre cost for following that primal submission.

She forced herself to look at him. She looked first at his hand and groin, saw that he was fully stiffened, wondered how that could possibly be, what it was about her demeanour that could possibly have caused that. Where was the impulse coming from which now stiffened him? From the picture in his mind of her with a Negro's black penis between her painted lips? She then lifted her eyes to his, expressing repudiation of him, and also demanding a return to the courtesy of two married people, realising, at the same time, that the courtesy of marriage was another illusion and that no two people could express more viciously, or have the craftiness for deeper discourtesy, than a married couple.

She held his gaze. Their eyes were in contest.

The courtesy she was demanding was the deadening courtesy which also killed passion in marriage but she didn't want to succumb and rearrange their marriage *that way*. It was too late for that.

She sensed clearly that to yield to him would be a true and animal thing but he was no longer the person with whom she wanted this true and animal thing. That was no longer possible. Had been lost, lost, lost.

His gaze was filled with lust. She could also see in his eyes a desire to punish and degrade her. As if the punishment and degradation would burn Jerome out of his heart. Affirm his own supremacy. But blazingly, it was lust. He wanted her to pleasure him. He wanted her. And she yearned for lust and, to her unnerving surprise, her body, at the sight of his stiffened cock, was becoming ready to receive him. She had deep urgings to kneel and take him to her mouth.

'No,' she said. 'No.' Her mouth was thick with saliva.

There was a burning silence and he did not make any other gesture but to hold his stiffened cock in his hand for her to take.

'No,' she said, thickly. 'No. Go.'

Without breaking their gaze, he made an ugly, frustrated noise, a man's noise which she had never heard before, a pained whimper.

From the corner of her eye, she saw his cock had lost some of its rampant stiffness.

Turning from her, he put it away and did up his flies, and left the room without speaking.

She was breathless with colliding emotions—of relief that he had not prevailed, yet a sense of a loss of the rising lust within herself, that she had not abandoned herself to the primal call to do what he had asked—and at the same time, a sense that something even more dreadful than anything which had gone before had happened between them, and to them. And that dreadful thing, as gross and as unjust as it was, came from her denial of his lust. And her denial of the animal lust within herself.

That form of sex had happened between them only once during the very early days of their marriage, as some levy he had imposed, perhaps, after her confession, and which she had been delighted to pay, to show him that she was entirely with him and for him. It had never happened again, as if it had become *something which had happened with another*, worse, with an exotic other, and did not belong in a decent marriage.

The confession from way back then must have been eating at him. Eating and eating at his spirit to become some chronic indignation. Or need.

Now something had broken irrevocably between them, her refusal to submit to it, to abandon herself, had caused a rupture from which she could see no recovery.

After a while she rose, finding that she was shaky. She had difficulty in moving steadily. She quickly drank a glass of sherry.

She had to flee from his proximity.

She went to the telephone and had herself put through to Jeanne, telling her in a low quiet voice that she must see her urgently, that perhaps they could meet at her place.

She had an inkling that Jeanne would understand, although she was unsure what it was she would tell Jeanne.

She went to the dressing room, hesitated about what to wear and, for the first time, felt fearful of being undressed in the same place as Robert.

She dressed for dinner, knowing that Robert must be listening to her movements. She packed some clothing and things for an overnight stay with Jeanne, and gathered her work papers. She had never gone to stay outside their marriage in this way before.

She then went to the door of his room, agitated.

He was now drinking whisky but appeared to be doing nothing else.

She said, 'I am going to dinner with Jeanne. I think it best that I stay with her tonight.'

'Perhaps you could both find yourselves a *rendezvous.*'

She could hear his rancour.

'Don't.'

'Go back to the gutter.'

'You have a disgust of the world. I don't wish to be poisoned by it. You abused my candour.'

They had never spoken to each other with such disrespect.

She felt her whole being deforming, warping, inside her.

He drank from his whisky as a way of dismissing her. He did not look up.

He seemed utterly without empathy, regret or kindness.

She stayed the night with Jeanne, explaining her surprise visit simply as a marriage spat, not feeling sure she could go to the heart of the matter with her just yet. Or perhaps ever. She felt scared of ever offering confidences again.

On consideration, she would never go to the heart of the matter with Jeanne or anyone.

Jeanne had been rather thrilled to have her as a guest and to provide a hideaway, and rose to the occasion with great tenderness, and with absolute commitment to her, as if her running away from Robert confirmed to Jeanne the supremacy of her own single life. They slept chastely together but she was glad of the near warmth of Jeanne's body and her sisterly caresses.

When she returned to the apartment, Robert and she seemed to avoid each other, although that happened in the natural flow of things, and communication was now mostly by businesslike notes left on the table, a sad reversal from the earlier days of marriage when the notes had been those of loving and witty exchange.

Over the next few days at the office, Edith followed the story of Edwina Mountbatten in the bits and pieces of tittle-tattle which came up in conversation.

All the English on the staff were following the case, but she did not wish to show to them any uncommon interest, a caution which came from an absolutely ridiculous fear of revealing her burning personal preoccupation.

She went daily to the League library and furtively checked

the London papers and saw with some puzzlement that Edwina Mountbatten had taken the *People* newspaper to court for libel.

This was something she would've loved to have talked to Robert about but there was no one really who could answer her questions.

In the court proceedings, Edwina Mountbatten denied ever inviting any coloured man to her house or of knowing any coloured man.

She read that on the day after the court case, Dickie and Edwina had lunched with George V and Queen Mary at the Palace. So the Palace was forgiving them or standing by them, it seemed.

Robert and she, alone of all the English people on the Continent, did not talk of the matter, although communication after a week or so resumed at a housekeeping level.

She wanted to know more and wondered who she could ask about the scandal who would be reliable. She could, she supposed, write to Ambrose who would *know all.*

Yet Ambrose was an approach not without qualms and snares either.

She had been in the company of Ambrose on that night in Paris when she'd been in compromising circumstances, to use the language of the newspapers, with Jerome.

Her own incident had arisen at a visit to a jazz club in Paris. Ambrose had come looking for her after she had been absent—probably for longer than was polite—and it was he who'd found her in the Room *Artiste* with Jerome.

How much Ambrose had seen, or what he had surmised that night had never been discussed nor resolved between Ambrose and herself.

For her to take an interest in the Edwina Mountbatten story now would perhaps inflame his imagination as much as it had inflamed Robert's.

Was there anything to be lost in inflaming Ambrose's

imagination? Ye gods, he *lived* for aberration. She could've told him back then. Of all the people in the world, it was he with whom she should have talked about it all.

Or were there things which could never be told to anyone without setting in play unforeseen repercussions of an unguessable magnitude? Better consigned to eternal silence?

Yet, in those earlier days, all the candour she had risked with Ambrose, and he with her, had created a fineness of life. Their mutual candour had exhilarated them.

God, how she now missed him.

It brought home to her how many boundaries there were to the conversations and friendships which she had around the League. Even among the progressives and the radical reformers. There was on the one hand so much propriety among those of conservative leanings and, on the other, so many things which were not worthy of serious moral discussion among the progressives.

There had been no taboo on the salacious with Ambrose. If something had been seen as salacious in the respectable world, it became a giggling lark in Ambrose's world.

It was Ambrose she needed to speak with and she began her letter to him—and, with a deep breath, decided once again to risk the candid approach.

'We, or at least I, are all agog at the Edwina Mountbatten scandal,' she wrote. 'I am dying to hear more. You must be close to that crowd. Of course, you will be saying to yourself, "Edith has every reason to be interested in that *affaire*" or is it more that it would be for me an *affaire de goût*. Recalling, of course, our infamous night in Paris.'

There, it was out and plain between Ambrose and her.

She had decided to write on the assumption that he knew what had happened that night between the black musician and herself. If he did not indeed know, she prayed he would enjoy having his suspicions confirmed. That he would relish it.

If he did not—if he were hurt or offended—then the possibility of finding their way back to their outrageously candid relationship was lost.

That was the risk.

It could be that she was asking too much of that former intimacy, just as she had asked too much of her marriage.

Her statement in the letter—'an affair of taste'—had such ambiguity in this particular matter. She hoped that Ambrose would enjoy the vulgar ambiguity of it.

She recalled that in Ambrose's and her affair, this particular carnal pleasure had been, for a time, a favourite thing for both of them. And he was the only man who had ever pleasured her with his mouth.

The more she thought about it, that particular sexual act had never gone out of season in their affair. In fact, it had seemed to be more the natural thing for their affair and its nature.

She then realised that the letter to Ambrose had other yearnings hovering about it—a yearning to tell him of the crumbling of her marriage.

She was not yet ready to tell of the crumbling of her marriage. That was, as yet, too personal and undigested a mess. She hoped their letters would in the future allow her to blurt out the sorry mess.

She finished the letter, though, with some of her yearnings expressed: 'I miss you dear Ambrose ... oh, how I miss you,' she wrote.

Tears fell to the page. She blotted them with her sleeve, glad to see that they had swollen the fibre of the letter paper. She hoped he would see the tear stains.

Unbelievably, in the days after she had sent the letter, her relations with Robert slowly healed and warmed, and even approached a cheerfulness.

They were able to resume eating together and doing things in public together. A marriage of appearances.

They did not mention the Edwina Mountbatten affair again.

In moments of reverie, her heart and mind were now more and more retreating into the world of her past to those times when she felt intrepid and free. Not trammelled in spirit, as now she felt.

She did not have the energy or time, though, to confront either her needs, nor the deceit of allowing routine and appearances to run her life.

Inevitably, Robert came to her bed again, and she pulled back the covers to let him in, and while in the bathroom inserting the diaphragm, she liberally applied the lubricating cream inside herself to compensate for her lack of arousal.

A reply came from Ambrose. '... I hear there was a gold cigarette case indiscreetly engraved by Edwina and given to the Black, known in some circles as 'Hutch' (as in 'rabbit'? Breeding as?) which he has shown to everyone in the world who can read. Discretion is not, evidently, in the character of the Black. Nor, now that I think about it, in the character of any colour I have known (and I've known at least three of the colours—how many are there???!!).'

He was hearing much of the case by being rather close to Peter Murphy who was very much in the Mountbatten entourage, '... but that is a story in itself ...' Ambrose wrote.

He told her that Edwina had so offended the Palace that she was now *persona non grata* despite the Very Public Luncheon on the day after the case.

The other story was that London's coloured artistic community, especially the opera singer, Paul Robeson, was outraged by Edwina's denial of knowing them when they had, in fact, been at Brook House many times by her invitation.

So there were convulsions of temper among the artistic and black crowd, as well.

He'd heard that Dickie's naval half-stripe was in doubt. 'Of course, he has always closed his eyes to his wife's "social" life but now he has had his nose rubbed in it. But that is all very well, after all, he prefers to mix with sailors. Don't we all? The word is: They May Not Last As a Couple.'

Edith could not help but feel the queer coincidence that now further identified her with Edwina. They both had marriages which were strained because of their relations with black men.

She laughed. She might write to Edwina. A girl from Jasper's Brush writes a personal letter about shared Scandalous Things and about Marriage, to a woman out of the top drawer of English high society.

'. . . There is a wonderful story going around. Following the scandale, Dickie whisked her off to Malta where he's based. The story is that there was a command ball, well, you see, it was ALL SAILORS—no women—what can I say? There was a long line of sailors formed to take part in the Palais Glide and Edwina, the only woman there, leapt into the dance. Dickie was not amused at having his wife, already the talk of London, now frolicking with 50 SAILORS. In a ballroom (how aptly named). Well. After Brook House and its "Fêtes Pour les Sauvages", and Wild West Parties, and Circus Parties, and Almost Naked Parties in St John's Wood . . . what is left for a girl to try? We hear she's planning to go to the US—alone—and for a long time. The best joke around London is that Edwina is going through "a very black time"—well, it sounds better after a few gins. A Prince Obolensky is also mentioned in connection with Edwina. Of course, George and Mary have a little problem with the heir—and a woman named Mrs Simpson—yes, Mrs Simpson. Of that More Later. Dear, sweet Edith, it is so good to be talking to you again even if by mail, and talking about Things That Really Matter. And you must tell me all the delicious details of that outrageous escapade of yours those years ago in Paris. Whatever I might have said or not said at the time, I was filled with admiration at your absolute audacity. Yours as ever, Ambrose.'

The letter charged Edith with loving delight and deeper longing for his company. She cried for it. She forgave him everything. She would forgive him murder. She needed a Rotten Friend like Ambrose, in her life, desperately.

Best of all—best, best, best of all—the letter told her that Ambrose had forgiven her for her hopelessly misdirected behaviour those years ago.

As she was pouring herself a port in her parlour one evening, Robert came to the door.

'Hello,' she said, 'did you get your copy off?'

'Yes.

'Did you write up the League's radio station?'

'With photographs. Including one of Sweetser broadcasting to the world. How was your day?'

'The Disarmament Conference seating plan. Final draft.'

They no longer touched, no longer kissed. She did not offer him a drink.

He no longer fitted into her room, her parlour, or the way she had rearranged it.

'I have news,' he said.

'What?' She felt on guard with him most of the time. Although his voice was not threatening, she prepared herself. In fact, if anything, he seemed sheepish.

It came out. 'I am going to China. To cover the war.'

She avoided showing any emotion.

Thank the gods.

Oh, thank the gods.

She concealed welling pleasure. 'Have you missed war so badly that you have to go all the way to China?'

'I may have. It's the best war we have at present.'

'When do you sail?'

'Still finding a ship. Matter of days, with any luck.'

'For how long?'

He did not answer immediately. 'For as long as it lasts, I suppose.'

She turned to fully face him and probed further. 'Indefinitely, that is?'

He looked away from her and cleared his throat, 'I suppose that's the word—indefinitely.'

She found herself nearly trembling. She was confused now in her emotions. Including her sheer guilty pleasure at the news. However, she could hardly hope for a long war.

'Is the paper sending you?' Her voice was firm, but it lied.

'I asked them to send me.'

There was something odd about his reply.

'They're paying you?'

'By the line.'

She took a deep breath. There had been no hint, and no discussion. And if they were paying by the line it meant that they had not sent him but that he had chosen to go freelance.

Then, they'd not been discussing much of anything at all.

She reminded herself that it was all for the good, regardless of how abruptly it was being presented. 'You'll join up with Potato?'

'Yes.'

'Who's taking over the bureau here?'

'James's coming up from Paris.'

'Until you return?' She wanted this confirmed again.

'James is permanently replacing me.'

'I see.'

She sipped her port.

So. This was something of a resolution of things.

He remained standing, as if he were just telling her about some household matter. 'Of course, I'll send rent money.'

She heard this and found the ground between them again unsure.

'Oh, no need—I can manage the rent. The League allowance . . .' Which did not, however, cover the rent of an apartment this size.

His 'paying the rent'—an expression of his husbandly role—had been something of a farce. He had borrowed from her in a frequent, haphazard and unrecorded way. Borrowed more than the rent. She had subsidised his life indulgences, limited as they were to betting on horses and losses at all-night card-games with his reporter mates—moderate but frequent losses.

'Better that I keep my end up,' he said.

What did that mean?

'Oh, you'll have expenses while travelling. I can look after the rent.'

'My responsibility.' He said this without conviction and as if it were still required of him to say it. 'Should send you something.'

He was trying to have a place in her life, a toehold.

'The rent is not going to worry me financially,' she said. She wanted that connection, at least, stopped. She wanted secure command of the apartment.

This did not sound like the beginning of a discussion about divorce. A task for which she had no heart or time.

'Will we have then a marriage such as that of Edwina and Dickie?' she said, trying to quip like a Modern Woman.

How she hated the nickname 'Dickie'. And, inadvertently, she'd raised the dreaded subject.

She didn't care anymore.

He cleared his throat again, and said, 'And how is that?'

'They seem always to be in different parts of the world. With different people.'

Edith liked the sound of that.

'I suppose it might be a bit like that.'

'You don't have to send money.'

'Doesn't seem quite right.'

'It's quite all right.'

'Will leave some stuff here.' His tone was halfway between asking her and telling her.

'I can arrange to store anything you have to leave.'

She was sure he didn't have storage in mind.

Leave it murky? Or have done with it?

'Good,' he said. 'Good to have a base.' He seemed to have ignored her reference to storage.

A 'base'? Was that the way a husband talked?

Yet something now stopped her from clarifying everything. Although she knew she was happy to have him away from her life, she was uncertain of how she wanted him gone. She could not clarify that to herself just now. To not clarify was best for her sense of self and to her advantage for the time. As it was, perhaps, for him.

It might be best clarified in writing at another time.

'And you'll be gone indefinitely?' she said, wanting to have that confirmed again.

'Difficult to say how long.'

He was fudging it.

Best done in writing.

'Good night, Edith.'

'Good night, Robert.'

He hesitated and then came over and kissed her cheek and took her hand. 'Think it's the best plan,' he said.

'Yes,' she said.

'For now,' he said.

She nodded.

She heard him go to his bedroom, heard him pour a drink and prepare for bed.

She could turn his room into a guests' room? Or should it remain there for as long as he wanted?

She would become by default now the lessee of the apartment. That, too, would suit her fine. She would have the contract changed. If she were, as a woman, permitted to sign a lease under Swiss law.

She found herself gasping, trembling. It was over, this uncomfortable domesticity with its disfigured sexuality. For the indefinite future, at least.

She was released. Or partly released.

She felt an urgent burning need to unburden herself to Ambrose.

To tell him that she'd flunked her marriage.

There was another nice parallel in her life, in a time of parallels.

She was present as an official witness at the small ceremony, representing Under Secretary Bartou, together with Under Secretary Marquis Paulucci di Calboli Barone and a few others to see the foundation stone of the new Palais des Nations relaid.

It had been wrongly placed back in 1929. The architects had made a mistake back then and now it had to be moved to its proper place.

The foundations of her life had also now to be repositioned.

Wrongly laid.

But where and how to relay her foundations?

Fare-thee-well

E dith stood at the window in the Palais Woodrow Wilson in the office of her friend Jeanne and looked out across the lake. In the office fireplace behind her the coal fire burned while the dreaded Geneva wind, the *bise*, swept the lake.

She rested her forehead on the chilled window glass and moaned to Jeanne, who lounged on the office settee.

She said that she dreamed for a year of having a 'Peace Picnic' but that would be out of the question in the bitter Geneva February they were experiencing. And with no break in the weather predicted.

'Have a *pique-nique en hiver*,' Jeanne said. 'In Paris we had winter picnics. I had a winter picnic on the floor of my Paris office once. One winter picnic I had in the back of a horse and carriage. Which was altogether too delightful.'

'And about which you will now talk—a picnic for two?'

'*Mais oui*, a rug over your,' she looked at Edith, deadpan, '... laps?'

'And you needed gloves?'

'It was cold but we kept warm.'

'One glove each?'

'Each of us wore one glove, yes,' Jeanne said, still straightfaced.

They both giggled.

'Edith! Sometimes you embarrass even me! You are becoming more bawdy than we French.'

Edith tried to picture herself as bawdy. No, she didn't think that was part of her picture of herself. That was more a word to describe a barmaid. The French word *risqué* sounded much better.

'I think I would rather be described as *risqué*, Jeanne.'

There was a time when she would have wished to be truly *risqué*. In fact, there was a time when she fancied she might become the Wickedest Woman in Europe. 'I want to have a winter picnic for one hundred.'

'For the delegates!?'

'Not for the official delegates. It'll be a picnic for all those people who come to Geneva to make sure the leaders of the world keep their promises. The citizens, Jeanne. *Les citoyens*.'

'Edith, those people are not *les citoyens*. They are in politics also, just waiting for their turn in power. And so dull! And you do not like them. Mrs Swanwick will be there. And Mary Dingman. Edith, you do not like them. A *risqué* person does not belong with these people, Edith.'

'I want the Disarmament Conference to be ... more embracing. It's time for involvement of all the people. It is more than a diplomatic thing.'

'Ah Edith, you are *scheming*. You are playing the crafty diplomat. You want to orchestrate these people?'

Not quite right. Edith wanted to channel the fervour of these well-meaning people who would be coming to Geneva. She wanted them to lose their tone of moral incontestability. And she wanted them to stop shouting. They were mostly ardent pacifists and, while she was drawn to pacifism, as a dreamy magnetic north to her politics, she had reluctantly accepted that pacifism was not a doctrine for this century.

She wanted these well-meaning people to formulate more astute tactics and more intricate positions. She wanted them to concede that there were times for taking up arms against evil, albeit only collective arms through the League. Knowing when to fight with all thy might. She wanted them to come to accept an armed League. She wanted them to adjust to the conditions of ever-present peril. To learn *machtpolitik*.

'I want to draw a larger box around their small boxes. To make yet another unit of persuasion. At present they are either in their own little box talking to each other or pretending that they are really the only box.'

'Edith, whatever you have in mind for your *Pique-nique du Désarmement*, let us—our crowd—have a picnic in a four-in-hand—'

She saw Jeanne stop herself, registering that given the situation between Edith and Robert, picnics might not be the right thing just now. Picnics were for lovers and the happy-hearted. Robert and she had forfeited the right to picnic. For now. Jeanne knew it.

'Will Robert still be here?' Jeanne asked, tentatively, as if asking about an ailing elderly parent, and without waiting for a reply, 'Just you and me, if you like, that too would be good. Yes? Or another couple? Or bring that nice young man who seems to dote on you. And I will bring ... mmmmm?'

Jeanne went through the act of considering a long list.

In her case, Jeanne was referring to a nice young man who seemed to be an admirer of Edith. He was not a young man who wished to romance married ladies—he was, she suspected, a young man who wished to have an older woman friend. She seemed to attract them, these nice young men who wanted older women friends.

Edith's mind was now drifting to the arrival of Ambrose. 'You know that Ambrose will be here for the conference?'

'He will? Well, that's good, Edith.' Jeanne searched her face, 'Or is it not good for you?'

'I don't know if it will be good for me.'

'Robert and Ambrose on a picnic? Possible?'

It had been three years since Ambrose had his breakdown and returned to England, and he and she had gone their separate ways.

She'd seen him off on the train back then and that had been the last time she'd seen him. He hadn't come across to Geneva for her wedding, and she'd been secretly glad.

The Edwina affair had brought them back into a more intimate letter exchange, the letters more frequent.

He was working in London for Fred Pickard at the Federation of International Institutions.

How would it be to see him again? Would there be physical attraction? She was still at ease with the idea of his errant nature and, musing in retrospect, she felt she had handled it rather well at the time.

Maybe she could regard it with ease only because it was far, far away.

Regardless of all that, she did want Ambrose to visit her life even if she did not need that part of his nature back in her life. She suspected that it may have gone now from his life, that the treatment he'd had back then may have worked and that he was cured of all that.

More importantly, how stable was he now? Obviously stable enough to hold a job and write merry letters. And he had said he went back to medical practice for a time.

'Yes, Jeanne. A farewell picnic with Robert would be a fine thing. But not with Ambrose. We may have to have two picnics: a picnic for him who goes and one for him who returns—returns, at least, on a visit.'

'How sad it is. When one of the old gang leaves I cannot bear it. First Caroline, then Ambrose and now Robert. Even if he and I were not always *sympathetique*.'

'Only for a time.'

'Yes, with Robert—just for a time.' Jeanne said, but Edith

detected that Jeanne was just agreeing with her. In Jeanne's voice was a hint that she thought Robert was going for good. And she knew for Jeanne that the hint was also something of a wish.

The next day over breakfast with Robert, she brought up the matter of Ambrose. Not that she needed a clearance from Robert now for anything. However, oddly, she sensed that there were niceties to be observed. 'How do you feel about Ambrose's visiting Geneva?'

'How should I feel?'

'He and I were lovers.' She imperceptibly winced as she again took one more of the sensitivities of her past out of the bag. Too bad.

He moved in his chair. He obviously still found it difficult to accept this as a conceivable fact. Her confession and revelations about Ambrose had been another part of her attempt at complete candour during the courtship.

'Some years back now,' Robert said, tightly.

He was trying to be civilised about it.

She wondered whether that was a clearance.

She stayed on her guard—prudently as it turned out, because Robert then said, 'I have never asked questions. Not after you told me about him and his nefarious predilections.'

She noted that he didn't use the word 'nefarious' jokingly. How she wished that she had been able to lie back then.

As it turned out, he hadn't deserved the deeper truths of her life.

'I appreciated that.' She granted him his virtue in not having brought it up before.

For all his paraded worldliness, she suspected that he'd never asked about her time with Ambrose because it was so incomprehensibly and sickeningly alien to him.

He then surprised her. Struggling towards a smile, he said,

'I think I will leave it at that. I've done enough dabbling in your past. I believe in our marriage, you know. Regardless of my going to distant parts. I still see us as a married couple.'

She'd hoped that he would have avoided saying things like that. It required her to affirm and, as yet, she did not know what it was, exactly, she wanted to affirm. She supposed that she saw it now as a partly relinquished marriage.

He seemed to have given it some thought. And regardless of the *scandale Jerome* and now the Ghost of Ambrose Past, he was persevering with some idea of a married life. Perhaps as his departure drew near, he had started fearing the separation.

She ducked giving the affirmation he seemed to want and instead said, 'I take it you don't wish to discuss the visit of the "nefarious Ambrose"?'

He shuffled a little and said, in his man-of-the-world voice, 'I'd be happy to say hello.'

She said she thought that would be fine. 'Jeanne was thinking of us all going on a picnic.'

'Ambrose?'

'A bunch of us.'

'That might be going too far. Hate picnics. Count me out.'

She was glad he didn't want to join it. Good.

They then went back to reading their newspapers there in the café.

Or to the appearance of reading. She continued with her thoughts of Ambrose and suspected that Robert continued with his thoughts, also of Ambrose.

Back in the old days, Ambrose had, at times, felt challenged by Robert's manliness and Robert and he had engaged with each other occasionally in a bantering bellicose café manner. Robert had hated what he described as Ambrose's pose of 'drawling detachment'. Robert, on the other hand, had conceded that Ambrose was a good administrator with important Foreign Office connections.

This had been before her pre-marriage revelation of the precise nature of her affair with Ambrose and its perverseness.

In her recent letters to Ambrose, she had, in the end, spoken only of the 'ups-and-downs' of married life and left it at that. It seemed to her that Ambrose had to accept that she and Robert were a married couple, regardless of what had happened within that marriage, and regardless of its state of disrepair.

She tried then to stop herself laughing at the ordinariness of their appearance there in the café, as a man and wife, sitting reading their newspapers, munching their toast and marmalade, in the only English breakfast café in Geneva, which Robert now asserted as his preference.

How bizarre it was that they pretended to be doing the normal things when they were feeling so far from normal.

She couldn't decide if these were the last dying days of a marriage or an interregnum or a new marriage arrangement. She was tired of it all. For now, apathy would have to do all the work.

She would not try anymore.

She would place herself in the hands of apathy.

Ambrose arrived two days after the opening of the Disarmament Conference.

Robert joined her in meeting him at the railway.

Ambrose came off the train and she realised that she'd forgotten how dashing and good looking he was now in his mid-forties. How slim. He was slimmer than she.

She sighed as they hugged. Ah, those strange, lost, wicked days.

'You haven't changed,' Ambrose said, stepping back. 'Either of you.'

He shook Robert's hand with energetic friendliness, 'No, I lie,' he said, looking at them through hooded eyes. 'You have both changed into a seriously happy married couple.'

She and Robert laughed together merrily like a seriously happy married couple, and for a second she felt seriously and happily married.

'I despise you both,' he said, laughing.

Robert and she laughed again as a couple, and she heard Robert say, 'We get along—more like cats and dogs than a house on fire.'

'Oh, much better to be cats and dogs than a house on fire,' Ambrose said.

She wondered if that was now how Robert wished to see them 'as a happily married couple who fought like cats and dogs'.

Ambrose hugged her again. 'I missed the beginning of the conference. Heard it on the wireless, nonetheless.' Ambrose was using his diplomat's voice.

Robert did not offer to carry Ambrose's bags.

Talking like a newspaper reporter, Robert described the opening of the Disarmament Conference to Ambrose, probably for want of something to say, to cover the need for conversation now that he was face to face with Ambrose.

Ambrose said he heard the church bells of Geneva ringing away via the wireless. 'Heard Arthur Henderson ask the assembled world, "Have we all genuinely renounced war as an instrument of national policy?"'

'Did you hear any reply to the question?' Robert said, laughing to keep the situation jolly.

'The whole world was, as you know, tuned to it on their wireless or waiting to hear that the world was disarmed,' Ambrose said. 'I suppose they were waiting to hear the clatter of guns being dumped in a heap.'

'They'll wait a long time,' Robert said.

'Quite surprising to get sixty-one countries together—including the US and the Soviets. Pretty much everyone who matters.'

'Sweetser takes it as an omen that President Hoover will soon join the League,' she said, keeping up the laughter.

'Dear Arthur has been predicting that the US would join the League now for twelve years. How is the old dear?'

She told him about Arthur wanting to go back to get his hat during the Manchurian crisis.

'As you must've heard, the whole disarmament show was an hour late starting because the Council was hearing about the Japanese invasion of China,' Robert said. 'A war gets underway as disarmament begins. Truly, there is a Laughing God.'

'Are you backing ratios?' Ambrose asked, still using his serious, diplomatic, man-to-man voice to Robert.

She observed that she was listening to Robert as if he had also just arrived on the train. As something of a stranger.

'If I'm backing anything.'

'It's probably the only way to go, that's what my pals at the FO think,' Ambrose confided. 'Lock together the big powers—Britain:Japan:US:France:Germany:Russia—to set ratios for their armies, navies, airforces, and their munitions production. And then over the years you reduce the ratios.'

'As long as there are no cheats. Don't see how you can catch the cheats,' Robert said.

'There is the incentive that reducing armaments saves each country money,' she put in.

'I'd keep Germany totally disarmed,' Ambrose said.

'Lost cause. They've secretly armed. Even under Stresemann they were getting their guns together. Which is why the Disarmament Conference will not work. As long as people can rearm secretly, how can it?'

The two men were fixed on each other, like two circling dogs.

Edith mentioned the idea of international inspection teams freely travelling in all countries.

'How will they know where to look?' Robert said, dismissively.

'I would biff them back into a state of disarmament,' said Ambrose.

Robert laughed in agreement.

She said that the inspection teams would have to be more cunning than those who tried to hide weapons.

'And what if they were bribed to look away?' Robert said.

She said that, as with eradicating all corruption, you had to make it more worthwhile not to be corrupt.

Ambrose chose to stay out of this argument.

The three of them walked silently to the car.

It was a long time since she'd heard Ambrose's real-man voice. Perhaps he had changed back into being a man 100 percent. If it were true, it would perhaps be for the best in this stern world.

She felt Robert had been very civil.

She fell then into deceit.

They dropped Ambrose at the Hôtel Richemond and she and Robert went on to their respective work places.

As soon as she was back at her office desk, she called Ambrose at his hotel and said that she would like to come around to the hotel immediately.

'Come,' he said, and it was not his diplomat voice, nor his man-to-woman voice, nor his voice for dealing with the everyday world. It was his Other Voice.

And her voice to him was not that of a proper wife. Or any wife.

In Ambrose's rooms at the Richemond, they held each other in a long embrace, melting from being an embrace of the upper body to an embrace of their entire bodies.

She stood there in his arms tearful with the relief of it and she felt his body responding to their physical cleaving.

She moved away and sat on a chair, her breathing broken.

He looked across at her, speaking with his eyes, a deep

craving look she knew from the old days, and one which expressed bodily longing for her and for the consolations of their former love.

She shook her head gently, slightly, but unambiguously.

She dried her eyes.

She rose, went to him and kissed his forehead. 'I must go now,' she lied, 'I just wanted to say a proper hello. I'm a married woman, dear, and cannot stay long—if at all—in a gentleman's room. I came so that we could hug properly, that's all.'

How false she sounded.

'Of course,' he said, rising quickly and resuming his friend-like voice, a voice of courteous understanding about the nuance of things, 'Of course, dear Edith. Fully understood.'

'May we expect you for dinner tomorrow, as arranged?'

He looked at her. 'May I be excused?'

She looked at his eyes and saw a miserableness, the miserableness which came from the unmeasurable distance between them now that she was a wife. As she continued her pose as a wife.

It wasn't just the pose of a wife. It was a fear within her about the whole nature of her former intimacy with Ambrose, the nagging question of what it meant about her if she desired a man such as Ambrose?

And she did, did desire him.

Dreadfully.

She was using the shell of her marriage to hold him off but sooner or later he must realise that her marriage had become a broken thing. What would restrain them then?

'Are you sure you won't come to dinner?'

'I am sure.'

'Then, dear Ambrose, you are excused. And understood.'

She was relieved. It would not have worked.

She looked at him. 'Remember, I love you in a very special way.'

'And I you, dear Edith,' he said. 'I would find the dinner party too full of jumping beans, demons, and sharp corners. I do not think I would survive.'

'I understand.'

Why was she talking of loving in special ways as if to classify it all, to put it off there in a file, and then back into the filing cabinet?

'When do you return to London?'

'Friday. I think the draft convention will have been adopted by then. It will all be over. Just a matter of tedious detail after that.'

'It's rather breathtaking, isn't it? That we should've lived to see the world disarm? And to have been part of making it happen?'

He nodded. 'And there's something else.' He was nervous.

'Yes? What?'

'While here, I'm charged with looking for accommodation for our Geneva offices. There's a possibility that I might be returning to Geneva—for the longer term. More international organisations have opened up their offices here. Geneva as the Headquarters of the World, sort of thing. The Federation feels that it should be here to help.'

His coming to live there permanently was not in her scheme of things.

Ambrose being around. Ambrose being around while Robert was not. That was not how she had seen it.

'When will all this happen?'

'Oh soon. Immediately perhaps. Would my being around worry you to death?'

'Of course not.'

'Would you welcome my presence? My return to the old crowd—the fast set—forgiven and feted.'

'And very fast?' She managed to make a joke but found that she did not have a ready inner response to the question of his returning.

'Oh yes, I am much faster now.'

Her heart was still preparing its answer. His living in Geneva would give her another quandary in an already quandary-filled life.

The contemplation of it was seductive and portentous.

He was not the man of her dreams but he was the man of her present *hankerings*, or the man who enlivened her shadowy side, a man who gave her inadequacies some sort of strange *competency*. Oh yes, he gave to her psyche a coherence, he infused its timid darkness and disarray with an irreverent confidence.

Her sense of courtesy answered. 'Congratulations, Ambrose. That'd indeed be fine. It'll be like the old days,' she said, and added, ambiguously, in this day of ambiguity, 'but you must be prepared to find so much changed. The League is huge now. I've changed: we've all changed. We are all so much older.' And she said with a false lightness, 'And you, yourself, you have changed, I'm sure.'

He considered his answer. 'Much. I am older but Wilde-r— as in Oscar Wilde-r. Without the wit.'

She laughed. 'And here I am—a dull married woman.'

Why did she say that?

'You should stop saying that you're a married woman, Edith. I'm well aware that you are a married woman.'

If he were so sensible of her married status, how then did he justify his suggestiveness of touch and embrace just minutes earlier?

How did she?

Their friendship was having difficulty finding its feet. If it had any feet.

'It's much in my mind. Being married. It has changed so much for me,' she said soberly with a dishonest emphasis meant for him.

'Edith—you aren't happy.'

She bridled at his presumption. Even coming from a special other person such as Ambrose. Of all the presumptions, presumption about one's unhappiness was the most unacceptable. It carried in it an assessment by the person of one's very success at living.

She did not show her displeasure, but simply shrugged.

He said softly, 'Your letter, your letter about Edwina Mountbatten. It was a *cri du coeur.*'

She tried to smile gaily, 'Oh come, Ambrose—it was a letter seeking gossip.'

'If you wish.'

'I do wish.'

'I apologise for my presumption,' he said.

This was no good. No good. No good.

She detested the duplicity. Ambrose and she must not make a false start.

She had to come clean. 'You're right. It was not a letter seeking gossip. It was a letter seeking . . . just seeking.'

He reached over and took her hands. He waited for her to go on.

She looked at him helplessly. 'Not very happy, no.'

'Is marriage supposed to be happy? I thought it was supposed to be, at best, comfortable. Give and take. Something like that. So I read.'

'It's supposed to be happy. That was what I was led to believe.'

'Maybe marriage is different now. Modernity.'

'Suppose so.'

'Enough of that. So dreary. And I am hardly an expert.'

It was far from being enough *of that.* She tried not to cry. Get the rest out of the way. 'And you? Are you all cured now?'

'Cured? Did I say I had been ill?'

'Have you been ill?'

'Nothing to talk about. I don't remember saying anything in my letters about being ill. Perhaps the odd cold. Rather good health, really.'

'I meant something else.'

'I know that you meant something else. Cured of being a spy?' He was joking with her.

'That might be somewhere to start. But what's the point? You would never tell the truth. Spies aren't expected to tell the truth.'

'I was a very poor spy. Very lazy. Too half-hearted. Really couldn't be counted as a spy. Just talking to old friends at the FO. That's how I saw it.'

She looked at him tenderly, full of yearning for his arms, his soft body, his breasts.

And what about his predilections?

It was not the time to speak of that.

She rose to leave.

She rose—and went to him. He rose from his chair. Resting her head on his chest, she lifted her face. 'What are we to do with you?'

They kissed deeply.

She then took off his tie and unbuttoned his shirt, wondering what she would find beneath.

And what her heart would do about it.

She pulled his braces off his shoulders and then took off the shirt, and allowed the trousers to fall to his ankles.

He stepped out of them. He wore a grey silk vest and grey silk undershorts.

Maybe he was, in fact, cured of his old predilections.

He sat down and removed his shoes and socks and garters.

She was relieved that he was, today, simply *male*. To do what she was now doing was enough of a demand on her very self, without the other.

She deliberately took off her skirt and blouse, leaving on her chemise, brassiere, and silk underpants, and together in their underwear they moved to lie on the bed where they kissed and their bodies embraced.

She could not restrain her craving, and pushed up his silk

vest, her mouth finding his nipples on his hairless chest.

His hands cradled her and she suckled, and began to rock in his arms. She found herself calming into a deep peace.

After a time, a blissful eternity, on his breast, she let go of his nipples, and looking up at him, said, 'Enter me,' and putting her hand on him she felt him grow larger. She guided him fully into her, holding aside her underpants and, to her absolute surprise, she reached the height of her pleasure almost immediately, and tears came to her eyes at the rarity of that in her life in recent times. She wiped them away with her hand, smiling at him, her tears like light rain on a sunny day.

He kissed her tears, as she tried to recover her breath. 'Oh my, oh my,' she said.

She then took his testicles tightly in her hand and coaxed his fluids with words, making him release them, allowing them to flow freely into her. She rose to his coming a second time.

It was strange that his infertility granted to them this freedom, the freedom for her to allow his fluids to flow into her without consequence or hindrance. She was glad that again she could have all this without any of the impediments of birth control.

As if her body had appreciated that she was again open.

They had champagne sent to the room. She hid in the bathroom while it was delivered.

And there in the bathroom, having reluctantly and gently wiped herself, she accepted that she had *committed adultery*. She held the stained towel to her face and breathed it in with a strange exhilaration as if it were air from another planet. Which perhaps it was. She then washed herself in the bidet, sad to feel the exquisite fluids leaving her body.

But that was that.

No washing would change it. She'd broken the contract of marriage. She'd failed to keep her end of the bargain. And it was no use her saying to herself or to the Court of Life that because it was with Ambrose, it did not count. He had entered her. He had flowed into her. That was that.

She was an *adulteress*.

She was starkly aware of this but not devastated. She did not know what it meant. She wished she had felt strongly enough about Robert to have kept the pledge. She had not. She had fallen from that grace.

That was the test of it all, the test of her pledging—as a Rationalist she did not care a hoot about religious vows—the test she'd failed, as a Rationalist and as a woman, was her pledging as a woman to a man. The pledge to commit 'to the exclusion of all others'. She had let it happen. Invited it to happen.

She did not feel guilt but, inescapably, she felt she had changed her life and her view of herself and she knew not whether it was for good or ill.

She was now something other than simply a married woman.

She looked briefly at herself in the mirror, mainly at her make-up.

And then, in her very much alive adulterous skin, she went back out, knowing that she was again going to join Ambrose's body.

There in each other's arms, afternoon drifted to twilight.

At some time, they removed their underwear, and Ambrose brought his small, firm, but not fully rigid penis against her, the unpenetrating penis which she loved, not completely entering her, but pleasuring her deliriously with a keen *frottage*, and they found again their twilight pleasure, belonging neither to woman nor to man, something else. Together they unlocked hidden pleasures.

During the ensuing hours, they talked of all things intimate and trivial and supreme.

At some point, she wept for her marriage.

She was not pleased with herself as a person of integrity but she was pleased with herself as a person who had regained something precious to her life, something she had almost lost, had believed lost, and, worse, had believed to be something which had no further place in her life.

They talked of the affairs of nations.

She even outlined her intentions for the winter disarmament picnic.

Ambrose said protectively, 'Don't do it, Edith. Have your picnic, but don't try to talk with them about their nature and their policies. Don't do it. They aren't listeners. People who are fanatical have lost the art of being listeners.'

She looked into his eyes, tracing his face with her fingers. 'I want to try to give them back that art. I do not believe, will never believe, that people do not hear *reason*—and while they do not change at that moment, they will one day, maybe years later, consider that reason if it had been true and genuinely put.'

Staring up at the high ceiling of the hotel room, with its grandeur, promiscuously shared by many anonymous lovers over decades, she quoted Pearson: ' "Hidden beneath diplomacy, trade, adventure, there is a struggle raging among modern nations which is none the less real if it does not take the form of warfare." Making the peace has to be more hard-knuckled than pacifism.'

'Who will pay?' asked Ambrose. 'Will Sir Eric cough up?'

'I will pay,' Edith said.

'Must pay my respects to Sir E. He drops me a note now and then. Rather good of him.'

'I will use my own money. Grimly enough, the war in the East has sent some shares up, despite the Depression. Rubber is especially good.' She had her main investment in rubber— Firestone stock. 'Remember, it comes from my mother's inheritance? I had always earmarked its earnings for this sort of thing. Allows me to be responsibly rich.'

'And what makes you think they'll listen?'

'That is my secret stratagem.'

'What is your secret stratagem?'

'It will be my picnic: they will be my guests: they have to listen.'

<hr>

She did not go to Marseilles to see Robert off on his ship. She said goodbye at the railway station in Geneva.

He had become renewed by the idea of travelling again and, it seemed to her, also by the idea of war. He showed no sign of wavering at his decision.

She had a stirring of hurt about his lack of regret or second thoughts and at the same time felt relieved that he had not changed his mind at the last moment. She scolded herself for expecting to be paid the ordinary emotions while grasping at the personal freedoms which came to her from his going away.

He had on his old greatcoat from the War, his Army Warm.

He travelled light, as if wishing to gain speed from the absence of luggage. He carried his new portable typewriter which she had bought for him as a going-away present and on the case she'd had his surname painted in small script. He had been thrilled. Even if she said so herself, it was a terribly fine gift.

He was cheery and she was lightly affectionate. She did not cry although some conventionally shallow part of her wanted to. To cry would have been a lie. It would have also given something to Robert which she did not feel he deserved.

She still could not determine whether she was letting him go from her life or whether she still needed to half-believe that he was still her husband who had simply gone to the war. There was something of a comfort in thinking that way. If she could believe that way.

A husband away at the war.

As the train pulled out she pondered the arrival of Ambrose and Robert's leaving and the symmetry it had brought to her life. Why was symmetry appealing, even endorsing? Was it because it suggested, however ridiculously, a deeper order to life?

Despite what had happened at the Richemond with Ambrose, she was still holding to her ambiguous situation as wife.

Maybe ambiguity suited her. Suited her just fine.

Ambrose himself was, if not ambiguous, then a personality of ill-connected parts. And had no claims and could never make claims on her.

And, ye gods, if all this suited her just fine, *what then was happening to her?*

In the landau, with a hired groom at the reins, they clip-clopped—or as Ambrose, in very high spirits, said, 'titupped', savouring the word, and repeating it, claiming it to be the more precise word—along the snowy lanes of Geneva, through the white fields now empty of cows.

With rugs over their knees, they sipped from Ambrose's silver travelling cups filled from his and her pocket flasks of cognac, holding the cups in their gloved hands. The picnic baskets tied on to the back, everyone chattering, singing.

The weather was sunny and they had both the back and front hoods down.

She had ended up with two picnics—her large special Disarmament Picnic still to happen and, taking up Jeanne's proposal, this small picnic.

What had been intended as the farewell picnic for Robert had, instead, become a welcome to Ambrose.

She had left it to Robert's journalist mates to organise his public farewells.

She'd invited Bernard Follett, proprietor of the Molly Club and a former friend of Ambrose's and someone from the old days. She was glad to see him again and to welcome him back into her life, wondering though, as she did, about the mixing of her categories of friends—League and Molly Club. This had never happened back then but the 1930s were a new world.

Edith hadn't see Follett during the couple of years after Ambrose had left the League. She had mixed feelings about him. Follett shared Ambrose's predilection and she suspected he'd been once a lover of Ambrose's. Despite his *louche* club Follett had always seemed to be well connected both diplomatically and in Geneva's closed social circles.

Today, as ever, he was charming.

Ambrose had wanted to make contact again with his old friend. It was perhaps evidence that the predilection remained and if Ambrose was to be back in Geneva the Molly Club would be part of his life. Her life?

From the League circle, Jeanne was there and so was Victoria, a remarkably efficient New Zealander from Registry. Jeanne was supposed to have brought one of her beaus but as sometimes happened with Jeanne, he failed to appear. Victoria was her determinedly hearty self, never having managed a steady beau and forever bemoaning her single life. Trying hard to be someone helping to make a good time while not herself sure whether she was having a good time. She brought along a generous donation of home-baked cakes.

And how were Ambrose and she presenting themselves at this picnic? A couple again united as the husband conveniently disappeared? And were those at the picnic celebrating this? Tacitly marrying them in some informal way?

Ambrose and she worked well as a socialising couple and fell back into their comfortable, companionable style. There was much smiling and touching between them as they titupped through the snow.

'Miss Coventry both drove a four-in-hand and smoked tobacco,' Ambrose said. 'And that was eighty years ago.'

'Who was Miss Coventry?'

'A character in a forgotten novel,' Ambrose said. 'I now read only forgotten novels. I have made myself the caretaker of forgotten novels. My job is to remember the passingly good forgotten novels.'

As they rode on, Jeanne said, 'Tell us all about the latest plans for your Disarmament Picnic for a Thousand, Edith.'

'Not a thousand,' Edith said. 'I want to have a gathering for the non-diplomats who've come to Geneva for the conference, with their petitions and pleas for total disarmament.'

'Edith wishes to mould them into her secret diplomatic corps,' Jeanne said conspiratorially to the others.

'Picnics must either be simple—one dish, one gateau, one wine, one cheese, one fruit—or very complicated,' Victoria said seriously.

'Which is the New Zealand way?' Jeanne asked her.

'Oh, we always have the most complicated picnics and every picnic I've organised in my life has given me a headache,' she said. 'I usually have to retire to the car with a cold cloth on my forehead.'

They all laughed. It sounded achingly true of Victoria.

Everyone's reaction to the disarmament picnic had been pretty much the same—razzing. They teased her mercilessly.

'What's your secret diplomacy?' asked Follett, but he alone did not indulge in the playful derision. He seemed genuinely curious.

'I want to introduce that pacifist crowd to champagne,' she said laughing, trying to lighten things up. 'They're so prudish. They're out to stop more than just war. They have a whole list of things to stop.'

'They seem to wish to stop every single one of my vices. Including some I will not list,' Follet said.

She did not want to talk about the picnic but she had to

say something. 'As you all know, the Disarmament Conference simply plans to reduce the armed forces of all countries to a level compatible with national safety. The pacifists and their lot want all armaments to go. And they want them to go now, *immédiatement*. Actually, I just want them to accept the idea of permanent and unpredictable danger.'

'Advanced weapons are the answer—not the threat,' Follett said, 'Old weapons are dangerous. Last month the Bedouins managed to kill two thousand people by wielding knives.'

Jeanne sprang into the argument. 'New weapons make new problems. The Bedouins could kill two thousand but that was probably all they could kill.'

'Until they'd had their dates and wine at the oasis and could begin again,' said Ambrose.

'Bombs are only another form of artillery,' Follett said. 'The projectile is carried and dropped instead of being propelled by a gun. And the artillery shell is only a new form of a rock thrown by a savage. Or by David's slingshot at Goliath. Both can kill. You can't ban rocks.'

'It seems to me,' said Victoria, reaching for the cognac flask, 'that it's an entirely different thing, dropping a bomb on someone's head from a great height.'

Follett continued his argument in favour of the new weapons. 'My point is this, the aircraft and the bomber can bring about a preclusion of war. Take the North West Frontier. Drop a bomb on warring villages and you stop them dead in their tracks.'

Edith felt delightfully woozy from the cognac, rolling along there in the crisp chill of the snowy landscape. Woozy or not, she couldn't help but note that the genial nightclub proprietor Follett had strong ideas—this man who'd created a club where the outside political world seemingly did not exist. His club was a place where the world and its dangerous madness had no place, yet where everything that was amusingly bizarre and darkly pleasurable had a place and a home. She remembered it as a club which banished the pain of existence for a night—a long night.

In fact, she had rarely if ever seen him in daylight or in a situation such as today, outside the Molly Club.

And they were more than ideas that he seemed to have— he had *information*.

She would keep an eye on this other Mr Follett.

'Dead in their tracks is correct,' Jeanne said.

'That's why we have to study how to improve weapons. It may give us the dream of the short war, at least.'

'Happier if we are the ones with the bigger bombs,' said Victoria.

'Of course,' said Follett.

'You should tell the pacifists that,' Ambrose said. 'Tell them that peace lies in the very opposite to their position.'

There in the landau, they all chortled.

'I wouldn't go as far as defending bombing,' Edith said, laughing, trying to keep it all light. 'But I do think that the pacifists have to see that abolition of all aircraft isn't possible.'

'It is possible!' Jeanne exclaimed passionately.

'Jeanne, you can't stop history and put it back to where it once was,' Victoria said. 'At least, I don't think you can,' she said, as ever immediately reconsidering her position.

Jeanne attacked Victoria gleefully. 'You *can* put the clock back. Mr Winston Churchill said that because of our military misuse of air travel, humanity had proved unworthy of the gift of air travel. He said it should be taken back from us.'

'Jeanne,' Follett said patiently, 'if something is invented it cannot be uninvented.'

'I have never seen the force of that argument,' Jeanne said blithely. 'We invented slavery and then abolished it. We invented the rack and now we don't use it.'

'There may be other examples in history,' said Victoria. 'I would have to research that.'

'The beauty of the abolition of all aircraft would be that

you would know immediately if someone had breached the treaty,' said Jeanne. 'The plane would be spotted and reported to the League. Every pair of eyes would be a keeper of the peace.'

The others laughed.

Victoria said, 'I would love to fly one myself. May become something of a pilot. I would be good at the controls, I suspect.'

'And I, dear Victoria, would be rather bad at the controls, I suspect,' said Ambrose.

Victoria had been quick to forgive Ambrose during the time of his disgrace in the Secretariat. 'Oh Ambrose, dear, I could teach you the controls.'

'I fear not, Vicki, I fear not. But if ever I were to learn control it would be to you that I would come.'

'Perhaps it is I who needs to come to you—for lessons in getting out of control,' Victoria said.

'The world was a very good place before aeroplanes came,' Jeanne said, 'and we made our life well enough without them.'

Follett was playful in the delivery of his ideas, but Edith felt he probably believed in this use of bombing. She suspected she might too. 'Who said that once nations had the weapons to annihilate each other in a second, war would cease?'

'Alfred Nobel—having invented dynamite, he had a vested interest,' Follett said.

'I suppose the aeroplane is a weapon of retaliation and of aggression,' Edith said.

'Which shows that the whole effort to separate defensive weapons and aggressive weapons and weapons of retaliation is rather slippery,' Ambrose said.

'Perhaps we should abolish military aircraft,' Edith said.

'That is not enough,' said Jeanne. 'I'm told that a civilian aeroplane can become a bomber simply by putting on a bomb rack and installing a bomb sight. To abolish bombs you must abolish all aeroplanes. All of them.'

'Oscar Wilde said that soon war would simply be one chemist approaching another chemist at the border, each carrying a deadly phial,' Ambrose said, in a voice which implied that he'd had enough of the disarmament arguments.

Edith herself had nothing more to say.

She leaned back with her flask in her hand. She drank deeply from it directly, rather than using her cup. It was *infra dig*, but what the hell. She let the disarmament questions play on around her like a tennis match. The flask was always a comfort, both the contents and the silver flask, embodying her memories of Jerome, the black musician in the Paris club years before, when she had behaved so scandalously. *Jerome's sweaty, sultry smell and smile rolling over to her, lapping her face. The sultry smell she knew was typical of the Negro. His fingernails were manicured. She felt entranced by their white moons. His lap, his groin.* Away in her distant consciousness she heard the other four go on with their interminable discussions of weaponry down ever steeper spirals of befuddling detail. Funny that it had been Jerome who had finally come between Robert and her ... *she was back there in the hot nightclub in Paris. Jerome had taken the flask and drunk from it, and passed it to her, she drank, the spirit in it tasting like milk. She handed it back to him and with it the offer of her hand, which he took and gracefully drew her to him, onto his knee. Time and movement then became slippery, as she gracefully slid, and without thinking too much at all about things, it seemed his warm dark hands were on her exposed and very alive breasts, which she had opened to him, it all seemed to happen in flowing, preordained movements, something like a waltz, except that they were not moving from where they were, she sliding from his lap, and then without any guidance at all and in no time at all, and with no impediment, with no thought at all, she'd slid between his legs, and it was all so warm, fleshly and flowing, it was*

*finishing, and she took her lips, tongue, and gentle teeth away,
and opened her eyes ...*

Follett's voice came through to her, 'What will you tell
them, Edith, at your Grand Winter Picnic?'

'What will I tell them?'

'You will make a speech?'

She rallied herself from her reverie. 'When they talk about
removing the causes of war, I will tell them that some wars
are about nothing at all.'

'Very good.' Follett seemed amused.

'Oh, I don't believe there is such a thing as a human conflict without a cause,' Victoria said. 'I've never read a theory
about that.'

'I thought you Rationalists believe there was a cause for
everything. Everything could be analysed,' Ambrose joshed.

'Montaigne said that any theory of human conduct
which did not take into account the irrationality of humans
was flawed,' she said. Something which came from family
discussions long ago. 'Maybe nothing has a cause,' Edith's
mind was drifting to nihilistic exhaustion. 'I will tell them
that there are not only just wars there are also inescapable
wars.'

'You won't be popular,' Follett said. 'They won't give you
a prize, I'm afraid.'

'Oh, I will say that war just, causeless, and even inescapable
is all finished. We can stop war in its tracks now with sanctions. They'll be happy with that.'

'They will all fall for the Soviet position of total abolition
of all arms except rifles,' said Ambrose, 'The lion looks sideways at the eagle and says wings must be abolished—'

'Oh, Ambrose,' Edith laughed, 'spare us that hoary fable.'

The others tried to shout Ambrose down.

He went on with it as if gripped in the trance of the story,
as if he couldn't stop himself. He knew they'd all heard it a
hundred times.

'—the eagle looks at the bull and declares horns must be abolished. The bull looks at the tiger and says claws must be abolished—'

'Ambrose! Stop!' They all put their fingers in their ears.

He went on, 'The Russian bear in his turn says all claws, wings and horns must be abolished. All that is necessary, says the Russian bear, is a universal embrace of fraternity. Come to me.'

'Like so.' He grabbed Jeanne in a playful hug.

'I knew you'd all heard that story. Do you know why I repeated myself?'

No one asked him why.

'For the enjoyment of *telling a story* as much as for *pleasing an audience*. And go on, admit it, there are some stories we tell *because we've all heard them a hundred times*. And that is one of them.'

They booed him.

They reached the chalet at Thoiry where they were stopping briefly and they all dismounted from the coach. Stamping their feet, running about in the snow with scarves flying and, inevitably, throwing snowballs at each other, there in the fine shining blue Swiss day.

Edith slipped, tottered and then fell backwards into the snow. She found she couldn't get up.

They all laughed at her.

'Help me up, someone.'

They laughed at her and didn't come to her rescue. She tried again to rise but she couldn't quite make it.

'Ambrose, help me. *Aide-moi.*'

Ambrose came over to help her. 'Edith, I think you're a little tipsy,' he said, as he helped her to her feet.

She realised that she was indeed a little tipsy and so soon in the day, but she laughingly blamed it on a patch of ice.

And, in all truth, her life in recent times had suffered One Very Great Upheaval. Let that be said.

Two Very Great Upheavals, if Ambrose's arrival were included.

And she knew that some of them there today, Ambrose and Jeanne, at least, knew it.

And let it also be said that she had not had a sober night since Robert had rolled away in the train to Shanghai.

She brushed the snow from her and took a deep breath, still holding on to Ambrose as they all went in.

On the trip home, she slept the uneasy and gritty sleep of inebriation.

Winter Picnic

E dith had had to book the American Library in Geneva for her indoors picnic because all other public halls were taken most nights and days for talks and lectures and meetings—even though the city of Geneva had built two new hotels and a special conference hall to house the Disarmament Conference delegates and others.

Geneva had been swamped by three thousand delegates, lobbyists, journalists, observers and others—including the armaments lobby, in panic and disarray.

Her picnic was set to begin at lunchtime on the seventh day of the conference, the day when public organisations from around the world were to have a morning to present their petitions to a conference plenary session.

The organisations had been given the time to speak as ordinary people to the diplomats and statesmen at the conference. She'd hoped to have had the picnic the day before this but that couldn't be arranged. She had to take what she could get as far as accommodation and timing went.

Edith briefed Tony, chef from the Perle du Lac, to carry on in her absence so that she could join the petition procession through Geneva in the morning. The city had fixed prices for meals and accommodation for the duration of the conference so that there would be no overcharging, and she wondered if Chef Tony would obey that in his calculations when charging her for the cost of the picnic food.

She made her way to the Old Town for the start of the procession wearing the green sash and white armband emblazoned with the word Pax which the International Women for Permanent Peace were handing out.

Officially, she was there on League business along with McGeachy, the League officer responsible for the non-government groups, but given that it was a League conference and that disarmament was part of the mission of the League, Edith felt she could wear the garb of the International Women for Permanent Peace without compromising her official position.

If someone complained that she'd identified herself on such an occasion with an organisation outside the League, it was hardly a hanging offence.

The sash and armband had, anyhow, almost become the official insignia for the conference.

At the procession startpoint, hundreds of women and quite a few men were gathered and most of them carried their 'Christmas presents' to the world—their petitions calling for disarmament.

Even the journalists accepted the estimate that the petitions contained more than eight million signatures.

As Edith arrived at the procession, she spotted Viscount Cecil from the League of Nations Associations, there in his long overcoat talking with Ambrose and Fred Pickering.

She went over and said hello. They were joined by Leon Jouhaux, who said he was there as a delegate for the fourteen million French trades unionists.

The Belgian delegate, Emile Vandervelde, the great internationalist and statesman, went by carrying a placard which said, 'We do not ask—we demand.'

'I wonder if that is an all-purpose slogan which he can carry in any procession for a good cause?' she said.

They laughed.

She left them to get on with her supervision. She said hello to the feminist Mary Dingman, the American who had told her that she represented forty-five million American women from many organisations.

Edith silently doubted the figure.

She chatted with a young man—an American student, James Green—who said he was not presenting a petition but an ultimatum from the students of America. His placard said simply, 'Disarm or else.' She wished him well.

As she moved along the procession, talking with the march officials, Edith came across the crippled and blind War veterans. Hundreds and hundreds of them.

They were trying to assemble in military-style ranks, shuffling on their crutches, the blind guided by friends. The marshals were even moving those in wheelchairs into lines as their leader called out military orders.

Some of their faces were virtually erased by injury. All seemed to have missing arms and legs. Noses and ears were missing, jaws were missing.

It was ghastly.

She was stopped in her tracks.

She turned back and got herself under control and then turned around again to face them but even then she kept looking away, both from a sense of propriety and distress, and then her eyes would be drawn back.

She'd not seen men with faces such as these.

An official told her that they were gathered there from most European organisations of former servicemen from the War, including Germans.

He used the French word for these millions of men who were mutilated by war—the *mutilés*.

They had, less than fifteen years ago, as virile young men,

fought against each other; now they tried to hug or touch as best they could and yet still be soldier-like.

She choked with tears and at the same time tried to close the tears off, causing a cramp in her face, trying to retain the composure expected of her.

She couldn't and she turned away yet again and went off into an alley to hide herself. She was wrestling to contain the tears, her face was spasming. She feared letting herself cry. She might never stop, she would be engulfed.

She stood there in the alley, fighting to control her emotions and her breathing. After she had calmed herself, she went back to the swelling crowd of mutilated soldiers and found that the journalists and photographers were now there paying attention to the *mutilés*.

From habit, she looked for Robert and then remembered he'd gone.

As she watched the newspaper men, she realised then that she was seeing something rather strange. Some of the photographers and the most hardened of newspaper men had begun to cry—even Norman Hillson was crying. So was Edgar Mowrer from the *Chicago Daily News*, one of Robert's mates.

She'd never seen press people cry.

The newspaper men were turning away with handkerchiefs at their faces.

A photographer had put down his camera and was openly bawling as they all watched the struggling attempts by the *mutilés* to be soldier-like and to form proud ranks with military bearing, trying to carry out the drills they'd learned as young men.

Some wore their old uniforms, some had pieces of uniform, some had only military hats, and many had ribbons and medals.

She saw then that many of the glasses they were wearing were mended in an amateurish way with wire or sticking plaster, that crutches badly needed repair, that artificial limbs were themselves sometimes broken. These would have been issued after the War and had obviously deteriorated over the passing years. It was heartrending.

Seeing the newspaper people crying brought her to tears again.

'They make their point,' Hillson said, his voice struggling to find control through gruffness, and then he gave in and wiped tears from his eyes.

'Journalists and nurses shouldn't cry,' he said.

'Or League Officials,' she said, allowing her tears to flow.

'Good luck with your picnic,' Hillson said, his voice changed by the emotions he was trying to suppress. 'I'll give it a mention.' There was a huskiness to his voice, a voice that sounded like that of a young boy.

She thanked him softly.

'Heard from Robert? Too soon, I suppose,' he said, turning away from the *mutilés*.

She shook her head.

'I heard from Potato—he's already there. Seemed to expect Robert any day.'

She told the two journalists that the Swiss telegraph service couldn't cope with the telegrams of good wishes coming to the Disarmament Conference from town councils, mothers' groups, scout troops, and all sorts of other citizen groups from around the world.

'The whole telegraphic system has been swamped for the first time in its history,' she said. 'We can't get cables out from the League—we're using our wireless station instead.'

Unable to take it anymore, she left the journalists and the *mutilés*, and joined the women's group further up in the procession.

The procession filed through Geneva, the women in their green sashes and white armbands, the trades unionists, Rotary, chambers of commerce, the school children, the scouts and guides, the mutilated soldiers, in its own dignified pace along the Geneva streets. Swiss men stopped and held their hats at their breast, women cried into handkerchiefs, some people waved, some men saluted, assistants from the stores came out to watch in their aprons, some people threw flowers.

The procession was slow and solemn, almost funereal.

There was no music.

The procession arrived at the Bâtiment Electoral, the most imposing of the halls in Geneva, where like some giant snake it was swallowed by the doors of the building.

Those marchers who could be accommodated filed into the hall and took their seats in front of the official delegates seated on stage, who were dressed in cut-away coats and striped trousers.

After the official welcome by the conference president, Arthur Henderson, each group came up to deposit its petition at the front of the hall where clerks recorded details.

The petitions were piled so high that Mary Dingman had to speak with a growing wall of paper stretching out either side of her, as yet more groups came in and placed their petitions, creating as it were a paper peace monument.

Edith told her aides to move the petitions away from the front of the hall before they obscured the speakers and officials seated on the rostra, although she hesitated to spoil the visual effect of it all.

Still the petitions arrived as more representatives came in and laid down their bundles of signatures, some of them mayors wearing the ceremonial robes and gold chains of office, bringing petitions painstakingly collected in towns and villages across the world.

Edith moved to the back of the hall, and found the sight astounding, something the like of which she had never seen.

Looking at the scene professionally, she concluded that the four-level rostrum was appropriate for this momentous occasion.

It was like a wedding cake.

The higher level was occupied by the President of the Conference, Arthur Henderson, backed by his personal staff, including Bartou.

At the next level down was the platform and lectern for the speakers and the shorthand reporters.

The next level was for Secretariat members serving the conference.

The final level was for official delegates and then at the side and back were special sections or 'tribunals'—for the press, for representatives of organisations, for visiting diplomats and statesmen observers, and then for the public.

'Yes,' Edith thought, 'this is truly the pinnacle of my days at the League. All our work, whatever tedious paperwork, whatever tiresome committee, had ultimately been for this—to this magnificent end.'

That lunchtime, there on the floor among the shelves of books in the American Library, Edith's caterers had managed to spread out twenty red- and blue-checked tablecloths and lay out on them a picnic. The tables had been pushed to the side and the chairs had been removed.

Edith herself preferred plain white tablecloths but had decided that she needed the checks to give colour to the occasion. Each tablecloth seated eight people; 160 people in all had been invited—two representatives from every peace organisation known to be in Geneva for the conference.

Ambrose was standing with her at the door.

'Red and blue check was right, wasn't it?' she asked.

'Oh yes, a splash of colour—definitely.'

Each of the tablecloths had a wicker picnic basket containing chickens and sliced hams, salads, breads and cakes and, despite the objections of the caterers, vegetarian rissoles. There were four bottles of wine on each tablecloth.

'I will put temptation in their way,' she'd said to herself.

Arranged around each of the wicker baskets were eight well-polished wine glasses.

She had decided against placement. She would obey Thomas Jefferson's view on placement. When he'd been President he'd introduced pell-mell seating at the White House. She hoped the British and the Europeans could cope with such informality.

Sitting on the floor could itself help relax them from the overall formality and solemnity of the conference atmosphere. She had provided cushions and rugs but still it would be a jolt, she suspected, when they realised they would have to sit on the floor.

What she did hope was that the seating might shake them out of their pious poses.

Change the chairs: change the *mentalité*. Edith's Rule. How many times had she said that people thought and argued differently if the speaker were seated rather than standing and that the practices by which policy is executed are commonly as important as the policy itself. Salisbury's rule, to be honest: the methods by which policy is executed are commonly as important as the policy itself.

She caught sight of herself again and thought that she should freshen her make-up. 'How's my face?' she asked Ambrose.

He examined her make-up. 'A touch-up, perhaps. Lips.'

'The puritans might turn on me.'

'All the more reason, darling. All the more reason.'

She looked at herself again in a hand mirror.

'I would make-up to the hilt,' he said.

'Of course you would,' she replied.

'Show them that modern woman has all the artifices and guile of Womanhood at her disposal. That's a lesson they need.'

'No. I think I'll let my make-up fade a little—recede, as it were. The busy woman look. I'm not on display.'

The guests began to arrive, still wearing their green sashes.

Guests were tentative as they came in but Jeanne, Ambrose, Victoria, Gerty, and the rest of her little team welcomed them and explained the random seating plan.

Her gang, despite their teasing of her, had all rallied to the flag, including Bernard Follett and four of his waiters from the Club.

Many of the guests exclaimed with surprised pleasure—or graciousness—at the arrangements.

A crippled ex-soldier in a wheelchair then presented himself at the door and she went over and welcomed him with joy.

He couldn't sit at the tablecloth on the floor but she seated him at the reading tables at the side.

As she turned from seating him, she saw more of his colleagues arriving in their wheelchairs and on crutches. She placed them also at the reading tables.

When she returned to the door again she saw Ambrose assisting a blind soldier in to the picnic. And then behind him came others of the *mutilés*. More than she had officially invited.

My goodness, she thought, the word is out.

She had invited the leader of the *mutilés* delegation but had specified only two representatives. In her mind, the picnic had been for the women's organisations which dominated the peace groups.

She glanced at Ambrose and saw that he was aware of the breach in the wall of the picnic.

In they came. All sorts, mainly the *mutilés*, invited or not.

The other helpers glanced at her and shrugged.

She gestured that they should allow them in.

She left Jeanne and the others to handle it while she took Ambrose into the small Library kitchen, where the two staff were preparing to serve *soupe provençale de légumes*. She told them to add more water.

'The word is out,' she said.

'You are popular with the *mutilés*, Edith.'

'Dear God.'

He then began to laugh and she was caught up in it and she too giggled. 'Free food,' he said, 'and hungry, tired and cold men.'

She got control of her laughter and asked Tony to put out all the contingency picnics held in reserve and to prepare some more. He went to the door of the kitchen and looked out. '*Mon Dieu.*'

'I want everyone fed. Send out for provisions if needed. Put out all the bread we have.'

'Of course,' Tony said. 'Of course we will feed them.'

Edith looked into her handbag and took out a bundle of bank notes which she had for contingencies.

Tony held up his hands. 'Non. It will be taken care of—you?—me? Whoever? That is not a question for this occasion. It is not a consideration.'

Ambrose and she looked out of the Library kitchen into the reading hall. 'It's really the most bizarre picnic I've ever been at,' Ambrose said.

In total, he counted twenty-seven *mutilés*.

The other delegates gradually seated themselves around the overcrowded Library. Edith looked around, thrilled that they had all shown up.

'When should I speak?'

Ambrose advised her to speak after they had eaten something. 'A little wine helps.'

Edith was too tense to eat, so she went out into the main reading room where she leaned down to shake hands and introduce herself as people ate the food and drank the wine. She realised that quite a few spoke neither English nor French, especially among the *mutilés*.

Bernard and Ambrose also went about helping with the welcoming.

Ambrose came to her and said , 'Now is the time—speak.'

Edith got out her notes and went to the low makeshift platform.

Edith began her speech of welcome in English: 'In some ways, you all, as individuals, represent seven hundred million people. There is no human being—whether his home is in one of the great centres of industry and population or in the deserts of Africa, among the jungles of the East, or amid the ice of the Arctic region—who has not someone here to speak in his name.'

She repeated this in French and then indicated that Jeanne would continue a simultaneous translation into French from a copy of the speech.

'I will not abuse my position as host by attempting to tell you your business. You have all spent many years thinking out your beliefs.' As she said this, she thought to herself, that is exactly what I am about to do: tell them their business—abusing my position as host.

'As someone who works for the League and has been privy to much of the argument in preparing for this conference over the last few years, I would like to share some of my observations. I will be brief.'

Most went on eating away at the food.

Many of the *mutilés* were ignoring her, perhaps finding her words incomprehensible in English or French. Though, understanding or not, some waved at her, chicken legs in their hands.

'You are all people with passionate beliefs and doctrines. Extremely principled political positions do identify social illnesses and connect those illnesses with the guilty, though, in my opinion, rarely contribute to a solution. I say this with respect.

'Finding workable solutions—albeit often imperfect human solutions for both the guiltless and the guilty—is left to the likes of me. Our work—my work—is to search for those procedures which make, and keep us, humane, and which accommodate the diversity of belief. Even if it involves the distasteful work of negotiating with the disreputable.'

She went on to urge them to shift from extreme uncompromising positions and join with those who work with the imperfection of the human condition.

'First, we must keep the armies—' there were murmurs of dissent, '—but transform those armies into world police, or into a different sort of army. An army which will have to learn new ways of diplomatic behaviour in countries not their own where they have been sent to quell violent unrest or evil. We have, though, to retain the will to bring force to bear when it is required.

'Every one of these new soldiers will have to negotiate and educate at the same time as they enforce the peace.

'To those of you women here today, I say that we must not surrender these deliberations to those who say that military matters are men's matters.

'And pacifists—which I know many of you are—have to learn about machine-guns and grenades and not turn away in moral disgust. Because this conference will be about which weapons to do away with and which to keep. There will not be a total destruction of all weapons.

'It is the weapons which are kept that will make for the success or failure of disarmament.

'Another paradox: the civilised states differ from the savage tribe not only in the use of less force through diplomatic restraint—at least since the War—but also, oddly, at the same time by possessing more force through the innovation of the human mind. Our job is to develop advanced diplomatic and planetary methods of oversight and supervision as fast as we develop advanced weapons.

'Civilisation is nearly to the point "when armies can destroy each other in a second" and, as Alfred Nobel said, this will be the point in human history when the world will decide to disarm.'

She nodded towards Bernard, acknowledging the contribution of his thoughts.

She mentioned Angell's plan for international 'pairing' of politicians, trades union leaders, business leaders and professors, and towns country by country, who could engage in correspondence and be the conscience of the other.

She had doubts about the value of this but thought it would make her sound less military-minded.

And, she said, the League must have its own army or at least its own airforce which could act quickly before a conflict spread or did too much damage.

This proposal also caused some stirring among the picnickers.

'The most important thing is for the League of Nations' International Control Commissions to be stationed in every powerful country to inspect what is happening there in military build-up and to enforce disarmament.

'These Commissions must have the power in every significant country to inspect armaments factories once the limits are set.

'We will only survive and disarm if we *never* base policies on trust.'

Small murmurings of dissent came from one picnic group and then another and another.

She stopped speaking as the noises of consternation began drowning her out.

One woman, a Miss Royden, rose and interrupted her, the others falling silent as Miss Royden took the floor. 'You are the hostess and I will not insult you by walking out. But we are here to assert one thing only: pacifism—the end of all armies and all weapons. Now and forever.'

There was general clapping.

Miss Royden continued, 'We must not be persuaded away from total disarmament.'

More clapping.

Miss Royden was campaigning for a Pacifist League of Nations.

Miss Royden went on, 'No preparation at all should be made for war—including listening to the sort of position being put now by you, which I see as itself a preparation of our minds for further war: trying to present war in a different costume.

'Most of us here have learned that to even *entertain* an argument against pacifism is to weaken it. Pacifism is the one position for which there can be no compromise. No argument can be heard against it. No challenge made to it is to be given the time of day. To accept compromise, argument or challenge is to shake the very essential nature of pacifism. We too are practical people, Miss Berry: for the next war we too have a new weapon: we will call for the peace-lovers in the world to fling themselves, if need be, in front of the troop trains.

'Troop trains will be unable to move anywhere in the world without running over the bodies of soldiers' mothers and daughters.

'If millions of men will go out to offer their lives up in war, surely there are millions of us who would just as gladly die for peace. We will march onto the battlefields between the combatants. They will have to shoot daughters, mothers and grandmothers if they wish to have their war.

'We will sabotage the munitions. We will stop the aeroplanes from landing on aerodromes.'

There was much clapping.

Miss Royden sat down.

Edith glanced down at the remaining pages of her speech. She thought she may as well finish.

She began again.

In a demonstration of her dissent, Miss Royden then turned her back on Edith.

To Edith's confusion, many of Miss Royden's followers also turned their backs on Edith. Others joined in this protest.

Mary Dingman rose to her feet from her tablecloth and

picnic and turned to the picnickers. 'Let us at least listen to the only official woman who has spoken to us here in Geneva, while at the same time knowing that she is wrong, knowing that to compromise is to fail.'

She sat down and turned her back too. Now nearly all the women and the few men had their backs to her.

The *mutilés* went on drinking and eating—mainly drinking. They appeared to be cadging bottles of wine from those picnickers who were abstainers.

A few of the women did not follow Miss Royden and clapped Edith, but they were a handful and their clapping showed how little support she had rather than giving a sense of endorsement.

Edith looked at the turned backs, decided that they might still be listening even if with disapproval, and went on. 'What I have to say may be in disagreement with you but I have had to say it: "I kept silence, and thou thoughtest that I was altogether such a one as thyself." To do that would be wrong. I wanted you to know what one woman, myself, that is, working within the League who has spent much of her life in and out of the Preparatory Commission for the Disarmament Conference has thought about such things.'

She was speaking to a wall of backs and to the incomprehension of the *mutilés*.

She stopped, deciding not to finish her speech. She thanked them all—to their backs—and went to the Librarian's empty office, shaking.

Jeanne followed her.

Ambrose was already at the office, having listened from there. 'Bravely done.' He kissed her cheeks, and hugged her.

'But not so *well* done, I'm afraid,' she said.

'You stood up and made them listen to sense,' he said.

No. She had blundered in her management of *mentalités*.

Edith took out her pocket flask and poured herself a drink from it, put the cap back on the flask, looked at the glass, took the cap off again and poured out some more cognac.

'Steady on, Edith,' said Ambrose, touching her arm. 'You'll slip on the ice again.'

'I have slipped on the ice, it seems to me.' She looked down at the sash. It seemed all so unnecessary. She removed it.

He reminded her that those who speak out from the floor of a gathering never speak on behalf of the entire audience. 'We never know the mind of a crowd or an audience. It's a hundred unknown minds. And we never know what it is that changes a mind or when that mind will change.'

'You fed the multitude,' Jeanne said.

'I felt I was back at my boarding school in Sydney being school captain again. And failing in my speech on Prize Day.'

'You *are* our school captain,' Victoria said, earnestly, then caught herself, adding, 'if you want to be school captain, that is.'

'And I skipped the last two pages of my speech.'

'I thought that there was a gap in the advancement of the argument,' said Victoria. 'But that isn't a criticism.'

'I don't think anyone missed it,' Ambrose said, bringing her a chicken leg and a piece of baguette. 'And at least there were no ants. Unless you count Miss Royden.'

'What sort of picnic is it that has no ants?' She looked out through the one-way window and saw that many were now leaving the picnic for the afternoon sessions.

Her gang, including even Chef Tony, sat around there in the Librarian's office and nibbled at some of the leftover picnic food, tired, obviously feeling for her, but probably thinking that it was all a great folly to begin with.

'They're all leaving. Perhaps we should say goodbye,' said Victoria, after looking out the door.

'To hell with them. I've done my bit,' Edith said, and laughed deeply. The picnic was over.

The *mutilés* were the last to leave, some taking the leftover bottles of wine. They were welcome to them.

Finally the Library was empty. The caterers and Bernard's staff went about cleaning up.

Soon the little party in the office was giggling. There was mimicry of Miss Royden.

'The *mutilés* will love you forever,' Bernard said.

'Maybe they could put on a show at the club,' Ambrose said. 'Get together in some sort of *cabaret macabre*.'

Jeanne and Victoria shouted in unison. 'Ambrose!!!'

She wondered if they had the faintest idea of what went on at the Molly Club. They had, of course, heard of it, although they had refused her one invitaion to accompany her there. But even she thought Ambrose's joke was perhaps going a little too far.

Latitude: Doorway to Chance?

Edith felt a light, giddy guilt about bringing Ambrose to the apartment.

But as they entered, the apartment felt airy—spacious.

Robert's going had created a spaciousness she could almost breathe. Maybe it was what was known as a breathing-space.

A second, surprise relief also came to her as she stood in the apartment with Ambrose: while Robert's absence had caused a deep disturbance, it had not left any sense of *void* in her life.

In fact, the ghost had left the castle.

As she saw the apartment through Ambrose's eyes she could see that Robert had left reminders of himself, and it occurred to her that if he'd wanted to really *go*, he would be all gone. He was not *all gone*.

'I feel rather mischievous,' she said, taking his hand, 'bringing you here. The corpse not yet cold.' *Marriage treason* was the expression perhaps, rather than mischievous. She found that this treason, if that was what it was, did not worry her. If she had a marriage.

'As long as it's the good kind of mischief,' Ambrose said.

'Not—not quite yet,' she replied, 'it is not of the good

kind, yet.' She smiled nervously. 'It will be of the good kind soon.'

She went to the sideboard and picked up a splendidly wrapped gift box.

'A gift,' she said, presenting it to Ambrose. '*Pour toi, ma chérie.*'

He showed genuine pleasure, as if it were some time since anyone had given him a gift. 'What's the occasion?' he asked, taking it from her, weighing it in his hand, shaking it lightly, playing the gift-guessing game.

What sort of gift was this? 'I am unsure what the occasion is. I've never given a gift for this sort of occasion. If it is an *occasion.*' She put on her thinking face. 'It *is* an occasion. But the occasion doesn't have a name.'

It was, in part, a gift to mark the miraculous resurrection of their liaison. She couldn't quite say *that*. It would sound too solemn.

'Perhaps we can find a name for it—for this occasion,' he said, holding the box, as yet still unopened.

She moved around the apartment. 'Perhaps we could.'

How hard some gift-giving was. To choose the gift to show a communing of spirits was hard, especially when, as in this case, the gift could either be the most remarkably appropriate gift or the most devastatingly wrong gift—that is, when the gift was audacious.

Though, if you were sure of the correctness of the gift, it was not audacity.

The gift could be a test, to see if the receiver was the person the giver wanted that person to be. Or to say that the person *was* the sort of person the giver wanted them to be. Affirmation.

The audaciously intimate gift was probably though the most effective—or at least the *fastest*—way to see if the receiver was the Right Person. If the gift were badly wrong the receiver, at least, would know they were not the Right Person for the gift.

Ultimately, a truth would have been hatched from the gift which would redirect the nature of the friendship. Despite all the dishonesty surrounding the reception of a gift.

Ambrose began to unwrap the box.

She watched with her fingers crossed.

And if the audaciously intimate gift was the best test, then this would be it.

Ambrose opened the ribbons from the box and took out from the tissue the yellow silk, lace-edged, full length, feminine nightdress.

He looked at her with a small smile, she might call it a *pert* smile.

She smiled back with a warm, special smile which said, '*That you* is welcomed back too.'

She knew instantly, from his face, that she'd chosen just the right gift for this occasion, whatever this occasion may be called.

'You like it?'

'Oh yes. Oh yes, dear Edith.'

He came over and they kissed.

'Your scandalous, depraved self is welcomed back, too,' she said. 'That is what I meant.'

Despite all they'd been through in the old days and all that they knew about each other, it'd still taken a lot of boldness to buy the feminine nightdress for him, to hand it to him now.

And it welcomed back something of herself as well. *That Edith* was coming back again, as well.

He held it full length before him, covering his dark blue lounge suit, looking down at it.

'Try it on!' she said, softly, urgingly. 'Go on.' She got the words out sounding just right, just saucy enough, just cheeky enough, just poised enough.

The words did not show any of the small remaining qualms.

It occurred to her as she watched him that perhaps he was so adept at the false response to an inappropriate gift that she was misreading him. If she'd indiscreetly misjudged him, their relationship may be forever, irrevocably *embarrassed*.

If he did not wish to try it on now, it would be a sign that the gift was wrong.

But Ambrose left the living room and made his way to her dressing room. By leaning back from where she sat, she could see him. He removed his jacket, tie, shirt, and then his shoes. He took off his trousers, looking around for a place to hang them, then folding them over the back of the chair. He stood there then for a moment in his socks and garters, and in his silk men's underpants and vest.

Perusing Ambrose, as he stood momentarily there in his undergarments, she thought how starkly this sartorial under-pinning rendered the male animal.

When growing up, she'd sneaked glimpses of her father and her brother dressed such as this—in this framework of Man. Somehow, it did more starkly render Man than did the naked man. The man in his undergarments was man caught between the state of animal nakedness and the presentation of that animal nakedness as the public man, before the full sartorial facade was in place. This intermediate state reminded her of drawings of man's evolution from the ape.

This drawing of man in his undergarments should come after the drawing of man in the loincloth, holding the club. How so farcical and unready Man looked in this underpinning of garments. Probably because it was not ever meant to be seen. Yet how severe and unknowable the fully dressed Man of the next stage looked, in his silk top hat and awards and medals.

Yet it was from this underpinning, these undergarments, she mused, that a man must sense himself throughout the day, the underpants and vest and garter and socks were next to the skin, and that must be how the man felt to himself as he moved about his public life. Certainly reminded him at the beginning of every day as he put these garments on. How those fabrics and the pressures of those garments on those parts of his body must subconsciously inform the man of his primitive manness and all that went with it.

Her gift today was then an *invitation*, too—an invitation to Ambrose to leave that state of being man, and to go to his other self.

Ambrose turned his head and caught her watching him. He looked down at himself still in the men's undergarments and pulled a face of displeasure.

She smiled and waved her hand which said, *Get rid of it—away with it all.*

She kept her fingers crossed behind her back.

He smiled at her and removed the socks and garters, the underpants and vest, and stood there, animal naked, naturally hairless.

He quickly slipped into the nightdress. Its silk fell well on his slim body, down to his ankles. The round silk straps graced his smooth shoulders. He turned in the nightdress, looking behind to see it on his body from the back, he wrapped it to his body, looking to the full-length mirror, absorbed for the moment with pleasure at the sight of himself.

And as she saw him admiring himself in the mirror she thought, oh yes, she had not misjudged.

He was still as she remembered him.

And for all its deviance, he was the way she would wish him to be with her.

She clapped. 'Perfect—exquisite.'

He came back to her from the dressing room, parading his slim, silk-clad body with seductive grace, twirling in front of her, and then holding up the nightdress from his knees, he sat beside her, tucking the nightdress and his legs under him.

He put his arms around her neck and kissed her, a kiss of lips, a kiss of passion. She felt his tears on her cheek. 'Thank you, Edith, for the mercy.'

'Mercy?' The word did not belong in their old jaunty ways. They weren't yet finely tuned to their old jaunty ways.

'Saying such a fine hello to what I am.' His voice broke a little. He quickly pulled himself back from this earnestness, back towards flippancy, as he added, 'Rather, I should say, thank you for your rather sultry taste in silk nightdresses— expensively sultry, silk nightdresses from Milan.'

She placed her hand on his mouth. 'You shameless hussy.'

'I am a hussy, I truly am,' he said, lightly, with a saucy laugh.

And his shamelessness, and his being a hussy, and his deep acceptance of the gift, *unshackled* her, there and then.

Unshackled her from ever being abashed by her own life or from ever being embarrassed by their friendship and its irregularities. Something was unshackled which had been missing from her conversation and her thought and her sense of self during those years he'd been gone.

She'd yearned to be *shameless* again.

And now was.

And she was as pleased as punch.

Both of them were now together in each other's arms, perfect and exquisite and comfortable.

'How did you become so?' he asked her. He was again pensive, but lightly and affectionately so. His voice was close to having the old right ring to it.

'You made me so,' she said.

'In there ...' He placed the palm of his hand on her breasts, and she shivered, aroused by his touch. 'There was always a person who could consent to all the strangeness of my life. And more. Could do so with joy. I simply came along and said hello to that person inside you. To the hussy inside you.'

Had such a person existed in her? She rested her head on his silken breast. Or had he groomed her to be such a person, to serve him?

Whatever—of one thing she was sure as she came to rest there, there on his silken breast—this was where her head yearned to be.

Oh, yes.

She could come to rest on a man such as this, whatever it might mean about her womanhood—so be it. It was here with this sort of man that she came to rest. It was a verity. Tears came to her eyes and she looked up at him. 'My darling, it's here that I come to rest.' She looked up at him. 'In the arms of a hussy.'

In the saying of the last part, she found their voice, the frolicsome, larky, lusty voice—the voice of their old relationship.

That voice was beginning to be heard now.

She saw now that the gift of the nightdress had also been a query about their quintessence. And her quintessence.

In the old days, she'd made their ambiguity the answer. Back then, she'd hidden inside that ambiguity. That is, she'd always told herself that Ambrose, by being something other than elementary man, had allowed her a halfway staging place, a place where she could appear to have a man in her life, a place from which she would eventually pass.

Not a place towards which she had been headed.

At the time, it had looked genuinely like that. One needed to document selected minutes of one's life so that it would be possible to look back and be reassured that one had not been as dishonest, or had not acted as badly as the memory sometimes unfairly suggested.

Now, it seemed it was not *a stage* at all but was, in fact, the place where she wished to go—if not *wished* exactly, then where she'd again found herself and beyond which she might not ever wish to go.

Or did she want to linger, still, in that ambiguity, to idle a while—a lifetime perhaps?—in an indistinct, borderline way of life, rather than in resolution?

And was *resolution* within the command of her will? Anyone's command?

The nightdress was also a Question. It was not just a Gift of Resurrection, the resurrection, that is, of their bond, it was an Interrogatory Gift—with the interrogation going both ways out from the gift: towards Ambrose and towards herself, and, if the answers to the questions were appropriate and coincided, as it seemed they had, it became then a Gift of Affirmation.

That they were together in each other's arms and that she was tranquil and that he was tranquil, and that she liked the look and the feel of him this way, there in the silk, lace-edged nightdress, that was one answer.

She suspected there were more answers. She was tumbling into the arms of the cosy answers.

'Don't,' said Ambrose, placing his warm soft palm on her frowning forehead. 'Cease.'

She smiled a perplexed smile at him. She knew he saw something of what was going through her head. 'How can I not?'

'You can entertain some ideas without thrashing yourself with them,' he said. 'Some ideas are to be royally entertained: some have to be shown the door.'

'Shouldn't we talk? Shouldn't we have ... an understanding?' she said. 'Isn't that what happens in these modern times?'

He didn't reply.

She said, 'I do know what we do need—we do need a drink.'

She wasn't quite into the cosy arms of all the answers yet.

Ambrose rose and went over to the butler's table. 'Scotch?' She nodded.

'Soda?'

'A flick.'

He poured them both a drink. His taking charge of the

drinks like that in her apartment was, she noted curiously, also part of an answer.

He said, 'I see that your taste in Scotch is still as good as your taste in silk nightdresses from Milan.'

'I learned both from you, darling.'

Actually, she'd learned Scotch from her father and John Latham.

Oh dear. What would these two Proper Men think of her now, here in her living room with a nancyboy? She rushed the images of their quizzical faces from her consciousness.

He came back and handed her the Scotch.

'You know ...' she said, 'I've spent more of my life in your company than in that of any other person.'

'You were always good at a certain "statistical reality", Edith.'

'As you, dear, were always rather good at a certain "fantastical reality".'

Before Ambrose could be seated, she drank down the Scotch and sighed, waiting for it to seep through her body and mind. She held out the empty glass to Ambrose who went back to the butler's table and poured her another.

She wanted the drink to heighten and celebrate the moment, to hold it securely in place.

'Is Robert coming back, do you think?' he asked.

Were they now fashioning an 'arrangement'?

She sang. 'Husband Robert to the war has gone, his faithful harp beside him.'

'And his Harpy left behind him?'

'I have *never, ever* been a *harpy*. And to quote an Australian poem, "Robert's gone a drovin', and we don't know where he are." Oddly, knowing I'm still here allows him to be solo. Something like that. To be partly a bachelor-journalist again. With his newspaper men mates in dusty, distant places and in exotic belly-dancing clubs.'

'What does it allow to you?' Ambrose asked.

Ah.

'I suppose,' she said, 'that Robert will go from one war to another, if there is another war, or one horror spot to another—plagues, earthquakes and *coups d'etat* are what he lives on. He'll visit home now and then. For clean underwear. Something like that. Once a year? Twice a year?'

Visit home?

Ambrose said, 'What a curious man he turned out to be. Not the marrying kind, perhaps?'

'Perhaps. Perhaps neither he nor I was.'

'To repeat: what then does it mean to you, Edith?'

Yes, that was a question.

Sipping her drink, she thought.

He waited.

She replied, 'Latitude.'

She saw that he liked the precision of her answer. She liked it as well.

'Which is not independence?' he said.

She again thought.

She replied, 'No.'

She thought some more and said, 'Latitude is not an open door to chance.'

Her answer pleased her immensely. But to her profound irritation, her clever reply curled itself, in her mind, into a question, 'Latitude: not an open door to chance?'

Her wretched mind had added a question mark.

'Latitude may be an open door to *permutation*,' Ambrose said. 'I look around the apartment and I see much of you. I see a little of Robert.'

'Robert never did really touch the walls. He doesn't alter the space he's in. He left all that to me, the interior arrangements, the pictures, the ornaments. And what there was of him has been removed. His army photograph—his company of the Lancastershire Fusiliers. I didn't mean for it to sound like that. No sneer meant to the Lancastershire

Fusiliers. Sorry, Lancastershire Fusiliers. He still seemed to leave ... deposits. As cats and foxes do. Squirtings in the corners.'

'It was his lair, too.'

'It was his lair, too. Robert is in that room.' She pointed at the door to his room with her drink. 'In what we called back home "the spare room".'

'Spare room?'

'To be precise, it is now the room where either the past is stored, or the present is in abeyance. Or possibly, where the past is awaiting collection and—removal.'

She saw that she was tampering ever so slightly with her answers to make them accommodating to Ambrose while trying to present no false promises.

'I see you still have that wretched Kelen cartoon on the wall.'

She looked at the framed cartoon having not 'seen' it for some time.

It was done by the cartoonist Kelen, and given to her and to Robert on the day they had first seriously flirted in public and had later become intimate.

It showed them both standing before a double bed saying, 'No, after you'. It was a take-off of another well-known cartoon.

She got up and went over and removed it. She opened the door of Robert's room, and placed the framed cartoon inside, and closed the door.

Ambrose made no remark.

She came back and sat with him again, and said, 'Do you know what I think, my dear Ambrose?'

'What do you think?'

'I think, that you should have the second bedroom. It needs some furniture. But has a westerly aspect. I seem to recall you prefer not to rise with the sun.'

'Have always been somewhat out of step with the sun.'

He pointed at the door of the second bedroom questioningly. 'That's the room?'

'Yes.'

He stood and lightly walked across to the door of the second bedroom, opened it and looked in. 'In the old days, you came to my apartment. Now I come to yours,' he called to her.

'It appears that way.'

He went into the room and then came out. He draped himself against the wall, gracefully, one bare foot on the wall, drink in hand, leaning back, his privates showing alluringly through the silk. She felt her body enliven at the sight. 'The room's fine. But what pray tell is that strange *chaise longue*.'

'The Woodrow Wilson chair? It can be changed to fourteen different positions. Mechanically.'

'Oh. It might have to go,' he said. He looked at her. 'Am I then to have the status of parlour-boarder?'

'More than that, perhaps. More like—two gals sharing an apartment.'

'Do these two gals share a bed on cold and comfortless nights?'

'These two gals share a bed whenever they wish.'

'And when the Husband returns from the Wars?'

She found something of an answer. 'Maybe there's room for three. One as the guest.'

'Which the guest?'

She had no firm answer.

Did she, then, now have a *mariage blanc*?

Or was it, perhaps, a *ménage à trois*?

Heavens.

Ambrose did not push for further answers on that front.

Did she really believe that was how it all would work?

'And public opinion?' he asked.

She made a dismissive noise. 'The old gang know us as a couple from the old days. God knows what they know or what they care to know. Anyhow, the League is so big now. Gossip doesn't matter as much. Too much of it now. And the people at the League are not a club anymore. If asked, we shall say that you are a house guest, living here until you find yourself an apartment. And time will pass.'

He looked at her quizzically. 'Are you happy with that formulation, Edith? Is that to be my *locus standi*?'

She frowned.

She thought about it. 'On second thoughts, no. I'm not happy with that formulation.'

'For a moment, Edith, I thought that you may have become duplicitous.'

'My trick has always been not to be duplicitous when others think I *am* being duplicitous.'

'If you permit someone to believe you *are* being duplicitous you are being duplicitous.'

'I will tell the truth to whoever asks, or ...' she smiled, '... or whatever part of the truth to which I think they are entitled—or able to comprehend without blowing a fuse.'

Ambrose returned to her and they again entwined into each other's arms, smiling, she aware of a stiffening in his groin.

He said, ' "By how we live, we show the way"?'

She sensed that he was quoting her, quoting a distant, more youthful Edith. It came to her mind. 'The quote from Stendhal of which I was once rather fond. I think Julien says something like, "I am convincing the world to make heaven on earth." And he asks himself, "How then shall I make that place visible to them?" And he replies to himself, "By the difference between my conduct and that of a layman." Something like that.'

'It might be a rather tiring way to live.'

'We might alter the requirements a little. *By how we live, we show some of the way—to some of the world—sometimes.* Not to all, all at once,' she said.

'We are not to live as another of your instructional picnics, I hope?'

'No more pedagogic picnics.'

Edith heard then in her voice a new resignation. But not a giving up. More a giving *over* to the imperfection of it all.

Imperfection seemed to be all that she had.

She decided now was the right time to ask him another question.

'You seem to like women—to like me—intimately, that is?'

'I do. When they are women such as you—which is rare.'

'And where do men fit into the picture?'

'Let me tell you something I have discovered'

'I am all ears.'

'I have dallied with men.'

'I know.'

'And I have loved you, and one other woman.'

'I know about *her.*'

'And more often, I've had dalliances now and then with men who dress as women.'

'I know that too. And?'

'All those dalliances and that loving—men and women and the other—were fairly glorious. And you were the most glorious of all.'

'You are required by etiquette to say that,' she laughed, covering her joy at his words.

'I suspect that the world of which I speak does not have an etiquette, as such. I meant what I said with all my heart—you are the most glorious of all.'

She was moved.

'Thank you,' she said quietly.

She considered the breathtaking gift of his revelations.

In a soft voice she asked, 'And what were you to those you dallied with? How did they see you? As man? As woman? As woman-man?'

'They knew me, I suspect, *as a man who dressed as a woman.* Perhaps, best described as a man who was *womanly.*'

'I see.' She was unsure of the degree of her comprehension.

'Perhaps I am your foible?' he said.

'Perhaps we are a couple who dares not speak its name? Or who *has no name*.'

'Nicely put.'

She decided to leave it at that.

But it raised one other last question.

'What if you should choose to bring home a guest—an overnight guest?'

He contemplated the question. 'I would not consider it good form to do that.'

'What would you do then if overtaken by desire?'

'Behave as a cat, perhaps. Find some dark alley. Some alternative accommodation.'

She left it at that. 'And are you sane?'

'Dr Vittoz thinks I am sane enough. My English doctor thinks so as well. Do you think I am?'

'Yes. Sane enough—and sane in the right way.'

They kissed again.

'I, too, have changed, perhaps,' she said.

'How so?'

'You may find that I have changed in such a way that you find nothing about which you need to fib.'

'How nice.'

'You can be my Rotten Friend, though, if you find you have to be. As well as my Strange Lover.'

'I have very little Rotten left in me, I hope. But, as you see, the Strangeness is still there.'

She stood to remove her outer clothing, wanting their bodies to be joined.

She wanted to feel his body through the nightdress, for them to be bodies in silk against each other.

And the nightdress—her Gift of Affirmation—would change, once again, this time into a Gift of Carnal Celebration.

She remembered one of their silly old games.

As she undressed herself before him, she whispered, 'Halt. Who goes there? Man or Woman?'

She removed her underpants and corset and left on only her petticoat, brassiere, garter belt, and stockings.

He whispered his reply. 'Neither man nor woman.'

She sat down again, going into his arms. 'Who then?'

'A brazen hussy.'

'Approach that we may recognise you.'

She opened her legs to him.

He moved onto her and kissed her. Her hand went lightly to him, under the nightdress and she led him to her, allowing him to enter her deeply.

Lying back under him, she whispered, 'Pass friend—all's well.'

Stiff Face

'Guess what job I've landed?' she said to Ambrose as she arrived to join him at the Perle du Lac, trying not to be breathless, putting down her satchel and the bundle of papers she was carrying under her arm.

'Gather your breath.'

'Eden and the Committee of Five. Liaison Officer. *Working with Eden.*'

'I wondered why we were eating flashily tonight. You know Eden is called "The Glamour Boy"?'

'And he *is*. At last we'll bang on economic sanctions. For the first time in the history of the world we are going to stop war by non-military means. Eden is being formidable. Italy is going to get a caning.'

Ambrose put away the newspaper he'd been reading and said, '*If* Italy is found in breach of the Covenant. And *if* everyone comes on board.'

'Ambrose, this is it—the defining moment. Yes, I know I've said this before and been wrong. This time the League strikes. Thump. Whack.' She slapped the table. 'Disarmament may have failed but this will not.'

'Liaison is rather a delightful fish,' he said. 'It's a role which can be, how shall we say ...'

'Augmented.'

'Precisely. We shall say *augmented*. Oh, yes. We can have fun with this—however, it sounds to me that it's not arbitration which has you so breathless but more the possibility of exercising naked power.'

'As something of an expert at naked power and also something of an expert at *la liaison*, you must coach me.'

'Many times have I been *l'officier de liaison*. And in the strangest of situations.'

'It'll be power, darling, if we get to hit Italy with economic sanctions.'

'You know who dreamed up this economic sanctions thing?'

'Cecil? Wilson?'

'No.'

'Who?'

'I should warn you—you won't like the answer.'

'Who?'

'Pope Benedict XV.'

'How infuriating. I suppose even popes can come up with a brilliant idea every century or so.'

'I dare say.'

'Darling, I'm on my way up.' She stretched out her arms and danced in her chair.

'Decorum, Edith. You may well be. Did Avenol appoint you?'

'He said, "I want you to report to me. If I put a French person in there, Eden will not talk freely. They will talk freely with you, the English. But, remember, you report to me."'

'To him? Not to the League?'

'I said, "Oh, absolutely, my loyalty is always to the League."'

'And he said?'

' "I am the League." '

'He didn't!?'

'He did. "*La Société, c'est moi*".'

'He was joking!?'

'He was joking, and at the same time, he was not joking.'

'What is the politics of this appointment? What is your analysis?'

'For a start, Jeanne whispered my name in his ear. Vouched for my absolute neutrality. And for my deep attachment to France—both at the same time.'

'The French affiliation. I keep forgetting about Jeanne's Important Uncle at the Quai d'Orsay.'

'Important Grandfather. Jeanne's loyal to the League. And more crucially, she's loyal to me.'

'I suppose these days one is loyal to The Good People. But how to know them?'

'*We* are The Good People.'

'That illusion is the first step on the road to conspiracy.'

'Well, after all, darling, conspiracy is your *field*.'

He ignored this reference to his irregular past. 'Who—apart from Eden—is on the Committee of Five?'

'England, France, Spain—Senor de Madariaga, one of the good people—Poland, Turkey. Madariaga is in the chair. But Eden's the prime mover. Alexis Léger will surely be there. Swoon.'

'Now that you're really in the diplomatic thick of things, I have one last lesson in diplomacy for you, Edith.'

'Yet another "last lesson". How many last lessons are there?'

'Of last lessons there is no end.'

'What is it then?' she said, chin on hand, pretending to studious attention.

'The Lesson of the Stiff Face.'

'The Lesson of the Stiff Face?'

'In all you've learned—and may I say, I feel at times you now are ahead of me in your understanding of statecraft—

the lesson you haven't yet learned is the lesson of the stiff face.'

'Pray tell.'

'You have a face which is too expressive, Edith—which is, in every human situation except that of statecraft, a wonderful, winning, and enchanting thing to have. You have *un visage expressif.* That's no good for diplomacy. No good at all. For example, there's tremendous power in the act of not smiling. You smile naturally and frequently. In statecraft, that is not always efficacious. Not smiling is a way of causing others some degree of quandary. They must ask themselves: "What is it that we have here—this unsmiling enigma?" You have heard it said many times that a diplomat is a mask for his country. A diplomat cannot smile or be pleased without the authority of his government. You must now learn to wear The Mask of the Stiff Face.'

Edith made a stiff face.

'Perfect.'

'And as a diplomat in high places you do not stretch out your arms and wriggle at the dinner table.'

She stretched out her arms and danced again. It was a long time since she'd felt in such high spirits. 'Now for a stiff drink. I can do a Stiff Drink.'

Edith hit trouble on her first day. The Italian diplomat, Baron Aloisi, presented to the Committee two volumes of reports and photographs of brutalities he alleged that the Ethiopians had inflicted on captured Italians. It was to counter Ethiopian allegations of Italian use of poison gas.

The volumes with the photographs were passed around but not to her.

When the men had finished, she reached over for them, but Aloisi without looking at her, simply moved them out of her reach. He said, 'Not, I think, for the eyes of a lady.'

The two volumes, however, remained halfway in the common part of the conference table but half in what could be seen as Aloisi's official space at the table.

She looked to Madariaga but he did not give her his attention.

Edith swallowed and said in a voice remarkably firm and quiet, and with a face diplomatically stiff, 'I feel I should be as fully informed as the rest of the Committee,' including herself by declaration to be *in* the Committee. She did not want to be classified as an observer.

She held out her hand.

And anyhow, they were tabled documents. She added, 'I would feel remiss if I were not to see your documents. At this Committee, I should, perhaps, be considered as the eyes and ears of the Secretary-General.'

And, there, she'd spoken, even if only as a functionary. How important it was to make oneself speak on such occasions, to breach the cage of one's personal silence and to dive into the committee's deliberations.

Aloisi said, '*Mais oui*, of course,' but in fact ignored her, and went on with his claims that the Ethiopians had used dum-dum bullets, hollowed to explode in the body.

She heard him refer, in French, to the brutalisation of the captured Italians and the 'loss of their manhood', the meaning of which she guessed.

Léger, the head of the French Department of Foreign Affairs, said something about 'a warrior tradition from times immemorial'.

Aloisi said, 'Not the traditions of a civilised nation.'

Léger said, 'Quite so. Civilised nations have discovered worse things to do to each other. We are more modernistic barbarians.'

About the documents, she felt she was about to suffer a defeat but could see no way of advancing her position. She was tempted to get up from the table, walk around to where the volumes were, and take them. But that would be a tad temperamental.

Eden came to her rescue. He reached over and took the books from their ambiguous location on the table and moved them in front of himself, into his personal space, and then opened one of them randomly, turning the pages, while Aloisi talked on. At some point, Eden then closed the book and pushed both volumes out into the common area of the table, but this time in her direction and within her reach.

He said, *sotto voce*, 'Ghastly stuff,' perhaps as a warning to her. Or perhaps as an invitation to her to look.

She realised she had his implicit support.

She reached over and took them securely into her space, but did not open them. She would spare the men their embarrassment and peruse them in private.

Aloisi glanced at this manoeuvre without pausing in his speech. 'Ethiopia is controlled by a ruling minority which has cruelly repressed its people. Ethiopia is not an organised state at all. It should never have been admitted as a member of the League.'

'Italy voted for her admission,' Léger said without looking up, addressing his remark to no one in particular.

When the committee adjourned for lunch, she was pleased that Eden invited her to join them, but she declined, feeling she should begin writing her report, sensing that the men needed to be free of a woman's presence. She knew things of importance would be said at lunch, but that couldn't be helped.

She had Eden on her side and she did not wish to strain it.

As Eden and the others put on their coats, she recited to them,

> *When the great ones go off to their dinner,*
> *The secretary stays getting thinner and thinner,*
> *Racking his brains to record and report,*
> *What he thinks that they think they ought to have thought.*

They chuckled. Even Aloisi.

'Quite true—and quite unfair,' Eden said.

As they trundled off to lunch, she immediately regretted having done the recitation. She'd put herself back in the subordinate role. But at least the doggerel referred to a secretary of the higher order.

She asked Gerty, who was acting as the stenographer, to bring her in some lunch on a tray from the café. 'And a *pichet* of their *vin blanc.*'

'Yes, madam.' Gerty looked to see that the men were out of earshot and said in her staccato, Dutch-accented English, 'Madam Berry—are you going to look in the book?'

She raised her eyes to Gerty, one wicked woman to another. 'When I've got my report on its way.'

'Could I have a look?'

'It's really a Committee document—but I think that we can find a time for you to have a peek, Gerty.'

'Thank you, madam.'

Edith had some qualms about the voyeuristic use of the material. And then had a qualm about her prudish protectiveness of Gerty. Gerty was no prude.

As soon as Gerty had left to get their lunch, she opened the Italian atrocity documents.

They were photographs of castration, of exposed wounds from where limbs had been hacked off, of stomachs exploded by bullets, of intestines spilling onto the sand. There was a photograph of an Italian soldier with a spike driven through his body from anus to mouth.

She came across a photograph which she at first did not understand, and then felt stunned. The Italian soldier had a penis in his mouth. His own penis had been cut off and put in his mouth.

To her surprise, she found that she viewed the ghastly photographs with a coolness, a detachment. Maybe those years of dissection in the science laboratories as a student were now serving a diplomatic purpose.

She wondered if they were 'doctored' photographs but concluded that it would be difficult to do that.

Before she'd finished looking at them, her detachment began to dissolve and she felt dry-mouthed and dizzy. She took a glass of water.

She put the documents back in their ambiguous space near Aloisi's chair, out of some deference to him. She did not wish to offend the Italian government nor the sensitivities of Italian manliness.

It was, she recorded to herself, the first time she'd seen a castrated man.

She continued to feel queasy about it but began writing her report. She had second thoughts about whether Gerty should see them.

But Gerty was hard to stop.

In the afternoon, the meeting was addressed by Gaston Jèze, Professor of International Law at the Sorbonne, who had been employed by the Ethiopians to present their case.

The Italians walked out of the room as he rose to speak.

Sadly, Edith felt that Jèze did not do a good job for the Ethiopians. They were a shaky little nation—the Italians were right about that—but Emperor Haile Selassie was trying to modernise it, and to bring it up to the European standards. It couldn't be treated as land up for grabs.

She was surprised to hear Eden ask Laval, the French Prime Minister, outright in front of the others, whether the French would join with the British in enforcing sanctions on the Italians. Perhaps he was taking advantage of the absence of the Italians.

Never walk out of a meeting. She remembered the saying she'd learned early in her days at the League: 'The League never walks out.'

She suspected that it was the first time a member of League

Council had seriously proposed the use of this new economic weapon.

'This is clearly a case for Anglo-French collaboration,' Eden said. 'If we fail to stand together now, the consequences will be calamitous for the League.'

It placed France on the spot.

Laval agreed. 'I have a divided Cabinet, as you are well aware, but I will ask for a mandate to apply sanctions, yes.'

'They should be substantial sanctions.'

'I agree.'

Edith regretted the absence of the Italians. She would've liked them to hear this.

Someone here would be reporting to them.

They must have known that they would learn what was said or they wouldn't have walked out.

Edith then felt she should both recover her position and enlarge it by speaking.

At first a question: men enjoyed answering questions from a lady. They would all rush to answer. 'Will Mussolini formally declare war? Or simply walk into Ethiopia?'

The men made comments which assumed that Italy would follow the convention of declaring war.

'I ask,' she said, 'because Italy, if she declares, would be then entitled to belligerent rights.'

Laval was astonished. 'I have never heard of such a thing. *Belligerent rights*—what are these?' Laval didn't address the question to her, but to Eden.

Eden thought for a moment and said, 'Berry has a point. If war is declared, for example, under international law Italy could stop French ships if she thought they were aiding Italy's enemy.'

'No one stops a French ship,' Laval said. 'Least of all, Mussolini.'

Edith cut in. 'If war is "declared" the belligerent also is supposed to adhere to the international rules of warfare.'

She continued, 'But I do not believe that a nation which has breached the League Covenant can legitimately exercise any belligerent rights.'

And she would say one more thing. 'Until now, technically, war didn't exist until "declared". We have a new situation where we, the League, can deem a conflict to be a "war"—and by so describing it we *declare* a war, in that sense.'

'Very interesting,' Léger said. 'Yes. You are probably right.'

She said lightly, though without smiling, 'Curiously, we have legalised war—in the broadest sense.'

Thank you, Robert.

Ah, but Robert, there is more to be said. 'I suppose that international law tries to ensure that nations do as much good as possible in peace and as little harm in war as possible.'

She stopped. The men were still looking at her, including Professor Jèze.

Léger said he agreed with her, but pointed out that the 'law of war' had really begun with the Geneva and Hague Conventions, before the League.

Professor Jèze rushed to display his historical knowledge by agreeing with Léger.

Edith kept her stiff face but inwardly beamed. The acknowledged master of French foreign policy had agreed with her, even if his agreement had contained a correction.

'True,' she said. 'It did begin with the Geneva and Hague Conventions in the nineteenth century, but what has changed is that with the existence of the League, we have for the first time a referee, as it were.'

She realised that the exchange was taking place between the bureaucrats—Léger and her—not among the delegates. This was that other level of participation at a committee—where the experts were expected to supply such material to the lay people. She liked the role.

But she realised with slight embarrassment that she had answered her own question.

Laval excused himself to return to Paris, leaving Léger to represent France. Laval turned to Edith and said, 'Thank you Madame for your lesson.'

The meeting continued its discussion until Eden intervened and suggested that a report be prepared *now*.

That day.

'We must act with speed,' Eden told the Committee, 'or we will lose the moment.'

Eden looked at Léger seeking advice, by his look, on whether that was now possible without Laval.

'I agree,' Léger said.

Eden looked around the table and received the agreement of the other members of the Committee of Five and their advisers.

Eden was behaving as if he were chairing the session, not Madariaga.

'We will consider the doors locked until we have completed our report to Council,' Madariaga said, as if reminding people that he was the chairman. 'No one will leave.'

Edith had Gerty ring for an additional stenographer and paper and afternoon tea.

Night fell on the Committee. Sandwiches, cheese, and fruit and coffee arrived.

After several more hours a draft was ready.

Edith's contribution was for her the most exciting sentence she had ever written or perhaps that anyone had ever written—at least in the history of the League.

Edith's sentence was: 'The Committee has come to the conclusion that the Italian Government has resorted to war in disregard of its obligations under Article 12 of the Covenant of the League of Nations.'

She read it and looked around at the members of the Committee.

There was silence.

Madariaga said, 'Agreed?'

They made noises of agreement.

After all the hours of negotiation they had no more to say.

Eden again pointed out that if the League as a whole adopted this report Article 16 of the Covenant would be automatically invoked. 'It may be best if we heard Article 16. Would you kindly read it for us, Edith.'

'I don't have to read it: I know it by heart,' she said. ' "Should any member of the League resort to war in disregard of its obligation under Articles 12, 13, or 15 it shall *ipso facto* be deemed to have committed a war against all other members of the League." That's the relevant part,' she said.

Léger asked for the rest. 'If you also remember that . . .'

She obliged, again reciting from memory, ' "the severance of all trade or financial relations, the prohibition of all intercourse between their nations and the nationals of the Covenant-breaking States, and the prevention of all financial, commercial, or personal intercourse . . ." '

Her memory did not fail her and she went on with it. ' ". . . It shall be the duty of the Council in such case to recommend to the several Governments concerned what effective military, naval, or air force the Members of the League shall severally contribute to the armed forces to be used to protect the covenants of the League." '

She went on to the end of the Article.

This time they lightly clapped her. The Committee was relaxing into tired jocularity.

'Well done,' Eden said.

'*Encore*,' Léger said, laughing.

'Really?' she asked.

'No, no. I joke. With a memory such as that, and such a voice, you could have been a stage actress.'

'Thank you, M. Léger. But is that really a compliment to pay to a lady?'

'In France it is—maybe not in England. I meant it as a compliment. I have friends who are actresses.'

Eden gave a small laugh. 'Don't we all?'

Madariaga asked whether the Committee were clear on the consequences of their report.

They all nodded.

She nodded.

The meeting then adjourned for the day and only Léger, Madariaga, Eden and she remained.

Edith hung about, giving some instructions to Gerty and the stenographer and arranging for a car to take them home.

She hovered, and then sat back down, joining in the tail-end chat of the meeting.

She loved the tail-endings of a good committee, the un-ceremonious comradeship of those who hang around after a meeting.

It was always the winners who stayed, the real inner committee.

Léger said that their report was unequivocal. 'In my expe-rience, no international dispute has ever been the subject of a clearer verdict.'

'You know, we are letting loose stupendous forces, hurri-cane forces. This will be the League's finest hour. This is the test of the will to collective action,' Eden said. 'I hate the expression—but history was made here tonight.'

'You seem to have confidence in the League,' she said.

He nodded. 'What I like about the League, as it is evolving, is that it ensures that negotiation is always used to its utmost limit.'

Outside, on the steps with Eden, waiting for their cars, now the even smaller last committee, the committee of two, Edith said, 'Will everyone hold together?'

'Laval is the risky one. But yes. I think the time has come for the world to pull together against the dictators. We can stop them in their tracks.'

'This is not pie in the sky—this is *realpolitik*?'

'Yes. I speak as an experienced politician privy to the

thinking of even more hardened politicians. This can be done. And this is the moment of trial.'

———◆———

The next day she went with Eden to meet with Laval, who had arrived back from Paris overnight. Eden wanted to clear the report with Laval face to face. Edith had had a copy sent to the Hôtel des Bergues so that Laval would have it on arrival.

In the lobby of the hotel Léger met them, kissing her hand as usual.

He looked worried.

'Could I speak with you privately?' he said to Eden.

'Of course,' Eden said.

'I shall wait in the lobby,' Edith said, hating herself for saying it. She should be present. She had the right to be present. But again, the old habits of diffidence died hard.

'Berry, I have known you longer than I have known Monsieur Eden. I would like you to be with us.'

'As you wish, sir.'

She was hugely gratified.

'I feel it is best we go to the privacy of my room,' Léger said.

He sounded grave.

They took the lift to his floor and went into his bedroom suite which had not yet been attended to by the maid.

He apologised. 'Hotel maids seem to come at unpredictable times. They seem to work to a clock from another zone of time.'

The room had the odour of a man's presence, the odour of a refined man. Léger's odour was of fine food, fine wine, fine tobacco, exquisite toiletries. And fresh flowers in vases.

She tried not to be too obvious as she breathed deeply of it. She felt she was almost pilfering it. To take in another's odour so deliberately was almost ... what? An intimacy of the nose?

Léger placed a couple of chairs together in the small sitting room and they sat. '*Thé? Chocolat?*'

They shook their heads.

'Laval is angry. He feels we went too far last night. Or to be more particular, that I went too far in giving French approval for the resolution.'

The French were going to back off.

'He will renege?' said Eden, showing no perturbation.

'I doubt that he will renege. It is more my position which is in jeopardy.'

'*You* in jeopardy?!'

'He may hold me responsible and if Cabinet rejects the report, the volatile Cabinet may also reject me.'

'That serious?'

'It is that serious.'

'You have been in the Department for years!'

Transfixed, she listened to this exchange between these men, perhaps two of the three most powerful men in the crisis—Laval being the third.

Edith admired Léger's quiet French composure. It seemed to her to be inconceivable that a man as cultivated and powerful as he was could be in jeopardy.

She'd read his poetry.

She wondered if Eden had.

'I am not a popular man in France at the moment,' Léger said. 'I dislike asking any man to be duplicitous, worse, an Englishman "to boot", even if that is the common perception of our craft. But I have to beg you, dear fellow, to be so for my sake.'

'Explain to me further your situation,' Eden said.

'Laval thinks we have gone too far in the report and he thinks that I should've restrained you. I should not have committed France. He perceives me as being weak with you and with England. Yet before we met that day he had foreseen the resolution and had wanted to support it.'

'And what do you think is required?'

Léger now lost poise, he was disconcerted.

'I need for you to convey to Laval that I offered, well ...
offered opposition to the final report. That I fought against
the report ...'

It was so abject a request that Edith had to look away to
the flowers in the vase at the desk. Had Léger bought the
flowers, requested the flowers? Were they a gift from a woman
friend?

She could not look at him—his abjection could not be
further removed from the image of the Léger that the world
knew.

Edith looked back to him and then felt so much empathy
for him that she felt tense.

She had never seen a man lose so much dignity.

And she felt for him that he should have to do it in front
of England. England, the traditional prickly partner in diplomatic competitiveness and distrust.

Léger went on, 'Convey, please, to Laval that you were
dissatisfied and angered by my "opposition" last night.'

He was asking Eden to lie.

In diplomatic reputation, she supposed Eden was junior to
Léger—Léger being the older bureaucrat of a great power—
but Eden was a Minister of the Crown, Léger a bureaucrat.
Politically, Eden had the power.

She felt no one could refuse to help Léger, yet she was
fearful of perversion of the record and of the unorthodoxy of
the meeting now taking place.

'Of course, my dear chap,' Eden said. 'I will do what you
need for you to hold your position. Inconceivable that you
could be in jeopardy.'

Edith wondered if Eden had thought this through.

And what should she report to Avenol? Had Léger included
her in this meeting so that her report to Avenol would also
reflect this rewriting of the meeting?

Léger said, 'I thank you. These are strange times in French politics. We have left behind the time of grand design, of grand realisation. We are into the time of a political *décadence*. Sadly.' He sighed tiredly. 'In the time of Briand there was never ambiguity in our position. Security for France, first, yes; but in step with the rhythm of the broader vision of collective action. Always.'

What he was saying may have been close to treason.

'Of course I will consolidate your position with Laval,' Eden repeated. 'The world needs your counsel. Politicians such as Laval and myself come and go. But you, you are the continuity of French national decency. And sound intelligence.'

'I thank you,' Léger said again. He then tried to regain his poise. 'I fear the days of international vision are nearly over; yet I feel now that I am a guardian of the guarantees of peace we put into place in the 1920s. The people believed us when we told them that these guarantees would bring lasting peace. We must act, preferably within the League, to prevent—or punish—treaty violations. Treaties must be made inviolate. Treaties are the handshake of world civilisation. Treaties are the walls of the city.'

He seemed to grow grey-faced.

He shook Eden's hand. He again kissed Edith's hand, saying to her, 'I have taken you into my confidence, Berry, because of our love for the memory of Aristide Briand. We have to keep the promises he made to the world.'

'Of course.'

Of course what? She was being encircled by this confidence. She was party to the perversion of the historical record.

'I was at his bedside when he died,' Léger said.

'It was a sad day for the world,' she said. He was using Briand as a way of tying her to him.

Léger held Eden by the arm at the door. He said, 'You understand, I am sure, that I ask for this unsavoury manoeuvre not because of personal need—it is not for reasons of career.' He made the French puff of dismissal. 'I do it because I fear the person who would replace me—I fear on behalf of the world.'

Eden looked him in the eye. 'I understand completely. Your position must be defended. In everyone's interest.'

'Go to Laval, now. I will wait until called.'

They left Léger in his room.

In the corridors, on the way to Laval's suite, Eden turned to her and said, 'Is it a French ploy?'

She was flattered and at the same time caught unawares. 'Léger seemed genuinely upset. I found it upsetting, to see him like that.'

'In your eyes he is not an actor?'

'No. It was genuine distress and dilemma.'

'I agree. I demean myself by suggesting that it may be a ploy. We can, however, use this situation to put iron into Laval.'

She saw how he might do that.

'You are, of course, off duty, Berry. This is behind the scenes—not for the report to A.'

Could Eden decide that? How could he decide her duties and where her duty might lie?

She nodded, with misgivings. But things were happening too quickly for her to find her proper position.

They found Laval in his room, fiddling with a wireless set. 'I have a financial interest in a Swiss broadcasting station but I cannot find it on the dial. Perhaps it is a fictitious broadcasting station. Maybe I have been duped.'

Eden then went into what Edith could only describe as a fabulous act.

He evinced annoyance. 'I have a serious complaint.'

Laval gave up fiddling with the wireless set and assumed his diplomatic posture. He showed them into his sitting room. 'Complaint? How so? Please—speak.'

'You and I agreed that France and England would stand

together: that we would reach a position together and stick.'

Laval nodded. 'Of course.'

Eden ploughed on. 'That being the case, at the meeting last night of the Committee of Five, Léger did nothing but make difficulties. He showed none of your reason and moral strength. Since you have been out of Geneva he has obstructed us. I am sure they were not your instructions. It is my understanding that the report of the Committee of Five would be an expression of your country and my country's positions of strength.'

Laval seemed not to know quite how to handle this.

Eden then said, 'I demand that you inform Léger of your moral and diplomatic position—that is, that we are together shoulder to shoulder, France and the United Kingdom.'

It was obvious to Edith that Eden still felt that Laval and the French had to be *dragged* into strong action. He was using the manoeuvre to do just that.

But people dragged into strong positions made the position less stable. She knew that also.

Laval took the bait and agreed to expressing displeasure with Léger's *obstructionnisme*.

He took them to his new wireless set and explained it. Its dial indicated that it could reach Berlin, Moscow, Athens.

As he fussed with a demonstration which did not live up to his expectations, she sensed that he was keeping them in the room so that he could further digest what they had said. After all it was not the first wireless set either of them had seen.

He was not letting them go just yet.

Perhaps he wanted Eden to let more drop. Perhaps he had not been convinced. But Eden did not reopen the subject and, after a polite length of time, excused them both.

Afterwards, when Eden and she had left Laval's room, they had tea in a private room off the lobby.

Edith thrilled at being *tête-à-tête* with such a glamorous figure. She felt that she was indeed *on stage*.

She even wished that someone from the office would see them there together taking tea.

She tried to prevent her tone of voice or demeanour from becoming too feminine, she tried to maintain a professional tone.

It was a matter of pride that she should not in any way flirt or be thought of as flirting.

But inside her was a silly girl, locked in her room hammering on the door, wanting to flirt. Wanting to flirt outrageously.

Eden said to her, 'The French will be only as strong as they are compelled to be.'

'Can you compel them?'

'I can only try.'

A messenger arrived with a dispatch for Eden. He read it and handed it to her. 'The Italians have bombed a Red Cross ambulance and hospital near Melka Dida. Where is that?'

Edith took out a map from her attaché case and spread it out and together they found Melka Dida.

'You know what we have to do?' Eden asked her.

'Yes. We have to dust off the economic sanctions plans of the Second Assembly so we can be ready to launch.'

'Quite so.'

'I have already called up the file.'

'I think we should draw up a special list of commodities which must definitely be prohibited to Italy.'

'May I raise a point, Minister?'

'By all means.'

She heard the locked-away girl who wanted to flirt groan at her oh-so-correct tone of voice. Lordy, why not say, *let's leave the affairs of the world for now and relax. Why not say, 'And tell me Anthony, what gives you most pleasure in life?'*

Edith said, 'The Second Assembly thought that every effort

should be made with the economic sanctions to avoid their effect falling on the civilian population—the women and children.'

'I am aware of that argument, but isn't the aim to use the Lesser Misery of sanctions to avoid the Grimmer Misery— the misery of war?'

'During the blockade in the War—which was very much like sanctions, I suppose—it was the poor and the children who suffered in Germany; the ruling junta and the army were fed. Many cases of rickets have shown up among children.'

'That's why the sanctions should be swift and total—before the Italians can arrange secret and illegal supplies and so on. The sanctions should cause a collapse of the economy. They should be automatic and terrible—make life intolerable to the ordinary man and woman. The theory of modern war is that the army and the people are one. Everyone is responsible for the war. Everyone a soldier.'

'Except the very young.'

'Of course.'

'I rather favour gradual strangulation of the economy. And that food and medicines should come well down the list.'

'Strangulation? You're both compassionate and rather cold-blooded, Berry. Glad you're on my side and not on theirs.'

She heard him say 'on my side' and savoured the words for all their other meanings. Or at least the locked-away girl savoured them.

'I am glad that I am on *your side*, Minister.' The words came out with a rather softer tone that she'd intended. She corrected her voice. 'Naturally we start by stopping war materials,' she said.

'Beg to differ. You are wrong. Swift and total, I think. Ton of bricks. The financial structure of Italy must be collapsed first.'

He then left that point, as being settled. 'I have to move assiduously. It must not seem that the British are pushing everyone on this—and my Co-Foreign Secretary, Sam Hoare, has been telephoning me asking that we not be seen as the initiator of all this strong stuff.'

He smiled at her. 'So you see, Laval and Léger are not the only ones with problems in their Cabinet.'

It was always other squabbles of politics which tripped up their feet.

'See if you can jolly the others along,' said Eden. 'Anything you can do, Berry. I'm sure that Laval wants to be friends with Musso, but I think we can frog-march him—no pun intended—into sanctions.'

She said, 'I will do what I can to get the Assembly moving rapidly.'

'Good. All the commotion will now shift to the special Assembly. Do you think we're too far out ahead of the pack on this?'

'No—not at all. I have been testing the water.' Edith began to tick off the members of the Assembly whose opinions she'd tested. 'We are backed by almost all of Europe, the Dominions, Holland, Belgium, Soviet Russia, the Balkans, Scandinavia, the Little Entente—they are all firmly against Italy and for the sanctions. Romania worries about its oil exports to Italy which are substantial.'

'Quite so. I suspect I will be hearing "*Encore du cognac pour les anglais, encore du cognac*" at dinner with Titulescu tonight. Did you know he always brings his own supply of brandy to Geneva?'

'I have been privileged to taste Monsieur Titulescu's brandy,' she said, with a smile. Her reply sounded somewhat indecorous—Titulescu, the brandy, and Edith. She qualified, 'I have been at an official dinner with the Romanians.'

'Talking of brandy,' Eden said, 'I was at a lunch in London with Lady Cunard and Nicolson—at Grosvenor Square—and others, just before I came across to Geneva. I'd just come from Cabinet. Emerald—that is, Lady Cunard—knowing full well I can't talk about Cabinet, simply pops out as her first question, in full hearing of the dinner party, "You are all wrong about Italy. Why should she not have Ethiopia? You must tell me what Cabinet's thinking." '

'What did you reply to Lady Cunard?' Edith asked tentatively, not sure how far to inquire into his social life.

'To make it worse, de Castellane from the French Embassy had to save me. De Castellane made the joke about *cocottes* and the *commandant de frégate*.'

Edith laughed even though she did not get the point of the '*cocottes* and commandants' and supposed it was the arcane talk of gentlemen to gentlemen and left it at that. Or gentlemen to gentlemen and Lady Cunard. Even if these days she were more familiar with the dinner talk of gentlemen and ladies of high rank.

She had enough in her life to puzzle about, without puzzling about *cocottes* and their commandants.

Despite their tactical differences, Edith was exhilarated that the sanctions instrument was now going to be tested. They would drag France along, and the Assembly was reasonably solid.

She heard herself say, 'I don't think I understand the joke about the *cocottes* and their commandants. Maybe I come from too genteel a background.'

'Oh?' He seemed disconcerted.

She should not have asked.

'Oh, I don't think it's really a joke at all—I think de Castellane was saving me from Emerald's indiscreet questioning, showing me at the same time that he knew I was in a hot seat. It's what diplomatic chaps do for each other. Sometimes.'

'Oh, I see.'

His face became bemused. 'Must be a joke in there somewhere though. I suppose.' He looked at her sheepishly. 'Could be that I missed the joke. In the fluster of it all.'

She smiled widely and fully for the first time in days. She felt her facial muscles relax.

Eden stumbled on. 'I will, Berry, endeavour to find out the point of the joke—if joke it be—and report back to you.'

'I would enjoy that.'

She dropped her report for Avenol in to the Night Officer so that it would be there for him first thing.

She did not report on the Léger incident and she implied his 'opposition' at the meeting.

She'd decided that, on balance, the protection of Léger was a priority.

She'd been manipulated, but not so unwillingly. She'd hardly had time to consider how she should handle the things which had happened that day.

She was too tired to care.

She was bone weary.

Was that how wars began? Because everyone was too tired to bother?

The Diplomacy of Bibulation

E dith got home to the apartment one night after a late meeting of the Committee, took her attaché case and papers from the League driver who had carried them to the door, said goodnight to him, backed herself in through the door, pushed it closed with her foot, went on into the sitting room—which Ambrose insisted on calling the drawing room—dropped her handbag, attaché case and papers on to the floor, went over and kissed Ambrose on the cheek, noting that he was wearing light *maquillage*, flopped into an armchair and took off her shoes.

Had he been 'out'?

She placed her shoes side by side, but then staring at them for a second, she tipped them over with her foot, looked at them again, and then bad-temperedly but lightly kicked them across the room.

She looked at the attaché case and handbag in matching leather. In a cupboard somewhere there was a travelling case as well. A sometime gift from Robert. Tonight it did not please her. Tonight it embarrassed her. 'Matching' was not one of the higher principles of aesthetics. She thought it was on a par with neatness. That was the limit of his aesthetics. Still, he had *thought out* the gift.

It was *too* thought-out—in the duller sense.

Or was she being an ungrateful harridan?

Yes. Ungrateful harridan.

In the early years at the League, she'd used her briefcase from university, until it had become too scruffed and would not respond to polish. She'd hung on to it—for whatever sentimental reason—for as long as she could.

She looked at Ambrose but couldn't find the energy to speak.

Ambrose had raised his head from his book and watched her testy entry but had said nothing.

Her entry barely expressed the ire she'd brought home. It was not in any way a rebellion against the shipshape order which Ambrose had brought to the apartment over the time he'd been there, but she may as well rage against that as well. They had, on his suggestion, let the housekeeper go. Even Robert, on his last flying visit home, had commented on the order of the place.

Ambrose's order would tonight have to stand in for all that beset her and take the brunt.

'Shipshape' was not an aesthetic for which she cared, either. Although she'd been relieved that Ambrose was no longer the slightly unkempt bohemian bachelor of yesteryear. If bachelor were the word in his case.

He was now, she thought, if anything, a little prissy. Perhaps prim.

Yes, he was now a little *prissy*.

She looked at him and he looked at her looking at him.

Prissiness was a defensible enough aesthetic.

Perhaps.

If it came with elegance.

In Ambrose's case, it did. How imperturbably elegant he always looked these days. So much composure.

Maybe it was serenity.

She was sure it was.

He should not be serene while she was *beset.*

Robert, on the other hand, had been downright slovenly.

Better prissy than slovenly, of that she was sure.

She was perhaps prissy herself.

Yes, she was prissy. With a touch of elegance. At times. When at her best.

> *Two prissy people*
> *living in a steeple*
> *known now and then,*
> *to occasionally*
> *tipple.*

Poor rhyming. Shocking.

Maybe that was what Ambrose and she were—one of nature's poorly rhymed couplets.

Or maybe *too* rhymed.

In personality, they were, she supposed, both by nature *aides-de-camp.* In a way, while she was an *aide-de-camp* in work, she felt she needed, well, a 'wife' at home. And perhaps that was what Ambrose had become.

While she, alas, had turned out not to be quite a wife. Not at all a wife.

You could, of course, be a Leader of Men at work, and a wife at home.

If you chose.

Or if you were chosen.

He was dressed in his knee-length, blue satin lounging jacket with flared sleeves and its fetching, high, round neckline—very Chinoise—over cream silk-satin trousers. Blue velvet slippers.

She coveted the jacket. It was always a fight to see who got to it first.

She admitted that his appearance, at least, pleased her. His calm did not please her.

Mr Femality.

They continued to silently look at each other.

If she left the shoes where they were, would Ambrose pick them up and put them away before bed?

She pulled a face at him.

Book on his knees, he continued to look at her.

She broke first. 'Do you think I drink too much?' she said, challenging him. Not quite recognising her voice. It was a difficult question to get out. Exposing. Well, it was out now.

'Why do you ask?' He sounded decidedly unchallenged by her question.

'Sweetser said something tonight about my drinking—jokingly, of course—but his jokes are so ponderous. It was obviously a stone wrapped in cellophane.'

Ambrose watched her, expressionless, but she had his attention.

'Well?!' she said.

He closed the book on the bookmark.

Don't lose your place just because of me, Little Miss Serenity. Mr Femality.

'What did Sweetser say, exactly?'

'He suggested I "hadn't come to terms" with Robert's "leaving" and that this was causing me to hit the bottle.'

'He said "hit the bottle"?!'

'He used some euphemism: "finding comfort in cocktails", I think it was. Hell's bells—Robert's been gone for ages. And he does return.'

'Sweetser said *that*?'

That wasn't exactly what had been said by Sweetser, but that would do for now. What he *had* said, she remembered precisely—in flaming letters. 'How dare he!'

'And what did you say to Sweetser?'

She sniggered, but the snigger did not in any way relieve her injured fury. 'Ah—what did I say!? I turned to him and held him in my gaze and said, "Arthur," I said, "if I drink a lot, it's because I have a lot to drink about."'

Ambrose laughed. 'Very good, Edith.'

'And while on the question of annoyance,' Edith said, 'I wish people—namely you, dear Ambrose—would stop expressing surprise when I make a joke. I make many jokes. Yet people—namely, you—refuse to see me as a dazzling wit. All my life that's happened, even at university. I have wanted, now and then, to be seen as a lovable clown. Instead, people see me as Earnest Edith. It's something about my hair. There are no red-headed clowns.'

'I seem to recall that there *are* red-headed clowns. Or red-nosed clowns,' Ambrose said. 'Maybe you're becoming a red-nosed clown.'

'Don't be cruel.' She tried for it to come out as a funny complaint but it came out just as a bald old complaint.

He glanced at her, showing that he'd registered her pique.

She looked over at the drinks table. She found herself arguing with herself about having a drink. 'The Good Edith and the Bad Edith are arguing now about having a drink. That's how piqued I am by Sweetser.'

'Listen to the Bad Edith,' Ambrose advised. 'Have a drink.'

'Hah—you're wrong. It's the Bad Edith who says not to drink; the Good Edith wants me to have a drink.'

He laughed again.

'And don't say, ''*Very good, Edith.*'''

'It's probably best that you not be seen as a clown,' he said. 'The problem with being a clown is that you can ridicule a chief but never *be* a chief. And, sorry to say, you are correct—you've never been seen as a clown.'

'A wit—do you see me as a wit then?' She paused. 'Well?'

'You *are* in a bad mood. Were you squiffed when Sweetser said this to you?'

'I'd had lunch and dinner wine, if that's what you mean. No different to any other day. A *pichet* or so of wine. For mercy sake, don't you start.'

'I wasn't "starting"—I was asking you what caused Sweetser to make this remark.'

'I think he has been observing me. He hates that Avenol has attached me to the Committee and that I'm buddies with Eden.'

'There is a theory,' Ambrose said, 'that it's not the alcohol that's bad for you: it's the late nights which accompany the drinking.'

'I never show my drink.'

Ambrose went to the drinks table and poured them both a port.

He came over to her, and handed her the drink and kissed her forehead, 'Have you eaten?'

'Yes. Thank you.' She drank from the glass and then added, 'Dear.'

He returned to his seat. 'Are you sure that you've eaten?'

'*Yes, I am sure that I've eaten. Sure, sure, sure.*'

'Mustn't skip meals.'

'And *you* mustn't become a *mother*. You can be a girlfriend, you can be a big sister. You can, if you so wish, be a chorus girl, you can be a hussy, you can even be courtesan. But do not, not ever, try to become a mother.'

'To that, dear Edith, I have never made claim.'

'You would never be good at it. Not at all. And do not ever become matronly.'

'Woefully, I dare say I will.'

She turned the idea over in her head and then said, wearily, 'I dare say that we'll both become matronly. What a sickening thought. Sickening.'

She was hiding in the chatter, hiding from the hideous encounter with Sweetser.

She returned to the burning issue. 'I do not show my drink.'

Ambrose examined his nails, picked up a nail file and worked on them. He said, quietly, as if taking a conversational risk, 'The Manual to the Diplomacy of Bibulation states that one should never assume that people don't know you've been drinking. It's the Drinkers' Grand Delusion. Sober people pretty much always know. And drinkers pretty much always know. Always assume that people know.'

'I am not a "drinker",' she said tersely. 'I am a person who drinks.'

She stared at him feeling unpleasantly annoyed. Annoyed by everything. 'Oh, put down the nail file.'

It reminded her of how bad her own nails were. Her grooming at present was a disaster. No time.

'Nancyboy.'

She didn't say it with good humour.

She knew that his rule was that youth let you off much of the boredom of grooming but at their age grooming was everything.

He looked across at her and did put down the nail file and gave her full eye attention, crossing his legs as if to emphasise the attention he was giving her. And then he said, 'Another precept of the Diplomacy of Bibulation is: Don't drink when with sober people; and don't stay completely sober when with drinking people.'

'Nancyboy.'

'Drinking is civilisation flirting with anarchy.'

'Pansy.'

He didn't respond.

'Nancyboy,' she said, staring at him, not really feeling any personal antagonism, more a free-floating antagonism. 'Pansy nancyboy.'

He opened his book and began to read.

She watched him read and then said, 'Stop talking to me as if I am eighteen years old. Drinking is a slight relaxation of discipline or it's nothing. It's to do with frivolity and frivolity has no rules. Pleasure maybe has rules. But not fun.'

He again closed his book and returned his attention to her.

'Nancyboy. Pansy.'

'Have I ever told you that in my part of the country the pansy is called "heart's-ease"?'

'Fascinating.'

He continued with his sermonising, 'The saddest thing of all about the drinking life is that when one was young and innocent and one drank to excess it appeared to others to be "enchanting", perhaps "daring", even amusing: now that we're older, we appear simply as, well, mundanely, people who've had too much to drink.'

'Is that what they taught you in the Foreign Office? The Diplomacy of Drinking?'

'As a matter of fact, they did give us some advice on drinking. Basically, it was that one should never be drunk at the wrong time of the day. Don't be seven o'clock in the bar when it is only five. We all scoffed, of course. Hence my downwards career. Hence the state of the Empire.'

She drank the port. 'I'm going to bed.' She stood up and went over to Ambrose, giving him a goodnight kiss, 'See you in the morning, darling. Sorry—didn't intend to be mean—I'm done in.'

'The more I think about the state of the Empire, it's curious—as long as we've had an empire it's been considered to be in a bad state. Bit like the jokes in *Punch*. Not as good as they used to be and always have been.'

She gave a weak grin of appreciation at his efforts towards good humour.

She glanced at her papers, attaché case and stuff dumped in the room and at her scattered shoes.

She left it all.

In her bedroom, she felt a desperate need to be free of all tightness: the earrings, the waistband of her skirt, the tightness of her underclothing—girdle, stockings, brassiere, the elastic waistband of her underpants, her garter belt—her stockings, the rings on her fingers, her watchband. The lot.

She pulled them off and let them stay where they fell.

Her body was bridling at constraint. Even her make-up felt tight.

She chose a flowing ankle-length crepe-de-chine nightgown which left her shoulders and arms bare and her breasts swinging free and, putting it on, went to her bathroom, washed her make-up off with a hand cloth, came back to her bedroom and fell with relief onto the bed. She did not put on night cream.

Only after breathing deeply and worming her way down into her bed did she let Sweetser's words fully return to her, and his words returned to her over and over as she lay there. He'd said more than she'd told. Sweetser had said, 'I heard Walters and Bartou talking about you and the question of your drinking came up, that's all. Thought I should mention it. Word to the wise.' She kept going over Sweetser's remarks and her clever rejoinder, a rejoinder which she knew had not nullified the situation at all.

Not at all.

His remarks implied all sorts of things which she couldn't quite bring herself to face. There were the implications for her professionalism. And implications about the way people must see her. She felt sick. Was she commonly seen as a tippler? And there was his presuming to comment about Robert's absence from her life. And furthermore, on top of everything, she wasn't ecstatic with Ambrose's observation on the so-called 'delusion of drinkers'—that people could always tell.

She suspected that he was wrong about that, but it added to her agitation. It dawned on her that he, too, was warning her. Why was he warning her? About what was he warning her?

The hide of Sweetser and Walters and Bartou to speak about her behind her back.

She would have it out with them.

Lying there seething, she heard Ambrose wash the glasses in the kitchen, and then go to his room.

She lay there stark awake. Realising that she wasn't going to be able to sleep, she pulled herself out of bed and went back out to the sitting room.

Looking into the darkened room, she saw that Ambrose had picked up her papers and attaché case and put them on the table. Her shoes were together. She smiled tiredly. She'd been going to do it herself.

She knocked on Ambrose's door.

'Come.'

She went in and threw herself on the bed beside him and began to cry.

'Darling, what is it?' he said, taking her in his arms and stroking her hair. She put her face to his. The make-up had gone from his face, replaced by the clean smell of night cream.

'The wretched Sweetser.'

'Come on, Edith, you've never let Sweetser get to you. And he's only trying to be, well, *superior*. He probably didn't give the matter a second thought. Just something to say in passing to make himself appear in-the-know with the *haute direction*.'

Ambrose continued to stroke her hair.

'I didn't tell you all,' she said, at last, through the crying.

'Tell me all.'

'I'd finished the meeting. People were hanging around as they do after a meeting, but I was exhausted and eager to get home. I said my goodnights and went to my office. I put on my coat and did my face, and realised that I felt edgy, the usual feeling of being edgy after a difficult meeting. Laval is dragging his feet again on full sanctions. I took out my flask and, well, had a nip. And who should come in through the door but Sweetser—he'd been at some other meeting, I suppose, he barged in without knocking—he looked in and said something about an action file he was searching for.'

'He caught you with the flask at your lips?'

'Precisely.'

'And?'

'It was, of course, an irregular request and he's done it before—taken a file before it's gone back to Registry.'

'And?'

181

'And, he said, "Finding comfort in cocktails?", in his joking voice, and then said rather seriously, "Not good to drink alone."'

'And you said?'

'I said—she put on an American accent—"Would you like a nip, Arthur?" He didn't. He then continued in a brotherly voice, saying, "I heard Walters and Bartou talking about your drinking. I told them you were going through a difficult time and all. I thought I should mention the conversation to you. A word to the wise." And, furthermore, he actually put his index finger to the side of his nose—he actually did.'

'Your American accent needs coaching, darling. And that's when you said . . .?'

'That's when I said, "If I drink a lot, *Arthur*, it's because I have a lot to drink about."'

She got no additional applause for her quip.

'That's all that was said?' The tone of Ambrose's voice had changed.

'He said more. He suggested that the Committee was too much for me. "Taxing" was his word.'

'He said that?'

'Implied that.'

'That's all—entirely all?'

'Isn't that enough?'

'It's enough. It is indeed enough.' His voice was serious.

'Why the interrogation?'

He was silent.

She filled the silence. 'And anyhow, the more I think about it, why on earth was Sweetser looking for a file at that time of night?!'

Ambrose ignored this gambit. 'On further consideration, Edith, your saying, "If I drink a lot, it's because I have a lot to drink about" was a shrewd reply.'

'I thought it rather good. At the time. On the spur. But I don't see what *shrewdness* has to do with it.'

'Sit up, Edith.'

There in the darkness, they both pulled themselves up, side by side against the bedhead, her head on his shoulder, their hands clasped.

'It was a tactical reply because it implies that you're under strain.'

'I am not "under strain" and I am not "taxed" by my work with the Committee. It's a simple matter—I was edgy after a meeting. I had a nip to calm me. I'll have it out with them all tomorrow—face to face.'

'How do you intend to do that, exactly—this "having it out"?'

'I'll storm in and ask them what they think they're doing talking behind my back.'

He didn't reply.

'You obviously don't agree?'

'You might shut Sweetser up. But I don't know if that is the approach with Walters. Bartou will never harm you. Bartou was probably defending you. He's your best ally as you know, a friend-in-club. But with Walters we will have to think up better moves. He is after all Deputy Secretary-General.'

'They're a bunch of gossips.'

'It has to be thought about some more.'

'You don't think Walters would have the hide to reprimand me!?'

'Walters *is* Deputy Secretary-General. He may call you into the Head's Office for six of the best. Is it Regulation 286? No alcohol in the office? Or is that the rule on dogs?'

'It's the regulation on dogs and their drinking. I'll have it out with Walters. I'll tell them all to mind their own b— business.'

'Edith, we'll have to talk about it. In the cold light of day. Not now.'

She felt suddenly afraid of his voice. She did not want to

ask why they'd need to talk about it more. 'May I stay the night with you?'

'Of course.'

She pushed in beside him and they snuggled back down in the bed.

'Go to sleep,' he whispered, and then quoted in his becalming, loving voice, as if to a child: 'It may well be that the bear you have seen is only a bush. Remember, "in the night, imagining some fear, how easy is a bush supposed a bear".'

'Say it again.' Edith closed her eyes, putting Ambrose's hand up inside her nightdress, between her legs. His wonderful, firm and knowing fingers began to move inside her. He whispered it to her again more fully,

The lunatic, the lover and the poet,
Are of imagination all compact:
One sees more devils than vast hell can hold,
That is, the madman: the lover, all as frantic,
Sees Helen's beauty in a brow of Egypt:
The poet's eyes, in fine frenzy rolling,
Doth glance from heaven to earth, from earth to heaven ...
Turns them to shapes ...
Or in the night, imagining some fear,
How easy is a bush supposed a bear!

In the silence which followed, his gentle fingers brought her to a small, comforting release which shooed away some of her tension. She drifted to sleep in his arms, fleeing to the comfort of oblivion, but as she drifted, she was vaguely aware that Ambrose was lying there, awake.

In the morning, as she went about dressing, she thought out a pointed remark for Walters and ripping riposte for Sweetser. And she would say to Bartou something about those in glass houses ...

She felt in better spirits.

She was finishing her make-up when Ambrose came back up to the apartment after having been shaved at the *barbier*. He stood and watched her make-up.

'How was Barber Didier today?' she asked. 'Did he have any more views on the Italian crisis for you to communicate to the League?'

'He still sides with Mussolini.'

'Why do you persist with him?'

'If I changed barbers he would know I was going somewhere else and stare at me every day as I passed his shop. Would ruin my day. And Arthur Norris once said to me, "Even in the wilds of Asia, I have never shaved myself when it could possibly be avoided. It's one of those sordid annoying operations which put one in bad humour for the rest of the day." '

'You shave yourself in the evening.'

'The second shave is different. The morning shave is to allow me to face the world. The evening shave is to allow me to face myself.'

She examined her make-up, moving her head from side to side. 'Do you know the first woman I saw make-up in public?'

'No.' He didn't seem that interested.

'The wife of the New South Wales Premier—Ada Holman. She was the most sophisticated woman—apart from my mother—I have ever met. She had her initials on her specially made cigarettes. And she made-up in public. New South Wales, by the way, is a state of Australia.'

They went to the café downstairs for breakfast.

As soon as they were seated and had ordered, Ambrose said, 'I want to say that I was rather preachy with you last night. Sorry. Didn't quite see the full picture. Sorry about all that stuff about diplomatic drinking. Must've sounded rather prefectorial.'

'Forgiven. Hang the precepts of drinking. The rules of gossip should be enforced. Whatever they are. Sweetser barging into my office. Sweetser! You know he once blew his nose while seated at dinner? And he dares to tell *me* how to behave.'

She sipped her tea. 'And he uses too much slang.'

'Has anyone ever mentioned it before?'

'Sorry???'

'The drink question.'

'No. Never. Would never have dared. And, there is no "drink question".'

'Go over it again for me.'

'For mercy sake, Ambrose!'

'Indulge me.'

She recounted the events of the previous evening. 'It's not as if I was staggering around the office. I don't drink any more than any of them.'

'That's the Second Delusion of the Drinker—drinkers always imagine that other people all drink as much as they do.'

'You drink as much as I do.'

He was quiet.

'Admit it!'

'In truth, dear Edith, you regularly have two or three more drinks than I.'

'Rubbish.'

He went on with his breakfast.

'Do you count?'

He didn't reply.

'Oh, stop being so damned impeccable. It's never affected my work. Never.'

Ambrose didn't say anything.

'You think it has?' she said, defiantly.

He was silent again.

She burst out, 'If you are thinking *something*, say it. Don't sit in sanctimonious silence!'

He took her hand. 'I'm on your side, Edith. And remember that I'm a doctor, as well as your dear friend.'

'Sorry. But I hardly need a doctor. I need a lawyer. I should sue for slander.'

'It was a nasty thing to have thrown in your face. And in the cold light of day, yes, I do think that it has serious implications.'

'What implications?'

'The perception that you drink too much.'

She coloured. 'I'm going to throw it back at them. I'm going to see Walters. Have it out. Clear the air.'

She looked at her watch and rose to leave, dabbing her mouth with the serviette, careful of her lipstick.

'Don't go— not yet. Sit down.'

'I have to go. The car will be here.' She leaned over and kissed him. 'Want a lift?'

'Yes.' He finished up and followed her on to the pavement.

'I am going to put a lid on the rumours—now. This day.'

They got into the car.

'I agree—but we have to find a way to do that.'

She dropped him off first and found that by the time she reached her office she had lost her momentum.

Ambrose's remark about serious implications was eating away at her.

She saw now that simple outrage would not necessarily do the trick.

She turned away from the League door and walked back to Ambrose's office. He had his suit coat off and was at work at his desk. He was startled to see her. 'What's happened?'

'Don't look so worried.' She sat down.

'Did you do anything about it?'

'No. I agree with you. We should talk more. Do you have a moment?'

'Of course.'

'Tell me more about the shrewdness of my saying "I have a lot to drink about"? How might it be useful?'

'It allows you to plead strain and special conditions. Robert and so on ...'

'He's been gone for ... how long? Who cares? Hardly a new situation.'

'It's a situation that people would understand.'

'Hang on—you're siding with them. If I say that, then I admit to being a tippler. Or worse.'

'You are not a drunkard, Edith.'

'Well, *thank you*. I will not plead "special circumstances"—that would be admission of guilt. Some sort of guilt. And what are the implications you alluded to? Do you think they might take the Committee away from me?'

'I don't know what they might do.'

'You could say something—boys together. You know Walters, you know Sweetser.'

'I could. I suppose I could say something *in club*. But I'm pretty much on the outer these days. Might make matters worse. Do you know what I think you should do? It might help for you to see a doctor who specialises in this sort of thing.'

Hearing him say this scared her. 'What "sort of thing"? A doctor who specialises in the treatment of inebriates?'

'I think you're suffering from the demands of everything. I think you took the collapse of the Disarmament Conference very hard. Your personal life has suffered an ... upheaval, shall we say. Avenol and the French taking over the *haute direction* has meant new ways of doing things. It's been trying for you. Then there's this Italian crisis. You're certainly suffering fatigue and strain.'

'Strain? That implies I can't handle the work.'

'You could plead nervous prostration. A "nerve storm". That's not as bad. All the American film actors have them.'

'I will not.'

'It shifts the blame away from the drinking.'

'You do think I drink too much!' She began to cry. 'You see me as an inebriate!' She stopped her crying and became angry. 'They all drink! Everyone in Europe drinks.'

He came around from his desk and crouched beside her, putting his arm around her.

'In a sense, that's true,' he said.

'What do you mean "in a sense"? They do! Agree with me for once!'

'Well, for the French, wine is simply food.'

'I am sick to death of the "French way". Don't talk to me ever again about the "French way". I've seen them staggering out of their *estaminets* drunk on pastis. Don't talk to me about civilised drinking. The French drink to get squiffed just like everyone else.'

'Edith.'

She looked him in the eye, still boiling.

'Edith, I think that your reaction to all this is a sure sign that you are seriously strained.'

Hearing him say that now brought it home with a bang. She *was strained*, she was strained near to breaking. She began to cry again. But that didn't mean she should give up. 'The sanctions are not moving well at all.'

He stroked her, comforting her.

He then stood up from his crouching position, and went to the window, staring out.

She watched him. 'Don't go into a thoughtful limbo!'

He turned around to face her. 'You should see a doctor who'll advise you on your state of mind and general health. And then you could perhaps present this medical advice to the office. Let it be known.'

'They will have to accept me the way I am. I'll brazen it out.'

' "By how we live we show the way"?' For the first time that morning, his mood seemed to lighten. 'That's rather audacious. I rather like that. But it's a tall order to take on yourself, Edith—teaching the world how to drink.'

She smiled through her tears, 'My life will be a demonstration of *la joie de vivre*, liberty for my *unwomanly* self. My contribution to the cause of emancipation.'

His seriousness returned. 'Edith, how others perceive us does matter. It's an unfair truth about the world, but to reveal our vices too readily is to give ammunition to our enemies. We do have to take care. Politically. And to feel that you need to prove you're strong is weakness.'

She began to come around to the doctor solution. 'I'll go to a doctor, then. But not to be certified as ill. I'll get a medical declaration giving me a clean bill of health and I'll throw that in their faces. A declaration of my fitness and reasonableness.'

'I think going to a doctor is the best move. I suggest you see Vittoz.'

She baulked. 'I would've thought that an ordinary doctor would be enough. I hardly need a head doctor. I am not cracking up.'

'I am not suggesting that you're in as bad a way as I was. I was off my trolley. But you'd be better off with someone who knows about nerves.'

'But he's a doctor who treats hysterics.'

'I myself rather liked the idea of being an hysteric. I was good at it—at hysterics. Seriously, he did very well by me. I may not be here today if you'd not arranged that, dear Edith. Let me return the favour.'

'Will he "analyse" me?'

'If you want.'

She thought about it. 'Could be fun.'

'I found it all rather labyrinthine.'

'Could be frightening, you mean?'

'How easy is a bush supposed a bear! And how sometimes, the bush doth, indeed, be a bear ... He has a long waiting list. Very fashionable now, this sort of thing. Being analysed.'

'Sweetser had analysis, you know,' she said. 'In Vienna—after his son suicided. Couldn't stop talking about it.'

'Oh yes. That's good. He'll be on your side about seeing Vittoz.'

She would throw the medical declaration in their faces. The procedure for doing this throwing would have to be worked out. But work it out she would.

Another matter came to her mind. 'Does this Doctor Vittoz know ... about your particular predilections?'

'He knows everything about me. That's part of it, Edith—telling all.'

'What did he say?'

'He recommended a very reasonably priced *haute couture* seamstress.'

'Seriously.'

'We decided that as long as I didn't go to Directors' Meetings so dressed, I might be all right.'

Something else followed from that. She had never asked before. 'Does that mean you told him about *us*?'

'In so many words ... yes. No names. Inescapable, I'm afraid.'

'If I turn up he'll know about *us*!'

'He may put two and two together.'

'I'll deny everything.'

'It isn't really a place where you are supposed to deny things, dear. *Au contraire.*'

'Maybe it's best that I see him rather than a stranger. He would be somehow a little in the picture. Friend of the family, in a sense. And he didn't censure you?'

'No censures from the good Doctor Vittoz. It was rather like doing a laboratory study of myself. Rather luxurious and self-indulgent, really, when one looks back. But not at the time, though. A few spiders. A few home truths.'

'Home truths?'

'Home truths.'

'Oh dear—that doesn't sound very attractive. Perhaps I won't do the analysis. I want him to write me a medical clearance. Something to throw in their faces.'

'Our first task is a medical examination. Then we will deal with office tactics.'

'There's a certain symmetry in all this: you sending me off to a head doctor—after I'd sent you off. Are you sure it's not retaliation?'

'We could do with some symmetry in our life, in the absence of any other conventions.'

'I guess that we are both show ponies.'

'I don't know that expression.'

'I suppose it's Australian; both of us are temperamental horses. You mean it, though—that I'm strained? That I'm not a dipsomaniac?'

'You are not a dipsomaniac, Edith.'

'You think they could reprimand me?'

'Perhaps. Lightly. The Raging Twenties are over, Edith. For the world and for you.'

'For the world, maybe. I will live as I choose. I will proceed as I intend to continue, as my grandmother always said. Sorry, I can't live as a prisoner of other people's expectations.'

'Shall I make an appointment?'

'Yes. But don't tell him that I'm barmy.'

'What you are will be obvious to Vittoz.'

She felt frightened again. Her mood kept changing. 'What will he see in me?'

'An elegant young woman, full of zest for life. Too full of zest, maybe.'

'I need to hear things like that. Those gossips must be made to see me as you see me. I will not bow.'

Ambrose didn't comment.

'Tell me something good about drinking,' she said.

'About drinking?'

'A happy story about drinking.'

'I can tell you about hunting and drinking—not one of my favourite stories perhaps but jolly in a certain way—if you like hunting.'

'I shot a rabbit once. Go on.'

'I hunted near Danzig—Sean Lester was the League Commissioner for Danzig at the time—a Shooting Party with some Austrian friends. We went in forest wagons; I fired twice during the day and hit nothing. This hunting though was rather hard work—starting at dawn with hot soup around big wood fires.'

'Did you drink?'

'Hot red-wine grog—and then later for breakfast we ate great dishes of split *brötchens* with fish meat and cheese, heaped up. Hearty breakfast.'

'And then?'

'By the end of the day we had a small bag—as things go— forty-eight hares, four foxes, and one poor rabbit. No deer. No *wildschwein*. But it was the ceremonials which I rather liked.'

'Such as?'

'At the end of the day, we had coffee and cakes at the Forestmeister's house and then a ceremony in the village square. The bag for the day was laid out in a long line on benches. The foxes had pride of place. The police band played hunting calls. Then we went to dinner. The dining rooms were decorated with fresh foliage and berries—they keep it all in the forest theme. The man who shot the most is elected King of the Hunt—*Jagdkönig*. People are fined by the King for various mock counts of misbehaviour during the hunt, fined in drinks. The man who shot the second best is called the Crown Prince and the man who shot the least—me, that is—was called the Poodle King—don't remember the German word—we all had to make speeches. As the Poodle King I had to speak on behalf of the hares.'

'You spoke for the hares?'

'I did with eloquence—even if I say so myself.'

'Tell me what you said on behalf of the hares.'

'Too long ago.'

She thought of the hares, of Ambrose speaking on their behalf, and she was suddenly weeping.

Precepts Five, Six and Seven

As the economic sanctions plan went forward, she would every day report to Avenol either by memorandum or face to face, depending on their individual daily schedules.

On this particular Tuesday, after a meeting of the newly enlarged Committee—known now as the Committee of Eighteen—which was overseeing the implementation of sanctions, she spoke with Avenol while he walked from one meeting to another through the new Palais.

She walked beside him in the wide corridor known as the *Salle des Pas Perdus* and brought him up-to-date on the application of sanctions.

'We are having trouble getting oil onto the list,' she said.

'We must not hound the Italians.'

Edith did not show her consternation. This was the first hint from the Secretary-General that he was not fully supporting the Council and Assembly.

'We are simply going by the Assembly sanctions plan,' she said.

'In the interests of the League I would rather lose Ethiopia than lose Italy.'

It would be good not to lose either. And better still not to lose our integrity, she wanted to say.

'You must understand, Berry, it's a quarrel between England and Italy for control of the Mediterranean.'

'There are other issues, surely.'

Impudence.

'There are not. We should make Ethiopia a League mandate. It should never have been made a member of the League. Thank you, Berry, for your report. Excellent.'

She went to her office, shaken by his explicit shift against Assembly and Council policy.

She wondered what she should tell Eden. That the Secretary-General was undermining policy? Or, at least, speaking loosely against it?

Earlier in the crisis, during the Committee of Five, she'd regretted the walkout of the Italians but realised that, of course, someone in the Committee would be reporting to them.

She now suspected that it was *she* who had been, indirectly, reporting to the absent Italians—through her reports to Avenol.

She gave a dark laugh.

'I owe my loyalties not to Avenol but to the League. The Council and the Assembly,' she said to Ambrose, as he tied his bowtie at the mirror of his dressing room.

They were on their way to a Delegates' Reception—to keep the spirits of the Assembly delegates high. After finishing their normal business, the Assembly had been held back to consider the Ethiopian crisis. The Assembly members hadn't complained at having an extended stay in Geneva. As she checked her make-up in the better light of Ambrose's mirror, she again resolved to get better lighting and her own magnifying mirror. An honesty mirror. How could she get the world in order if her personal life was not in order? There were so many things to have fixed in the apartment.

'On the Committee, you are a representative of the Secretary-General's office,' he said. 'And as such you must keep your line of responsibilities clear. Otherwise you'll get into a pickle.'

Edith reflected that because Avenol couldn't be present that night at the reception, she would be representing the Secretary-General. 'In a loyalty conflict, my higher loyalty is, probably, to the spirit and intention of the Covenant.'

'Your personal interpretation of the Covenant?'

'Yes.'

'If the League collapsed? To where would your loyalties scurry?'

She had not considered that.

He pursued her. 'To Australia? The British Empire?'

'I would become a citizen of the "country of lost borders".'

'That sounds like the Molly Club.'

She laughed. 'I might very well shift my loyalties to the Molly Club.'

'You could do worse.'

'This is not a laughing matter. Help me define my loyalties!'

'I am more worried by the Other Matter.'

'To hell with that.'

'As for the loyalty question—dodge it as long as possible.' He turned to face her, his bowtie perfect. 'How do I look?'

'Perfection—but for mercy's sake, put on a happy face.'

He made a clownish face.

Ambrose and she were finding that they were now invited to the same functions and increasingly went as each other's escort.

Ambrose followed Edith into the sitting room. She went to the drinks table. 'A shoehorn?'

He looked at her. 'I am going to say one more thing about

the Diplomacy of Drinking. As a diplomat you do not begin drinking before everyone else. And even if you think that everyone else in the world has a 'shoehorn' before going to an official function, *you shouldn't.* If you are right—that everyone has a drink before a social function—then your not having a drink makes you one drink more sober than the others. For an observer that's an advantage.'

She looked at him with amusement. 'I do believe you're becoming prudish, hiding it behind your precepts.'

He didn't smile. 'I am trying, dear Lord, to save you from your brazen self.'

She poured herself a drink. 'Are you sure that you won't have one, Nanny Ambrose, or should I call you *Mademoiselle de Garde?*'

'I'll have one. I need it more than you. *I'm* the nervous one. And I'm not the one on trial. It's bloody unfair that I should be the one who is nervous. Pour me a Scotch.'

Out of the arms of an arrogant husband into the arms of a bossy wife?

'Don't become a bossy squaw, dear,' she said, handing him his drink and kissing his cheek.

'I did see a recent photograph of Louise Brooks dancing as an Indian squaw which was quite fetching.'

'I'd be happy if we were known as Geneva's most heavenly *bon vivants,*' she said. 'Shall we go?'

'I have not finished my drink. Being a grand *bon vivant* does not involve excess. A true *bon vivant* has the other keys to the pleasures. And to drink too quickly is unpleasant: to drink too much is a waste.'

'I find it absolutely astounding that you should know so many rules to a pastime which is, at its heart, *truant.* Honestly, you astound me. How do I look?'

'You know that outfit is one of my favourites.'

She looked again at herself in the mirror. It was a splendid evening dress—gold coloured silk-satin, ankle length, halter neck, vee-shaped front, bias cut. 'You don't think I've worn it too often?'

He thought. 'Not with this crowd.'

'Is the tapestry shoulder bag acceptable?'

'We have definitely seen that bag before.'

'I know.' She examined it. 'Unfortunately it doesn't show any signs of wear. I wish some things would wear out faster.' She looked at him. 'Where are your medals?'

'Can't be bothered.'

'Oh, go on.'

'You think so? They seem too martial.'

'It adds glamour.'

'In that case, I will. Anything for glamour.'

He went off and came back with his medals.

She pinned them on. 'In the Secretariat, not only are we not permitted to wear decorations, but now you men can't use your military rank in the office.'

'Never did.'

'You did! You loved being called Major Westwood.'

'Only when it was useful.'

'I like you in your medals,' she said. 'Now give me a fun face.'

He gave her a funny face, and finished his drink. He came over to her and hugged her, but it was a hug that seemed different—it was a lovingly protective hug, perhaps even a prayerful hug.

'Mind my make-up.' She found she held to the comfort of the hug.

'Let's go,' he said. 'The car will be waiting.'

As they went down the stairs, Ambrose said, 'I agree with you in a way—we can be *too* careful about life.'

It was the usual affair held at Bâtiment Electoral. Next year the Palais would be completely finished, and the Assembly business and receptions would be held there.

Soon after arriving, Ambrose and Edith parted to circulate among the guests. How consummate Ambrose and she were at socialising together. How poised they were, how well they mingled. They had their private signals which they used to tell the other that they needed to be rescued or that they needed support or that they were ready to go, and the signal which said to stay away. The wonderful way they kept an eye on each other from a distance. If ever she looked around for Ambrose, it seemed his eyes would turn to her.

Socialising had always been her forte. She enjoyed all its masks and artifices, much of it learned from her mother, who also, when in a sociable phase, had loved public functions.

But at a deeper level, socialising did not really sit that well with her natural inner self. Maybe it didn't sit with anyone's true inner self. Maybe socialising with strangers was an unnatural human act, regardless of how far the human race had progressed. The unnaturalness of it could be enjoyed, but that required the practice of artifice and it was *that* which had to be enjoyed, although there were the occasional connections and exchanges. Still, she did not wish for affairs of state to depend on the accident of personal association. But she supposed they sometimes did. As did personal affairs.

She looked around at the smiling, laughing, chatting, gesturing people—some of the most poised people in the world—and knew yet that within each of them was some social unease, an *effort* made, and all that effort created the appearance of a glittering crowd.

Socialising at functions such as these was where the international fraternity began its first faltering and awkward steps from suspicion towards amity.

No wonder, she thought, that we take a few drinks to make it happen smoothly.

She spotted Mr Huneeus and Mr Toptchibacheff from the Azerbaidjhan government-in-exile, still hanging on in Geneva despite having been refused admission to the League and having then been swallowed up by the Soviet Union.

At the last Assembly it had suffered the final blow of seeing the Soviet Union admitted to the League.

Against protocol, she'd left them on the invitation list. She felt for them and had a long-standing personal link with Mr Huneeus.

Their dinner suits were looking threadbare but they both still wore them with some dignity. They were standing alone taking a feigned interest in the string quartet.

Edith mused that an unrevised social list could bring about diplomatic disaster. Even an invitation list had its politics.

She made her way to them, greeting them warmly, and patted herself on the back for having got the names out correctly.

'Greetings, Madame.'

'Good to see you still socialising with us.'

Toptchibacheff spoke little English or French and Huneeus, as usual, did all the talking. He waved at the crowd. 'I come to these things to show that we are still not defeated. I still have the national seals.'

'It's bad for Azerbaidjhan but perhaps good for the rest of the world—having Russia in, that is.'

'Your view, Madame, your view is as an internationalist. While I still see the world as a nationalist—worse, a nationalist without a nation. A dismal one.'

'I feel for you.'

'Thank you, you have been a long-time sympathiser. And I suspect that it is to you we owe the invitation tonight.'

She saw that they both wore the national emblem on their gold cufflinks. The decorations they wore seemed now to be antique, lost in history. The decorations too had lost their nation and their history.

Social manners required that she should introduce them, join them to someone, rescue them from social isolation. But to whom should she attach them? She guessed it had to be either the Dutch, Swiss or Portuguese, the only nations who'd voted against Russia's entry last year. She looked around and spotted Giuseppe Motta speaking with Jeanne and a few of the Secretariat. The old Swiss diplomat would be a safe haven.

'Let's go over and speak with Monsieur Motta,' she said.

'Delighted.' Mr Huneeus offered his arm and she took it. Mr Toptchibacheff followed.

Motta seemed surprised to find them there at the reception.

Huneeus said to Motta, 'I liked you saying that Russia only uses the League as a propaganda station.'

'I am sorry about the fate of your nation,' Motta said. 'But we must leave that all behind us now.'

'Unfortunately, it is my duty to not leave it behind.'

'Will you continue with your delegation here?' she asked.

'All is uncertain. As always, questions of money. We will go on. I cannot return to my country, of course.' He made a gesture indicating that it would mean death to him.

'You are welcome here in Switzerland,' Motta said.

'Thank you.'

Only as long as the Swiss and Russians were at each other's throats, Edith thought.

The conversation then turned to other matters, in which Mr Huneeus tried to take an interest, but as people with a single cause, all other matters seemed to be a waste of time.

Then Mr Huneeus turned to Edith in a side conversation, and said, 'That club where we first met, the Club Molly? I do not get there in recent times. It is still open?'

She did not particularly wish to talk about the Molly Club but said brightly, 'Oh yes, it's still there. I've been back once or twice.'

Ambrose had reintroduced her to the Club and she was liking it more than when she had been there with him in the old days.

She felt she was part of it now, if that were a good thing.

Bernard was, she felt, a guardian angel to them both, to their partnership. To their whatever. And the Club habitués treated her as one of them. Was she one of them? There were other women such as she, companions of the *true* habitués. She chatted with these women in the Ladies Room but although they knew what their role was they never mentioned its peculiar nature. But there was a bond among them. In some ways the Club was truly a refuge. Its dim rooms, the regular satirical burlesques, the inversions of the conventional world where men were women and women were men, all comforted her whereas once it had discomforted her.

She returned to her social obligations. It was time to move on. 'Sadly, I see someone gesturing to me. Will you excuse me? Duty calls. Nice seeing you again.'

He looked at her rather plaintively but smiled and gave her a small bow. Mr Toptchibacheff did the same.

Edith extricated herself, receiving a champagne from a waiter as she passed, at the same time returning her empty glass. 'Two', she noted, counting her drinks for the first time in her life. Or three, if she was counting the drink she'd had at home.

She saw Eden gesture to her. He was with some of the Committee.

She approached him and held out her hand. 'Minister, how good to see you relaxing.'

He briefly took her hand.

She greeted the others.

'Good to see you relaxing also, Berry. But are these things ...' Eden gestured at the crowded room '... are these things really time off? Really relaxing?'

'They are a form of work. But the form of work I prefer,' she said, laughing.

'Is our Secretary-General with us tonight?'

'I represent the Secretary-General tonight.'

'Splendid. How is he or she?'

'The stand-in Secretary-General is fine and the real Secretary-General is fine. I talked with him today. The Ethiopian thing is a pain for him.'

He turned her slightly from the group, so that they could speak *à deux*. 'What does he feel about the situation?'

That was direct.

Eden was speaking to her as his equal and his ally. She felt charmed by that.

To dodge?

It came out. 'He thinks as Lady Cunard thinks.'

'Does he now,' he said with emphasis. 'Does he indeed.'

She felt her stomach tighten.

Eden looked at her. 'Thank you, Berry. Thank you for that.' He touched her elbow.

Eden then moved the conversation away to lighter matters and they turned back into the group.

If she were there tonight as the Secretary-General, she had, in fact, betrayed herself.

She pushed it aside. *I serve the Covenant.* Yes, but . . . She'd have to think through her action later.

After an interval she again excused herself. 'I must speak with my compatriots.'

As she moved over to greet the Australians, Stanley Bruce, Frank McDougall and Mrs Rischbieth, she caught the eye of Frank Walters across in another group. She felt she was being spied on. How ridiculous. She wanted to mouth to him, 'Only my second.'

Third.

She would, though, have to talk with him about it all. Give a rumour twenty-four hours start and you will never catch it.

Then why bother?

She felt the third drink feeding her spirit, giving her poise a surge of exuberance.

She made her way to the Australian group, trailing through the crowd with smiles and touches, feeling like the princess she sometimes was on such occasions, known to many who came to Geneva only once a year, a familiar face. Once or twice she stopped for a word, at times almost flirting as she moved through the crowd.

She reached the Australians. Bruce was rumoured to be in line for Presidency of the Council next year.

'High Commissioner Bruce, I present the compliments of Under Secretary-General Bartou.' She held out her hand, and he took it and held it. 'And also I present the compliments of Secretary-General Avenol. Tonight I am three people.'

'Edith—please return my compliments to Auguste. And to Avenol. And to your charming self. We've all heard of your work on the Committee of Five and the Committee of Eighteen. You're certainly in the thick of it.'

'I *am*.'

And I have just done a bizarre thing with Eden which I cannot yet explain to myself.

She and Frank McDougall greeted each other. They'd met at other League functions over the years.

She was introduced to Mrs Rischbieth whom she hadn't got around to meeting during the ordinary session of the Assembly.

'I really came over to break up this little group of Australians, to make you circulate,' she half-joked. 'And the Presidency next year?' she said to Bruce.

'I don't seek it. I really didn't want to land in the Council, as wonderful as it is for Australia to be represented there. I'd rather work behind the scenes.'

'We'll be taking a strong stand against Italy?' she asked. 'Australia, that is,' she said, smiling.

The Australians looked less than comfortable with the question.

'We must, surely? After Hoare's strong speech against Italy? And Eden's consistent stand?' she persisted.

McDougall leapt in. 'We thought our tactics this year

should be to talk up wider world issues—nutrition in particular.'

'Still trying to sell dried fruit, Frank?' she said, lightly.

They all laughed.

She pushed on with her urgings. 'The League stands or falls on what it does about Italy's aggression. Japan was too far away for us to do much—but Italy is in our own backyard.'

Mrs Rischbieth said, 'Which backyard? The Far East is our front yard, I suppose. Is Europe our backyard?'

Point taken, Mrs Rischbieth. She smiled and nodded at her.

'Mustn't drive Italy into the arms of Germany,' said Bruce. 'But yes, we must see the thing through now. Hoare's right. Eden's right. For good or for ill, we must follow the Covenant.'

'Italy will at least put a stop to slavery there,' McDougall said. 'Something of a plus.'

She said, 'Slavery was being put to an end, so I'm told.'

Bruce returned to the earlier subject, seemingly eager to convince her of the Australian approach, 'There's a strong case to be made on nutrition and we made it. A world food policy is critical. Unsaleable surpluses, destruction of food—ridiculous.'

'Better health means better people better able to solve their problems,' Mrs Rischbieth put in, following the line.

'We're seen as the radicals for advocating equal distribution of food as a human birthright,' Bruce said. 'And for suggesting food should be seen as a public utility the way clean water is. A birthright.'

'And yes, Edith—to return to your earlier jab at me—as an agricultural country it is in our self-interest,' McDougall said, winking at her. 'We have food to sell and the hungry people have no money to buy it. We need another way.'

She knew all this. They were talking about this to avoid Italy.

She thought she would have one more crack at the Italian question, in an attempt to strengthen Australia on it. 'Don't you agree that if we let Italy get away with it, Germany will then know that it can do pretty much what it likes in Europe—can disregard the League? Hitler must be watching with interest.'

Always make your statement a question, her mother had said.

Bruce looked around to see who might be listening, and then ventured to say, 'I think we should move ships about and make threatening noises and bluff Italy out of it. If not, we should let well enough alone.'

'But if Italy calls our bluff, sanctions will never have credibility.'

'It's the risk,' said Bruce, impatiently, wanting to move away from the subject.

She conceded to his tone. She'd pushed enough. 'Have any of you seen John Latham recently?' she asked the group generally.

'Now he's on the High Court, he's out of reach of mere mortals,' McDougall said.

'Out of politics, lucky devil,' Bruce said. 'As High Commissioner I seem to be neither in politics nor out of it.'

Edith said, 'I saw him at the Disarmament Conference briefly. His last job as a politician. I had the feeling that he saw the hopeless way it would go and quietly slipped away.'

'When America said it would never allow disarmament inspectors on its territory, the thing was finished,' Bruce said.

'What country would?' Mrs Rischbieth said.

'The best the League can do is make war more difficult,' Bruce said. 'But I am with Eden on sanctions—we must push on with them.'

Edith came in then against herself, trying somehow to show

that she was analytical, not simply a League crusader, 'John said another thing to me in a letter, which I took on board. He said, "Always remember that economic sanctions are themselves an aggressive act and likely to lead to conflict as much as stop it." He thought that economic sanctions could be *casus belli*. I don't—I feel they should make it impossible for an aggressive nation to fight.'

She enjoyed letting the Australians know that she had a personal correspondence with John Latham.

She thought she might as well throw in another good piece, 'Of course, you could adopt Baldwin's position—that in diplomacy, any firm stand is a danger.'

They laughed.

'I can tell you confidentially that the Australian Cabinet is for automatic sanctions against any aggressor,' Bruce said.

It was a little gift to her.

'Good,' she said. That pleased her.

Edith became conscious that someone had joined them at her right elbow. She glanced and saw that it was Huneeus and Toptchibacheff, smiling broadly. She knew that they were going to follow her throughout the night. Ugly ducklings were her specialty.

She introduced them to the other Australians. Again, she pronounced Toptchibacheff's name correctly.

'Now I know more Australians than I know of any other nation apart from my own,' he said, laughing.

'And you, sir, are the first Azerbaidjhani that I've met,' said McDougall.

The conversation became general, and they chattered about Bartou and his failing health.

Howard Liverright from Translation came over to them with a glass of champagne in each hand. '*Pour toi*, Edith'.

She laughed, but for the first time would have preferred not to have Liverright hanging around. He was known as a notoriously heavy drinker.

'I have a drink already, but thank you, Howard,' she said, holding up her glass.

'Have another.' He more or less forced her to take it.

She was now holding two glasses, laughing to cover the annoying inconvenience of it—and, truth be said, the look of it.

She hardly needed Ambrose's voice in her head to know that having two glasses of champagne, one in each hand, was, for a lady, definitely a breach of some rule of etiquette.

She turned and handed it to Huneeus, wanting it out of her hand.

'No, no, no, I too have a drink.' He held it up.

Until tonight, she would've taken the glass from Liverright without a thought.

She became bothered. 'Howard, please take it back,' she said, handing the glass back to Liverright.

He chose to treat it as a game, 'No—no,' he backed away, laughing, 'It's your glass. I am not an Indian Giver. It was my gift to you for looking so splendid tonight.'

There was general agreement on her appearance from the group.

She then saw Frank Walters making his way over to the Australian party.

Damn and blast it.

She drank down the least full glass and then poked the empty glass into Liverright's dinner jacket pocket. He barely noticed.

She felt she accomplished the manoeuvre before Walters arrived.

Then the dreadful thing happened. Edith took it on herself to introduce him to the others in the group and had accomplished the introductions perfectly when her champagne glass slipped from her hand and smashed at her feet.

She stared down at it, aghast.

Huneeus on her right and Liverright on her left both went down to pick up the pieces.

She told them to leave it, and looked around for a waiter.

'Yes, leave it,' said Walters, also looking about for a waiter.

Huneeus and Liverright stood up with pieces of glass in their hands.

The spilled champagne was a small puddle at her feet, and some had splashed on the men's shoes.

'Oh dear,' she said. She could've wept.

'We've all had it happen,' Walters said. 'We have all dropped a glass, at some time or other.'

He didn't sound convincing.

McDougall rushed in to tell of a similar embarrassment which had occurred in his life. 'It was at a Country Women's Association function near Hay.'

The CWA was not the League. Geneva was not Hay. And Frank Walters had not been watching.

'Always curl your little finger under the glass, that's the trick,' Bruce said to her, as if she were a debutante.

More Precepts From Wise Men.

As a group they moved away from the mess.

'I'll find a waiter,' she said.

She went off and found a waiter and brought him back.

'Some of the gentlemen may have some champagne on their legs,' she said to him.

They all demurred, glancing down at their trousers, saying that everything was fine.

The waiter used a napkin to mop the puddle and then collected the pieces of glass into the napkin.

She apologised once again, and then detached herself from the group, heading for the toilet.

In the toilet, she cursed herself.

She felt ill. She wanted to get out of the reception, to flee.

She did her face, breathed deeply, and then returned to the reception to seek Ambrose.

She was close to tears when she found him.

'You look shaken,' he said, detaching himself from the cluster he was with.

'A dreadful thing has happened.'

'What?'

She took his arm. 'Let's get out of here.'

'Tell me what happened?'

'I wish to leave.'

He did not question her further, turning back to the cluster of people he'd been with to say his farewells, while she stood off to the side of it, not looking to the right or to the left, not wanting to be reconnected to the evening.

They collected their coats and took one of the waiting taxis.

'Right. Now tell me,' he said.

'The one thing which I wanted not to happen to me at this time happened tonight.'

Ambrose waited to be told. 'Well?'

'I dropped a glass of champagne at the feet of Frank Walters.'

Ambrose was silent, and then said, 'Tell me that you're joking?'

'I dropped a glass at the feet of the Deputy Secretary-General.'

'No.'

More crushing silence.

'Where would you like to go?' Ambrose asked, in a soft, uncritical voice.

'Let's go to the Molly.'

She found the idea of the Molly appealing. A place where few rules existed.

'Yes, let's.'

Ambrose gave directions to the taxi driver.

He took both her hands in his and smiled. 'Oh dear.'

They reached the Molly Club and went down to the door with its spy-hole, were recognised, and admitted into the dim anonymity of the large cellar with its stage and private rooms.

The burlesque was finishing and with a display in unison of scantily clad bottoms and silk stockings the 'girls' tripped off the stage and the curtain closed, to much applause.

Ambrose ordered two large Scotches.

'Oh dear,' he said, again touching her glass with his own.

'Yes, "oh dear".' She said, looking at him with a small, helpless smile. 'Oh dear.'

'Look on the bright side—at least it wasn't at the feet of the Secretary-General,' he said, trying for lightness. 'Just the Deputy Secretary-General.'

'The only saving grace is that it happened in a group of Australians who wouldn't see anything unusual about a young lady throwing champagne glasses about the hall. But will, nevertheless, find it an amusing story to tell back home.'

'Happens every night there does it?'

'Social custom.'

'You should always crook—'

'—your little finger under the glass. The High Commissioner gave me that advice. Thank you.'

'It's really all my fault—I forgot to teach you the little finger rule.'

'And by forgetting to tell me the little finger rule you have destroyed my career. I think I'd been taught the rule long ago and thought I was too grown-up to need it anymore. Shoot me.' She shook her head in self-disgust. 'And there's something else ...' she looked at him.

'What!?'

'I told Eden where Avenol stood on Italy. I carried tales. Broke confidences. Took sides. Betrayed my office.'

'Did he ask you where Avenol stood?'

'Yes.'

'If Avenol is taking sides against the Council, you were probably justified.'

'Do you think it was a blunder?'

He looked at her. 'When you make a move such as you

have you must always bear in mind that it may very well change the course of events. Best you know how it will change them before you make your move.'

Ambrose left the subject at that. He said, 'And you say that Huneeus was there tonight?'

'Looking like Charlie Chaplin. And Liverright with two glasses of champagne. Looking like ... the Michelin man.'

She buried her head in her hands.

'It sounds as if you were Charlie Chaplin.'

'Oh, Ambrose—it's a mess, isn't it?'

'Oh, it was just an accident. Walters will see it that way. Could happen to any of us.'

'How big a mess?'

'Any situation is not finished until it has run its course. And in the running of the course anything can happen. This Drinking Question has not run its course. It could turn our way yet.'

She looked at him. 'Or not.'

Before he could answer, Bernard came over and greeted them, kissing her on both cheeks, calling her 'my heroine', as he always did. 'Aren't you the Princess Marvellous tonight! Gold suits you. I want to be fully informed about the Ethiopian situation. I want all the juicy gossip. I once knew an Ethiopian. *A Nubian slave.* Rather young, and rather handsome. Rather *too* young and rather *too* handsome. The eye is more elongated than the Egyptian eye, rather fetching. Rather *too* fetching.'

Bernard was dressed in a splendid gown, fully made-up, earrings. But for some reason, no wig.

He kissed Ambrose. 'Oh, the medals are out too. How martial.'

He then went off to have some light food prepared for them.

He returned. 'Your supper will be here shortly. Now tell me all.'

Edith forced herself to leave aside her own disaster and to make conversation.

She told him about the problem the League was having applying the oil sanctions.

Bernard said, 'That speech at Assembly by the man with the delicious name, "Hoare"—can that be right? Is that the pronunciation?—it was the strongest position England has ever taken. I nearly stood and applauded.'

'You were there?' she asked.

'I peeped in.'

He often surprised her. She always saw him as being from another world.

'And you have been liaising with Anthony? How strange the English are with their names—Hoare and Eden. We have a Whore and an Eden—the Whore and Paradise—oh, what I would give to liaise with the glamorous Anthony, a Cabinet Minister and so young ... What does Anthony think?'

'Eden believes he has won over the British Cabinet to collective action.'

Ambrose came in, 'Hoare's speech was the strongest I've heard— the stuff about "precise and explicit obligations" and "my country stands for the collective maintenance of the Covenant in its entirety".'

Bernard said that the speech demanded a similar commitment now from France and so on through the other powers. England had ruled a line in the sand. 'He even threatened Japan if she goes on with her naughtiness.'

'Eden thought that was going too far,' Edith told them. 'He tried to get that out of the speech but Hoare wanted everything in—boots and all.'

She concentrated and thought back to Hoare's afternoon speech. She had a sickening realisation. 'It was *too strong*. There was something fishy about the speech.'

They both looked at Edith for explanation.

'I see it now—Hoare has made the speech a manoeuvre,'

she said. 'The British are banking on a massively strong speech to do the trick. It is not a commitment to deeds. If the strong words don't work they'll walk away from the crisis. I see it now. It's not a line in the sand as much as a line over which they will not go—the speech is as far as they intend to go. It was too strong.'

Edith hated to have to say it, because she'd wanted so to believe it. 'Hoare has never been so strong before. I want to believe it. But, but ...'

'Doesn't Eden believe it?' Bernard asked.

'Oh, yes. But he's like me—he *wants* to believe. Until this moment, I wanted to believe it. I think Hoare hopes that strong words will do in place of strong action.'

Ambrose said that the speech must have gone to Chamberlain and Cabinet or senior Cabinet members.

'It did. It is just that I suspect suddenly, sad to say, that it's a bluff. And nothing more than bluff.' She felt ill.

'If it's really just a ploy but Eden believes it, that would mean that Eden is out of the decision-making circle,' Ambrose said. 'Could that be true?'

Bernard said, 'Mussolini is himself a bluffing man—don't bluff against a bluffing man or you will both end upside down.'

'I know. I know,' said Edith. 'The Italians will say what I have said—this is too strong, it is not meant—those references to Japan. They know they are not meant. That means that the first part of the speech is also not meant.'

Bernard touched her hair, adjusting an unruly strand. 'Edith, you are becoming too much the Machiavellian. It is this wretch who is turning you into a Machiavellian.' He pointed to Ambrose. 'Don't listen to him. He sees malady everywhere.'

'She is something of a Machiavellian without my help— I'm actually convinced that the British'll back the Covenant,' Ambrose said. 'The Peace Ballot showed that the British public were strongly for it. Backing the League is good politics back home. I think we've got a government willing to give collective action a try. I really do.'

Edith said, 'I hope I'm wrong. It's been a dreadful, dreadful day. If Hoare is lying then all is lost.'

'You are becoming so hard, darling,' Bernard said. 'Ha, it's true, though, that the Catholics run the League. Those South Americans are all Catholic; France, Spain. So nothing will be done against the Vatican or Italy. Perhaps that is where the problem lies.'

Ambrose said in his languid voice, 'The Vatican is not Italy.'

In a way, Edith welcomed her suspicions—if the League did not go with sanctions and collective action now, it was lost. And the fact that she herself was lost in disgrace would then be of little consequence.

Bernard was still gung-ho. 'I believe Britain could do it alone. It doesn't need France. Or the League. A British squadron could scoop up any Italian transport ships bound for Ethiopia. Take them back to the wide anchorage at Aden. Impound them. *Finito.* The Italians wouldn't risk a naval war with the British.'

Edith wondered if that were so. And even if it were—it was not collective action.

The supper arrived but she was too exhausted by events to eat.

'In all international situations, no one person knows what is happening,' she said. 'No one knows.'

Bernard said he must go about his hostess duties and regretted not being able to go on with the discussion. 'Before I go, I have some literary gossip. I hear that Proust's Albertine is not, as we thought, a Syrian waiter but, in fact, a beautiful boy from the Lycée Condorcet. So there. And the boy simply delights in driving Marcel insane with jealousy. I hear this on the very best authority by one who has *been there.*'

They laughed.

Bernard left to go about his duties, and Ambrose and she spent the rest of the evening going over and over the evening's embarrassment and its consequences and the whole stupid situation.

She did not feel there was much of a way out of the mess. She saw that she had compounded a situation which she now accepted was fraught.

Ruinous. There would be a reprimand. Perhaps no further promotion.

'Do you know the only high point of the whole day?' she said, trying to find comedy in the mess.

He shook his head.

'I pronounced Toptchibacheff's name right three times.'

He smiled at her.

'And,' she said, 'I think I have a new Precept of Bibulation, for you to add to your list—and it contains a saving grace. May, in fact, save me from this disastrous evening.'

'What is this new Precept?'

'That everyone who has taken drink is a little mad.'

'A very good observation. But where is the saving grace?'

'The saving grace is that as long as everyone in the circle is drinking, the madness is shared and therefore may not seem to be madness to those in that circle. My precept is that the drinkers will think nothing of the madness of the dropped glass.'

'A very intricate precept. Was Walters drinking?'

'That,' she said, grimly, helplessly, 'I do not remember.'

Again and Again

S he waited at Doctor Vittoz's waiting room with great apprehension but, thankfully, alone.

She did not like the idea of being seen there by other people waiting, who would speculate about her personal problems.

She would've probably turned on her heel if there'd been others waiting there.

The appointment itself was terrifying her. What if this Doctor Vittoz saw through to some dark and murky self of which she was unaware? What would he 'see' when he scrutinised her and listened to her secrets?

If she ever revealed her secrets.

If she had any real secrets.

She supposed she had.

Ambrose—for one.

But then he was no secret to this Doctor Vittoz. Only *her* bit of the Secret Life of Ambrose was secret. Or was it? And if it was, did that have to come out too?

She knew bits and pieces about the Freudians and the science of analysis but did not really know its arts.

She'd gone to the library and read a little.

It was, from another point of view, quite intriguing and rather, well, *chic*. It was perhaps *chic* as long as one did not have what could be considered a serious problem.

One should have an amusing problem or perhaps a glamorous problem.

What would be a glamorous problem?

For a start, it would help to be a 'creative genius'. If one were a creative genius one could have any number of problems which would be seen as artistic.

She supposed that the Strain of Momentous International Work might be glamorous enough.

These doctors, she suspected, had techniques of getting to what Ambrose had called the 'home truths'. She wondered if the expression home truths in any way connected with the emphasis that analysts were said to place on childhood experiences.

One would think that childhood was well and truly behind one—hardly of use in helping out as an adult. Things of childhood, she would have thought, belonged with childhood.

The doctor came to the door and beckoned to her.

He was without a beard and seemed younger than she'd expected, only slightly older than herself.

He gestured to her to come but did not smile.

Nor did he return her anxious smile.

As she passed him, as he held open the door, she said, '*Bonjour.*'

He said, 'Good afternoon' in English.

They seated themselves in his office.

The office was decorated with African masks hanging on the wall alongside otherwise bland paintings of the English countryside.

There was a couch in the room. Would he make her lie on it?

And if she were to lie on it, should she take off her shoes? Her hat? Her gloves?

Apart from the masks, it was a very dull room.

He suggested that they talk in English and then waited for her to speak, glancing only casually at some notes on his otherwise clear desk.

She opened by mentioning the African masks.

'You find them curious? They are curious. They are from darkest Africa—from the *Côte d'Ivoire*. I like them looking over my shoulder.' She was then relieved to hear him chuckle. 'We deal with darkest Africa here.'

The chuckle was reassuring but the reference to 'darkest Africa' was not reassuring. Not at all.

'Darkest Africa? Do you mean ... the "unconscious" mind?'

She wanted to sound intelligent, but the way she said it sounded as if the mind had been knocked 'unconscious', rather than whatever the Freudians meant by unconscious mind.

'You know of the unconscious mind?'

'I have a layperson's knowledge of Freud's work. And I studied science at university.'

What had that to do with it? They had not studied the unconscious mind. But by saying that she supposed it let him know she was reasonably educated. That she was somehow *more his sort* than his usual patients.

What would that gain her? Immunity? On the grounds that educated people could not be mentally unbalanced? Parity? She supposed it was parity that she sought. She wanted him to consider her something of a social equal, at least. A cerebral equal.

More silence as the doctor looked at her. Inquiringly?

Was she another mask, a League of Nations Mask for his collection? What was she supposed to say?

He looked down at his notes and without looking up, said, 'How is Major Westwood? Doctor Westwood?—man of two titles. He writes to me as a doctor, so we will call him doctor.'

'Fine—just fine. The Ambrose of both titles is fine.'

She smiled at her own jest. He nodded. He looked up but did not particularly smile at her jest.

She felt compelled to go on talking. 'He's here in Geneva again. With the Federation of International Societies.'

Another silence.

Edith again felt compelled to break it, although she knew about that conversational ploy which forced the other to speak. 'The Federation helps coordinate all the different international societies which are here now in Geneva. They all want to have dealings with the League. He coordinates things.'

'I see.'

He saw *what exactly*? That therefore he was her lover?

The doctor spoke. 'And he has written to me asking me to see you.'

'I wanted to talk with you about strain of work. "Nerves"? Ambrose—Doctor Westwood—pointed out that I was under strain.'

'How are you under strain?'

'Italy invading Ethiopia—I work at the League, I deal with these things—I was the Secretary-General's liaison officer with Anthony Eden.'

'Will sanctions work?'

'The Assembly has held firm—except for Switzerland and Venezuela on oil. And except for the Americans, of course, who, as you know, still haven't joined the League. They say they'll impose bans on arms sales but not on other trade. One more turn of the screw and Italy will collapse. But I ramble on . . .'

'It is interesting. I am interested in what you do.'

'But it is better for a country to lose money by imposing sanctions than to spend money on war.' She felt she should return to her own problems rather than those of the world. 'Long hours at work. Failure of the Disarmament Conference to make headway has saddened me. I fear trouble brewing in Spain. Germany and Japan have left the League. Everything's going wrong.'

As she described things, she felt very seriously that everything *was* going wrong. She had babbled out all this stuff. She feared she would cry.

'Everything's going wrong? I read that the British have moved the battle-cruisers *Hood* and *Renown* to Gibraltar. That shows the British are serious. No? Have you lost faith?'

She was not going to engage in the endless talk about diplomatic tactics and Italy. The diplomacy of moving of ships about. Was he going to engage in amateur diplomacy? Maybe at least that would let her off the hook about herself.

'I haven't lost faith. I was close to losing my faith.'

He seemed to become aware that in his political inquiries he had asked an irrelevant question, too removed from their purpose. 'You are married? Do you have children?' he asked.

No, she did not have children. And soon it would be too late.

'I have no children.'

'No children.'

The dog was back on the scent.

'I see in this letter from Doctor Westwood, that you are living in the same residence. By the way, the Disarmament Conference has reconvened, yes?'

'It's limping. Japan and Germany have walked out.'

'You see no hope for disarmament?'

She considered her answer. 'Not with Hitler rearming. No. None.'

'Too bad. And apart from the burdens of a troubled world?'

'My husband is away.' She said that rather quickly.

'How so?'

'He's a foreign correspondent for a London newspaper. Travels a lot.'

My minstrel boy to the war has gone.

'How long has he been away?'

'Oh, months now.' She tried for a less bewildered voice, tried to make it all more commonplace, for a husband to be away, and for her to be not sure how long he'd been away.

'And he will be returning?'

'To be precise, he's been away for a year—he's been gone for more than a year.' She tried to make it sound as if it were simply a matter of mathematic calculation which she was now correcting. 'Returning? Oh, yes, he'll be back. One of these days.'

She tried to make it sound light, forcing herself to grin.

Silence. He stared at her. It was, she supposed, acceptable for such a doctor to stare.

'You seem to be uncertain—your voice. You seem not to know how long he will be away, your husband?'

'I don't, really . . .' She again felt tearful. 'But you see, there are two answers to your question—when did he leave the first time, decide to be a foreign correspondent, that is, rather than working here in Geneva, and when it was that he last "visited"—which was nearly a year ago.'

'It is hard, his being away?'

'Oh yes, I miss him.'

Silence. A silence, provided, it seemed to her, to give her an opportunity to elaborate, revise? Change her statement?

She didn't feel ready yet to mention that whenever he returned Robert usually took the husbandly rights and comforts without asking. And about which she was only mildly pleased. He seemed to get a lot out of it, though. Oh well. It wasn't a great demand for him to make in itself. Although during it, she worried a little about catching foreign diseases. She could hardly tell the doctor *that*. Nothing to be done about that, they were, after all, husband and wife. And if she couldn't get this little thing right, what hope was there for her?

This doctor's silence was not in the give and take of negotiation.

This was a silence which sucked up things from within oneself.

And the doctor was being silent because it was the patient who had the things to say—he was not there to speak.

She knew enough about it all to know that the doctor was there to read what she said rather than just take it in at face value.

She thought she might as well be honest about her marriage, that at least. 'I think he's away indefinitely. Modern marriage. We thought a break would be best. His newspaper work and my diplomatic work don't fit well together. Something like that.'

Was that the truth?

'You don't miss him, then?'

She tried to smile a wry smile, and shrugged. 'I don't really. No.'

Again she was near to tears. 'I suppose I should. But I don't.'

She looked inside herself. 'I don't, really.'

That was now a little untrue in the opposite direction. There were days when she missed him. Hard to be precise. But this revised answer was more true than her first attempt.

The doctor didn't smile back, he refused to be complicit. 'Has the marriage ended, then?'

'I don't think so. I don't really know.' She was uncomfortably close to tears.

'Has he left you?'

The words 'left you' caused her heart to clutch. She had never put it in those words. In the vague shape which her marriage now took, if anything she preferred somehow to see herself as the one who'd 'left'—even if she'd been the one who'd, literally, stayed in the matrimonial home.

She'd been the first to leave, emotionally.

Or was it really that Robert had left her?

She felt cold. Their parting words in all their airy ambiguity and breezy affection had never quite added up to anything much in the way of a plan for their lives. On reflection, it had never been clear what was happening.

'You seem distracted?'

'I prefer to refer to it as a separation. We have never discussed divorce. A separation.'

'And Doctor Westwood?'

And Doctor Westwood.

'He is sharing my apartment—while my husband is away.'

Silence. Doctor Vittoz stared at her.

She blushed. She had thought that blushing was out of her life.

Oh well, here goes. 'We are lovers.' She managed to get it out, in a rather small voice.

'You were lovers before. When I saw Doctor Westwood. Do I remember that correctly?'

'Yes. Yes, we were, before I married.'

'And now you are lovers again?'

'Yes. Again.' She made her wry face, trying to say, well, these are novel times.

Again and again.

'Again,' she repeated, and this time it came out sounding very strange indeed.

'You repeat the word?' His voice seemed kindly, at last.

She looked at him and shrugged. They held each other's gaze—his face was kindly. 'Again, yes again, lovers again,' she said, feeling compelled to utter the word 'again'. But the word she wasn't saying was 'forever', together again and, she suspected, forever.

She now began to cry, scrabbling in her handbag for a handkerchief.

He offered her a laundered and pressed handkerchief from his drawer. Did he have a drawer full of handkerchiefs for weepy ladies?

A copious male handkerchief.

'Oh dear.' She pulled her voice together, and dabbed her eyes dry. 'Oh dear, I didn't mean to cry. It's not as if my life is a tragedy.'

'You may cry here. This is a place to cry.' As he said this, she began to cry again. 'Everyone's life, if not a tragedy, is lived on the precipice of tragedy. In fear of tragedy and loss.'

When she was again in control of herself she said, 'Yes, we are again lovers, Doctor Westwood and I.'

'Again.' He smiled.

She smiled, and nodded. 'But that is not why I am here.'

She put on a strong voice, trying to keep to what she thought was a safeguarded point, and to keep her life simple for the doctor, and for herself, and for the purposes of explanation. 'I am here about strain. Work strain. I really need to be examined for ... work strain.'

'How do you suggest that I do that?'

She was surprised. Wasn't it his job? 'Oh, I didn't think that you would have an instrument which measured it,' she smiled and sniffed and used the handkerchief to wipe the tearful moisture from her nose. 'I suppose—I suppose by me telling you about the hours I work and so on. The dreadful problems we face at the League. Statistically. Perhaps.'

She felt a tiredness, a deep tiredness.

'What brings you here this day—particularly—at this time of your life—apart from the demands of work? An incident? Something has happened to bring you here?'

'Not Ambrose—not being lovers. That is not why I am here.'

Silence.

She found herself with nothing to say.

'Your husband understands this? Your being lovers with Doctor Westwood—again.'

'It was understood, I believe, before my husband and I ... separated ... that Ambrose was living in Geneva again. And

I wrote to my husband about Ambrose—Doctor West-wood—moving into the apartment.'

'Still, this part of your life is somewhat, how to say it? Somewhat "nebulous"?'

'To outsiders, perhaps, but not to those of us who are intimately involved. I believe we all understand.'

Much had been left unspoken about the arrangement.

'Be that as it may, that is not why I am here. I was told something by a colleague at work,' she stumbled, 'which led me—and Doctor Westwood—to think I was under strain.'

'Tell me about the something which was told to you.'

'It was gossip and I resented it and I wanted to rebuff it. That's why I am here.'

'You haven't told me what it was—this that the colleague said which touched a nerve?'

'It didn't touch a nerve so much as it annoyed me. And it brought home to me how frazzled I was.'

How very weary.

'Everything you say to me is confidential. And we are not here to judge—only to remedy, if we can.'

'This colleague referred to drinking, which is not what I am here for. I don't see drinking as the problem.'

To her relief, the doctor seemed to accept what she'd said and returned to her marriage. 'You cried when we mentioned ... Doctor Westwood, Ambrose ... and your husband's absence—but that's not what you are here for?'

'I suppose everything is connected,' she finally admitted. 'One might have to say that—that everything is connected.'

She cried again.

The doctor again softened his voice. 'That's a big leap for us to take. To allow that everything is connected, it lets loose all sorts of fears that seem unmanageable. But they are manageable. Often everything is a symptom of everything else.'

Crying into the handkerchief, head down, she nodded.

'Never fear. We can come to an understanding with these

phantoms. Fatigue distorts yet it also serves us by allowing things to capture our attention. Things which we had tried not to see. Which we block out by everyday matters. Fatigue allows serious things to break through sometimes. The dam bursts.'

'I suppose it does, the dam does burst.' She tried to laugh about her tears, struggled to make a joke about the dam, struggled to control her tears, but gave up. 'I suppose, though, that specifically, I am here so that you can verify my state of mind as being, well, frazzled. Something like that.'

She tried to seal off her tears and to find control again. 'And I would rather not let everything become tangled together, even if they are connected. I would like to deal with one thing this time. Maybe the other things at some other time.'

He didn't laugh. 'You mention drinking, your colleagues mentioned your drinking?'

She felt herself colour. 'That was annoying but that was, well, just that—annoying.'

She felt herself sinking into heartache, sitting there, trying to keep things from becoming tangled. 'Very annoying. Very affronting.'

'It cannot be very good, for your colleagues to talk about you that way?'

'No.'

'Do you, yourself, worry about your drinking?'

'Not at all. Not that is, until this annoying business of them talking about it.' She found a clever formulation. 'It is not my drinking which is the problem: it is their talking about it which is the problem.'

That was suddenly clear.

'Why do you think they talk about it?'

Her self-defensiveness was giving her insights. 'I suppose, because I am a woman. If I were a man they wouldn't care two hoots. Women who drink ... only loose women drink. Every man can drink.'

That it was only gossip wasn't strictly true—Walters, Bartou were not gossips. Sweetser was perhaps a gossip. How much gossip was there and for how long had there been gossip?

This idea distressed her further. She saw Florence and the others talking about her, whispering about her as she went by. Did her friends also gossip about her?

'You drink more than a woman should?'

She looked directly at him, 'How much should a woman drink?' she said, aggressively, at last gaining some strength to resist. He didn't respond to her question.

She said, 'It's seen as unwomanly. That's the problem.'

'As unwomanly?'

'Yes.'

'Do you feel unwomanly.'

'Not at all.'

What an odd question. How would she feel if she felt unwomanly? She wondered if this connected to Ambrose. If this doctor was to see everything as connected, then perhaps unwomanly and womanly and so on were all churning about in his head? And Ambrose's womanliness was also there in this doctor's head. Oh dear. Where were they? 'It is seen that way only in some circles. Not in sophisticated circles, not in liberal-minded circles.'

'Is the League a sophisticated circle of liberal-minded people?'

She was shaken. 'That's not quite how the League is at all. It is a mixture. Some are, for example, very religious.'

'Yet you had tended to look at it as a circle of liberal-minded sophisticates?'

'I think I had. I think I had wished it to be that way.'

She was shaken a little by having to accept that, to realise how wishful her thinking had been about the nature of the League. Her group was not the League anymore. The League was now bigger than simply her circle.

'Does it affect your work?'

'Drinking?' He didn't answer her query. 'I don't consider that it does.'

'Your colleagues do?'

She resisted admitting this. Presumably that was a conclusion that the gossip could lead to. 'This isn't the issue. The issue is . . .' She'd lost track of the conversation. 'The issue is my need for a doctor's assessment from you. Relating to strain.'

He again left her stewing in silence.

She said, 'As far as it affecting my work, I get to the office before any of the others. I work longer than others.'

'You feel that this is saying something to the others? This getting to work first?'

'It says that I am serious about my work. My work is my life.'

'Does it say anything else?'

She thought. 'That I am dedicated to my work?' It was as if there was a correct answer which she was expected to find.

Silence. 'Anything else?'

Why weren't her answers enough for him? She scratched around to find something else to throw to him, 'My coming to work early is a game, I suppose—to beat the others. Also as a personal standard—that regardless of whether I may have caroused the night before I still get to work first.'

'What does this show, what does it say?'

'Please?'

'It would seem to me that you are proving something by getting to work first?'

'Proving that I am as good as the men, perhaps? Is that how you see it?'

'I ask *you* how do *you* see it. What is it you are proving by working harder? Yes, perhaps. And more.'

'What?'

They had both fallen off the conversation.

Silence. He wanted her to say something, whatever it was. Something did cross her mind fleetingly but she let it go. She shook her head. 'Why can't you take me at my word?'

'We don't take anyone at their word here, the African masks and me.'

He was almost cruel.

She glanced at the fierce eyes of the masks. She was growing tired of this conversational trickery.

She sat, determined not to play anymore.

He said, 'Tell me, does it perhaps say this: "I may drink more than others but I work harder to make up for it?" '

She coloured. 'I work harder because I am dedicated to my work.'

He stared at her. 'You are not working harder because of guilt about your drinking?'

Guilt?

Why should she be guilty?

What an impertinent question.

Still, he was the doctor.

She should give him some credit perhaps. Concede something to keep his morale up. 'Maybe. In a way. I don't think I feel guilty. They should feel guilty for gossiping.'

'What do you have "to make up for" by getting in early?'

'I don't follow?'

'Going to cabarets, as you say, doesn't mean that you take time off from your work, does it? You do not lose work time?'

'No. Maybe the occasional longish lunch.'

'You do not then have to work longer hours as a rule, to give back time taken away from your work?'

'I work most days and many evenings. They owe me time.'

'So getting to work earlier than all others is not required of you? You are not repaying any hours lost? Are you then saying: I am guilty about my drinking but it is all right because I punish myself by getting to work first? So I am to be excused? Is it guilt and punishment perhaps?'

She didn't like that formulation.

She sat on it for a few seconds. 'I don't see it that way.'

But yes, she did see it that way. Suddenly.

She did see that. She wasn't ready to say it. Yes. But it wasn't everything. Being in at the office first was perhaps part of it all too. She couldn't quite see it. But she felt it.

Was perhaps the *all of it*. She coloured again. Why had she even mentioned this getting into the office first?

'You are thoughtful. Silent. Did I touch a nerve?'

'No.' She felt herself closing up on him. 'I have no reason to be guilty.'

She was not ready to say it yet.

'You may have no reason to feel guilty but still may feel guilt. That is more galling, is it not? To feel unreasonable guilt? To be made to feel guilty?'

'Yes. But my being here isn't about my drinking. It is about what people are saying about my drinking.'

She liked that point.

And then she found her way back: 'I told you of my getting to work early to show that it doesn't affect my work. That is, I am not getting to work late every day because I have a sore head from drinking.'

There had been days. But they were rare. They didn't count.

She made it clear that she was losing patience with having to repeat it. 'It's about having something of a clean bill of health from you, of the health of my mind.'

She was annoyed that he was not taking this down on a notepad. 'You are not taking notes. Shouldn't you take notes of what I am saying?'

'That is part of the confidentiality. You and I talk—there is no other person. There is no record. It is sacred. And if I took notes, how could I listen closely? Tell me—why then do you drink?'

The question pulled her up.

'For the pleasure of it.'

'What is the pleasure for you in drinking?'

'It relaxes my nerves. It makes me jolly.'

'Do you find that you need more alcohol than others do, to reach these relaxed states of mind?'

'I think my crowd all drink the same.'

'Not all people drink as your crowd do?'

'I suppose not.'

'And some in your line of work find they have no need for alcohol at all?'

'I suppose so.'

'Why do you?'

'Perhaps I am more strained in my position or because of just how I am.' She sort of shrugged. 'The way brandy is used in medicine. Maybe I use it as a medicine.'

'You see it as medicine?'

'Only now—in one sense. I really see it as a pleasure. It is a quick and easy pleasure—a bit of a break from work.'

'If you saw it as medicine then it implies an illness?'

'*Touché*. The illness I would see myself having is only the illness of the fully led life. The pain of being alive. Every day, through my work, I witness the afflictions of the world.' She looked at him. 'As you must.'

She contemplated the difference. 'Though you see single people and their personal problems, while I see the problems of people in large groups. That is the difference, I suppose, between us.'

He nodded. Did his nods mean agreement? Of which part?

He seemed to ease off his interrogation. 'If I could give you this assessment of the health of your mind? How would it be of use to you?'

She didn't know. 'I suppose that I feel that it would be good to be assessed, clinically, and cleared of the allegation, so as to speak. For my self-confidence. I could use it to scotch the rumours.'

She couldn't now see how she could use it.

He didn't say anything.

'Something like that,' she said. The idea now sounded hopeless.

'As you know I treated Doctor Westwood a few years back.'

'Yes. That is why I am here,' she said impatiently, glad to be able to be impatient with him. She saw a tricky ambiguity in what she'd said. 'In the sense that he recommended you, as a good doctor.'

'He's a man with personality contradictions, as you must know. I say this with his authority. He states in his letter that my knowledge of him must not be withheld from you.'

'He is, yes, a man of contradiction within his personality. I have always known that.'

'Do these contradictions persist?'

Was he checking on the results of his work?

She nodded, hoping that they were talking about the same things.

'And how do these contradictions affect you?'

Affect? She felt deep waters around her neck. 'We get by. We are comfortable with the "contradictions", as you put it. I prefer the word "predilections".'

'As lovers?'

She bridled at this. This was a long way from the point.

He pushed. 'It must be strange for a woman?'

'I am accustomed to his predilections . . . from the old days. I suppose I see it as part of life's rich tapestry. Part of his rich tapestry.'

'Is that all that it is?'

'How do you mean?'

'Are you perhaps drawn to him because of these contradictions?'

He was sticking to his word against hers.

'I was drawn to him as a friend, firstly. His predilections came out later.'

'Here you are, now years later, back together. Again. As lovers. Even though you know about his contradictions and predilections you are still drawn to him?'

He had now conceded her word.

'You think it discloses something about me?' She felt she'd caught him *up to something*.

'Do you?'

'I think I am a modern person, a free-thinking person.'

'That is very generous.'

'Do you think so? It is not seen by me as an act of generosity—it is more an act of affection.'

'I meant generous to yourself.'

Was he being cruel? 'You are being critical of me?'

'When we describe ourselves as being virtuous in some way, we sometimes conceal that it is also in our interests to be "generous", as we put it. I am not here to hurt you. I am here to help you find the truth about your inner world. Nothing more, nothing less. I am not here to flatter you.'

'Of course.' She bristled. She found an escape along the path of curiosity, 'Did you try to cure him of what you call his contradictions?'

'Cure? I suppose we tried to interpret his condition. I don't know if cure is the right word. Yes, it was an attempt to either eliminate the contradictions or ... accommodate ... them into the household of his personality. And into the realities of the world.'

For the first time Doctor Vittoz seemed unsettled. He had wavered on the word 'accommodate'.

She had truly 'accommodated' them. Literally. She decided to say that. 'I have accommodated him—and his foibles. Literally.'

He genuinely did smile this time at her humour. 'Yes, you have, it seems, literally "accommodated" him, in your household.'

He laughed again, seeming to be pleased with her little

witticism. 'Into the household of your personality, as it were, also?'

He didn't let the word 'foibles' pass. 'Foibles? How do these express themselves in your life as lovers?'

'Am I required to answer that?'

'Required? You must help me understand. I am interested also clinically, scientifically. As a student of human nature.'

She didn't answer.

He seemed to let her off the hook. 'Tell me, what does your husband think of Doctor Westwood living with you as a lover? Does he know of Doctor Westwood's contradictions? Foibles?'

She looked at him helplessly, 'I told him about Ambrose before we married.'

'That required some courage?'

'Yes,' she said, with slight bitterness.

'And you say you told him, more recently, about Doctor Westwood's coming to live with you again?'

'Yes.'

'And when you told him—he replied?'

'He didn't mention Ambrose ... Doctor Westwood.'

'Not at all?'

'Not at all.' She felt close to tears again.

Oh, what did Robert think of her now? He'd always been free-thinking, but this may just have been too much. The idea of her living with a nancyboy. When Robert visited, he and Ambrose circled about each other in the apartment but remained perfectly civil and Ambrose always presented himself as a regular man. But it was perhaps all too much, too much, for Robert. Perhaps if he had not left her when they parted in Geneva, he had left her now.

Perhaps something had happened in their marriage *after* her letter telling him that Ambrose had moved in. Although affectionate postcards still came. Lightly affectionate. And he still visited and took his rights as a husband.

'You seem to be thinking?'

'I don't really know what my husband would think—about me living with a person such as Ambrose.'

She was cold and tearful. She found she held the doctor's handkerchief tightly in a ball in her fist.

'Perhaps it will help if I say something about myself, at this point, in these matters,' he said, breaking off his inquisition.

He considered his words, and then spoke, 'I am a professional correspondent with an institute in Berlin—the Hirschfeld Clinic—which is interested in these matters, matters of human sexuality—'

She said rather eagerly, 'I know of the Hirschfeld Clinic.'

'Through Doctor Westwood?'

'Yes. And they have informed the League of their work.'

'As you would know then, the Clinic is interested in sexuality from a scientific point of view—not from any persecuting motive, which seems to be more common. As a way of knowing and perhaps accepting human sexuality. I correspond professionally also with the World League for Sexual Enlightenment in Stockholm. It's run by Elise Ottesen-Jensen. You know of that also?'

'Through the League, yes.'

The doctor was telling her not to fear him. She relaxed, somewhat.

Edith said, 'Not very popular at the League—not among the Latin countries, Catholicism and so on. Birth control is not discussed at the League. Ambrose has visited the Hirschfeld Clinic.'

'My support for Hirschfeld is why your case interests me.'

'Am I a case? I thought in these matters, Ambrose, Doctor Westwood, was the case?'

He smiled rather condescendingly. 'I use that expression from habit. I want to put you at ease. I am not shocked by human behaviour. I am not a persecutor. Indeed, not. *Au contraire*. The richness of human behaviour fascinates and pleases me.'

Au contraire? It then came to Edith that Doctor Vittoz was perhaps a man who loved men. Or was he *as* Ambrose? Surely not? He was not in the Molly circle, Ambrose would have told her.

This flustered her. Ambrose had not said anything about this. She couldn't very well ask Vittoz. Did it make any difference? She thought it might.

The flustering went away and then, oddly, she felt suddenly more able to talk with him.

If he'd been a properly married man, as she'd first assumed, then he would have perhaps looked down on her as something of a married failure. A failed wife. Even, a failed woman. If he were not a properly married man, it would be a little easier to talk about it all.

What tangled web was she flailing in now?

He changed his voice back to that of the interrogator. 'Isn't it a little ... disingenuous to say that it is his case, not yours? When you are his lover?'

She looked at him. She was floundering.

'Earlier you avoided my suggestion that you were perhaps drawn to him because of how he was. To be attracted the first time may have been a misunderstanding, but to be drawn to him once again must be illuminating of you too?'

'I could like him *despite* the way he is. Isn't that a possibility?'

He looked at her quizzically. '*You* must tell *me*.'

'I suppose Ambrose—Doctor Westwood—and the way he is, makes me feel calm. Tranquil.'

She had a flash of recall of always feeling somewhat sweaty and tense with Robert at times of sex.

Doctor Vittoz then broke the gaze. 'Our time is up. Let us pursue that further next time.'

Up?

Next time?

'We can make another appointment,' he took out his appointment book. 'We have much to talk about, it would seem.'

Would it seem?

She asserted herself. 'I was hoping that we could more or less complete our arrangements, business ... whatever ... today.'

'Tell me again,' he said calmly but, she felt, tendentiously. 'What is this business we are to complete?'

'As I said ...' she was again exasperated by what she saw as his doctorly stratagems '... a statement by you, a letter from you, of some sort, that I might use ...' she tried her winning smile, '... attesting to my normality, but to my strain.'

'Do you see yourself as normal?'

'Why, yes, as normal as most.'

'Yet you live with a man who is not your husband? Who has personality incongruities? You seem to have worries about your drinking habits or, more precisely, what others think of your drinking habits? You take the woes of the world on your shoulders? You choose to live away from your country of birth? Are they signs of the norm? Of the average?'

'Not of the average—no ... but I am not ... monstrously abnormal.'

She looked at him helplessly. 'Am I?'

'In one appointment, you wish to find out all?' He said this in a kindly, comradely way and shook his head and smiled. 'At our next meeting, I should perhaps explain my method of working. I will give also some physical tests. Of your blood and so on. But be reassured you are not insane. And I am sure a letter can be written—if you feel it would help you deal with your life.'

He smiled. 'You are not "monstrously abnormal"—but nor are you an average woman by any measure: and rest assured also, I admire your work—your mission.'

'When I was at school all we wanted was to be average—I think that is an Australian wish: to be the same as the others.'

'Or of all children. And again, please rest assured that I do not find your way of personal life a matter of censure. We must be sure that it is a way of life that you want, and not one that has been the result of a series of accidents.'

'Aren't all friendships an accident of meeting?'

'As you probably know, in my profession we rarely concede that there are accidents.'

'I am not really here for analysis.'

'We could perhaps explore that as well, at the next appointment; examine, then, what is the best way to proceed.'

Proceed? Proceed where?

'How is the same time next week?'

She nodded, but with resistance. 'That would be possible.'

'Good,' he smiled at her.

'Tell me, doctor—are you a married man?'

'Oh, the details of my life are of no consequence here in this room, neither here nor there—the more I am just the neutral *docteur* the better. Just think of me as a *docteur*. But since you ask, no, I am not married.'

He was standing up to show her out, holding out his hand. They shook hands across the desk and he came around to where she was and took her elbow.

Before she knew it she was out in rue Mont Blanc feeling buffeted and distinctly chilly, awash in awkward recognitions and ill-shapen comprehensions about her frayed life.

It was as if Doctor Vittoz had begun a charcoal sketch of her life which was only partially finished and slightly smudged. And it was as if, in the few stolen glances over his shoulder at the sketch, she did not really quite see herself in his sketch. Or that she saw that it was *her* but not quite the way she might have wished to be sketched.

She stood stock still then in rue Mont Blanc.

Had Robert been the one who had left? Had Robert left her? Why did that send a tremor through her?

Was she still not prepared to let go of him?

Was he, for her, a touchstone of normality?

She wanted desperately to go back up to Vittoz and ask him more.

Gossip and the Hazard of Unwitting Collusion

'Tell me what happened with Vittoz,' Ambrose said, as they sat at their dinner table in the apartment, having one of their rare home-cooked meals.

Ambrose had cooked. He'd insisted that she—they—stop their public life for a few days and think out what she was now to do. She was owed the usual three days off after the Assembly and had a few other days owing.

They'd become homebodies, cleaning and fixing and re-arranging the furniture, hanging two Tamara de Lempicka lithographs, *Spring* and *The Young Ladies*. What would Robert make of them? Advertisements for the Modern Woman? Decadent? Terribly advanced even for Geneva. Maybe two Lempickas in one room was too strong? They matched her lithograph of *Les Deux Soeurs* which was in her bedroom.

And they talked about all manner of things.

What *had* happened during her appointment with Vittoz?

'Well?' Ambrose said.

'He was very clever. But isn't it supposed to be all confi-dential—between a doctor and patient?'

'I am your doctor, in some sense.'

'The Good Doctor Ambrose? Yes dear, you are my doctor, in a sense. Well, he pronounced me sane. Or normal, but not average. Or at least, he thought my life was very unusual but normal. Something like that.'

Like what?

'*That*, we more or less knew.'

'I pointed out to him that all the gossip about drink was happening because I was a woman. He seemed to agree.'

'He "seemed to agree"?' Ambrose sounded sceptical.

'I know what you mean about our Doctor Vittoz. But, yes, I think he nodded.'

'Nothing can be assumed with Vittoz. His silence should not be taken as agreement. Or comment. I sometimes think talking to him is like fortune-telling: we tend to remember anything that the fortune-teller says which is vaguely connected to our lives, usually something generalised such as *mourning a loss*. Everyone is mourning a loss of some kind. And we forget the rest. Then we remake it all in our heads to make it tell us what we want to hear. We wish to believe the fortune-teller. But we do the fortune-telling of ourselves. Although the home truths do get through with Vittoz.'

'You hardly need to tell a Rationalist about fortune-telling. I'm now inclined to think that we might be placing too much importance on the whole thing.'

'I don't. With the gossips at the League I think we still have what I call unwitting connivance—an unintended conspiracy—an accidental conspiracy, if you like.'

'Vittoz doesn't believe in accidents.'

'Gossip can unwittingly cause disasters. And it could well be that you have risen in the organisation to a point where you attract hostile gossip—that you're a target now for resentment. You know that achievement gains you enemies as well as admirers.'

'I thought the wisdom was that when you gain an enemy you also gain the enemy's enemies as your allies.'

'Perhaps not with gossip. The gossips are not enemies—they don't intend you harm but will accidentally do you harm. They know not what they do.'

'How do we erase this view of me from the minds of people—so that it doesn't keep coming up when the *haute direction* are considering me for a position or a promotion or whatever?'

'I think it can be done. During the last few days you've led me to a new position. You have identified things which I did not see. First, you are right, Edith. Drinking, as such, is not your problem. And yes, it is because you're a woman.'

'Regardless, I'm perceived to be a tippler,' she said.

'There are different kinds of drinker,' Ambrose said, speculating as much to himself as to her. 'Liverright is a drunkard. He's so boozed by evening he's not worth talking to. You're a different drinker. But there is not much fine distinction in gossip. I'm inclined to think that you should become, formally, a non-drinker.'

'I can't see that happening.'

'Hear me out. We have to change their conversation—by getting out of the gossip. And we, as you say, have to erase the image of you as a tippler that some might have.'

'If I let it be known I am not drinking it will seem that I have had to give it up—that I have a difficulty with drink. And I rather like drinking.'

'Drinking is not that important in your life, Edith—it is a very, very minor activity. And anyhow, drink should be your friend—not your colleague. And something else, Edith.'

'What?' she said tiredly.

'The world needs you.'

She looked over at him.

'Edith, we don't want a drift to a situation where you are forced to leave.'

'You think that could happen?' Edith could hardly believe his words.

'Remember that they forced Dame Rachel out because of drinking. And there is your countrywoman, the legendary Jocelyn Horn, dismissed for "dancing too much". And we pretty much can guess what that meant.'

She felt disturbed.

'You'll find the first part of the plan the most unpalatable. I propose that you do not drink at work or where your colleagues will see you. Stay away from people such as Liverright who will urge you to drink at any given moment of the day. No drinking at official occasions.'

'Ambrose! That's the only thing which makes much of it bearable.'

'The drinks afterwards in private will be all the sweeter.'

She could see that what he said was the inevitable outcome of their discussions.

She had some new thoughts. 'About the medical document—I've changed my mind about it. I do not think that it is ever a good idea to inform people of medical conditions of the mind. I think that anything to do with a doctor such as Vittoz should not be mentioned at all—except perhaps to Sweetser who sees going to such a doctor as a progressive thing.'

She felt embarrassed then as she realised that this lesson applied in some way to Ambrose who had left the League because of such a medical condition.

She realised that his own wounding back then with his departure from the League played a part now in his fears for her. Perhaps he was driven by his own anxieties and was overstating the problem.

She ploughed on. 'I think Sweetser was looked at differently because of his having been treated in Vienna for mental problems. Because of that, I don't think he'll get promotion now.'

'Agreed. And my nervous collapse, as you well know, forced me out and they still look at me sometimes as if I might still be a little daft. Of course there was the great Sixtus V and his use of the tactic of ill-health.'

'I wish you'd stop reading about the popes. It worries me.'

'He was a rather zealous and ruthless reformer—in the Franciscans, I think—and he was in many ways an obvious candidate for Pope. But he was penalised time and time again for excessive zeal. So he decided to pretend to be of poor health, no longer having the energy of a reformer. He became passive and this was seen as a kind of wisdom and serenity. They made him Pope. And lo and behold, once installed as Pope, he returned to his former self and became the ruthless reformer again.'

'How does that apply to me?'

'I don't quite see how it does.'

They laughed.

'It does in one small way,' Ambrose said. 'You should perhaps "disappear", as it were, from gossip. Quieten down. Become dull for a time. If you don't wish to use Vittoz, go to see Weber-Bauler and say you are run down. And then I suggest you ask for leave. And then really disappear from the landscape of gossip for a time.'

'What if Weber-Bauler says I'm unfit to hold my position? Sees me as a spent force?'

'You're not. And he won't. Just have a physical examination. Get him to diagnose that you're just run down. This will be seen then as evidence of how hard you've been working—as you have been.'

The League doctor was something of a friend.

'And you have now to act your position—as a senior member of section.'

'You really mean that I have to act my age? How ghastly.'

'Edith, You're no longer a wild young thing in your twenties. You must now become a sober administrator.'

'What about the other Edith—Edith the madcap!?'

'Edith, you are a sober administrator—that is the new you. Save your wildness for the Molly Club.'

'The Molly Club?' she said. 'Are we to be confined now to the Molly Club?'

It was slowly sinking in that she could be sacked. 'I'm terrified. I see yet another key to the plan.'

'Which is?'

'I'll go to Sweetser and ask Sweetser's advice—make him an ally. With Bartou, I'll simply seek his advice about my life and strain—but I won't tell them about my seeing Vittoz. Bartou will pass on what I say to Walters.'

He thought about it.

'It's a master stroke. Very good indeed. You get them on board as advisers—they become protectors. If you can pull it off it will be a *coup d'éclat.*'

He laughed. 'And, Edith, may I add one more thing. Two things.'

'I listen,' she said in the tone of the chastised schoolgirl.

'You will improve your grooming.'

She knew what he meant. She looked at her nails. 'I know, I know—I've not had the time enough in a day, to attend to myself the way I should.'

'While on leave and when you come back, you must make time for your hair, your nails, your waxing, your facial cleansing, you must ... bloom! And you'll buy a new wardrobe. Maybe when you're on leave, go to Paris and buy new clothes.'

'You just want my old clothes.'

'I shouldn't mind some hand-me-downs. It's important not to let life coarsen us. Working long hours can coarsen one. When you return everyone should compliment you on your wholesomeness, your radiance, and then you must keep it that way.'

'And the second thing?' she asked.

'You will get rid of that wretched drink flask.'

She coloured. What did he remember about the flask?

She said, 'The flask will remain out of sight.'

He stared at her, forcing her to say more.

She hoped that it was not going to blow up as it had with Robert.

'It's something of a talisman. It's from the trip we all made to Paris years ago,' she said.

'All I know is that you disappeared backstage with a black musician, that you didn't have the flask when you left us, and that you had it when you came back. I suppose it to be a trophy of sorts.'

'A trophy of audacity.'

'Perhaps the circumstances surrounding the winning of that trophy are better left to my imagination.'

'Given your rich imagination, yes.'

So. He did not glimpse what was happening when he'd come looking for her back then in the Room *Artiste*.

She left the table and went to his side and kissed his head.

'It was all a long time ago. Sorry.' She sighed. 'The only good thing that I can see coming out of the plan is that I'll never have to pretend to be sober when I'm not.'

'I agree—pretending to sobriety is the most disagreeable of all the social demands.'

'You are a wonderful nanny.'

'A nanny who's also a vamp.'

'Yes. A vampish nanny. Should I continue with Vittoz?'

'That's up to you. Just do it for yourself if you think it interests you.'

'I think it'll be good for me to have some more appointments with him. During the period of the emergence of the New Edith. I'm curious about where he might lead me. You think I'm a bit barmy, don't you?'

'Strain is a sort of barminess, Edith.'

'I don't want to be seen as being a person who is unable to stay the distance.'

'The Committee of Eighteen is in abeyance. You were successful in what you did.'

'If I'd known that getting older was so much trouble I wouldn't have bothered.'

'Different ages: different pleasures.'

'And different pains?'

She went about implementing the plan.

She first approached Bartou.

She contemplated taking him to lunch, but the plan now excluded drinking in work circumstances and so instead she took him to afternoon tea.

'We did all we could with the sanctions. We put all we could into it. I think we were successful as far as we went. Now is a good time for me to take a break,' she told him.

'Good. You have done your job with the Committee of Eighteen. You've earned your rest.'

'The leave will give me back my old spirits.'

'I know it will.'

'Weber-Bauler gave me a medical examination and my health is good. Could you mention that I'm taking leave to Walters? Keep him informed—tell him that all is fine, that I'm not deserting the ship, not losing my nerve?'

'Of course, we all appreciate you and your work. May I be impertinent and ask if the strain is in any way to do with Robert? It is perhaps no secret that many of us find your union with him ... unusual. I take it that you consider it a marriage still?'

She considered her answer. The arrangement no longer seemed unusual to her. Did that show how unusual she herself had become?

Bartou was something of a father figure. What to tell him? 'In many ways it has to do with Robert. All things are connected.'

'Of course. Is the marriage ... over?'

She again considered her answer. She said. 'We have not pronounced it over.'

Auguste looked at his *petits four* as he thought about her answer. 'You have made a personal treaty to cover your marriage? And the treaty holds?'

'It hasn't been negotiated in detail. It has evolved.'

'And Ambrose Westwood is to continue as your *escort*?'

Bartou had been a close witness of the collapse of Ambrose in the old days, and her connections with him back then.

'Yes.'

'I always liked Westwood. He fell from grace but he seems to be recovered. That you two are together again is a remarkable turn of events.'

He didn't pursue the matter of Ambrose. 'You must take your home leave.'

Home leave? She hadn't thought of home leave.

'I was thinking more of a break to London.'

'Go home. Walters will be glad that you're having a long break. You know we talked about this in the early days of the League—the need for officers to go home from time to time, the dangers of being cut off from one's *patrie*— and the dangers of living here in the artificial atmosphere of Geneva and the League.'

She wondered if Auguste and Walters, maybe others, had talked among themselves about her taking home leave?

She enlisted Sweetser's advice about her strain and confided in him her visits to Doctor Vittoz. He was complimented by her confidence in him and enthusiastic about any form of psycho-analysis.

'You have my support, Edith. The analysis in Vienna saved me. And we should talk about a proposal I have. You can join me in it. An institute to study the psychological dimensions of political life.'

'When I come back perhaps, Arthur—and when I know more about this psycho-analysis.'

'Of course.'

'You'll keep this confidential?'

'Naturally.'

He stood up and came around to her and hugged her.

She went to Nancy Williams in Personnel and asked about leave.

Nancy took out her file and flicked through it. 'I see that you've carried over much of your annual leave. You have rather a large slab of leave owing.'

'Dr Weber-Bauler says I'm run down, but in good general health. He feels I should take a break.'

'You hardly need a doctor's certificate to take leave, Edith. You are long overdue,' Nancy said. 'Go home to Australia, Edith—all expenses paid. Go.'

As she left the office, she wondered if Nancy was in a plot to send her home.

But her anxieties were melting away and she was beginning to feel that people were thinking of her and her welfare.

She waited until they were together in bed before telling Ambrose of the new possibility that she should go to Australia on home leave.

'That would be for three months?'

'Three months yes, but with some additional leave and the time of the travel there and back tacked on, closer to six months. I have the feeling that Walters and the others want me to take a long break. Auguste seemed to have considered it before I talked with him. And it's time. It's time for me to go back. My father is alone and growing old. I missed seeing my mother before her death. I suffer remorse because of that. I must not miss seeing my father before he goes.'

He took her hands. 'Go. But I will miss you greatly.'

'I'll be back.'

'What if you choose to stay?'

'Why should I?'

'Didn't you say that Australia now had a Department of

External Affairs—Australia is handling its own foreign policy? Maybe you'll be offered a position?'

It hadn't crossed her mind.

'You would be a jewel in their crown.'

She wondered if that was how they'd view her? And what followed then?

'But then I would have to live in Canberra. I hear that it is a couple of buildings in a paddock. I would be a jewel in a potato patch.'

'What if they do offer?'

'Then you can come to live in Australia.'

He pulled a face. 'Really? Barely imaginable.'

'There are bohemian types there, you know. Even people of your bent, I dare say.'

He was silent.

She touched his face with her fingers, 'No long faces. Come on, I wouldn't desert you and I wouldn't desert the League. I'm an internationalist, remember.'

He was serious, 'I would hate to lose you, Edith. We've come a long way, and have a long way to go.'

'I, too, believe that,' she said.

They kissed.

'However strange this partnership is, Edith,' he said. 'It's a very fine thing we have. We should not lightly treat it nor risk it,' he said.

She had never heard him show emotional nervousness in this way.

'Dear Ambrose, I'm aware of what we have. It's safe—believe me. Trust me. But you must see it's time for me to go home? You see that?' she said, searching for his blessing.

She sought it not entirely in good faith. She was not really sure what would eventuate from her return to Australia. But she needed the blessing, selfishly. 'You agree?'

'Yes.' He looked at her shrewdly. 'This will be a momentous visit for you. A return. Maybe you should not be making promises about the future at this time. To anyone.'

She saw what emotional bravery was behind this gesture. A generous offer of 'latitude'.

'Thank you, Ambrose. Thank you. Of course, you'll stay on here in the apartment.'

'If you so wish.'

'This is your home. Of course you'll stay on. Guard the fort.'

'And when and if Robert comes to Geneva?'

'As usual, you two will get along, I'm sure. I'll write to him and let him know I'm going home.'

'By the way,' he said, 'do you know he has rooms in London?'

It hit her like a slap. She was strangely offended that Robert had not told her.

Why should he tell her?

'I didn't know—who told you?!'

'Someone casually mentioned having visited him there—a journalist.'

'How interesting.'

'Probably for convenience. I assumed that you knew.'

'Probably. His postcards still come from exotic places.'

'He probably needs a place in London.'

'Yes, probably.'

She wondered if this told her anything about Robert's attitude to the marriage.

'Anyhow, they can't dismiss me while I'm on home leave.'

'No. And out of sight, out of gossip. And Edith, one other thing.'

'Yes?'

'Take your hip flask—as a talisman.'

'Thank you, dear Ambrose. Thank you.'

———◆———

Edith experienced a growing excitement from her decision to return home. She did not wish to lose Ambrose from her life but the return would be a time of reassessment—the time on the boat going over, the time among her country folk.

It would normalise her life for a while. She wouldn't be a married woman living with a man not her husband.

And she would not be telling them back home that she'd flunked her marriage.

Maybe she should see Robert while on leave?

She thought it should be mentioned. 'I could well bump into Robert,' she said casually one night. 'If he's in my neck of the woods.'

'Where is he?'

'Last address was Ethiopia. I wouldn't mind rendezvous-ing with him somewhere. To find out what we should do with what is left of our marriage. Perhaps consider divorce. Perhaps on my way back through London.' She mentioned divorce because she sensed that would calm Ambrose.

He made no comment. She could see that Ambrose had been made to feel vulnerable by the idea of her taking long home leave and the mention of Robert.

She continued her appointments with Doctor Vittoz up to the time of her departure. She now felt at home on the couch under the gaze of the African masks, kicking off her shoes, lying back and letting her mind float.

Her appointments with Vittoz at first concentrated on the idea that Robert had perhaps, or indeed, left her and they gradually reached a point where she saw that she was fearful of Robert's strong male nature and following from that, she feared, in some sense, marriage itself. And motherhood.

Their conversations—if that was what they were—also drifted further towards her earlier life back in Australia.

Her talking to Vittoz about her father and mother and her distant, wandering brother was like some preparation for her return to Australia, a going over of the ground and ploughing it before she landed back there.

She glimpsed something else about it all. It may indeed be a break from things but it could also very well be a fleeing—a fleeing from all of her life here in Europe as her coming to Europe had been a turning of her back on Australia.

If it were a fleeing, would she also be leaving Ambrose?

On the matter of Ambrose, Doctor Vittoz had suggested the possibility that she was suffering *chagrin d'amour*—the tendency when disappointed in love to turn against the opposite sex. Hence her turning to a man not quite a man. But this interpretation denied the friendship which preceded her sexual involvement with Ambrose. And it ignored the ongoing, undiminished pleasure that this part of him gave her.

The Vittoz observations did, however, cause her to ask seriously if Ambrose was the right person for her. He was, apart from the irregular side of their sexual matters, just a little too much older than she.

As they would say back home—'couldn't she do better?'

Because she'd be catching the boat in Marseilles there'd be no streamers, no on-board entertaining on sailing day.

On the day she was to leave, Ambrose gave her a gift.

It was his second gift to her in all the years that she'd known him.

He gave her a silver medallion on a fine silver chain to go around her neck. On one side of the medallion was her name and her address c/o the League, and position at the League, and on the other side, his name as next of kin. He gave his address as White's. She'd noticed that he still had mail forwarded to him from the club.

He had assumed the role of next of kin.

'Wear it so that you can be found,' he said simply. 'If ever lost.'

She kissed him and held him.

They let go of each other and she looked into his eyes as if trying to say with her eyes that which she couldn't find to say in words.

'It is a beautiful thing,' she said.

She raised the medallion to her lips and kissed the cold silver.

'It's modelled on the Red Cross soldier identification tag, better crafted than those they give the soldiers—pure silver. Well, sterling silver—as good as it gets.'

'And I will wear it so that I can be found.'

What were the implications of this particular gift? Was it another form of marriage? Or was it a command to return to him?

She had no contract with Ambrose. It had been a coming together without calculation.

There were implications in the gift but they were loose. More liberal than a ring, for example. More in line with the generous release he'd given her from making promises for the future.

What pledges were exchanged by the giving or by the wearing of this?

She offered her neck to him so that he could put on the chain and the medallion.

As she bent forward she felt that there was some meaning in this gesture too but she felt safe about it. It was security without bondage.

It was simply an affirming of an uncommon connection.

An expression of an exquisite form of loving.

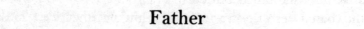

Father

A ustralia 1936.
As she stared out of the railway carriage window at
the coastal bush landscape, Edith felt a low revulsion.

Appalling, she thought, the bush is simply appalling. It
appeared to her to be grasping and twisted. Grasping for
water, grasping for soil—the way the roots of the eucalyptus
clutched rocks and clutched the soil.

She turned her eyes back to the food laid out on the narrow
first-class carriage table. She had declined the refreshment
service and had spread out her own picnic to the rather
amused glances of the few others who occupied her section.

She remembered enough about travel outside the cities in
Australia to know that to eat well, one had to be gastronom-
ically self-reliant.

In Sydney she'd bought fresh fruit, leg ham, English
mustard, Bodalla cheese—which she had yearned for in
Geneva—and bread, albeit of doubtful quality.

She poured herself a small cognac from her flask to aid the
digestion.

She had Lawrence's *Kangaroo* on her lap—the first chance
she'd had to read it.

The disloyalty of her thinking about the bush registered. What sort of falsely superior person had she become, what dreadful snobbish disloyalty had moved through her mind, causing her to dislike the bush? It was not an aesthetic judgement. She knew that much.

As Vittoz would say, she was projecting something onto the bush. She was using it as a screen on which she was saying something about herself. She pushed the messy awareness down and then, obeying Vittoz, allowed it back again.

She had to confess to whatever lay behind her powerful revulsion to the bush, admit it to her mind and examine it.

What was it about the bush? She stared back at it, trying to stare it down.

It seemed that there was no way into it, no invitation coming from the bush suggesting that a person might walk in it. It was sullen, closed and resistant. And it was dull in colouring and dreary in shape.

She turned back to Lawrence. It was all very well for Lawrence to describe it as an '... invisible beauty somehow lurking beyond the range of our "white vision"'.

What, may one ask, is 'invisible beauty'?

She smirked. Lawrence was struggling to find something, anything, to say about it. 'For the landscape is so unimpressive, like a face with little or no features, a dark face.' Yes, he was struggling to find something nice to say, like a polite English visitor.

She agreed with the character Harriet in *Kangaroo* that the landscape did feel as if 'no one had ever loved it'.

She thought then of her friend—former suitor?—George McDowell burning a gumleaf when he visited her in Geneva years back and remembered the genie-like fragrance coming up from the ashtray in the ambiance of the fine restaurant in Geneva that night.

The smell of the burning leaf had made her gag.

It was on that visit that he told her that her mother was

dying. The smell of eucalyptus had been welded to the death of her mother.

Just off the ship, strolling in the botanical gardens, she had crushed a gumleaf, and the smell of eucalyptus had reminded her of death.

There in the railway carriage she was suddenly in fear for her self, her *placement* in the world.

It was more than death that the eucalyptus brought to her, it was, as she had earlier observed, that no invitation came from the bush. Was there no way *in* to Australia for her now?

Australia felt closed to her.

She looked away from the train window.

Or did it mean something more dastardly? That she had abandoned her country of birth?

How could she not react to the Australian bush with sentiment? Where were her sentiments? What had she done with them?

I'll be shot, she thought, that's for sure.

She consumed what remained of her picnic, wrapped the food, and wiped her hands on the napkin provided by the NSW Railways Refreshment Service. She had accepted that.

I will not resile. I will *own* my feelings—the bush *was* grim and the bush *was* dull to the eye. And dangerous.

She let her antipathy rampage.

It wasn't gothic, it was *grim*. It wasn't gothic in the way of the European forest. It wasn't grim in that rather exotic and shivering sense.

It was grim in its barren repetition.

Yes, yes, she knew from childhood play in the bush that each tree was different. And yes, the pine forests and birch forests of Europe were sometimes repetitious but, on the whole, there was more colour and contrast.

She and her brother had played in the bush throughout their childhoods. It did not scare her. She'd even had her favourite trees. She'd even given them names, although her brother didn't believe in naming the trees. She'd also learned their scientific names. He hadn't done even that. In her bossy way, she'd told him that naming was a way of seeing. He'd said angrily that naming was the wrong way of seeing. Now that she'd forgotten the names, she began to see what he meant.

Still, looking back, the trees—regardless of names—were not her friends, never had been her friends—they had been dull, hot and dumb to her affection. And even then she'd been disloyal to them, been disloyal to the bush when at night, reading her *Girls' Own Annual* and studying the botanical plates of oaks, elms, chestnuts, conifers and birches, she'd yearned to have such trees as her friends.

The Australian bush did not emphasise its difference but sat stolid in its sameness. She recalled how sharp, brittle, gnarled and dry it really was. It had always been difficult to find a comfortable place to sit in the bush. And then there were the aggressive insects. As a child the insect kingdom had almost defeated her.

The European forests, though, were comfortable and comforting. There was a cool softness about the European forests.

There was nothing comforting about Australian nature, nothing cool, mossy or kind which invited you to lie back and allow the pine smells and the murmuring of the breeze in the tall treetops to lull you to dozing. The bush prickled, insects nipped and flies stung, and the noise of wind in the trees was vaguely threatening. And branches sometimes fell.

How disgustingly disloyal she really was. What was to become of a person who thought as she did? Her disloyalty was an embarrassing and gaping hole in her heart. She hoped, and supposed, that time and reacquaintance with her country would eventually mend her and that she would feel wholehearted about her habitat and her place of birth, her patrimony.

She did have sentiments about the railway station names—

an odd confusion of the Aboriginal and the European, Thirroul, Austinmer, Coalcliff, Fairy Meadow, Wollongong, Kembla Grange. She laughed. Who in God's name thought of calling the place Fairy Meadow? There were no meadows and there were no fairies at Fairy Meadow.

The railway stations had their neat platform gardens, the four-gallon oil drums and forty-four-gallon oil drums, painted and used as garden pots. That caused a moistening of her eyes. There—she wasn't heartless or without sentiment. She wasn't that detached from what she now saw as her previous life.

The stations with their tended gardens of geraniums and daisies and roses seemed more like remote botanical forts of civilisation surrounded by the bushland screeching in fury at them and the invading train.

The train left Gerringong and she began to gather her things—she always gathered her things too soon.

And gathered herself for her meeting with her father.

Her father, too sick to meet the ship, would have dragged himself to the station.

She stood now at the door of the carriage staring out at the more English-style freestone fences of the district and the rolling green hills and the sea.

Then Jasper's Brush.

There he was, on the small lonely station, leaning on a walking stick.

Standing with another man. One car parked at the station.

The other man, who turned out to be one of the Abernerthy boys, helped the guard unload her trunk from the guard's van and then shouldered it himself with one superb heave.

My, my.

She went to her father.

She held him in a deep and long embrace, both of them weeping, he weeping with the freedom of an old man, with no masculine reserve left or masculine pride to prove or protect.

The train moved on, leaving them standing alone, embracing on the lonely unattended platform.

Opening her eyes she looked out from their embrace and saw the Abernerthy boy, discreetly some distance off, leaning on the Dodge, rolling a cigarette.

'I've missed you something dreadful, Edith,' her father whispered hoarsely, holding to her, 'something dreadful.'

'And I you, Dadda, and I you.'

She looked out across the paddocks. The trees too tall, the cattle too small, the land too wide.

She looked to her father there on the verandah.

He was fussing over a bottle of beer, trying to get the crown seal off but his arthritic hands were failing him.

'Here, Dadda, let me.'

'Opener is worn out. Like me.'

She reached over and took the opener and the bottle of beer. She levered off the top with a frothing, fizzing spurt.

The frothing spurt pleased her. It somehow affirmed her aliveness. Womanliness. I must be in the grip of something, she thought.

Oh yes, I am alive, she thought, as her attention went up and down her body from thighs to breasts, I am very much alive.

In that regard, the return to her home had given her unfamiliar feelings indeed. It had made her feel that the whole country of men was hers for the asking—something she'd also felt on board the ship. Although, from tiredness, she had resisted the overtures and had not had a ship-board romance.

She felt no intimidation from men here in Australia, but she hoped she had sufficient respectable reserve not to run amok.

She felt no fear of the working-men either, but they were

more beyond her than ever before. They appeared to her as a different breed, as it were, and they did not affect her or draw her to them or offer any thrall, with their laconic, familiar ways, which she knew from the old days simply masked their shy fears.

The well-spoken men were very much in thrall to her, both on the ship and in the few instances since landing, and a very strange feeling of power had invested itself in her.

It came not only from her age and the sense of being in full bloom—for she had to acknowledge that she was no longer the debutante. No, indeed, not a *debutante*. A married woman—of sorts. And more.

'Shouldn't have to open bottles, being the guest of honour,' her father said.

'Indeed, I shouldn't.' She poured the two glasses. 'Dadda, your good health.'

'What's left of it. And to your return, daughter, to your one and only native home.'

Halfway to a speech. She smiled. They toasted with the beer.

She hoped that he would relax and stop fussing about her with his bumbling concern.

She saw that he surreptitiously wiped away another tear.

The flies gathered around the beer bottle and she kept shooing them away.

The flies, always a few inside despite the flyscreen. Flies, of course, bred inside the house as well as outside the house. She, the one-time scientist, knew that much about flies.

'Where's Robert. How's that all working out? You seem to have gone quiet about him in the letters. And I see you aren't wearing your wedding ring.'

Her father did not beat around the bush.

The wedding ring. 'You wouldn't believe it—but I took it off because of some skin problem and in the rush to leave for the ship, forgot it . . .'

She wondered if he had appraised her figure, half-expecting her to be with child. Maybe hoping that she'd come home to have her child in Australia.

She had been vague in the letters. She smiled at him. 'He's in Ethiopia, covering the war. What's left of it.'

'I read that Haile Selassie has fled to England. The Italians seem to have won.'

'We heard the news on the ship. Sanctions came too late.' She couldn't bear to think about it.

'Looks as if I am not going to get a grandchild,' her father said.

'Come on, Dad, there's still time. I'm not over the hill yet. But, yes, it doesn't look promising, I grant you that. Unless brother Fred comes good. Robert and I have no immediate plans.'

Was there still time?

She sometimes wondered what would happen if she accidentally fell pregnant to Robert after one of his visits. Diaphragms were not 100 percent.

'I wouldn't bank my money on Fred. Doesn't look like we can expect any progeny from your brother.' And then added, without bitterness now, as a kindly humour, 'Never have been able to expect anything from him.'

'Do you hear from him?'

'Once a year. As I presume you do.'

'What's he doing?'

'Seems to drift from town to town.'

'What work does he do now?'

'Whatever he can get. He's fallen in with the sideshow crowd.'

'Performing?!' She showed interest.

'Assistant tent master.'

'Is that a good job?'

'Driving the marquee pegs, most likely. He was never a labourer, he was always the assistant surveyor.'

She laughed. That was true. It sounded as if she wouldn't see him. Would she ever see him again? The lost other half of her childhood?

'Perhaps he could become a circus magician. Will Andrade taught him a trick or two. How is Will?'

Her father laughed. 'Andrade—the name means magic, did you know that?'

He had told her that many times over the years.

'Does he still run his magic shop in Melbourne?'

'Oh, yes.'

'Still in the Rationalists?'

'Very much so.'

Why had the lives of both children been childless?

She'd been meticulous about birth control with Robert. Not so with Ambrose. That she'd not fallen pregnant to Ambrose was a murky mystery which he had only partially explained but he had told her not to worry and she hadn't and despite the many sexual encounters with him over the years she hadn't fallen pregnant. Mumps, he said.

Somehow, sometime, imperceptibly, she'd passed by the yearning for children. But why had she been able to do that? Was it because no man qualified as a father to her children? Or was it that she'd not qualified as a mother? She knew she didn't have the qualities of a wife. What then was she? Vittoz suggested 'displacement' of her maternal drives onto an organisation to care for the world. She was trying to be a Mother to the World.

She didn't find that convincing. It surely didn't feel like mothering.

Her father moved back to her marriage, absent-mindedly asking the same question he'd asked before. 'How's Robert?'

'He's covering the war for his paper.'

How he could cover such a thing from one side she didn't know.

'Looks as if things are blowing up in Spain. Is the League to do anything?'

'No. It's within the boundary of one country. I suppose he'll go there.'

'The League's finished, isn't it, Edith? That's why you've come home?'

'Some people say so. I came home to see you, Dadda.'

'Will you stay home?'

'I'll go to Canberra to see if they want me.'

'Could John get you a position?'

'Don't know what would be available to a married woman. And he's on the High Court. Out of politics.'

Should she stay with the League until the bitter end?

Sometimes it was harder and braver to take the decision to quit than it was to obey the principle of 'staying to the end' or not being a quitter. Sometimes the use of these maxims was itself mental cowardice, an avoidance of difficult analysis.

Instead of being game to get out while the going was good.

Another rough maxim.

'He travels a lot?'

'Yes.' She knew he was still gnawing at the bone.

'Didn't want to see Australia?'

'He thinks Spain could be the beginning of another world war.'

'Could be.'

'He's often right.'

She found that hard to say.

She could see her father was both curious and restive about her marriage to Robert. He wouldn't want to know. He had been rather keen on Robert. He liked the idea of having a son-in-law. A replacement for Fred perhaps. But Robert had become a Fred, an absent husband, an absent son. Robert and her father had played golf together in Geneva on the League links. They had gone out together to some burlesque show looking for something *risqué* in the French style.

Her father had never met Ambrose. Knew of him only as Edith's friend.

He became rather serious. 'Hasn't gone bung has it, Edie?'

He reached over to take one hand in both of his.

She smiled at her father. 'Doesn't go as well as yours and mother's marriage. But it still goes.'

She stood up to ease her inner discomfort about her marriage and to deflect her father's inquiries.

She wandered along the verandah, her hand trailing along the flyscreen. Her mind found the form of words. She turned back to her father. 'Our married life suits me fine.'

She went on to change the subject. 'I see you still take *The Rationalist* and *Ingersoll's Magazine*.'

Copies were lying on the verandah table.

'I take them but do I read them?'

'Don't tell me you're drifting away from Rationalism? Fear of what's on the other side of the dark divide?'

He laughed. 'That'll be the day—the day that I worry about the God business. If there's something after death then I'll be happy to be surprised,' he laughed. 'I don't get to read them because the print is too small. They seem to have reduced the size of the print.'

She laughed and looked again at his physical condition.

Six years earlier when he'd come to Geneva for the wedding he'd seemed sprightly, unintimidated by Europe. Now she could tell by his face, his movements, his excuses, his inability to get to the ship, that he was declining.

The loss of his wife, the absence of both children. He would need looking after in the years ahead.

And during the hour or so of their reunion he had muttered a few times about the 'collapse of everything' which ranged from the watertank stand to the international situation.

He feared Japan. He was fearful in a childlike way.

He thought the weather was changing.

But she was happy to hear his spirit still bridling at the idea of him becoming religious.

'Speaking of the Rationalists, the Melbourne lot and the Sydney lot are fighting among themselves,' he said. 'You'd think they'd have a few clues about how to talk and how to resolve their differences. Think they're the brightest people in the world but they're at each other's throats like a bloody political party.'

She felt that her father's way of speaking had become more countrified and broader since her mother had died. At least it was broader than she remembered. Her mother had been the educated one in the family, although her father was a reader.

'What's the problem?' she asked.

'Some want to go with Japan and Germany, and the other lot want to be Russians.'

'At least the communists are atheists.'

'Atheists are only right about one thing—about God. They're not necessarily correct about anything else. I see Stalin has permitted Christmas this year.'

'I saw that. Hitler's pulling the churches into line too. At least he's doing that. Telling the Roman Catholics to get out of politics.'

He laughed darkly. 'Great people to have on our side.'

Her father's face darkened then with memory. They were both remembering the family fight over Christmas. As a Rationalist he had decided that the family wouldn't celebrate Christmas. She and her mother had argued for it: her father and her brother had been against it.

For two years there had been no Christmas, which made Christmas Day one of the most dismal days of the year, with the family divided and gloomy.

Voltaire's birthday celebrations did not make up for it.

After two years, the family began to follow the Christmas Day traditions and to enjoy the day.

'I was a bit of a Stalin,' her father said, bitter with himself. 'About Christmas Day. Do you remember that?'

'Vaguely,' she lied, trying to help him over his memory.

'I was a bit of a fanatic. I feel sorry about that.'

'It's all right. I remember we eventually agreed it was great to celebrate. We didn't believe in Christmas but we believed in celebration.' She laughed.

He laughed with her.

'A man can be a bloody fool about big ideas.'

She went to his side and gave him a hug. 'Ideas have always been your treasures. You had a huge treasure chest for us.' He had often delivered ideas to them—not as arguments—but as small discoveries, as if he'd found them in the garden and was handing them around to be examined with curiosity. 'So the Rationalists are becoming political?'

'Isn't the whole world?'

'I suppose so. But the Rationalists?! I thought they'd have a larger view of things.'

'You'd think so.'

'Langely? Is he caught up in it?'

'Oh yes. In the thick of it. They'll be tossing him out before long.'

'Really?'

Langely had been the powerhouse and the leader, the first General-Secretary and full-time lecturer for the Association in Melbourne.

'And John?'

'Being a High Court judge, he's not in public life but he's very much in the Melbourne end in a behind-the-scenes way. Miles is bringing out his own magazine. *Australia First*. I've washed my hands of them.'

How sad that the good old Rationalists were at each other's throats. That her father had lost that too, the merry, wine-loving, forever-talking bohemians. Her father, often the whole family, had gone weekly to Sydney to attend the meeting and the picnics. They were his clan. What did it say about the supremacy of reason? Where was the safe-track of the intellect which supposedly led through the shallow misunderstandings of politics?

Her days in Sydney and then in Melbourne with the Rationalists had been her happy days. After graduation, especially when she'd gone to Melbourne, the Rationalists had been her club and her family. Working with John Latham on his political career, helping to organise the visit of the great English Rationalist, Joseph McCabe. Attending WEA lectures. Free love. Well, free love in theory. She had been too reserved for free love. Then.

And now? She had put it into practice for a time, she supposed. Supposed? And what did she have now in her life— a *ménage à trois*? And with a man who was not quite a man.

'I told you in my letters that I've been analysed.'

'Was he taught by Freud?'

She laughed. 'They all claim to be colleagues of Freud. A Doctor Vittoz in Geneva.'

'What did he find out?'

'Oh—that I was too sane.'

'Doubt that.'

Her father looked at her, knowing that the analysis was evidence of something 'being wrong'. 'What was up?'

'I did it as a bit of a lark.'

'It's all the rage, isn't it?'

'Americans and others come to Switzerland and to Vienna to be analysed.'

'You're older and wiser, Edith,' he said, perhaps for want of anything left to say to her.

'Older and wilder, perhaps.' She laughed to herself and with Ambrose whom she heard in her head saying 'as in Oscar Wilder'. Her father might appreciate the joke. Might not. Might lead to places she did not want to talk about.

'I think we've always known deep down that reason is the weaker of the faculties,' he said. 'There was a problem in the design of the human species.'

He then seemed to go back to her humorous remark and said, 'You were never a wild girl.'

And she supposed that she was not a wild woman. Yet she'd been punished for it back in Geneva. She'd had her fun. Her wonky marriage. Her teaming up with Ambrose. She supposed that was Wilde enough.

She was wild at heart. But she preferred the company of dispassionate people.

'How's the new Palace of Nations?'

'Our offices are fine. The Council room is a bit of a disaster.'

'Why so.'

'They've done away with the horseshoe and set up the Council on a type of stage facing the audience. Everyone is inclined now to make pompous statements—less discussion— less real argument. It's all too stagey.'

'You still think the right table might change the course of things,' her father teased. 'Like your mother. She thought furniture changed the way we felt.'

Edith smiled too. 'The right setting does help. But like reasoning, aesthetics too is one of the weaker human attributes.'

She became conscious of her bedroom door opening and her father standing at the door as she unpacked.

She turned away from him, a little embarrassed that she had taken off her travelling dress and was only in her short black satin petticoat which was gathered under the breasts and showed her figure.

'You make a pretty picture,' he said.

She moved to find a robe to put on, but delayed putting on the robe, allowing herself to move around in her satin petticoat, her cleavage very obvious, allowing her father to watch a little longer, feeling that it was a pleasure for him, and wondering if there was necessarily anything wrong with a father enjoying the sight of the body of his grown daughter in lingerie. She must remind him of her mother at her age in some way. She pulled on her robe, smiling at him.

'Sorry,' he said. 'Didn't expect to find you half-undressed.'

'That's not an embarrassment.'

He was particularly interested in her new travelling writing box.

She showed him the stationery holders, the screwtop ink-wells, the pencil case.

'It even has a secret compartment,' she said. 'It opens if you push this divider.' She showed him.

He laughed with boyish pleasure. 'Very nice piece of woodwork.'

She stopped her unpacking when she came across a drawer of her childhood things.

She held up some of her wooden animals, made by her father. He was something of a woodcraftsman.

'Want me to throw away any of that junk?' her father asked 'While you're here, you'd best sort out what you want to keep.'

'These are not to be thrown out. Not these—not ever. I might throw some of the other stuff away.'

'Keep some of it for your own kids.'

How much did parents feel the absence of grandchildren?

How to choose what to keep? Well-chosen memories—was that possible? Perhaps in what we chose to remind ourselves of about ourselves. Much like the facts of history. Who chooses what is to be remembered?

Be careful about which memories you surround yourself with.

At the graveside, she wept a little while her father pulled at stray weeds which were encroaching onto the stone slab.

He stopped and put an affectionate hand on his wife's tombstone which read, with perfectly chosen words,

Of all the wonders that I yet have heard,
It seems to me most strange that men should fear;
Seeing that death, a necessary end,
Will come when it will come.

Her mother had decided the words.

'They are the right words for her,' she said.

'Your mother became more atheistic as she approached death. You know, she was very strong.'

'She wasn't that much of a Rationalist when she was alive, was she?'

'She was a bit like Ella Latham. She came to it gradually. She began as a secularist, thinking that, even if there were a spirit world, then the material world, as we know it, demanded our whole attention and service. Then she became an agnostic, feeling that the human mind would never understand the origin of the universe so there was no point in worrying about it, except as a rather early part of a long scientific inquiry. And then she realised that religion was a story people told to keep fear at bay and not a very interesting story at that. And that she didn't need it. She was an atheist in the end.'

She laughed out loud. Her father had always placed people in his many divisions of free-thinking, each with their attendant definitions, each held in different esteem, all graded. The Rationalists were like Believers, they had their categories, heresies, and hierarchy of righteousness. She'd forgotten that. 'I'm laughing at your wonderfully endless definitions of people's positions,' she said, as her father showed surprise at her laughter.

'Differences exist. Why not know them? Helps to find your true friends and enemies.'

Sometimes his comeback was quicker and cleverer than she ever expected.

'Before it's too late,' he added.

'How did the locals take a non-religious burial?'

'As I told you at the time, there was a great to-do. The Reverend Baker rang me and wanted to carry through the service. He said it would avoid any scandalising of her death. I told them that her wishes were to buried with a Rationalist service. The crowd came down from Sydney for the burial,' he said.

'I've put some of the earnings from Mum's inheritance in the League International School. And I spent some on a gathering at the time of the Disarmament Conference. A picnic, actually. Tried to drum some sense into the pacifists. Didn't do any good. A b— disaster, in fact.'

'Those causes would have met with her approval. What went wrong at the picnic?'

'They turned their backs on me—and all the cripples of the world turned up.'

'Cripples?'

'Those crippled in the war.'

He left it at that, as if his daughter's life were now beyond his reach.

She stood then in the insect-noisy afternoon at the grave, brushing away the flies from her face, her father still finding weeds to pull as if trying to keep busy and as if trying to reach out and care for his departed wife.

Mother, father, patrimony. She remembered something that Huneeus had said to her in Geneva when asked where he came from. He had said, 'I come from the belly of my mother and from the belly of my country.'

She had a dead mother and a country which seemed resistant to her.

'I am plagued with regret about not coming home before she died.'

'She was happy that you stayed. She was proud that you worked for the League.'

'I should've come.'

He found another weed to pull from the adjoining grave.

'The doctor in Geneva thinks that it was a big issue for me. It was a revealing action.'

'Is he smart, this doctor?'

'I think he's smart. On some days.'

'I wished you'd come back before she died,' he said then but it was without rebuke. He was speaking for himself, about his need to have her with him at the time of death. She should have come back for him. And for herself.

'I was wrong.'

'Nothing to be got from fretting about it now.'

'No.'

He said, 'When I look at the beauty of nature I think how it has come out of the dust of all the dead plants, animals, insects, humans, and I think sometimes it's Mother grinning back at us through the flowers. And so forth.'

They moved away from the grave and started for home.

'Don't suppose you and Robert are ready to retire to Jasper's Brush?' he asked, suddenly.

'Retire?'

'You could have the house. I could be the handyman about the place.'

She tried to laugh it off. 'What on earth would we do in Jasper's Brush?'

'Didn't think so.'

She saw clearly what she would do in Jasper's. Look after him. It was a looming problem. What to do about caring for him. Take him to Geneva?

She linked arms with him, and tried to say lightly, 'You could come to Geneva,' hoping she wasn't promising something she couldn't give. 'Or who knows? I may well be in Canberra. You could come up there.'

That was feasible.

'Might like that. Too old to travel to Geneva. Good place to raise kids, Jasper's Brush.'

She wondered if that were true. Everyone fancied country life for children. Wasn't there more for them in a city?

She saw now that the care of her father was another mission arising from her visit home. She would speak with George and Thelma about it.

Or did a daughter belong with her failing father at the end of his life?

'Let's go home—have an *apéritif*.'

Her father lightened. 'Sounds better than just having a drink.'

Edith wanted to feel at home, at least in her childhood home, if not in the country at large.

Didn't the Secretariat believe in home visits as a necessary therapy?

She wanted to feel like an internationalist at 'home', which should be a very special feeling—a special new and powerfully felt association to home and the world—but instead she felt very much adrift.

And, indeed, she was.

Very much adrift.

I am not home, I am at sea.

Dinner with George and Thelma

H er first social engagement in the district was with her old friends, Thelma and George.

The dinner party began badly.

She had brought an arrangement of cut flowers from the new Nowra florist for Thelma who said, laughingly but point-edly, that Edith must come over in daylight and inspect her garden one day, meaning that flowers were the last thing the McDowell Family needed as a gift.

'Daresay the bringing of flowers is a very Continental prac-tice but it hasn't caught on here. And perhaps isn't necessary. Every Australian has a garden. I would guess that the bringing of flowers has to do with living in flats. I don't think the Nowra florist will survive.'

Thelma was quite correct, realised Edith. The bringing of flowers to a country home was fatuous. Her father's garden was abandoned and there'd been no flowers there. But she'd hardly thought to look.

'You're so right, Thelma,' she said. 'I'm a fool.'

Modesty always stopped a conversation dead.

She scratched around, and came out with, 'I'll come over tomorrow and look at your garden, if I may?'

That sounded as if she were doing so with condescension.

It was just the three of them. If it had been a large dinner party, Edith would've known to avoid bringing flowers, that the arrival of a guest carrying flowers simply added another little task to the hostess's evening—that of dealing with the flowers amid the arrival of guests, unless, of course, servants were on duty. One should assume that the flower-arranging for the house had been done.

Thelma and George showed Edith through the house, leaving her holding the unwanted flowers until Thelma felt she'd punished Edith sufficiently and took them from her, carrying them to the kitchen as she would a dead rabbit, by the legs, or in the case of the flowers, by the stems with the blooms facing down to the floor, shamed.

'How was the trip out?' Thelma said. 'Did you have fun and games when you crossed the equator? Everyone always says that's a high point? George said it was.'

'Oh yes—we did all that. Someone dressed as Neptune and we got up in fancy dress. Hula girls, mermaids and so on.'

'Were you a hula girl?' George asked with a wink at Thelma.

'I considered coming as Queen Victoria—but settled on being a Gypsy.'

She had a trip story ready.

'You will love this. At our table on the ship there was an American who'd never been to France—a Mr Goldberg—and we had a Frenchman at the table—a wonderful man, M. Motte, who knew very little English. When M. Motte came to the table the first time, he sat down and said politely "*Bon appetit*" and Mr Goldberg said "Goldberg" and offered his hand.'

Please, let Thelma understand this story.

'This happened at the next two meals'—she looked at Thelma—'the Frenchman always said "*Bon appetit*". Finally, Goldberg asked me why the French always introduce themselves at each meal. I had to tell him what the misunder-standing was. He laughed and at the next meal said to M. Motte, "*Bon appetit*" and M. Motte said, "Goldberg".'

George turned to Thelma and said, '*Bon appetit* means have a good meal in French.'

'I know that! I may not have travelled but I'm not com-pletely ignorant.'

The last part of her story was lost.

'I did the plan of this house myself,' George said.

'I wouldn't have thought otherwise.'

'Turned out well, if I may say so myself.'

'Splendid. A very efficient house.'

The three of them had been at school together right through infants' and primary schools.

She knew that Thelma had been piqued by Edith having then gone away from the district to boarding school and then to university while Thelma had stayed on at Nowra and left school at the Intermediate Certificate and worked in a bank. A pretty good job for a woman to get.

Edith had gone to Melbourne and then to Europe. And, in Thelma's eyes, she supposed, ever higher.

She'd bought a silver hairbrush and handmirror as a gift for their daughter Gweneth, who was four.

Thelma had again laughingly reprimanded her for buying something 'too expensive for a child'.

She laughed along with Thelma, hiding her exasperation. 'It does no harm for a child to have a few fine things,' Edith said, and then wondered if this would be seen as a criticism of Thelma and George's style of providing for their child. She hoped they did see it as criticism. 'She'll grow into it.'

Edith found the child Gweneth winning in her ways and pleasing in her appearance, and thought, as she played with her, that if she'd married George this would have been her child. She watched the child and fantasised. She tried to create the feeling of how it would be for her if she had taken that path. How her womb would've felt? How would she look now? Thelma and George would've been married nearly ten years. She wondered why George and Thelma had waited so long to start their family. Perhaps the Depression had worried them. Or were the early years of marriage a little unsettled, causing them to wait?

Thelma's voice broke into her reverie there with the child. 'And when do you and Robert intend to start your family?' Edith observed that Thelma's voice was more posh than she recalled. She must have attended elocution classes. Perhaps George thought it good for business to have a wife who was a bit more posh. George was always strong on self-improvement.

Or was Thelma putting it on for her? Oh, she hoped not. That would be miserable.

'We'll get around to it.' How the mouth could so convincingly and simply conceal a tremor of the spirit, the tremor which the question and answer set off. 'Do you intend to have a large family?' Edith asked.

Thelma had a formula. 'The fashionable three: one for each parent and one for the nation,' she announced. 'Now that we've started.'

'Three is nice. Manageable.' 'Nice' wasn't one of her words. She was reining herself back to the vocabulary of her hosts.

'But we're spacing them.'

Thelma then took Gweneth from Edith, and said it was time for her to go to bed.

They all went with Thelma to the nursery. 'How long will you be in Australia?' Thelma asked, pushing questions and statements out in a breathless way as if she feared that any silence would smother them all.

'I intend to look at the possibility of a position in Canberra.'

'In Canberra?!' George said, laughing, 'Who would go there out of choice?'

'Have you been to have a look?'

'I went up to see if there were business opportunities. You can't spit without a permit.'

'I should hope so,' Thelma said.

Edith laughed, taking it as a good joke by Thelma.

Thelma looked somewhat confused by Edith's laughter but came back saying, 'How would one go about finding out "the possibilities of a position" in Canberra?'

Thelma's voice carried a fearfulness, the fear that Edith once again would soar to great heights above Thelma. This time closer to home.

'I thought my League experience might count for something. The Public Service is recruiting people for the new Department of External Affairs.'

'Are they taking on women?' George asked.

'I suppose not,' she said and then laughed wearily. 'I don't have high hopes. Not a married woman.'

'That's hardly like you, Edith,' Thelma said. 'You always seemed to have high hopes.'

'We need to get into the Public Service—keep the Roman Catholics out,' George said.

Her father had said something like that too. Seemed that they all feared the Roman Catholics getting control of the Public Service.

Oh dear. She looked down at her second sherry—how well Ambrose had instilled in her the need to count, although it would be the last count she would make this night as she realised that Thelma and she were not going to get along. Back at school they'd been so close. But there seemed nothing left of their merry, racing-about, flurried childhood fun and games, or the other elaborately invented games of complicated rules and penalties, resulting in disputes and temper.

Maybe the making of the rules and the disputes were the real game.

And as Edith remembered, it was always *she*, of course,

who laid down the law, interpreting the labyrinthine rules of their childhood games.

'Edith is rather high up in the League now,' George said, as if defending Edith.

'Not really,' Edith said. 'Not really high at all. I do have some influence, I suppose, by now.'

'Well done,' George said.

'So you're back,' Thelma said, looking at her watchfully. 'And your husband? Robert. Is he coming to live here? If you find this position in Canberra?'

'All my—our—plans are very tentative at this stage, Thelma.'

'Are things not going well for you then, back in Geneva?' Thelma persisted.

'Oh no. Everything is going just fine.'

She wondered when—or if—her contract renewal would arrive. It was overdue. Ambrose was to cable her the minute it arrived. If it arrived.

'This will be my third five-year term. They seem to like me.'

'Congratulations,' Thelma said.

'Yes, well done,' said George. 'Good for you.'

There was a silence. Boasting and modesty both stopped conversation.

'I see you aren't wearing your wedding ring,' Thelma at last blurted out.

Edith gave her explanation.

'Oh.'

'Of course, the League could always change their minds— decide they've had enough of me ...' she added.

'They wouldn't do that,' George said.

'We have a French Secretary-General now—Joseph Avenol—anything could happen to those of us of British descent. Felt it was a good time to go to Canberra, with the Department of External Affairs opening up. Australia'll have its own ambassadors. A good time to show my face. Get the lie of the land.'

'Do you think you'd be made an ambassador?' Thelma said, her voice on the edge of mockery and envy, unsure of what Edith might be capable.

'Hardly. Something in the office, more likely.' She would dearly love to be an ambassador. It was one of her favourite words. It was a position she yearned to have.

'I'd vote for Edith as ambassador,' George said, loyally.

'Your husband's career? What is to become of that if you up stumps and come back here to live?' Thelma snooped on.

'It's all very tentative.' Thelma was probing. Somewhere in the conversation she'd said something which had alerted Thelma to the irregularity of her life. If Thelma knew only the half of it she would shriek with shock and relish. Or more likely, crow with triumph, that she, Thelma, at least had a home and family started, while the high and mighty Edith was in a mess.

'You'll have, of course, to think about your father now,' Thelma said.

'I wanted to talk with you both about that.'

'He's getting on.'

'I'm going to arrange for a housekeeper.'

'You could do it yourself—if you were coming home.'

'I think a local woman would meet his needs. Don't think I'd be much good at that kind of housekeeping.'

'We went to your mother's funeral.'

And you, as the high and mighty being you now are, you could not spare the time.

'I will regret for the rest of my life my not coming home to see her before she died.' She looked at them both with an expression of remorse.

They respected this confession with a silence. Thelma reached over and squeezed her hand, and then withdrew it, the hand like a mouse darting across the table.

George cleared his throat and said, 'When I was there in

Geneva, I saw that you were close to the Secretary-General.'
Turning to Thelma, he said, 'Edith and I had an interview
with Sir Eric Drummond, Secretary-General of the League.'

'I know that,' Thelma said, with a hard laugh. 'I don't
have to be reminded of that. Heavens, I've heard you tell the
story a thousand times.'

George laughed at himself, 'I suppose you have.' He smiled
across to mollify her.

Edith felt again, passing gently through her, those ambiguous carnal feelings she'd had for Sir Eric, which she was sure
he'd also harboured for her. That was all a long way back
now. The good old days.

'Sir Eric is now British Ambassador to Rome,' she said.
'He's Anglo-Catholic.'

'The Catholics are all on Mussolini's side, I suppose,'
George said. 'The Vatican.'

'Oh, Musso and the Vatican have strong differences. The
Vatican feels it should run Italy. Or at least run Rome.'

She must be careful not to be forever correcting people.

George returned to his Geneva story, ignoring Thelma's
earlier objection to the retelling. 'Edith arranged for me to
see Sir Eric Drummond and I put a proposition to him.' It
was one of those stories which she suspected that George just
had to tell once it was upon his lips.

Or was it to nettle Thelma?

He turned to her, 'Did anything come of that meeting?
Was there follow through?'

She had trouble remembering what it was that George had
put to Sir Eric. She had been embarrassed that while in
Geneva, George had demanded a meeting with Sir Eric. He'd
wanted her to arrange that appointment but she'd stalled and,
in the end, George had achieved it himself. That had
impressed her.

'As I remember, George, you arranged that appointment
yourself.'

'That was a grand trip,' he said with relish, turning to Thelma. 'We had such grand food.'

Thelma rolled her eyes, 'While I was stuck in the bank counting coins.'

Had George concealed that Thelma and he had been engaged when he'd come to Geneva? She had thought at the time that George seemed to have come to Geneva to court *her*.

Although Thelma had a light, bantering softness to her complaining game, Edith felt that over the coming years the lightness would drop away and George would live a life listening to her constant complaint. Edith felt for George, 'I have good memories of the visit,' she said.

Thelma continued. 'While I was stuck back here wondering if George was ever going to return home.'

George looked at Thelma as if speculating about her in some way, or was it with affection?

George tried to go on reminiscing about his visit to Geneva. Edith did not want to appear to be forging private and exclusive bonds with George before the very eyes of his wife, so she steered away from the subject of George's visit to Geneva and instead asked about old school chums. 'What ever happened to Fay?' and 'What did Peter end up doing?'

The meal dragged on to its completion, the conversation a trail of inconsequential childhood memories and district gossip.

She feinted Thelma's further questions about her marriage. They knew almost nothing about Ambrose and didn't ask.

Edith felt she had so much to tell, so many adventures— had met the greats on the world stage, had witnessed the making of history—yet she felt inhibited, concerned that any such telling would make her seem superior, boastful, snooty.

She tried to twist the conversation back to the shared part of their lives. But they in turn seemed to feel their lives were petty and negligible and tended to trail off from their stories and in turn tried to get her to talk about Europe. But when she did she felt they were envious, and she would cut her stories short.

'It's a long time since I've eaten roast lamb and baked potatoes.'

'Not very French, I'm afraid,' Thelma said.

'That's why I enjoyed it.'

They were all returning to being so frightfully formal. Oh, where was their old childhood irreverence and merriment?

'Must get you to speak at Rotary. That would cause some raised eyebrows. But we did have another woman. Enid Lyons spoke to us. A surprisingly good public speaker. Good diction. Everyone could hear her quite clearly.'

'I see in one of the papers that she is to be made a Dame of the British Empire. Only thirty-nine,' Thelma said.

'She deserves it. She does a lot of public speaking.'

'Her husband is PM so I suppose he can give his wife an honour if he wants,' Thelma said.

Edith said. 'I see that Joe Lyons wants a Pacific non-aggression treaty—USSR, China, France, Netherlands, US and Japan. Can't see Japan being there. Can't see why we should team up with them.'

George seemed to have an opinion on that. 'I was always against economic boycotts of Japan—can't talk things out if you're refusing to trade with a man. Trade is pretty basic to life, isn't it?'

'I rather see economic boycotts as a way of bringing a country to the discussion table,' Edith said. 'Which is another way of saying that trade is basic to life.'

Thelma got up to make coffee, saying, 'You know that Joe Lyons was thirty-five and she was only seventeen when they got together?'

While Thelma fussed with the coffee, making it with a percolator which seemed never to have been used—it had the newness of a wedding gift—she went with George out onto the verandah.

He offered her a cigar which she declined. 'Thought that women on the Continent might smoke cigars these days,' he said.

'Not this woman,' she said.

He sat in a cane chair and smoked his cigar, looking out on the night, frogs croaking in the swamp. Green and Golden Bell frogs, if she remembered rightly.

Standing behind him, she put a comradely hand on his shoulder. 'You seem content, George. The factory is a fine achievement. I was impressed this afternoon. So gleaming. So polished.'

'It's hard to keep up standards. As soon as you turn your back the men let things slide. Content? I suppose so. Sales are up. The house works well. I designed this house, did I tell you?'

'It seems a very ... efficacious house,' she said, again. 'Quite large.'

In fact, she found the rooms themselves too mean. The ceilings a little too low.

The covered entry porch at the gate to the house was an imposing structure. An attempt at the baronial, perhaps. 'I liked the gate entrance—a touch of drama.'

George put down his cigar and reached back to her and took her hands, at the same time glancing into the house.

At first she thought he did so warily, but she saw defiance in his eyes. His taking of her hands was more than comradely, but might just pass as comradely. In polite society.

He spoke in a loud whisper and his voice was vehement, 'Edith, I envy your life ...'

'Don't think like that, George. It's wasteful.'

'Edith, you *did it*. You left the town and you went out there into the world. You have achieved your wildest dreams.'

He gripped her hands tight, raising them, and, at the same time, turned around in the cane chair and put his forehead on her hand.

Oh dear.

'I had stepping stones. I did it in small jumps, George. It wasn't heroic.'

'But I lowered my sights,' he said. 'I lowered my sights. You shot for the moon.'

'George, all your life you always said you wanted to manufacture. You said you wanted a factory. That's what you wanted from life and you have it! And before you were thirty.'

'Oh yes. Just.' Then his voice seemed to carry with it a cry from the heart. 'I wanted a bigger life. A much bigger life.' His words were heartbreaking. 'Edith. You and I know that.'

'Hush, George. Your factory means something.'

'I shouldn't be here in this town. I should be ... I could be in New York ... Chicago.' He savoured the city names. 'I backed Pacific City. But that's not going to happen. The railway line from here to Canberra isn't going ahead.'

She'd forgotten the great plans for Pacific City at Jervis Bay. Following the Canberra design, Pacific City was to have had a great 200-foot-wide main boulevard with very wide streets and avenues radiating off from it. It had been laid out with designated spaces for a racecourse and a university. They had all gone out to look at the laid-out city.

George had believed in it. Had bought land there.

His head gestured towards the house and its creature comforts with a small grunt of baffled consternation.

The house was the shape and size his life had taken. There was no Pacific City with which he could've grown.

No Australian Chicago.

He then raised her hand to his lips and kissed it. 'Let's go away together, Edith. Together we could conquer the world.'

She was taken aback. She tried to find words to reply, words which would save his pride.

He must be a little soused.

At that moment Thelma backed open the screendoor, carrying a tray of coffee cups, cream, sugar, the coffee pot and a cake and biscuits. As she backed though the door, she turned to see George kissing Edith's hand.

Although Edith had tried to get him to let her hands go as soon as she'd heard the noise of Thelma at the door, George had held on.

Thelma dropped the tray.

Edith broke free from George and moved to help.

George did not. He did not even continue to look at the mess but picked up his cigar and turned his gaze back to the croaking swamp which stretched away from the house.

'Here, let me help.' Edith stooped to pick up the things spilled from the tray.

'No. Please, allow me to do it. Please leave me alone,' Thelma said. 'Go away.'

Edith stood back up and wondered if 'go away' was a request to leave the house, the country, or simply to leave the spilled tray be.

Edith looked back to George who, cigar in his mouth which seemed to have gone out, was staring away, in some sort of slump.

Thelma gathered up the coffee things and broken crockery onto the tray and backed into the house again, disappearing to the kitchen, leaving a mess of coffee, milk, and cake.

Edith went to the door and called into the house, 'Thelma, don't bother with fresh coffee.'

'I'm not.' Thelma's voice had an hysterical force.

She turned back to George. 'George? Shouldn't you go in to Thelma?'

George turned. 'Let her be,' he said, with great exasperation.

She let the wiredoor close and walked to the verandah railing. Her face was flushed.

'You know what I am saying, don't you, Edith?'

She looked at him, trying to find a response, but before she could, he said, 'I should've married you.'

Oh God.

'What would you've done in Geneva, George?' she laughed, trying to extinguish his seriousness.

'You don't think I would've been up to it?'

'I don't mean that. I mean you would've found it hard to get a business going there.'

What a ridiculous conversation to be having at this moment.

He stood up, came across to her, and tried to embrace her. 'That was my wrong turning—not marrying you.'

She backed off, holding him away with her outstretched hands.

'George—I couldn't give you a bigger life or whatever it is you are bemoaning. Another person can't do that.' He came close to her again. 'And you're doing just fine.'

This time she let him hold her. He closed their bodies together, breasts, groin and hips closed together and she let it stay that way. 'No, George,' she whispered. 'Let me go. Remember yourself. You're doing just fine. You are where you should be and I am where I should be. Now let's go in to Thelma.'

'I don't want to go in to Thelma. She drives me mad,' he whispered with frustration. 'I'm trapped now.'

His body was still against hers. In panic she expected Thelma to appear again, but she did nothing about separating herself from him.

He was right about himself—he could've achieved just a little more than he had. What was sad was that as a young man he'd always put himself forward as the great achiever.

There was nothing she could do for him. The embrace was awkward. He was a handsome, virile man and his desire for her was palpable. But no.

She released herself from the embrace, kissing him lightly on the lips, tactically avoiding the deep kiss that he wanted.

She went inside without George.

Thelma was leaning on the sink, transfixed.

Edith's flowers were on the floor.

Edith put her hand on Thelma.

Thelma shrugged it off.

'What you saw on the verandah wasn't what you think it was,' she said.

It was exactly what Thelma probably thought it was.

'Please leave this house,' Thelma said, without looking at her.

Edith felt cold with shock.

Again, without looking up from the sink, Thelma said, 'You're a snob. You're a seductress. You fancy yourself so superior. You come prancing into our lives. I'm not going to suffer it. Please go. Go.'

'That's unfair, Thelma.'

'Go.'

Edith went out to the hall and found her things.

She didn't go back out to say goodnight to George, still out on the verandah. She would call in on him at the factory before she left the district.

Outside, in the coolish night, she sat in her father's car trembling with distress. The inside of the car was heavy with leather smell and the odour of petrol and oil. She wound down the windows.

She yearned for the chill winter air of Geneva and the warm, gentle body and tender arms of Ambrose.

The dinner party had been too small—other people being there would've stopped it going mad. Blame it on the claret.

She was a little soused herself.

What was she doing back here? What was she looking for?

Instead of driving directly home, she drove to Jamberoo, her favourite place on the coast, and she sat there looking down the dark valley to Minnamurra House which she'd once dreamed of owning one day.

Or of being the wife of the owner?

Although she thought that her family home was also one of the finer homes of the district.

But Minnamurra was the oldest and had such comfortable elegance. Would have even more if she were mistress of the house.

Norfolk pines and cabbage palm trees. Hardly any gums. Take away the cabbage palms and oddly enough it reminded her of Chateau d'Oex, back in Switzerland, favoured by the British, where she and Robert had gone occasionally to find English company, away from Geneva. It was where English prisoners of war had been interned during the War.

Thelma was somewhat correct about her 'prancing into our lives'. But seductress? She didn't know about that. Given the right circumstance, though, she would have given herself to George. For a night. Partly from curiosity about them as lovers.

Thelma was dead right about her.

And she didn't give a damn that Thelma was dead right.

She still wanted in some vague way to connect with home and to be corrected by it so that her life could return to being more in tune with the conventions.

To somehow adjust the mechanism and get back on track.

To be back on track *as a woman.*

That was partly what she was here for. And it wasn't working.

The natural life seemed to repel her, to push her away and hold her away. And as she sat there, she tried to think of ways to make amends to Thelma and George but she realised that there was no way to recondition their friendship. George was eaten by disappointment with his life; Thelma by a sense of distinction between them, a sense of Edith's rank and privilege—which again, Thelma had correctly perceived. As unflaunted as it had been.

And on top of it all, George's stupid advances.

She wouldn't go to George's factory again. She could see where that might lead.

She had only one other obligatory dinner party—with the Hennekinnes, the French bakers who, as a child, had taught her French words and told her about France. But they had had to back Australian bread.

And then it was back to Sydney where she had to give a talk at the University. And then on to Canberra.

She wanted to say to Thelma and George, 'Come on—you can both have another life. There are things of the mind you may be missing. You can have a great life here where you are. You don't have to move. You can expand what you have.'

For whatever reason, they couldn't. They had a good life but failed somehow to give it due appreciation and had lost the way of expanding it.

There were just different worlds one could inhabit, no better no worse, but absolutely different and with unmistakable borders.

She knew this now. There was no superiority in it. Indeed, she was unsure about whether her own life was in any way on a proper course.

Very much unsure. Perhaps she had been born into the wrong generation. Perhaps she belonged more properly with the next generation of Australians?

She wished she were back on board ship—at the beginning of the voyage—when one was suspended from ordinary life and time seemed endless.

She couldn't fix George: and she couldn't deny her difference.

She had to let it all go.

Tonight, life's cogs had moved, ratchetted around a few notches, and the three of them were all in different places now.

And her skin had been caught in the teeth of the cogs, and bruised.

For comfort, she felt her nipples through the georgette of her dress and the silk of her brassiere. They became erect and the good feeling came, and then the good feeling moved down through her body and as she played with her nipples she imagined them being suckled by a baby, as Ambrose had suckled her breasts from time to time, and she his. She crossed her legs and found the right position and rocked her leg and, slipping her hand into the brassiere to her breasts, she fondled them around the nipples, gently squeezing, and then uncrossing her legs and still squeezing her nipples, she put her other hand up inside her skirt and pleasured herself in a small way.

The Crash of *rebus sic stantibus*

E dith stood in the quadrangle cloisters of the university caught in a gale of recollections from her prickly student years.

She felt again the inadequacy of that time and shivered. At least the Quad was finished now.

She recalled the downright fear of being wrong about everything while at the same time trying to maintain an air of certainty about all things.

A feeling of downright ineptitude which could never ever be shown and confessed.

Each day had been a quandary, even about what to wear, about her hair—long or short, back or forward, up or down, about her make-up or absence thereof. She'd stood out as a girl who had been taught about make-up by her mother, she had dithered and bothered about her personal appearance for years. As her social group changed and her friendships firmed up or fell away, a subtle change of appearance seemed to be required, to be got right.

Not that she'd ever aspired to be, or had any desire to be, a glamour puss. Well, for one term maybe she'd entertained strange notions of her beauty. She'd dared to varnish her nails for a time.

As she walked about the university, she caught again the smell of the laboratory which, as a student, she'd feared would penetrate her skin and remain with her forever.

She stood and smelled the laboratory, the formalin, the sulphur.

And then the false release of graduation, which had not brought to her the certified competency she'd so much needed.

In the last year of her science degree, she'd finally and consciously turned her back on any idea of a scientific career. She'd admitted to herself that she was not going to become another Madame Curie. Consequently, the degree brought to her none of the assurance of direction that it had for the other girls in her graduation year. Although the girls with science degrees had less assurance of career than then those from arts, who were nearly all destined for teaching careers.

The science girls had all considered themselves pioneers. But teaching was usually where they went too.

The degree had been very close to being a waste, although she'd fought away that idea—the thought of having wasted three years of her young life was simply too appalling.

In reference to something else, her mother had once told her never to dwell on what you felt was a waste in your life because the 'dwelling' itself became then a second waste of time.

Back then, she'd told herself that, after all, they were all living in a scientific age and that the degree equipped her for that scientific age.

There'd been a lot of Darwinism, Mendelism, and Pearson and, of course, Galton, which she supposed had given her an edge in some arguments and helped form her world view.

She loved Galton's experiments to prove the inefficacy of prayer.

Galton had discovered the use of fingerprints for identification. He and Pearson had been her heroes.

Walking towards Women's College, she remembered her 'path to go' from Women's College to the lecture rooms and labs. She'd worked out the most pleasing walk even though it was longer. Alva and the others had sometimes indulged her, but mostly they left her to walk her own way alone, while they went the short cut.

She'd also devised her own 'way to go back' to college, that too chosen for its pleasing trees and because it gave her time to calm down after the day, before facing college life.

She had always devised ways of coming and ways of going to the places where she'd worked or lived.

She stood outside the college and decided not to go in. Maybe later in the week she'd go in and look at her old room. All she seemed to remember at that moment were the frantic efforts to keep up her grooming, to get the creaming of her body and hair plucking done, in the rush and bustle of shared bathrooms and the college timetable.

Her gang, had not been only from Science but included also some of the Arts people at Manning and the Union. That and the Public Issues Society had been her real university life.

It was in those places that she'd begun to somehow turn her provincialism into a suave questioning—a style of urbanity based on curiosity.

She thought that she still held civility and curiosity as her highest personal values.

Standing there in the university grounds, she again felt herself as a perplexed young undergraduate who concealed her perplexity by behaving loudly.

Oh God, her laugh! Back then her laugh had been so false. It had been too loud.

They'd all been putting on an act to get by.

At least, now the Quad and the Harbour Bridge were

finished. Two things at least. Almost nothing had been finished in Australia when she'd left.

She had the sort of mind which yearned for, and in fact, lived in, projections of some idea of a *completed future*. She was always impatient with incompletion.

That was what she loved about Geneva—it was a finished city, old and solid.

Finished, that is, except for the Palais des Nations—but almost finished.

She felt a coldness pass through her at the idea of living in unfinished Canberra, of going back to another unfinished, imaginary state of mind and place.

And the world the League was trying to design was certainly far from finished. She'd expected the newly designed world to be finished by now.

The joke at the League was that when the world was perfect they'd be out of a job.

Had she lost faith?

One day, she'd have to sort out the whole business of political faith. Faith came into play at that point where statistical information no longer pointed the way forward and some sort of belief was needed—or if not belief, perhaps a Grand Wish.

Did she live by Grand Wishes?

She'd once thought her view of things was historically inevitable. She now saw that she belonged more with the crowd who thought that there were identifiable things which could be won or lost, that everything was always in the balance. That there was no inevitability.

And you never knew which gesture, word, or action won the day. Which silence, which acquiescence, which inaction lost the day.

She guessed that there was also the poignant position of belonging to a lost cause.

The League?

And then there was the more complicated position, of

belonging to a lost cause while welcoming the justice of a new regime. Karen in *The House in Paris*, speaking of the socialist revolution, had said, 'I should always work against it, but I should like it to happen in spite of me.'

She headed towards the Student Union.

Time to meet the organisers from the League of Nations group.

It was somehow more daunting to speak to those who'd known you when you were immature. And she assumed that some of her old teachers and friends would be there.

An audience of strangers was alive only to what you were saying.

A familiar audience, especially one from one's past, was alive to your person and to your background—they saw too much of you as you spoke. And in this case, they would be seeing that younger version of herself, not the new improved version.

And, in so many ways she'd been such a queer young undergraduate and today they would probably still see her as such.

Maybe she was.

As such.

At the Union refectory, she was met by two of the academic staff, an A.P. Elkin, and an Irishman, Enoch Powell, who was younger than she but was introduced as 'Professor'. So young?

Hanging behind them was an undergraduate introduced as Rob Follan.

They were joined by a Hermann Black—handsome, with a fine voice, from Economics—who brought with him a couple of other undergraduates.

She did not remember any of these dons from her days nor they her. Too much time had passed.

She wore her wonderful wide-brimmed felt hat with a feather tucked in the band. She'd once been told a French proverb, that 'when a person wears a hat it is impossible to tell what is on their mind'.

She felt she needed any shielding of her mind that a hat might give.

She had on a black suit with a hip-length jacket, a box-pleated skirt, and belt. Two-toned blue and white shoes. She rather liked the two-toned shoes although on men she considered two-toned shoes to be cad's shoes. As a general rule. The rule had not applied to Jerome—but he was another sort of person from another time.

And she wore soft kid-leather gauntlet gloves.

And a cape.

The gloves, she thought, were rather swashling. The swank hat was perhaps excessive, although when she'd put it on that morning, she'd thought at first that it suggested the sheep station. But on second thoughts had seen it, simply, as swank. For Sydney.

Give them *splash*, Edith.

Perhaps, there was also something defiant in the hat.

She wore no jewellery, apart from Ambrose's necklet which could not be seen.

She realised that most of those present were younger, and she had to remind herself that this was only natural. And then, hovering in the background, she saw dear Alva, whom she'd asked to be included at the official lunch table.

She excused herself from the greeting party and went over to embrace her. She'd been closer to Alva than anyone else in the last year at university.

'It looks as if we're the only two women at lunch,' she said to Alva, leading her back to the greeting party.

She introduced Alva and then asked the men, 'Will there be a turnout?'

'I think the League group is still the largest society on campus,' Elkin said, turning to Black. 'Would that be right, Hermann?

'Oh yes, by far,' said Black.

'And I think Camilla Wedgewood, Principal of Women's College, will join us—to even up the sexes.'

'Support for the League is holding?' she asked.

'Own up,' said Powell to the other men, and then turned to her. 'Dwindling, I'm afraid—in attendances.'

'But not in dedication,' said Black.

'Can't be sure of that, either,' said the man Powell.

The Harsh Realist.

'Disheartening times,' she sympathised. She asked what their activities were. She felt momentarily as if she were a member of the royal family in a cinema newsreel visiting a factory. *And your work is to sweep up the iron filings—how interesting that must be.*

Elkin said that Black and he were doing broadcasting work and talks to trades unions. 'And we organise model assemblies for the brighter high school students.'

'Broadcasting! Splendid,' said Her Royal Highness. 'Duncan Hall, of course, invented the idea of the model assemblies—an Australian idea.'

They then turned the questions to her and she felt herself sink as she tried to make answers for them which would hearten them. She ached to be able to tell them that something grand, noble was about to flow from Geneva directly to the world and to them.

She said that there was a feeling that the League had to leave aside sanctions and a collective military force for now. Moves were afoot, to let go of the idea that the League could police the world. Time to concentrate on good works. Relieving suffering.

The undergraduate Follan asked a question about citizen sanctions as his way of making a rather strident statement— 'the trades union can stop goods moving from one country to another,' he said. 'The workers can choose to stop buying the goods from another country, sanctions could be done by the people, not only by governments.'

'The trouble with citizen sanctions is that you could have one foreign policy pursued by the trades union and another by the farmer organisations. Confuses everyone abroad,' Edith said. 'But, I agree that they are a new form of diplomacy. And more diplomacy seems to be done outside of government. The Peace Ballot, the Red Cross, and the international conferences of citizens. Can't be sure it's a good thing.'

She saw Follan had not accepted her answer.

Bolshie.

He began another foray. She held up a hand, laughing. 'Don't make me give my talk twice. I'm going to argue sanctions this afternoon.'

Follan unwillingly withdrew.

Black, the economist, said, 'Sanctions could make the marketplace more devious—make traders cunning at finding ways around the blockades and so on.'

Powell said in a staccato voice, 'And I'm worried about the hollow value of treaties. Hitler has killed the Locarno peace treaties now that he's invaded the Rhineland. One could ask what value there is in treaties?'

He was irritated with the world. Maybe with the League. Maybe with her?

Edith had long pondered the enigma of treaties.

She was about to reply when Black said, '*Rebus sic stantibus,*' as if pulling it as a rabbit from a hat. 'When the circumstances change the treaty no longer applies.'

'You make my point,' said Powell, impatiently.

They looked to her. She was being paid respect. She was also being seen as a bearer of the latest from Europe. The Latin term brought with it a crowd of memories for her. It had been one of her first lessons in the arts of diplomacy.

She had also once lived by it. 'Diplomatically, most of us now consider the doctrine of *rebus sic stantibus* a rather immature doctrine,' she said. Hoping it didn't sound offensive.

'Which doesn't prevent some nations applying it,' said Powell.

The Pessimist.

'The doctrine lends itself to misuse by politically irresponsible nations,' she said. 'We—the more responsible diplomatic community—have tossed it.'

She went on, 'The advanced nations do not accept that one party can just up and terminate a treaty.'

There were smiles showing that they knew which nations these were.

She turned to Powell, trying to win him. 'I'm reminded of what Alexis Léger once said to me. He said, "We must act within the League to prevent, or punish, all treaty violations. Treaties are the handshake of world civilisation. When the trust of the handshake has gone so has civilisation." He said that the only way treaties will be kept is reward and punishment.'

'One wonders, if treaties are so unreliable and so much trouble, why we need so many,' Powell said.

She batted back. 'Well, things are changing about treaties. At last, all treaties are public. They are all registered with the League and open to inspection by all parties. In fact, for the first time in history, the world is a party to every treaty—the League, in a sense, is now a signatory to every treaty. The recent Anglo-Egyptian Treaty of Alliance allows for revision if necessary, but only by the League Council. That's the new thinking on treaties.'

Bring them up to the mark on treaties.

Discussion was robust here in Sydney, to say the least. No small talk here.

And what about your marriage contract, Edith? There was perhaps no safety even in the contract of people pledged to love. That contract was nothing more than a signing up for the effort or intention of the two people to avoid risk, to find safety. Or could one only find safety with those who knew that there was no safety?

The partnership of the frightened?

She didn't feel that much at risk though, with Ambrose. But she supposed they *accepted*, both of them, that there was no contract, that they lived from day to day. Another hopeless manoeuvre to avoid putting the heart at risk.

In the refectory, they sat at a reserved table. After much shuffling around, she was placed facing into the dining hall, in the middle.

'Of course, there's the Doctrine of Frustration,' Powell said, buttering a slice of bread as soon as he'd sat down. 'Where circumstances arise between two parties which neither party to a contract could have foreseen, the contract is then set aside.'

'That applies, as I understand it, only in civil law,' she said. 'And the contract still cannot be set aside by the action of one party.'

She knew that much law, if they were all to play lawyers.

'*Mutatis mutandis*—other things being equal,' said Black, having found another Latin tag in his bag of tricks. 'And with those things being changed which must change.'

They all laughed knowingly.

'Many things in civil law are not to be found in international law,' said Elkin.

'Contracts signed by force?' said Follan, sounding like a smart student rushing out an answer. 'In civil law if a contract is signed because of threat of force it's invalid. But internationally, many treaties are imposed on defeated nations by force.'

'Treaty of Versailles, for one,' said Black quickly.

'At the end of every war—and some of these imposed treaties last,' she said.

My goodness, she thought, although they were not against *her* as such, it did feel as if she were in a Hollywood cowboy picture with the baddies and the goodies shooting up and down the streets.

The students at the end seemed to be sitting in some awe at the exchange.

All those at the table, she decided, were taking her measure.

She added, 'I do agree that treaties on matters of war and peace seem to be simply descriptions of a prevailing mood—which can soon change.'

'Everyone signed the Kellogg-Briand Pact and the Locarno treaties to end war forever,' said Powell. 'That was done with great confidence. People trusted those treaties. Now Germany and Italy have just torn them up.'

'But the treaties supervising the airwaves and sea waves, postal service and so on, seem to be useful rules of the game,' Edith said, trying to salvage some respect for international diplomacy. 'Florence Nightingale once said that people who will keep a vow would do their duty without a vow; but people who will not do their duty without a vow cannot be relied upon to do it with one. But I don't agree. We need rules and agreements to keep us on track. They're usually the distillation of long past arguments. Wisdom of the tribe.'

'I can't see why we bother with treaties at all,' said Alva, finding the confidence to join in.

Edith smiled encouragingly at Alva and said, 'I once asked the same question of Under Secretary-General Auguste Bartou. And I remember that he replied, "Because they sometimes work." We make treaties because they might be kept.'

That sounded too *instructional.*

These were university dons she was talking with. Perhaps deference might be a better demeanour.

'Give me a good example of a long-lasting treaty,' Black asked.

That was easy. 'The Rush-Bagot Treaty—one of the oldest in the book,' she said, also sounding too much like a bright girl in a classroom. Though she reminded herself that she was older than most of them and more experienced perhaps than any of them. It was being back in the university grounds that had caused her to shrink like Alice in Wonderland. She was growing back to her right size.

'The United States and Canada,' said Black, his memory having thrown it up. 'The disarming of the Great Lakes?'

She was touched to see him seeking her approval.

'Yes,' she said. 'Between Canada, America and Great Britain. After the Canadians and the British burned down the White House. A treaty which has lasted.'

She'd learned a thing or two in Geneva and she may as well promenade her learning.

'Rather than *rebus sic stantibus* ...' she said, deciding to lighten things and to round this discussion off '... I prefer, for the likes of us, the motto *sidere mens eadem mutato*—"though the sky be changed our spirit is the same ...",' putting in the translation quickly with just the right tone to suggest that, of course, they would all know it, the tone suggesting she was simply refreshing her own understanding of the term.

Two of the men patted the table in approval.

'Oh gosh—it's the university motto and you remember it!' said Alva.

One of the undergraduates—McAuley?—ventured a quip, 'My translation is "although the facts may changeth: our opinions remaineth the same".'

Much laughter.

The food was served. Ah, Union food, but the superior menu perhaps? It was really Windsor soup, two joints and mixed vegetables, and wine trifle. Only two bottles of wine among them all.

She removed her gloves, placing them in the handbag glove loop.

They were perhaps too fashionable. She wouldn't wear them during her talk.

Black said, 'Let's have a lighter conversation before we thoroughly depress ourselves. Tell us about the Palais des Nations.'

'That's one thing the League has started and will complete,' she said, laughing. 'We have moved house although the Assembly room is still being completed and a few other parts. I love the Palais. Dignified and practical. But ...'

'What's the "but",' Black asked.

'I won't criticise the first building the world has built together.'

'I think you should tell us your "but".'

'For my tastes, the Assembly hall is too ornate,' she said. 'But the Assembly will try it out for the first time next year. By the way, the rostrum is made from Australian woods. We were the first nation to make a gift to the League.'

She made a gesture of bleakness. 'In the days when we were really achieving things we were in the shabby Palais Wilson which I also loved. Now in these inglorious days we are ineffective and frustrated—but living in a Palace. And I'm being gloomy again.'

Again, some dark laughter.

'And,' she announced, 'I'm going to order another two bottles of wine—on my account. To say "happily returned" to my alma mater.'

She felt the undergraduates deserved it. She'd wait for later.

'Hear, hear.'

'A generous gesture,' said Elkin.

Then with vehemence, a demand, a cry, from the man Powell, 'Italy's as good as out of the League. Germany's out. Brazil is out. Japan's out. The US is never going to join. It's all over. Admit it. It's all done for. Disarmament Conference has died. Rearmament has begun.'

'Costa Rica has also withdrawn,' added Black.

She felt compelled to keep up morale. 'We have gained the Dominican Republic, Ireland, Iraq, Mexico, and Turkey.'

'And the USSR,' said Follan. 'Which shows that the USSR at least remains international in its thinking even if the Americans do not.'

'Yes, and the USSR. A rather important new member,' she said.

'To what end have they joined?' Powell said to Follan.

She hadn't told them that Guatemala and Honduras and Nicaragua were all pulling out because they couldn't pay. 'I think the League gains are still ahead of the losses. On last count.'

Powell wasn't to be placated. 'We have to admit that disarmament is dead.'

He stared at her, waiting for her response. The others were obviously uncomfortable but not surprised by Powell's persistent irritation.

To give the official line or to speak her heart?

In a measured voice, she said, 'If it were all over, I wouldn't still be there working for it—nor other Australians such as Duncan Hall and this year Australia's chair of the Council, Stanley Bruce. We all believe there's something to be done. There are all the health projects—and even the US is enthusiastically contributing to those—there's lots of good things still going on.'

She hadn't answered his question.

'But it cannot keep the peace!' the man Powell almost shouted.

'Easy on, Enoch,' said Elkin. 'It's a lunch, not a rally.'

'And we're all on the same side,' said Black.

Again, Edith spoke quietly and slowly, with control, 'Disputes, yes, admittedly minor, are still settled by the League. The Moslem countries are using Geneva as a meeting place to deal with their problems and emerging as nation states out of their mandates. Iraq is now a nation and a member of the League. Things like that.'

Alva then spoke up. 'You have to agree with Mr Powell that one of the great illusions of the League is already flat, the illusion of disarmament. It may still be "peace for all nations", but it'll have to be an armed peace.'

It was something Alva had obviously been burning to say and had, by the sound of it, prepared somewhat before coming. It sounded like she'd decided she should have her say. It all came out in a lump.

And, Edith noted, it was, possibly, a speech against her. It was—she further noted—also Mussolini's newly stated position.

Edith looked at Alva, smiling but quietly wondering about her.

Since coming back she had not had a long talk with Alva about her politics. And their letters had been so sporadic and light-hearted they'd given no clear view of what Alva had been thinking over the years.

'Mussolini sometimes makes sense,' Edith said, showing that she recognised the line of thought. 'But I don't think we should quote him.'

The men laughingly agreed. Alva laughed half-heartedly but appeared squashed.

She hadn't wanted to squash Alva. She'd make it up to her later.

Despite her confident clubby manner, Edith felt enfeebled as she heard the disheartened tone of the luncheon group. What could she say? How could she be Doctor Cheerup?

'The nutrition report is very good,' she heard herself say.

Oh God, was that the best she could do?

'Treating illnesses, feeding the children ...' She felt her head drooping—she was speaking to the breadbasket.

Head up, shoulders back, Edith.

'Health is a foundation for order—through people who are healthier, through their well-being.'

Oh, it was all so limp. Edith felt like McGeachy from Information Section struggling to interest reporters. It was rather pathetic to base the hope for peace on free Oslo lunches and milk for school children and getting people to eat breakfast.

Oh dear.

'Maybe,' she joked, 'Italians wouldn't go to war if they ate breakfast. We are trying to get them to eat a proper breakfast. The coffee may irritate their stomachs. Lead to troublesome digestions.'

They laughed.

Elkin asked politely what interest there was in the Australian initiatives on fairer distribution of food in the world.

'Very little, I'm afraid,' she said. And then looked at them and grimaced, 'None. No interest at all.'

Dr Cheerup said, 'We've produced tables recommending diets according to occupation. World-wide.'

Oh dear, it was getting worse.

Hay-rake diplomacy.

Abruptly, she felt as if she were Ambrose—Ambrose and the hay-rake fiasco. A few years ago Ambrose, in the midst of what turned out to be a nervous collapse, had seen the solution to the world's ills in more efficient agricultural machinery—in fact, specifically, in a new design for a hay-rake. Ambrose had cracked up after making this submission.

Perhaps she was cracking up.

The League was cracking up—the League was close to having a nervous collapse.

That was the truth of the matter.

'Did the League determine how much a professor should eat?' Elkin joked, trying to lead them out of their gloom.

Everyone laughed.

'Should be less than a student,' one of the undergraduates said from the end of the table. 'Students have much healthier appetites.'

They all laughed and heads looked to the student who blushed with the success of his quip. The student, suddenly aware of all the attention he had captured, added, 'I would've thought.'

'We're doing nutritional surveys of Australian families,'

Black said. 'For the first time, we will have a picture of what Australians eat. They don't eat enough greens. We know that much.'

Elkin tapped his watch and indicated it was time for them all to stroll across to the lecture theatre. 'Don't know what happened to Miss Wedgewood.'

Edith's confidence and sense of mission had dwindled. She felt flat.

She felt hurt, too, that the Principal of Women's College hadn't shown up to have lunch and given support to an old girl.

But as she stood up and excused herself to go to the Ladies, she thought that as a good Women's College girl, she would gird her loins and go into the fray.

The Beautiful Instrument

For all her experience at public speaking she was, this time, as well as being flat from the lunch, unsure of herself. She felt she was back in the Public Issues Society. She'd grown small again. For the first time in her life she was taking the role of lecturer in her old university.

She knew that once started, she would become caught up in the talk and the flatness would go and a spring of energy would arise, but one still had to live with the nervousness of starting. And with the fear that there would be no voice with which to *start*.

The banked seating of the history lecture theatre was full.

They hadn't installed microphones. Behind the times.

She began with a few of the old jokes about the League, 'The world's wastepaper bin' and so on.

'The joke I like best came from the Prime Minister of Canada, Mackenzie King, who called us "The League of Notions".'

The laughter gave her strength. Laughter from an audience was sweet music. The spring of energy began to flow.

She then turned to Italy's invasion of Ethiopia.

'Confronted by the invasion of Ethiopia by Italy—with both countries being members of the League, and with Italy a permanent member of the League Council—this is how the League went about its business.

'Firstly, it had to determine whether a state of war existed.

'Swiftly, the Council decided that Italy had breached Article VI of the Covenant of the League and was, under international law, an aggressor state.

'The matter went then to the League Assembly. Voice after voice spoke for strong action. It seemed that after years of uncertainty and timidity the League could act.

'Australia spoke out against Italy.

'I was in the Assembly for this debate. I was moved by the voice of our smallest member state, Haiti. Its delegate, Laired Nemours, said he spoke not only for the smallest member state but also for the oldest black republic on the continent of America. He said, "Great or small, strong or weak, near or far, white or coloured, let us never forget that one day we may be somebody's Ethiopia."

'At this point in the crisis it was obvious what must happen: Italy was wrong; the League was obliged to take collective action against Italy.

'We decided to use our newest weapon—economic sanctions. Something for which careful planning had gone on for years.

'I want to explain this new method of stopping wars.'

She stared out at them. The laughter of the opening jokes was fine but she'd plunged perhaps too deeply, too soon. It sounded like a lecture. It was a lecture. Ask a question.

'I assume that you all understand what we mean when we talk of "sanctions"?'

She searched the faces, some nodded, some shook their heads.

She explained the new sanctions system. 'The Covenant includes all methods of collective action to stop war—military and otherwise—available to the League for bringing an aggressor to heel—all described as sanctions.

'Increasingly, in diplomatic circles the word sanctions is used to describe the non-violent economic weapons which can be turned against an aggressor to stop that nation from waging war.

'We have come a long way in creating these economic sanctions as a non-military answer, although they have never yet been properly tested.

'So at the League we wheeled it out, as it were, from its hangar—gleamingly sharp and well designed.

'We set up the Sanctions Coordination Committee, a new organism for the League. I was the League's liaison officer on the committee.

'This was a gigantic step forward. Never in history had this new united form of economic action been taken against a country.

'There are two views on the use of this instrument: one argued to me by the British Foreign Secretary, Mr Anthony Eden, during the crisis, was that economic sanctions had to be applied swiftly and totally. What he called the Ton of Bricks approach.

'The other position is the Turn of the Screw, that they should be applied gradually so that they do least damage to those countries applying the sanctions—remember that by joining in the sanctions, innocent countries lose exports they would normally have made to the aggressor or they lose much needed imports from the aggressor.

'The screws get tighter and tighter until the aggressor submits.

'The first action under the gradual sanctions plan is to stop the flow of arms and munitions to the aggressor nation.

'If this doesn't work, you tighten the screws another notch—you stop all financial credits and loans.

'If this doesn't bring the aggressor nation to its knees, you stop the flow of exports from that country—all countries agree to stop buying the goods of the aggressor country. This means all League members close their ports to Italian shipping.

'And now, if that doesn't work, you stop the flow of what are called first list raw materials. These are rubber, tin, aluminium, manganese, nickel, rare minerals and transport animals, all associated with war industries.

'And, if by now this doesn't work, you stop the flow of second list materials, which are oil, iron, steel, coal and coke.

'If this still doesn't stop them, you prevent all travel to the aggressor country, and finally, if all this fails—which is hardly conceivable because no country is that self-sufficient—you can stop the flow of food and, in some cases, water, to the country.

'And I'd also like to see the leaders and the top circles of an aggressor country being stopped from going abroad on expensive holidays to the French Riviera and to fashionable clinics in Switzerland or shopping in Paris and so on.'

She received some claps and chuckles from the audience.

At least they were listening. She outlined in more detail the other mechanisms which the League had up its sleeve.

As she went on she felt she had their interest. She was interested in what she was saying, which she always took to be a good sign. She had spoken about this before but as she went on she became convinced once again that sanctions were the way forward.

'While doing this, though, it is important to keep diplomatic channels open until all else has failed. You do not break diplomatic relations.

'You use this as the final step when you cut the aggressive nation off from the world community entirely—diplomatically, by travel, by mail, cable and telephone, and by expulsion from the League.

'They become an outcast nation.

'Now isn't it a beautiful way to avoid war? Such a fine instrument of non-military peace-making?'

Her enthusiasm was there in her voice, and her hands were in the air, she realised. Maybe she was becoming an orator?

'Someone is sure to ask about those nations which were not members of the League and neutrals who might want to continue trade with the aggressor nation regardless of what the League wants to happen.

'In the case of Italy, some of the neutrals and the US were willing to go along with the League sanctions on military equipment. But America increased its sale of oil to Italy and thus broke the oil sanction. I suppose for the Americans, business is business.'

Some cynical laughter.

'So ultimately, to make sanctions work might require a League naval blockade and the interdiction of any ships attempting to trade with the aggressor nation. Although moves have been made to ban all submarines, I would favour the League having its own fleet of submarines, as a way of imposing embargoes.

'But yes, all nets break—some things will get through to the embargoed nation. But not enough to sustain that nation in its aggression.

'This beautiful instrument of peace has other parts to it: the scheme of reverse sanctions, that is, ways of economically helping that nation which has been attacked; the Treaty of Financial Assistance for Victims of Aggression, to provide funding and materials for the attacked nation. This Treaty has not yet been fully ratified.

'But when in place it will mean that while economically strangling the aggressor, we strengthen the victim.

'The League very early on recognised the importance of having the machinery of sanctioning in place so that it could be quickly applied as soon as bloodshed begins.

'So over the years we prepared the plans made for just the situation which occurred with Italy.

'Because some of those countries applying the sanctions are

hurt more than others, we have tried to statistically evaluate the degree of burden—country to country.

'Those nations which suffer from having their trade with the aggressor suspended are compensated from a fund administered by the League.

'By the way, another possible economic weapon being discussed is for the League members to buy the entire production of strategic materials needed by an aggressor nation—for example, all of Sweden's surplus iron ore production which normally would be bought by, say, Germany. And to then hold this stockpile of materials for sale at a later date.

'This would then render a country such as Germany impotent. I am speaking hypothetically about Germany, of course.'

Knowing laughter.

She went on for a while with more detail on ways of stopping aggression and then glanced at her watch.

She had a joke for the end.

'The world renowned cartoonist, Emery Kelen, who spends most of his time in Geneva, and whom I have the good fortune to call a friend, said this to me about sanctions.

'He said that the only people who should not boycott Mussolini are the cartoonists and the satirists.'

There was strong laughter.

'If Ethiopia had not collapsed and if we had acted fast enough—used the Ton of Bricks approach—we might have stopped Italy in her tracks. As it was, Ethiopia could not hold out.'

She then said her concluding sentence, with great emphasis, 'I think, at last, we might now know how to stop war without military action.'

She left a silence now for emphasis, and there were murmurs of appreciation in the audience.

'Thank you.'

As she sat down she said to herself, 'Yes, but we didn't stop Italy.'

At question time, one young woman asked why, if sanctions were such a fine new instrument to stop war and everything had been thought out beforehand, they had not been brought against Italy fast enough?

Edith took a deep breath and felt for the young woman with her wish to be reassured. 'It was not sanctions which failed but the question of political will.'

And what, Edith, is political will?

The same woman half-rose from the seating, and said, 'And how do we find this political will?'

'The political will to act is a strange and mysterious thing. I don't pretend to know how to analyse it.

'Political will seems to depend on political timing—there seems to be a time when moral concern, political vigour, and political gravity are concentrated and resolute.

Her mind found a joke.

'There is a diplomatic joke—"Last month it was inevitable; this month it is possible; next month it will be out of the question."

'But when it comes to the time for action, time passing allows impedance and torpor to develop. The passing of time is the enemy of political action.

'If this gravity and vigour are not effectively used at the time, they dissipate and political attention shifts to other matters. I suppose that is why we have the expression "strike while the iron is hot".

'There is a moral moment, it seems, when the issue is clear, the remedy obvious, and people are prepared to act.

'But if time is allowed for the aggressive nation to stall, diplomatically obfuscate, make false declarations, move in secret—that is, fritter away time and diplomatic energy—the moral moment can be lost.

'This was what happened in part, back in October. The League did act—the Sanctions Committee swung into action.

'Within weeks, Italy's financial difficulties started to appear and confusion and fear were showing in the Italian economy.

'Then Italy moved troops to the French border—a bluff, but it caused France to talk of the matter as a national security problem for them.

'This required talks and further talks—outside the League—between France and Italy, and France and its ally, the UK, which took France's attention away from the Ethiopian issue. Governments have only a limited amount of political attention or energy for a matter.

'France and England then said that they would make one last effort diplomatically to convince Italy to desist.

'The League Sanctions Committee was asked to hold off from full implementation of the sanctions.

'This hiatus allowed Italy to make diplomatic war while getting on with its real war against Ethiopia. Italy also threatened other military action, claiming, for instance, it would consider the applications of the sanctions to be an aggressive act and that Italy would attack those nations which applied them—the Italians argued that sanctions would "spread the conflict".

'So we had this new argument against sanctions—that they would spread the conflict.'

Edith found that the whole room was deathly silent. Had what she said brought about a sense of defeat?

'However, the beauty of sanctions is that if an aggressor does choose to retaliate or "spread the conflict" they at the same time "spread their resources"—their already dwindling resources—thus further weakening their economy and their military resources.

'The more they spread their resources, the more they reduce their resources.

'But for the League, the moral moment had been dissipated, the momentum had been lost—diplomatic impedance had brought sanctions to a halt. Political will melted like an ice cream in a little boy's hand.'

She looked out at them; she saw they were dismayed.

A few were shaking their heads.

She was not here to dismay them.

'The problem with France—and with any country—is not the principle of putting "national interests" above everything. The problem is that "national interest" is a lazy formulation, is rarely obvious and never unanimously perceived.

'Paradoxically, national interest can mean the subjugation in the short term of one national "interest"—say, a trade in a commodity. Making these judgements is the test of diplomatic wisdom.'

The chair took another question from a woman. 'You mean that sanctions can work only in a perfectly wise world?'

Edith looked into the woman's eyes and said, 'Even imperfectly applied sanctions can work: the instrument has within it a tolerance for imperfection.

'The world has to have things in position so it can act fast.'

The woman sat down, and then stood up, remembering to say 'Thank you' in a weak voice.

As Edith spoke with strong conviction, without nervousness, she realised that she loved—almost to obsession—the instrument of sanctions and desperately wanted to see it tried.

She didn't care so much about the particular issue anymore: she felt the need of an inventor to see the invention tested, whether it blew up or not.

Perhaps she'd become preoccupied with *technique* rather than with international morality.

She pushed aside this new self-observation and returned her attention to the woman who had sat down and was now standing again.

The woman said, 'Then who should have forced what you call the moral moment? Who should have called the bluff?'

'A resolute international leader can engender political will—in his own country and in the international forum.'

She knew that was a circular argument. Where did 'resolute leaders' get *their* will?

She had no ready answer for that.

She then said, 'All is never lost. Once a diplomatic chain of events has occurred, whether the chain leads to success or failure, that diplomatic chain becomes part of the institutional memory of the world, lodges itself, as it were, in the diplomatic memory, and the next time a similar situation occurs that memory will cause people to behave differently. Perhaps the next time they will use this memory of failure to forge the political will—to call the bluff of an aggressor.'

If situations which arose were ever the same. Bartou thought not. And if you could identify them as the same.

Was that really correct? Was there a world memory.

Maybe the League was the world memory.

A man stood up and asked, 'If a country can bluff the world by threatening to spread the conflict, how do we ever know that it *is* bluff and that the conflict would not be spread in some frightful way?'

Edith knew the horrible answer.

She heard in her head the voice of Ambrose giving the answer he had once given in their bedroom during a discussion. She had never used that answer.

Now she saw no way of avoiding it.

'There is something called the Dilemma of Preventative Action. If you take strong and successful action—be it military or economic—to prevent some *predicted* dreadful thing happening, history will never ever know if that predicted dreadful thing really would've happened. If we had wrecked the Italian economy for a time, caused some hardship there before they were able to properly invade Ethiopia, we would never have known if they would've spread the conflict or done the brutal things we feared they would. History cannot tell you that you were right to act; it can only tell you when you were wrong *not to act.*'

The man remained standing waiting for more of an answer.

She was sucked on into the question. 'And there will always

be those who condemn the preventative action if it is successful—the surgery—and there is often very little conclusive evidence that can be given afterwards to say that the dreadful things would've happened had there not been the surgery.'

The man said, 'Does that mean that we'll always go to war when the dreadful things are underway, can be seen to be happening—that we will only act when it's too late?'

She thought and said tiredly, 'It could be that democracies will always go to war too late. Because they have to pause for debate and listen to qualms. Yes.'

'Is that your complete answer?'

While saying this Edith was hearing for the first time the true meaning of this political truth.

She saw clearly that the members of the League and the democracies would always have trouble taking joint action. She saw that nations were falling back on defending themselves alone or in alliances. They were falling back into the dark ages. Away from the vision of a single sensible world of decent nations.

'Is the League dead then?' the man insisted.

She looked at the intent faces yearning for her to say something which would keep the faith. To lift the meeting.

She had never seen faces so craving for reassurance.

The chair cut in and said, 'Each person is entitled to one question I think, Mr Tierney. You have, if I count correctly, asked three.'

She could hide behind the chair's ruling.

She looked out at their eyes.

Regardless of the chair, they wanted an answer to the deep and existential question on the political condition.

Before she could try to answer, the chairman then called on Hermann Black to move a vote of thanks which was seconded by someone she didn't know and the meeting was closed with loud applause.

She had been relieved from giving the answer.

She decided then that she had to answer. That the question went to the very core of the human political condition.

She went back to the podium and said, 'Please. Please may I beg your attention for a second?'

The audience paused in their postures of rising from seats and the gathering of things.

'I haven't answered the last question. I don't want you to go away thinking I'm an artful dodger.'

Their faces once more turned to her.

She knew that only a second-class mind cannot adequately and comprehensively explain the opposite of what one personally believed. You were either involved in inquiry or you were involved in making propaganda.

She decided she had to go in against her argument.

'I would be simply a publicist if I put only the case for the things I believe. I would not be a true inquirer. And universities are for inquiry.

'There are three things against sanctions—that they could spread the conflict; that they could be seen, *in themselves*, as an act of aggression; and they hurt the poor or those who are unable to protect themselves from being injured by the sanctions within the country.

'The leaders are always quarantined from the impact of sanctions by their control of food and medicine. Only the powerless suffer.

'But sanctions as a preventative action—and as distinct from military action—at least, do not cost people their lives.

'I think you want me to tell you what I believe about the future of world politics from my experience at the League.'

She saw that no one was leaving. They were standing listening to her.

'I believe that no significant international injustice remains forever,' she said. 'That Ethiopia will regain its independence.

'That Mussolini will answer for misusing his country's resources in war.

'That a failure of will at one time is not a failure of will for all times. That democratic countries are self-examining and self-correcting.

'And that sometimes that will, having failed, can at times, reassert itself. That democratic will is *resurgent*. I believe that democracies can come together with great force. And will learn how to do this.

'Democratic states in combination are still learning the hardest lessons: when to act and when not to act; how to act; which instruments of collective action?; and how to act swiftly. There is an old Indian proverb—it is good to help; but it is wiser to know *how to help*.

'The League of Nations is a college as much as it is a political instrument.

'We are all learning.'

The audience began to clap and it grew into massive applause.

She saw belief in the eyes of the audience.

She wondered if her answers were a sham.

Whether they would survive the test of the cold light of day.

Everyone was still standing and clapping.

On stage, Elkin, in the chair, was clapping. Chairmen were not supposed to clap.

Even Mr Powell and young Follan were clapping.

It was pleasing and she was flushed, but her relentless punishing mind was already saying sardonically in her head, 'Explain again what constitutes "political will", Edith.'

She told her relentlessly punishing mind to go away—to let her have a moment of triumph, let the League have a moment of acclaim. It could be its last.

It was applause for her belief in the ingenuity of the human political mind. She had won applause for the visionary and inventive nature of higher politics.

The applause died away and people left. Follan came over

and shook her hand, and others of the committee came over to thank her. The appreciation sounded genuine.

She gathered her notes and put them in her handbag. The best part of her speech had not been in her notes.

Perhaps today there'd also been the confrontation of herself with her student past, a confrontation with her days of inadequacy.

She had come back to face that inadequacy.

Perhaps, today, she'd at last graduated.

Old Friends

After the thanks and the congratulations, Edith saw Alva waiting patiently at the back of the lecture theatre, as arranged, and she excused herself from the well-wishers and went over to her.

They hugged again and then took a taxi to Mockbells coffee shop, one of their old undergraduate haunts.

When they were seated, she said to Alva, 'Well? How did I go?'

Alva seemed confused. 'How did you go?'

'With my talk? How did it go?'

'You want me to tell you how your talk was received!?'

'My going back like that after the talk was all over and having a second go. I've never done that before in my life.'

'They applauded. It was an ovation.'

'But was it just politeness?'

'Isn't it rather immodest to ask me to praise you ... to your face?' Alva looked down at the table.

Alva was irritated.

Edith was taken aback.

Edith put her hands on Alva's hands but realised that Alva was not responsive. She searched Alva's face for additional meaning. 'I suppose it is a seeking of praise. Public speaking is always nerve-wracking. I want to know.'

'You just want me to say how brilliant you are.'

'Alva, deep down I'm seeking reassurance. Plain and simple reassurance. That I didn't make an ass of myself.'

The paradox of it—she had been trying to reassure the audience and now desperately needed to be reassured herself.

Alva seemed to disbelieve her. 'You don't need reassurance from a plain old laboratory assistant like me.' And then she laughed unpleasantly. 'And anyhow, politeness would prevent me telling you the truth.'

Alva's agitation now seemed to imply there'd been some nasty failure in the speech. Applause could never really be trusted, nor the remarks of the organising committee afterwards. Nor the vote of thanks. Even laughter from an audience was a qualified acceptance.

Edith said, 'A friend can tell the truth.'

'A friend?'

Was she also presuming Alva's friendship? 'It's rather frightening to be with someone after a talk who doesn't mention it. I'm sitting here thinking you found it all dull propaganda.'

Edith was now embarrassed, floundering. Of course, if it had flopped, Alva might not be able to find the words. Edith could see then how it must seem to Alva—that Alva didn't think her own reaction to be important to Edith.

Edith said. 'Alva, you've talked in public—you must know the feeling?'

'I have never talked in public' she said, with some irritation. 'Not in the way you talk in public. I can't imagine doing it. Furthermore, no one gives me an opportunity.'

Edith thought back to the Public Issues Society and yes, she couldn't remember Alva speaking.

Edith kept back her spontaneous retort—*then get up on your hind legs and talk!*

She did not remember this whining attitude in Alva.

Edith kept this all back and softened her voice, tightening her hands on Alva's, 'I find it so demanding,' Edith said. 'Every time I get up to speak.'

'You don't show it.'

'It's there.'

Alva stared back at her, 'You're brilliant and composed and assured—all those things. And you know it.'

The words came out almost resentfully.

'Alva. I see now I shouldn't have asked. It was unfair. I apologise. You don't have to say anything.'

'Now you want me to stop because you realise that my opinion doesn't count for beans?'

'No! I do value your opinion—but I should never've sought it. I felt today in the talk that I had so little to give—so little true soundness. That perhaps I was bluffing. I had only sad stories to tell. I felt the League had let the world down. Oddly, I felt I had let everyone down. As if I was sent from this country to set things right with the world and have come back as a flop.'

'That's a rather big-noting way of seeing yourself.'

Alva was being impossible. Edith began to bristle, 'Alva! I wasn't being that serious. I don't see myself that way—it was just a caricature of myself. A caricature of my dreams.'

Alva seemed to respond to Edith's stronger tone. 'To tell you the truth, I expected you to be more critical. To say honestly that the League had crashed.'

Hah. So now there was some true criticism of the talk.

Edith restrained herself from falling back into the role of Champion of the League. Edith softened her voice. 'I thought I was bleak enough.'

'I can't see why you say sanctions and blockades are any better than war. Surely it means starving the population into submission? And it's the children who suffer. There are always rations for soldiers.'

'I said that in the talk.'

'And why turn on Italy? Mussolini is a source of hope, surely?'

Edith recalled Alva's remarks at lunch. 'Mussolini? How so?'

The coffee arrived. Edith, in a conspiratorial way, took her flask from her handbag, and gestured that Alva might like some brandy in her coffee. Alva was flustered. 'Go on—keep me company— I'm desperate for a drink.'

Without waiting for an answer from Alva, Edith poured brandy into both their coffees.

'Golly,' Alva said. 'You really live the emancipated life.'

Edith grinned and lifted her coffee cup, 'Cheers.'

Alva took up her cup. 'Cheers.'

'In Geneva we say *santé*—health.'

Shouldn't have flaunted Geneva.

'*Santé*, then,' Alva said, lapsing back into a discontented frown. 'Isn't Musso a force for order? Vera Brittain said she'd rather fascism than war.'

'I like Vera Brittain but I'm not a pacifist.'

She wanted to find agreement with Alva—she needed the comfort of friendship now. 'I went to Italy—I loved it.'

Alva lit up. 'Tell me about Italy.'

Edith felt she had to give something positive to Alva. 'I was in Italy on League business.'

Was that big-noting in Alva's book?

'As you know, it's not that far from Geneva—it's really just down the road. Italy is more . . . well, sanitary now, I'll grant Musso that. And tipping has been banned.'

Hell's bells. Her travelogue would have to be smarter than that.

'A police attendant was attached to me at the border to look after me because I was travelling with a *lettre de mission* from the Secretary-General. But I felt more under observation than under protection.'

'That sounds so grand, Edith.'

Edith detected begrudging admiration. How difficult it was to talk while taking into account all these sensitivities.

'Oh, really? Standard practice when you do these sorts of things.'

'Did you meet *him*?'

'No—I am far too lowly for that. Anthony Eden told me a story about *him*.'

'Anthony Eden!'

'He's Minister for the League, so we see a lot of him at Geneva.'

'Gee, that's fairly grand too—meeting him. Is he as good looking as his photographs?'

'Yes, he certainly is. I was working for him and we became rather close—he told me that Mussolini goes into dinner *ahead of the ladies*.'

'Well, he *is* the Ruler of Italy.'

'No excuse for poor manners.'

'Go on.'

'I rather think that the police escort was a spy to see who I talked with and about what.'

'Why do you always think ill of the Italians?'

'I don't think ill of the Italian *people*—but I had a bad experience in Geneva a few years ago. Not with Italians but with fascists. Fascists who modelled themselves on the Italians.'

Edith thought she would leave it at that.

'Sorry to sound querulous,' Alva said.

At least Alva was bending a little now.

'Tell me more about Italy,' Alva said. 'I really would like to know.'

'Oh, I wasn't there doing anything really important. Just delivering a document to their Foreign Office which couldn't be entrusted to the mails. At Milan the train was delayed for a few hours and my fascist escort called the local police for a car and this long black car arrived to take me sightseeing until the train was ready to depart. The train couldn't, in fact, depart until we had returned.'

Everything she said seemed to come out with a boastful ring to it.

'Edith! You live like an ambassador. I suppose you speak Italian?'

'A little—Geneva gives you a smattering of Italian, I suppose. If you want to be smattered.'

'I think I'll learn Italian,' Alva said.

'I will say this—if the Italian police hated being servants to a woman, and a woman from the League, at that, they didn't show it.'

'The Italians respect women.'

The more Edith thought about it, it was a flirtatious civility which had been shown her. Behind the flirtation there was perhaps a discomfort. They had to hide their servility behind this flirtation so as to be able to stomach the idea of a woman travelling alone and doing a man's job.

'Oh, there's a wonderful detail which I forgot. The fascist escort had to ride a push-bike behind the car when we were sightseeing because the District Chief was my official host at this point, and the fascist escort was of too low a rank to travel in the same car. We had the sight of this man pedalling as fast as he could to keep up with us.'

'Doesn't sound very fair.'

'They have other values—other values than fairness, I suppose. Rank, for a start. They value rank.'

'I suppose so.'

'When I'd completed my mission—I had to deliver the document and also to interview some Italians in government departments to collect some figures, so I had an interpreter— I tried to give the escort a gratuity, some *lira*, because he'd run messages for me and got tickets and all that sort of thing. He refused the money, gave a fascist salute and said . . .' Edith put on her actor's voice, ' "*It is my duty, signora.*" '

'It sounds like a marvellous country.'

That was hardly the point of the anecdote. Never mind.

Edith decided to tell her another story to give Alva what she wanted to hear. She wanted Alva to relax, to be on side. 'A peddler trying to sell me some trinkets became very insistent and rude as peddlers can be in these countries. My escort was off doing something else but another blackshirt came out of the crowd and told this peddler to return to his stall and to stop pestering me.'

'Surely that sort of thing is good for Italy and an example for the world?'

Edith had been through a number of arguments in the Bavaria and elsewhere about Mussolini.

'I don't think so. As I've said, you find Mussolini-style fascists even in Geneva. Called the Action Civique. A nasty, nasty gang.'

She told Alva how she had been at a nightclub when they had burst in and how they pushed around people including herself. Edith felt the painful qualms of that night pass through her as she relived the grim and dirty details in one part of her mind while telling Alva a milder version of the story which she had often used for general telling and to illustrate a political point. 'I defended an ambassador from Azerbaidjhan from the crowd and suffered an indignity at their hands for my trouble.'

'Perhaps they were provoked?'

'You don't understand. This was a nightclub where people went to have fun.'

How to describe to Alva the sort of club the Molly was. Oh dear. All these evasions. Oh well. She must keep it light.

'The outcome was fascinating,' she laughed. 'For my efforts to defend him, I have had a river named after me in Azerbaidjhan.'

'A river named after you?' She did not seem to believe the story. 'And you go to nightclubs?'

'Not every night,' she laughed. 'On some occasions we go to the casinos in France, usually to take visitors—the border isn't so far, you know—or to nightclubs, yes. But I hate gambling.'

The conversation was a mess, all the wrong things were coming out. It was out of control.

'Such a life,' Alva said. A resentful admiration. 'Europe is so far ahead of us.'

'Oh, the only thing that I think Australia has to learn is to install bidets,' Edith said, trying to lighten things.

Alva looked as if she were drowning. 'What's a bidet?'

Edith laughed. 'Oh, I was frightened you might ask me that.'

'Well?'

She leaned over to Alva and whispered, 'It sends a jet of water out to wash the private parts in the lavatory.'

Alva shook her head. 'I remember now, I've heard of it. Don't see it taking off here, somehow.'

Edith leaned over and said, 'Well, apart from hygiene, I rather like it—the bidet—as something of, well, a *refreshment*. And, let's face it, paper alone hardly does the trick.'

They both giggled in their old way.

'Edith! There, you see, you are *Continental* now.'

'Perhaps only in *that* way.'

They laughed again.

Alva frowned and returned to her fascination with the fascists. 'I imagine that some of those European clubs could do with a clean-up. Maybe there's a place for fascists in places like that, surely? We need more self-policing, don't you think?'

Edith perceived the dreamy state of admiration for fascists in Alva, something which she'd encountered in others back in Geneva. Even in the League. She felt like shaking her. 'It's not the Australian or British way, Alva. Things should be researched, talked out and voted on. Give and take.'

'What about your League of Nations stuff? Isn't that a faith? Which a gang of countries is trying to impose on the world?'

She had not expected to find herself so far apart from Alva.

'The League is not a movement. It's an instrument. A political arrangement.'

'Frankly, Edith, it sounds like a movement to me. I tend to agree with Mussolini—that the League's only fit for the scrap heap and that nations should clear the table of all illusions and lies. And live with the hard truths of life.'

Edith poured herself another cognac and put some in Alva's cup as well. Alva didn't object.

Alva went on, 'How could you ally yourself with people who want to starve Italy into submission? Italy, to whom the world owes some of its greatest achievements, the greatest poets, artists, heroes, saints, navigators, aviators. Marconi— the inventor of radio.'

'Al, is this why you stopped writing to me?'

Alva looked away with some embarrassment. 'I think that I felt I hadn't much to tell that would interest you. My life in Sydney seemed rather dull.'

Edith stared at her. She thought, Alva, you've become childlike in your political faith. As had so many in the world. Believing in political fairy stories.

Edith said, 'Oh, Alva—that isn't right at all. I thought of all of the gang all the time. You're part of my living memories.'

'I should've kept up the correspondence, I know. I felt bad about it. And I was angry about the sanctions.'

Edith found her mind wandering to the memories of their university days. 'Alva, remember going to Miss Williams for exemption from college prayers?'

Alva nodded.

'We bucked against religion then because it was not part of the spirit of inquiry? Nor is fascism. The faith I was talking

about was faith in our intelligence. And our political ingenuity. Ingenious democratic solutions.'

Alva came out with a different tone, close to sarcasm.
'Good old Edith. Always trying to correct the error of everyone's ways.'

Edith was embarrassed. Was that how she'd appeared to
others back then?

'Was I always doing that?'

'Correcting the error of other people's ways? Oh yes. You
were always against souping. You were against using the fresh-
ers as servants. You were against this: you were against that.
The rest of us mostly wanted to fit in. You wanted to rewrite
all the rules.'

Edith was losing the point. 'What I wanted to say was that,
although we never got official exemption from prayers, she
did say that we didn't have to *go* to prayers, remember? But
Williams said it would still be considered to be cutting and
we still had to go and apologise to her at the end of each
term. Even if it were a formality. I thought that was an ingenious political solution.'

Williams had created a diplomatic solution to the problem.
An example of political ingenuity. Not bad at all.

Alva also ploughed on. 'Frankly, Edith, I didn't think going
to prayers was such a big issue. It was all part of college life.
Part of our world. All you did was to make our gang into
rather ridiculous pariahs.'

Edith decided to leave the discomfort of this and lifted her
coffee cup in a toast, needing the brandy. 'To the Newtown
tarts.'

'*Newtown tarts?*' Alva presented a puzzled face, but still
raised her cup in the toast.

'Remember? The boys at the Union used to call us
Women's College girls the Newtown tarts?'

'It's not something I would care to remember.'

'You must remember. After they began calling us the

Newtown tarts—a sort of undergraduate joke in bad taste—
our gang decided to adopt the name, turn it back on the
boys, and called ourselves the Newtown Tarts. Surely you
remember that?'

'Not really.'

'I rather liked being called a tart back then,' Edith said,
feeling rather *risqué* and wanting also to say it as a way of
pinching Alva's arm. 'And I liked being identified with
slummy Newtown which I privately thought of as *demi-
monde*, a world of devilish mysteries.'

'Edith! We never went there,' Alva complained.

'That made it an unexplored place. A metaphorical place.'

'I seem to remember that we weren't allowed to go there,'
Alva persisted.

'I thought of it as The Underworld,' Edith said, wondering
what Newtown had really been like.

'It all seems long ago. I suspect going away to Europe kept
all of that student stuff in aspic for you.'

'Could well have, I suppose.'

Would nothing succeed in this conversation with Alva?

'The rest of us had to get on with our banal lives,' Alva
said.

Alva then made an effort—perhaps it was the brandy
working at last. 'I do remember when the No Smoking and
No Drinking signs went up in the college rooms we all rebel-
liously adjourned to your room—the headquarters of rebellion—and had a cigarette and a drink of sherry. For some of
us, the putting up of those silly signs was the first time we
had a cigarette or a drink. Not for you, Edith. You always
claimed that your family had wine with your meals.'

Edith laughed, remembering that evening of insurrection.
'We were a very rebellious year.'

'*You* were.'

'It's funny hearing you describe my room as the headquarters of rebellion. Some days I used to curl up there in

utter confusion and not want to leave the room,' Edith said. 'It was sometimes like a hospital room where one had been sick for a long time.'

'I don't believe that. I used to get jealous if I was passing and heard laughter coming from your room.'

Alva seemed to be finding her tongue. 'The human is not strong enough or smart enough for democracy, Edith. That's what I think.'

Alva picked up the cup and took a big sip. 'If we're honest with ourselves we can't really rely on the sort of people who have the vote now. Not educated enough.'

'Having the vote forces people to confront their lives. That's why I was for compulsory voting,' Edith said.

'Ah, see—you are happy to force some things on people.'

'I don't mind forcing them to think. No. Not *what* to think but *how* to think. At least encouraging them to.'

'H.G. Wells doesn't think democracy has much of a future,' Alva continued, as though ignoring Edith. 'I believe that the world's population will go on expanding, putting those who rule further and further from the control of the populace. And more self-governing nations will have to be created and the more nations you have, the more conflict you have. I think, deep down, people would rather serve than dissent all the time. Even Australians. That's where I found your rebellion at college so tiring. You were dissenting all the time. I would rather belong in a great cause than be a lonely spoiler.'

In confusion, Edith realised that she had the same feeling, the same desire to be part of a Great Cause. 'But the great cause, Al, has to meet the requirements of our reason.'

Before Edith could find an extended, more robust position in the messy conversation, a strange male voice intruded. 'Edith, Alva—haven't seen either of you for years.' It was like the voice of a gramophone with a worn needle.

They looked up at a man dressed in a faded, brown

corduroy suit and beret, a returned soldier badge on his jacket, and with a face that looked like that of a mummy. It had obviously been surgically rehabilitated. The skin was tightly stretched, emphasising the cheekbones which seemed about to poke through the unnaturally brown skin. The eyes seemed to be glass but he was obviously not blind. He had no eyebrows or eyelashes.

They both stared at him and then Edith glanced at Alva for help in recognising the man.

'You're a fine couple of friends—not remembering an old mate.'

The voice was sardonic.

Edith remembered the voice, even if a damaged version. But couldn't find a name for it.

'Scraper Smith,' he said.

'Scraper!' Edith said, furiously trying to find the old university friend in this spectre, rising to her feet and shaking his crumpled hand. 'It's been so long I didn't recognise you at first.'

Alva also rose and shook his hand. 'Scraper—good to see you.'

'You don't have to be so polite. I know I look like an Egyptian mummy. It shouldn't be good to see me.'

Edith and Alva stood, rendered mute.

'Oh, sit down, sit down, no need for all these Red Cross faces—stop being solicitous.'

They sat down in a shot, like schoolgirls. He dragged over a chair.

He seemed to have to close his eyelids more often than normal. His hands were bent and buckled, also reconstructed in some surgical way, looking like hen's feet.

Edith's mind flashed to the *mutilés* at the Disarmament Conference in Geneva in '32.

She couldn't remember his first name. He'd been nicknamed Scraper because of his height—skyscraper.

'Skyscraper,' she said to Alva. She caught herself talking about the student boy, Scraper, as if he was unrelated to the form of this disfigured man seated with them.

'Half the students thought it was skyscraper and half thought it was bootscraper,' he said. 'Useful. Let me know who were my friends and who were not. Scraping the bottom of the barrel is another way I think of it. Scraping the bottom of life's barrel.'

'Sit down with us,' Edith said, unnecessarily, bringing herself back to self-control, and taking him at his word about excessive politeness, adding, 'though you seem to have done so, already.'

Laughing from unease.

Scraper ordered tea. The waitress seemed to know him well.

He looked Edith over, a disconcerting experience because the appearance of his face made him seem to find looking an act of some effort. His neck did not move freely. 'You're a big wheel in the League of Nations, Edith—that's what I hear.'

'Edith gave a stirring talk this afternoon in the history lecture theatre,' Alva said.

Was this Alva being sarcastic?

'Would've come if I'd known. Interested in the future of war.'

The three of them lapsed into another silence. The tea arrived and when the waitress had left them, Edith offered cognac and he accepted with alacrity. She gave Alva and herself another boost in their now empty cups.

'Tell me what you've been doing, Scraper? You did law?' Edith said, now slowly recalling the student named Scraper. 'You were a couple of years ahead of us?'

'Well done, Edith! I practise law in a small way. A very small way. I practise away from the public gaze. Whatever scraps of work are thrown on my plate. And I write, you know.'

'Novels?'

'Verse.'

'I'm sure my father warned me about lawyers who practise a little law and who write poetry,' Edith said, laughing, trying to be light-hearted in the presence of such physical tribulation. 'Married?' she asked, immediately regretting the almost certain insensitivity of the question. No one could live with that face.

He laughed darkly. 'Stop being conventional, Edith. You never were before. Or was it a cruel question? And, no. The answer is no.'

'Alva hasn't married either,' she said, disobeying his rule on convention, and realising that, in a more conventional situation, it would be a horrible joke towards matchmaking. Oh dear, what a day. She couldn't get control of her conversation.

He seemed to examine the question and the additional statement for possible motive. And then he became black as a storm. 'Don't pretend I'm normal. And don't pretend to flirt. I have no stomach for that.'

Flirt! Edith could not imagine anything more remote from her intentions.

He then changed immediately, the black cloud passing, looked at them and laughed, ' "The Newtown Tarts." '

'You remember!' Edith exclaimed. She turned to Alva, 'See, he remembers.' She turned to Scraper, 'We were talking about that just now. Alva claims not to remember. I think it's because she's a reformed woman. Putting her wicked past behind her.'

'I may indeed be a reformed woman,' Alva said laughing, but her voice indicated that she too was heartily dissatisfied by the way the conversation had gone and with the inclusion of herself in the repeated references to tarts.

Scraper slurped down his tea, holding the cup in both hands, wanting the brandy, impervious to the heat of the tea.

Alva chose at this time to excuse herself, looking deliberately at her watch and saying, 'Time flies.'

The coward. How could she!

Edith had also enough social life for the day. Regardless of how callous it seemed, she also grabbed at the opportunity to leave. 'I suppose I should go too.'

He looked at them with a cynical smile. 'Don't like the look of the face of war?'

Alva and she both coloured.

Edith made no effort to leave, knowing that it was now impossible. 'The war is a long time over,' she said, rather harshly.

'For me it's never over.'

'*Touché.*'

Edith gave in to the idea that she was stuck.

'Please stay,' he said in a more courtly tone. 'Conversation is hard to snare these days. And you are just as I remember you, Edith. If you take away the conventional gambits.'

Edith now began to picture Scraper before his injuries—the boy Scraper was now back in her memory. He'd been so cocky, and so much a son of the sheep station.

Alva held to her resolve to leave, gathered her things, shook Scraper's hand and then held out her hand to Edith. 'I hope we can all get together again before Edith goes back to her fine life in Geneva. And, Scraper, you must look me up—I'm working at the Commonwealth Laboratories. Call me some time.'

'I do hope we have another chance to talk, too,' Edith said, feeling trapped and abandoned.

Alva left, saying to Edith, 'I'll contact you at the Victoria Club tomorrow.'

'Do that, Al, please.'

'I will.'

War Work

S craper turned to Edith. 'Don't stay from compassion.'
'Why not from compassion? Won't that do?'

He moved his mouth in what was probably the shadow of a grin. 'That's better. Edith, the implacable foe of cant and humbug. Compassion will do. Anything that wins me a conversation will do. Some days I feel I would be happy to pay for conversation.'

'You aren't married?' he asked.

Edith to her consternation again found herself considering her answer.

'I am,' she answered, as firmly as she could.

'Australian?'

'British.'

'In the War?'

Must the War remain the pivot of all their lives? Yes. 'Dardanelles. Lancastershire Fusiliers.'

'Rank?'

'Captain. He was wounded at the Dardanelles. Shrapnel.'

'Are you happily married?'

She again considered her answer. Some people did not deserve to be trusted with the truth. Could this freakish man be trusted with her truths? She decided that she had better carefully lie to him. 'Yes, perfectly.'

He looked down at his tea. 'Perfectly.'

He made a smile with his tight, unnatural mouth. 'Why no ring?'

She gave her explanation about having forgotten to put it on after hand washing.

He smiled his twisted smile. 'Have you read much Freud?'

She nodded. 'I've been analysed,' she boasted.

'You must know about forgetting things and losing things—they are signals to ourselves.'

'Sometimes.'

The waitress cleared away the things. 'Leave them,' he said. The waitress shrugged as if accustomed to his ways, and went off. 'Have you any more of that cognac?'

Edith took out the flask and poured them two more drinks in the cups. She left the flask on the table.

'I like a little harsh honesty. It's how I remember you. Given the way I am, I'm denied anything to do with honesty. Except by the mirror. Are you back here because the League is finished?'

How astute he was. He was not so far submerged in his self-pity that he was unable to see what others were doing around him. And by praising her honesty he was demanding it from her.

He pointed his question more sharply. 'Jumping ship?' he said.

She would have to work out soon—in reasonably honest conversational form—just what it was she was doing with herself back here.

'Very interesting. Your answer is a long time coming and I can't read your mind on this,' he said. 'Ah, we have an interesting case here in our dashing Edith. You can have time to answer and you may also revise your answer to the marriage question.'

'I can't read my own mind. I'm here on home leave. I'll go to Canberra to look at the possibilities of working there. Yes.'

'From Geneva to Canberra?' He seemed to find this incomprehensible. 'You may be the first person to go to Canberra voluntarily.'

She grimaced slightly. 'I may return to help build the nation.' She tried to make it sound sardonic.

'It'll need some help.' He said this through the circular black, seemingly toothless hole of his mouth, a joyless laugh.

'I could give it a push,' she said.

They then chattered lightly about the university days which helped her remember further, his brilliance and his gangly sort of handsomeness coming back to her. And the arrogance of an older student.

He looked across at her and smiled, his smile now appearing like a crack in a plaster wall. He touched the flask, which she didn't like him doing. 'An elegant flask. I like a woman who carries a flask. Of all that crowd you would've been the one I'd expected to carry a flask. And to wear a cape and gauntlet gloves.'

'Really?'

'You were going places even then.'

'I thought of myself as a rather earnest undergraduate.'

'You were that—and more than that. You were dashing. Dashing is the word.'

She was rather flattered to have a glimpse of her younger self and to have been remembered so. She looked down at her flask.

'And the flask?' he asked.

She touched it. 'A special memento.'

'And not of your husband.'

She smiled at his observation and at the same time had a flash of recall about Scraper. 'I remember now—you were friendly with Arthur Tuckerman.'

'That's right,' he said softly. 'Poor old Arthur.'

Ye gods, what dreadful thing could have happened to Tuckerman that would make Scraper feel sorry for him?

'He was so good looking and he got those impressive marks for essays as well,' she said.

'He was a rare spirit, old Tuck. He's dead you know, Edith.'

'I didn't know. What happened?'

'He did himself in.'

'But potential always *gleamed* out of him! He shone with it.'

'He had a breakdown remember, and then he went back a few years later.'

'I went to Melbourne—lost touch—and you were both older.'

Tuckerman came rushing back to her mind. 'Everyone wanted to be around him and to talk with him. For him, each conversation was a playlet and everyone had a part.'

'He was doing brilliantly and then broke down again and went to work the land. He built something of a pretty little orchard out of nothing near Windsor. He thought simple work might save him but he slipped into the mental shadows and never recovered. He took his life with a shotgun.'

'I didn't hear.'

She found herself wondering why Scraper hadn't taken his life.

'You are thinking why is it that I haven't taken my life?'

She opened her eyes wide. He was impressive. 'Oh Scraper, you're dangerous. I know nothing of your life. Tell me.'

'It's a rotten life. And I often think of joining Tuck.'

'It must be hard. How'd you become a mind reader?'

'It does me no good—mind reading.'

'But it means that there's no need for me to speak. I'll sit here and think and you can read it.'

He stared at her. 'You want to know how and where I live?'

That wasn't on her mind. She said, 'Ah, you have two sorts of occult: you can read minds; and you can implant thoughts.'

'I've a third sort of occult, as you call it, but that will be revealed.'

She didn't care for occults of any sort.

'Let me show you my poet's garret. I live around the corner in Macquarie Street.'

He stood up fumbling for money with his bent fingers. She thought it was probably exaggerated to avoid getting the money from his pockets. Don't be like that, Edith.

'Let me pay,' she said, reaching for her purse.

'Let the world pay? I like that idea. But a gentleman pays, crippled or not.' He found coins and a note in his pockets. He appeared to carry no wallet or coin purse. 'I'm not poor. I'm rather well off. I do not play a musical instrument on street corners and I do not have to operate a lift. Or run a tobacco shop.'

She apologised that she couldn't visit his garret that day—perhaps some other time? She was fagged from the talk and the whole damned day.

'Where are you staying, Edith?'

'At the Victoria Club. Which is also just around the corner.'

'I'll walk you home.'

She laughed.

'That's about all I'm capable of—walking.'

'What happened to you during the War?'

'I was blown up in France and when I landed, everything was broken or missing. The War only lasted another two months.'

He was a walking entitlement for charity and indulgence. A requisition on humanity. He *was* the damned War.

'Macquarie Street's hardly a starving artist's garret.'

'Inherited the flat. Come on, Edith, pay me a visit—for old times' sake. I want to hear about the League and France. And let me in on the secret about when the next war is to start. I may rejoin. I have precious little to lose. A pre-dinner drink and then you can go. I haven't had a chance recently to talk with someone fresh from Europe.'

'I couldn't face a dinner table, I'm afraid.' The word face had jumped into her conversation.

'You mean to say you couldn't face me over dinner. I won't press dinner on you, promise.'

She let that pass. His bullying of the conversation was becoming tiresome. She was sick of his guesswork as well.

Scraper went on, 'We were talking about Tuckerman. He was a manipulator of glamour. I'm a manipulator of the gruesome. And I manipulate through close observation.'

His candour made her laugh genuinely and with relief. She reversed her idea of him—for the first time she could see the possibility of liking him. But only the possibility. 'That is the first time I've ever heard anything honest about Tuckerman. When he was alive he was constantly given what he sought so desperately to get—popularity. You are so right.'

'Popularity instead of love. Charm instead of fame. I'd settle for it. Either.'

She tried to remember how popular Scraper was before. Not very. 'You had friends but you weren't popular,' she said.

'At university, no. In the army I was accepted. If you didn't shirk you were accepted and that was something special. It meant you were taken in and you belonged regardless. The army life was good for me. The belonging. I miss it more than anything. I think it was the nearest I got to marriage. Living with a platoon of men.'

She turned to him, 'Please, I don't like calling you Scraper and I can't think of your first name.'

'Warren.'

'I shall call you Warren. It's a little more grown-up.'

'No one ever calls me that. I am forever Scraper. It's perhaps easier for people. Makes me something other than a man.'

'I will call you Warren.'

His flat was surprisingly pretty. He had done much the sort of thing she would have done if she had been living in the flat. Curious. It had the smell of male hair oil and strong soap and shaving lotion.

'Oh,' she said involuntarily.

'What is it?' he said.

'Nothing, I like the place—it's what I might do with it. If it were mine.'

He was opening a bottle of cognac and pouring out large drinks for them both.

'That's more than enough for me. I was dosing the coffee all afternoon.'

He didn't accede to her request and went on to fill the glasses generously.

'That wasn't why you gasped,' he said. 'You gasped at the lithograph of *Les Deux Soeurs*. Why did you gasp?'

'I like the lithograph. I'm surprised that you have a Laurencin print on the wall.'

He looked at her, head to one side, and with his damaged smile. 'You have the same lithograph!'

She was reluctant to confirm it but said, 'Yes.'

She sometimes thought of the faces of the two sisters as Ambrose and herself. Ambrose's feminine self. At least Scraper had not been able to read her mind about that.

'You like her work?'

'Yes.'

She did not want to establish another connection with this man. This man who was once a boy and then disappeared to reappear as a ... wreck. 'May I ask why you are attracted to her work?'

'When I was in France.'

'You had time for art as well as soldiering?'

'I had time for art. During convalescence. Much time for art. I like her hardness. I suppose I like the idea of hard women.'

She sat, deliberately choosing a chair rather than the couch. She had one sip of her cognac and then stood up again and walked around. 'I think you've made the flat a work of art.'

'By fastidious decorating of the flat I'm compensating for what I am.'

She looked again at the flat—its resemblance to her own taste and its painful contrast with his disfigured self appalled her.

'I should be off. I've had a rather straining day.' She put down her unfinished drink.

'Please stay. Indulge me for a few more minutes.'

She sat back in the chair. The flat was, in fact, another way he drew attention to himself, to his disfigurement.

He went on, 'Don't sit all the way over there. Come and sit beside me, here.'

'I'm comfortable where I am, thank you.'

'I am hard of hearing.'

She thought it a lie but there was no reason to think it a lie.

She tried to find a way of responding to this monstrous visage which, in turn, had become something of a monstrous personality.

Reluctantly, she stood up and went to sit on the couch with him, as a nurse might.

'You are like Tuckerman. You are right to compare yourself with him,' she said.

Harsh.

'Manipulators?'

'Yes.'

What she had intuitively but not consciously suspected but had dismissed as beyond the bounds, now began to happen. Something so far from being humanly legitimate or acceptable as to be, itself, monstrous.

He had moved his leg next to hers.

She plunged into a confused swirling of feelings, of

compassion and of indignation. And, just as unacceptably, she felt a twitch of carnality in herself from the touch of his leg.

She moved her leg away and said, 'Regardless of how life has treated you, Warren, you should perhaps hold on to the conduct of a gentleman. And of an old mate.'

'I long ago jettisoned all that. It did not serve me. I thought you might play the tart for me, Edith?'

'I am not a tart in any way, shape or form, Warren. Please remain courteous.'

He then took her kid-gloved hand and placed in on his lap.

She felt him rigid under her open palm. He held her hand there as she tried to move it.

'Please Edith. We're both people of the world, you and me. You've been in Europe long enough to know the ways of the world. We are miles away from Alva. And I'm forever placed beyond the boundaries of conventional nonsense. You know that people shun me. Have you ever been shunned?'

'Don't appeal to me, please, Warren.' She again tried to move her gloved hand, but he held it, and she felt his penis rise further and thicken into her hand.

'You were the sophisticate even back at university, Edith. As a married woman, you must understand the needs of a man—as *something* of a married woman.'

She had no time to deal with his observations about herself as she tried to find equilibrium in what had turned into a bizarre human skirmish.

She stared unseeingly at the Laurencin print. He was undoing his flies.

She closed her eyes.

She said, 'Turn off the light.'

He rose and went to turn off the light.

This was her chance to stand up and leave.

She didn't.

He returned to the couch and released himself from his trousers and replaced her gloved hand on his privates.

She opened her eyes but did not look at him or at her hand.

Looking at the Laurencin print and without taking off her glove, she worked his privates with her fingers—it felt so stiff, so hard. Sometimes she yearned for that sort of stiffness and hardness inside her, sometimes Ambrose could be like that and Robert had always been very hard, sometimes too hard— and in a very short time she felt Warren spasm and finish.

She glanced at him. He had his eyes closed.

She felt none of the secret pride she sometimes felt when one of the men who'd been in her life had become erect for her and had then given out his semen to her.

She looked down at her hand and was relieved to see that nothing of his fluids had touched her or her glove. In the dimness of the room, she wasn't sure where the fluids had gone.

She stood up, took her handbag and went to the door of the flat. He stayed seated there in the half-darkness.

At the door she said, 'I hope your life eventually finds some proper peace.'

How unnecessarily polite she was.

'Please leave me your gloves.'

Was there to be no end to the bedlam of this day?

She took them off and laid the beautiful gauntlet gloves of kid-leather on the arm of the couch. Wishing them well in their new life.

'My life has pleasures,' he said. 'But, usually, as you see, I have to steal them.'

She closed the door behind her. In the lobby of the apartment block, she again searched her clothing for any sign of the fluids.

Oh God. There was a stain. It had come on to her sleeve. She felt her stomach clutch.

She walked out into the street, glad of the night air, the smell of the botanical gardens. But the purity of the air scarcely kept her distaste under control.

She was rushing up the stairs of the Club when the receptionist called to her and she had to go back.

There was a cable waiting for her from Ambrose and, surprisingly, a letter from her psychiatrist, Dr Vittoz.

She opened the cable and read it as she mounted the stairs. Ambrose told her that her contract had been renewed. And there were some loving words in cablese, words which she found she needed dreadfully. She kissed the cable.

No promotion but there was a raise in pay.

But was she going to renew her contract with the world? Out there so far away?

She took off the suit—one of her favourites bought on her Italian visit—and her underwear and put it all in the brown paper laundry bag and wrote on the bag, 'Please dispose.'

She kept her cape and hat.

With resignation, she realised the maid would probably take the clothing and wear it.

Oh. Such was the world. She wanted to think no more of the matter.

She saved Dr Vittoz's letter for the bath.

Sighing, immersed in the hot water and lavender oil, she opened the letter.

It was simply a clipping and his professional card with the word 'compliments' written on it in his handwriting and with his signature. The clipping was from the English magazine the *New Statesman*. It was a letter signed by three hundred psychiatrists from around the world—including Vittoz—who had declared war to be a form of disease which infected communities, much as an epidemic would. The declaration proposed various treatments which should occur if such epidemics broke out. That teams of psychiatrists should go to such places and work with those who had war fever.

No personal message.

She put a finger on his signature. She found his communication rather cold.

And what would Dr Vittoz have to say about today?

As she bathed she wondered whether she had lost the joy of the Laurencin lithograph. Would there be an intrusive third face there now? A disfigurement?

After a while, as she soaked and felt clean again, Edith was able to laugh—albeit, bleakly.

There in the tiled bathroom she said aloud, 'It's a far, far better thing I have done than all the knitting.'

It had been a kind of war work.

Eighteen years after the war.

But still, war work.

La Séance Continue

A wakening in the spartan room of the Victoria Club to the view of a water stain in the right-hand corner of the ceiling, Edith's first thoughts were of her gloved hand on Warren's privates in his dim apartment.

Today, she felt no revulsion.

It had happened.

That was that.

Then her mind wandered over the hectic day—her revisiting the university, Alva, the lunch, the talk, the postscript to her talk, the fractious afternoon tea, and then the outlandish finale: her gloved hand on Warren's privates.

She allowed it all to play through her mind, almost with disbelief, and then, hoisting herself from the bed, went to the door and picked up the *Sydney Morning Herald* left by the porter.

The Stop Press item caught her eye: *Jewish film director, Stephan Lux, kills himself at League of Nations.*

There were no further details.

Stephan Lux. Their Stephan Lux?

She'd met a Stephan Lux at the Molly Club with Ambrose and others. She didn't really know him but he'd been one of the refugees who had drifted to the Club for whatever reason, perhaps finding the decadence or bizarreness of the Club congenial, a grotesque burlesque of their own exile and relegation from normal society.

As she recalled, Stephan had been more part of the artistic set around the Club, not a dolly boy but perhaps a friend of the dolly boys. The artistic set and refugees now outnumbered the dolly boys.

She remembered an argument with him where she'd taken the side of the talkies against silent movies. He thought that the silent movie was the true art form.

Edith felt then an overwhelming need to speak with Ambrose and be connected back to the world of Geneva, and decided to go to the expense of a radio telephone call to Ambrose in Geneva. She booked it and then went out and bought all the papers, but there were no further details of the suicide.

Eventually, after breakfast and hours of lying around, the call came through. Half-dozing, she jumped when the call came. It was rather thrilling to be talking across such distances.

'Ambrose?!'

'Edith!—so good to hear your dulcet voice. I can hear the waves. The fish.'

'It's radio telephone, not cable, so it's not waves—maybe air waves?—the wind?—don't really know how it all works— but it costs a fortune. Routed through London.'

Oh, how good it was to hear his voice and to be connected, as it were, with the outside world again.

'My cable reached you? About your contract renewal?'

'Thank you, yes, a relief to know they still want me.'

'Oh, but they do—very much. Everyone asks after you.'

'What's this dreadful news about Stephan Lux? It's mentioned briefly in the stop press of the papers? It *is* the Stephan I met at the Molly?'

'The same. Very sad, very grim. Kelen was there in the Assembly when it happened. Stephan went to the front of the Assembly which was in session. There was a crack like a whip and when people looked around Stephan was lying there bleeding, gun in his hand.'

'Oh no. Why? The papers here have no details.'

'It's very moving. He left letters for Avenol, Edward VIII, Eden, and one for Paul du Bochet—you've met him at the Bavaria, a Swiss journalist. The note said—hold on, I have it in front of me in *Journal de Geneve*—it said, 'I do not find any other way to reach the hearts of men ... to pierce the inhuman indifference of the world.''

'Indifference to what?'

'The treatment of the Jewish people. He said the world had to face that Hitler was preparing for war.'

'He was Jewish?'

'Oh yes.'

'How is it that I am the only one who never knows if someone is Jewish?'

'It's not a failing, dear.'

'I thought things were improving for the Jews? I told some people here that evidence shows that the worst of the anti-Semitism is over. That the regime is reining in its extreme elements and that the Jews arrested in 1933 who were in concentration centres have been released.'

'Well yes, that's true. We have to wait and see if it's all over. The Olympic Games of course have played a part. Trying to present a happy face to the world ... He died in hospital. Can't hear you ...'

'I'll speak up ...'

'He put a pistol to his head in full view of everyone. He fell down next to Eden. Eden didn't know what had happened, evidently, until he saw blood and the police came over.'

'Kelen told you this?'

'Kelen was there. Saw the whole business.'

'What did Eden do?'

'He was very cool. He was reported as saying, "He sealed his message to the world with his death."'

'Who was in the chair?'

'Van Zeeland was in the chair and was heard to say, "What's happened?" over the microphone, which was still on. Someone said there'd been a suicide. Van Zeeland then said— everyone could hear because of the microphone—"Are people now coming to the League to suicide?" And added, "This chamber is becoming a showplace of fatal events. It was only a matter of time before we were bound to witness death."'

'He said that aloud?'

'He said it without thinking that the microphone was on, I think.'

'Then what?'

'Evidently he followed the French tradition in these circumstances. He and others stood while the body was removed, and then he said simply, "*La séance continue ...*" And the meeting went on.'

'*La séance continue!?* And they went on with the discussion as if nothing had happened?!'

'Probably not as if nothing had happened, exactly—but it is, I am told, a form of honour, to go on with important things regardless of what has just happened. The French way. I went to the funeral.'

'He's been buried so quickly?'

'Before sunset of the day of death—the Jewish custom.'

'Oh. How sad it is. I remember him from the Molly. We had an argument about cinema.'

'Only a handful of us were there at the funeral. Bernard, Kelen, Beer, the German journalist, Dell from the *Guardian*, someone from the Jewish community. That was it.'

'How odd. Why were all the cynics the only ones to go to his funeral?'

'They all have hearts of gold. On that point, a beautiful thing was said by Kelen ...'

'Speak up.'

'A most beautiful thing was said by Kelen later—at the Bavaria, we had a bit of a wake—Kelen said something along these lines, "There were only a few of us there today because there are only a few left who think it remarkable or sad that a man should stand in the palace dedicated to making peace and take his life." Let down the cynics' side, a bit, I thought. Shed a tear or two myself.'

'Oh dear, darling, it's all so sad. I want to be there. I belong back there. I don't belong here anymore. I really don't. Strange disruptions occur all around me.'

'Come back, then.'

She realised that her remarks about not belonging had been simply throwaway lines, unthought-out.

She found herself now at the point where she had to face the question of staying or returning—truly—and to answer truly.

'I am going to Canberra—the meeting is all arranged. But I think I should book an early passage. I miss you. I didn't want to miss you but I do.'

'Why didn't you want to miss me?'

'I wanted to get over you a bit. You know ...'

'See where your life was going?'

'See where I fit in the world. Where things fit in my life. You are a difficult thing to fit into a life.'

'I don't fit into my own life very well.'

'Oh, you have worked it all out. You do fine.'

'Doesn't always feel that way.'

'I suppose after all this time we have worked well enough. Fitted together somehow.'

'I think so. What if you're offered a tremendous job in Canberra?'

She had to face this.

Big questions to answer on the radio telephone with its odd background noises. But now was the time.

'It's so unlikely—but a possibility.'

'You know I would come to Australia to join you—if you wanted me so to do.'

He had not said that before. 'Would you really?' How would he fit into Australia? Where was the life of the Molly Club here? She supposed there was such a crowd hidden away somewhere in Sydney. 'Thank you, darling. That's a big thing to offer.'

But they would be living in Canberra. She had no real picture of Canberra. 'What about the life of the Molly Club?'

The pause was at his end this time.

'I am sure I can find friends with my tastes.'

'I suspect so. But you have to be sure that you can survive here.'

'We can but try.'

He was being brave.

She then made her decision. 'I want to say this—that you are in my life, like it or not, Ambrose. We have found each other. We stay together.'

'I think that might be the truth of the matter, Edith.'

It was the most serious thing they had said to each other about their life.

'Are you sure?' she asked him.

'We're not bolters. And we might have to go far to find a better . . . arrangement.'

Or was that exactly what she was—a bolter? And was Ambrose labelling her as *not a bolter* as a manoeuvre to stop her bolting?

If she had come to Australia as a way of bolting, she now felt convinced that she would not bolt. At least from Ambrose.

She said they should see what Canberra had to offer but that she thought her work with the League was not finished, 'Even if they didn't promote me.'

'They raised your pay. You are paid as much as a *chef de bureau*. As much as I earned when I was at the League.'

'But still no title.'

'There is no title which describes you, Edith. You are unique.'

'Pooh to that.'

'Edith, do the things you have to do over there. Test the waters. Events are moving fast here. Europe is gathering storm. Needs you. Everyone asks after you.'

'Do they mention my Bad Habits?'

'No one has mentioned anything to do with that. Or your marriage. They mention only you. We all love you.' There was a pause and then he said, 'I love you, Edith.'

They had never said that to each other.

'And I you,' she said.

'Maybe it doesn't count on a radio telephone?' he said, his voice finding its way back from the seriousness of it.

'It still counts.'

'I think it counts,' he said. He again tried to move away from the suddenness of their declarations. 'This call must be costing you a fortune, Edith?'

'We have valuable things to say to each other.'

'I will be as Ruth in the Bible.'

'You know I don't know the Bible.'

'Whither thou goest, I will go.'

'Thank you, Ambrose. Thank you. Even if it is a quote from the Bible.' She was trembling. 'I'm still wearing the identity medallion.'

'Oh, you must do that. Couldn't bear it if you became lost.'

'I look at it now and then to see who I am.' She touched the medallion inside her gown. 'Keep the faith,' she heard herself say to him—and to herself. Which faith? Did the declarations require now for them to be *faithful* as in marriage? Or was that against the spirit of their kind of love? 'Have you been out *playing* much?'

'Oh—no time for hanky-panky.'

'Maybe you should. To keep yourself happy.' She found it hard to say but was proud of herself for saying it. The declarations must not change things. They must not lose their, *shamelessness.*

'Thank you. I am more interested in dogs at present, than in strangers in the night.'

'Dogs!?'

'Thought we might get one when you come back—or wherever.'

'How strange, I had the same idea. We must study the breeds. I will buy a book of breeds.'

'Do that. And I will keep the faith.'

'But we mustn't change anything,' she said, strongly.

'I hope not.'

'Bye, I love you.'

'Bye, I love you.'

It was the first time they'd ended a conversation with those words.

The telephone clicked. Out of reach again.

He had not asked if she'd been up to any hanky-panky. Anyhow, what had happened in that line was only ... by default. And it seemed that they were not asking for that sort of faithfulness from each other.

Maybe what had happened with Scraper would undo them? Be a confession too dark?

Oh God.

She would tell Ambrose. There could be no secrets. She did not want to live that sort of concealed life.

Edith lay down on the bed and wept for Stephan, for Ambrose, for Scraper, and for herself.

She had committed herself to Ambrose. Just like that.

On a radio telephone connection.

Just like that.

Today she would see no one.

No people.

She stopped crying only when the maid knocked on the door and she shouted, 'No servicing of the room today, thank you.'

She remembered the bag sitting in the middle of the room and jumped up, grabbed the bag, opened the door, called to the maid, and gave her the bag, saying, 'Please get rid of this.'

The maid looked into the bag.

'You could keep the clothing—if you find it to your taste.'

The maid said she would need a note 'to that effect' from Edith.

Oh God. Edith went back into the room and scribbled a note on the Club stationery authorising the maid to take the clothing.

'There,' she said, giving the maid the note.

She felt sick at the idea of the maid wearing the stained garment.

She closed the door on the world and locked it.

No one at all, today.

No one.

To the Unfinished City

From the front door of Beauchamp House as far as you could see stretched a paddock without a fence, and then the paddock became a wall of wretched bush.

Of course, she knew that one day a grand street would pass the front door. With an appropriate historical name.

One day.

The taxi had failed to arrive despite the clerk making a second telephone call to the taxi office. She decided to walk to Parliament House but it was so hot.

There on the steps she decided that she couldn't face any of it.

She went back inside the whatever it was in which she was staying—she looked around at the lobby—what was it, this Beauchamp House? A guest house? Quality accommodation for women public servants, she'd been told. The other guests seemed to be and were, of course, typists, though surprisingly fashionable in their dress, she thought.

'Forget something?' a man in the lobby asked.

'Yes,' she said.

And to herself added, 'My sanity.'

She went up the stairs to her room, pulled off her hat and

gloves and seated herself, breathing deeply, suffering prickles of agitation through her skin and the feeling of iron bands across her chest. Her perfume smelled too strong because of the heat. She felt indigestion rising from her stomach, bringing with it the taste of bacon and fried eggs and the hard brown lace of fat which had surrounded the eggs.

She calmed and then went to the mirror, checked her make-up once more, put her hat back on and pinned it, and pulled on her gloves, repeating, 'Do not throw French expressions around' and 'Do not say "The way we do it at the League is . . .",' took a deep breath and, with shoulders back, forayed out again.

This time the man in the lobby said, 'Got everything now, have we?'

She looked at him without expression as she passed.

She again stood at the 'front' door of Beauchamp House. She was uncertain to what front Beauchamp House faced. It seemed to face the paddock. The back door was the door used by everyone.

The Palais Wilson, she remembered, had a confusion between front and back door which she had later learned had to do with the closing of the lakeside door during the *bise* wind, but not until after she'd made a rather naive suggestion that the League of Nations decide once and for all about which was the front and which was the back door.

She cringed at the memory. She then reminded herself that embarrassing moments are remembered only by the person who suffered the embarrassment.

Usually.

Other people remember their own embarrassing moments.

If other people had embarrassing moments.

From Geneva, one of the civilised world's oldest cities, she'd travelled to the world's newest, most unfinished and unhewn of cities.

Capital of one of the still uncompleted nations. Although she was beginning to think that all nations were incomplete.

Had changes yet to be made. Had to continuously evolve.

But she had come to the world's most *baffling* city, baffling by its not *being there*.

The city was just not there. Nor was there what you would call even a town or a village. It did not have the shape of a town or a village. It was something else. It was a plan perhaps, marked out by random structures scattered across the fields.

Sorry. Paddocks.

In a way, she would like to be part of something just beginning, as she'd been at the League. It would be a chance to be young and hopeful again. Perhaps.

John Latham had arranged for her to stay the remainder of her visit to Canberra with the Watts but they had children and had themselves just arrived and were still settling in. They'd asked for a couple of days to get ready to receive her.

Which was a nuisance. She hated arriving in a place and having to change rooms or change residence. It was bad enough having arrived in a strange place *once* without, as it were, arriving twice.

As she made her way along what might be called a footpath or at least a path towards the bridge over the Molonglo River, she looked again at Canberra through narrowed eyes, trying to reduce as best she could the blinding impact of that sun, brushing the flies away.

She hadn't expected much of Canberra at this point in time but, truth be told, she had expected somewhat more. My God, there was a herd of sheep grazing.

Canberra had pockets of people in isolated structures spread across the paddocks, centred—if one could discern a centre—on the provisional Parliament building and the administration offices.

She could see that.

How had this been conceived? And how had Australia made such a breathtaking decision? And what if it failed? What if people did not come to live there?

What if it just didn't work?

What would they do with it? Pull it down and put it some-where else? She'd been told that some of the newspapers were arguing that the Canberra idea be abandoned now before it was too late.

A man came by on a bicycle and stopped.

He said, 'Headed to the offices? Want a lift?' Brushing the flies away from his face.

'A lift?'

'I can double you over, if you can put up with it.'

'Double' was a word from her childhood.

'On the bike?'

'Yes.'

She hadn't doubled on a bike since childhood. Her initial exasperated recoil from the idea of it changed to happy thoughts.

'All right then,' she said, finding a hearty, horsey voice, and hoisting her skirts, she mounted the cross-bar of the bike, remembering to hold on to the handlebars without steering or attempting to steer, a special loose hold which came back to her instantly.

'What's your name, by the way?' he asked.

'Edith Campbell Berry. Edith. And yours?'

He gave his name—Theo Matthew—which meant nothing to her.

'I'm going to External Affairs,' she said.

'You're in luck—so am I,' he said in her ear.

It was good to be in the arms of a man, however innocent. She could tell that Theo Matthew certainly didn't mind.

She worried that the heat made her perfume too blowzy.

What a way to arrive for an appointment, what a way for a mature woman to travel. But it seemed right, in a way. And Theo Matthew seemed to think it acceptable behaviour for Canberra.

He turned out to be a junior officer there and he showed

her to the outer office of the Secretary of the Department where she spoke with a clerk. She told the clerk that her letters of introduction from Stanley Bruce and John Latham should have preceded her.

Although a trifle early, she was shown in immediately to meet the Department Head, Colonel Hodgson.

As they shook hands, she was put at ease by seeing his dog sitting in the office on the other armchair.

Perhaps the dog was applying for a position too.

It reminded her of the old days at the League when each Section had a dog mascot and dogs abounded in the Palais Wilson.

There was a decanter of what she guessed was whisky, a soda siphon, and glasses on a silver tray on a butler's table.

A good sign.

'How lovely to see a dog in a bureaucratic office,' she said to Colonel Hodgson.

She went over to the dog, pausing and glancing at Hodgson for reassurance about the temper of the dog before patting him.

'Go ahead, he's susceptible to affection,' Hodgson said, implying that he, Hodgson, was not.

'When I first went to the League every Section had a mascot and we took our dogs to work. But as the League grew—and the number of dogs with it—eventually an edict came forbidding dogs.'

'Oh, there's always room for a dog.' Hodgson had a rather Australian accent. She'd expected, for no good reason, that he would be more plummy. 'I'll give you a good reason for having a dog in official life—do you want to hear it?' he said.

She waited but he didn't speak.

'Do you want to hear it?'

She'd forgotten about this Australian practice in which the storyteller made the listener *ask* for the story.

'I'd like to hear it.'

'I learned this from Keith Officer. When you're entertaining officially in your own home it can become rather tiresome because you always have trouble getting people to leave. So you get the dog trained to come to you at about 9.30, wagging its tail. The dog gets everyone's attention there in the room and you say in a loud voice, "Yes, Rover, I know it's getting late and you want to be put to bed. Or taken for a walk—whatever. Won't be long now." People present get the message.'

She laughed. 'I'll remember that.'

He looked at her as if wondering what official entertaining she might do back in Geneva.

When might she have a dog?

She badly wanted a dog, or any animal.

She talked on, about dogs, 'I remember that a memorandum came around before the meeting of Assembly—don't remember which it was, maybe the Seventh Assembly—that dogs should not be brought into the building. Evidently a delegate, I was told, had a phobia about dogs.'

Oh dear, was that a how-we-do-it-at-the-League story?

'Might have been the Chinese delegation,' he said.

She wondered what he meant and it must have shown on her face.

'Made them hungry,' he said, deadpan.

She smiled. No one had made *that* joke at the time the dogs were banned. Not even Liverright. She would certainly tell it when she got back.

If she got back.

He said, 'The dog reminds me that there is life outside this office.'

He complimented her on her rather imposing letters of introduction and then they chatted about the news from the League.

She'd written to Colonel Hodgson outlining her background with the League and had suggested that it might be useful to exchange views.

In the letter, she'd said she was considering returning to live in Australia.

She hoped that by bringing these two ideas together in his head, she would create a third idea—that of using her in a position in the new department. She hadn't mentioned, in her brief curriculum vitae, that she was married. And today, she was still not wearing her wedding ring. But she could not be sure that John or Frank hadn't mentioned her marital status.

She went through the formalities, and asked about the new department. 'I gather you are recruiting under S.47 of the PS regulations—taking people from outside the Public Service?'

'That's really for duties which cannot be performed by others already in the Public Service,' he said.

She moved herself to another attitude about the interview—when, and if, she was invited to accept a position, she would then ask herself if she *wanted* the position, whether she could live here in the Unfinished City.

She brought some energy to the interview.

'I've heard that you are going to bring out a bulletin—*Current Notes?* Gertrude Dixon did the same job back at the League.

'Yes.'

They then went into general conversation about Canberra and about the new League Palais.

He closed the interview rather abruptly, by standing and extending his hand, but not before she'd managed to get in that she'd worked closely with Anthony Eden on sanctions.

'I very much want you to talk with some of my staff,' he said.

He then buzzed for his secretary who came in and she was taken to meet two men from the International Co-operation Division.

Again, the two men, maybe older than she, chatted to her about her opinion of Canberra, this time over tea and biscuits. Rather good porcelain.

She realised after a time that she was being humoured.

She realised that she, in turn, was relaxing into a supercilious aloofness. The patronising attitude of the men and her superciliousness were locked in the midair of the conversation, both increasingly unbending and stubborn.

'Sinking ship' was one of the expressions which had now been used twice by one of the men.

'Rat leaving' was left unsaid.

Behind all these generalities and exchanges, were they assessing her?

Or just putting up with her visit?

'Your education is in science?' the thin one said.

'That was a fair way back,' she said, in reply. 'And I've more than ten years now in diplomatic circles. And I've done a number of odd jobs around the League. Special missions. I even had a bomb go off outside my hotel while in Lebanon on refugee work.' That was enough about that. She didn't want to overwhelm them with her adventures. In fact, she'd fired shots from her revolver.

'That was truly an education,' she said, knowingly.

She might as well give them a little more of her life. 'One of the loveliest letters I've ever drafted was to the Commissioner for Refugees and it had in it the sentence, "I am engaged in compiling a list of the names of three hundred Assyrians together with the names of their animals, who are to cross to the Ghab during the winter."' She then added, 'I was there briefly filling in for a sick officer.'

This whiff from her adventurous life did not seem to engage them.

'You have not been promoted as such?'

The questions were thrown at her like shies at a fair doll.

Surely these two were not the appointments committee?

Oh, well.

'I am now in the A Division. However, my actual position is much more complicated than it sounds. I work as a sort of private secretary—in the parliamentary sense—to Under Secretary-General Bartou.'

'That is not a gazetted position?'

'You must understand ...' how she loved that expression, '... that even within an administration as structured as that of the League, there are some of us who fulfill duties not perceived by the original administrative planning. Arthur Sweetser, for instance, handles liaison with America—surely one of the more important roles—yet he's not listed as such.'

'And you handle Australian matters in the League?'

'No.'

Then she added, 'There are not that many Australian matters.'

That sounded a little *wrong*.

'I suppose, in another role, I could be considered *Chef du Protocole*. And I act sometimes as a sort of Inspector-General—seeing things are done properly in the Sections and so on.'

That was stretching it a bit.

There was a brief silence. She broke it. 'The Public Service is taking on university graduates at last, I understand?'

'At last. The returned servicemen are starting to retire. Making room for us younger ones.'

They didn't seem that 'younger'.

But she recalled the resentment of some of her university friends at missing out on jobs after the War because they hadn't served.

'How do you feel about the High Court ruling that Australia, and not London, should now handle its relations with the International Labor Office?' the not-so-thin one said.

'I have always thought that Australia should handle its own relations with the world.'

'Everything?'

She thought about this. Before she could answer the thin one said, 'Obviously relations with the other Empire countries should be coordinated through Westminster, for example? And when the Empire should go to war?'

She sensed it was a controversy within the new department and she was being asked to take sides.

'I realise that we need the protection of the Empire. I realise that it's very much to our advantage to sidle up to London. But ultimately, we alone should decide if we go to war.'

'You think the Chanak matter cleared that up?'

She did not know what the Chanak matter was. She kept coming across references to Australian issues and personalities which she did not know. She had to admit she was somewhat out of touch. She'd tried to catch up by browsing in back issues of newspapers at the Mitchell Library but one couldn't anticipate everything. She'd learned the names of the state premiers and the cabinet ministers.

She hated admitting ignorance but there was no way out. 'Chanak?'

'Back in 1922, Great Britain nearly went to war with Turkey and simply assumed we would go up the hills of Gallipoli again without consulting us.'

She felt caught out. And she had been in Australia when that had happened, working with John on his campaign for a seat in the House of Representatives. How could she not remember this Chanak matter?

Then it came to her—she realised that it was resolved by the Treaty of Lausanne. It came to her now from her League experience. Out of another box entirely. She knew the matter by another name.

'Oh yes, of course, the Treaty of Lausanne. I know it as part of the Treaty.'

They exchanged glances. 'For us here—known more as the Chanak matter.'

'Do you believe the League is "the great shipwreck of Wilsonian ideology, only fit for the scrap heap?",' the thin one said, laughing off the question to show he wasn't expressing his own opinion.

Or was he?

How bizarre. Was everyone quoting Mussolini? Was it fashionable?

'I do know who said it,' she said. 'And no, I don't believe it's a shipwreck.'

They were stuck on this shipwreck metaphor.

Edith looked out the window and across the paddocks to the arcaded buildings of what she thought must be the Civic Centre shops. How nice to have the arcades rather than country town verandahs.

Or was it?

'And you agree or disagree?'

She brought her mind back to the room.

It was hard for her to say it, but she did. 'I agree with Mussolini that if there is to be peace now it has to be an armed peace. We can assume that the Disarmament Conference has failed.'

'We should be glad that Italy is with us, I suppose,' the one who wasn't thin said.

'If she, in fact, stays with us,' she said.

'She was with us in the last war against Germany,' said the thin one.

'You have doubts?' said the other.

'I have doubts,' she said.

'They may have enough on their hands with Ethiopia,' one said.

Since returning, she had learned that the labour movement, for one, was opposed to sanctions against Italy. It was said that it was because of the Roman Catholic bloc within the Labor Party and in some of the unions. The unions were split.

She knew that the Department was not RC so she took a risk and said, in a clubby way, that she would, herself, rather 'be an Ethiopian of whatever religion ruled by Ethiopians, than a Roman Catholic under Mussolini'.

They guffawed.

Obviously Protestant. She'd got it right.

They then asked her about Japan, now sounding somewhat more friendly after her daring revelation of her religious preferences.

She said that she had doubts that Japan could be brought into a non-aggression pact in the Pacific, which Prime Minister Lyons was urging.

She said she did not trust Japan since Manchuria.

'Some in the unions here argue that it's the workers of the world who will stop war.'

'I suppose I believe that loading ships should be left to those who load ships and diplomacy to those who practise diplomacy,' she said glibly. 'And I've noted that the labour movement is split on the issue. Who speaks for the workers? Who speaks for Australians?'

They smiled in agreement.

The Diplomats' Union.

'What hours do you work at the League?'

'Eight to six, different in winter—some of us work all the time, it seems to me. We do have one-and-a-half hours for lunch.'

They nodded. 'We work 8.30 to 4.50 p.m. With half an hour for lunch.'

'We have the long French lunch in Geneva.'

'Lucky you.'

She thought she would amuse them. 'I've heard that the British Foreign Office enjoys a rather long lunch too—they are like the fountains in Trafalgar Square, they play from 12 to 3 p.m.'

They laughed. The atmosphere had melted.

The thin one looked at his watch.

She thought she might use up the remaining thoughts in her head.

Push her barrow. Get in Eden's name.

'I still believe sanctions are the answer to war. I worked with Eden on the Committee of Five and the Committee of Eighteen. I found it very illuminating.'

They asked about Eden and she told them snippets of information and gossip. They lapped it up.

The interview seemed then to be over, if interview it was, and the men were standing as if by mutually agreed signal.

She placed her napkin back on the table, and stood.

'You mentioned sinking ships once or twice,' she said, smiling at the thin man. 'But you did not mention rats. Thank you.'

They laughed loudly. The thin man blushed.

She felt the three of them had ended up liking each other. She could see herself working with them.

But would she forever be seen around the Department as the 'rat who jumped'?

On Sunday, a young officer from the Department, Noel Deschamps, took her to play tennis at the residence of the Secretary to the British High Commissioner, who had a tennis court.

This Noel Deschamps was the secretary of the tennis club, she learned. And had read politics at Pembroke College, Cambridge.

He seemed to get that into the conversation rather too soon. He also pointed out to her that he was christened 'Noel' because he was born on Christmas Day. 'As in "Nöel",' he added, in a passable French accent.

She found she liked him almost immediately. She supposed he told her so much so quickly because he was young.

'I've come good at tennis rather late in life,' she said. 'However, not *that* good,' she lied.

'Oh, you'll find some good players here,' he said. 'You'll get a run for your money.'

'We'll see about that,' she said to him.

He laughed.

The two men from the Department greeted her like an old friend but said nothing about any response from the Department to her fishing for a job. Would not be proper, she supposed.

She met the British High Commissioner and managed to get Eden's name into the conversation and had what she considered to be a genuine conversation on genuine matters with him.

She knew that he was the only diplomat yet to be appointed to Canberra.

Maybe she stood a better chance of a job with the British Foreign Office?

In the general chat at the Residence, she remarked how much the setting up of Canberra reminded her of the setting up of the League.

'How so?' said Watt's wife.

'The working out of things for the first time. It was still like that when I arrived there. Allocating rooms. New appointments. All that sort of thing. We then went through it again last year moving into the new *Palais des Nations*.'

Someone picked up the conversation. 'The photographs of the Palais look very grand. Sad that the Palais is completed just when the League itself is so shaky.'

'I do wish people would stop saying that,' Edith said, laughing, 'or I will be talked out of a job.'

'I am sorry—I shouldn't be so negative.'

'I see the Palais as a re-commitment to the League in a way. A re-dedication,' she said, sounding pompous. 'Or it's the world's last great folly,' she added, saving herself. Winning a few laughs.

Throwing it back at them, she asked about the newspapers

who said that Canberra was a failure and doomed. 'Menzies doesn't seem to believe in it,' she said.

'Too late now,' someone said.

'Menzies got us the golf course,' someone said.

Another laughed, and said, 'You must come to a meeting of the Kangaroo Club.'

'And what is the Kangaroo Club?'

'Our citizens' committee—its job is to "keep Canberra hopping",' the wag said.

She laughed along with the others. She sensed it was a joke they had enjoyed before.

She positioned herself out of the sun and became an appreciative and noisy spectator of the tennis until it was her turn to play.

She was fitting in all right, she felt.

She played very well. The sun—the whole atmosphere—made even the playing of tennis something of a struggle against nature and against the rawness of it all, but this brought out new power in her.

She beat Noel 6-2, 6-4 in a singles game. He took it rather well.

And later over cakes, tea and barley water, she overheard that someone else had been appointed editor of *Current Notes*.

She swallowed her disappointment and showed no emotion.

Unless something else was offered, she was to return to Europe. And, if everyone was right—to return to the maelstrom.

And to Ambrose.

They would get a dog.

She received a long-distance call from John Latham in Melbourne, which she took in the telephone booth in the foyer of Beauchamp House.

'Recovered from the train journey to Canberra?' he asked.

'It was worse than the whole trip back from Europe. And seemed to take longer.'

'They leave the road bad and the rail link impossible as a way of stopping people leaving. How did it go at the Department?'

'Hopeless,' she said.

'You didn't drop your champagne glass?'

'Who told you that?!' She was glad he couldn't see her blush. 'Did Bruce tell you that? Or Frank McDougall?!'

'A Little Bird.'

On no, why did they gossip like that?

She kept her end up, 'I haven't had a glass of champagne since arriving in Canberra. But how dreadful that they brought that gossip back.'

'My Little Bird said that you handled the situation with aplomb. He was impressed. Has happened to everyone. I think you got marks for your handling of it.'

She hoped that were true. 'I suppose they remembered the dropping of the glass but didn't remember any of my remarks on matters of import?'

'As a matter of fact, one of your opinions has travelled around the world.'

Dare she ask?

'Which nugget was that?'

' "Still trying to sell your dried fruit, Frank." '

Oh. 'More a quip than a nugget.'

'And also your belief in sanctions.'

'I'm flattered to be quoted.'

'Tell me what went wrong?'

She described the interviews. 'It's really a case of *nul et non avenu*.'

'You mean, you delivered them a message and they returned it unanswered?'

''Fraid so.'

'You know that being married is the problem.'

He must have mentioned it in his letter of introduction. 'I know. But I was married in a church.'

He got the joke and laughed. 'You mean that for Rationalists a church marriage doesn't really count?'

'Yes.'

They both chuckled.

'I had a call from a mutual friend of ours,' John said.

'Who was that?'

'Scraper Smith—said he'd bumped into you in Sydney.'

She felt sick

'Small world,' John said.

'Small world.'

John went on, 'Scraper said that you were a treasure and should be grabbed by the Department.'

Grabbed.

'How do you know Scraper?' she managed to ask.

'He did some work for me on a case—a few cases actually. As you see, he can't ever appear in court—does devilling. You impressed him.'

She tried to control the nausea rising inside her.

'I agree with him,' said John.

'About what?'

'About how Australia should grab you and put you to work somewhere.'

'Oh well, thank you, John,' she said. 'We tried. I appreciated your letter to the Department. Being married is probably the biggest obstacle.'

'You'll go back to the League?'

'I think they still need me.'

'I am sure they do. Australia's loss.'

Robert Comes Home

1 938

'Ambrose,' she said, waking him, holding on to his arm. 'Someone's just let themselves into the apartment.'

Ambrose sat up in the bed, listening.

'Must be Robert,' she said.

'He didn't telegram?'

'No.'

They listened and heard two male voices. The sound of luggage dropped to the floor.

The light in the front room came on, and showed under the door of Ambrose's room.

There was a silence as she heard what she knew was Robert at the drawer where any mail for him was put.

The sound of a drink being poured.

Then Robert called her name and she heard him go to her bedroom and knock. She heard the door of her bedroom being opened and then heard him return to the living room, calling out both for her and for Ambrose.

Ambrose put on the bedside light. 'It's two in the morning,' he said.

She made the sickening admission to herself that this had had to happen sooner or later.

Ambrose was *en femme.*

That everything between Robert and Ambrose and her had been left horribly vague now came crashing down on her. She'd tried at times in letters to make it clear that the marriage was over and that something else now existed between them, better described in her mind as a friendly, bohemian arrangement about accommodation.

That hadn't quite stuck, nor been quite true.

'He can go to his room—the bed's made up,' she whispered.

And it was no longer his room, it was a guest room.

'There is someone with him,' Ambrose said.

Damn, damn, damn.

'You stay here,' she said, leaving the bed, finding her robe and slippers.

Damn.

And then Robert, without knocking, opened the door to Ambrose's room, coming face to face with her as she tied the sash of the gown around her waist. She closed the gown across her breasts barely concealed by the lace of her nightgown.

Light from the front room streamed some way into the bedroom.

He stood there and behind him she saw Potato Gray.

He and Gray both peered in behind her.

She couldn't believe their crassness. Both, of course, were under the weather.

She glanced quickly to see what it was they could see. Ambrose, lying on one elbow, was mostly covered by the bed clothing, but it was clear in the glow of the bedside light that he was in a feminine silk nightgown—well, boudoir satin, to be precise—and that he had traces of make-up, his lips definitely had lipstick on them and he wore black eye make-up, giving him Egyptian eyes. The one hand which showed had its nails painted crimson. He wore three silver rings. After their coupling, they'd both fallen into sleep without properly removing their make-up. There were two bedside tables and both had jewellery on them.

Robert's eyes went from Ambrose's bed to her and then back to Ambrose.

He turned to Gray and said in a crude voice, 'Potato, have you seen anything like this in all your born days?'

Potato made an amused, embarrassed noise but avoided a reply.

'Oh, this must be Shanghai, Potato—we must be back in the bordellos of Shanghai.'

She moved forward, pushing them out of the room.

Her mind was racing with thoughts about the situation as her anger tried to find expression.

She closed the door behind her, still shepherding both the men into the front room.

Robert had 'known' about Ambrose only in the abstract, had never witnessed it. During all his other visits he'd seen a very respectable and conservative Ambrose.

The impact of what he'd seen now showed on his face as the three of them stood facing each other in the front room.

'Why didn't you telegram that you were coming?!' she almost shouted.

And she'd forgotten whether she'd ever made it clear that Ambrose and she had resumed a physical relationship. Or whether Robert had ever asked. Or whether that was taken for granted. Or whether she'd considered it none of his business. Or whether he ever considered Ambrose as being eligible for the category of lover.

Robert probably dismissed him as a rival of the proper male sort.

She was afire with angry embarrassment. And guilt. That this had happened was inescapably her fault.

Way back at the beginning of the separation, there'd been

bedroom nonsense with Robert coming and going, a few days at a time, with each of them—Robert, Ambrose and she—sleeping in their own bedrooms, although, in Robert's and her case, not altogether decorously. In those early days, he'd taken his husbandly rights now and then. But that sort of thing had not happened for some time.

In those days, Ambrose had silently accepted all this, behaving with absolute correctness in matters of dress and conversation, with everything very pally and clubby in the apartment. And she'd hid deep down in her confusions, allowing the confusions to drift on.

Why, oh why, hadn't she cleaned it all up and had done with the empty marriage? Why the nonsense of leaving him all that time with a key? Why the symbolic suit hanging in the wardrobe?

It was the weakest thing she had ever done in her life. Dishonest in every way.

And there'd been silly play-acting about her marriage back in Australia. A game which no one close to them in the League and diplomatic life now believed or expected.

And then, within the empty subterfuge of the marriage, there was the real subterfuge—the game within a game—because of Ambrose's secret life and the secret intimate life which had grown out of it which lived itself out in the privacy of the Molly Club and occasionally at dinner parties in some apartments with friends from the Molly who were in the know or themselves players of the same game.

Now this secret intimacy had been appallingly revealed in the most embarrassing and uncouth of ways.

With the gross Potato Gray as the witness at the funeral.

She wondered if she had the odour of the night about her. Too bad if she did.

Gray was, at least, ill at ease.

Good.

She regained her composure.

'Well, well, well,' Robert said. It was clear to her that he was in an ugly mood.

'Perhaps we could find a doss at a friendly inn, old man,' Gray said.

'No, make yourself at home, Potato—this is *my home*—you're welcome here,' Robert said. And looking then at her, said, 'Isn't he, my love?'

She looked at him. He'd declined. What age was he now? In his mid-forties? His decline was ahead of his age.

'Both of you should leave,' she said, coldly. 'I'll call an hotel and book for you both.'

'How about a welcoming kiss?' Robert said, approaching her, his breath heavy with alcohol.

She pushed him away. 'Get out. You have no rights here.'

Even for Robert, this behaviour was really beyond the pale and out of character.

'Control yourself.'

'We're still married, remember,' he said. 'Have rights.'

Probably true in Swiss law, she thought. She was chilled and frightened by his tone and the whole mess.

'As a civilised person you have no rights,' she said. 'Please go.'

Gray was now standing at the bookshelves of the apartment, feigning an interest in the books.

Robert and she glared at each other.

There was the click of the door of Ambrose's room opening, and they all looked around.

Ambrose had not changed into male attire.

He was in a feminine silk robe—black, plain enough, but clearly feminine. He had on embroidered velvet slippers. The lipstick was still evident, his eye make-up quite striking.

Silver rings on fingers of both hands.

She thought that he looked tasteful, exquisite.

She could only shudder about how he must appear to Robert and Gray.

She was somewhat startled by his coming out of the room but then felt hysterically pleased and released.

By his appearance Ambrose had broken through all the hypocrisy of it.

Perhaps it brought with it ruin and disaster, but it also brought with it a special kind of splintering relief. She smiled at him and went to him, taking his hand, taking it up to her lips, kissing his ringed fingers for strength.

Strength for both of them.

Robert was disconcerted. He turned to Gray and said, 'May I introduce Miss Westwood?'

The schoolboy joke sounded weak and uncouth.

Gray tried to laugh, holding in his hand a book taken from the shelf, now obviously embarrassed by it all. For once he seemed not willing to play Robert's game. His eyes went nervously back to the book, as if he'd been interrupted in his reading, and then up from the book to Ambrose for a surreptitious glance, and then back to the book.

Ambrose said, 'Hadn't we all better settle down, darlings? Get some sleep?'

She was impressed by his composure.

She said, 'Why don't you leave, Robert? I'm sure you can find an hotel that'll put you up.'

'I intend to stay,' he said, in a voice she hardly recognised. The voice, she guessed, of a fierce male, fighting for what he saw as his marriage or even his home.

She saw that Robert was trying to hold his ground—or what he saw as his ground. 'For God's sake then, go to your room—' she immediately repudiated her use of the word 'your' and corrected herself—'sleep in the *guest* room, the bed is made up. Gray, you can sleep on the settee, Robert knows where the bed linen is. Both of you get to sleep and you can find accommodation in the morning. And stop gawking like schoolboys. Surely you men of the world have seen things more incredible than this. Try to be urbane. And good night.'

'Good night, Robert. Good night, Gray,' Ambrose said sweetly, but in the almost theatrical sweetness of his voice there was a barbed strength.

Gray's head came up out of the book again and like a polite boy he said, 'Oh, yes—good night all.' And then he went back to staring at the open book.

Ambrose and she went to his room, closing the door behind them. She turned the key.

They took off their robes and lay down in a loose embrace. She was trembling.

'I apologise. I am so sorry,' she said. 'I am so sorry.'

'Don't be sorry. They're both soused. We know he's not a bad fellow. Generally speaking.'

Ambrose then managed a chuckle, a strained chuckle, but a chuckle nonetheless, 'And he's had a nasty shock.'

She smiled in the darkness. 'A very nasty shock. But was it nasty enough?'

'They will probably awake as if from a dream,' Ambrose said. 'It's their Midsummer Night's.'

She chuckled. 'With Gray as Bottom.'

'Have you ever told him?' Ambrose asked.

'Told him what?'

'For a start—that we were lovers.'

'I *thought* I had. But that wasn't the nature of his shock tonight.'

'No.'

'Perhaps I hadn't quite prepared him for that. For the reality of that. He *knew*, but I don't think he ever quite *imagined* it. Not in fine detail.'

'Difficult thing to put in a letter. Difficult for a chap such as he is, to *picture*, I would think.'

'The word will be around the traps tomorrow, I suppose.'

'He may feel that he should keep silent. Because of you. Maybe he'll think *his* pride is at stake also.'

'Let's hope so. And that dreadful Potato Gray.'

'Potato'll probably think he dreamt it. Maybe one of his better dreams.'

She chuckled. 'Oh, what a dreadful thing to have happened.'

'Not something one would've chosen to have happen at 2 a.m.'

'And why are these two rats here in Geneva? Surely not for the Assembly. Something must be in the wind.'

'The Spanish war? Czechoslovakia?'

'They've smelled something.'

Ambrose and she eventually got back to a restless sleep.

In the morning, Ambrose and she lay awake, dreading the breakfast confrontation.

'I don't have to rush,' she said. 'The Assembly can do without me this morning. I'll get up and deal with Robert. Sadly, I'd rather face dreadful Robert than the dreadful Assembly.'

'If you want, I'll hang about—moral support and so on.'

'No, no—it's my mess. I have to sweep it up once and for all.'

There was a knock on the door.

'Awake?' It was Robert.

'Yes,' she said, formally.

'Offering apologies. Buy you both breakfast?' There was some contrition in his voice.

Ambrose and she looked at each other. Ambrose raised his eyebrows.

'I accept,' she said. 'Late breakfast—at nine down at the café.'

'Fine. I'm going out for a walk.'

They heard him talking to Gray and then the front door opened and closed.

'It has to be divorce,' she said.

'Probably best,' he said.

'I'll make an appointment with a lawyer today. Do you think Gray went with him?'

'I'll look.'

'No—I'll do it.' Before she could leave the bed, Ambrose rose, removed his make-up as best he could there in the bedroom with cold cream, wiping it with a bedside towel. He put on a male lounging robe over his nightdress.

'Wear the black satin,' she said.

'Might inflame him with lust.'

She giggled. 'Could very well—what a fearful idea.'

Ambrose went out into the apartment and then came back. 'All clear. Gray and his luggage seem to have gone.'

'Thank heavens.'

He went then to his bathroom.

She lay there in the bed exhausted rather than rested.

Ambrose returned and dressed.

'Want me to come to breakfast with you—moral support—immoral support?'

'Thank you, dear. I have to do this on my own.'

They hugged and kissed and he left for his office.

She eventually dressed and joined Robert in the café.

Robert stood up as she came to the table. Being the gentleman.

Awkwardly, he shook her hand.

Embarrassment was making him awkward.

They sat down.

She was trembling but did not think that it could be noticed.

He'd had a coffee but ordered again when she did.

'We were rather tight. I'm sorry,' he said.

'I accept your apology.' She wondered if she really did. 'You were outrageous.'

'We were.'

'Has Potato gone?'

'He's out finding some rooms.'

'Might be difficult because of the Assembly,' she said, trying to make normal conversation.

She hoped he didn't take that as an invitation to stay. 'If you have trouble with hotels let McGeachy know—she'll find you something.'

They remained silent as the waiter brought the breakfast.

Robert said, 'Dull agenda.'

She decided to dump their attempts at companionable conversation.

She said, 'The marriage has to be tidied up.'

'I did notice you're not wearing the ring.'

'Haven't for some time.'

She was confused about the ring. For the purposes of the world at large it sometimes seemed better to wear it.

But it had no sentimental meaning for her.

She said, 'We have to settle things. I'm happy to pay whatever the law requires me to pay to you, as it is I who owns the assets.'

'No need to get into legal issues.'

'What do you mean?'

'Happy to leave things the way they are—neither of us is going to marry. Why bother? Or are you planning to marry again?'

It was dawning on her that he thought they had a marriage of a kind. He was *holding on*. This had never occurred to her.

She looked at him, at the ageing, at the attempted correctness of his manner.

She saw a small, smoky wisp of desperation.

He spoke again, 'You and Westwood seem to be more than chummy.'

'Oh, don't pretend you didn't know. And it's none of your business.'

'My business—in a theoretical sense, perhaps.'

His voice was still trying to be companionable. To be somewhat worldly.

'I'd like the key of the apartment back.'

'Rather need a base, you know. A place to hang my hat.'

'It's not your home anymore.'

'We'll call it a bolthole, then. I'd be happy to pay something.'

'I'd rather we settle the matter and make a clean break. It's long overdue.'

She sipped her milky coffee without shaking. 'I'd like your things out of the apartment.'

'Edith—no need for this formality.'

'I think a return to formality is long overdue.'

'Surely you're not intending to go on living with West-wood indefinitely? That's hardly a proper set-up.'

'Leave Ambrose out of the discussion.'

'You don't see this *ménage* with him as being acceptable, do you?'

He always pronounced his French with an English into-nation. As if giving up his English intonation would Frenchify him and he'd be diminished in some way.

'It's been a satisfactory *ménage* for some time now. I see no reason why it shouldn't continue. That is not the issue here.'

She found that she wanted temporary relief from the inten-sity of the subject.

She asked him why he was in Geneva. 'Surely the Assembly isn't hot news?'

'We've heard that Chamberlain is going to Bad Godesberg. Or Munich. To meet Hitler again. We're on our way up there. Thought we might check things here first.'

'Are you trying to scare up a war?'

'There'll be war. Chamberlain will give Hitler what he wants. And then there'll be a war, anyhow.'

He was *willing* a war. But arguing with Robert had passed from her life now. 'How was it down in Spain?' she asked.

'Haven't you read my dispatches?'

'I haven't had much time. But I'm going with the League Commission to Spain and then to New York for the World's Fair.'

'My, my, you're becoming the regular traveller. What's the Commission?'

'The Assembly has agreed to supervise the repatriation of foreign combatants—from the Republican side.'

'That seems all the League is capable of.'

She shrugged.

'Thinking of getting out?'

She shrugged. '*Tertius gaudens.*'

He laughed to himself, 'Still playing the diplomat, Edith. I don't know that tag.'

She considered not telling him. Oh, she wasn't interested in point-scoring anymore. '*Tertius gaudens*—we will wait upon the turn of events in hope of advantage.'

'Not much of a policy.'

'Not much of a world. As a policy it will do.'

He looked at her, assessing her.

'I see that the Assembly has abandoned sanctions and collective security.'

'That's right. We're to be a forum of consultation and nothing more. More realistic.'

'A talking shop.'

'There's still work to be done.'

'Such as putting on an exhibition at the World's Fair?' His voice was drifting away from the companionable.

'Yes, like putting on an exhibition at the World's Fair.'

He laughed. 'The theme of the fair is "Tomorrow's World".'

She didn't laugh. She played with the sugar. They had to return to the matter of the marriage.

'And you'll be at the League exhibition in New York?' he asked.

She nodded.

'When do you leave?'

'After Christmas.'

She took a deep breath. 'Should we go to the lawyers together?'

He drank the last of his coffee, and said, 'I don't particularly want a divorce. Don't want the trouble of it.'

'I do. I shall go to the lawyers myself. No need for you to bother yourself. I'll find out how it is to be done.'

She stood up. 'I want your luggage out of the place today. Anything you leave I will put in storage. And put the key on the mantelpiece after you're gone.'

He remained seated. 'I am still *in law* your husband.'

'Technically.'

She then felt she had to guard Ambrose. 'I hope you will respect both Ambrose's and my privacy.'

He looked at her quizzically, 'You mean, will I make a good bar-room story out of my wife's perverted tastes?'

The companionable tone had gone entirely now.

She coloured.

He went on, 'Will I put it around about her and her nancyboy?'

In a quiet voice she said, 'I expect you to respect our privacy and to tell Gray to do likewise.'

He didn't say anything.

She tried a wild card. 'You might consider that if you put it around in any way whatsoever, it could enter people's minds that being my former husband, you yourself may have had similar tastes.'

'I don't think my virility is in question. Not in this town.' He laughed meanly. Was that meant to imply that he had an affair in Geneva while married to her? Or after they'd separated?

She'd never considered that possibility. With whom did he have an affair? One of her colleagues?

But the jibe assumed, too, that she still had feelings for

him and that those feelings would be wounded now by that.

She was slightly wounded. She didn't show it.

And she was not going to ask and would, presumably, never know.

With quiet deliberation she said, 'If I hear a breath of rumour about Ambrose which could've come from you or Gray I will certainly make some remarks which will change the way people view your so-called *virility*. After all, you did not father a child with me.'

'That, as you well know, was never on the cards,' he came back. But his voice was not confident.

He smiled at her in a tough way, trying to smile her threat away.

'Goodbye, Robert. I'm sorry that it has come so abruptly. But you brought it on. And it's long overdue.'

He looked away.

'And I mean what I say.'

He didn't respond.

'You'll hear from the lawyers. Should we send it care of your newspaper?'

'That will find me.'

'Or to your rooms in London?'

He was taken by surprise but recovered quickly.

'No—send whatever to me care of the newspaper.'

She took what she thought would probably be her last close look at him. He appeared as a stranger.

How could all that passionate love have disappeared? Where were all those fine conversations? Where had the tenderness gone? Where had all their mutuality and empathy gone?

Gone, gone, gone.

Was there a black chasm in the ground somewhere, a chasm where all the lost love of the world was dumped?

Outside the café, she was visibly trembling, truly upset.

She had been inwardly affected by having said that they'd

not had a child. The words were so potent. Charged with life.

She was affected too in a way she had not expected, by the actual acknowledgement that the marriage was at an end.

She had never felt such sickening anger before in her life and the anger was directed inwards against herself.

But at last she was cleaning up the mess of her life.

She looked out at the traffic of the street, to the life of the shops and stalls, and people buying and selling, coming and going.

How distant she felt from all this buying and selling and coming and going.

The Flag Will Fly

At the New York World's Fair of 1939, by the Lagoon of Nations, Edith Alison Campbell Berry sat down and lightly and privately wept.

Thankfully, the Fair's gawking, hungrily expectant crowds ambling with fairground weariness, hoping for a flash of sensation around the next corner, did not pay any heed to her and her private tears.

She kept her head down and away, looking out over the lagoon, her weeping concealed by her arm.

At this, the Fair of world harmony, she was already in discord and in tears.

And what made it worse, she was up against Sweetser. And she was one of those who appreciated Sweetser. Sweetser was one of the old gang. Sweetser was true blue.

Although, over the years in Geneva—at, say, the League Tennis Club and so on—while appreciating him, it was true that she had not always warmed to him.

The crisis was now over the flying of the League flag.

It was Sweetser who had actually designed the flag. He'd personally taken it to a tailor in downtown Manhattan and had it hand sewn.

Now he'd lost his nerve and wouldn't fly it at the opening ceremony for the League Pavilion at the Fair.

He felt that flying the flag would be provocative to the US because it was a non-member state. He was suddenly frightened about raising the flag of another, perhaps higher, entity in his own country.

Pure funk.

Her brain told her that it was a trivial matter on one level but it had become for her highly symbolic at a time rich in symbolic conflict. Swastikas, uniforms, torch-lit processions, banners and bands.

God knows there was not much else left for the League but symbolism.

There was another part to the problem.

Sweetser felt it was his decision to make.

It wasn't his decision to make.

It was her decision.

Sweetser had always seen himself as the doctrinist, the strategist. An *éminence grise* in the Secretariat.

Well, he wasn't.

She'd even caught him calling himself Counsellor, when the League no longer used that title—and his claim to it, anyhow, had always been in doubt.

And these high and mighty views of himself had now led him to be insubordinate to her. A flaming row had ensued.

Unlike Sweetser, she did have a base of authority within the League, even if it did not flow from an official appointment. Arthur Sweetser had made himself a role as the odd-job man for anything to do with America—but his authority was circumscribed by his job in Information Section. Her authority, on the other hand, was expansive, free-ranging and not circumscribed by any Section.

She, at least, was someone who had the use of the bow, arrows and quiver of power.

Even if her authority was not in the wall-chart of

organisational structure, her authority was as known as the brightness of day. She was a Diana.

Since Bartou's decline and illness, she'd spoken, acted, and thought for Bartou. For all intents and purposes, she *was* Bartou. From this office her line of authority was directly to the Secretary-General.

But hell's bells, she outranked them *by aura alone*—all of them: Sweetser, Ben Gerig, and all the other self-important little men.

And they knew it.

They knew it, they knew it, they knew it!

With those thoughts, Edith pulled herself together, took out a handkerchief and carefully dabbed her eyes, and checked her make-up in the compact mirror. Her eyes showed some strain.

She stood up. She turned to examine the seat of her skirt, dusting it with her hand.

Then, head down, she made her way back through the swarming people to the League Pavilion.

Outside the League Pavilion, she passed the chairs which were filling with guests for the opening ceremony, the young American official guides in their blue satin sashes showing the early arriving visitors to their seats.

She moved into the Pavilion noting with pleasure the crowd inside, pausing to stop a small boy picking at the exhibit which showed the League's success at setting international names and dosage for sera and toxins.

She went straight in behind the exhibits to the staff toilets.

She stood before the mirror.

As usual she avoided seeing the complete picture of her face until the end, concentrating on the particulars of her fastidious new routine of make-up, luxuriating in her new American cosmetics. She'd gone into Manhattan last week to a 'Beautician' and asked for a completely new approach to her make-up. She'd been in there nearly two hours and came

away feeling very pleased and renewed and with a very expensive package of new cosmetics.

She'd gone back to the hotel and thrown away all her old
cosmetics and stuff.

In recent years she'd become insecure about her make-up.
What she knew she'd learned from her mother and through
rather secretive experiments within her inner circle at
Women's College although most of them had been against it.
She'd even gone without make-up for a year.

Apart from things Jeanne had told her or she'd observed
in other women, she had never really known about make-up
fashion. It was something of a confusion in her head. She'd
stuck to the older ways of her mother for too long.

Now she felt she was fully renewed. American or not, she
liked the look.

Her lipstick was brighter. Her eyes larger.

After she'd repaired her face, she closed her eyes and
repeated her intimate litany, saying soundlessly to herself:
Edith Alison Campbell Berry, you are thirty-nine years of age;
you are comely; you are radiant; you are a woman of precious
authority in this world of strife: *go forth*.

She then opened her eyes and looked at herself, fair and
square.

Yes, Edith Alison Campbell Berry, you are thirty-nine years
of age.

Do you wish to be younger?

Did she wish to be younger?

Thirty-nine may be a fine age but for one thing, it did not
proceed—at least as far as she could observe in the nature of
things—to yet more glamorous ages. It was the Last Gorgeous
Age to Be. Although she did know some glorious older
women.

Yes, one could still be glorious into the older years.

But not glamorous.

Make A Wish.

If she had a wish she would wish to be one year younger. To have thirty-nine always ahead of her.

Wish Not Granted.

Well then, she would go and do wonders with this her last truly glamorous year.

She studied her re-enlivened face again, stepped back to see a fuller reflection of herself, turning her head left and right. Comely, radiant, perhaps even *striking*.

She turned away from the mirror, washed her hands and primed herself to have it out with Sweetser.

She had only an hour or less before the opening.

She went to Sweetser's office which she'd walked out of after the flaming row and its stalemate. She'd left his office telling him that she was going 'to consider her position'.

She had acknowledged that in the old days Sir Eric Drummond had not wanted the League to have a flag, did not think it proper for the new world organisation to cloak itself with the appurtenances of a nation state.

The world had moved on since Drummond's days and flags were not only for nation states.

The League, anyhow, was something of a state, although not a nation, as such, it was perhaps a new form of state.

And in these darkening times, she wanted the League to declare itself more stridently, in a state-like fashion. A flag would proudly display and proclaim the power of the League—whatever power resided still within the noble institution.

The League should be an inviolable refuge for all.

People should be able to stand under the flag of the League and feel protected by it. It should provide a sanctuary for those standing under it—the flag should be a fearful warning: 'do not harm this flag or those it represents or those who gather under its protection.'

It should be a declaration of a mighty, forbidding other-worldly power.

She'd considered just going ahead and flying it herself but that would be seen simply as a petulant act, to be laughed about by the men.

She stopped at the door of Sweetser's office, thought about her approach, and then turned away and went back to her office.

The strategy in a stalemate was that you had to introduce a *new factor* to break that stalemate. You could not simply go over old ground.

She would issue Sweetser with a written instruction.

That would be the *new factor*.

She sat at her desk and summoned the stenographer through the intercommunication device.

The neatly folded, newly made flag with its virgin white rope and shining brass eyelets was still there on her desk.

The stenographer came in, dressed for the opening ceremony, surprised—perhaps grumpy—at being summoned to work on a day which was to be something of a holiday, but carrying her notebook and pencils.

'I'm sorry, Frances, I have an urgent memorandum. Two memoranda. One to Mr Sweetser and one to Mr Gerig.'

'Ma'am, are they for tomorrow?'

'I want them typed now, immediately, and delivered by hand.'

No.

She changed that. 'I will deliver them myself.'

'Typed before the opening?'

'Before the opening. Now.'

'Yes, ma'am.' Frances looked at her watch and then took a position of alert readiness with her notepad and a pencil, swallowing whatever irritation she felt.

'I want this done with great urgency.'

'Yes, ma'am.'

'I've changed my mind, they will not be memoranda.'

Frances crossed out whatever she'd written and looked back to Edith.

'They will be headed DIRECTIVE in capital letters and then OFFICE OF UNDER SECRETARY-GENERAL, then, "Temporary Office, League of Nations Pavilion, World's Fair, Flushing Meadow, New York, New York." Use the embossed letterhead and heavy cloth paper. The directive will begin: "My dear Sweetser, My dear Gerig. With the authority of the office of Under Secretary-General, Auguste Bartou, I hereby instruct you as follows:

'Item One) The flag of the League of Nations will be displayed at the opening ceremony along with the flag of the United States. The American flag to the left and the League to the right on the hand-held poles already purchased.

'Item Two) The flag of the League of Nations will fly at the same height as the American flag.

'Item Three) Until raised, the flag will be held during the ceremony by a boy scout or state trooper or, failing that, by Arthur Sweetser.'

Edith laughed to herself.

'Item Four) After today, the League flag will be raised on a permanent pole (to be erected) perceptibly higher than, and between the two poles already in place. The poles already in place will fly the American flag and the flag of the State of New York.

'This directive overrides any pre-existing national flag protocols.

'Please note, this is not a request but a directive.

'It is to be executed forthwith.

'Nota Bene: No excuse will be accepted for failure to observe this directive.

'Signed: E.A. Campbell Berry.

'Date it and also type in the time.' Edith looked at her watch: '10.36 a.m.' Now go, Frances. Quick sticks.'

'Ma'am? Quick sticks?'

'As fast as you can.'

Frances then said, 'Ma'am, may I ask a question?'

'Go ahead.'

'With respect, that is . . .'

'Yes, Frances?'

'Are you really able to tell Mr Sweetser and Mr Gerig to do these things?'

'Yes, I am.'

'Pardon my ignorance, but are you then *their* boss?'

'I am their boss.'

'Well.' She looked at Edith with uncertain regard.

'Go to it,' Edith said.

Frances moved quickly from the room.

'I will come with you,' Edith said, grabbing the flag and going with Frances to the typing office. She watched over her shoulder as Frances expertly typed the directives.

Edith took them as they came from the typewriter, proof-read them and signed them. Flawless typing.

'Thank you, Frances. Excellent typing.'

'Ma'am, will I be needed again?'

'I don't think so. You can get ready for the Opening.'

As Edith turned to leave, Frances said, 'Ma'am?'

Edith turned back, 'Yes?'

'I'll watch for the raising of the flag.'

Edith smiled at her conspiratorially, 'Can you raise a flag? Were you a Girl Guide, Frances?'

'Oh no—I can't do that. Oh Lord, don't ask me.'

'You're free now—enjoy the ceremony.'

Frances said, 'Go for victory.'

They exchanged kindred smiles.

At least she had one person on side.

Edith licked and sealed the envelopes, gathered up the flag, then dashed down the hallway to her office, put on her hat and gloves, grabbed her handbag, and half-ran to Sweetser's office, knocked and entered without waiting.

He was standing at a small wall mirror adjusting his tie.

'Arthur.'

He turned away from the mirror and fixed his fine smile on her. 'Calmed down, Edith?'

'I am calm, Arthur.'

'Feeling better?'

She was trembling but it was inner trembling and she did not give a damn. She said to herself, I'm trembling because it's natural to tremble.

'Arthur, about the flag ...'

'Don't apologise, don't give it a second thought. Matter closed.'

He went back to the mirror, making another adjustment to his tie.

She had observed that here on his home ground in the United States, Arthur was an even more confident person. On home ground he was able to present himself with mystique—as an officer of the distant international institution with unknown authority—among people who had never seen the *Palais* or been to Geneva.

Back in Geneva he was just a familiar face about the place, known for what he was.

From his mirror, speaking without turning to her, perhaps watching her in the mirror, he said, 'In the flow of history the matter of the flag will be nothing.'

'Arthur, I am not here to apologise.'

He paused at the mirror for an instant, and then slowly turned to her.

Now that she had his face-to-face attention, she said, 'I am herewith instructing you to raise the League flag at the ceremony this day at noon.'

'I thought we went through all this. There is to be no League flag. It would be an error of judgement. Drummond would not have tolerated it.'

'Drummond is long gone, Arthur. And yes, we did go through it. I said that I would consider my position. I have considered my position. I have made my decision.'

Breaking their eye contact, Arthur looked at his wall calendar as if maybe he had got the day wrong—the year, the century. '*You* have made a decision?' he said to her, still without looking at her.

'I have made a decision and I have here in my hand a directive.'

Arthur looked back to her. His look had a merry smugness. 'In normal circumstances, and as a matter of courtesy, I would study your suggestion and consult with Ben, but we haven't the time.'

He then made to tidy up his desk. Again looking away from her.

'I agree,' she said. 'We haven't time.'

'Leave it be, then, Edith. When we're back in Geneva and if you still think that it's important, I will raise flag protocol with Avenol. God, we could even form a committee to consider it.' He then looked at her, smiled his dazzling smile, and said, 'Happy now?'

'Arthur,' she stared unblinkingly back into his smile, 'Arthur, it isn't a matter of whether there is time for discussion. *I am issuing you with a directive.* By my hand.'

He leaned on his desk, looking down at the desk, as if pushed to the limits of his patience.

'Here it is in writing.' She held it out to him.

He did not take it or look at it although he could not avoid its presence thrust out there into his field of vision.

She felt a wave of indecision. If he didn't take it, the situation would collapse onto her.

Then what?

She hadn't thought it through.

Then what?

Humiliation, that was *what.*

'I'm issuing the same directive to Ben.'

He remained there, leaning forward on his hands.

'Arthur. Take it.'

She gave the directive a slight flick.

He remained leaning on the desk, eyes down.

The Living Statue: adopt the pose of any well-known personality.

Was he doing a Mussolini?

She was tempted to drop it onto his desk in front of him.

That would not work.

It was important that he take it from her hand.

'Arthur—I have resolved this matter. Take it.'

He looked up. 'Surely you do not have the authority?'

She could tell by his voice that the fight was still there, but that he was now also slightly unsure of himself.

He'd asked a question.

His error.

'I have the authority, Arthur. If you do not take this, I will suspend you and I will suspend Ben.'

He tossed his jaw up and woofed back, 'And then what? Ship us back to Geneva in disgrace? You're a big girl, Edith, but I don't think you could take on Ben and me.'

He laughed and tried to throw his laughter over her, like sand into her eyes.

It was an acted-out, insecure laugh.

He was cracking.

She gave a small tight smile which in no way went along with his laughter, a *managerial* smile, 'Arthur, if you do not accept this directive I will call in the State police and have you removed from this office, from this site, and from this fairground.'

As she said it she felt all breath leave her lungs. She did not quite recognise her voice.

She tried to remember how to breathe.

Her mind then rushed to question the linkage of her authority.

Did it really stretch from the League in Geneva to the police force of the State of New York?

How would she convince the State police of her authority? Would they believe a woman? Would she need a cable from Bartou? How would she establish her command?

Probably through Grover Whalen, President of the Fair Corporation, who had rather liked her when they'd met at meetings and receptions.

It would be all monstrously hard.

Edith. *It would be impossible.*

She had gone too far. And she knew it.

Go further, Priestess of Delphi—'I feel assured of Grover Whalen's backing on this.'

That was ambiguously put.

It was a desperate throw.

Sweetser then looked up from his desk. His eyes expressed an unaccustomed, stunned look.

The Statue Awakens. He stopped leaning on the desk, straightened up, did up the top button of his suit coat, and took the directive from her hand.

He'd taken the directive. He'd obeyed her.

Make your will, Arthur.

He opened it with his Fair-crested ornamental letter opener and took out the directive, holding it as if it might bite.

She waited until he had read it.

He folded the directive and replaced it in its envelope.

He did not hand it back to her.

That was important.

He put it on his desk.

It was delivered, read, and received.

She held out the flag to him.

The ultimate submission.

Crossing Niagara. If he took it, he was done.

She held his gaze. Her trembling had stopped.

He looked at the flag in her hand, hesitated, and then took it.

Snap.

Time for reconciliation. 'Thank you, Arthur. I take full responsibility.'

'You?' His poise had crumbled before her very eyes and the crumbling was there in the limp tone of his voice.

She was about to repeat the wording of the directive about 'acting in the name of Auguste Bartou', but she held it back. She was a thousand miles from Geneva.

She was Johnny on the Spot.

'Do it, Arthur.' She said it in a voice the like of which she had never heard from her mouth. It was not harsh but it was inflexible. It was soft as well, maybe the voice of a strong mother. Or an elder sister.

He stared at her, flag in hand.

'I take it that I have your compliance, Arthur.' The voice which said this was also inflexible but not hard. And it was not a question.

'Compliance?'

'Compliance.'

He wiped his face with the back of his hand.

It was almost over.

He moved his head as if refitting it to his shoulders and said, 'Because we have no time to take this to Geneva, I will do as you ask.'

It had happened!

She said in a firm but placating tone of professional courtesy, 'Thank you, Arthur. Find a Boy Scout.'

'The flag won't stop the Nazis,' he said.

She looked at him. 'A million diverse deeds will stop the Nazis, Arthur. This is but one. We never know which deed brings the victory. Every important word we speak and deed we do designs our future. Or as my uncle, the shire president, would say, "Enough maggots can destroy a horse".'

That lightened things a little.

He sniffed. 'And you take responsibility if there's a backlash about this in the press?'

She knew that he had to say this.

'Absolutely and totally,' she said.

She wondered if it were a tactical error to leave the flag in Arthur's hands. Was Sweetser capable of retortion?

She thought not. It was also now his *duty*. And perhaps more importantly, she'd relieved him of responsibility.

'I will get Ben and we'll come back to get you. You stay here.'

That way she could follow his every move.

She left the office and went to the office of Ben Gerig, the Pavilion Manager.

He would be a pushover. She was giving him the directive simply as a matter of bureaucratic tidiness.

She found Ben leaving his office, locking the door as he left, spruced up for the Opening.

'Ben, I've just issued this directive to Arthur. I am now issuing it to you as Pavilion Manager. It's about the flag.'

She handed Ben the directive. He took it, opened it with his finger, and read it.

Staring at the document and not looking at her, he said in a small voice, 'Did Arthur agree?'

'It's not a matter of agreement, Ben. It's a directive.'

'I'd better talk with Arthur.'

'There's no time to talk to Arthur. More importantly there is no point in talking to Arthur. He has the flag and he has accepted the directive.'

Ben stared at her.

'It is a directive to both of you.'

She saw disbelief on Ben Gerig's face.

'And Arthur agrees?' he said again.

'Ben, this is not a matter for discussion among us any longer—this is a directive.'

'I see.' He made as if to read it again. 'Very well,' he said, glancing at her, perplexed.

'Fine,' she said, 'That's that. Now let's go to the ceremony and greet the guests. Let's enjoy the party.'

'I suppose so,' he said, his voice sounding dazed. He didn't know where to put the directive. He unlocked the door of his office again, and went back inside.

She wondered if he would try to call Arthur on the inter-communicating device. She stood at the door looking in just in case.

Ben had a clean desk and hesitated about putting the directive on it. He put it neatly in the in-tray.

Out in the corridor, she said, 'Come on, Ben, let's have a good time.'

'Yes,' he said, looking at her. His face showed the relief of submission.

Ben Gerig was glad to be told what to do.

Impulsively and tactically, she linked her arm through Ben's, and said gaily, 'We'll join up with Arthur.'

His body was less than willing to be entwined with hers but he did not pull away.

So linked, they went down the corridor.

They opened Arthur's door to find him examining the couplings on the flag.

'Come on, Arthur,' Edith said, with Ben still entwined, holding out her other arm in an inviting way. 'We're going to the party.'

Sweetser looked at them with their arms linked. Edith felt Ben Gerig about to disengage and pull away from their physical alliance. She held him lightly with her arm.

Taking him with her, she went around the desk and entwined Arthur with her other arm.

The linking of their arms was instinctively the perfect move.

Here we go gathering nuts in May, nuts in May.

'Here we go gathering nuts in May, nuts in May, nuts in May,' she sang.

Arthur was an unwilling dance partner but she hooked him up firmly and led them out into the corridor.

She kissed both men on the cheek.

They moved along the corridor together out into the sun. Nearly all the seats were full.

Dutol the architect was there, and she saw Sweetser's daughter and tried to remember her name.

Duncan Hall, also from Information Section, the only other Australian in the Secretariat, came over.

He saw the flag under Sweetser's arm. 'You're going ahead with the flag idea, then?'

Before the men could speak, Edith said simply, without granting any room for discussion, 'The flag will fly.'

Duncan Hall looked at her. She saw that he was about to say something flippant and Australian, but her gaze stopped that too.

'I'll find a trooper or scout for the flag,' said Sweetser with a small, businesslike voice

'Good. Ah, what a fine and glorious day for it,' she said. 'Isn't it?'

She made them all agree.

She looked across to the part of the Fair known as Gardens on Parade.

'In this world, we live in parks which grow in dangerous jungles,' she said, but no one heard her.

The general public were coming over to stand behind the reserved chairs.

The trumpeters were arranging themselves for the Chorale from Beethoven's Ninth.

American federal government cars arrived.

Roosevelt had promised to send three personal representatives, the Secretary of Agriculture, the Assistant Secretary of Labor, and the Surgeon-General.

She moved over with Ben to greet them, and out of the corner of her eye, and with a shock she caught sight of the figure of Robert, lounging in a chair at the back of the assembling crowd, hat down on his forehead, legs out-stretched. He could've been asleep.

Her heart jumped with surprise and caution. She made herself disregard him and concentrated on the duties at hand.

What in God's name was he doing here?

As the ceremony began, she again glanced over at Robert who gave her a small wave.

Secretary of Agriculture Wallace began his opening address. 'Perhaps no other edifice on the grounds of the New York World's Fair is more symbolic than that of the League of Nations building—here, as nowhere else, is symbolised the hope of man in the world of tomorrow.'

An Art, a Cause, and Motley Friends

After the formalities of the opening of the Pavilion were finished, she turned to look for Robert, half-expecting him to have disappeared as strangely as he had appeared.

He was standing alone off to the side, staring across at the crowds in the Court of Peace.

She took a deep breath—in a day of arduous duty she now had yet another—and went over to him. He took off his hat politely.

They shook hands.

'Surely not your line of thing? Fairs?' she said.

'Might cable a line or two.'

'No wars left?'

'No wars left. There was no fighting in Prague.'

'Poor old you.'

He played with his hat and then said, 'Could I invite you to dinner?'

She explained that she was engaged in an official function that evening. She looked at her watch. 'I have to go to my hotel and change now.'

'Where're you staying?'

'The Algonquin on 44th Street in midtown Manhattan. Not that far by the Fair train.'

She rather liked saying the American address, the glitz of it.

'Lunch tomorrow then?'

She made herself firm. 'Do you think getting together's a particularly good idea? You have the papers from the lawyer in Geneva?'

'They found me. I see in the settlement that you've been generous to me.'

'I own the assets. The Swiss have rules about these things—about the division of assets within a marriage.'

'I'm the penniless reporter who married a millionaire.'

'I'm hardly a millionaire.'

'You didn't have to admit to adultery. I'll do that.'

'How gentlemanly. But it's done now.'

'I'd like to discuss the divorce with you.'

'Shouldn't all that be done by the lawyers? We pay them so that we don't have to talk about sordid things. At least to each other.'

'Don't be so hard, Edith.'

'Not hard—busy.'

It occurred to her that he might have come to New York from wherever just to see her. If so, what did that mean?

He persisted. 'I thought we could have a grand lunch or dinner and see the sights together.'

How could he possibly think that she would want to see the sights with him.

'Never knew you as a sightseer, Robert,' she laughed. 'Thought you were above all that.'

'Wouldn't mind seeing the city from the Empire State. Radio City. I'm not absolutely blasé. Maybe you'd prefer a supper club?'

He was trying to 'date' her, as they said in New York. That's what he was trying to do.

'I believe we have a supper club here at the Fair—*Le Pavillon*, no less—but thank you, no. No time for supper clubs.'

'Lunch for old times' sake then?'

She'd observed that associates—even ex-husbands—who one met in exotic places such as New York did seem to be less mundane, more appealing than when back in their everyday lives. In Robert's case, even less threatening. Worth an effort, she supposed.

'I'll check what I have on tomorrow. Let's go into my office.' She was buying time, trying to think what to do with him.

They went into the League Pavilion, behind the exhibits, and to her office.

The desks were tidy, the typewriters covered. Frances gone.

'Did you see our flag?' she asked him.

'I did.'

'What did you think?'

'Did you make it? I've never seen you work a sewing machine.'

She laughed. 'Sweetser had it made and then lost his nerve, worried that it'd offend the American Congress if we flew it—would ruffle Roosevelt.' She laughed to herself about her victory that day. 'That's not for publication.'

She found her diary. Robert browsed through publicity material stacked along the wall, picking up the leaflet publicising the League.

He read it and said, 'Did this go through the Council?' waving the leaflet at her.

'I doubt it. Why do you ask?'

'I don't think they would all agree with this statement. 'The sweep of history through the clan, the tribe, the mediaeval state, the nation, towards federation ...' I didn't think world federation was what the League had in mind? Don't think the Americans would like that.'

He *would* pick on that. 'It was the American League of

Nations Association who printed the leaflet and wrote it. They didn't check it with us.'

'Surprises me. Wouldn't go down well here at all.' He read out something else from the leaflet, '"Mankind's common action against common ills"? Sounds like the search for a cure of the common cold,' he said.

The old tone of scorn was there.

Did she have the stomach for that?

In her diary she saw that she was free for dinner the next day.

But she had no wish to sit through a meal in which he sniped. Nor did she want to discuss the divorce papers.

She went over and took the leaflet out of his hand. 'They're amateurs—they were doing their best. I'm sorry, I'm not free for dinner. Give me the telephone number of where you're staying and I'll call you when I have a free moment. As you must realise, I'm shockingly busy.'

He stared at her. 'The Americans have an expression for this.'

'For what?'

'For what you're doing.'

'What am I doing? And what is the expression?'

'"Playing Hard to Get."'

'I know the expression. And I'm not. I'm genuinely busy.'

And what presumption on his part.

'May I take this?' he picked up another of the leaflets.

'Not if you're going to make a song and dance out of it. But I suppose it's a public document now.'

He took out a notebook and wrote down his hotel and telephone number, tore out the page and gave it to her.

She took it and walked back out with him.

She almost relented at the door—perhaps for old times' sake—but managed to hold to her policy of cutting all links with him.

'We may get to see each other,' she said, sweetly. 'But don't depend on it.'

She held out her hand, which he held for a time, glumly smiled, tipped his hat, and disappeared into the crowd. She watched him go, noting how quickly he dissolved into the throng.

Something from her childhood encyclopedia drifted across her mind as she watched him going. *Deer have no permanent homes, dens or bedding sites.*

She went back to her office, disconcerted. Why *was* he hanging around in New York?

She couldn't believe that he would be writing about the Fair.

And why had she kept looking at him and saying to herself, 'Well, he *is* still my husband'? And why did she think that this should still determine her behaviour towards him?

He telephoned three times.

She was nonplussed as she picked up messages both at the Fair and at the hotel. She kept asking herself what he thought would come of such a meeting? Surely he didn't expect to exercise his husbandly perquisites as a yet-to-be-divorced husband?

When he did get through to her on the telephone, he again asked for a meeting with her. 'Edith, you always believed that meetings incubate ideas.'

She replied, 'Yes, but ideas about what and to what end?'

'About us.'

'Robert, we are concluding our lives together. We are not in the incubating business anymore. That's it.'

He went on about the meeting being a tidy conclusion. And he mentioned sentimentality about old times.

Finally she agreed to meet him in the lobby-lounge of the Algonquin Hotel for cocktails.

As she waited for him, she thought she'd like to be a smoker. It would give her something to do while waiting—and would look *trés chic*. She might take it up. She would have to find someone to teach her how to do it properly.

He arrived looking dapper. His hat had been cleaned and pressed. He'd made an effort.

She was still in her clothing from work and hadn't bathed.

Ye gods, he had flowers.

He was courting her.

She supposed that was flattering in its own ridiculous way.

He presented the flowers and she was forced into exclaiming her appreciation. She kissed him on the cheek.

After the drinks and nuts arrived she said she could only really stay for an hour or even less, she had yet another reception.

He said, 'Then I'll skip the small talk and come to the point. Now that I have you face to face.'

'Please do. We were never a couple for small talk.'

'I don't want to divorce.'

She looked around the lounge while gathering her thoughts, returning her gaze to him. 'And why on earth not?'

She selected a single nut and ate it slowly, looking at him.

'I believe once you marry, you marry and stay married. And more. I think we could make a success of it, still. We're older now. Might even have matured. I'll travel less.'

What he said about the contract of marriage hit home. She too believed in the contract. And she also believed the marriage contract could be made once and once only. You could pledge 'until death do us part' once. Perhaps again after the death of one's spouse but only after the death. But not after divorce. There should be a different form of service for divorced people.

Did this count as the fourth proposal in her life? She believed that George had proposed to her. Ambrose had once,

out of desperation when faced with incipient disgrace. And
Robert had originally proposed to her. And that time, she'd
accepted.

She felt that he was proposing to her again.

How odd. How very odd.

She realised she hadn't answered and that she was staring
at him as she chewed the nut.

Before she could speak, he said, 'And we could have children. I want you to have my child.'

She coloured slowly, overcome by a reaction which she'd
never felt before in her life. And, indeed, no one had ever
said that to her in all her life. No man had asked her to bear
his child. Not even Robert in the early romantic days of it
all. They'd broached the subject but never with conclusion
or commitment.

The feeling which came over her now from hearing his
words seemed to begin way down in her and move up slowly
to her scalp, as the mercury of a thermometer might move.

He said, 'I mean we should have a child *soon.*'

*They roam an area called a home range in search of food and
mates. They may live in groups or alone, depending on their age.
Males generally stay with the females only during the breeding
season and do not assist in raising the fawns.*

'A child?'

She felt a tremor somewhere in her stomach.

'Start a family,' he said.

'At my age?'

'Women do. I was a late child myself. My mother was
forty-two.'

She took a small scoop of nuts this time, filling her mouth.

She chewed them like a ruminating cow.

She had to face that she was pretty much beyond being a
mother now. Surely. Too many medical complications. She
knew them all, all the complications of her age. Never discussing
it with anyone, Jeanne or anyone, just privately knowing the

increasing risks of motherhood, carrying them around like frightful secrets. Like dangerous radium in her mind.

'How could you be serious?' she said rather impolitely through the mouthful of nuts.

The nuts reduced the import of it all nicely.

She could see from his face that this was not the response he'd expected.

'And why not?' he said, insistently.

'We are supposed to be discussing a divorce and you're talking of starting a family!' She began to laugh. 'Only in New York,' she said, using an expression currently in vogue at the Fair.

She could see that he was discomfited by her laughter but then managed a laugh himself.

'I see the funny side of it,' he said. Laughing more sincerely.

'Thank God for that,' she said.

The laughter did not send away the unexpected maternal tingling she felt through her very being.

She should be more tender with his feelings. After all, it was a rather momentous—even courageous—thing for him to have said. 'I suppose I'm honoured,' she said. 'Honoured that you'd consider me now—after everything—to be a suitable bearer of your offspring.'

'That's right,' he said, as if she'd somehow partly agreed to it all. 'That's right. You're of good stock, I'm of good stock—there's no reason why the child or children . . .'

'Children?!'

'You start with one and then go on till you have enough. Isn't that how it happens? There's no reason why they shouldn't be very fine children.'

'Stop,' she said weakly, as much to herself as to him as she felt herself sinking into a warm fantasy.

He stopped talking. She made an effort to pull herself out of the fantasy.

'Robert, the marriage is finished. To put it bluntly, I am living with Ambrose.'

'Ambrose? I don't consider that to be ...' he trailed off.

'Don't consider it to be what?'

'A proper situation.' He looked for words. 'A situation which could possibly be compared to a marriage.'

What he said scratched across a nerve. She was still, from time to time, discomposed by her arrangement with Ambrose. This was hard terrain.

'It wasn't as if you *chose* to live with him. After all, it was something of a haphazard sort of arrangement.' He looked at her. 'Wasn't it?'

Robert could be so brutally right.

She said, 'I suppose that because we find ourselves washed up on the shores of life with someone, it doesn't mean that it doesn't suit. Or that there's something better out there in life.'

'I thought of you as a careful planner of life.'

'I once thought of myself that way, too. Still do, I guess. But there are other parallel things in our lives which happen and which move alongside the plan, in an unplanned way, so as to speak. It seems. Or maybe the plan simply brings in things it needs without us having to think about it.'

He then said with some emphasis, 'You can do better. You don't have to accept second best.'

She bristled. 'Don't be impertinent. You show how little you know of my inner being.'

He fell silent, realising he'd made a false move.

She said, 'And, why would anyone think about having children when there could be war?'

'What has war got to do with it?' he said.

'For a start, you'd want to go to war.'

'I think it's time for me to put all that behind me. To settle.'

'It would be irresponsible to have children at this time in world affairs.'

'Edith, you don't wait until all things in the world are

perfect before you have a family. If you did, the human race would never have got started.'

'You make sure some things are in place.'

'You can't wait until the League has got everything set up in the world ready for the baby.'

She smiled and laughed a little. 'You're right' she said. 'You're right.'

And suddenly, the having of a baby was very appealing as a misty, rosy contemplation. To do something in the face of all odds.

She played along.

'What would be your plan then?' she said. 'Hypothetically.'

'We would leave Europe and its woes. Go to Canada. Australia?'

'A farm?' They had once fantasised about a farm, she seemed to recall.

'Somewhere out of the world's way. I really had New Zealand in mind. Cooler.'

What madness.

'New Zealand!? What would we eat? Sweet potato? Lamb every night? What's wrong with Jasper's Brush?'

Her father would be delighted. Thelma would be vindicated.

'Your almost mythical Jasper's Brush? A "close, caring people", people who read books, go to public lectures, play music, and dance and sing, all set in idyllic surroundings?'

He was quoting her from some time in their life, long ago.

She felt warm and glad that she'd grown up there although some of the description was more of the Rationalists' Association than of Jasper's Brush.

'Go on.' She wanted to hear the fantasy out. She let her mind drift with his dreaming.

He rose to what he must have seen as her warming to the idea. 'You could write a book about the League and then become a world expert on it all.'

'And raise children at the same time?'

'You'd have hired help.'

'I'm not a writer.'

'You wrote poetry once. You could learn the ropes. Do writing for newspapers. Be the Vera Brittain of the southern hemisphere.'

There was a distant feasibility about it. He seemed to have thought about it. He'd worked it all out.

'But wouldn't I be a bit out-of-date about things European, by the time the kids were ... weaned?' She'd never used that word about her own body. And it was too intimate a word to use with Robert now.

'We could visit Europe so you could get up-to-date.'

'What would you do? Milk the cows? I don't believe it for one moment.'

She laughed.

He didn't.

He struggled to keep the matter serious and alive. 'I'd write detective novelettes.'

'The first one didn't do very well.'

'I'd be more thrilling. Have some adventures to write about now.'

She'd never told him what she'd thought of his book—she'd been a good wife. His book was less than brilliant.

'Had a good review in the *Manchester Guardian*,' he said.

'By an old mate.'

'I could try for an editorship. Of a daily newspaper. If we went to New Zealand, say. Make it as good as the *Manchester Guardian*—coming out of a provincial place—so good that London would take notice. They'd say in *The Times*, "However, the *Auckland Guardian* takes a different view", and they'd quote me from time to time. You could write special articles.'

She found his vision charming enough, even if it were a rather egocentric fantasy.

He could never be an editor in a provincial city somewhere in the far-flung empire.

And she could never be a mother weeding a vegetable garden.

'I'm approaching forty,' she said. 'In a few years it'd be pretty much too late for children.'

She heard herself say 'in a few years' and could hardly believe she'd said it. She was putting her age down. She'd scorned other women for doing that.

What was more disgraceful was that she was making herself attractive to him. She was still inviting his crazy courtship.

She glanced at him to see if he knew her age. They'd known each other's age of course, but it was away back now. And he'd always shown so little sentimental interest in such things as birthdays that she was sure he would have forgotten. She also knew that at some time she'd consciously stopped mentioning her age. She had exercised the woman's privilege even if doing so wasn't considered modern by the *Reader's Digest*.

He mused on. 'I think you could write. Your reports are fine. Your poetry was quite good,' he said.

Ah, flattery.

'One poem published,' she said. 'Well, actually, two. And committee reports are a long way from readable journalism.'

'The poetry was quite good. I remember "The Pirouette of Knowing".'

She was pleased and surprised.

He quoted a couple of lines.

> *Knowledge without reach*
> *is a no-ing, not a knowing*
> *is a retching not a reaching.*

She couldn't believe he'd remembered it.

She looked over at him with suspicion. 'You dug it up and learned a few lines—for this little show.'

'I remember it.'

'I don't believe you'd remember it after all this time.'

'I do.'

'You hate poetry.'

'Some—most—but I know your poems, bits of them.'

Time for a splash of cold water.

'What about last year? When you burst into the apartment? How could I put that sort of behaviour out of the equation?'

'I have apologised for that.'

She remembered an exchange about his virility which had happened around that incident. Maybe this fantasy had to do with questions of virility? Maybe she'd stung him when she'd threatened his virility?

Was she done in her life with manhood and virility? And if she was, could that be a sign of her passing out of womanhood, at least full-blown womanhood? She still menstruated. For how much longer? She was hazy about that. She supposed she had a few good years yet.

Won't think about *that*.

She had a primitive fear, a superstition, about drying up as a woman. Because of not having children. Although it was a fear more connected to not having a full physical life in marriage—but she had a sufficiently physical life with Ambrose. She was not 'drying up'.

'So,' he said. He looked at her expectantly.

'So?'

His fantasy had flattered her. And it had made her womanly instinct put its head up. Briefly. As if awakening from a quiet sleep.

The waiter was there. 'Sir? Ma'am? Anything I can get you from the bar?'

'Champagne?' he said looking across at her. 'Edith? Time for champagne?'

He looked at her with his most winning smile, an endearing smile from this spruced-up Robert. From a younger Robert long ago.

If she said no to the champagne, the fantasy would blow away like so many pieces of coloured crepe paper taken in the wind of the big pedestal fan there in the lounge.

'I can't drink champagne anymore. Except now and then when I have to—in a toast. It's heavy on my chest. Sometimes like lead,' she grimaced, as an apology for refusing the gesture.

This admission made her sound old.

'You refusing champagne?! Edith!? You who once said that it was one of the only reliable things in the world?'

'I've changed. I enjoy the odd glass of almost anything else alcoholic,' she laughed.

Edith, it is time to put a stop to all this.

Or was it a time to grasp the grand fantasy and hold it to her breast, this chance? This moment of destiny.

This chance of a proper womanhood.

To be swallowed up into family life. Would it mean that her life had then come out right after all?

And would she live happily ever after? Was this what she had been waiting for? For her life to come right?

The only thing which was not feasible was living with Robert. Or had he matured?

As if reading her mind, he said, 'It can work. It can happen.' He reached over and took her hands in his.

The waiter coughed. They'd forgotten him.

The waiter said, 'Champagne is it, then?'

Robert let go of her hands and turned to the business of drinks, he again looked to her, 'Champagne then? For a special occasion?'

She shook her head.

'No champagne. The same drink for me again, please, waiter.'

The waiter went away and they were back now in the land of Scotch and soda.

'I suppose we could've tried one of the fancy American cocktails,' she said.

He looked at her. 'It's too late then?' he said.

She felt tears at the corners of her eyes and she looked for a handkerchief in her bag.

He offered her his from his lapel pocket. She shook her head, took out her own and dried her eyes.

She noticed that his handkerchiefs seemed to have gone up a notch in quality.

'We missed the boat,' she said, trying to laugh.

'I'll leave the offer on the table,' he said.

Oh no. Oh God, don't do that, don't do that. She couldn't live with such an offer on the table of her life.

But wasn't she also carrying on the fantasy by that reaction? Still pretending that the offer was a possibility if it were left on the table?

'You have a reception to attend?' he said, his throat husky.

He'd let the fantasy go. He'd given up on it.

Given up just a little too soon?

She said in a comradely way, sounding a bit as she did in the old days, 'I invented that in case things got out of hand here between us—an escape hatch.'

'Oh.'

'And things did get a little out of hand.' She laughed.

She drank down her Scotch. 'All too late, Robert.'

She took his hand. 'Thank you for honouring me with your ... proposal. The dream. Very beautiful. Very enchanting.'

'It's Ambrose Westwood, is it?'

She looked back at her life in Geneva, saw Ambrose and his elegance and his new quiet dignity and his—their—strange intimate life and their shared living, with its artfulness, spun from within its limitations—an intimacy so against nature. Or against the nature of what Robert had offered. Yet there *was* an art—if not a passion—to the life Ambrose and she had made around them. And they shared a great cause. And they had found like-minded friends.

Motley friends.

She watched the hotel cat wind its way through the legs of chairs.

She ached for a dog or a cat. She would get both when she returned. Ambrose and she had still not got around to the dog despite endless discussion of breeds and size.

She looked at Robert. She realised then that he wanted so badly for it not to be about Ambrose.

In all this his manhood was at stake. Womanhood, manhood. Oh yes, that was at stake.

For both of them.

'Thank you, Robert, for honouring me. But it cannot lie on the table. It's not the way for me to go now in life.'

'Leave it on the table overnight.'

He was urging the fantasy on her again. She could have it for another day. The chance would still be there for her in the morning when she awoke.

She could lie awake with it, play with it, savour it, hold it up in her arms.

She could imagine her belly with child. Could imagine a playpen with a gurgling child wearing only a nappy and a smile. With effort, she said, 'I won't leave it overnight. The answer is, no. The marriage is over, Robert.'

He stood up, drinking the last of his drink as he stood. How she hated that.

'Goodbye, Edith. I'll sign the papers and send them back to the lawyers tomorrow.'

'It's not about Ambrose,' she said, feeling that she had to save that in him. 'It's about me. Things lacking in me, I suppose, as a woman.'

She took the blame—to spare him. Gave him the half-truth. Patronising, she supposed. But an act of kindness.

'I knew it couldn't really be about him,' he said.

He believed that too readily.

She didn't stand up.

He stood for a moment, hat in hand, and then walked out with a good stride. She saw him stop and give the waiter money, and then he stood as if calculating, and then gave the waiter some more money—the tip, she guessed.

And, putting on his hat with a decisive movement, pulling it low over his eyes, he went out through the door, held open by the doorman, into the busyness of 44th Street still bright with the late sun of New York City.

How had she come to marry him?

She breathed deeply, and lay back in the chair, gesturing to the waiter for a drink.

Perhaps she would write to Robert and say that there would always be a room for him at the apartment in Geneva.

If Ambrose were agreeable.

A kind gesture to a former husband who had been spurned.

No.

She would not.

It was all over.

She had passed across some great line in her life. She had tendered her resignation from motherhood.

More, she had acknowledged—and accepted—her perhaps less than complete life. A life which was not going to change.

Ultra posse nemo obligator, as Bartou would have said. 'No one is obliged to do more than he can.'

The Entwining Coils of Conspiracy

1 940
When, some months after her return from New York and the World's Fair, Bartou took Edith to the Hôtel de la Paix for summer evening drinks and an *échange des vues* and she found Deputy Secretary-General Sean Lester and the Greek Under Secretary-General Thanassis Aghnides there, she deduced that something consequential was happening.

She had met socially with each of them, indeed with combinations of all three, but not all three at once. And, in fact, rarely with Under Secretary Aghnides.

And not at a hotel lounge.

From the window of the hotel where they were seated they could see the lakeside machine-gun nests at the bridge Mont Blanc, surrounded by sandbags and manned by highly trained, earnest Swiss soldiers, who seemed to her to be somehow unsoldierly, still looking like clerks and schoolteachers in uniform, their binoculars scanning the lake for German hydroplanes and scanning the sky for parachutists.

There was something unconvincing about 'neutral soldiers', although she tried to take reassurance from their weapons, which were real enough.

Aghnides offered around cigarettes in a silver cigarette case, 'Turkish on the left, Virginian on the right—*blonde et brune.*'

She had only recently taken up smoking. She took a Virginian, although tempted by the Turkish.

'No,' she said, putting back the Virginian. 'I'll be bold and try a Turkish.'

'Bravo,' said Aghnides.

There in the Hôtel de la Paix with this wartime backdrop the first talk was, as always, about the war—about whether Norway would hold out, whether the British forces there were strong enough. And there, among the men and the talk of war, she drew carefully on the Turkish cigarette, and found that it did not cause her to cough.

With her second draw on the cigarette, she was in control of it.

Lester thought that the Anglo-French force belatedly assembled to fight against the Russians in Finland could be sent to Norway, given that the Finns had capitulated to the Russians.

Everyone had some scrap of information to throw into the stew of gossip and anxiety.

'Mrs Leland Harrison told me that she wouldn't care too much if the British got it in the neck,' Edith said. 'Which is fine when you're packing to go back to America and can put it all behind you.'

The Americans on the staff, especially, were getting out and going home. Sweetser was going.

She'd miss Arthur.

Bartou said that he had good reason to believe that the British blockade of Germany was now beginning to bite and it would not be long before Germany was out of iron.

And of course Italy. If Italy joined Germany in the war then France's back was threatened by the Italian dagger.

'I wonder what meaning we can put on the arrival at the Palais of the armillary sphere as a gift from Rome?' Lester asked.

'I suspect that Mussolini was barely aware that it was being manufactured.'

'It was promised by Mussolini years ago when the Italians were in favour,' she said. 'Now it might contain a bomb with a timer.'

'Where's it going to be placed?' Aghnides asked.

'In the Court of Honour, or near the Library—somewhere there. In the garden.'

'Court of Honour for an Italian sculpture. That would be a nice irony,' Aghnides said.

They laughed.

'The English children are being evacuated from the International School,' Lester said.

'I was told by one of the teachers,' Edith said, 'that those leaving promised the other students that they would be back soon. I found it rather touching.'

Some of her mother's inheritance was invested in the school.

This was the most serious gossip of Edith's life and it gave electricity to being there in Europe. Underlying it was the not-so-distant thought which surfaced from time to time that one's very own life could quickly be in danger.

Despite the declarations of war by France and England last September, during which not much fighting had occurred at all, the League Commissions had disregarded the war and had held their annual meetings and had set meeting dates for this year.

The Assembly had held a special meeting in December, and had taken its strongest action ever by expelling the Soviets for their invasion of Finland, although most countries abstained from the vote.

Life at the League had been so eerily normal until now.

They were sleepwalking through their business. They clung to agendas and budgets and details of administration to avoid seeing the beast coming out of its lair.

Lester introduced a lighter note.

He said he'd been invited to join the Shoe Club of the USA, which collected pairs of shoes worn by notables from all walks of life. 'Is this American recognition of the League?' Lester joked. 'Or only recognition of my shoes?'

'Did you send them a pair?'

'Elsie wanted me to get rid of a few pair. But no. Didn't think it added to the dignity of the League.'

It was Bartou who opened the discussion about why they were there at the Hôtel de la Paix.

Without looking directly at her, he said, 'Edith, we have a mission for you. We want to move you to Avenol's office. As you know there's a convenient vacancy. And he can't hire anyone from outside with such a tight budget.'

She knew what the gathering was all about then.

'You want me to keep my eye on Avenol.'

Lester said, 'Precisely.'

'You'll work in with Vigier,' said Bartou.

She stared down into her drink and felt the irony of it. How righteous she'd been those years ago when she'd discovered that Ambrose was passing information to the British Foreign Office. How he would enjoy the account of this meeting.

'I don't really see myself as a fifth columnist. And Vigier— what do we think of his loyalties?'

'He's decent. A good international civil servant,' Lester said.

'He won't be in on it?' She may as well say it. 'In on the plot?'

'No.'

'Who is? Who are the Baddies and who the Goodies in our plot?'

'We are not writing a novel, Edith,' Bartou said.

She realised that Bartou, for the first time in her long experience with him, had slightly misunderstood the English word 'plot'.

No one was going to correct him. 'What precisely are we doing?' she said. 'I detect a whiff of insurrection.'

Bartou coloured, and mumbled to the others, 'Tell Edith.'

Lester named people who were concerned about Avenol's loyalty to the League and his judgement in the crisis.

'And I am one of them, of course,' said Aghnides.

'We think he's losing control of the situation,' Lester said.

Sweetser and some of the other Americans were named as being worried about Avenol. There were, it seemed, two groups: those who were in on the plot and those who, while not in on it, were considered to be on side.

'Would he have me around the place? Wouldn't he want a French person?'

'There're no French available.'

'He got along well with Bruce, your fellow countryman,' Lester put in. 'He thinks Australians are all anti-British—that you're all Irish. By the way, I won five francs from your former Prime Minister at bridge once. I seem to remember that Bruce and his wife regard themselves as no small beans.'

'Back home he was ridiculed for wearing spats,' Edith said. 'He was the first Australian Prime Minister to have a valet.'

Aghnides asked, 'What's happening to the Bruce Report?'

'What can happen?' Lester said, 'It's hardly time to begin reforming the League. Sweetser is making the report known in the right places in the US. That's about all we can do.'

'What *is* your attitude to the British?' Aghnides asked. 'Simply as a matter of interest.'

'Being of British stock made me a better Australian,' she said. 'My family read the *Round Table*. I often thought the Empire was a forerunner of the League. We could've had a community of equal nations within the Empire. Still could, I suppose. We're a long way from any friends, down there.'

Turning back to the matter at hand, Bartou said, 'That you're close to Jeanne will help ease you in to Avenol's favour.

We want you to try it, Edith—and yes, he may reject you.'
Bartou fidgeted. 'There's a hard part, Edith.'

'Yes?'

'I'm going to "drop" you from my office.'

She made histrionic noises of protest.

He held up his hand, 'Of course, not for incompetence.'

She laughed sourly. 'For overstepping?'

As the three men laughed, she crossed her fingers and hoped that he was not going to resurrect the drinking question.

'I think we could mount a case for that, Edith,' Lester said.

'For reasons of political unreliability,' Bartou said, watching her reactions as he went about the business of lighting his pipe. 'You can see the strategy?'

'I can't say I'm happy about it all,' she said. 'It may come as a surprise to everyone but conspiracy does go very much against my nature.'

She was worried about involving Jeanne in the situation. She assumed that Jeanne could not be told of the scheme. She was then being asked to use Jeanne.

And she didn't know whether to trust Jeanne with word of this plot. Whether to place the burden of it onto her.

She really had to talk with Jeanne. 'What about Jeanne? In or out?'

The men looked at each other and shrugged. Lester then looked to her. 'What is your assessment of her position vis à vis Avenol?'

'I really don't know, now that France is under threat. The beast of nationality has sprung to life,' she said.

She could not believe that Jeanne would be other than loyal to the League. Just as she was. But then, her country was not under threat.

Being part of the inner gang was nice, but what was not so nice was that the League was breaking into gangs and groups as the crisis around them became more frightening.

At first, she'd expected that the crisis would draw them all closer together. Instead, they were dividing into three groups, those who were pro-German, those who were anti-German and the Neutrals—usually dishonest neutrals who secretly supported one side or the other.

The pro-Germans divided into those who hoped for a benign outcome from the German victories and those who had no concern one way or another for any evil which might come with a German victory.

In fact, they saw no evil.

'You can probably find out easily enough—without giving the game away,' Lester said.

Again, the finding out would be an abuse of her friendship. She bridled at the suggestion.

'I don't think the situation is exactly a plot,' said Bartou. 'A plot is an activity of a politically criminal nature, surely.' The little bell in his head must have rung about the confusions over the word plot.

'Quite so,' said Aghnides.

The men gave some nervous laughs.

She didn't feel that it was a joking matter. She was the one who would be jumping into the fire.

Lester came in, 'By putting you out of the British camp you can be seen by Avenol as a potential ally. Thanassis is seen as acceptable by Avenol by reason of being Greek.'

'We have a social life together,' Aghnides said, apologetically. 'And he thinks the British have too much influence even in Greece.'

'Won't it mean that I won't be able to be seen with my friends? And what about Ambrose?'

Lester said, 'For a month or so, that's all we ask—by then the situation will have cleared; Hitler may feel enough is enough. Until then, we need a set of eyes and ears in Avenol's office.'

'But I will not be able to mix socially with those who are seen as being in the British camp?'

' "I do desire we may be better strangers",' said Bartou.

'I don't recognise the quotation,' Aghnides said.

Nor did she. Nor, she could tell, did Lester.

'*As You Like It.* Rosalind says to Orlando—a girl dressed as a boy, remember—that it would be better for the time that they meet as seldom as they can. Orlando replies rather nicely, "I do desire we may be better strangers".'

As if this had been somehow discussed at another time, Bartou then said, 'I think you may safely share what we say today with Ambrose.'

The other two nodded.

Was it because they knew he was no longer trying to be a spy for the British? Or because that was no longer an offence in their eyes?

'We want you at the keyhole,' Bartou added.

'*That* would be a criminal act,' she said. 'And worse, it would be unladylike.'

They smiled.

'I can't see it working,' she said.

And she couldn't see herself going back to taking shorthand.

'Which part of it?' Lester asked.

'My French shorthand part,' she said. 'I'm very glad to say that my shorthand is rusty.'

She pondered the legality of it out aloud. 'His appointment *was* confirmed by fifty member states. His authority is not in question.'

'Only his sanity,' said Lester. 'His competence. And, of course, his loyalty.'

The strength of Lester's attack made her look to Bartou and he looked across at her with unspoken connection.

Everyone in the higher levels of the Secretariat was aware that Lester had become a vehement opponent of Avenol. And he had most to gain—if you were to think that way. The Secretary-General's job would fall into his lap.

But Lester's loyalty to the League or his sound-mindedness was not in question.

Only, perhaps, on the matter of Avenol.

'He won't even speak with me,' Lester said. 'Consultation has broken down.'

That Lester, as Avenol's deputy, was finding it impossible to consult with Avenol was itself, *prima facie*, a crisis.

She thought that fact alone might be sufficient basis for her to enter into a conspiracy. Or at least convince her to try to protect the League.

It seemed to be a growing opinion in the Secretariat that Avenol was unstable. Because she'd been absent in New York most of the previous year, she was a little out of touch and hadn't been able to assess Avenol's behaviour.

The word was that Avenol was set on disbanding the League Secretariat.

Mental instability was perhaps sufficient ground on which to depose an elected official. The only other justification she could think of for turning on a democratic regime was if the regime itself was turning on democracy and its rules.

Maybe by not consulting with Lester, Avenol had breached his democratic responsibilities.

Was it a breach of office to be taking steps to disband the organisation—or was that an administrative necessity?

On whose authority was he acting?

The plot was feasible. As the size of the League staff shrunk, officers found their functions were doubled. This made the moving of her to Avenol's office more understandable.

The boundaries of work duties were fracturing and collapsing.

'I did think he was going crazy with that invitation business some time back,' she said, remembering an old incident.

'What was that?' Aghnides asked.

Bartou laughed. He knew about it. 'Avenol's famous

standing instruction that he, and he alone, would decide who should speak for the League and on what.'

Bartou asked Edith to tell the story.

She began, realising as she did, that this was her act of treachery against the Secretary-General, her stab wound, and would join her to the conspiracy. 'I was invited by the British Commonwealth League to speak on something—our work on public nutrition, I think, and the letter named me as the person they wanted to address them—probably because Cornet Ashby remembered me and liked me. Or maybe it was Mrs Rischbieth, who's the Australian representative on the BCL. Anyway, in came the invitation specifying that they wanted me. Before I see this invitation, it gets shunted across from Avenol's office to Loveday—of all people—for advice. As if Loveday and Avenol didn't have better things to do. And then, ye gods, it also goes to Pelt for his remarks.'

Everyone laughed.

They were laughing themselves into their conspiracy.

'Then it goes to Wilson who writes to Cummings in London asking that he explain Avenol's policy to the BCL—that is, he alone decided who spoke for the League. In the end, I think the file had ten letters. The BCL had to write again cancelling their two earlier letters which had specified me as the speaker. It was nothing against me, I was told. It was that Avenol ruled that no organisation could dictate to *him* who spoke, and on what, for the League. So to get the invitation approved it had to go through six League officials, most of them at senior level. That is a sign of neurosis in an organisation. It's not as if the BCL is bolshie. Its real interest is in equal status for women. Perhaps Avenol thinks that's bolshie.'

'You eventually spoke at the conference?'

'Avenol himself finally approved it. There was a problem with the cost of accommodation in London in the spring season, I seem to recall.' She laughed. 'I think I ended up out-of-pocket.'

There were chuckles.

She saw the matter afresh and was shocked by it. She felt she had to say, 'Looking back, it was an indictment of all of us as much as of Avenol—a sign of an organisation going mad.'

At the time she'd simply laughed at it. 'This was happening during the Ethiopian crisis, remember—and it shows that the whole procedure was seriously diseased. Avoiding the frustrations of those far greater things that we couldn't change. It's a sickness which can infect everyone in the organisation. I was part of the disease too.'

'Yes,' said Lester, stopping his chuckling. 'You're correct, Edith. It is a sign of an organisation going mad.'

Oh God, yes, the organisation was sick, maybe mortally ill. She saw it now, both in this procedure and in other things which were happening.

Something *did* have to be done.

As they sat there talking seriously but still laughing too readily, she saw the entwining coils of conspiracy curling around her.

Edith realised how much she was now one of them. She saw that she was considered to be part of the Good Gang.

But she had qualms. 'I still worry about the legality of this. What does the fidelity oath say?'

No one could remember the exact wording of the oath. As senior officers, those in the room had sworn it before a meeting of the whole Secretariat. She had sworn it before the Appointments Committee.

Avenol himself would've sworn the oath before the Assembly of the League.

'Ultimately, we are formulating an action not so much against the Secretary-General but in protection of the Covenant,' Bartou said. 'You are not a conspirator—you are more in the role of an internal League police officer.'

She had the impression that Bartou was worried about the

legality of it too and was turning it over in his mind as they sat there talking.

'And who appointed us the guardians of the Covenant and the executioners of its enemies?' She laughed.

Had she heard the laugh coming from another woman, she would have described it as overloud. It demanded that those listening should join in the laughter.

And they did.

'Who's mentioned an execution?' Lester said wryly.

They laughed again. The nature of this laughter did not please her. Too self-assured, too pitiless.

'It's not against the office of Secretary-General—it's against a man who might be misusing his post and the Covenant,' Aghnides said, clouding into seriousness.

Drawing on his pipe, Bartou applied another argument, 'Meng-tzu preached in his Politics of Royal Ways that the heavens bestow on a king the mandate to provide good government. If he does not govern well the people have the right to rise up and overthrow the government in the name of heaven.'

'As a Rationalist who has no understanding of heaven, I have a little difficulty with that,' she said, smiling.

'The will of the people could be seen as the will of heaven, perhaps,' Lester said.

'My larger reservation is, then, whether members at our level of the League of Nations Secretariat represent the people.'

They all looked at her and seemed to ponder this.

'Thanassis and Auguste are of course in there,' Lester said. 'This is not an Anglo-Saxon clique.'

She looked across at Aghnides. She did not know what to think of him. Apart from the fact that he was with them.

As for cliques, at times some of her own discarded and suspect patriotic sentiments came scampering out, like dogs pleased to see their former owner.

'And you say I am to do filing?' she laughed. 'I'd hoped I

was beyond that at my age.' And by saying that, she saw that she had agreed to play her part in the conspiracy.

'It is a guise, Edith, nothing more,' Bartou said.

'None of you men would ever lower your rank to do dirty work,' she said, easing it with a generous smile, relieving them of the need to take her complaint too seriously.

Bartou smiled. Her protectiveness of her status was familiar ground with them. It was he who replied, 'Not so, Edith. When an operative is parachuted into hostile territory so as to do espionage—male or female — the operative often adopts a guise, say, as a farm labourer.'

She nodded, 'Point taken,' and stubbed out her cigarette.

She'd got through the cigarette without coughing and she thought that her putting out of the cigarette was perfectly executed. 'Somehow this scheme of ours doesn't have the glamour of being parachuted into hostile territory dressed, say, as a whore.'

They laughed at her earthiness.

'At least we aren't sending you to Avenol as a mistress, Edith,' Bartou said laughing. And then, perhaps sensing that his remark was in bad taste, added, 'No offence meant.'

'No offence taken, and I thank you for not asking that, gentlemen,' she said.

'You never know, Edith, you may be invited to La Pelouse,' Lester said.

'As Mistress Number Two?' she asked. 'He may be anti-British but he seems to like his mistresses to be British.'

They all laughed. Each time they laughed, the coils of conspiracy became tighter.

'What if he unmasks me? What if I'm dismissed?'

'We will reinstate you.'

'What if he dismisses you lot too?'

They laughed.

'Nice point. He might very well try,' said Lester. 'He may very well try.'

'And,' she said, trying to blow smoke from her second cigarette at the right time for effect, 'he has the authority to dismiss you all.'

'And then we would all be out of a job—with no diplomatic privilege and surrounded by the German army,' Aghnides said.

The discussion dwindled to an end.

Everything had been agreed, she supposed, without formality.

Bartou suggested a whisky and called a waiter.

'You've taken up smoking?' Lester said to her.

'It's supposed to sterilise the mouth.' She laughed. 'I liked the look of others smoking. I hope I look as *chic*.'

'You seem very accomplished at it,' Lester said.

'Hitler has banned smoking—so there must be good in it,' she laughed. 'But I'll show you some numbers. They're the case against smoking.'

She took out her notepad and wrote down '3000'.

She handed the number around.

'That is the number of forest fires in California caused by cigarette butts in the last ten years.'

She took back the pad and wrote the figure '1500' and again passed it around. 'That's the number of fires in homes caused by cigarettes.'

Finally she wrote, '$2.5 million'.

'That's the value of the automobiles destroyed at the motor show fire in Chicago after a cigarette was dropped near a petrol tank.'

They all laughed.

'An American on the ship coming back from New York showed me the figures. What I liked was his method—the writing down of the numbers and so forth.'

'Most people don't put out their cigarettes properly,' Aghnides said.

'To do it elegantly is a real skill,' she told them, even

though nearly all of them were experienced smokers. 'The same American on the ship showed me how to do it. Like so ...' She showed them her way of stubbing and twisting the cigarette butt.

'Talking of America—I have only recently heard the story of the flag, Edith. You must tell us the whole story.' Lester had an amused look.

'Some other time,' she said, blushing. 'Some other time.'

The conversation returned to war strategy and the discussion of military tactics.

When she returned to the apartment that night, she looked up the fidelity oath.

'I solemnly undertake in all loyalty, discretion and conscience the functions that have been entrusted to me as (rank of official) of the League of Nations to discharge my functions and to regulate my conduct with the interests of the League alone in view and not to seek or receive instructions from any Government or other authority external to the Secretariat of the League of Nations.'

'I solemnly undertake ...'

She did that.

'... in all loyalty ...'

She did that.

'... and discretion ...'

Was she exercising discretion now? To what extent and with what meaning was she exercising discretion?

'... and conscience ...'

Perhaps she was now exercising discretion and conscience by entering into a conspiracy against Avenol. But there was no way that was the intended meaning of the oath.

Leave that.

'... the functions that have been entrusted to me as an official of the League of Nations ...'

Her functions were so self-defining and self-inventing that she wondered whether being another set of ears and eyes in the office of the Secretary-General could very well be one of her functions as a League official. Or as Bartou had said, was she some sort of internal police officer for the League?

Leave that.

'... to regulate my conduct with the interests of the League alone in view ...'

Of that she was sure. She had always done that.

'... not to seek or receive instructions from any Government or other authority external to the Secretariat of the League of Nations ...'

She was not seeking or receiving instructions from any authority external to the League.

She recalled how that clause had caused a kerfuffle in the United States and Italy. In the US it was said by the opponents of the League that the fidelity oath required a renunciation of loyalty to one's own country—the Hearst newspapers had called it the Traitor's Oath, the work of a super-government which sought to rule the US and all other nations and which made a mockery of patriotism.

The US State Department had ruled that it was not an oath of allegiance and therefore did not conflict with the American oath of allegiance. The Americans who worked in the Secretariat had been permitted to stay on.

Those from whom she was taking a lead, and perhaps instructions, were not in any way external to the League.

In her heart, then, she felt that she was not being disloyal to the Covenant.

Still, still, still—there were questions of propriety.

It then occurred to her that if she were to play the part of being dumped by the English camp and thrown into the French camp, as it were, then Ambrose would have to somehow be seen to be against her.

She heard the key in the door. Ambrose came in. Bowler hat, umbrella, Burberry raincoat.

Each day he went to work dressed as an English public servant, to work below his talents, in the darkest, smallest office in Geneva.

He came over and kissed her.

He went to the drinks table.

'Drink?' he asked.

'Yes, please.'

He flopped down. 'Wretched day. I see more gun emplacements and sandbagging. The Swiss must be convinced the Germans are coming.'

'Darling, I think it's time for you to leave.'

'Leave—flee the enemy? Think not.'

'Leave the apartment.'

'Why so?'

He brought over the drinks.

He was unflappable, of course.

She knew, however, how to flap him if she wanted to flap him. He did look at her quizzically.

He had his *hello-what's-going-on* look.

'Not seriously. It's part of a small conspiracy. I told you I was having a strange meeting today—*l'échange des vues*. It was, of course, much more than that. They'd been talking among themselves before I arrived. The upshot is that I'm to go to Avenol's office. As a watchdog.'

That was a better word for it. Less damning.

'Watchdog?'

'Watchdog.'

'Who wants to put you there as a watchdog?'

'Lester, Aghnides, Bartou.'

Ambrose stared at her, taking it in.

He whistled. 'I see.'

'Yes.'

'It's a coup.'

'Not quite. Not yet.'

'Tread carefully. Avenol is not stupid.'

'He's lazy. And blind to the things happening around him.'

'He could bite back.'

'I'm not doing this without misgivings. I'm frightened.'

'It's a time to be frightened. You are to insinuate yourself into his office?'

'Something like that. And as part of it, you're to go to stay at an hotel. Or with Bernard. For the time. To create an impression of rift.'

'Rift?'

'Rift between me and the British camp. In Avenol's eyes.'

'I see.'

'Do you think I should go along with this?'

Ambrose sipped his drink and thought. 'In these times— yes. But you'll be at serious risk. If he finds out what you're doing you're finished for good. Gone. Everything you have devoted yourself to, worked for—gone.'

'I know.'

'When am I to move out?'

'I'm not sure yet.'

'For how long?'

'I am not sure of that either. A month or so. All will be known by then. In the meantime you're part of the plot and you're to seem to be furious with me for my pro-Avenol stand.'

'How curious.'

' "I do desire we may be better strangers".'

He smiled, 'How well put—an elegant quotation for a nasty situation. I don't recognise the quotation. Shakespeare?'

'*As You Like It.*'

'Very good, Edith.'

'Thank you, dear.'

'Don't fancy moving.'

'You'll be a free man again.'

'Maybe free is not the way I wish to be.'

'You don't have to go. If you wish not to go. I am not yet truly committed to the plot.'

'These are times of manoeuvres and stratagems. I think we have to act. It's good to see someone doing so.'

'Yes. It's time to act.'

Jeanne's Response

I n the new Palais dining room, now virtually empty of the
ever smaller lunch crowd—although she'd noted that the
lunch crowd, what was left of it, was staying longer and drinking more—she sat with Jeanne, hiding her new conspiratorial
role under a pile of endless chatter.

Jeanne broke into the chatter. 'What is going on, Edith?'

Edith stopped her babbling and looked up from her fiddling with a cigarette case.

Jeanne looked at her searchingly. 'You haven't been dismissed by Bartou—I simply don't believe it.'

She smiled tiredly. 'I can't say just yet. Something is going
on. I have to keep it to myself for now.'

After much discussion with Ambrose, her decision had
been to tell Jeanne but not just yet. *Salus populi suprema lex*—
security before principle.

'Edith, the world is falling apart—this is no time to hold
things back from me. From a friend.'

'I have to. For reasons which I cannot explain. Sorry,
Jeanne.'

After a silence, they both stood up to leave.

Jeanne was far from happy.

Fortunately as they walked back to their offices they were joined by a couple of other lunch stragglers which precluded any more irritable interrogation by Jeanne.

Edith sat there in her office. Around her were the boxes into which she was packing her personal things, her dictionaries, and some private files ready to move to Avenol's office suite.

She knew she was now involved in multiple betrayal—the trust of her position as an officer of the League and probably the betrayal of her friendship with Jeanne and betrayal of some of the others in the wider circle.

Many were asking her searching questions about what had happened between her and Bartou. Some were hurt that she was throwing in her lot with Avenol.

She was being, at the least, misleading, but more brutally, she was now lying to a number of people.

And when it came down to it, she worried about why she was not trusting Jeanne.

In a crumbling, threatening world she found that she increasingly asked not only 'Who is my enemy? Who is my friend?' but more, who of one's friends could be relied upon in a crisis? Why could she not rely on Jeanne? Why was she placing her allegiance to the conspiracy on a higher order than her friendship with Jeanne? Hadn't she herself been the victim of all this sort of thing with Ambrose and his spying in the old days? She'd been excluded from his secret life by him— presumably by something he saw back then as being of a higher order than their friendship. She, in turn, had squashed her friendship with him in the interests of her higher order— the League.

She had never been able to resolve this eruption in their friendship. Or was there no strict ethical rule about all this? Lovers above friends? Friends above loyalty to a set of beliefs or to a cause? Group allegiances above patriotism? Country above cause?

Was the highest allegiance to those around one who shared an abiding belief? To be like a communist? Noel Field had said to her one drunken night—talking, she thought, about himself, but generalising it all about some of the Reds they knew in his circle, 'To say the truth and not to say the truth, to be helpful and unhelpful, to keep a promise and break a promise, to go into danger and to avoid danger, to be known and to be unknown. He who fights for communism has, of all the virtues, only one: that he fights for communism.'

Could she substitute the League for communism as her higher allegiance?

And then, one rarely knew the reliability of friendship. Did one's friend hold you in the same esteem that you held them?

Or did the friend also have hidden allegiances which would out-rank the friendship in a crisis? Religion, for example?

She liked Ambrose's formula about having Rotten Friends. But would the Rotten Friend formula permit one to continue a friendship with someone who became a Nazi?

Maybe in life there were only slippery rules and tricky judgements. Or decisions with equally unpalatable possible outcomes.

Should one be guided by what one would prefer at the end of the day when all outcomes had eventuated, even if you were there in the ruins of life?

To have lost a dear friend and to have lost the League? Or to have kept a friend and lost the League?

Jeanne was no pal of Avenol but having been told of the conspiracy, Jeanne would then have to make her own odious moral judgements about the League, about her Secretariat oath, and maybe about her loyalty to France, to a French colleague, despite all their high talk of being above nationality.

That last was the uncertain part.

What would she, Edith, do if the Secretary-General who was behaving dangerously were Australian? Certainly not support him—but would she conspire against him? Outside their own country, isolated in a foreign country, would she feel some protectiveness towards him?

She supposed she would.

Jeanne was not always rational in her judgement of people or in her placing of trust. She used too many superstitions and intuitions—the colour of a person's eyes, their astrological sign and so on. In fact, Edith sometimes wondered how it was they had remained friends.

Language was a bridge to trust and even though Jeanne and she spoke each other's language they could never truly be sure that they were in each other's language club—the club of subtle meanings.

The League Secretariat had thought it was above all extraneous and petty allegiances. Had worked to be better than that.

And many times they had managed to rise above nationality and language. Some of them at some times had risen above those obstacles.

The others in the conspiracy had entrusted her with this judgement. She could no longer maintain the position of *salus populi suprema lex.*

There was absolutely no way she could determine whether Jeanne would betray the conspiracy. But she would take the risk.

She stirred herself from her thinking.

At that moment, Jeanne burst into the room.

Jeanne was ablaze.

She burst out, 'It is not good enough, Edith, it is not good enough for you to say you cannot tell *yet.* After all we have seen together. Not good enough.'

She leaned forward, two hands on the desk, as though resting her anger there.

Edith leaned back on the sprung chair, as if making distance between herself and Jeanne's temper, trying to find words. 'Sit down, I'll tell you all.'

'Edith. No. I do not want to know. No. That is no longer at issue. What is at issue is that you would not tell me until now that I confront you. You would not tell me out of friendship.'

Edith rushed to say, 'These are horrible times. We find ourselves behaving badly—behaving strangely.'

'*You* find *yourself* behaving badly, you smug one. Not everyone is behaving strangely. Look at you—leaning back in your chair so arrogantly.'

Jeanne's abuse crashed through and struck her.

She leaned forward to refute the charge of arrogance. 'I was simply leaning back, Jeanne. Don't be silly. I was just leaning back. I am not arrogant.'

Jeanne walked angrily about the office.

'Jeanne listen to me ...'

Edith stood up and came around the desk to Jeanne.

Jeanne turned to face her and said angrily, 'I will not *listen*. You have a superiority about you which is not justified. You live a strange life—you *dénatures* yourself with Ambrose West-wood. I have never really understood that liaison. What you are doing with him? You had a good husband even if I did not like him. And you go off to places without your friends— let me finish—you are a secretive, snobbish person. And you parade as the great lover of the peace and of the world yet you find everyone around you *imparfait*. And you live with a man who is *imparfait* as a man.'

Jeanne had never, never spoken to her this way.

'You know nothing of my friendship with Ambrose. Don't speak that way. You know nothing.'

'I know. I can tell.'

Edith found fighting words leaping to her mouth and she shouted back, 'Surely it's you, you with your Frenchness—it's you who parades superiority. Pretends to know the secret ways of the world. Looks down on the rest of the world, looks down on Australians such as me. But look at your country now!'

'Don't you dare talk with disrespect about France. We will repel the Germans. You will see.'

'If the British Empire does the fighting for you—as per usual.'

Oh how silly. She was saying silly things. They were both saying silly things.

Edith was not sure who hit whom first, the first slap—perhaps they both went to slap each other at the same time.

She felt the incredible pain of the slap which seemed to be something so much more powerful than a hand and at the same time felt her own palm hit Jeanne's ear rather than the cheek, failing as a slap.

The pain in her cheek drove her to try again to slap Jeanne but Jeanne pushed her away roughly and she fell against a chair, which tipped over. She recovered herself and lurched back at Jeanne and hit her shoulder with her hand and this time Jeanne went backwards.

Edith felt all self-control go, and she hit out at Jeanne with both hands, trying to slap both sides of her face, but the slaps went wild and hit Jeanne's neck and chest.

Jeanne lunged forward and grabbed Edith's hair, dislodging the hair clip, and jerked the hair, pulling her head down, the hair paining at the roots.

She went on flailing her hands trying to hit Jeanne although she couldn't get her head up to see her.

They were both breathless with fury as Edith now tried in turn to grab Jeanne's hair, getting hold of it so that they were both pulling at each other's hair with one hand and slapping with the other.

Jeanne stumbled against a chair and fell backwards onto the arm of the couch and then off the arm to the floor, her hair pulling free of Edith's grip, at the same time. She herself lost her grip on Jeanne's hair.

Edith glared down at Jeanne.

Edith dropped to her knees and went for Jeanne again, getting down and kneeling on her arms and gripping her throat, not to choke so much, more to shake her, to bang her head against the floor.

All her fights with her brother and others in the playgrounds of Jasper's Brush came back to Edith and she heard herself shouting, 'Give up! Give up? Give up! Give up???' first as a command and then as an interrogation.

Jeanne was trying to bang her with clenched fists but her arms were pinned by Edith's knees.

'Take it back! Take back what you said about me and Ambrose!' Edith said, her voice made high pitched by her temper. 'Take it back!'—fleetingly wondering if Jeanne would know what 'take it back' meant.

'False friend!' Jeanne said. 'Traitor! Traitor!'

Edith then sat back on Jeanne's stomach, and let go of Jeanne's arms, her ears hurting from the clouts of Jeanne's fists. Jeanne was gasping for air, her body still struggling.

Edith felt her fury subsiding.

Jeanne spat at her.

The wetness of spittle hit her forehead.

Edith's tears came—a different sort of tear, as if from a different part of her eyes, tears from a different emotion.

Tears of violation and insult—she wanted to spit back but her mouth was dry. She wiped her face quickly with the back of her right hand and, drawing her hand back, slapped Jeanne with force, a slap which began way out and which connected perfectly and powerfully.

Jeanne gave a cry of acute pain and stopped struggling, her hands going to her face.

Edith looked down at her, fearing that she had injured her, the slap being so powerful, so perfectly landed, so fierce.

She saw that Jeanne had given up fighting.

Edith stood up, brushing her skirt, tucking in her blouse, straightening her hair.

Her breathing was so rapid it was difficult for her to catch her breath.

She went over and picked up her hair clip, keeping one eye on Jeanne who remained on the floor, sobbing with pain.

Well, she'd asked for it.

Edith found her feelings changing to concern for Jeanne and for the French, and for herself, a confused sense of shame jostling with feelings of base satisfaction about what had just happened.

Jeanne got to her feet.

They stood opposite each other at a safe distance, both with uneven breathing.

Jeanne fixed her clothing, looking down at a huge ladder in her stocking, putting a finger to it, her tearful eyes all the while looking cautiously back at Edith.

Jeanne then straightened up, threw her hair back and strode out of the office, slamming the door.

The sound of the slam of the door seemed to go on and on.

A mess.

A bloody, bloody mess.

She hadn't explained the situation to Jeanne.

Her fingers explored the swelling on the left side of her face and a scratch on her neck. She went to the washbasin annex to her office and examined the scratch in the mirror. She remembered the spittle but did not feel disgusted. She washed her face and hands thoroughly for the sake of her appearance, dried herself gently, and then redid her make-up, putting foundation and powder over the scratch, and buttoned up her blouse, pulling up the collar. The scratch still showed a little.

Back in her office, she stood unable to grasp quite what had happened in the bizarre whirlwind.

She found it so hard to believe, as if it were some bad dream which had leapt into the room from her childhood. A feeling too, that it was part of the total disintegration of things around them.

Trembling still, although her breathing was returning to normal, she righted the chair, and sat down on the couch.

Oh, how bloody awful.

How bloody awful.

The door swung open again.

Jeanne burst back in. Edith rose from the couch and brought her hand up in fright. But Jeanne was not attacking. She came straight to Edith, embraced her and she embraced Jeanne back.

They held tight in the hug.

They let go a little and looked at each other and looked into each other's eyes and then without hesitation they kissed each other, a kiss which began as a kiss of sisterly forgiveness, and which then changed, and their lips opened to each other. It became a kiss as a man might kiss a woman.

The kiss was short and then they looked at each other again. They embraced, kissed again, and this time the kiss was long and Edith melded into it and into Jeanne's arms and her knees became weak.

She broke apart from Jeanne after a time, continuing to hold Jeanne's hands, giddy, lowering herself on to the couch.

Jeanne sat down with her. She looked into Jeanne's eyes and said, 'Did that really happen?'

And Jeanne said, smiling, her breathing uneven, 'The kiss? Or the fight?'

'The fighting.' Edith smiled and added, 'And the kiss.'

And Jeanne said, softly, without recrimination, 'You are conspiring against Avenol.'

Edith nodded.

'I don't want to know.'

Edith nodded and made a small face, 'Lester thinks we have to.'

'I don't want to know. It's all too dreadful. Do what you have to do but do not expect me to be part of it. And do not tell me.'

'Agreed. And, Jeanne—I'm so, so, so sorry.'

'Edith, it is all right now. I love you, you love me. We will be all right.'

It was not all right—not just yet.

She did not know what it was. This thing between herself and a woman had happened once before. An American woman, years back, whom she'd thought about often. Who had touched her breasts once at a party. At least, Edith remembered it that way. Maybe it hadn't happened quite that way. A full and proper kiss certainly had happened between the American woman and her at that party. And she had gotten to know such women at the Molly Club where two or three came sometimes dressed as men. She sometimes watched them and wondered about their lives.

And then there was what went on between Ambrose and her, too. The femininity of it.

She had gone some of the distance down that road with the American woman because it was *alluring*.

But too much was spinning through her head now.

She gave a sheepish glance back up at Jeanne beside her there on the couch as they sat there holding hands.

Jeanne, sitting beside her, holding her hands very tightly, said in a low voice, 'You know, Edith, we could be lovers.'

Edith at first thought Jeanne meant that the way they were sitting together was a bit like the way lovers sat when they were together.

Then she realised that Jeanne had made some sort of a proposal.

A proposal that they become lovers.

'We could—but we can't,' Edith said, looking down at the carpet, her hands still captured by Jeanne's hands. 'I am not able to cope with that, or to contemplate that. No.'

It had never crossed her mind in all these years, that Jeanne might be *like that*.

Jeanne had men. Were there women too? Why hadn't

Jeanne told her? She'd told Jeanne about her love life, quite a lot. Although not very much at all about Ambrose—Jeanne had guessed about that.

Maybe she was the first *woman* Jeanne had professed love for.

There was no response from Jeanne.

'I really couldn't, Jeanne. I'm not up to it. I am with Ambrose.'

'It's all right,' Jeanne said, quietly. 'I don't know what I was saying. It is the hysteria.'

'I can barely cope with my life as it is.'

'It's all right,' Jeanne said. 'I was not myself. I spoke madly.'

She let go of Edith's hands.

Edith took hold of Jeanne's hands again. 'We are both on the edge. The war . . .'

'It's all right,' Jeanne said, and kissed her lightly on the cheek, and letting go of Edith's hands, she smoothed Edith's hair, touched her inflamed cheek, saw the edge of the scratch, undid Edith's blouse, and touched that with her fingertips. 'It's all right, Edith. Shush. And I take back what I said about Ambrose—he is a good man. And I enjoy him so much. I was just angry. Angry. *C'est la guerre.* The war is making us mad.'

'I may be doing something dreadfully wrong—with the Avenol matter.'

'We have to take risks of being wrong.' And Jeanne kissed her lightly again and said, 'Even you, Edith Alison Campbell Berry.'

Edith sniffed her running nose, and smiled, looking up. 'It's just plain Edith now.'

'Edith Berry.'

They looked into each other's eyes. She again tried to find a place for Jeanne's profession of love—that kind of love—but couldn't find a place for it in her life.

'About our fighting ...' Edith tried to find something to say. A way of erasing it. There was nothing to say.

They both began giggling.

'It was so so dreadful—how could we?' Jeanne said. 'How *could* we???? Behaving like schoolgirls!'

Their giggling, as juvenile as their fighting, overtook them and, locked in each other's arms, they giggled until they cried. But even then, as she came up out of the depths of their giggling, part of Edith's mind told her that another part of the world had slipped, had become unsteady.

When the giggling did stop and became smiling, she was aware there on the couch that Jeanne wanted to kiss her again.

And that she wanted to kiss Jeanne.

But, by whatever subtle distance she managed to keep from Jeanne, or whatever her mouth showed, it did not give any invitation to the kiss.

It was true that she had willingly joined with Jeanne's first kiss and it was true that she'd felt weak in her knees when they had been in that kiss.

It told her something about her life with Ambrose more than it told her about her feelings for Jeanne.

Coils of Office

O n the first day at her new posting to the Secretary-General's office, Edith came to the Palais to find maintenance workmen painting red arrows on the walls.

She asked them what they were for.

'*Abris*,' the foreman said.

'Shelters from what? *Attaque aérienne?*'

'*Oui—les bombes.*' The workmen made gestures and whistling noises of how they imagined the bombs falling.

Amused, they seemed to find the dropping of bombs unlikely.

She understood from the scraps of information they threw to her that the arrows were to lead to basements designated as gathering places during attacks from the air.

The paraphernalia of warfare came ever closer. In a shivering way it heightened her senses. It was as if she were coming closer to the very nature of the human species. As if an unreality was being stripped away. She also felt that she was now in it—the war—and she marvelled at how things around her had begun to prepare for it—to administer the war and its destruction. How the wording of signs was being discussed by Swiss committees, how paint was being ordered—which colour for this? Which colour for that? And how the costing of shelters and the furnishing of shelters was now the daily business of people throughout the world.

How long, though, did the administrative responses remain in place and working? When did these also fall apart? When did the civic administrators decide that it was no longer possible to administer the war? When did they decide to lock their offices and flee, leaving the population to fend for itself?

How dreadful it must be when the signs were still there but the people who had written the signs had fled or been killed. Or when the shelters themselves had collapsed. And when the signs kept on saying shelter or first aid or hospital and there was no shelter, no first aid, no hospital.

That was when war truly began, perhaps, when all had collapsed and it was every person for themselves. She'd heard that a collapsing army was a dreadful sight to witness.

That must mark the end of something too. Military discipline was the last line of anything resembling civilisation.

Would they become animals? Would they scramble over each other and loot? It would be a strange freedom to be able to go into the fine Geneva stores and take what she wanted. To her consternation, she found that the thought of going into a fine shoe store and being able to take what she wanted was tantalising.

Even the petty freedom of being able to go behind a bar and take what you wanted seemed a tantalising fantasy.

She frowned. Part of her was hankering for it, hankering for the freedom which flowed from catastrophe. Not just to see it but for its release from routine and the humdrum of order.

From constraint.

It would be like being let out of school early. Or the absence of the teachers. The sudden absence of rules and supervision.

She was slightly disgusted to find such hankerings within herself.

She met Sweetser in the corridor, who stopped to explain the way the shelters would work. 'There is an irony,' he said. 'The Palais—a building constructed to procure peace—is now protecting itself from war. The populations of the cities will huddle in these shelters until the bombing has stopped and then come out of the shelters to find no electricity, no water and the telegraph destroyed. The whole thing will take a week.'

Dear Sweetser, always looking for tragic ironies, grand allegories, turning points in history.

'Don't make a sonnet of it, Arthur, you'll be out of it all,' she said. 'When do you leave?'

'May 15. Regrettably. It's cutting me up. But ... the kids.' He looked at her for approval.

Her resigned smile and touch to his arm gave him the approval he needed.

'You wouldn't like to buy Gerig's car?' he asked.

She contemplated it. Maybe Ambrose and she would need a car for escape or emergency?

'I'll think about it. I'll let you know.'

She then reminded him, as one of those in on the conspiracy, that he should be cool towards her.

He winked in compliance but said, 'You've had a fall?', gesturing at her bruised face.

'Slipped on a banana skin,' she said, with a tone of womanly mystery.

He nodded as if he understood and went off in his characteristically urgent way.

Further along the endless corridor, she met a worried, bewildered Loveday from Economic Section.

His fear of bombs aroused, he wanted to find a safe place for his card index. 'I have records of all the trade figures of all the countries of the world since 1920,' he said. 'Their value is incalculable. Edith, you must get someone to do something about it.'

She told him to contact Hadyn at the ILO. 'He has a small cinema machine which can make photographic copies—3000 copies in an afternoon. So I'm told. You could send a copy of it to London or somewhere safe. Put a set of the cards in a Swiss bank.' She laughed. 'Maybe not. Maybe even the Swiss banks aren't that safe anymore.'

Ye gods, what was safe? 'Maybe Australia or New Zealand would be better,' she said weakly. She didn't want to add to his fearfulness.

'That far away? Do you think so?'

'Perhaps.'

He thanked her.

She said, 'Your figures might help us put the world back together again.' She probably shouldn't have said it. It sounded too ominous.

Unsettled by her reply, he stared at her as she walked off.

She turned and called to him, 'Send a copy to New Zealand—that would be my advice.'

He called to her to wait. She stopped and turned while he came back to her.

'Could I ask your opinion on another matter?'

'Of course.'

'If we were captured and tortured—'

'Really, Loveday, I don't think that will happen to you. I don't think it will come to that.'

'There is always a possibility.'

'Go on. What is it you want?'

'Do any of your friends have pharmaceutical knowledge?'

'How do you mean?'

'I believe there is a tablet which can be concealed about one's person and swallowed.'

'Suicide tablets?'

'Precisely.'

Ambrose and she had discussed it and Bernard had found some for them. She had a duty, she supposed, to help others.

'I suppose I could ask around.'

'Thank you. You're the only person I could come to—on a matter like that.'

Why her? Was her role also to dispense death?

Such grim business now occupied fine minds. 'I'll contact you tomorrow about it,' she said.

He scurried off.

Her corridor manner belied her inner commotion about her move to Avenol's office. Her inner commotion was not dissimilar to her first day at the League fifteen years before, a day which returned to her again and again, a day of nervous glory.

The new girl.

Avenol was welcoming from the first. Perhaps it was her recently acquired reputation in the *haute direction* as having pro-Avenol sentiments and her being a friend of Jeanne.

Jeanne and she had never discussed the matter again after the day of their scrap. On the surface, everything was as before with Jeanne—and Jeanne was the only one of her old friends with whom she could openly fraternise.

Both of them preferred to take the surface friendliness as the reality and perhaps hope that what lay underneath that surface friendship would properly heal. And Jeanne had not referred again by word or behaviour to her 'proposal' after the fight.

She suspected that Jeanne had planted things in Avenol's mind which would have given Edith further favour in his eyes.

She simply assumed that Jeanne had not spilled the beans to Avenol.

Avenol asked about her face. She muttered about slipping over and he took no further interest.

As she and her co-conspirators had predicted, the fact that she and Bruce, the chair of Council, were Australians helped.

'I liked your countryman, Bruce. Bruce and I see eye-to-eye.

We agreed that sanctions against Japan would've been wrong. We agreed on the need for a Central Controlling Committee for the League. To separate the political and military business of the League from the social and economic business. If we'd done what Bruce had argued earlier many countries would have joined up with the League for the social and economic business who were frightened of the political and military. Even the Americans. Now is the time for *un directoire*. That is what we need here in the Secretariat. *Un directoire* to replace all the endless wrangling in the Assembly, the Council, the committees.' He punched his hand. '*Un directoire*.'

He stood about the outer office where she was to work but did not offer to help her unpack. She would have to get used to not having an assistant. Gerty had remained in Bartou's office and kept back her tears when Edith had left.

'I find it interesting that you do not see yourself as British,' he said.

'I've been here so long now,' she said drolly. 'I'm perhaps international, or perhaps Genevan.' She smiled, charmingly. 'Aren't Geneva and Vienna two of the cities which one can claim without having been born there?'

'I've heard that said.'

'Or perhaps I am one of the new international aristocracy.'

He didn't respond to that idea.

How well she performed the masquerade and how she hated how well she did it.

As for the Bruce Report, she felt that there was a lot of politics in the 'social and economic' and a lot of the social and economic in the 'political'. But that argument was now buried in history. At least until after the war.

She would oppose turning the League into an international department of social services. She still wanted it to be a police station. But she agreed that the international enforcement of peace was a political art still to be learned.

As Avenol left to go back to his inner office, he said, 'I ask that you remember only that you work for me now and not for Bartou.'

'*Mais oui.*'

During the next week, never had Avenol's private filing been more meticulously done—nor as slowly done and re-done, as she invented excuses to be in and around his office as he talked endlessly on the telephone.

To her advantage, she found that within the first week Avenol began chatting to her casually.

He liked her company.

Over the days, her unceasing use of French, even on the telephone, also began to put him at ease. But more than all this, she sensed there was another affinity between them which came from her having had, for a time, unusual marital arrangements. So both he and she had an absent spouse and another arrangement. Although so strictly conservative in his politics and administrative style, Avenol was not so in his personal life. His wife was in Paris refusing him a divorce and he had, regardless of opinion, installed Vera Lever in La Pelouse as his mistress.

He was curious to know where Robert was and how she and he saw their marriage although he had difficulty approaching the question directly.

The hopelessly vague, indirect questions restricted by decorum allowed her equally vague and indirect replies.

The unsatisfactory nature of the answers only extended his curiosity and it returned at odd times in the form of yet other indirect questions about her life. Avenol had known Ambrose in the old days, had seen Ambrose crash and leave the League, and had seen Ambrose return to Geneva and had seen them again become a duo.

He was curious about Ambrose and had obviously been party to the gossip that they were a *ménage*. He had also heard on the grapevine that Ambrose had rather publicly moved out of the *ménage* to live in a hotel.

He even sympathised with her about this but his sympathy did not go so far as to accept that her working with him might be the cause.

Ambrose and she still saw each other secretly—after dark, as it were. But they had put it around on the gravevine that he'd been furious that she was siding with Avenol's group and working for him.

In dribs and drabs she let small details of her private life come out, chatting with Avenol although she knew that she was using her very personal life as part of the conspiracy. That she could do this so skilfully somewhat alarmed her.

She had tried at first not to be untrue to herself by her remarks and had then found that this was easier than she would have thought, because she found that she and Avenol actually agreed about much, at least about the stupidity of the conventions for the likes of them and about administrative method, if not about higher policy.

She began to find Avenol quite judicious.

On the day that they heard of Germany's invasion of the neutral states Belgium, Holland and Luxembourg, Avenol called her in to take dictation of a memorandum to staff.

He began the dictation: 'I have heard from the Staff Committee that some members of the Secretariat are in doubt as to the effect which the latest development of the war might or ought to produce in respect to their course of action. Those who desire to do so are free, both morally and administratively, to ask for the suspension of their contract; or if they so wish, to resign and every possible action has already been taken to provide for the security of the staff pensions fund and staff Provident Fund ...'

They were interrupted by a telephone call which Edith handed to Avenol. When he put it down he said, 'Chamberlain has gone—Churchill is Prime Minister of Britain.'

Her spirits soared. But she did not show her reaction. She looked at Avenol and saw no indication of what his reaction was to this news.

She became cautious, sensing that this could be a crucial test of her position. To cheer, which is what she felt like doing, might be too British.

Perhaps he was watching her.

He did not ask for her reaction.

He then said, 'With Churchill it will now be total war. I wish to meet with the Permanent Delegates. Arrange that.'

'Returning now to the memorandum. Add this: The Headquarters of the Secretariat will remain in Geneva. The Administration cannot accept any responsibility as regards the practical possibility of travelling, nor as regards the safety of officials and their families whether in Geneva or elsewhere.'

By not cheering Churchill she had made a silent lie. She observed that she was able to enjoy the success of her dissembling. It had within it a prowess which could be enjoyed for its own sake. The way a criminal, perhaps, enjoyed his skill as a safe-breaker or confidence trickster.

And she was impressed by how cool she was as she took such ominous dictation.

As she typed it up she saw that his memorandum was the beginning of the end.

And the war was moving significantly closer to Switzerland.

The closer the end came the freer she felt from ethical or other restraints.

Out in the general office, the staff were behaving like nurses by not crying and not panicking, going about their business with the appearance of normality—although in a few cases, she knew that relatives and friends were increasingly in the war zone.

Later that morning, Lester came into Avenol's office without an appointment, passing her by in the outer office without a comment or glance.

There had been no communication between the Secretary-General and his Deputy for months.

It occurred to her that Lester might need a witness, and she went into Avenol's office on some pretext and was hardly noticed.

Avenol was arguing against Lester's demand for an evacuation plan for the League.

Lester said that it was time for the Secretariat to have a plan to move to safe ground and to go on working.

As she pulled files from Avenol's personal cabinet and dawdled, she realised she enjoyed the invisibility of a clerical worker—she came into focus only when he needed her for work or to relax and talk with, but at all other times she was invisible.

Part of the furniture.

She heard Avenol accuse Lester of funk. 'The French are more disciplined: the safety of families has to be ignored. In France the family and the head of the household go down together. So it will be with the League.'

Emotionally, she found herself rather agreeing with Avenol.

Lester kept saying that a plan for evacuating the families, at least, was necessary.

Avenol refused, 'For the families of the *haute direction* to be seen to be scurrying for safe haven is bad for the morale.'

'All right then,' Lester, said turning to leave. 'That is easy then: if there is no plan then I accept no responsibility.'

Edith thought Lester was rather petulant.

Avenol stood and walked with Lester to the door—not, it seemed, from any politeness but from a need to continue to make his point. 'We must accept the fate of the Swiss people who are our host nation. We accepted their protection in peace: now let us join them in their fate.'

Edith found herself impressed by Avenol's rhetoric and dissatisfied with Lester, even if the rhetoric made no real sense.

She also knew that rhetoric was something of a sign that the person using it was unsure of what to do.

After Lester had left, Avenol noticed her in the room and said, 'You heard? You agree?'

'I do agree,' she said. 'For the League to run is to invite all to run.'

'Lester is a scared dog.'

She didn't comment.

She looked at him. He was leaning back in his Napoleonic pose.

'Do you have your haversack packed with chocolate and tinned food?' he asked her, his voice carrying a note of derision about the idea.

'I should, I suppose. But I don't,' she lied.

Her reply pleased Avenol. 'All the English have their haversacks of chocolate, clean underwear, wax matches, candles, and soap.'

He laughed to himself.

That evening in their dark banquette at the Molly Club where she and Ambrose were continuing to meet, Ambrose said he believed that by the new offensive against the neutrals, the Germans had begun their decline.

'Overstretched,' he said.

She wanted to believe it but so much of what they'd all said over the last few months had turned out to be wrong.

She felt they were sunk in half-information, misinformation, fantasies, and the distortions of fear—and that all their intelligence could not find a way out.

The Molly had lost a few of its regulars, those she'd known only by their party names—'Madame de Stael', 'Maisy', 'Delores' and so on, fluttering about in the dim light in dark flirtations. The one or two South Americans, she knew from accents alone, were still there, protected, they hoped, by neutrality and commerce.

Bernard kept on with the cabarets and their satire became even more grim.

Newcomers continued to arrive—still more refugees—and sometimes they too came in the masks and garb of the anonymous night. How did they come to know of the Molly? How did people from across Europe know of it and its strange ways? Coming down the stairs for the first time, uneasily, warily, until absorbed into the low hubbub and occasional screaming laughter and hysterical humour.

Sometimes, she noticed, Bernard seemed to be expecting the newcomers, or knew them, or had been warned of their coming. How did it all work?

And more often now, Bernard would be found in the Club annex or in one of the small upstairs rooms, deep in serious discussion with people she did not know.

She returned to the war, the never-ending discussion. 'The taking of the neutral countries has cost them very little militarily,' she said to Ambrose.

'But the Germans now have to garrison these countries.'

'That's true.'

The exchange was typical of the sort which she and others *wanted* to believe. She could recognise them now.

Ambrose leaned in and said, with special emphasis, 'It is not the *loss* of blood—it is the presence of blood which will undo the Germans now.'

'Explain, darling,' she said. 'No enigmas tonight.'

'Roosevelt has Belgian and Dutch blood in his family line,' he said, with a flourish.

She giggled at yet another example of Ambrose's miscellany of little-known facts. 'I hope, dear, that you are perfectly correct,' she said. 'I keep forgetting that you are an expert on bloodlines.'

Bernard came over, his usual stylish, feminine self. 'My darlings! What's the gossip?'

'Bloodlines, Bernice. But there is no gossip. All gossip has dried up.'

'Of one thing I am certain in this most uncertain of worlds: there is always gossip. *Par example*, you are now very close to M. Avenol—mysteriously close to him. And *she* has already told me of the bloodlines theory. We'll see.'

She looked at Ambrose.

Ambrose shook his head at her, denying that he had passed on anything about the conspiracy.

Bernard was astute and an ally, but he could not be made one of those in the know.

As usual, she reported to her co-conspirators on the Saturday morning at their prearranged rendezvous in McGeachy's apartment on the rue Bourg du Four.

They seemed amused but not worried that she found herself somewhat in accord with Avenol.

'He seems to me to be keeping his nerve,' she reported.

'You know, I think he uses artificial aids,' Lester said.

'A drug of some sort?' Bartou asked, surprised.

'Some serum or other. It's a feeling I have—his manner, it seems to swing.'

She said she had seen no evidence of this. She found it an unlikely idea.

Lester rather uneasily announced that his wife, Elsie, was packing to leave that night.

'The children are in Ireland,' he reminded them. 'One parent should be there.'

'Of course,' said Aghnides.

As usual the loss of anyone was seen as disturbing, a loosening of the timbers of the ship.

Lester said that all Americans had been instructed by the Consul to leave Switzerland.

The Sweetsers' farewell party was that night.

Lester seemed to be implementing a policy of evacuating families regardless of Avenol.

She reported that Avenol was not doing anything untoward, and that he was taking the usual steps to allow staff to return to their home countries, arranging internal matters. 'We have booked alternative accommodation for the Secretariat in France, in case of an invasion of Switzerland,' she revealed.

It was accepted without much comment.

The talk then turned to the continued German advances.

She did not report that she had a growing inner conflict about being a traitor to her office—that is, to Avenol's office. There was an ethic about what one owed an office, both in the sense of the position and in the physical sense of the bonds of the people who worked together.

Such qualms seemed self-centred in the threatening atmosphere which surrounded Geneva like a fog.

Avenol and she began to draft a protest for Council against the German invasion of the neutral countries.

As she dutifully took down the draft, she felt now how impotent the words of a League of Nations protest were against the relentless rolling forward of the German tanks with their fresh, clean, crews in their new uniforms.

Later that morning, Avenol went to talk with M. Pilet-Golaz, the Swiss President. He returned grey-faced.

'Forget the protest. Tear it up. The Swiss think that such a protest coming from the League on Swiss soil would provoke the Germans. Worse, the Swiss wish for us to leave. They want us off their soil.'

Until now this had been a hypothetical discussion among hundreds of alternative hypotheses about the war and what would happen to the Swiss.

If Germany no longer respected the neutrality of Holland and Belgium, why would it respect Swiss neutrality?

'They say we jeopardise their neutrality. By our very existence we invite German or Italian intervention in Swiss territory. They are in terror of the Germans. Or awe,' Avenol said, in a voice which showed confusion. Showed perhaps the very terror and awe that the Swiss felt.

He asked her to book a call to Léger at the Quai d'Orsay and to the places in France where she had arranged options on accommodation for such a contingency.

Late in the day, calls came through from the French government in Paris agreeing that the League might make its headquarters in France.

She ordered the staff to begin hiring lorries and buses to take the archives and staff, and to book seats on the trains.

A general meeting was called of Aghnides, Lester and the remaining Heads of Sections.

During the meeting more news came by messenger and was shared among those at the meeting. News came of a Swiss general mobilisation. German forces were manoeuvring on Lake Constance.

The message said that Swiss refugees were arriving from Basle and Zurich. The *bourse* had closed and there were queues at the banks.

It began to seem clear that the invasion of Switzerland was imminent.

Walters, Loveday and Wilson were excused from the meeting to allow them to arrange for the immediate evacuation of their families.

After they had left the meeting, Avenol abused them to the others. 'We French have more discipline. French families suffer their fate together.'

Those remaining were stunned by the outburst.

She thought it was aimed also at Lester and she saw him chafing under the remarks.

Surprisingly, no one, not even Lester, protested at Avenol's remarks. Respect for his office still restrained them publicly.

Those who remained seemed unwilling to leave the meeting, as if being together was something of an action in itself. It was also the place to be if one was to know what was happening.

Gerty knocked on the door, but this time did not have a telegraph or message to hand over. Instead she reported that resignations had begun coming in by internal messengers from junior staff throughout the Palais.

'We no longer have time to read and authorise these,' she said.

Messages came from the Permanent Delegates who wanted to know if accommodation was to be provided for them in France and were they too to be evacuated along with the Secretariat?

Avenol had no answer.

He looked at her. She said, 'We had trouble finding accommodation for the Secretariat. No accommodation was booked for the Permanent Delegates.'

The meeting was finally closed and everyone went about their business. What business? What business was worth doing now?

She went about preparing for the evacuation. Even if she were a watchdog in Avenol's office, she was still an officer with duties. She was working normally, albeit in circumstances she had never before experienced. Her day was still made up of documents to be drafted and typed, telephone calls to be booked and made, cables to be sent and petty cash to be accounted.

Next day, she told Avenol that the remaining staff wanted to have a wireless set in the Library so that they could follow events.

After half a day of consideration, he agreed.

There were rumblings of complaint among the staff about

being asked to move from relatively safe neutral ground in Switzerland to France, a belligerent country.

Meanwhile, Germany drove deeper into Belgium and Holland.

She was taking shorthand from Avenol when a special announcement was foreshadowed on the wireless set kept on during the day at low volume in his office.

'Turn up the volume,' he said, agitated.

They heard some of the 'Marseillaise' and then an urgent-voiced French military attaché read a message from the President of France stating that as of four o'clock that morning France had been invaded.

Avenol began to tap his fingers on the desk.

He asked her to leave him.

He then called her back and beckoned for her to sit. She sat while he booked calls to his relatives in France with the wireless in the background. She offered to do it for him but he seemed to need the activity.

As he booked the calls and as the calls came back, having been given official priority, he would mutter to her personal details about the particular relative to whom he was speaking, classifying them according to their *courage* or their *poltronnerie*.

All over Europe people were trying to telephone to warn, to calm, to reassure, to plan.

His hands were now shaking and his voice was strained as he gave out advice and listened to information.

From time to time there would be a knock on his door and she would answer it, shielding him from callers.

He then asked her to call Securitas and hire an additional personal bodyguard for him.

'It will be where the Germans are stopped,' he said. 'This is the moment of truth for the Germans. The French and the British armies will bring them to their demise.'

'I am sure they will be stopped.'

As they were both leaving that evening, he told her that during the night he would be contactable at an address across the Swiss border in France, which he gave to her. 'I fear that if I sleep at my home I could be kidnapped by German agents.'

He had made these arrangements himself. Was it a sign that he did not trust her?

She gave no hint that she thought the change of address was strange. She saw him as a man straining to be the administrator of a great international organisation which he had somehow both to protect and at the same time to also dismantle, while his own nation fought a war for its survival, and his friends and relatives were sucked into the war zone.

Avenol was a man bending in a gale.

She felt for him. She was perhaps swinging to his side. She did not want to be false to him. For all his stiff posing, she did not want to deceive him.

She damned the others for having put her in this position. She would've rather given herself whole-heartedly to the protecting of the organisation, to the whole question of what was to be done as the world fell apart.

And as a woman working with a man under huge and unique pressure, she could no longer deny that she was forming sentiments of attachment, the special bond of the office.

At first, when she'd changed offices, her daily close contact with Avenol had made her feel as if she were being unfaithful to Bartou. She had been changing partners in a vocational marriage.

Or, more accurately, becoming bigamous.

With Avenol, she was in part playing the office wife in a very faint and restrained way, but because of the peculiar plot which lay behind her presence there, she was also at the same time being unfaithful to him.

She could not now fully involve herself in the pleasures of

either role—that of the clever confidence trickster or that of virtuous subordinate which came from professional fidelity and from the special restrained intimacy created within such an office.

That night, she and Ambrose had a personal emergency meeting at the Molly.

'I am loading trucks tomorrow,' she told Ambrose.

'So the move is on.'

'I'll have to go with the others to France.'

'France will probably fall,' he said. 'The Americans are not coming to help. Bloodlines do not seem to be working.'

'Won't it be more like the first War—trenches and years of fighting?'

'That's not what they're saying. It's all *blitzkrieg*. Tanks. Rapid movement. No trenches.'

'The French have tanks.'

'They do.'

'And what should we do then?'

'What do you want to do?'

'Loveday and Walters are getting out, it seems. Wilson is going to England, and then probably back to New Zealand—if he can get a boat.'

'Heard from Robert? He might know what's happening.'

'Nothing.'

She didn't know where he was.

'Sit tight is perhaps the policy for the moment. What is your favourite saying these days—"We will wait upon the turn of events in hope of advantage"?'

'You will sit tight, with me? I think you should come to France.'

'Of course.'

'Call Bernard over—I must keep him up-to-date on events. Although he seems always to be ahead of us.'

She took her apron and work gloves to the office, plus others for those staff who might not have thought of them.

She helped select and then supervise the loading of archives into the lorries, glad of the physical work.

She sent off the first convoy.

Avenol visited the Permanent Delegates from the Latin American countries—who seemed to be about the only ones around—and asked them to take into their custody some of the other archives.

Towards lunchtime, she received a hand-written instruction from Avenol to stop the removal of the archives and to recall the lorries already dispatched.

The instruction said that the Swiss government had reversed its position. 'It now fears that for the League to leave will create panic among their citizens who will also try to flee.'

Ye gods, the Swiss government was in panic.

She went to his office for further clarification.

As she stood there in her apron and gloves, they both laughed at the Swiss reasoning and from a certain relief.

'Recall the archives from France. Unbook the accommodation,' he said.

He even placed a comradely hand briefly on her arm.

That evening at the Molly Club, she told Ambrose, Bernard and a couple of others that Avenol had inquired about whether she was kitted-out to walk from Switzerland back to Australia.

She told them that the Staff Committee had advised those who still remained not to buy new walking shoes. For walking of long distances, it was important to have shoes which were walked-in.

Ambrose said he would do it in high heels.

Bernard thought high heels would be appropriate for them all. 'Style above comfort, always,' he said.

She was also able to report that she'd heard from Robert, who'd moved to Arras along with his dreadful friends Potato Gray, Moorehead, Philby and some other reporters.

His card had said, 'We are drinking out the now not-so-phoney war.'

She had a new fellow feeling for him in the turbulent times but she felt no desire to be in his company.

She imagined that he and his newspaper friends would now be scooting down through France, perhaps to Amiens.

Avenol kept her about him, talking to her more, at times talking to himself in her presence, but wanting her to be there nonetheless.

To be around him.

There were moments when she told herself to be cautious, thinking with suspicion, 'He actually wants me to report back all he is saying—he knows I'm a traitor in this office and is now using me against the conspirators.'

She thought him cunning enough to do this.

But she relaxed from this suspicious position, deciding that his tone and manner were too naturally like that of a Secretary-General with his female personal aide.

That tone and manner invited certain things from her—comfort and support—and she felt inclined to respond. For all his difficulties of demeanour, or because of them, she was warming to him.

She moved into subaltern positions too well, too snugly.

And so, as Edith sat there in the dim office, waiting for him to find his words during dictation, she was astounded at times to feel this snugness through her body. As she looked at this French man with all his power and trappings, regardless of the future outcome for her and for them both—for all of them in the League—regardless of the appropriateness of this to her career, to her age, to her relationship with Ambrose—she felt through her body the glimmering possibility of a surrender of herself to this Secretary-General, to the power of his office.

The daily exchanges between them, the cups of coffee and biscuits, the occasional glass of port at the end of a day of long hours, the special tensions which they were sharing, the unusual hours which they spent together, all of it was entwining her spiritually with him.

When he would lock the office door behind them for security or reasons of privacy and they would be alone inside the locked room, her spirit would begin to melt towards him, giving up all resistance to him. It was a state which she hoped remained unknown to him.

However, however, however—whatever her body told her, in her mind she knew that it was not within the scheme of human alliances and the tempo of the times for her to allow this ever to happen.

What she felt was just a very distant bodily glimmering and to give in to it would be a debasement with untold consequences.

Even if she were now too senior—say it, Edith, yes, too old—to adopt that subaltern relationship there was, she saw, another, older version of that subaltern love.

Where two were equal in the importance of their talents and acumen but where those talents and acumen were not identical and where, in this twosome, one was required professionally to subordinate for reasons of appointment or temperament or sex, there was for her as a woman, a dreadful pull towards surrender.

And so it had been with Bartou—daily she had silently offered herself to him, knowing that it would not happen but still, regardless, making the silent offering. And he had probably used his discipline of self to hold her at proper distance until he had, in the last year or so, grown old and ailing, had weakened, and she had become his guardian. He had become dependent on her opinions, unable himself to lead or contribute. And the risk of any physical surrender had passed and the silent offering had ceased.

In New York with Gerig and Sweetser, she'd tasted a new experience—the wielding of power, which showed her that she had the inherent will and confidence to take the position of power. Did it follow that if she ever took power, would she then have offered to her this special—limitless?—devotion from a subordinate?

Frances, her stenographer in New York, drifted across her mind as someone who might have developed into a devoted assistant, if time had permitted.

With Avenol she'd partly gone back in time to feeling younger because of the false reduction of her status and the devotion was there as well—sometimes during the day or in bed at night, she almost ached to be able to perform, totally, all that devotion could be asked.

But Avenol, too, would never ask more than he was at present taking.

And, for the good of her soul, she was glad of that.

Those in the conspiracy were having difficulty in finding a way to act.

Aghnides believed that Geneva could be the rallying point for Europe and the whole world against the Nazis.

He saw a role for the League as a global moral spokesman.

She was unconvinced.

She did however want to stand up to the Nazis somehow. Other than running up a silly flag.

She held to the position that for the League to flee was to invite all to run.

'Surely, though, you only stand where you can fight?' Bartou asked.

'Can't we fight here? Not militarily but, well, morally, diplomatically?'

'By being taken prisoner?!'

'By being here and yes, even by being taken prisoner. The Nazis may be uncertain of how to act towards us. And we would be a very special kind of prisoner and would be diplomatically—a symbol,' she said.

She felt she was now required to buck them up. She had to buck up Avenol during the day and then turn her hand to keeping up the spirits of her co-conspirators, Bartou especially.

'The Germans have shown precious little uncertainty.'

'When the idea of leaving Geneva comes up, Avenol has fallen back on the legality of Article VII which says that the seat of the League shall be Geneva until Council decides otherwise,' she said.

'If there is ever going to be another Council meeting,' Aghnides said.

'The Supervisory Commission is supposed to take control. But even they can't get together now. It's physically impossible to hold a meeting. In reality, Avenol has all power. There is no controlling instrument any longer. He is virtual dictator of the League,' Edith pointed out.

'I would think though that we must keep the nucleus of the League functioning—here where we are, in the midst of it—and perhaps initiate a cease-fire. Or negotiate the peace settlement,' Lester said.

Having removed his family, Lester was now prepared to stay and fight.

He had risen to the challenge.

The Fall of Paris

June 1940

Edith had never seen such an agonised identification between the very being of a human and the nation state as she saw in Avenol on the day that Paris fell to the Germans.

He wept openly in his office.

He could not control his demeanour nor find coherence of speech before his staff.

He was a man broken apart.

Edith suggested to him that they both stay by the wireless in his office and suspend meetings and clerical work of any consequence and he agreed.

Some of the French staff were permitted to use the office telephones to seek news of relatives, and anyone who wished was allowed to gather in the Library to listen to the broadcasts.

There in the office alone with Avenol, she poured him a cognac but did not pour one for herself.

The office was dim. He had taken to closing the curtains which she usually opened in the morning. It was as if he were hiding.

She wondered how Jeanne was faring. She wanted to call her but felt she should not do it right then.

He chose to sit on his settee and she sat in his comfortable
Leleu armchair, a seating arrangement which normally would
be reversed, but he was in that condition where he was
unaware of where he sat, alternately needing to stand and
walk about and then to sit.

They listened to the news coming in over the French radio
broadcast spoken by the announcer in a voice artificially
raised to an urgent pitch by patriotism.

It became clear by Avenol's attempts to ring out that although
the lines were down here and there and overloaded, they were
not totally disrupted, and telephone calls came to him from his
friends and relatives in Paris. Avenol spoke in short urgent
sentences as if time on the 'phone line was precious.

A friend of Avenol in the French government called in and
said that the government had fled to Bordeaux.

He called Vera a number of times, talking in a personal
code to her which Edith was able to decipher as being about
arrangements to flee and about money matters.

When the telephone bell rang she would answer and
announce the caller and he would come to the desk to take
the message or not as he chose.

They heard on the wireless that Churchill had offered
amalgamation of Britain and France—had offered common
citizenship in an effort to bolster morale. The French would
be English and the English would be French.

Avenol was on the telephone again to someone in Paris.
'The army has almost collapsed,' he called to her, relaying the
information he was receiving.

He continued to relay to her the news from Paris over his
shoulder. 'The roads are jammed with refugees from Belgium
and the north, wounded soldiers are mingled in with them—
officers' cars are forcing their way through those fleeing, for
the sake of Jesus!—cannons have been left by the roadside,
motorcycles smashed and abandoned ... Is the army running?
Some parts? Mother of God.'

Yet French radio was still talking of a counterattack. The solemn, patriotic voice of the announcer said, 'The Germans have not yet stood the final test. We are the old opponent of the Marne, the old opponent of Verdun. General Weygand brings back to us the genius of Foch.'

The famous fort at Verdun had fallen days earlier.

The Germans had bypassed the Maginot line which was still fully manned, the troops on the line now cut off.

Only the young cadets at the Cavalry School at Saumur still held out.

'The cadets of Saumur hold out!' he said, tears in his eyes. Edith also cried as she saw in her mind the boys fighting with their training guns, rallying to the Tricolour.

At other times, Avenol was oblivious of her presence in his office, sometimes speaking to himself, declaiming and gesturing, and then at other times staring at her in bewilderment at the situation, as if, perhaps, he expected her to take some action, to suggest a policy.

She worked to control her weeping and found herself coolly observant, as she sat watching him swing between crying and anger.

The telephone calls then stopped.

The announcer said that German units were on the outskirts of Paris and that resistance had collapsed.

The wireless began to play sombre music. Avenol finally brought his agitation under control and seated himself at his desk, and arranged some papers which were on the desk.

'The British stink in the nostrils of the world,' he said. 'They abandoned France at Dunkirk.'

He requested that she bring Aghnides to his office, but not Lester.

She went to Aghnides' office and found him grim-faced, listening to the wireless.

'Avenol wants you.'

'How is he?'

'He was distraught. He's now in a rage.'

They said little else as they walked back to Avenol's office. She poured Aghnides a cognac.

When the two men were seated, she did not ask for permission to stay, but simply sat herself on the settee.

'That's it. It is done,' Avenol said to Aghnides.

'What is done, Joseph?' said Aghnides.

'That which England has for three hundred years prevented France from achieving—leadership on the continent of Europe—Hitler has now achieved.'

'All is not over,' Aghnides said feebly and then found his stronger, official Under Secretary's voice. 'The fall of Paris is not only a French disaster,' he said, 'the fall of Paris is a disaster for civilisation. I heard today from Athens by long-distance telephone that people there are weeping in the streets for the fall of Paris. But the war is not finished.'

The office sat in silence, Avenol staring at the wireless which was calling for calm and continuing to play sombre music.

To relieve the silence, Aghnides went on to say that people were crying in the corridors of the Palais—all nationalities were weeping. They were weeping in the streets and stores of Geneva. 'For all people, Paris is the capital of the civilised world.'

'The crying matters for nothing. The war is finished, Thanassis,' Avenol said, banging the table.

He kept banging the table with his hand but without much force.

Edith's heart went out to him and she felt she should go over and calm him. She had a flash of Sir Eric and his despair at the time of his first great defeat as Secretary-General when, on the first try, the Assembly had failed to admit Germany back in '26.

She had shaved Sir Eric in the office as a way of calming him and giving him back his self-control. She wouldn't be shaving Avenol.

'England will last fifteen days and then the war will be finished. Italy will simply pick up the spoils. She will destroy us from the south.'

She wondered how he'd arrived at the figure fifteen.

'Perhaps,' said Aghnides, 'but then there is the United States.'

'The United States stays clear of danger. Roosevelt has declared that the United States will never enter the war. Their Congress will never enter the war.'

'And there is Russia,' Aghnides said, desperation slipping back into his voice.

Avenol looked at him with disgust. 'The Russo-German Non-aggression Pact took care of Russia. You know that. The war is finished. Accept it.'

She could only watch the force of what Avenol said crash against the feeble counter-arguments put up by Aghnides. And against her own speechless spirit. Her heart was beating and the voice in her head kept saying, 'Remain calm, be calm.'

She realised that with France gone and with Italy in the war on Germany's side, neutral Switzerland was now isolated and surrounded.

'The Russians may break the Pact,' Aghnides said.

Even she didn't believe that.

Avenol didn't bother to reply.

'The Americans will be in for the spoils,' Avenol said. 'And the Russians. Or perhaps the Americans will join with the Germans against Russia? Who knows? That is what will happen, you'll see—the Americans will now come in with the Germans and attack Russia.'

She and Aghnides stared at him, the ooze of his defeat seeping over them. It seemed there in that dim office that Avenol was perhaps tragically right.

Now and then there would be a government announcement on the wireless. Sometimes a message to mayors, sometimes to army units, sometimes to the people at large. At the sound of an official announcement, they would cease talking and listen; the music and the announcements were the sounds of a collapsing army and behind that, a collapsing nation.

A cable was brought in to the office by messenger. It was from Arthur Sweetser in Washington.

He looked at the cable. 'Sweetser ...' Avenol made a dismissive noise. 'The Americans ...'

He held it out to Edith and asked her to read it out.

She tried to stop her voice breaking as she read the message from dear old Arthur, which she knew was in part addressed to her, or at least to the true blue League group. 'I cannot let this day pass without just this briefest word about the tragedy facing Paris. American opinion is more deeply stirred than I have ever known it, for America is also frightened. People are living by the radio, praying for time. Armed we now certainly shall be ...'

She tried to hide her emotion by saying, 'At least the Trans-Atlantic cable line to America is still open.'

Avenol left his desk and paced about the room. 'Sweetser always sees hope,' Avenol said, although he too was trying to hide his emotions. 'He is the travelling salesman of hope. Safe and sound in the States. I think I will also go to the United States. I think I have a role there.'

She and Aghnides glanced at each other with puzzlement. Did Avenol see himself fleeing to America?

Avenol railed on, his mathematical mind now organising the news. 'The Germans have destroyed two great European armies. Gobbled up four smaller armies, and inflicted an immense loss on the English army. Four empires have dissolved overnight—the Belgian, the French, the Dutch and the British. The French and British together controlled over half the landmass of the world. All lost. We wouldn't let Germany have back one colony after the last war. Not one colony. Now they have every reason to punish us.'

The British Empire is not lost, Edith said silently. They were still there and they would fight.

Or would the collapse of Britain mean that the Empire too was out of the war?

She had never contemplated such a thing.

She felt that she might now be witnessing the character of Avenol which had, in part, been concealed, but which her fellow conspirators had suspected. She thought he would now show his true colours.

Or maybe he would rally?

'Hitler did it in twelve weeks. Twelve weeks. And it is over. Germany has won,' Avenol said, looking to her as if again remembering her presence, as if anticipating opposition, or looking to her for something else ... feminine solace? Her affirmation?

She offered no reaction.

Aghnides said in a desperate, tired and discouraged voice, 'We have a word in Greek—that word is *hubris*.'

Avenol did not look at him, but shrugged to show he knew the word.

'It means that those who grow mighty with pride and power the gods will strike down. One day Hitler will be struck down.'

'How?!' Avenol shouted. 'How?!' The tone of his question said that he would not believe any reply which challenged this.

'I do not know how. I know it's in the nature of things that he must eventually fall.'

'In two hundred years?!' said Avenol. 'A moment in history has occurred. The democracies have failed. Their role in history is finished. Even if the English hold out they will still have lost the war.'

She found no comfort in Aghnides' hopeless words.

Avenol's pacing seemed to change. He was almost marching about the office. 'A new order of things is appearing. I feel it. I sense it. History as we knew it is finished. Something very serious has changed in the nature of things.'

She felt that she was watching a man crossing a line in his mind, finding his way to a massive leap.

He paused, staring out the window as if staring across Europe. 'It is, perhaps, time that we began to think in a new way. To see how it is that we should now bring ourselves to the service of a new world. A world reorganised on new foundations.'

She listened with cold clarity to Avenol's words.

She was strangely relieved to hear them. They freed her, at last, from any bond she had formed with him. At last, she could be a true enemy. At last, the point of the watchdog group was confirmed. Avenol had in half an hour gone from a state of collapse to an obsessive surrender, and then to seeing himself allied with the victor.

He was finding himself a role in Hitler's New Order.

'Hitler will fail,' Aghnides said again, and again it lacked conviction.

Avenol paid no heed to this reply but went over to Aghnides and put a hand on his shoulder, saying, 'My dear Thanassis, it is all over. Our duty now is to work to achieve unity in Europe. The people will want order now. We must help bring order. England is finished on the Continent. The British officials must now leave the Secretariat. I believe in following the direction of history's arrow.'

Again, Edith felt a surge of release from anything to do with Avenol.

She only needed the word and she would join any rebellion against him. She herself would strike him down.

'Surely you will keep McKinnon-Wood on as legal counsellor?' she said, unable to remain silent, freed from any sense of her proper place. McKinnon-Wood was the legal conscience of the League.

'No.'

'You can't just single the British out and send them away,' Aghnides said.

Avenol smiled, a smile without pleasure or humanity. 'I won't have to send them away. They will go, you watch—they will run like rabbits.'

Aghnides shook his head.

'Charron would make a good treasurer,' Avenol said, his mind now reshuffling the staff to meet the new situation. 'You know, Hitler is not really against the League. He admired our work in the Saar.'

This was why she was there in her conspiratorial role—she was there to hear this.

She was there to bear witness.

If Aghnides had come to them with this story she might not have believed it. And perhaps not one of them would have believed each other's version. They would've suspected Lester's version. She was the key witness to what was happening there in the office.

Aghnides stared at him for a few seconds, looked at her to perhaps confirm to himself that there had been a witness, and then left the office without saying a word.

It was not wholly a gesture of disgust, it was also a gesture of frustration.

Aghnides was a man who desperately needed to have answers, to always be armed with arguments, but in this moment of crisis he had failed to convince even himself—had found himself with no arguments against the enemy.

She sat there staring at Avenol who was now making notes to himself.

She too then left.

He appeared not to notice.

At the door, she heard him go back on to the telephone, this time to the head of the League couriers ordering him to retrieve his personal trunks from his secret safe residence in France. '*Immédiatement!*'

He had become another sort of man, a man taking firm command of a detailed vagueness, a man ordering the details for want of a larger strategy.

In the outer office she made a quick shorthand note of what Avenol had said and then collected her personal things from her desk drawer. There was no work to be done today.

Or ever again in that office.

The conspiracy was over. They would now all declare themselves as Avenol had declared himself.

She nodded at the bored bodyguard from Securitas sitting on a chair outside the office. He had an automatic pistol in a hip holster.

On her way out of the building, she looked into Lester's office. 'You were all correct about Avenol.'

'I've just heard from Aghnides.'

'Something has to be done fairly quickly.'

He said, 'A meeting tonight, usual time, usual place.'

'I think I'll go now.'

'Go home.'

'I'll go first to Ambrose's office and then home.'

'Fine.'

As she went down the corridor people stopped her and asked what she knew. She told Giraud and one or two others whom she could trust and hurried on.

She looked in on Jeanne who was weeping.

'The Americans will come into the war,' she said to Jeanne, for want of anything to say. 'And the British Empire is still fighting.'

'Are you going to leave Geneva?' Jeanne asked.

'No. Are you?'

She said she didn't know what to do.

'Many are leaving. Perhaps you should go to your family?'

'I hear everyone is fleeing Paris.'

'Go to the South.'

'I think I'll just stay here.'

'Good, stay.'

They hugged. She wanted to give more comfort to Jeanne than she knew how to give. She held to the hug but even that had to finish.

They let go and wiped their tears. 'I'm going to see Ambrose. We'll all have dinner tomorrow?'

'Yes. Please.'

She left Jeanne.

She couldn't find a car with a driver—probably the drivers were in the Library listening to the wireless—so she decided to walk to Ambrose's office at the old Palais Woodrow Wilson.

Some people were gathering around the gates of the Palais des Nations, as if expecting an announcement to be made from the League.

The streets seemed full of people—as if everyone needed to be with other people—and, for Geneva, there seemed to be much more clustering together. It seemed that people were lingering in the streets and around the shop doors, not wishing to go home.

Strangers appeared to be talking with strangers.

She reached the old Palais Woodrow Wilson, the building she most loved in the whole world. True, the new Palais was her temple, but this shabby building was her spiritual birthplace where she had arrived as a fresh young woman to a fresh young organisation, formed to save the world.

It was the old homestead.

Ambrose was in the corridor speaking to Dot Arnold from the Women's Peace and Disarmament Committee, which had an office down the hall from his.

They were talking about the latest BBC broadcast on shortwave and piecing together what they had gleaned despite the interference of German jamming.

She and Dot kissed and hugged.

Ambrose went to get his coat. She wanted to go with

Ambrose but felt she had to stay to comfort Dot, whom she hadn't seen for a while.

'How's it all been, Dot?'

'Correspondence has just stopped dead,' Dot said. 'I'm afraid we will have to close up shop. Not one letter in over two weeks. I thought it was the international mail but it's just that everyone's simply given up writing or answering letters.'

'Have you had any interesting information at all?'

'The last private thing I heard was that peace talks would begin in September.'

'Peace talks?'

'To bring calm and order to the Continent.'

'Who said? And isn't that a trifle defeatist?'

Dot became wet-eyed and shrugged. 'We don't want more bloodshed. The Committee is trying to call peace talks.'

'Churchill won't be talking peace with Hitler,' Edith said strongly, speaking for Churchill.

'The last I heard is that there are some in the Commons and in the Lords who want to make peace.'

Edith didn't want to hear this sort of talk and changed the subject by asking after some of their mutual acquaintances.

'The last I heard was that Mary is still a pacifist. But I'm not. Not any more. All that we have which is of any value would be swept away under the Nazis. All I am saying is, I think there should be peace made with the Germans for now. That's all.'

'Never.'

'You are so strong, Edith.'

'Not really. Just desperate.'

'Miss Nobs wants to wire Madame Ciano and ask her to approach Mussolini and ask him to withdraw from the war. Do you think it's of any use?'

'None.'

'Nor do I. When I took this job I promised myself two

things: that I wouldn't quarrel with anyone and that I wouldn't compromise the Committee by foolish action.'

'You haven't, Dot.'

'But Miss Bauer wants me to send a telegram to America urging them to participate in the war but I am not clear whether to send it directly to President Roosevelt or to our affiliated organisations, asking them to bring pressure on the President. What do you think?'

'Do nothing.'

'That's Mrs Morgan's position and she is working to have both ideas quashed by the executive.'

That wasn't right. Anything could help. 'No—send it. Who knows what will tip the balance?'

'You think so?'

'I should think it best to go home, Dot—to England.'

'I can't really because we have an emergency meeting in June—Miss Bauer's doing again. I suppose as long as Mrs Morgan's still here everything is under control. She's a pillar of commonsense.'

'Go home, Dot.'

'I still believe in an evolutionary future.'

'Good. Don't lose your nerve, Dot.'

'What's happening at the League?'

Edith felt she couldn't show her feeling of hopelessness. 'We will rally around.'

She couldn't say that the League too was disintegrating. The Assembly and the Council had failed, and now the Secretariat was disintegrating.

She joked. 'We have *des masques gaz* and we have *l'abris*, Dot. What else do we need?'

Dot began picking wool balls from her cardigan, a lost English idealist in a crumbling Geneva. Her office gone silent. Her work petered out. Her pacifism renounced.

She touched Dot's arm. 'I must go, Dot. Ambrose will be waiting.'

'Go?' Dot was apprehensive.

She feared that Dot would want to stay with Ambrose and her. That wouldn't work. She had to stop herself inviting Dot to join them.

She hugged Dot again. 'We'll keep in touch.'

'Please do.'

'You know the gathering point for the English?'

'Yes. I've pinned it on the office wall.'

'It might be best to go there now. See what the next move is.'

'Yes.'

Dot looked at her watch as if unsure whether to close the office early or not.

Dot, usually so capable, was now a beached dolphin.

She couldn't look after Dot. 'Go, Dot. Go now to the gathering point. Take your haversack and gas mask.'

'I think I shall.'

Edith walked to Ambrose's office. Looking back, she saw that Dot was still standing in the corridor.

Oh dear.

Nothing to be done.

She entered Ambrose's wretched little office.

Ambrose had the two emergency haversacks and the gas masks ready on his desk.

'Planning a walking tour?' she asked, going to him and kissing him.

'I thought Australia via India. I got some tablets today to keep us awake. Everyone says we should also have our Pervitin tablets. And I have a bottle of cognac.'

'Morphine?'

'I have morphine.'

'Who will work the needle?'

'We will have to ask someone to assist when the need arises.'

'I have never given a needle. I daresay I could learn. Junior Red Cross should've taught us that.'

'Heard on the BBC that about three million people have fled Paris. The Germans found Paris closed up and deserted. The Parisians have gone—on bikes, pushing baby carriages, horse-drawn carts. Anything that moves. Three million of them. Germans found there were no fresh baguettes.'

As they locked up and walked out of the Palais Wilson, carrying their haversacks and gas masks, she described Avenol's collapse and his talk of surrendering the League.

'He could very well give the League to the Nazis,' Ambrose said. 'How remarkable. How unexpected it always is. Always.'

'Giraud said that Avenol is discovering Hitler's virtues even before a surrender is signed.'

'The war's not over. My contacts at Buckingham Palace tell me that the Queen does not intend to evacuate and is learning to fire a pistol.'

'*Your contacts at the Palace?*'

'Well, my *one* contact. I thought that I might be able to get one call out before it all went dead and decided that it might be useful to know exactly what the King was doing. You know, as a way of knowing what to do next. So I called my one friend at the Palace and was told the Queen is learning to shoot.'

'We must pack my pistol—if I can find it. You should have offered to be the Queen's instructor.'

'We must clean that pistol of yours. And find some more ammunition. Do you recall how much ammunition you have?'

She was surprised by the seriousness with which he took the pistol matter.

'No, I don't.'

'I wonder where we could get another pistol?'

'Didn't you say that pistols were being sold at the Molly?'

'Not the only thing sold at the Molly—and yes, I did. I might follow that up.'

'Do we really need an arsenal?'

'Who knows? In a life-threatening situation, the rule is use all the violence you can as quickly as you can.'

'There is a meeting tonight of the conspirators.'

'You plan a *coup d'état?*'

'We will have to remove Avenol from office, surely?'

'And how, pray, will you do that?'

She realised that she didn't know how they would remove him. 'Haul him out into the *Cour d'Honneur* and shoot him.' She frowned. 'I don't really know.'

'Must be something in the standing orders about fitness for office.'

'Must be. Will have to study it. He has to go.'

'Drinks?'

'Quite right. When in doubt—drinks.'

They went to the Hôtel Richemond for drinks. They found that they were alone in the lounge. No staff were about. A wireless set could be heard coming from an office.

From the public telephone cabin, she rang Lester and told him where she was, while Ambrose went in search of a drink.

When she came back, Ambrose was opening a bottle of champagne on the terrace.

He said, 'The Swiss franc had fallen so far that there was no reason not to buy the best champagne. And every bottle we drink is one less left for the Boche.'

Perhaps this was a time to drink champagne. Maybe the disaster of the day would give champagne back its zing for her.

Ambrose toasted, 'To dear fallen France and to dear fallen Paris.' His eyes were moist. He pulled himself together, 'And to the fallen franc. And to a fallen League.'

'No,' she said, 'not to a fallen League. Not yet. To a fallen Secretary-General—without a doubt. It is time for us to say "In the name of God, Avenol, go".'

Their glasses touched and they drank, saying 'In the name of God, Avenol, go.'

To her, the sound of the glasses touching reminded her of a pistol breech closing on a bullet.

'When we drink champagne, we must always remember that we drink the tears of the world,' Ambrose said.

'On this day, we surely do.'

They drank their first mouthful silently, looking into each other's eyes, and she felt unspecified frightened meanings in their glance. She felt their binding dependence which was now beginning to grip them like iron.

They were alone together in a disintegrating world.

She had never felt so bound to another person.

He spoke first. 'London cabled me to pack it in,' he said. 'My salary expires at the end of the month. Of course, I wish to stay. But no funds in the old bank. Suppose I could work at the Molly.'

'As a cigarette girl?'

'Mistress of the *corps de ballet*,' Ambrose said.

She looked at him and had a thought. 'Would you like to work for me?'

'How so?'

'As a kind of private secretary. You know the League has no funds to employ anyone. I think that I will need *fortifying*. And I have some private schemes. There will be things to do. You will be needed.'

'Schemes?'

'I want to find out about the opposition in Germany, if any. We can help refugees. All sorts of things apart from League business.'

She thought about it while they watched the sparrows play among their drinks, searching for biscuit crumbs on the terrace.

'You aren't thinking of leaving then?'

'No. And I want to be double my size,' she said. That was it. 'I want to double the size of my army. I want to be twice as strong. So I'm recruiting you.'

Ambrose stared at her. 'Edith Campbell Berry—sorry: Edith Berry—you are remarkable. You really intend to stay?'

'If Switzerland holds out, I think the League will last. As you know, some of us are going to Princeton although Avenol thinks this an American plot to steal the best parts of the League. Treasury's going to London. But I'm sure some of us will stay here to man the fort. Make the peace.'

'Would you be a hard taskmaster?' Ambrose asked.

'Oh, very hard. As hard as you like.'

They smiled at each other.

'You accept, then, my offer of a position on my personal staff?'

'I see no other job offers on the horizon. One proviso.'

'Yes?'

'If Bernard offers me Mistress of the *corps de ballet*, may I accept that instead?'

'How could I stand in the way of an artistic career.'

He reached over to her. 'I really require no salary. Only bed and board.'

'There has to be a salary, otherwise I can't boss you about. I shall need a private office for our informal operations.'

'I suppose I could rent the office I'm in.'

'I want you out of that wretched office. You need something more your size.'

He stared at the bubbles rising in his champagne glass, his finger running around the rim of the glass.

He then looked up at her. 'We've travelled far since we met on that train to Geneva.'

'We have, dear Ambrose, we have.'

She felt herself begin to weep again.

'Adding to the tears of the world?' he asked, placing his arm around her shoulder.

'Just twenty or so.'

She kept crying.

'God counts the tears of women.'

His words caused her to cry harder. 'I'd hoped he might be able to do more than just count them,' she said, through the tears. 'And how come you know so much about tears? Or God?'

Her tears changed to a small, light laughter, 'Dot ...' she sniffed, wiping her nose, '... Dot still believes in an evolutionary future.'

'That's reassuring.'

She managed a giggle and they then smiled deeply at each other, gripping each other's hands.

Coils

Again the conspirators gathered, this time in a bedroom of the Hôtel de la Paix. This time Ambrose was present at her request.

Coffee and *galettes* arrived up from the hotel kitchen as she'd ordered but there was also a bottle of whisky and glasses on the sideboard, Irish whisky which she hadn't ordered. Edith supposed the whisky was Sean Lester's contribution.

Again the meeting began with war talk.

Since their last meeting on the day of the Fall of Paris, Germany had divided France into two parts and allowed the French the pretence of an independent government based at the town of Vichy.

Everyone wanted to believe that some of the French spirit and at least a token government had survived the German invasion. But in another part of their heads, everyone knew that, as an independent government, it was a farce.

For a start, the French government at Vichy had refused to hand over the French fleet to the British.

To prevent the fleet falling into German hands, the British had yesterday, without warning, bombed it at Oran and Mers-el-Kebir and hundreds of French sailors had died.

There could be no pretence now that France was a potential ally, except for remnants of its army which had ended up in England after Dunkirk and which remained in the unoccupied French colonies.

The bombing of the fleet had shaken the world. Churchill had turned on France. Ally had turned on ally.

The United States was still resolute that it would not join in the war.

In fact, some said that because the United States had such sentimental attachments to the French, the British bombing might have alienated them even further from coming to the help of the British Empire.

And now Roosevelt had recognised the Vichy government.

The Soviet Union had congratulated Hitler on his capture of Paris.

Avenol was still occupying the office of the Secretary-General but the Secretariat—what was left of it—was reporting to Lester, behind Avenol's back.

Things were grim.

Edith noticed that much smoking was being done.

'Not smoking, Edith?'

'Having mastered the art, Sean, I have now abandoned it. Had a frightful cough from it.'

That wasn't true. She'd used the cough reason to avoid stating the truth. She'd stopped because she felt it was not something a woman in her position should do. She supposed that this sort of thinking let the suffragette side down because smoking was seen by Florence and her bolshie crowd as being a rather progressive thing to do. As well as being *très chic.*

But Florence had gone home to Canada and most of her crowd had also dispersed.

Smoking did not seem quite right. Not in public anyhow. Maybe she was getting old.

It wasn't as if she had always maintained a high standard of decorum in other areas of her life. Still, one didn't have to have *every* vice, and cigarette smoking was one vice she felt she could drop.

And she didn't want to give out the suggestion that her smoking showed she had a case of nerves.

The way people were smoking these days around the place gave the impression of near panic.

After the war gossip, Lester said he would like to read a letter he received from Sweetser, 'If that's agreeable to all? It's typical Sweetser prose.'

They all nodded. Lester read from the letter, ' "So at 12.40 p.m., we said goodbye to Geneva which had been our home for twenty rich years. We passed out of the Rigot courtyard, down past the League buildings and the International Tennis Club, down by the Labor Office and off onto the Lausanne road. Never, as long as I live will I forget that ride. Switzerland at its most perfect season. The mountains stood out firm and strong on the horizon, their tops still capped with a glistening white snow; the lake was its deepest and richest blue; the fruit-trees were in their fullest bloom all about; the manifold little gardens were just springing out of the ground. Nature was giving everything she had to give ..." '

They were chuckling. Ambrose said, 'Indeed, Sweetser at his purple prose best.'

Lester, regardless of the joking, seemed quite moved by it, and read on, ' "Yet war was all about us, even here in Switzerland. Not once, or twice or thrice were we stopped by the military on this beautiful ride, but no less than ten times. First we would be slowed by a warning sentinel, with machine guns set on either side of the road, then a guard would look at our papers, another would examine the baggage for chance guns or munitions. It was done very efficiently and thoroughly with grim determination but democratic good humour. The country teemed with soldiers and they were a fine upstanding manly group of people ..." '

Lester looked up just as Ambrose and she glanced at each other and suppressed giggles.

Lester ignored them like a tired schoolteacher. 'Sweetser now says something here which we, the League, should take steps to look after. He points out that twelve thousand Spanish Republicans who fled Spain after the civil war and were housed in France under our auspices ...' Lester looked up. 'Edith, you had something to do with that—you went down to Spain with the Commission in '38?'

'I did.'

And she had had a strange, short fling down there with an anarchist.

My, my. What *had* she been doing!?

'Sweetser says that we have the personal records of these Republicans with us here in Geneva. Is that correct?'

'It is. They're in the Registry basement.'

'Sweetser points out that the Germans might want to get their hands on those—if the Germans ever overran Switzerland. We may have to ship them out or even destroy them. Could you look into that, Edith?'

She nodded. 'You think we should burn them?'

'Might be best.'

'Or we could bury them.'

'Whatever's best. You look after it. I'll read on. He says that the ship from Genoa was nightmarish, overcrowded, and those on board gathered around the radio to listen to the BBC every night. He says that the journalist Dorothy Thompson was on board and was receiving radio telephone calls from New York. Her assessment of the situation was that it was hopeless and that Germany would soon be in total command of Europe. Sweetser said that those on board thought it wouldn't be long before England went under. He goes on. Rather depressing ...'

'He seems to have been infected with defeatism,' Bartou said.

Bartou was losing heart.

'Not Sweetser,' said Lester. 'Just gloom.'

'If not defeatism, perhaps American isolationism,' Bartou said, with some animosity.

'You probably don't know this, but Sweetser offered to accept a forty percent reduction in his salary if Avenol would allow him to stay on—did you know that?' Lester said, looking around.

'Remarkable,' said Aghnides.

'He didn't even get a reply. Avenol just wanted him out.'

'It's true that he brought in more money to the League than any single individual in its history—millions,' Bartou said. 'He even got the money to buy La Pelouse where Avenol sits brooding and plotting every night with his mistress.'

'I've some other news,' Lester said. 'The Registrar, the President and ten officials of the International Court have arrived in Geneva from The Hague.'

'At least they got here,' Aghnides said.

'They used the diplomatic immunity of their League papers, which seems to have been honoured by the Germans. Which is interesting.'

Lester reported that Avenol had offered him unlimited leave back home in Ireland in an effort to get rid of him from the office. 'The idea of fishing my way through the war was tempting. It shows you what sort of man he is: first he tries to freeze me out by ignoring me; then he tries to get me to resign; then he tries to bribe me to leave with his indefinite vacation offer.'

Despite his bravado, she could tell that Lester was rattled.

Everyone was a bit rattled.

Aghnides said that Avenol thought it possible that the Germans might parachute into the Palais and make it a fortress. He said that Avenol had asked him to make contact with Wolfgang Krauel, the German Consul-General in Geneva. 'I think that further confirms all we have feared.'

'He must think you're still on his side,' Lester said.

'He calls me in. We never talk politics. And of course I haven't acted on his instruction.'

'Dear God,' Lester said with disgust. 'I'm surprised he hasn't hoisted the swastika as a flag of welcome.'

Lester pulled himself together and addressed himself to Ambrose, perhaps showing some deference to Ambrose's Foreign Office background and the informal connections he still had with it. 'Let's hear your summation, Westwood—would you object to us using first names?'

'By all means—first names are fine with me. You would like me to start?'

'If you don't mind—will give us all a fresh point of view.'

'I hope I don't add to the gloom of Sweetser's letter. We have to accept that France is well and truly out of the war. It's just the British and the Empire now that are still fighting. As for the League, there are the Scandinavians, the South Americans and the Empire left as countries still on the membership list—still in the club, as it were. The Scandinavians are neutral, so they're shy of the war. The South Americans—well, as Sweetser used to say, in his colourful American way, "They don't have a dog in this fight."'

There were chuckles.

'Quite so,' Lester said. 'And the Irish remain neutral. I suppose we don't have a dog in the fight either.'

'And Greece,' said Aghnides.

'Sorry, Ambrose—please continue. Afraid our discussions here are often a bit disorderly,' Lester said.

Ambrose went on, 'The League, I'm afraid, doesn't quite enter anyone's picture. It could, of course, at a later time, enter the picture. Could be that the League will make the peace and so forth.'

Lester turned to the others. 'Any disagreement with that?'

Bartou had grown red and seemed angry. 'I see the neutrals including Switzerland playing a part in bringing a cessation to hostilities. You discount the neutrals too quickly.'

'If Germany lets you remain neutral,' Ambrose said. 'They didn't let Belgium and Holland remain neutral.'

'Switzerland can defend itself against any invader.'

Edith was surprised to hear Bartou letting his patriotism express itself. It was the first time he'd ever shown it. Nerves. And age.

'I'm not saying that it couldn't, Auguste,' Ambrose said. 'I am saying that Switzerland and the other neutrals may not have much time to think about the League. Or be able to do anything with it.'

'Disagree,' said Bartou irritatedly, trying to find his composure.

Lester tried to calm the jittery atmosphere, saying, 'Let's stay calm. Let's put national allegiances aside as best we can.'

'You don't see your posturing as a mask for being on the British side?' Bartou shot back. 'National allegiance is a bit like bad breath—everyone can smell other people's bad breath but not their own.'

They laughed.

It dispelled the jitters a little.

Lester said, 'How are we to get rid of Avenol before he makes some sort of contact with the Germans? He's sacking Jews. Two poor devils have gone from Opium Section. I tried to countermand it but I'm afraid Avenol still holds the office.'

Edith spoke up, impatient with Lester's rambling from the point. 'It's time for us to put our efforts into holding the fort at the League—above the conflict, as it were.'

'The peace effort or the war effort?' said Bartou, calmer now. 'Isn't that the choice most are making?'

'I think we are all agreed about who we wish to have win,' Lester said, glancing around. 'Even if we should as international civil servants try to stand aside, as it were, from the war.'

All nodded.

'I can't see how that's possible—to stand above the conflict,' Bartou said.

Edith spoke up, 'I think there can be a happy overlap of positions.'

They all looked to her.

'How so?' said Lester.

'As I see it, the British—all those who want to defeat Germany and its allies—need something to fight *for*.'

'You mean war aims?' Lester asked.

'That's what I mean, precisely. The League might be one of the things people would consider fighting for ... well, a bright, new and better League. We might see ourselves as a war aim. Ostensibly, this should be the preferred outcome whatever side wins, but we know that only one side would consider it truly admirable.'

There was an odd silence.

'As I understand it from the dribbles I get from home,' Ambrose said, 'there is precious little time at present to think about After the War. It's all that Churchill can do to keep fighting on.'

'That gives us a job to do. We should communicate to Churchill our thinking on life after the war,' she said. 'And After the War is something *we* could think about. We have the time if Churchill doesn't.'

'To do that we need sane leadership,' said Lester, 'Which brings us back to getting rid of Avenol.'

'As members of the Secretariat we have no authority: the member states will have to force him out.' Bartou said. 'But there's no way that the members of the Supervisory Commission can meet: Norway, Canada, India, UK, Mexico and Bolivia—impossible.'

Lester said he would get back to the British and to Hambro in Norway. 'Hambro's still Chairman of the Supervisory Commission and President of Assembly.'

'May I again interpose?' Ambrose asked.

'Of course,' Lester said. 'You're one of us.' He laughed, 'That is, if you want to be one of us.'

'Thank you. As a non-League person I cannot really be one of you—but I realise now, listening to you all, that I know something which I had assumed you all knew. And which may take the worry out of much of what you say.'

'Which is?' Lester said, sounding disconcerted by the bumpy way the meeting was going.

'The French government in Vichy is going to leave the League and it's asked Avenol to resign from the League.'

'The French have asked Avenol to resign?!' Bartou was astounded.

Edith was stunned for a double reason. It was a surprising move—and why hadn't Ambrose told her!?

'That's what my informants tell me,' Ambrose said. 'I was talking to someone very close to the French government in Vichy.'

The group was seriously surprised.

Her stomach was churning with the emotional reaction to Ambrose's silence about this with her.

'I gather that the French feel it's inappropriate for a Frenchman to be Secretary-General given the circumstances,' he added.

'That makes sense and it means it's over—the crisis,' Aghnides said. 'Avenol is out.'

'If he takes his instructions from Vichy,' Ambrose said. 'That we don't know.'

'Yes, he will take his instructions. Vichy has no foreign policy other than that which pleases the Germans. He may well wish to be part of the Vichy government,' Aghnides said.

'From what I've heard, that may well be,' said Ambrose.

Ambrose had been withholding things from her. He was leading a secret life again. He had been sitting on this information which implied that he was, well, seeing people and hearing things and not passing what he heard on to her.

And she employed him.

True, they'd lived apart for a month or so. But still, they'd seen each other frequently.

She struggled to dismiss her sense of betrayal.

She'd hoped never again to feel as sickened as she had years back, when she found out that Ambrose had been passing information to the British while working at the League and while being her friend. And had not told her.

What he'd done back then had been wrong and clandestine, and she'd felt betrayed. She'd thought that was now all behind them. She now felt betrayed again.

'What happens,' she managed to get out, 'when Avenol resigns? Who appoints his replacement?'

'The resignation would go to the Chairman of the Supervisory Commission—Hambro. We assume he has power to appoint a replacement,' Bartou said.

'And that would be you, Sean,' said Aghnides.

'Or you, Thanassis.'

Oh God, were they going to fight over the bone now?

'We are both from neutral nations—but you are Deputy Secretary-General,' Aghnides said. 'Furthermore, it would upset Avenol more if you become S-G. That is reason enough.'

Chuckles.

While paying attention to the discussion, Edith's mind kept returning to the sense of injury she felt from Ambrose's withholding.

She was scarcely able to think.

The meeting seemed to have had the wind taken from its sails by the news of Avenol's imminent demise and fell silent.

Events had decided the day: not them. Just as it had been with the League.

We can't even make a successful conspiracy, she thought. We weren't even able to manage a *coup*.

She had envisaged calling in the League *huissiers*—or perhaps people from Securitas—to have Avenol forcibly removed from the office. Instead, he'd fallen like rotten fruit.

She would have preferred the dramatic removal.

And now, for all their plotting, it seemed she alone had been betrayed.

Lester tried for humour. 'I suppose all that remains now for us is to arrange his farewell party. Perhaps that will push him along. Maybe we should just go ahead and organise it. Surprise him with it.'

There was much relieved laughter, except from her. She wasn't going to organise a farewell.

Lester said that it looked as if this would be their last meeting.

'And congratulations to you—Mr Secretary-General elect,' said Aghnides.

The meeting broke up.

She and Ambrose remained on at her suggestion. She said to Lester that she would close up. The others went off in a happy mood.

Lester gave Edith money to pay for the room. She waved it away. 'They have given us this room, compliments of the management.'

'Well done, Edith.'

The whisky had not been opened. Lester looked at it, smiled at her and left it where it was.

Ambrose and she remained.

She got up and went over and opened it and poured herself a drink. She didn't pour Ambrose a drink.

To hell with him, too.

He got up and poured himself a drink.

She waited to see if he would comment on the situation—whether he was even aware of it.

He was. He said, 'You're hurt?'

Sounding like a young girl, she denied it.

'You are—about the information I had on Avenol's resignation.'

'Why didn't you tell me?!'

He reached over to her, 'Don't be hurt. It's a messy situation.'

She avoided his hand. 'Tell me, then. Explain why you wouldn't let me in on it?'

'It was information which came through Bernard.'

'Oh, the Molly telegraph—the Molly Gossip Circle,' she said with derision. 'The Buggery Club.'

'Edith, Bernard, as you well know, is a very good source of information and I can't always break the confidences he asks of me.'

'Am I, then, out of his confidence? Because I am a woman and not a bugger? Why?'

She stood up, drink in hand, and went to the window. 'Is it because I can't bugger?'

'Now, now. I know that you're sensitive because of the bloody silly things I did before—in the old days. This is not like that. I've apologised for that. And I've paid for it, God knows. I lost you for a time. I lost my position. You know that I would never put our friendship at risk, Edith, ever.'

'It's not just a friendship.'

'Quite right. It's not just a friendship. Edith—we're living in dangerous times and all information has to be handled carefully now. Gossip is deadly and dangerous. People's lives now depend on this information and we must make sure that it goes only to those who must have it. Today at the group meeting here, for example, are people who should have the information which I had. You alone—maybe not.'

'Why not me *alone*?!'

'We can all make slips of the tongue. And remember that you yourself were, until recently, in a strange game of double deception with Avenol. With those around you.'

'I feel betrayed. You promised no more secrets.'

'There are no personal secrets: there may have to be secrets of war.'

'Bernard usually tells me everything,' she said, still

sounding like a sulky girl. 'My little heroine,' she mimicked.

'He admires you enormously.'

'But can't trust me?'

'He does. The situation is changing daily and information becomes more dangerous and more fraught. And there is something else you should know about Bernard, which I will tell you even though it's confidential. Highly confidential. Seriously confidential.'

'What? More secrets of the Buggery Club?'

What was the full extent of Ambrose's private relations with Bernard anyhow? She had never questioned them until now. They seemed to be simply close friends. Maybe they were more than that? God knows.

'Bernard is a delegate for the International Red Cross. He goes on missions for the Red Cross to gather facts about, say, treatment of political prisoners and others—to the prison camps in Germany—and reports back here to the Red Cross. This is not a public fact. If it were he would be jeopardised. He is not supposed to share his information with anyone.'

She was surprised and impressed. 'I didn't know he was a delegate.'

'Delegates are not supposed to be publicly known. We have to be careful not to compromise him. What he gathers as a delegate is not available to the public. But he sometimes chooses to pass that on to people who might be able to help in some private way.'

She had not calmed down.

'Think of it like this,' he said. 'The public—the voters, if you like—have the right to the truth from every minister except the Foreign Secretary. Maybe the Secretary for Defence, as well, is exempt from always telling the truth.'

'Why the Foreign Secretary?'

'All citizens realise that in a military or international crisis you have to take what is being said as an interim statement of affairs. That more will come later. That all cannot be told now.'

'I do not accept that.'

'Because in foreign relations the telling of the truth is not always in the national interest at a given time. The truth must ultimately be told but cannot always be told there and then. Sometimes the Foreign Secretary has to leave it to history to tell the truth, because telling the truth in the heat of a situation could, for example, endanger lives, or make negotiations impossible to complete successfully. It is the unspoken understanding between the public and the Foreign Secretary. Of course, when he lies he must have damned good justification for that lying. And almost always, he will be held accountable for that suppression of the truth. But withholding is part of the responsibility of his office, at times.'

'Give me an example.'

'Oh, I don't know—say if one's nationals were to be secretly evacuated—from some country and that to say so would endanger the evacuation—the Foreign Secretary in this situation might deny that an evacuation was taking place.'

'And you see yourself in the position of Foreign Secretary of the Buggery Club?'

'Please stop using that expression. Maybe yes. I'm your Personal Secretary but I also play a role in the secrecy of the Molly Club.'

'The other palace. The Buggery Palace.'

'Perhaps you and I are both Foreign Secretaries—on the same side, but from different countries.'

'I thought I was a member of the Molly circle?'

He pondered this.

'You are as close as anyone to Bernard, but you cannot escape your other position, your position as member of the League inner circle. I suppose the interests of both overlap but are not identical. Damned tricky at times. You do this with Bernard too, you may not be aware of it. Sometimes you duck or mislead in your answers to him.'

He had made his point. Things were messy.

'Couldn't we form an overriding alliance—an alliance of two?' she said, calmer now.

He smiled but looked perplexed.

She went to him and kissed his hair, then stood near him, her arm on his shoulder. 'There's some sort of other thing isn't there, with Bernard and the Molly? It's not only the Red Cross—it's a ...' she tried to find the words for it. 'You're bound together because of your way of life, shall we say? A brotherhood of sorts?'

He looked at her. He seemed to have considered things and come to a decision, 'I think you should consider yourself part of that brotherhood, as you put it.'

'As a woman?'

'As a woman.'

'What caused you to change your mind?'

'As I said, the situation is changing daily.'

'We haven't seen *those women* who used to come some nights to the Molly. I suppose they have gone. They worked at the ILO. All sent home.'

'You are another kind of woman.'

'And what kind of woman am I, pray tell?'

'I don't know what kind.'

She smiled at him. 'What a mess it all is.'

'It is a mess and it's going to be a bigger mess.'

'Can you trust all at the Molly?'

'Not all.'

'There are many new shapes for friendships, alliances and bonds,' she said.

They were all in webs of strange allegiances.

Sticky webs.

He poured them another drink.

She suddenly laughed.

Ambrose looked at her.

'When you were asked to give a summary of the situation they all thought you would tell them insider Foreign Office thinking,' she said, laughing. 'If only they knew. If they knew where you got the information. Which Foreign Office you really represent now.'

He smiled. 'I don't get all my information that way, Edith.'

She went on laughing. 'Oh hell, we could give up on the world—go to South America,' she said. 'The Peruvian Permanent Delegate offered me a posting there this week.'

'It's tempting.'

'However, I made up the A List. So I have to stay.'

'The A List?'

'We now have four lists in the League. A List is the sixty-nine people, including me, who are to stay on as a nucleus whatever happens. The B List is a smaller group who will now go home but remain on call, the C List is most of the League personnel who have now been given choice of suspension or resignation, and List D is some Swiss staff who would become caretakers of the building if all of us had to go or were arrested by the Germans or whatever.'

'The A List are those you would invite to your party, I presume.'

'And the circular reminds those staff being sacked to leave the keys of their apartments or houses with their *régisseurs*. Avenol is on no list.'

They looked at each other.

'So the League dwindles,' he said.

'The lights are going out in the offices. It's becoming darker. Victoria is going across to the Red Cross. At least she'll still be around.'

She sat down beside him, her arm around him. 'I don't think my parents raised me to be a member of the Buggery Club.'

'I hate that expression. Would they mind?'

She thought back to her father and mother. 'Perhaps. We always think our parents have a childlike innocence. I guess they don't.'

She stood up and faced him, and taking his hands pulled him to his feet and led him over to the bed in the room.

'Edith Berry, you amaze me.'

She folded down the bedclothes.

She took off his jacket and began to undress him. He in turn began to undress her.

And they made love as a very conventional couple would make love, very simply, and Ambrose, she found, was rather manly.

Afterwards they lay together in silence.

Ambrose spoke first. 'What about the rumpled bed?' he asked. 'Given that the room was rented for a private meeting?'

'Ah yes, the bed.'

She looked at him and laughed. 'Let the management speculate about it. *C'est la guerre.*'

'You entertain four men in a hotel room? Edith, you will certainly be remembered in Geneva.'

She blushed. 'I will have to take the risk of that rumour. May enjoy *that* rumour.'

As they dressed, she wondered if perhaps Ambrose needed to have secrets in a childlike way as part of his sense of his own specialness and for his own sense of importance in the world.

If so, perhaps she should let him keep some of those secrets.

Only Night

O n her birthday, October 10, 1941, Edith met Ambrose for dinner at the Perle du Lac, at his invitation. 'I've decided it's to be my last birthday,' she said, as she sat down.

'Oh, nonsense to that,' he said. 'Let's stare age in the face.'

'You can stare. I'm looking away. And I don't thank you for going to all this trouble to remind me of my age.'

The table had been especially arranged, the best table overlooking the lake, with acacia decoration. 'And thank you for not putting a stuffed kangaroo on the table.'

He laughed, 'An oversight—I've almost forgotten what nationality you are.'

'Australia has never looked more attractive . . .'

Her favourite wine, a sparkling shiraz, arrived and Alphonse, the maitre d', obviously alerted by Ambrose, expressed the management's best wishes and brought a bouquet of flowers. And then M. Doebelli himself came over and wished her *joyeux anniversaire*. There was a hand-written menu which she glanced at and saw was a selection of her favourite dishes.

When Doebelli left, she looked across at Ambrose and said, 'This is not going to be a happy birthday celebration, I'm afraid. I really should've called it off.'

'Can't call off your birthday. Only thing you can't call off. Oh, there is another important event you can't avoid but we won't dwell on that. Did you have an office function?'

'The usual cake in the Library which Lester turned on at morning tea. It was all rather touching. So few of us there now. Let's stop the birthday talk.'

'I will not be deflected from my duty as birthday host. We will stare age down. We will defy it.'

'It may be a birthday we never forget—when you hear what I have to tell.'

He chuckled, 'My dear, what incredibly wicked thing could you possibly have in mind!'

When she refused to join with him in his jolliness, he looked across at her face. 'Unforgettable? How so?' he said, reverting to seriousness.

'I've heard some strange news.'

'We hear nothing else but strange news. Family?'

'Not family. This news is more than strange—more dreadful. Or more dreadful than any we've heard so far. I'm sorry to bring it to the birthday party but I heard it only today. It has to be talked about.'

'What is it!? Let me guess ...' he pretended it was a guessing game. 'New Zealand has fallen?' Part of him was still resisting all serious talk. 'Am I warm ...?'

'It's serious, Ambrose, and it concerns you. Concerns us.'

'Tell me then.' He seemed frustrated in his role as host.

'I was called over to Red Cross headquarters by Victoria. She introduced me to a young man who is seeking help to stay in Switzerland. Or that was what we assumed he wanted. It wasn't altogether clear. A German.'

'So? They come in every day—we are all approached by these people.'

'This was different. At first we thought he was simply another refugee with a sad story. It seemed that he wanted to tell us something. It was as if he didn't know quite how to say it.'

'Edith, get to the point.'

'He wanted to tell us that the Germans have begun murdering people ... *en masse.*'

'It's wartime. That's what war is about.'

'This is hard to describe and I haven't quite understood it.'

Caviar arrived, preordered by Ambrose. Beluga. More than she'd seen for some time. In the earlier days at the League there'd been much caviar but the killjoys had put an end to that.

'Thank you, Ambrose! You know I've been yearning for caviar.'

She had to force herself to be appreciative, although it was, in the circumstances, probably the only food she could digest.

'You've talked of nothing else for months. I took the hint, as they say. It's becoming impossible to get—thanks to Germany invading Russia.'

She exaggerated her savouring of the first spoonful, eyes closed. 'Bliss.' It did taste wonderful, but it was not accompanied by true gastronomic abandon. 'Thank you, darling.' She dabbed her mouth with the serviette. 'I'm sorry, but I have to go on with my bad news.'

'If you must.'

'It's more than just individuals—they're rounding up specially designated parts of the civilian population.'

'To be killed *en masse?*'

'Yes. It seems that way.'

'*C'est la guerre,*' he said. 'Go on.'

'This isn't just warfare. There is a weird and frightening sound to it.'

'*Go on.*'

'Civilians such as those who frequent the Molly Club are part of it.'

'*Who go to the Molly Club?!*' He laughed.

'Even the word murdering is too imprecise. Annihilating. The Germans are it seems planning to annihilate the likes of you. And others. Jews. And others.'

He looked at her. 'Surely you mean that they're ill-treating them. We know that. You mean they're forcing them out? We know that.'

'I'm not talking about those sorts of things. I'm talking about mass shootings and working people till they drop. Worse, he told of plans to electrocute them *en masse*. All.'

'All—all at once?'

'As fast as they can manage—with these newly devised methods.'

'How can we be sure?'

'I don't know. I heard it from this man only today.'

'It sounds highly improbable.'

'It does.'

'And you hear this through this one German?'

'Victoria believes it.'

'She's not always the best judge of character.'

'She's hard-headed and practical.'

'True. And can that be done—electrocution *en masse*?'

He sounded determined to doubt her.

She shrugged. 'The Germans are rather good at technical matters. So we are led to believe.'

'Edith,' he said, 'leave this till tomorrow. Eat your caviar—forget it for tonight.'

'I can't forget it. Even for a night. It was in this man's face—he seems connected with the Nazis. These are your friends who are being killed. Our friends. People we met in Berlin in the old days.'

'Why would they bother?' he said.

'It's crazy.'

'Why would the Germans do that? And why the likes of us? And why don't we have a name for ourselves?!'

'The Germans say—sexual vagrants.'

'How in God's name did this German get onto the subject?'

'He mentioned other civilian groups that the Germans are

killing—Jews and so on. And he mentioned *urnings*. Which Victoria and I interpreted as "half-women".'

'He actually said the word *urnings*!?'

'Is that what it means?'

'He actually used that word!?'

'Yes.'

She looked away across Lake Léman. She looked back to him with deep perplexity. 'Until I came to Geneva I'd never met a Jew. Or, for that matter—your lot.' She rolled the word 'urnings' in her mind.

'You'd never met a Jew?' he asked, carefully spooning a morsel of caviar into his mouth.

'Did you always know Jews?' she asked.

'I've known Jews all my life.'

'I think Liverright was the first Jew I ever met. And Rabbi Freedman who came to the 14th Assembly from Australia. He was the first Rabbi that I'd met.'

Ambrose looked away from her and out of the room as if he were caught on a hook, twisting, not wanting this sort of conversation.

'What are Jews like?' she asked.

It was, she saw, a rather silly question.

He answered flippantly showing his impatience with her question, 'The men carry their money in a purse. The married women wear wigs so that gentiles cannot see their hair. What else do you want to know?' He laughed to himself and muttered, 'Some similarities to the Molly crowd.'

'It was a stupid question.'

He drank his wine and said with a low voice, 'There are those at the Club who pretend there's no day—only night. I have to say that I'm more and more inclined to be like that.'

'Also to pretend that there's no war?'

'Precisely.'

'And no women—only men dressed as women.'

'Yes—only a make-believe world.'

'Feel free to go. Go now, if you like.'

She was becoming annoyed.

'Edith.' He reached over to her. 'I might pretend there's no war and no day. But the sad thing is I have to pretend to pretend.'

'I know you do.' She persevered. 'Let me tell you the rest of the story.'

He drank deeply from his wine glass. A waiter came over and refilled his glass.

'This German says he's a steward in the service of Heinrich Himmler. He tells us that Himmler and his staff have been instructed to plan and prepare something of a party, some time in the next month.

'This planned party caused gossip among the staff because Himmler rarely leaves Berlin. The party is to celebrate the opening of a new sort of plant or factory or whatever they call it, for the beginning of these killings.'

'I really still can't see why the Germans would bother.'

'I can't explain it, nor can our young German friend.'

'How young?'

'Say twenty—it's below-stairs gossip. And what's more reliable than below-stairs gossip? The villa is owned by Schulte's company—we've *met* Schulte, haven't we?'

'Yes, we both met him here in Geneva at the Molly.

'I remember.' What in God's name was this important German doing at the Molly? How mysterious that place had become.

'His lodge is in the forest of Katowice. I've actually been there.'

'When?'

'Oh, before I came back to Geneva. It's near Krakow. It's not what you, Edith, would call a fashionable "spot".'

'Do I call everything a spot? What a lazy little word.' Ambrose's connections also weighed her down. Why had he been to this man's lodge before the war? She couldn't be bothered pursuing it.

'You do use the word rather a lot.'

'I may use it but I don't believe I use it *a lot!*'

She hated most his correcting of her English.

'Oh, doubtless it's etymologically sound. I suppose Milton and so on used it that way. I happen to think that it's time the word was confined to meaning a pimple or a stain. I can't help but think of a pimple or a stain whenever you use it.'

'I do wish you would consider before you decide to correct me, Ambrose. Correction shows poor breeding.'

'Or true friendship. Apologies.'

'Don't *stop* correcting me, just find a more tolerable way of doing it. Write to me. Or become more the discreet friend who whispers nicely that your stocking seam is crooked.'

'Consider it done. If you'll always tell *me* when *my* seam is crooked.'

'I still have Jeanne correcting my French. Although I'm now beginning to think that she's sometimes wrong.'

They sat silently while she allowed the annoyance of the spat to pass—she didn't like the word 'spat' either, and she was sure Ambrose would grimace if she used it.

She returned to the news. 'It doesn't add up,' she said.

'They've been killing pockets of Jews here and there. That's been in the press,' he said, at least making an effort to discuss it.

'It seems that they now wish to kill them *all*—systematically. That this, this factory or camp or barrack has been constructed to do just that. What've you and the Jews done? What sort of trouble have you all been up to?'

Ambrose dipped at the caviar and drank resolutely as if trying to avoid the matter.

'Why are you connected with the Jews?' she asked, wearied by her ignorance.

'There's no real connection at all. Some of us are Jews and vice versa. Some of us also carry purses and wear wigs.'

'Is it about unnaturalness?'

She supposed that some of the things Ambrose and she did were in the realm of the unnatural.

'Could be. If the Jews are unnatural.'

'Undesirable behaviour?'

'Something like that, I suppose. People Not Wanted by the Reich. The folk see it as unhealthy.'

'A rage against those who are different is also defending everything that is unique about ourselves. Isn't that also the case?'

'Too philosophical for this time of night, Edith.'

'There has to be a reason for them not being wanted by the Germans. Wouldn't they just let them all go? Push them over the border?'

'That's what they'll do—they'll get fed up and just push us all over the border and be done with it,' he said.

'Which border?'

'Which border would want us, you mean?'

'Remember Avenol was against the League being the organisational centre for Jewish immigration? Said it would offend the Germans and close the door on Hitler rejoining the League.'

'Tell me about this German boy.'

'Dieter. Victoria and I think he's one of those who could be put in this camp.'

'Jewish?'

'No, one of your lot.'

'How'd you tell?'

'We took an educated feminine guess.'

'*Victoria* is educated in these things?!'

'Well, I certainly am. And Victoria is something of a woman of the world.'

'A woman of *which* world precisely?'

She felt that peculiar tiredness which came from once again being confronted by something about which she could do nothing. She said silently, we showed the world how they might have lived and been happier, if they had so wished.

They chose otherwise. It should no longer be my concern.

She said, 'It's illegal in Germany, I suppose.'

'It is. But widely practised even in the highest circles.'

Something then occurred to her which had never occurred to her before. 'Is what you and I do—do in bed—is that illegal then?'

He looked at her. 'What an interesting question. Under Swiss law? Under British law? German law? Not mentioned in the Bible as far as I know. I think you'd be safe, Edith. I suppose I might be in trouble. Engaging in lewd acts would be the charge, I suppose. On second thoughts, you might go to the clink for it, Edith.'

'For lewd conduct?'

'Precisely.'

'I rather like the sound of it. And conduct unbecoming to a lady?'

'And unbecoming also for a man dressed as a lady.'

'Are you suggesting that there's nothing to be done?!'

'Can hardly go to Churchill and Roosevelt about *our lot.* Wouldn't quite make the business paper.'

Then he said, 'Hirschfeld used the word *urning.* Demi-women. I've told you all this.'

'As you well know, there's nothing that can be done at the League,' she said. 'Sumner Welles? Isn't he one of you? He's Roosevelt's foreign policy adviser.'

'I doubt that he would talk about it and I doubt that Roosevelt would listen. You could, of course, try the Pope.' He laughed. 'Pius XII seems to get along with Hitler.'

'I don't see myself talking to the Pope. This man Dieter said that the place could kill hundreds a day or something like that. They've evidently already tried it out. And there may be other places being constructed.'

'Why'd you believe his story?'

'I believe it because it has a ghastly preposterous ring to it.'

She again looked away in a sort of pain. 'I want you to

meet this Dieter, tonight. He's here on holiday and is supposed to return to Germany for this party Himmler has
planned. He's frightened that he may be more than waiting
on table at this party.'

'See him *now*?!'

She felt her heart sink into a bog of tiredness. 'I know it's
a rotten thing to ask after you went to this trouble for my
birthday.'

'You want us to trudge up to the Red Cross!?'

'I arranged to meet him at the Molly Club—thought he'd
feel at home there. I can't eat tonight.'

'Let's at least eat something. Eat up the caviar—at least do
something extravagant.'

'Please? Let's go now.'

'Why now?!' He sounded like a spoilt child.

She looked across at him, suddenly worried. 'Ambrose,
you're changing.'

'I would hope so.'

'You're hardening yourself against it all.'

'How else to be?'

She looked at him as much as to say, if you don't know I
can't tell you.

'All right then.'

He made no move to go.

'I need your appraisal of this man,' she said. 'I have to be
sure that he's believable.'

'And how will I *know*? Do you believe that there are ways
to tell if someone is lying? Do you still believe that?'

She felt sick.

'Do you think you can tell a person's lying because they
can't look you in the eye?'

'Ambrose, stop.'

By taking Ambrose to Dieter she was simply passing over
the responsibility of believing or not believing.

Around them the other tables laughed and were charming

in candle-lit elegance. Out across the lake the war went on. With binoculars you could almost have seen the German sentries at the border at Veyrier, rifles slung on shoulders, pudding basin helmets, feldgrau uniforms, black kneeboots, pacing, pacing, raising and lowering the border boomgate.

The white-coated waiters with blue epaulets leaned towards the tables serving with two spoons held in one white gloved hand from wide white dishes.

Switzerland was a candle-lit world flooded with macabre news and rumours from the dark forests beyond the light. The abnormality of the rest of the world seeped across the borders making their life seem itself reversed, brightly unreal—attractively and brightly unreal.

She increasingly wanted to escape into the make-believe life of Switzerland. She truly wanted to stay now in the candle-light and not go into the dark forest.

She sensed that Ambrose was already beginning to escape, to go into hiding from reality.

Without waiting to call for the bill, she went to Alphonse, explaining their abrupt leaving of the meal in the midst of a *menu composé de ses plats préférés*, telling him '*c'est la guerre*', which he would resent perhaps, or to the contrary would love to believe—perhaps it would make him feel that the war mattered even in Switzerland.

She realised that she had no idea what Alphonse thought about the war despite the numerous times they'd been to the restaurant and exchanged pleasantries and even chatted with him.

'Madame Berry, is something the matter with the dinner as arranged?'

'Oh no—it's perfect. I am not feeling very well.'

She may as well add that onto the excuse.

'*L'addition* has been paid in advance,' he said, nodding towards Ambrose still seated at the table. 'There's a special dinner prepared and waiting to be served.'

'Sorry. What has come up is all so unexpected.'

'There will be an adjustment,' Alphonse said. 'A refund.'

'Don't worry about that now—Mr Westwood will deal with that tomorrow.'

'As Madame Berry requests.'

Ambrose had remained seated.

She went back to the table where he was savouring the caviar.

'Should've had vodka,' he said. 'Vodka is the correct accompaniment for caviar.'

'Shall we go?'

He didn't move.

She looked out at the lights on the lake. Saw the ferry *Italie* moored at the quay.

Her birthday.

He then called the waiter with his hand. *'Deux verres de vodka, s'il vous plait.'*

'Ambrose, don't. This is something we have to face now tonight.'

'Have a vodka and then I'll go. We should've had vodka from the beginning. Sparkling shiraz was wrong.'

She stood there, distracted.

The vodka arrived almost immediately.

She said, 'You can't drink vodka while drinking the sparkling shiraz. Won't do.' A hopeless attempt at humouring him.

Perhaps they were all cracking up.

He then said, 'I'll come later. You go.'

'But it's about *your* appraisal. We have to do it before this man gets hopelessly drunk or disappears.'

He looked at her standing there and must have seen that she was close to tears.

He began to gather himself together.

This would be the last time she bothered with this ugly world. The very last time.

She was finished with it.

She, too wanted to sit down and give up.

He rose from the table, drinking not only his vodka but hers also, in a few gulps as he stood up.

She'd never before seen him uncouth.

We are falling to pieces.

She was done with panic, alarm, hysteria, fear, rumours. Done with it.

Alphonse had wrapped her bouquet and now handed it to her, and helped her into her wrap. 'Thank you, Alphonse. Again, I'm sorry to have caused this disruption of your very fine planning.'

'Another night, perhaps, Monsieur? Madame?'

'I'm sure, Alphonse, that there will be another night.'

But she wasn't sure at all.

Hens Which Do Not Lay Eggs

At the Molly, she looked around for Dieter, the unwilling Ambrose trailing behind her like an unhappy child. She could not see him in the dark club with its many corners and nooks.

After all the years of coming to the Club, she was still loath to go looking and prying—one never knew what one might find happening in a dark corner.

The hungry-looking bowtied Bulgarian pianist played on, ever observing his surroundings. Probably part of Bernard's private guard.

They were not alone long before Bernard arrived with Dieter. Bernard carried an ice bucket and another bottle of Bouzy and was as usual *en femme*.

'My dear Edith,' Bernard kissed her hand and gave it a squeeze of true affection which she returned. He wished her a happy birthday. He leaned over and smelled the flowers. 'I'll have those put in water.'

'Thank you, Bernard. And, of course, you knew it was my birthday.'

'But of course. And this is the gentleman you asked me to look out for you? I was taking special care of him.' Bernard turned to Dieter and smiled maternally, a hand on his shoulder.

'Thank you, Bernard. Please, join us.'

Introductions were made.

Among all its diverse functions as a corner of jolliness in an ugly world the Club was, as Ambrose had said, a place where most people pretended that there was no war—just as, before the war, they'd pretended that there was no puritanical Switzerland outside the door. And that there was no day, only night.

The Club of Forgetful Pretence.

But it was also, conversely and increasingly, a place where life and death were being fought out. Intelligence information passed, fates decided. There was a core of regulars who were very aware of the war. The newcomers more so.

The regulars were closer these days and kinder. Or were the bonds of affection among them caused not by the war but simply by the passing of time, of growing older? The fraternity of age?

On her second viewing of Dieter, she saw that he was effeminate in a more exaggerated way than Ambrose. How did that fit with his Nazism? Was he one of those who liked their men in uniform?

If so, he wouldn't like Ambrose.

His English went in and out of German, and he was a little drunk, although she'd asked Bernard to try to keep him sober until they arrived.

'And again, we meet,' he said, emulating Bernard by kissing her hand, something she could have done without.

Dieter was voluble and most pleased by Ambrose's presence and moved his chair to be closer, even putting his hand over Ambrose's for a moment.

She guessed that Dieter assumed Ambrose to be important and, in his well-cut English suits, Ambrose *did* look important.

As they chattered, she noticed that Dieter also touched Bernard from time to time, for emphasis or connection, but he did not touch her.

Bernard had a waiter open the bottle and pour four glasses and instructed him to put the flowers in water. He then proposed a birthday toast.

Dieter joined in, which she also found disagreeable.

Over at the Red Cross, Dieter had treated Victoria and her as mothers, but now Dieter seemed overconscious, even unsettled, by her presence at the table.

Too bad.

She asked Dieter to tell Ambrose and Bernard his story.

He seemed nervous. 'Instead, let's talk of prettier things,' he said.

Ambrose, still disgruntled about being there, did however sense Dieter's reserve about her presence and moved to explain that she was one of them, whatever that might have meant to Dieter.

She sat quietly, pretending by her demeanour not to be the prime mover in the situation.

Bernard also worked to relax the conversation with light talk, *risqué* and amusing. Ambrose joined in, having, it seemed, decided to make the best of a night gone wrong.

Ambrose manoeuvred the conversation around to the matter at hand.

'So you wish for this information from the Reich?' Dieter said.

Bernard said that he found it an intriguing subject—the plans of the Reich were astounding.

'Indeed the plans of the Reich will astound,' Dieter said.

In the Club he was no longer the uneasy young man with something distressing to tell which he'd been at the Red Cross.

Before going on, Dieter now looked at Ambrose and then looked about him. 'We should speak in private,' he whispered, but he was speaking more to himself as a director of his personal theatre. 'Now that we have come to the matter at hand.'

Bernard said in German that the club was the most private place in Geneva.

Dieter shook his head conspiratorially, touching his chin in thought. 'To speak in public is perhaps to be without suspicion? A good ploy?'

He was enjoying the drama of his role. 'Yes,' he said to himself, 'we will remain here.'

Thankfully Bernard said, 'In English please, if you wouldn't mind.'

He told again of what he had heard about the plans for regulated mass executions, but now he spoke as someone breathless with the wonder of the information. 'I do not make a defence of the Jews. To hell with them. It could be said by some that it is hardly honourable warfare: others say it is but a *different* warfare. The Jews wage an economic war: we will wage our war in return.' He laughed. 'Herr Himmler says we are immigrating the Jews "into the air".'

Dieter pointed upwards and then, perhaps catching sight of their unlaughing faces, said, 'But I don't say this. Let's see, however, who history rewards. That's all. To hell with the Jews.'

Ambrose asked about the plans for the other groups.

'That's more mysterious,' Dieter said, leaning forward. 'Why would they bother with the likes of us? Some of the leaders are as we are and *love* us?'

He exchanged knowing looks with both Ambrose and Bernard, ignoring her. 'Can you explain? But it is happening. The round-up is happening.'

He looked around, pausing for emphasis. 'Is it because we are hens which do not lay eggs, do you think?'

He giggled, looking at Bernard and Ambrose, glancing to her to see if she understood the joke.

She said quietly in an aside to Ambrose, 'There's a label for your lot—non-layers.'

'Lacks a certain glamour.'

Bernard, who'd overheard the aside, smiled.

Dieter assumed that they had loved his joke and repeated it. 'The Reich needs children and we are hens who do not lay eggs. So ...' Dieter made a throat-cutting gesture.

She saw herself, too, as a hen which had not laid eggs.

What was she doing sitting around a table with hens which did not lay eggs on her birthday?

Oh God. Had she really crossed *that* border?

Dieter rambled on, giving out more of the information he'd given to her and Victoria earlier in the day.

By being excluded from the spotlight of the conversation, she was able to further observe this German.

He was not what she would have called an impressive witness. As he talked, it was clear that he was assuming that a consensus existed there in the conversation, perhaps a consensus in Switzerland, that approved of what was happening in Germany, at least to the Jews.

Dieter kept putting his hand on Ambrose's hand in an effort to involve him more or to gain his confidence, which perhaps he could see was still being withheld.

Dieter obviously felt that any official entrée into Switzerland would come from Ambrose.

Ambrose said, 'Could that part be wrong?'

'How I heard it makes me inclined to prolong my holiday,' he laughed. 'That's all,' he repeated. 'Prolong it indefinitely.'

He turned to Bernard, 'M. Bernard, a drink, please, if you would be so kind.' He held out his glass towards Bernard, without looking at him.

Bernard poured a glass from the birthday bottle.

Bernard gave Edith a private glance which she took to be scepticism about Dieter.

Dieter drank and said, 'Now, is not this information worth something?'

She stared at Dieter again. Victoria and she had missed the point of it all—money.

But that Dieter felt the information was worth money also gave it credibility.

Bernard said quickly, 'Let us talk about that later. There'll be a payment.'

'May I say something?' Edith said.

'Of course,' Dieter said, turning to her as if she had just arrived.

She asked Dieter how the staff had decided that the party was to be for the opening of such a place? She repeated the question in her stumbling German and also asked about the sort of food which was to be served, to disguise the intention of the question.

In answering, Dieter addressed himself to Ambrose. 'Himmler's personal orderly told me. But we clean the place and we see secret papers left lying around. We hear telephone talk. We hear table talk.'

There was perhaps hearsay in all this.

She tried once more the womanly line of questioning, again asking about the sort of food to be served.

This time, Dieter looked at her and answered with surprising animation, tickled by the sharing of domestic tattle with a woman.

'We have a First Class menu and other menus. This was our First Class menu—for very special occasions.' He said, 'I have a joke in English!'

They gave him their attention.

'It is not the *menu* which is important: it is the *men you* have beside you.'

They all gave out obligatory laughter.

'It is a good joke, is it not?'

He laughed again.

He then went on about the catering plans. It did sound like a very special party was being planned.

They talked more, going over the same ground. Dieter again alluded to payment and his coming to live in Switzerland.

'I would be happy to live here with my new friends,' he said looking at the two men, putting a hand on the hand of each of them.

She had another insight into him. While he sometimes identified with his Nazi bosses in his boasting, he was, at the same time, frightened.

Dieter excused himself to go to the toilet and while he was away from the table, Ambrose suggested she might go home.

If she left, he might say more.

Bernard seemed to agree.

She saw their point. 'He's frightened, you know, frightened of his Nazis employers.'

They then spoke quickly, analysing his information while Dieter was away from the table.

Bernard said, 'What if this Dieter is sent here to spread such information?'

'To what end?' she asked.

'To have it reach official circles, for the alarm to be falsely sounded—and then for the Germans to blame the Zionists for spreading alarmist propaganda. Cry wolf a few times and the world will stop listening. And then they can do what they will.'

Ambrose added, 'The Allies would be accused of atrocity propaganda.'

'If this were true, wouldn't they have sent a more convincing rumour-monger?' she asked.

'So you think he's unconvincing now?' Ambrose said.

She laughed. '"Grubby" is the word I had in mind. Grubby—but not unconvincing. That he thinks the information worth money is important.'

'You would think that the Germans would be more likely to expel the Jews—to give the British a headache in Palestine and divert British troops there,' Ambrose said.

'What of this about extermination of sexual vagrants?' Bernard asked. 'What do you make of that?'

'I think he has that wrong,' Ambrose said.

'I think he believes it,' she said. 'The man is scared.'

'I think he feels we are part of something bigger—a network—or that we represent the British government,' Bernard said.

'Are we going to pay him?' she asked as she began to get her things together to leave.

'As much as I find him rather distasteful, yes,' Bernard said. 'If he's correct, "we" have gone from being a colourful part of city life to being petty criminals and finally, now—to being ... well, *dispensable*.'

Dieter returned to the table.

Bernard asked one of his waiters to go out and find a cab for her and when it arrived, she said her goodnights.

As she went up the stairs she was, in a way, relieved to be free of Dieter's grubby presence although slightly miffed at Bernard's and Ambrose's suggestion that she leave.

Some birthday party.

In her bedroom, she awoke to hear Ambrose preparing for bed in his room, although she'd not heard him come in. She looked over at the clock—it was almost dawn. She must have been only lightly asleep or already awakening.

She called to him to let him know she was awake.

He came to her room in a silk nightgown and she opened the bedclothes to invite him in.

As he slid in beside her, she smelled the smoky odour of the Club, the liquor on his breath.

She asked him to tell her what had happened after she'd left.

He was brief, saying that Dieter had rambled on mainly to show how close he was to the men of power—even if only by waiting on their tables and in their beds—salacious stories from the Nazi court, a nice story about Hess, known as Fräulein Anna. 'Of all this, more later,' he said tiredly.

He said that Bernard had paid Dieter.

'How much?'

'I don't really know. Or care.'

'I suppose it means that we get to hear other things.'

'It means that every drunken little steward from Germany will find his way to the Molly Club looking for a pay-off. Yes.'

'You believe him?'

'As bizarre as it all is, yes, I now do believe him.'

Ambrose was inclined to think nothing could be done with the information.

She disagreed.

After talking around in circles about what to do with the information, Ambrose and she lay together in an uneasy bed, with only tired politeness keeping her from asking him to go to his own bed.

Underlying the discomfort of their bed, she found that she still resented having been excluded at the end.

And she was edgy in a vague way about Ambrose's odour of the night.

About that, she didn't want to know.

He eventually reached over to her and held her. She accepted him and they folded into each other.

'It's not been what you might call a spectacular birthday for you,' he said.

'My own fault.'

'I'll make it up to you.'

'May I make a joke in bad taste?' she said, sleepily, glad that they were reconciled, glad that a joke had come to her which she could wrap around them. 'It's really in bad taste, given the ghastly nature of the whole business.'

'Any sort of joke in any sort of taste, please. I need a joke.'

'If the Germans are really doing this, this rounding up *en masse* of your lot, it'll only encourage others to think that if this kind of *pleasure* has attracted such a huge penalty from the Germans—it must mean that it's a very remarkable pleasure indeed.'

He chuckled. 'The Nazis will grab you for making jokes like that.'

He held to her, a desperate hug, a hug looking for an end to all the ghastliness. He seemed to want to hug himself to another place within her.

Their embrace became an enveloping of each other, their bodies made an oblivion of warmth and enclosure in the world of the bed.

In the morning, they again argued about what to do with the information.

'Would it matter that much if we went to the Foreign Office or the State Department about the planned *en masse* execution of the Jews, and it turned out to be wrong?' she said, as they breakfasted downstairs in the café.

The newspapers, hastily flipped through, were piled on the floor beside them.

'It'd panic those Jews already in occupied countries, for a start,' he said.

'Or warn them.'

'Why warn people who can do nothing to escape their fate?'

'How do we know they can do nothing about their fate?'

Gloomily, they ate their breakfast.

A niggling thought surfaced in the bright morning light.

'What did you all do, until dawn?' she asked.

'Prattled on.'

'I trust that was all you did.'

It didn't come out right. It sounded querulous.

He looked at her. 'Edith?'

She flinched.

She found she couldn't stop herself. 'Well ...?'

'There are more pressing matters than Dieter's vices.'

'Or *your* vices?'

'Or my vices.'

She realised that there was something of an answer in his reply.

Was he implying that he had, well, *caroused* with Dieter?

She then found she wanted to scream, *did you or did you not carouse with him?*

She just restrained herself.

She hated herself for this wife-like jealousy, the shark which sometimes surfaced in their life.

After all, Ambrose had put up with Robert's comings and goings and her acquiescence to Robert's sexual needs in the past.

And her fling in Spain. And the bizarre episode with Scraper.

She'd always accepted that he was sometimes tempted by *amourettes* of the sort which, he'd explained, could only occur between strangers. That he hungered sometimes for those strange and dark experiences which the loved one could never give. Although it hadn't happened often. In fact, it had become rare in his life. He always told her of these *amourettes*.

It was not the loss of Ambrose which she feared: it was *exclusion.*

She was excluded when he entered that other world, a world which by its very nature was one which she could never enter or realistically be part of.

Yet despite her realistic understanding of it all, it still at times hurt. She tried not to retreat to the position held by The Married who felt that a person should forgo one existence to secure the other.

She wanted them both to have all possibilities of existence.

And who among passionate people really believed in forgoing one way to secure another? Didn't most people want to have *everything* that life offered?

And there was an answer to her jealousy—a solvent, which they used at times. He sometimes told her of his dark encounters, often at her urging—and she found his telling about the *amourettes* suggestive and provocative. Sometimes the telling caused heightened sexual feelings in her. For him to bring these dark affairs into their own bed this way, she found, was the best way to deal with this side of his life.

It was by his erotic telling of his adventures that she was re-embraced by him.

Perhaps her insecurity now was because of the war. Blame everything on the war. Perhaps the war was leading her to cling.

Everyone was clinging to those others who could offer, however intangibly, the chance of preservation while at the same time avoiding those encumbrances and those people who were flappable, who would hamper a swift flight.

The wavering people and the paralysed people were being pushed away. Excluded also from political arguments and plans.

She breathed deeply, trying to restrain the ugly thumping jealousy in her heart. She returned to the issue of Dieter's information.

She said, 'I think I would rather lose credibility than be negligent in the face of this information.'

Ambrose said quietly, 'It could cause a reaction which might be rather ugly?'

'Surely it would cause revulsion throughout the world?'

'Not necessarily. As unfortunate as it may be, we may find that many people side with the Nazis on this question.'

This had never crossed her mind.

He went on. 'There are some European countries which might think that driving out the Jews was not such a bad thing—and some individuals in our own countries might think likewise.'

She found this beyond her comprehension. 'We aren't

talking about driving them out. We're talking about some sort of slaughter.'

'The argument could well still apply.'

'You believe that?'

'It's a possibility. What I'm saying is that if we make this war a crusade to save the Jews we might find a weakening of resolve among some of the Allies, and in the attitude of some of our citizenry. We might find some of the fighting men saying, "Well, if this is all about saving the Jews—to hell with it. Let's go home."'

'What's the war all about, if not about saving people from the Nazis?'

'It's about not letting Germany dominate us. Staying afloat.'

'I think that we have to take the risk of adverse public reaction—and, if it occurs, argue against it.'

'And if we find that people are anti-Semitic in our own countries?'

'I have never thought about it.'

She'd never even contemplated these sorts of consequences. 'You think that one should avoid confronting those things about which one can do nothing? Or if what you do might possibly have results as bad as the injustice you wish to redress?'

'I probably do, yes.'

She said, 'But you can never be sure of the consequences?'

'You can be fairly sure.'

'I still want to take the risk. I could telephone Eden.'

'That would be an interesting conversation.'

'You think he's one of those who does not particularly care for the Jews?'

'I was fantasising more about you raising the other matter—the question of *our lot*. By the way, sorry again about your birthday. It was a dismal affair.'

'Oh, ye gods, did I really spend my birthday with a Nazi?!'

They both laughed in a subdued kind of way.

'At least you didn't want to leave the dinner,' she said.

'I certainly did not.' He frowned. 'There in the Perle du Lac, I really felt it might be our last night on earth.'

'What brought that on?'

'Just a premonition. Russia's crumbling. The Germans will be in Moscow soon. I really think they're going to win the war. India will probably jump ship to the Germans. Switzerland will probably be overrun soon. The Americans aren't joining in to fight. I had a dreadful premonition of the end.'

'It looks bad.'

'And then on top of everything, you brought news that the Germans were coming to get *me*.'

'And we agreed that they would probably take me as well.'

'And worse—there at the Perle I was struck by the thought that the Nazis may be right: that unreason is a higher order of reason; violence is a healthy cleansing energy; morals are for the weak. Nazism suddenly seemed to be a vigorous— vehement—position into which one could dissolve and happily lose one's mind.'

'Ambrose . . .'

'The Nazis are showing that their way of thinking breeds power—and they can brawl, smash, plunder, all for the hell of it. No stuffy rules for them. No tedium. And you get to belong to the superior bunch and swagger around.'

'And how do you feel this morning? Do you feel like smashing?'

'It was a false premonition. The feeling has passed. Sorry. Temporary thing. The German armies will overextend. But what I should say is that this morning, while I don't believe that we will *lose* the war, I somehow think that we could spend the rest of our lives *fighting* it. We may never see the end of the war in our lifetimes.'

'We'll just have to wait upon the turn of events in hope of advantage.'

He laughed. 'Edith, you're probably the only person in the League who still knows the diplomatic language—but someone should remember it.'

'And what are you doing today to win the war?' she said.

'I thought I would duplicate some of your office files—set up an independent record of what's important. Put them into smaller boxes which could be stored. Or could be carried in the luggage compartment of a car.'

'Lester buries his diary in the garden each night. Perhaps we need a hiding place for our files.'

At the Palais des Nations, as she went through the cool, empty corridors, she passed the doors of hundreds of empty offices.

She silently said hello to the ghosts as she passed offices where former friends once worked.

She stopped at the Council room and looked in at the green covers fitted to the curved dais and benches where once five hundred delegates and others would have gathered.

She glanced yet again at the murals: 'The End of Pestilence: Strength: Law: the End of Slavery: Solidarity of Peoples: the End of War'.

All closed now. All unseen and unbelieved.

The murals spoke only to themselves. They were tied up there like hungry pets.

She remembered the official opening of the Palais in '36.

The Spanish Civil war was raging. M. Gallardo, who, on behalf of the Spanish government, had made the gift of the murals said, 'These are some solace to us at this tragic hour of our country's history ...'

She remembered the grand, glittering opening party—the only party ever held in the new Palais. The Aga Khan had paid for it.

She closed the door and remembered that one reporter had

written recently that the Palais had become a 'magnificent mausoleum'.

She guessed that it had.

She went on to her office.

During the day, her jealousy about Dieter and Ambrose resurfaced and she found herself unable to bring her mind back to the business on her desk.

Surely Bernard would not have condoned it?

She trusted Bernard and Bernard's mature understanding and his protectiveness of her and Ambrose's attachment.

She stewed. Where did they go? To Dieter's seedy hotel? To somewhere grand with Ambrose paying?

At last she found herself compelled to telephone Ambrose at their other office.

After he'd answered, she blurted out, 'Did you bed this Dieter? Was there some carry-on last night after I left?'

There was a momentary silence. 'I did. There was some carry-on.'

She took a deep painful breath.

'You *bedded* him.'

'I did.'

'After he boasted about those ghastly things?'

'Yes.'

'It made no difference to you?'

He didn't answer at once. He then said, perhaps with the hint of shame. 'It made no difference as it turned out.'

'That's disgusting.'

He tried for a joke, 'Know the enemy.'

'*That will not do.* You cannot joke about this. He disgusted me. He disgusted Bernard.'

Ambrose was silent.

Would it absolve him if he had done it to confirm this Dieter's story? As some sort of *tactic*!?

'Did you do it to confirm his story? Is that why you did it?'

As she said it, it sounded like a pretty thin reason, anyhow.

'To be honest, no.'

They were both held there in painful silence.

She thought something had gone wrong with the line. 'Hello?'

'Hello.'

He was still there.

'Thought we'd been cut off,' she said coldly.

'I am still here, Edith.'

She filled with pain and jealousy. She could no longer contain it or control it. It overran her.

She suggested icily that he should pick up a few things from the apartment and go back to staying at a hotel for a while.

She said she did not feel like his company.

It was not jealousy, she told him. It was the whole nature and context of the act.

She said goodbye and rang off.

Alone in her office, she wept.

What had happened was a brutal reminder that Ambrose perhaps had no scruples and that this could cause him to endanger her, endanger everything, endanger himself.

It was Ambrose's sheer indifference to morals or to character or, more, to *personal aesthetics* which she found incomprehensible.

Beyond the pale.

He seemed to be able so easily to put aside all that was decent and sensitive so as to indulge his proclivities. He disregarded all that was fine about his class. His mind. His taste.

She simply did not understand it.

Above all this, infuriatingly and paradoxically, she was already feeling demeaned by her jealousy.

Her telephone call to Ambrose had demeaned her.

She was demeaned in a myriad of ways which now collapsed in on top of her—by Ambrose having gone with Dieter, by her having an outburst of jealousy, by allowing her personal feeling to interfere with such a potentially ghastly and momentous matter.

All these things. All.

Head on her desk, she cried—sobbing, smothering tears.

She saw her tears absorbed by the desk blotter.

All these things.

Crying, she went to the door of her office and locked the door and even closed the inner door.

Falling into the armchair, she gave herself over to crying and sobbing.

After a time, her crying subsided.

She dried her tears, but remained slumped there in the armchair.

Did it mean that Ambrose just didn't care? Where did they all stand? Was he becoming ill again?

She did not know how to save Ambrose or how to save their hopeless love—yes, their hopeless, hopeless *love*.

Tennis Court Oath

Heavy-hearted, she put on her pleated cream tennis skirt and white stockings, examined the skirt and stockings for dirty marks, sponged out a tennis-ball smudge on the skirt from last week, dried it in front of the gas fire, and then forced herself to go to tennis, wondering if Ambrose would turn up.

He hadn't called at the apartment to pick up his tennis things, so she assumed not.

When he didn't show up for tennis the others asked her where he was.

'Off colour,' she said.

'Aren't we all,' said Jeanne.

The others booed Jeanne, crying out, 'Bad for morale!'

The tennis club struggled to keep up morale and to give the sense that life was going on with some normality, or more exactly they kept it going so that when and if the war ended, they would still remember how to behave.

They were practising normality.

The club was down from sixty-three members to seven. She had continued to turn up during the Avenol charade despite some odd looks from some of the others. But they all placed tennis above office politics.

'I might be just a spectator today,' Edith said, slumped on the bench.

'Off colour too?' asked Irene from the ILO.

'I feel spectator-ish,' she said. 'I'm just not up to it today.'

She knew they wouldn't let her get away with it. The rule was you had to play, whether you felt like it or not.

'You know the iron rule,' Victoria said. 'You made the rule!'

'I did,' she said, getting out her racquet.

It would take her mind off things.

She played a rather lackadaisical game, her play so poor that she did not need to conceal her tennis skills at all. Since rising to the top of the club competition—and that was before the numbers had dropped—she'd learned to play clubbable tennis, concealing her natural ability and the coaching which had turned her into something of a champion. To win too often was not good diplomacy. Or good club practice.

She did sometimes go all out, and would win hands-down to show herself that she could do it and, well, to wipe the floor with the others out of a sheer desire to win and to check that the talent hadn't gone away as surprisingly as it had appeared.

After her game she went to the clubrooms to have some barley water.

Victoria came over and said confidentially, 'How did it go with the German?'

'Ambrose and Bernard think he's sound. I don't want to talk about it now.'

Divining that Edith wasn't happy, Victoria looked at her quizzically, put a hand on her shoulder and then left her alone. The hand on the shoulder was something she could not recall Victoria ever having done before.

From time to time she'd be swept with a sense of ghastliness about the whole business, horror-stricken by what Ambrose had done and sick at the idea that again their relationship had come undone.

It must have showed on her face because Jeanne also came over, 'Seriously, are you not well?'

She made a face at Jeanne which conveyed to her that it was to do with affairs of the heart rather than the body and Jeanne patted her back but did not pry.

Again, as in the old days, Ambrose had proved devious.

Perhaps not devious.

What then, if not devious?

He had again proved to be hurtful to her.

That was not precise enough either.

The others who weren't playing slumped around the club-room engaged in endless desultory chat about the war, rising prices, and what to pack in the escape haversack. And then the last game was over.

A special cake came out accompanied by a chorus of 'Happy Birthday!'

Inwardly she groaned. She'd thought she was going to get through the day without any of that.

Irene produced a bottle of cognac. They all cheered and a small party began.

At least no one asked her age.

Before the war they would never have drunk cognac at tennis but there was a for-tomorrow-we-might-die feeling at many occasions now, regardless of the nature of the occasion.

They even sang a couple of songs there in the tennis house, which she noticed badly needed paint. The International Tennis Club was all that had ever been achieved of Sweetser's grand plans for The International Club with his vision of games rooms with billiard tables, small lunches and dinners, the League Swimming Club, lakeside facilities, boats.

He'd dreamed of an American-style country club there in Geneva. To improve the way we live and play, he'd argued.

Ah, dear old Arthur.

They had begun to pack up when Jeanne said, 'Ambrose must be feeling better,' and gestured over to the gate of the club.

She saw that Ambrose had come to the gate of the court and was standing waiting for her, obviously not wishing to come in. A taxi was parked at the kerb.

'Why doesn't he come in?' Irene said, and then called to him and beckoned, demanding by her gestures that he come in.

Jeanne looked at her for an explanation. She simply shrugged.

Ambrose waved and then strolled up to the clubhouse, saying hello, fielding joshing about his having missed playing, responding with a careful vagueness to the questions about his health.

How could he be so collected?

'You've missed the cognac. All packed up,' said Irene. 'And the birthday cake. All eaten.'

Edith wished he'd not turned up like this.

She was caught. They held back, separating from the others as they left.

'The clubhouse needs painting,' he said.

'It does.'

He said that he had a taxi waiting.

'I'm not sure I'm ready to talk with you,' she said. 'Or if I wish to.'

'I have a lot to say.'

'I can't imagine what.'

'You could go home and change and we could go to a café. Have drinks and then an early dinner?'

She had learned a lesson about love and restaurants. When she'd broken off their affair the first time, before she'd married Robert, she'd learned that breaking off should not be done in a restaurant. It acted out a sad occasion in the ambiance of happier days; it prolonged the agony over the length of the meal; and it spoiled the dinner.

And there was nowhere to cry.

'Let's talk here,' she said.

'Here?'

He went to pay off the taxi.

They sat outside on the benches, looking at the pine trees in the cool of the fading afternoon, looking at the empty courts which also needed maintenance.

'This is rather austere.'

'Speak,' she said. 'Let's get it over with.'

She leaned forward, resting on her racquet, the silver chain of her identity necklet cold on her neck, her body seeking the warmth of the weak afternoon sun.

He tried to take her hand. She withdrew it from him.

He put his hands in his pockets and stretched out his elegant legs with their elegant unribbed long black silk socks, elegant black handmade shoes.

He spoke first.

'I would never betray you. I might *disappoint* you—but never betray you, never,' he said.

'If the disappointment is grave enough, it comes close to betrayal. Betrayal of expectation. A betrayal of your good taste.'

'I agree with the last—abysmal lapse of taste. Part of the appeal of it, I suppose.' There was something a little unserious about his tone.

'I'm seriously hurt,' she said.

'I don't accept your level of gravity.'

'You will have to. Ambrose! How could you have done it!?'

'I will try to explain. It was nothing more than an impulse. And I refuse absolutely and categorically to be downcast about it.'

'I am downcast.'

He made a restless movement of his body. 'It's to do with abnegation. Abnegation of all that we live by. The urge to fall into the black abyss. I just had the impulse. The impulse to throw off all the boring things of decorum—the things we really value. When I fall down into the abyss I believe momentarily that I'll never have to return to these things—

that somehow I'll be free of the mundane demands of life. And the agonies around us.'

'I don't see that what we have together could be described as mundane?'

'Oh, there's a deadly regularity—even in our lives. And anyhow, I felt that we had an understanding about these strayings of mine.'

'It was more than a straying—it was my birthday. You went creeping off with a despicable person.'

At first, she saw that the compounding of all these relatively small things—the lapse of taste, her birthday—changed the nature of the thing into something gigantically grotesque. Of course there'd been nights when he'd gone missing—but she'd considered that these had not been her business, given that they each had their own bedroom, and often slept alone, and were not married.

And the missing nights had been quite rare.

And after them, he would tell her the details of his escapade and usually it would be rather sensually stirring for her to hear the dirty details.

The telling in all its detail had been a gift to her and had raised their relationship above anything else that had happened, above any casual encounter.

The birthday night seemed an altogether different matter. And there had been his unsettling behaviour at the Perle du Lac. His irresponsible turning away from the world. His refusal at first to meet this wretched Dieter.

There'd been a certain collapse of character which had disconcerted her.

True, he had tried to explain—that he'd been overtaken by a premonition of doom and so on.

But still.

Then, as she ran through this review of her feelings, it all seemed suddenly to be just a pile of inconsequential things.

But they weren't. They weren't inconsequential.

Beside her, Ambrose continued in his quiet, placating voice. 'The birthday had been postponed on the night—I thought we'd abandoned that, at your request.'

She had silently to concede that to him. 'But it was—underneath it all—still my *birthday*.'

He laughed at her. 'Indicting me for a crime against birthdays?'

She nearly smiled. She stood up to maintain her indignation. 'I'm leaving if you continue treating this as a joke.'

'Sit down, Edith.'

He reached out and held her in place. She struggled, relented, and sat down again.

'He was disappointing in bed, as well,' he said. 'Lacking.'

He was trying to recapture her with his brazen remarks.

'Glad to hear it.'

She shouldn't have said that. Saying that was to join up with him a little in his devil-may-care attitude. It was not in keeping with her indignation.

He seized on it. 'He wasn't despicable in the good sense. He wasn't really able to do his duty.'

'Could've been your fault.'

Again she shouldn't have said that. She was being caught up in his brazen current.

'True—I wasn't wearing lacy lingerie.'

She pulled back from this kind of talk. 'This is not what we're here to talk about. We aren't here to talk about your lingerie or lack of it.'

She put on an angry voice.

'But it's the *interesting* part, is it not?'

Again she had to suppress an unwanted smile.

Oh, this was hopeless. She was succumbing to him.

She lapsed into a dissatisfied silence. Her indignation wasn't getting its due.

She had a burst of pain inside her. 'Dear God! Did you really need to bed him!?'

'It's a branch of espionage—bedding.'

'That explains your expertise in the field of espionage.'

Ambrose kept on, disregarding her fury, 'Given that we now trust Dieter, the question still remains about what we're to do with his information—and with him.'

'I'm no longer interested.'

'Dieter wants to stay in Switzerland and wants our help. Or to be precise, he wants *our money* and *our help*.'

'Send him back.'

'We have an obligation. He'll be a deserter from the army.'

'An obligation? Or do we simply need him around to satisfy your appetites?'

'I've lost interest in him—the unwholesome shine had gone by morning.'

'You are a very decadent person.'

His face became contemplative. 'Do you really think so? God knows, I try.'

'And you have muddied the mat.'

'What a horridly apt turn of phrase. Who then the mat, I wonder?'

'Ambrose ...' she said, with exasperation which wasn't quite positive enough.

It was hopeless. She was succumbing both to his amoral charm and to her crying need—the almost desperate need to return to a happy bonding with him—at the expense of her grievances. At the expense of her outrage. At the expense of pure decency.

She needed him—he alone in all her world.

Hell.

'What do we do with him?' she said abjectly, exhausted by it.

'We can find a visa for him—through Bernard. Send him up to Zurich where he will fit in with the Swiss Germans.'

'And what do we do for all the others?'

'I have given it thought.'

He'd changed his position on it. Maybe he was making a concession to her.

She looked at him, still trying to hide the love which must have been there in her eyes despite all. 'And what conclusion did you reach?' she said, trying for a businesslike voice.

'We can get some visas. Or forged visas. They'll have to get out as best they can. Bernard and I went to the Jewish Agency this morning. There've been other reports.'

He had listened to what she'd said. And he'd done something.

'Can't see that what we can do will make any difference,' he said.

'You do not know if it's your shot which wins the war,' she said.

She began to weep.

She was nearly at the end of her tether. 'You did wrong with Dieter, didn't you? Tell me. I can no longer see wrong or right. Tell me?'

'I did wrong by hurting you, but what I did, I did not do to wrong you. Never in my mind did I feel I was wronging you.'

She looked into his eyes, trying to find her way back to their strange logic, the strange logic which underlay their life together.

He held her chin in his hand. 'You are forever secure. But you know that for me not to follow the beast within would be disloyal—to us. And for *you* not to follow some of your impulses would betray yourself and betray us. Remember how we sometimes say that the highest way of life is to be above respectability.'

'You sophist.'

'With Dieter it was the bad taste of it that appealed. You alone in all the world understand that—that is what makes you my one and only soul mate.'

'I do understand, most of the time —most of the time I've relished it. Most of the time. This time it was hard.'

'I see that. This time was hard. But I will try to make you relish it.'

'Please—please make me relish it.'

She took both his hands, bringing them to her cheeks.

They kissed then, in reconciliation. When the kiss had finished she was without any resilience or sense of grievance or so-called rights of self. She simply ached to kiss more. To go on kissing.

'There's one other thing,' he said. 'When we were talking to Dieter I realised that Dieter was right—we *are* hens which do not lay eggs. That in the eyes of the world—how to put this? This dreadful masquerade with life that I play—this pretence against nature, this argument with nature. What I do *is against nature*. I realised this and it devastated me.'

She held him, comforting him, bewildered by the impenetrable nature of people, by the way they were able to be inwardly devastated and yet not show it as it happened, as Ambrose must have done during the Dieter conversation.

She was just able to feel and comprehend his state of mind that evening.

'We are hens in a big barnyard.' She struggled to find comforting words which had some solidity to them. 'More a zoo, perhaps, than a barnyard.'

She tried to laugh. He smiled gratefully at her, understanding her efforts to comfort.

He said, 'Can't seem to make a go of being a man. Rather unsuccessful—one way or another.'

She again struggled to find words. She put a hand to his cheek. 'You live *well*.'

'Hitler might be right—might've hit the nail on the head.'

'People who think like Hitler aren't to be *countenanced*.'

He smiled at her through his eyes. He was close to tears. 'That's right—they are not to be countenanced.'

'Oh God, let's go,' she said, after they kissed again. 'I need a hot bath, to get out of these clothes—I'm becoming chilly. And then a stiff drink and a good dinner.'

He leaned over and whispered into her ear, 'I will tell you the unsavoury *details*.'

She could hear from his voice that his bravado was weak.

'I insist,' she said, trying to bolster their feeble bravado.

But she knew, as she heard herself say it, that she was free again, free of the jealousy and was relaxing again, relaxing back into the soft silk cushions of their lurid life.

Her jealousy now seemed so pedestrian, so affronting to their all-encompassing, wonderful, lascivious alliance.

As they walked away from the courts, arm in arm, she said, 'I'm sorry for having become so pedestrian.'

'We all become frightened. Just have different ways of dashing it.'

'Tomorrow I will call Eden,' she said.

And how would she do that?

The Call to Eden

I t was against all the rules for her to call Eden, but all the rules were now scattered about on the floor of their world, underfoot.

Lester had most of the staff working in the Library, burrowing into statistical work, trying to keep a semblance of organisation or, as she sometimes felt—hiding.

Serious disquietudes did not fit into the monkish world of the Library—except over morning tea, and then tentatively and speculatively, everyone careful not to bring up any tension which would mar the sociability of morning tea.

If anyone had a serious rumour, it had to be one which could easily be calmed or dismissed. No one wanted any more bad news. Everyone sought signs that the enemy was collapsing.

So as she sat there in one of the empty offices, she stared at the telephone number which Eden had given her when they'd had their farewell drink at the Beau Rivage after the Committee of Eighteen had concluded its unsatisfactory business.

That was way back now. She had never used the number.

Maybe the number no longer rang.

She felt that it was probably a number she could call *just once* to ask for a favour or use to get his ear. But only once.

If what Dieter had told them turned out to be just a preposterous rumour—it was a war of preposterous rumours—she would have then burned her bridges with Eden.

Would be something of a laughing stock at the FO. And she would have done damage to the image of the League Secretariat.

She would certainly never be able to call him again.

She went to the window and leaned her forehead on its icy coldness. The person who doesn't make mistakes doesn't make anything. Her father's saying.

If the Swiss political police listened in to her call, and everyone at the League assumed they did, it would do no harm for them to know the content. If the Swiss police were sympathetic to the Nazis and passed it on, then it would be good for the Nazis to know that their secret was out in high places. And Vichy would listen too, she supposed, on the telephone lines which crossed through France.

Perhaps her call to Eden would be in itself a useful tactical move, simply by achieving that—by being *listened* to. She would not be mentioning Dieter's name.

She could see no harm coming from the call.

And in happier, stronger times, the matter would have been formal League business.

She went back to the telephone, picked it up, and booked the call to the British Foreign Office using the office of the Secretary-General as the authorising code number.

It was done.

She put down the receiver, her breathing irregular, and sat in the office awaiting the call to London to be connected. Given the turmoil she expected it would be a long wait.

After about three-quarters of an hour the telephone bell rang. She picked up the handpiece and a voice asked, 'Is that Geneva 50-381?'

'It is.'

'Hold for London.'

Edith knew it would still take a while for the connection; she put down the handpiece on the desk, and went to lock the door. When she returned, the connection had still not been made but after a few more minutes a telephonist said, 'Geneva, are you there?' She replied. The telephonist then said, 'Connecting London. Go ahead London.'

An English male voice came on the line. The voice said, 'Who is this calling?'

'Edith Berry, League of Nations, Acting Secretary-General's office, Geneva.'

'Good afternoon, Berry, what is the nature of your call?'

'Confidential to Foreign Secretary Eden.'

'This is Oliver Harvey, Mr Eden's private secretary. Do you have Acting Secretary-General Lester on the line?'

She wrote down Oliver Harvey's name and imagined him at the same time also writing down her name.

'I am speaking from the Office of the Secretary-General. It is I who is making the call. Is it possible to speak with Mr Eden at this time?'

She glanced at the outline of the steps of the call which she'd planned out on a sheet of paper.

'You realise that you've come in on the Foreign Secretary's reserved line?'

'I was League liaison officer on the Committee of Eighteen and the Committee of Five with Mr Eden. I am known personally to Mr Eden and I wish to speak with him on urgent matters.'

'You wish to arrange to speak with him yourself?'

'This number was given to me personally by Mr Eden.'

She had somehow to overcome this Mr Harvey. For the first time, she wondered why Eden had given her his number.

'Are you at liberty to explain your call, Miss Berry, so that I can pass on a summary to Foreign Secretary Eden?'

She pondered whether to broach the matter with him. She decided that she had to. 'It concerns reports we have received about a serious change in the way the Nazi government is treating the Jewish population in occupied countries. And others in the civilian population.'

'And?'

'I feel that these reports show a bizarre change in the conduct of the Germans and must be brought to Mr Eden's attention as a matter of urgency.'

'Reports or rumours?'

'This is tested information. I use the term advisedly.'

She grimaced at her use of the word 'tested'.

There was a stony silence.

'How would the Foreign Secretary come into the matter at this point?'

'Perhaps some measures could be developed to forestall or curb this German behaviour. I would prefer, if at all possible, to speak directly with Mr Eden.'

Her palms were sweating, leaving moisture on the handpiece which she wiped with her handkerchief, holding the handpiece then with her handkerchief.

'You would like to request a telephonic conversation with the *Minister*? I could put your request to him and call you back. I cannot promise anything.'

'I would appreciate your doing that.'

Blocked.

Push.

'Could you tell me if your return call would be today?'

'Nothing can be promised. I will put your request to the Minister. As soon as possible.'

A man who was not accustomed to being pinned down.

'Thank you, Harvey.'

Mr Oliver Harvey checked with her the spelling of her name and the Geneva number he should call and they hung up.

She put down the telephone, tense around her shoulders and neck from having made the call.

She dabbed the back of her neck with the handkerchief.

She became sickeningly aware again of how weakly based the information really was.

There had been some sort of vague confirmation from other reports received by the Jewish Agency.

And Ambrose had tested him *closely*.

Would she have ever slept with a man to determine his veracity? She preferred not to face that question.

She determined to sit out the day in the office awaiting the call but she didn't have to wait long.

The bell rang and she jumped.

The telephonist said, 'London calling, Geneva, please hold.'

She held. How gratifyingly quick.

'Connecting you.' She heard the telephonist's voice say to the London end, 'You may go ahead now, London.' Mr Harvey's voice came on. 'It's Harvey here, is that you, Berry?'

'It is.'

'The Foreign Secretary will speak to you in around thirty minutes. Will you be able to take the call at that time?'

'I will.'

'I will book the call for that time and we'll call back.'

He hung up. There had been a collegiate tone to his voice this time.

She waited the thirty minutes and the call came in—precisely on time.

The connection was made. 'Harvey here, I have the Foreign Minister on the line and will hand him across to you.' She heard Harvey say, 'Go ahead, Minister.'

'Berry? Eden here.'

'Good afternoon, Mr Eden. I hope you are well?'

Eden and she then exchanged pleasantries. He sounded genuinely pleased to hear from her and eager to know how they were surviving there in Geneva. She told him how the skeleton staff were working away in the Library, and another few, including herself, at the office of the Acting Secretary-General.

'Is Lester there now?'

'No, Minister, he's not.'

'I see.' He asked after Lester and a couple of the others. He expressed his support for them. 'Holding the fort,' he said. 'Gallant effort. Your time will come.'

His voice became brisk and he asked her to explain her concerns.

She picked up a pencil ready to take down his remarks and questions in shorthand as a record of the call.

She began to give an outline of the matter but he stopped her rather quickly and asked, 'Are you calling on Lester's behalf?'

She held her breath, crossed her fingers for luck, and said, 'On my own initiative.'

'I see,' he said. There was a slight pause and then he said, 'Always admire initiative. Continue. In three sentences.'

He gave a small laugh to cover his brusqueness.

She began again but had not gone very far when he stopped her. 'This is obviously a grave matter.' He then told her he would put someone on the line from his office to take down from her all the details, which he would then consider.

'I hope you don't mind doing it this way? I myself do not take shorthand.'

'I don't mind at all,' she said.

'Better for accuracy. Before I go—do you have any ideas about what we might do if what you say turns out to be the case?'

'I suggest a condemnation be broadcast—by Mr Churchill and President Roosevelt—warning the Nazis that if they continue with these acts they will be put on trial after the war.'

'From what I know of the Nazis it would only harden their hearts. And another thing, Berry, it's important in this war situation not to fixate on the Jews. Big picture, remember. Give your information and your ideas to my man. Good luck, Berry—and call if you ever have matters of urgency to report. You will do that, won't you?'

How sincere was that offer?

'I will, Minister.'

She was thrilled to have her direct access renewed, as it were.

'I'll hand you over now,' he said.

A male member of Eden's staff came on the line. Not Mr Oliver Harvey.

This staff member was less formal. He said he took short-hand but it wasn't so good and could she speak fairly slowly. 'Sorry.'

She outlined the information, reading from her telephone plan and notes.

'It is the word of one man?' he queried gently, after she'd summarised Dieter's story.

'One man we have tested well. And the Jewish Agency here has reports which back it up.'

'Good-oh. I'll have this all typed up and put before the Foreign Secretary within the hour.'

'Before you go . . .'

'Yes?'

'I have some proposals for what might be done.'

'Proposals for His Majesty's government?'

'Mr Eden requested them.'

She was glad he couldn't see her blush. 'Proposals for the Allies generally, including His Majesty's government and the members of the British Empire and the colonies. And for the United States as well.'

'What is the precise status of these proposals? Shall I say they come from the Acting Secretary-General? I understand that it's been impossible to hold a meeting of Council—or the Supervisory Commission?'

She hesitated. 'We haven't been able to hold any meetings. The proposals I will outline arise from internal discussion here.' She wondered if she would get away with that.

'Internal Secretariat discussions. Very good. I'll take them down. I'm ready ...'

From her prepared notes she read out the random ideas which Bernard, Ambrose and she had come up with.

'First, I suggest a condemnation be broadcast ...'

'You?'

'We ... we suggest a condemnation be broadcast by Mr Churchill and President Roosevelt warning the Nazis that they will be punished as criminals for their acts; secondly, that the possibility of an exchange of German prisoners of war for Jews and the others so threatened be offered; that an international fund be established to buy the liberty of the Jews ...'

The FO officer interrupted her. 'The second and third proposals run against Allied war policy—what you are in effect saying is that we give the Nazis resources and or personnel which could be turned against British troops, prolonging the war, and simply exchanging the death of British soldiers for the lives of the Jews.'

This brought her to a halt. Ambrose, Bernard and she had thrown together whatever they could think of which might help. All she could say was, 'I cannot argue out these proposals on the telephone. They are ideas for your consideration.'

'Please go on.'

He sounded conciliatory.

As they went on with the call, she guessed that in the FO he was probably equivalent to her rank or lower. Mr Oliver Harvey had probably found out her status from whatever League staff documents they had in the FO. Or maybe they had taken her standing from the willingness of Eden to speak to her.

She continued, 'Or that consideration be given to either the holding as hostage those Germans interned in Allied countries—as hostage for the Jews—and if the worst came to worst, the public execution of those Germans who still profess allegiance to the Nazi regime.'

'Strong. Yes. More?'

'The next proposal should perhaps be seen as informal and should not constitute part of any official report.'

'Tell me what you have in mind.'

'It should be considered how best to corrupt lower-ranking German civil servants and officials by bribery in return for helping with the release of Jews and others threatened with execution.'

'I will see how best to put that to the Minister.'

'Thank you.'

'Is that the end of your message?' His voice sounded carefully neutral.

'We have one last proposal—that selected German cities be leafleted explaining that the civilian population will be bombed because of this new German behaviour towards the Jews and other civilians.'

'Civilians bombed?'

'Yes.'

'May I say one thing—on a person-to-person basis?'

'Of course.'

'You probably know that, as a general rule, the Jews are inclined to magnify their persecution?'

She didn't know this.

This again stopped her in her tracks. Were there things about the Jews which no one was telling her?

Was that the failing of poor Stephan Lux? That he magnified his persecution? And what of the non-Jews? Did they magnify their persecution?

Or maybe this was the FO's pro-Arabist position speaking. Something Ambrose had alluded to at times.

She didn't know what to say.

He went on in what she heard now as his advisory tone, taking advantage of her hesitation, 'In dealing with the reports from Poles especially, you have also to keep in mind the Slavic imagination.'

She found her position. 'I can see that there may be a political motive for the Jews to exaggerate their plight to put pressure on the British government to open up further immigration to Palestine,' she said, wanting to show that she knew something about FO politics. 'I am aware of that. What we are saying in this report is that this is a new development. And furthermore, I would've thought that it was difficult to exaggerate the plight of the Jews, even working from what we know to be true to date—before any of what I am telling you. The Evian conference established the persecution of the Jews.'

She hoped that wasn't too strong a response.

'Sorry to sound as if I'm debating—I'm trying to alert your people to prevailing sentiments over here.'

As he referred to 'your people' she saw Bernard, Ambrose and herself in the Molly Club, sitting around making policy recommendations for His Majesty's government *et al.*

He seemed to be raising these points as if they were not really *his* views. Was he fishing to see precisely where she stood?

'I understand that's what your report is saying. Don't misunderstand me.'

She added determinedly, 'And this new development involves people other than the Jews.'

'Who does it involve other than the Jews? I don't think you identified the other groups?'

Her man at the FO had become curious.

'Politicals and others. People designated socially undesirable by the Nazis.'

There was a brief silence at his end. 'I see.'

She heard a sound from the other end which she could not interpret. Maybe it was the telephone cable.

Perhaps she shouldn't have muddied the report by raising, however obliquely, the question of the others.

She could not interpret his 'I see'. Maybe the fate of the socially undesirable did not concern him.

His voice came back on the line. 'It doesn't seem to gel with the facts of a war economy. To murder part of your labour force. Perhaps there's a misunderstanding? Maybe it's the use of these people as slave labour your source is talking about?'

'Perhaps it's not a normal government we're dealing with here. We've certainly had other evidence that it's not a rational government.'

She decided to ask a question which she knew was undiplomatic for her to ask, and to which she could hardly expect an answer, but she felt she had to ask, even if it made her sound inexperienced, a trifle green. 'Have you received other reports of this nature at the FO?'

This time the extended silence came from his end.

The silence meant yes.

She was elated.

He cleared his throat. 'I'm not authorised to say.'

'Of course.'

His voice was low but still comradely. 'If that's all, we should close this conversation.'

'Thank you.'

Before he hung up, he said, 'There is another thing. On a personal note?'

'Yes?'

'You know Ambrose Westwood, I believe?'

He sounded tentative.

She was surprised. 'I do. Yes.'

'I understand he's still over there in Geneva?'

'Yes.'

'Would you tell him hello from Allan. He'll know who I am.'

'I will do that. And thank you, Allan.'

'He's well?' he asked, as if reluctant to end the conversation.

'Very well.'

'Good. Still working with IFIS?'

'No. He works independently now. For the League, indirectly.'

'Good.' His voice changed even more to the tone of an ally. 'You know, I felt I had to put to you some of the positions floating around the FO—as background to your thinking. So that you wouldn't expect too much to happen here, at our end. You do understand? Things you might run up against?'

'Of course.'

He'd been briefing her.

'Goodbye and good luck, Edith.'

'Goodbye, good luck, Allan.'

They finished the call.

Well, well, well. An Ambrose connection. And this Allan was, after all, on their side. She felt that Allan's remarks meant their report would now certainly go to Eden.

She'd done it—she'd made the call.

And now had yet further confirmation—unspoken but indisputable—that this Dieter had been telling the truth. They had assessed him correctly.

There was little more she or any of them could do now, apart from the forged visas plan.

They'd done all they could.

Fired all their shots. She hoped Voltaire was right that 'Dieu n'est pas pour les gros bataillons, mais pour ceux qui tirent le mieux.' God is on the side not of the heavy battalions, but of the best shots.

Forget God.

She had done the best shooting that she could.

Back at the apartment she told Ambrose that she had a surprise for him.

'Which is?'

'I spoke with a friend of yours today. In London.'

'In London?'

'At the FO.'

'At the FO, no less? You made the call to Eden?'

'Oh yes, him too,' she said casually. 'I spoke with Anthony on a range of matters.'

She knew Ambrose was dying to hear what Eden had said.

'But I also spoke with one of your old flames.'

'And how did you know it was an old flame, as you put it?'

He was only just restraining himself from asking about Eden.

She smiled. 'By the fey little note in his voice.'

'And what was his name?'

'Allan.'

She watched him. His face brightened. *'You spoke with Allan?'*

'He was the officer designated to take our report.'

'He was? And how did my name come into the report? I thought you were planning to use your name and fudge in the League?'

'I didn't bring in your name. He asked after you—outright—at the end of it all.'

'He did? He's a good man. And you spoke to Eden?'

'Allan asked after your health.' She was enjoying her teasing.

'Tell me about Eden.'

'Allan seemed *very concerned* about you.'

'Edith! Tell me about *Eden*. You *did* speak with him?'

'Yes, well, no.' She looked back on the telephone call and how it had been handled. 'I did talk with him—briefly. But in the end I suppose, I talked with a minion. Allan. Allan Minion.'

'He's a biggish minion.'

'As big as me?'

'You might be the bigger minion. Go on, tell all.'

She then gave him the full story. 'And Allan took down our proposals for action, although he conveyed to me that the attitudes around the FO were somewhat against them.'

He made her go back over the telephone call.

When they'd both looked at it from every point of view, he said, 'It seems to have gone well.'

'We've done as much as we can at that end.'

She asked about the forged visa plan.

He said, 'You realise there's a limit to the number of those we can possibly manufacture and get away with without being caught out?'

'That means we'll have to select to whom we give them. Maybe we should just go to the border and hand them out? Maybe that's the fair way.'

'Or we could see that our friends and connections get them first.'

'What ghastly decisions.'

'And if we get them here to Switzerland, we'll have to keep them alive. I suppose Field and the Unitarians or one of the other welfare funds would help. The Jews do have their own organisations and their own plans. We'll have to look after the others.'

'Field seems to favour certain politicals and not others.'

Was everyone just looking after their own? What rules were they working with now?

Ambrose then said, 'Well done, Edith. Well done.' He rose and came over, took her hands, and knelt before her chair. 'Well done. Only you could've done it.'

She thought, sadly, that what she'd done was to shift the responsibility to Eden. It was not quite action.

And in reality, all they'd done so far was to save this man Dieter.

Not How Long But How Wide

The war rolled on. Switzerland lived in a nervous normality wondering if the Germans would consider them worth the effort of invasion. The citizen army still manned the anti-aircraft guns and roadblocks but became casual about it and played cards and sometimes sunbaked, their identity tags glittering in the summer sun.

All Europe was at war around them but the citizens of Geneva, despite their nervousness, shopped, wined and dined and took vacations.

At night on the BBC world service they heard of the nightly bombing of Germany, the grinding up of the German army in Russia and the consensus of opinion was that the Germans could not continue to sustain such losses, although there was an irrational fear that, some way, somehow, they might be invincible.

Because of the closing of Switzerland's borders, the Council and the Assembly couldn't meet. The members of the Supervisory Commission, scattered through a number of countries, made key decisions by cable or telephone with Lester in Geneva.

Jacklin managed the League treasury from London.

Money for the budget came mainly from Britain, the British Empire, and the neutral countries, although Switzerland, frightened of offending the Germans, had stopped paying its dues.

The Swiss also closed the League radio station and stopped the League printing its own postage stamps.

This saddened them all, because these were some of the ways of showing the League flag, showing that it was still there waiting in the wings to bring about a peace.

But at least the Swiss hadn't thrown them out or taken over the Palais as a hospital.

The staff at the Palais were down to about thirty, mostly working from the Library, with another seventy-odd guards, cleaners and clerks.

Walters and most of the *haute direction* had gone but Aghnides and Vigier stayed on to give support to Lester in his role as Acting Secretary-General.

Bartou retired and Edith found herself working more closely with Lester.

With Lester's blessing and encouragement, Ambrose, while still employed by her as a personal assistant, moved in with the Library group and looked after the work she would have done in normal times. Everyone was doing more work to fill the gaps made by the staff who'd left.

The skeleton Secretariat tried to keep some of the journals going, they tried to keep the statistical work up-to-date and many countries, even though at war, dutifully sent in their figures on literacy, iron ore production, VD cases, and so on.

Even the Germans still sent in some statistics. Clerks here and there in the German bureaucracy probably had it as their job from before the war and had not received instructions to do otherwise.

Maybe the clerks just assumed that the League belonged to them. Maybe some clerks saw it as an act of defiance against their Nazi masters.

After Pétain's Vichy government withdrew France from the League, Lester made contact with the French government-in-exile in London under General de Gaulle, and de Gaulle declared that the withdrawal of France from the League by the Pétain government was not valid and that France 'continued as a member of the League'.

With written approval from the Council members, Lester accepted de Gaulle as the true authority of France.

It was the League's only political act during this strange isolated time.

Lester's daughter, Ann, had used her neutral Irish passport to get into Geneva to be with her father and Edith had found her work around the office. Ann, helped by Edith, became the official hostess at La Pelouse for the little diplomatic social life that still existed, although they had closed off the main part of the mansion to save on upkeep costs.

The rare social occasions slowly drank away the official wine cellar.

Fearing overnight invasion and capture, Lester began a secret diary which he hid in the garden. Edith and Ann were the only two who knew its location.

Jeanne became increasingly depressed and withdrawn as her country collaborated with the Germans, yet she felt that the world had let France down. Any criticism made of France by Edith or others was resented as being easy to say for those who were not there under the Nazis. Even criticism of the rounding up of the Jewish people in France to be sent to concentration camps in Germany was brushed aside by Jeanne.

'You are not *there*,' she would say. 'We don't *know* how it is to be there.'

And she was bitter about the Allied bombing of Paris, even if mostly of railway lines and factories.

But, along with her compatriot, Vigier, she remained with the League although the Intellectual Cooperation Section, with its offices in Paris, had gone. She opted to stay doing menial clerical work rather than leave the League.

As a personal rule she would not eat bananas or oranges because they were not available to the French people.

She remained a member of the gang but without her old exuberance. And sometimes, when Edith and her eyes met, Edith wondered about what might have happened between them if they'd been women with slightly stronger unconventional tastes. And if she hadn't found Ambrose.

Of all of them she felt closest to Jeanne, but this was now rarely expressed.

Victoria worked on at the Red Cross and tried to believe that good administrative work was, itself, a work of compassion, as much as applying bandages to wounds.

'Of course it is,' Edith agreed. 'But we find it hard to *feel* it that way. Maybe as women we feel a need to be out there in the battlefield tending the wounded.'

'If we are not permitted to fight and not good at bandaging, at least we can *administer*. And anyhow, it takes ten people behind the lines to keep one person fighting. Or eight by some counts. But don't hold me to either of those figures.'

Cards from Robert were very rare. She had lost track of him. But from time to time she thought about how she could have made such a mistake of judgement about such an important matter in her life. It continued to shake her confidence about her close relations with men and her assessments of them.

She sometimes wondered if her employing Ambrose was a way of having a relationship in which she had more control, if it were a way of setting up of an arrangement, other than marriage, which she could understand.

The Molly Club prospered as refugees made their way legally or illegally into Geneva.

When the Swiss tightened border restrictions, especially against the Jews, quite a few midnight border crossings from

France through the Jura mountains ended with hot coffee, cognac and rolls in the Molly Club.

Edith noticed that the Club was never raided by the Swiss police. When she mentioned this to Bernard, he told her that the Club was protected by a couple of highly placed civil servants in the Swiss federal government and the canton. 'They sometimes come here—you can recognise them—they have the most expensive frocks.'

He added, 'If the Germans get control of Switzerland then we will expect changes.' He sighed. 'All that leather and black shining boots.'

As the war went on she sometimes saw Bernard's high-pitched, extravagant public mask slip and a more serious and harried self showed through the make-up and from behind the elegant costumes of his Club persona.

He studied and got to know every newcomer who came through the doors.

He kept on with the Club's satirical cabaret and because some of the arrivals from Europe were from the entertainment world, the standard of the cabaret, in fact, rose and the cabaret attracted a much wider crowd although the Club was never advertised. And it had become somewhat more scandalous as well. Ambrose was still an occasional stand-in chorus girl.

One day, she received a call from Lester. When she was inside his office, Lester locked the outer door and closed the inner door and asked her in a conspiratorial way about her connection with the Molly Club.

She was a little surprised that he knew of her links with the Club but she supposed she'd mentioned it over the years or perhaps Ambrose had talked about it in passing.

'I have been there,' she said. 'Ambrose and I are friends with Bernard Follett who runs it.'

She felt herself colour slightly. Edith, at your age, *really*.

'I have a vague idea of what sort of club it is,' Lester said, showing discomfort. She wondered what he knew about what went on there. And what he imagined.

Surely he wasn't going to reprimand her for conduct unbecoming to an officer of the League?

Those days were long gone. It had to be something else.

She sat poised with attention.

'I have a favour to ask,' Lester said.

Edith fleetingly entertained the *risqué* thought that maybe Lester had been separated from his wife for too long and needed 'company', but she would never have conceived that he would have sought the company that the Molly offered.

Who's to know? More likely he might want tickets for the cabaret show. But even that seemed unlikely.

'Of course, Sean, anything you ask—if it's in my capacity—anything—you know that.'

Oh. Had that come out sounding odd? She stopped herself from adding, 'and anything you ask will be held in confidence'.

Lester was trying to find the words for his request.

She waited.

'I am not a man who finds this easy,' he said.

She tried not to raise her eyebrows.

She continued to wait patiently for him to get the words together.

He came out with it—'I believe that certain things can be found there which are not readily available elsewhere in Geneva?'

That otherwise unobtainable things could be found at the Molly was certainly true. Perhaps he wanted a pistol? But the Secretariat had a small armoury of pistols for their guards and, at one time, for those senior officials who felt the need of such self-protection. Sean could have signed one of those pistols out.

It crossed her mind to find out who was now officially in

charge of the armoury and where the keys were. Who was taking care of that?

Did he want suicide tablets? There had been a brisk trade in those, she'd been told. But he was not the sort of man to suicide, and he had a family back in Ireland. Morphine?

She looked at him, 'You would need to be a little more specific, Sean.'

'Of course.' He cleared his throat. 'You know of the Irish writer, James Joyce?'

'I have read his book *Ulysses*. Something of a *cause célèbre*. He has a growing reputation, although more for his notoriety and the difficulty of his writing.'

'If you've read *Ulysses*, you are better read than I. All I can say is that I have *tried* to read *Ulysses*. Will leave it until after the war. But I did review one of his other books favourably several years ago. Sadly he has no reputation of a good kind in Ireland.'

She said, 'I tried *Ulysses* twice and put it down but on the third attempt I found that it gave me great pleasure. Although I am sure there is much that I missed.'

'I hear that there are sections which are rather *controversial*?'

'Naturally I left those unread,' she said, smiling.

He grinned back. 'Naturally, a lady would.'

Again, he seemed to be searching for the appropriate words or considering whether to make his request at all. Where could this be leading?

'The thing of it is, he has a daughter in a clinic in France and there are difficulties about her being released into Switzerland. Lucia, the daughter is named.'

'What sort of clinic?'

'She is ill in a French clinic near La Baule. Mentally ill, I gather.'

'I am sorry to hear that.'

'Joyce himself had trouble getting the rest of the family

into Switzerland. They thought he was Jewish. He had to deny that he was. Although he said that he took it as a compliment that they thought him Jewish. And then the French detained him because he had an English passport. And he has a son of military age whom the French wanted to keep as a belligerent. Things like that.'

'How confused it all is.'

'Indeed. I will be talking with him about the matter of his daughter and I was wondering if the worst came to worst, if all else failed, your friends at the club might be able to "obtain" a *permis de sortir* or other document—which would facilitate her being removed from France to Switzerland? Evidently she has a terror of bombardment as well as her mental illness.'

She wondered how the knowledge of this sort of Molly Club service had reached him. She felt a little apprehensive. It was dangerous if word was getting around about the illegal visa activities at the Club.

She wondered how much she should say? How authorised was she?

She was not directly involved in that part of the work. That was handled by others and she knew only that it went on. She was not even sure of Ambrose's role. It was part of the rules that everyone kept what they were doing to themselves and to their co-workers. 'If you don't know, it can't be tortured out of you,' Bernard had told the inner circle.

She remembered Olivia, one of the more outrageous of the circle, had cried out, 'Oh Bernice, please tell me something so that it can be tortured out of me!'

Edith did know one thing. She knew how important Olivia, a printer, was to the whole illicit business.

At the Molly, she'd become a source of diplomatic information for Bernard and others which, when necessary, she passed on, especially about changes in regulations and procedures and promotions in the Swiss bureaucracy.

Lester must have seen her pondering and guessed about her

reservations. 'I understand that I may be wrongly informed about this service being available there. I appreciate that you may not be able to answer at this point. But if there was a possibility I would be pleased to know of it. In due course. And only as a last resort, of course. There are still official channels to be explored. I have been talking with the Irish Minister to France. But we are pessimistic. Joyce has refused an Irish passport which would've made everything easier. He said he wouldn't accept in wartime that which he refused in peacetime.'

'And Mr Joyce has approached the League?'

'More that he approached me as a fellow Irishman who may have influence. More that than an approach to the League, as such.'

'This is not official League business then?'

'Does that worry you?'

'Oh no. I was simply sorting things into their correct baskets.'

He smiled. 'As always, dear Edith.'

She said, 'I suppose it's the League's old problem—how to be involved with the irregular without losing our probity: how to participate in the murkiness of events without losing our "noble" identity.'

'Precisely.'

Why had she said the word 'noble' so cynically? She was still fighting that sort of attitude.

She would have to raise this with Bernard before telling Lester anything.

'I will make inquiries,' she said. 'As soon as possible.'

He stood up to show her out, 'I would appreciate that.'

As they reached the door, he said, 'You couldn't imagine Avenol, in the old days, making such a request?'

She laughed. 'No. Never. Nor Sir Eric.'

'These are different times: the rules are bent now.'

'Yes—we live in times bent out of shape.'

She arranged an appointment with Bernard at the Club during the day, outside the Club's usual trading hours.

She realised that she had never been to the Club in the daytime.

She went down the steps and found the door open. What windows there were to the Club were open to allow airing and some light streamed in, but it still had the comfortable, decadent smell of stale alcohol, of cigarette smoke, of perfume, and of perspiration.

A cleaner worked away at the wooden tables with furniture polish and the smell of the polish smelt like it was attempting to *renew* the atmosphere.

That sunlight which did get into the Club from the light well and through the transom windows was feeble and seemed reluctant to enter such a decadent atmosphere.

There in his office, in this semi-daylight, Bernard was just another businessman. He was dressed in a business suit and tie, albeit a rather colourful tie, working away on figures, order books and invoices, with an adding machine in front of him, the enamel worn from the lever.

'Catering supplies and coal, questions of dancers' fees, costume makers behind in their schedule, a shortage of silk— the life of a nightclub proprietor. As you see, behind the scenes there's no flamboyance and no romance.' He rose to greet her.

Even his voice was more manly and everyday.

They kissed on both cheeks.

When seated over coffee out in the empty Club, their voices were drowned out by the noise of a woman dusting the carpets with a vacuum cleaner.

Bernard called to the woman to stop the vacuuming and to find some cleaning in the kitchens.

Edith explained Lester's request.

Bernard remained silent, considering it.

He then said, 'If the papers were used by Monsieur Joyce for his daughter and some diligent border guard or police officer found them to be forgeries, then what? What would Monsieur Joyce say about their origin? The trail of origin might be too obvious. The Irish connection for a start. And if it were traced back to Lester, what then? What would Lester say? How would it look for the status of the League? What would the Swiss government do? Would we all be at risk? Not just the Club—but Monsieur Joyce and his family. And the League as well. Unlike our other transactions, this one could leave a rather damaging trail. And is the moving of his daughter from one hospital in France to another in Switzerland of such priority to be raised above all the other matters we deal with here?'

'I understand the question of people who are well known, I get it at the League—they hope for special treatment but they also bring greater risk. The refugees come to us with their framed doctorates, their letters of commendation from governments long gone, their certificates of honourable mention.'

She thought about it. 'In some ways, it would be better to handle things on a first come, first served basis. But I suppose that is very Australian.'

'We would think of it as being very democratically Swiss. The French would think it was a matter of *égalité*.

'The Joyce matter would involve important people: Lester— and you—and a writer with a narrow reputation but considered to be important. The Swiss or the Germans may make an extra effort to trace the forged documents in this case. They may feel the tug of big fish. They may use harsh means to get their information. Nothing might protect us then.'

'What do you recommend?'

He thought again.

'If Lester's efforts through the official channels fail, I suggest that he signal this to you. And he should be circumspect in any visit he makes to Joyce. Not that Joyce would be watched. But we know about Swiss neighbours . . . And he should turn his back on the matter, making sure that he writes official letters to Joyce saying that nothing can be done. I will take it over from there. And the less you know about it, the better. My emissary will find out from Joyce what is needed to be known and I suggest that it be handled behind Joyce's back as well. If possible, the girl will simply arrive at his doorstep.'

She nodded. 'I'll tell Lester. I gather also that the daughter is troublesome.'

'How so?'

'Violent. During any travelling, she would need attendants who could handle her.'

'Mother of God.' Bernard ran a hand through his hair. 'Is there no end to it all?'

He was harried.

She said, 'At this stage it is all hypothetical.'

'Yes,' he said, tiredly.

Bernard changed the subject. 'How are things at the Palais?'

She shrugged. 'We pretend that we are still at the centre of the world. We pretend that we are not forgotten. Ambrose is working away at the Library.'

'Will the League take him back?'

'After the war? Maybe—no one is being employed at present, of course. I think Lester sees him as part of the League again. Seeks his advice. Uses him for indirect connection to the British Foreign Office.'

'Good. It is a bizarre position for you all to be in— isolated—reduced—to be so frustrated.'

'We spend our time planning the New World—the world after the war—and we will be involved in the peace negotiations. There is another peace conference to be planned.'

'But this time it is unconditional surrender? Isn't that what Churchill insists?'

'That is what he says. Though we will have some role in the grisly end, I daresay.'

'The Germans seem to have made their first mistake with the invasion of Russia. It may not be long now.'

'I see that even some of the Swiss are painting the V for Victory signs on walls and railway cuttings as Churchill asked.'

'I am told the street women in Paris see the opening of their legs in a V as an anti-Nazi act,' Bernard covered his mouth with his hand and winked. 'Oh, that is a rather vulgar thing to say. Apologies.'

Edith smiled. 'Tch, tch, Bernard.'

As she left his office, they hugged, hugged longer than for a parting hug. A hug to give each other strength.

She met Lester on a street corner away from the Richemond where Joyce and his family were staying. To her surprise he wore a beret and a cravat and looked like a caricature of a Swiss artist.

She did not know whether to laugh.

'I thought I would not dress like a Secretary-General.'

'You certainly don't look like a Secretary-General.'

'Do I look artistic?'

She made a play of examining him critically, 'You look like a Secretary-General disguised as an artist.' She laughed.

He joined in the laughter.

'Perhaps we should act as a couple involved in a clandestine assignation of a romantic kind,' he said, light-heartedly, as they walked towards the hotel.

'I think that the secret police here in Geneva know us well enough by now.'

'I think so.'

She suspected that he had dressed that way to fit in with Joyce as a writer.

As they walked she glanced at him again. She had never thought of Lester romantically. No. He was a family man and not her type. And he had been a journalist before he became a diplomat and she had had her experience with a journalist.

'If we feel we're being watched by the police we could, I suppose, act as lovers, if you wish,' she said, not really knowing what that might require.

'No, I don't think we want that on their files.' He smiled at her. 'But don't think that isn't an attractive proposition for me.'

They asked for Joyce at the reception desk.

His wife Nora came down to greet them and took them up to the room.

Their son, in his late twenties, joined them.

'I read a very early book of your poems, *Chamber Music*, and *Dubliners*,' Lester said. 'Do you remember the notice of *A Portrait of the Artist* in the *Freeman's Journal*?'

'I remember it was a fine notice.'

'I have to admit I am responsible for the notice.'

'Well, I thank you again.'

'You're generous. I'm sure the notice was inadequate. I haven't read the book for fifteen years but I remember vividly the first chapter which describes a typical Irish household in the crisis of 1890.'

It was obvious that Joyce had poor eyesight. His wife found something for him and put it in his hand rather than passing it to him.

She went about preparing tea.

Lester went on nervously, 'I tried to read *Ulysses* but didn't finish it. I remember that it gave a fine impression of Dublin's beauty but the Dublin argot beat me. I don't know how foreigners got along with the argot.'

Edith put in that she had enjoyed *Ulysses* but had something of a struggle with the Irish argot.

Joyce seemed pleased that she'd read it but gave his attention to Lester.

Joyce said that it had been translated into French, German, Czech, Russian, Japanese, and he thought Italian as well. 'I sometimes wonder what a monsieur in Tokyo made of it. Have you read *Finnegans Wake?*'

Lester said he hadn't seen it yet. 'Is it a big book?'

Edith felt embarrassed by the naivety of the question.

Joyce chuckled, 'You remind me of the story of the two drunks on the road to Dundalk who kept falling into the ditch on the side of the road. A stranger came along and asked them how far it was to Dundalk. One of the drunks said it wasn't the length of the road that worried them, it was the width.'

They all laughed.

Joyce told them of a peculiar publication of some of his poems set to music by twelve composers of different nationalities—'an international type of thing'.

She supposed that he assumed that might interest them.

Edith noticed that the family spoke to each other in Italian. Joyce saw her interest in this and said, 'The children were all born in Trieste and grew up there. Didn't speak English until they were grown.'

Joyce said the family and he enjoyed the wireless and listened to the quiz show on Sunday nights.

'On one night they asked the contestant—a labourer from Dublin—who had won some literary prize and the labourer said that he thought it was James Joyce and he was adjudicated correct. I stood up and bowed to the wireless.'

Lester and Joyce spent some time talking about common acquaintances in Dublin.

Tea was served and Joyce then outlined the problems of getting his daughter out of France.

Edith took notes.

'How was Mr Joyce?' Ambrose called from his study after she had let herself into the apartment on her return.

She went to the door of his study, 'Oh, it's rather disappointing to meet an author—though thrilling at first. Authors shouldn't talk about ordinary things such as the weather and postal difficulties.' She added, 'He praised Swiss wine.'

Ambrose turned in his chair, pushing back his typewriter, 'You talked about wine?'

Ambrose was dressed immaculately and conservatively *en femme* and she again wondered how it was that she could find it so *normal*—Ambrose as *Carla*, the name by which he was known at the Club.

'Joyce said he preferred the Swiss white wines to the French.'

She straightened the emerald brooch at his neck. 'He likes the wines of Neuchâtel. And said we weren't to tell the French. He says he always drinks white.'

'The Swiss wines *are* rather good. As we well know. What else did he say?'

Out in the living room, they sat down and she told him other snippets, her head on his shoulder, legs stretched out.

'We expect serious authors to speak with golden tongues,' she said. 'To speak wisdom and never to stoop to the banalities of us mere mortals.'

'Oh, you *know* authors—Robert was an author.'

'Of one book. And a detective fiction at that.'

'And you knew Caroline.'

'Caroline was a beginner when I knew her. And even she has written only two books. It is, I suppose, the older writers who should speak only wisdom. They should speak only in aphorisms.'

'I imagine that even authors have to buy groceries. Put out the cat. Unless they can afford servants.'

She looked at him with warm feelings. Tonight even his make-up seemed so perfect and his hair well brushed and stylishly feminine.

He was more a girlfriend now than anything else. Sometimes perhaps a big sister.

Sometimes a *courtesan*, although their love making had become more a comfort than an adventure. Still, they sometimes ignited each other's dark and rich desires and were, at times, surprised by the passion which sprang from their bodies. Perhaps it was his two identities which created the passion, allowing Ambrose and she occasionally to become intriguing strangers to each other. And also allowing her to become a stranger to herself. It allowed out to play a part of her which she had difficulty describing.

Sometimes after the long, deeply intimate fondling and fingering, and the aroused playing with their breasts, and bodily *frottage*—sometimes full penetration, but not always—they fell apart exhausted and sated. Their bodies seemed always to suggest their own personal ways and needs.

She had never talked with her mother about the matter of married love, even though they had been a free-speaking family. The nearest they came to it was when she was a young woman and her mother had let it be known that she possessed a rare, privately printed copy of the *Kama Sutra*—but this revelation was made only when Edith was at university. And, handing the book to her after she had asked to see it, her mother had said that it was a marriage manual and asked her not to glance through it in front of her but to read it in private, 'And return it—although I think I am familiar enough with it by now.'

In her bedroom, blushing scarlet, she had devoured the book. Even though she was at university and considered herself *widely* read she found the *Kama Sutra* breathtaking. Her mother and she had never discussed the book, and a few weeks later she reluctantly put it back in her mother's bedroom, unremarked.

Ambrose had shown her copies of erotic German and French magazines which had revealed to her other astounding things about the nature of human coupling. At her request, he had bought a copy of the *Kama Sutra* through an agent who handled such books. The *Kama Sutra* and his magazines still aroused her.

There were times when she asked that they look at them together, which led to love play.

And sometimes when alone in the apartment she delved into them, although there was no reason why she should be secretive about it, given the candour and character of their relationship. This secretiveness was perhaps some leftover, ineradicable modesty or maybe it was the thrill of furtive pleasure. And, she had to admit, the thrill of solitary self-pleasuring.

It was also erotic for them both when they shopped for clothes together although he had to play the bored husband to prevent the shop attendants becoming suspicious, a role which he sometimes forgot or rather *overflowed.*

They were fortunate that their sizes were the same. And their taste. Their favourite lingerie shop must have considered Edith extravagant in her needs, especially now during war when silk was expensive. But they continued to spend rather a lot on lingerie. They shared that indulgence.

These sorts of shopping expeditions and trying on the clothes at home inevitably led to love making of a special kind, too.

'Is Joyce to live in Zurich?' he asked.

She smiled at him. 'Could look up Dieter,' she said.

'Oh yes, Dieter—I had quite forgotten him.'

'You forget your ... friends ... rather quickly.'

He kissed her cheek, 'Now, now—and remember he did desert the Germans—and he was right about everything he told us, sadly. He's out of the war now. A neutral. At least I presume so.'

She'd kept going back over that episode in her mind and hoping that she'd done as much as she could at the time.

Dieter had passed out of their lives. Through the Club they had secured papers for his residency in Switzerland and he'd moved to German-speaking Zurich. And yes, he was no longer an enemy.

'War is between states and not individuals,' she pronounced. 'When an enemy lays down his arms he is no longer an enemy? Is that what we say?' She remembered the pain of it all back then.

'Something like that.'

'I seem to remember that was part of your argument back then. Or your *excuse.*'

'Was it? How clever of me.'

'How sly, darling.'

James Joyce died in Zurich. His daughter stayed in the clinic in La Baule. Switzerland was not invaded. And there in the Palace of Nations they watched the Germans gradually face defeat.

War's End

1 945

They continued to hear news of the war's end although Churchill hadn't been on the wireless to make it official, so there was some part of Edith—and probably some part of most of the small band at the League—which held back their belief. Paris had been liberated and the end had been coming for months but still some fighting went on.

Frustratingly, the end didn't seem to be coming in a single definite pronouncement.

The world conference to plan the peace was about to begin in San Francisco and Edith thought that might officially mark the end of it all.

She was already packed for it; they were simply awaiting confirmation of their sailing times.

Edith found something strange about her reaction to the end of the war.

Perhaps it was because they'd all become expert at living in a time of war. Now that expertise meant nothing. Their special status of being the Geneva staff holding the fort at the League would also now mean less.

They were now required to remember how to be expert at

living in a world *after* war. And that seemed an exhausting idea after all the dreaming of it and planning for it.

Life after the war seemed to have fallen on her and those around her as some perplexing burden.

In war, so much had been put on hold in one's life and in the life of the world and, of course, the future of the League and their futures.

All those decisions, for so long on hold, were now lit up, and from them new uncertainties were glaring.

There'd been something strangely carefree, if not irresponsible, about living in a time of war. Anything could happen in a time of war—parachute invasion, enemy administration, death from the sky or from poison-gas bomb—which made one feel that personal decision-making on a serious scale was not possible, and this limbo granted a careless freedom.

But now one had to begin to be *serious* about one's personal life.

They'd all been called to the Library to hear an announcement from Sean Lester but she doubted that he'd heard anything new about the end of the war since she'd chatted to him earlier that morning and he'd said nothing about it.

Though one never knew.

He clambered up on a chair.

Grave-faced, M. Vallery-Radot, the librarian, banged a teaspoon on a cup, 'People! Your attention, please. *Silence.*'

Lester had some notes in his hand.

Maybe the war had ended.

Maybe at last, the Library would cease to be the League's central office and M. Vallery-Radot would be back in charge.

At last, he would have proper silence in the Library.

Ambrose came around from his desk in one of the back book bays and stood with her.

What would happen to him? He'd been working in with the League staff recently but that arrangement would have to be either formalised or terminated.

They all moved in around Lester.

When everyone had quietened, they could hear a woman talking on the telephone. She became conscious that she was not in private and they heard her say clearly to the person on the other end of the line, 'Must go now, the Secretary-General is about to speak to us.'

The telephone, now free, began ringing and stopped only to begin ringing again.

Lester waved at them, indicating that they should let the telephone ring.

Lester said that everyone knew the war was coming to an end any day now and that he would be leaving to lead the League delegation to the world conference in San Francisco.

In fact, he said, this would be the last time he would have a chance to speak to them.

'When I return it will be with the arrangements for the New League. And everyone will soon get some well-deserved home leave—including, I hope, myself, and, in my case, some fishing—before we take up the task of rebuilding the world.'

He consulted his speech notes.

'Before I—and one or two of you—' he looked at Edith 'leave for San Francisco, I would like to say some words to you all.'

He looked down at his notes. 'Here in this fine Palace of Nations we were an important part of the political frontline against the Nazis and the world will not forget that. Your names will be engraved in stone. School children will know your names as well as they know those of great generals. Our vigil was made tolerable by two facts: that we kept busy at the world's work; and that we were doing something of great consequence symbolically. Alone in a warring world, we held high a banner through these terrible times which said "There is a possibility of reason and sanity in the world." I am proud—and you should be proud—that we held up that banner.'

His sincere Irish voice and strong words already had some of them tearful.

The ringing of the telephone sounded now like a type of modern musical accompaniment.

'I have already been privy to the plans for a New League, of which I promise you all will be a part. This time, this time, *we will make it work.*'

'Hear, hear,' M. Vallery-Radot said, standing beside the chair on which Lester stood, as if it were expected of him, and perhaps as part of his reclaiming of the Library.

All there in the room clapped vigorously.

'You should be proud that we kept the flag flying by publishing, without missing a single issue, *The Monthly Bulletin of Statistics* and *Wartime Rationing and Consumption.* The weekly *Epidemiological Record*—going now for nearly twenty years—the *Health Bulletin*—forgive me for not listing all our work, but we did keep working and we showed the world that we were still here by publishing and circulating our publications as best we could.'

More clapping.

'Yes, it may seem to some to be simply a bureaucratic thing that we did. But what could be more important than to have fair and reliable servants to the world giving fair and reliable information upon which fair and reliable decisions may be made? Never before in the history of the world were people willing to dedicate themselves to this trust above national allegiance. Isn't that a momentous offering?

'Now I want to make one thing very clear—and I have said this privately to some of you and now I wish to say it publicly and unequivocally: all the talk you've heard about the Supervisory Commission preparing to liquidate the League is nonsense. *There is to be no liquidation of the League.*'

Vigorous and prolonged clapping. Ambrose and Edith smiled at each other.

'There'll be all sorts of discussions—legal and administrative—about the shape of a New League. But there *will* be a New League. There is no talk of us "selling up" the League.

I need simply quote to you the words of the American Secretary of State, Cordell Hull, who spoke recently of a "bigger and better League". Our own President of Assembly, that valiant Norwegian, Carl Hambro, in a magazine article published in the United States says quite unequivocally that "talk of *reviving* the League is false ..."'

Lester paused dramatically, as people looked up again, uncertain of what they'd just heard. 'President Hambro says, such talk of revival is false ...' Lester continued with wonderful Irish emphasis, ' "because the League is very much alive". There can be no reviving of the League because the League is very much alive,' he repeated.

There was general clapping.

'And you here today are the living embodiment of the League and have been for these long grim years ...' Edith fancied Lester looked straight at her. 'You are the proof that it is *very much alive.*'

She felt tearful. She looked at Ambrose who had also touched the corner of an eye with a finger.

'During the war there was no meeting of Council—no meeting of Assembly. There was no meeting even of the Supervisory Commission. What *did* continue was the Secretariat—*you—you* continued.'

He paused and looked around at them all, moving from one pair of eyes to another and then back to his notes.

'At the world conference in San Francisco your interests will be looked after. And the US will be joining us now, for certain. Of that there can be no doubt this time. As we know, the Americans have been a part of the Dumbarton Oaks proposals; America is going to remain part of the world community now the war is won. The days of the Americans withdrawing into isolation are over.'

Hearty clapping. The telephone ringing and stopping and ringing again.

'And the Soviets will be there.'

More clapping.

'The Germans and the Japs may be missing ...'

Cheers.

'But only for a time. They will ultimately be brought back into the world community.'

Only light clapping for this.

'I have other news—and it is perhaps just as important.'

His voice changed to a lighter tone, and he pushed his speech notes into his coat pocket. 'The news is this—the Bavaria is about to reopen.'

Cheers.

'I was actually invited to see the renovated Bavaria only this week by its new owners. It may not be quite the way we remember it from before the war—well, the Bavaria has a swanky new ceiling which I think we all would agree, if our memory serves us well, was overdue. There are now rather grand chandeliers, which allows me to show off some Latin: *post tenebris lux*—you Latin scholars will know that means After Darkness, Light. Very appropriate for the new Bavaria of our new world.'

The word 'lux' passed sadly across Edith's memory. Brave Lux. Maybe he'd be heard now in the emerging new world.

'So it won't be long before we'll see statesmen, newspaper reporters, League staff, shoulder to shoulder again in the good-natured atmosphere of that much-loved historic tavern.'

Cheers.

'I remember—and many of you here will remember—when the German Chancellor Stresemann and the French Prime Minister Briand rubbed shoulders with us in good comradeship over ales at the Bavaria after the first war. International comradeship will return. In due course, with the passing of time ...'

'Hear, hear,' said M. Vallery-Radot and a couple of others, but this sentiment of universal comradeship was left in abeyance by most of them. Too early for that.

'Our colleagues will be returning shortly to Geneva from their far-flung outposts—from the Labor Office in Montreal, from the Economic and Finance section in Princeton, the Drug Organisation from Washington. And the Treasury from London—I hope they bring our money back as well!'

Laughter.

'In our League staff the world has the best interpreters, précis-writers and internationally trained stenographers that the world has ever known. And the best organisers of international conferences—something we invented—and the best international administrators.'

Cheers. Some of the staff patted each other on the back.

Seeing this, Lester said, 'Go on—you deserve it—pat your backs!'

Cheers and hearty patting of backs.

'Enough speech-making.' He was roundly clapped but then held up his hands for one last silence. 'To celebrate the imminent departure of our delegation to the San Francisco conference, I declare today a half-day holiday and invite you to join me for lunch at the Bavaria where I can say farewell to each of you individually.'

There was sustained clapping as Lester stood down from the chair, helped by M. Vallery-Radot.

No one picked up the ringing telephone.

'Good speech,' she said to Ambrose, wiping a tear with her handkerchief.

'Yes, good speech. Though he's forgotten that Cordell Hull's no longer Secretary of State.' His voice was husky.

'Oh well, we've been a little cut off over here,' she laughed.

They both went over to Lester and they all shook hands for want of any other way to express the drama of the hour.

'Has the Bavaria really installed chandeliers, Sean?' Ambrose asked, clearing the huskiness from his voice.

'Indeed it has,' said Lester, also trying to clear his voice of emotion and to find his everyday voice. 'In a strange way, I see the renovations as a vote of confidence in the future of the League. A good omen.'

She, too, found her businesslike voice. 'The old-timers will be taken aback when they return and see the chandeliers.'

'The caricatures of League dignitaries still there?' Ambrose asked.

'Still there. We may, of course, see Derso and Kelen back.'

'You, of course, will go as soon as you can to Ireland and see your family ... How long has it been?' she said.

Lester became a little husky again. 'You know my youngest has grown from being a girl of thirteen to a woman of eighteen and I wasn't there ...'

He pulled himself together. 'Anyhow, I can get my secret diary out from under the stone in the gardens.'

'It'll be a bestseller,' she said.

He looked at her with interest. 'You think it might be publishable?'

But before she could answer, he shook his head, 'Too many strong opinions. I let off a lot of steam in that journal.'

'It might be a time for strong opinions,' Ambrose said.

'Could well be,' Lester agreed.

Lester shook their hands again, emotionally, 'Thank you both. Thank you for being here during the bad years—or were they the good years?'

He turned to Ambrose and said, 'As I've said before, I'm very glad that you'll be with us in San Francisco—we shall need you.'

Lester thought for a moment. 'Hope you can find your way clear to coming back on staff eventually?'

'We'll see,' Ambrose said.

'There'll be a place for you.'

'Thank you, Sean.'

Lester then moved off to talk to others.

'You'll have a position after San Francisco,' said Edith. 'Otherwise Lester wouldn't have authorised your coming along with us.'

'Maybe.'

'You've been rehabilitated. Forgiven. Darling, you're back.'

'Sounds like it.'

'That speech made it feel like the end of the war, didn't it? Where were you when the other one ended—on Armistice Day? Everyone remembers where they were on that day.'

'I was at the Front in France. It was a very strange day indeed.'

'Tell me.'

'I was travelling up to a field hospital with an ambulance unit of the 56th—the London Division—and in that last hour before the Armistice was signed and the cease-fire occurred we had a Lance Corporal stretcher-bearer shot dead. We all thought at the time that it was the last shot fired in the war and that he'd been the last person to die in the war— the worst possible luck. We found out later that all along the line there were cases like that, of men killed in the last minutes.'

Ambrose drifted away into his memories momentarily and then pulled himself back with a smile. 'Oh, another thing— I cried with anger on Armistice Day.'

'Why *anger?*'

'Along with Marshal Pétain and others, I thought it shockingly premature.'

'The Germans should've been thoroughly beaten?'

'Yes.'

'I think it's the only time that a war has stopped too soon.'

'And you, Edith? Where were you on Armistice Day?'

'Nothing as remarkable as your Armistice Day.'

'Tell me your Armistice Day.'

'By Greenwich Mean Time our 11th of the 11th of the 11th was really in the evening but we celebrated it anyhow at our morning time—perhaps the news was withheld to synchronise with Europe. I was at Sydney University studying science—my second year. We were in the lab and Elkin, a member of the

Public Issues Society, came in and said that the war was over. He cried. It's disconcerting to see a teacher cry. We stood in our places in our white lab coats, test tubes or whatever in hand, until he waved us out of the room, saying something about there being no lectures that day. Oh . . .'

'What?'

'I've just remembered who was beside me during the celebrations later down in Martin Place—a student named Arthur Tuckerman.'

Scraper's friend.

'You all right?' Ambrose asked.

'Oh, memories from when I was back in Australia and Armistice Day—all a little too much for me.'

He put an arm around her.

She looked at Ambrose. 'The man Scraper—I told you about the shocking incident. He came back to mind.'

Scraper had joined the day.

'I suppose we've to take whatever memories are handed out to us.'

'It's sickening. It's as if he's still manipulating me.'

Edith looked around at the people she'd worked with during the war years.

It would be the last day, really, that she would see them in this setting. After San Francisco everything would be back to normal, everyone out of the Library and back to their offices, some of them gone forever and newcomers arriving.

She hesitated. 'Going to the Bavaria will be one of our good memories of this day. I think I should try to control the memories of this day. Maybe do things which will crowd out other parts.'

Jeanne joined them.

'We were just telling each other about where we were on Armistice Day.'

'I will tell you where I was!' Jeanne said. 'But only over drinks.' She winked.

'Let's go to the Bavaria,' Ambrose said.

Jeanne said. 'Come on, Edith, it's our half-holiday. You're appointed Leader of the Fun Club. Let's go.'

Jeanne had hoped to go to San Francisco but wasn't in the team.

Having piled into whatever cars were available, they arrived at the Bavaria and were welcomed in by the new owner and the new staff. There were no staff from the old Bavaria. God knows where they'd ended up.

Everyone exclaimed over the renovations.

Privately, Edith yearned for the smoky, dingy old Bavaria.

She was pleased to again see the Derso and Kelen caricatures of League personalities from before the war.

'I met Robert here,' she said to Ambrose. 'He pursued and, I suppose, courted me here.'

Was that a good memory to have today?

Couldn't be stopped.

She smiled as she recalled one time early in her career as a newly arrived young officer at the League. She herself had designed some stationery stands for the delegates' tables, and had them made and put in place. They'd all been souvenired by the delegates.

But she'd gone to the Bavaria clutching two of the new stationery stands, to find Ambrose and instead found Robert who was writing at a corner table.

'It is going to happen,' she called to him as she pushed through the crowd.

'What's going to happen?' He was deep in self-preoccupation and had, for whatever perverse reason, obviously not been at the concluding meeting of the conference which had renounced war.

'What, Edith Campbell Berry, is going to happen?'

She tried to bring her voice to a level of diplomatic calm.

Unpredictably, she felt protective of the worried journalist. She saw him as a person who had a gloomy pessimism about life. She felt sorry that she had to break the news to him and spoil his hopeless view of things. 'There is going to be a renunciation of war—the Kellogg-Briand Peace Pact has been initialled.'

He smiled at her. 'Bierce said peace is a period of cheating between wars.'

'Ah, you think nations will cheat on the Pact—I see you are a follower of rebus sic stantibus,*' she said, saying it for the first time. But by saying it to him she had, she thought, neutralised him. She also saw that she was displaying her new diplomatic maxim, seeking his approval.*

She must not sit with him. His gaze was transfixing and his manner always reached out at her.

'Rebus sic stantibus,' he repeated, looked up at her again, focusing on her, smiling with approval. 'I am relieved that you know rebus sic stantibus, *Edith Berry, very much relieved.' He returned to his drink. 'Very much relieved.'*

'You miss the importance of all this. For the first time, nations are talking about the end of war. Don't you see? With this Pact of Peace a change has happened in the psychology of the world. That is what has happened.'

He did not seem convinced.

'And here—here is a memento of this historic occasion.' She gave him one of the stationery stands.

He took it, surprised and pleased. He turned it around admiringly.

'I thank you, Edith Berry.'

She broke away from his gaze and left him to go over to Ambrose.

'They are going to do it,' she said to Ambrose, 'going to renounce war.'

'I heard. It was buzzing all over the Palais an hour ago.'

'Buy some champagne.'

'I will.'

Edith reminded herself that history was being made and she

*was where it was being made. She laughed wryly at her contri-
bution to history—stationery stands.*

Tears came to her eyes again, this time for the wasted effort
of her marriage to Robert, for her bad treatment of Ambrose
back then, for those innocent days of error.

Was that recollection of Robert going to be part of her
memories of this day?

She turned to Ambrose. 'You never seemed jealous of
Robert?'

'I was.'

'You were?'

'To Robert,' he said.

'To Robert,' and they touched glasses.

'In the long run, it turned out you didn't have anything
to fear from him.'

'In the long run? In the long run we are all dead, Edith.'

She hugged Ambrose and then moved off, hugging each of
her old friends and colleagues.

She hugged Jeanne and said, 'It's not the same, is it?'

Jeanne looked at her and said, 'Between us?'

She'd meant the Bavaria.

She held Jeanne's hand and looked into her eyes. 'My old
university motto is *sidere mens eadem mutato*: "though the sky
be changed our spirit is the same ..." We are the same,
Jeanne.'

'Are we, Edith?'

Edith felt cold. 'Yes, yes, yes.'

But as she said it, the words fell to the floor.

Jeanne looked wistful.

They hadn't been the same since Avenol. Despite every
effort on both their parts to act as if nothing had happened
to them back then.

Their masks had remained in place during the war years,
and now the masks had fallen off.

Oh hell.

Oh hell.

'We will make something different now, Jeanne, we will try—you'll see. New skies above us now, we will . . .'

They looked into each other's eyes and Edith saw that it was not going to happen.

Another outcome of war. The war had been a time of unfinished business, business buried because of the crisis.

Everything was going to change. Not only with Jeanne.

She looked around the outwardly merry crowd.

Not with Ambrose, that was safe—but perhaps it, too, would be different?

Some of the crowd began to sing.

She still held Jeanne's hand as she looked around the crowd, but Jeanne's hand seemed cold.

She knew which of those in the crowd would stay on and which would now go home never to return—go away to start their ordinary lives which had been postponed during the war.

Go to their banal and happy lives.

Her eyes came back to Jeanne. She'd lost Jeanne.

That couldn't be helped.

They let go of each other's hands.

'Going back to Paris, Jeanne?'

'As soon as I can.'

'Good.'

'Go well, Edith.'

'Go well, Jeanne.'

They were both tearful.

Edith turned away from her.

She went back to Ambrose to assure herself that he would not change. There he was in his sardonic, elegant self, chatting with urbanity. He would not change. She kissed his cheek and said that she was going to mingle, and she pushed her way through the crowd to find another drink as she had so many, many times there in the Bavaria, and also to find some more strong, good memories to paste onto the page of this unsettled day.

Long Day's Journey Into History

As the UN train pulled in to San Francisco, Edith looked out of the carriage window and searched for Sweetser's face.

She saw him wearing a red carnation and holding up a placard, saying 'Welcome to the League of Nations: Part Two', with their names on it.

He had printed his name at the bottom in large letters.

Perhaps in case no one remembered his face.

She smiled. He was surrounded by others she took to be from the United Nations conference, although she didn't recognise any of them.

The platform was jammed with reception groups meeting the train from New York.

Other conference officials held placards identifying themselves as meeting points for national delegations. Uniformed chauffeurs held name placards or offered limousine service. She turned back to the others.

'There's something of a reception. Dear Sweetser is holding a placard with our names on it. And his own. How very American.'

'Sweetser always feared he would not be recognised,' said

Ambrose, rising to get the briefcases from the overhead rack. 'He reintroduced himself every time one met him.'

Ambrose handed the briefcases to their respective owners.

'Sweetser, what a curious man,' Loveday said, rising from his seat, dusting his trousers. 'Indispensable, but where does one put him within any given organisation?'

'Undoubtedly he's found a title,' Ambrose said. 'And while you all discover what that title is, I'll lure a porter or two.'

'I'm glad to have him here—after all, he's one of us,' Lester said, also rising from his seat and stretching. 'Makes one feel a little more at home.'

'Remember that he's now an employee of the State Department,' Loveday said.

'But looking after *us*, I hope,' said Lester. 'He and Ruth always had a magnificent table.'

They found their way down the steps, assisted by the black train attendants, out onto the platform.

'Ambrose,' Lester said, 'would you look after any tipping that's necessary, please? I find American tipping something of a puzzle.'

'Of course,' Ambrose said and went off.

Why would he think Ambrose knew about American tipping?

'Gerig and Gilchrist are supposed to be here too in some capacity,' Edith said, looking around the platform as they moved towards Sweetser.

She wondered whether there would be the usual bodyguards and all the other American fuss.

She rushed ahead of the others and hugged Sweetser, his placard hard against the back of her head as he pulled her towards him. 'Oh, Arthur ...'

'Thank God you're here, Edith. Nothing can go wrong now.'

They parted and looked each other over.

'Let's thank the gods that you're here, Arthur. None of us speaks American.'

Her breathing was constricted with emotion. 'It's so grand for us all to be together again,' she said. She felt tearful with the joy of it.

'And was that the enigmatic Ambrose I saw darting about?'

'Oh yes, Ambrose is very much here.'

'I am told through the grapevine,' Sweetser said, 'that you and he are ... companions, still? And he's working with the delegation?'

'Not *with* the delegation as such. He's my *aide-de-camp.*'

Sweetser put on his face of discretion and nodded knowingly.

'Oh, there are no secrets, Arthur,' she said. 'He's more an *attendant lord,* I suppose.'

They both watched as Ambrose herded up porters. 'He's been magnificent behind the scenes—his remarkable connections and so forth. With me, the office really gets two for the price of one.'

'I remember him in the old days when we began the League—he was almost second-in-command. He came over to Geneva on the League train from London in 1921. Now he repeats history by coming to San Francisco on the UN train. He's a damned fine fellow.'

'He is, indeed, a damned fine fellow.'

'And still a spy?' Sweetser said, grinning.

'Oh, indubitably.'

'Feel in retrospect that he was badly treated,' Sweetser said.

She linked arms with Arthur. 'The English never believed he was a spy.'

Arthur laughed. 'And now, as it turns out, everyone was a spy during the war. We all ended up being spies.'

Lester and Loveday reached them. Edith could see the joy in the reunion of the men, the aching bonds which gripped them as they shook hands using both their hands in that positive men's way, and then thumping each other's backs. They had put civilisation together after the first war and had then seen that civilisation fall apart.

Now they were here to put it back together again.

The men talked excitedly with much laughter.

'Not only is America in the League: the League is now in America!' Sweetser said, as usual implying that he'd at last brought it off. Maybe he had—at last.

'Well said.'

She was still tight with emotion and tears, but she turned back to business and looked at the other people around Sweetser and then realised that perhaps they were not all with Sweetser, that some were simply part of the throng. There were officials and people in military uniforms galore still milling about on the platform.

'Which are our people?' she asked Sweetser, quietly.

She could see that Lester and Loveday were also interested in who was there.

Arthur said, 'For now, I'm it.' He did an imitation of a tap dance and bowed. 'I'm your reception party—the formalities come later.'

'That's a relief,' said Lester.

'We're working with an improvised staff,' Sweetser said. 'This is not Geneva—no well-oiled machine here—*yet*. There is great chaos, as you would expect.'

Lester and Loveday were looking about them. 'We saw Victor Hoo on the train. Only face we knew.'

'Naturally there'll be the official stuff, but not on the railway platform. I have cars waiting. I'll find a porter.'

'Ambrose is on that mission. And here he comes,' Edith said.

Ambrose arrived carrying newspapers and magazines, followed by two black porters with red caps and trolleys.

He and Sweetser embraced, which she found touchingly intimate, holding the embrace, their cheeks touching, Arthur patting Ambrose's back.

Then Arthur pulled away, saying, 'Enough is enough, Ambrose—people will talk.'

'You look well, Arthur,' Ambrose said, his voice tinged with emotion.

'Oh, I'm still overeating.'

'Since the end of the war we are all overeating.'

Ambrose said that the porters would get their luggage and the boxes of official documents and so on.

Loveday said, 'Have they provided cars for us?'

He probably expected brass bands, Edith thought.

Sweetser overheard him and said, 'It's all hell here at present, Alex—I collared some taxis to take us to the hotel. It's sheer hell in this city at present. Let's get you settled.'

She decided to let things just happen. 'Yes, let's get to the hotel—I'm dying for a hot bath.'

'I could do with a gin,' said Ambrose.

'We'll find you some gin, Ambrose. Instead of tonic or whatever pretence of moderation it is you put in your gin, we'll just drop in an olive and a dash of vermouth and call it a martini.'

'Sounds fine to me,' Ambrose said. 'Though I doubt that I need the olive.'

Sweetser ushered Loveday and Lester towards the exit.

Ambrose shepherded the porters as they made their way out of the station.

In the drive to the hotel, Lester told Arthur about the UN train trip across from New York. 'It was very moving. At every stop people gathered to cheer us on. I don't mean that they were actually cheering the League. They wouldn't have identified us as such, but the whole idea of the new United Nations—citizens, the mayor or city manager, were all out at each station. We sometimes got out to stretch our legs, talk with them. Wonderful to see.'

'We're making history here,' Sweetser said fervently.

Everyone laughed and Sweetser looked at them, not under-standing the source of the humour.

As they pulled into the hotel, Sweetser, obviously heading off their disappointment, said, 'Now remember, accommo-dation is scarce. The Soviets demanded the best, the Ameri-cans took the best, the French found the best—chaos, a dreadful scramble—but this is a decent enough hotel, and much better than it looks.'

'And the British are made think they *have* the best,' said Ambrose.

'Right!' said Sweetser, laughing.

Loveday asked whether Lester and he needed to be briefed.

'All that comes later, Alex. The official stuff all comes later,' Arthur said. 'For now, relax. Take in the sights.'

Edith and Arthur and Ambrose exchanged bleak glances. The hotel was less than first class. In New York they'd stayed in style at the Taft.

Sweetser said, 'I know the manager personally—Tremain Loud—you'll be well looked after. You'll be treated like royalty. Which you are.'

Aged bell boys helped Ambrose with the luggage. 'You'll be heartily tired of American hospitality by the end of it all, believe me.'

They went into the hotel lobby which smelled of the human comings and goings of many years.

'Get washed up, refresh yourself, get rested,' Sweetser said. 'I'll see you all tomorrow some time. Anything you need—ask for Tremain. Mention my name.'

Edith lay in the bath, glad of the oodles of American hot water, a gin and tonic water on the bath ledge.

They had not taken Sweetser's advice about martinis.

'Would you have expected someone to be either at the

railway station or in the lobby?' she called to Ambrose in the other room.

'As Arthur said, General Chaos was there to meet us. There'll be the usual banquets and balls. As Jane Austen said, "All those balls."'

'I don't believe she said that. At least there are flowers in the room.'

She heard him repeat 'All those balls.'

She smiled. 'I heard it the first time, darling, and not for the first time. I hope you are keeping in mind that Americans are never *risqué*. Was there anything at reception when you registered us at the reception desk?'

'Nothing official. Just a sewing kit from the management. One for each of us. Lester and Loveday took theirs. I left ours. Didn't see us doing much sewing.'

Over breakfast on the first day of the conference, their spirits were high. The four of them ate their American breakfast heartily.

'Have come to enjoy an American breakfast,' Ambrose said, 'At least, that is, once a day.'

'There is more national difference expressed in breakfast than any other meal,' Lester said. 'Must say something about how different nations view the demands of a coming day.'

'I cannot understand the strange idea that it's the most important meal,' said Ambrose. 'Surely dinner is the most important meal of the day? Or one could argue that all meals are equally important. I would've thought that it could be argued that the results of a good dinner carried over to the next day, so to speak.'

'We should have had Health Section do a study of breakfasts,' Loveday said.

'They did,' Edith said. 'The Nutrition Report, 1937.'

'The more I think about it,' said Ambrose, 'I have never

done anything important at breakfast. Lunch, yes. Dinner, yes. Breakfast never.'

'Is Arthur picking us up?' Loveday asked.

Edith said she understood entry passes for the seating at the opening session of the UN Assembly would be hand-delivered.

'Are they not calling for us?' asked Loveday peevishly.

'I have a feeling that we are to make our own way,' Edith said.

'Surely they'll send cars?' Loveday said again.

'Oh yes,' she said, making a note to herself to call Sweetser about transport.

'I'll go check with reception to see if the passes are here yet,' Ambrose said, sharing with Edith a glance of amusement at Loveday's fussing.

He returned, shaking his head. 'I'm inclined to think we should perhaps make our own way. Couldn't raise Sweetser on the telephone.'

Edith said, 'It'll be like one of the pre-war Geneva assemblies. Or the 1932 Disarmament Conference. Remember the problems with seating? Those different categories—the Diplomatic Tribune, the Delegates' entrance, the Press Gallery, the International Organisations Tribune, the Public galleries—all those different sets of seating, different tickets and different entrances. State Senators from America expecting diplomatic seats.'

'The Women's Organisations demanding their own seats and special passes,' Lester said. 'There was a very demanding Miss Dingman, I recall.'

'Assemblies were always hectic times,' Edith said.

'I remember a story about Arthur from the those days,' Ambrose said. 'He and Cummings were looking for a cab after some Assembly party. They found one with a driver asleep in the backseat. The story is that Sweetser got in and drove them both home without waking the driver—left the cab and the driver still asleep parked outside his house.'

'You know that Arthur was regularly censored at the League?' Lester said.

'How do you mean?' she asked.

'When Comert ran Information he couldn't trust Arthur's communications with the world—his letters, press statements and so on. Couldn't trust Sweetser's runaway diplomatic enthusiasm, shall we say. So all Arthur's official communications with the outside world were secretly routed and discreetly checked and edited. This led, of course, to the outsiders having a rather different view of Sweetser to that which we had, we who had to live with his rather exhausting enthusiasm.'

Lester then turned to her and said, 'What position do you want in the new organisation, Edith?'

'I might retire,' she joked. 'Might grow roses.'

'Can't see it,' Lester said. 'You must tell me what you would like to do. And you Ambrose, you've got a few good years left. Put something in writing which I can slip to Cardogan. Or maybe it's Hiss who handles the higher level appointments?'

'I wouldn't mind doing some welfare work in Europe, some reconstruction work,' Edith said.

'Put what you want in writing,' Lester repeated. 'And mention the salaries you would expect. Don't be modest.'

While waiting for the passes to arrive, they sat around the breakfast table after the other guests had gone, telling stories of the old times.

Then they moved to the lounge which reeked of a thousand cigarettes smoked by a thousand guests of times past.

'Ambrose, go to see if the passes have arrived,' Edith said. 'Time's passing.'

'The official opening isn't until 4.30,' Lester said. 'There's no need to become jittery. Though there'll be things to discuss with Hiss and the others.'

'I'd like us to have the damned passes and have all protocol correctly in place,' Edith said.

'Typically Edith,' Lester said, smiling.

She called after Ambrose, 'Call Arthur again, or maybe Gerig—he's part of the conference.'

Ambrose saluted.

'I don't quite know what to prepare for,' Lester said, suddenly troubled. 'I don't know what they will want to know about. I've made a selection of files but I keep thinking of things they might want answers on.'

'It would be unlikely that we'll be needed to go into depth on anything on the first day. It will be mere formalities,' Loveday said.

'I've prepared a general speech—the history of it all,' Lester said.

'Obviously you'll be called early,' Edith said.

'And there's the damned Russian problem. Am I to say something about welcoming them back into the fold? After all, we did throw them out. Now they're half-running the show.'

They separated then to go back to their rooms or to take a walk, leaving Ambrose as duty officer 'minding the shop'.

Edith strolled around the neighbourhood, finding it rather grim.

They met again at the hotel for a late lunch.

Over lunch, they speculated about the post-war world.

'Would you accept a joint Secretary-Generalship with a Russian?' Ambrose asked Lester.

'I want only to go back to Ireland and fish.'

'I think you should stay for the initial year. Help get things established,' said Loveday.

'Maybe for a year.'

'One thing is certain,' said Ambrose, 'there's no shortage of plans for the post-war world. It will be the best planned world we've ever known. Hope I fit in to someone's plan.'

They laughed.

'I think we should dust off the Bruce Report and table it at the conference,' Loveday said. 'That report said it all. The basis for restructuring the organisation is all there.'

Edith had almost forgotten the Bruce Report on reform of the League—it had been lost in the tumult of war.

'In my opinion, Bruce was the best Council President we ever had,' said Lester.

'He was good,' said Loveday.

'Better than Briand?' Ambrose asked.

'I think so,' said Lester.

They chatted but the good mood dwindled as they waited.

At 3 p.m., despite a number of telephone calls, the passes had still not arrived.

Loveday was grey-faced. Lester had ceased to be patient.

Edith considered calling the Australian delegation but she'd never met Evatt or Forde. Despite her visit home, she realised that she was now just too out of touch with Australian politics to ask favours.

All their calls and messages to the organisers were taken by efficient army voices, but no one returned the calls. It was obviously a chaotic situation over at the conference hall.

'Should we perhaps just land there?' Ambrose suggested. 'And take our seats?'

'It's a possibility,' Lester said, after a minute.

'I refuse to be put in a position which might embarrass us,' Loveday said.

Lester said, 'I agree, Alex. I don't want to have to be pushing through crowds to get to our places.'

'I could dash over, collect the passes, and then return,' Ambrose said looking again at his watch. 'Might be time enough.'

Edith looked at her watch. According to the front desk they were fifteen minutes by cab from the conference.

She went out and stood alone in the lobby, unable to take

the tension now smouldering among them. They should have gone to the Opera House much earlier, as Ambrose had suggested.

Now they were stuck.

She knew that it was an immense organisational task to run the first conference of a new world organisation. She knew all that. But still, the organisers should have had time for the usual diplomatic courtesies.

As she stood there fretting in the lobby, a military motor-cycle messenger arrived.

At last. Impatiently, she watched him park his cycle, remove his gloves and goggles, and take a dispatch from his saddlebag.

She followed him over to the front desk and heard the corporal asking for Lester.

She intervened. 'If it's for the League delegation, I'll take it.'

The corporal looked at her and then handed the packet to Edith.

She signed for it.

She told the clerk to call a taxi—urgently.

The clerk called the bell captain over who then walked out to the street and began blowing his whistle.

She almost ran to the lounge.

It was nearly 4 p.m. The official opening was in thirty minutes.

At the door of the lounge she cried out, 'The passes!' and held them high in the air. 'Arrived this minute by motorcycle.'

'Thank God for that,' Lester said.

They all stood, the tension falling away. Smiles breaking out.

Lester and Loveday picked up their briefcases.

'I'll arrange a taxi,' Ambrose said.

'I already have,' she said. 'It's on its way.'

She handed the envelope to Lester. 'It's addressed to you, Secretary-General.'

He opened it as they reached the door to the lobby.

He stopped and looked up at them. 'There's only one ticket.'

They all stopped.

'Perhaps it's a general pass for the whole delegation,' Ambrose said.

Lester read it again. 'It says clearly, "admit one" and there's a seat number.'

Lester looked at Loveday.

Edith asked Lester if she could see the pass, as if it were he who were making an error, an error which she alone would clearly see.

He was obviously dazed as he handed her the pass.

She read it. There was no error. It was a ticket for one. She handed it back, speechless.

She couldn't fathom it. 'It's a bungle,' she said.

'You must go, Sean,' said Loveday. 'Most obviously you must go.'

His voice was a brave attempt at control, at being businesslike.

Lester handed the ticket to Loveday, 'Alex, you go—I want you to be there. You've technical things to say. I'm more, well, symbolic.'

'Isn't it more appropriate that you go—as the Secretary-General?'

'If they'd wanted me there as Secretary-General the pass should have said so. Why should I need a pass at all ...?'

Edith was trying to get her head together. After all, the steering committee knew they were in San Francisco. They'd provided the accommodation. For the first time, she sensed a serious problem.

'It is my prerogative to nominate you to go,' Lester said. 'You can be my designate.'

Empathically, Edith felt all the dismay that Lester was showing.

'I would rather none of us went,' Loveday said. 'Let's make further contact with the steering committee. Let's sort it out. Let's find out what's gone wrong.'

'We can't boycott,' said Lester. 'That would be as rude as they have seemingly been.'

His movements and his voice were stiff with tension.

'It's surely an organisational blunder,' Ambrose said in his best calming, controlled voice. 'We all know these things can happen.'

To bungle on such a day, to bungle such people as Lester and Loveday was unforgivable. She felt sick to her soul.

'You go, Alex. I have no stomach for it now,' Lester said.

She and Ambrose stood watching the two legendary survivors of the League squabbling over the ticket.

She felt a protective duty but she was paralysed by panic. It was between these two men.

'You go, Alex. I would rather it that way.' Lester was already moving towards the elevator.

'I'll sort it out with the steering committee as soon as I arrive,' Loveday said, 'I'll see Hiss.'

They stood and watched Lester moving as if injured by a blow to his body, great spiritual pain showing in his effort at maintaining the dignity of his stride.

The elevator doors opened, he entered, then they closed and he was gone from sight.

Edith placed a hand on Loveday's arm. 'I'll come with you to the Opera House and sort this out.'

A bell boy came to tell them their taxi was waiting.

She turned to Ambrose. 'You'd better stay with Sean.'

Ambrose nodded. His face also showed severe shock. 'An abominable error. Must be an explanation.' He shook his head. 'I'll go up now. Take some tea perhaps.'

'Or Irish whisky,' she suggested.

648

'Maybe it's a time for Irish whisky.'

Of all of them, it was always Ambrose who one expected to somehow know the worst that life could deliver and always to be ready for it. That was his strength.

But she could see that he, too, was finding this moment testing.

She got into the cab with Alex.

They hardly spoke on the journey except for odd comments to ease the silence.

At the Opera House there was the usual milling of hundreds of delegates and others, searching for the correct entrance, searching for assistance, searching for papers, searching for associates.

It was clear that the opening was running late.

Press cameras flashed relentlessly.

Edith and Loveday pushed through and found the lobby of the conference.

A Marine sergeant on the door examined Loveday's pass, glanced at Edith, and pointed out that it was for one person only.

'We know that,' Loveday said with annoyance. 'But a seat must be found also for Miss Berry—at the delegation table. She is my associate. We'll be joined later by Mr Sean Lester, Secretary-General of the League of Nations. You must find his pass and hold it for him.'

'This is not a ticket for the delegation floor,' the sergeant said. 'It's a ticket for one person only in the auditorium.'

'We are the League of Nations delegation, sergeant. I am Alexander Loveday, director of the Economic and Financial Section.'

'I am sorry, sir, this ticket is not for a delegate. It is a pass for the top visitors' gallery.' The sergeant pointed upwards. 'This is an observer's ticket, sir.'

She and Loveday followed his pointing hand. He was

pointing to the second gallery high up and away from the great hall and the delegates and missions on the ground floor.

Tightly and coldly, in a voice scarcely concealing a raging indignation, Loveday asked the sergeant to take him to the Acting Secretary-General of the United Nations, Alger Hiss.

'At this time, sir, that is not possible. You are holding back the line—please stand aside.'

Edith and Loveday looked back and saw impatient faces of mission staff behind them. She recognised none of them.

They backed off out of the queue and the sergeant became occupied by the next person on the line, and Loveday and she went from his attention.

Edith broke back into the line and took the sergeant's arm and asked where the entrance to the top gallery was.

'You have to go out of the building and around to the side.'

He too was trying to keep his patience.

'Are you sure there's no mistake?' Edith said. 'Will you check with the Secretariat? Could you find Arthur Sweetser for me?'

'Ma'am, I have no time to check anything—the whole business is about to start. I simply read tickets and direct traffic.'

She went to Loveday, who was like some floundering insect in a stream, being edged towards the side. 'I'll try to find someone who can rectify it,' she said. 'It's some sort of stupid error.'

'I'll take my seat until I hear from you,' Loveday said.

She wrote down the number of his place in her notebook and he went off towards the visitors' gallery, struggling against the flow of arriving delegates.

Edith pushed through the queues waiting to talk with the besieged Marine clerks at the reception tables. Ignoring the other people queued for attention, she confronted a different Marine sergeant.

Standing before him, she took out her *lettre de mission* from the League, her League *carte d'identité*, and anything that in any way officially identified her. She laid the papers on the desk in front of this sergeant, explaining the significance of each document.

She then asked the sergeant to check the League of Nations seating allocation.

The clerk went through his list. 'League of Women Voters?'

She told him again. 'League of Nations.'

The sergeant did so and confirmed that one seat had been allocated in the top gallery.

Edith asked that the allocation of seating be changed. 'My name is Edith Berry, and I am *Chef du Bureau* to the Secretary-General.' In a sense, she was.

She pointed to her papers.

The sergeant glanced at her papers.

He refused to touch the papers as if fearing that his touch would give them some official recognition.

'I'm sorry, lady, these papers mean nothing to me. And I can't allocate seats.'

Edith demanded to see someone who could alter the allocation.

'The officials are all inside the conference hall. Maybe you could take it up with them tomorrow.'

'I want to take it up with them right now,' she said. 'I demand to see someone senior from the Conference Secretariat, from the steering committee.

The sergeant broke contact with her and began talking with another delegate. She stood there for a minute but his attention did not return to her. 'Excuse me—could I have your name, rank, and status?' she said.

He ignored her, now occupied with another person who also held official papers in his hand, written as far as she could see in Arabic.

Manoeuvre according to circumstances, Napoleon said.

What manoeuvre remained to her?

She couldn't very well lean across and take the sergeant by the collar, which she felt impelled to do.

Then, at last, she saw a familiar face in the crowd.

Judge Manley Hudson from the Court of International Justice. 'Thank the gods,' she said. 'At last some authority.'

She gathered up her papers from the desk.

She even made a private joke as she pushed her way to him, 'At last, justice,' she thought.

'Manley!'

They warmly grasped each other's hands.

'Edith—I am so glad to see you.'

'Manley, I urgently need your help. We're having dreadful trouble with seating. Alex is up the back row in the gods. He isn't even on the conference floor. Sean is back at the hotel because we haven't been given enough passes.'

Judge Hudson's face was close to rage.

'The Court has no tickets at all,' he said with anger. 'We have been excluded. The Court is excluded entirely.'

'What's happening here!' she cried. 'Why are they doing this!?'

Just then Gerig came up and greeted them. She hadn't seen Gerig since the World's Fair. From what she knew, he was now with the American delegation to the conference.

He seemed pleased to see them both.

She told him the situation. 'There's been a huge blunder! We have no tickets—not the League—not the Court—none of us.'

Gerig was uncomfortable. 'Not my area. I'm really hugely busy with the US delegation. But I'll do what I can.'

'What's the problem, Benjamin?' Judge Hudson cried out to him. 'Why are we excluded like this?'

'I fear it's the Russians, Judge.'

'The Russians?!'

'They are down on neutrals. The Irish, for example, who they think were too nice to Hitler—that excludes Lester.

They're down on Olivan from the Court because he's Spanish and they don't like Franco. And, of course, they are down on the League for expelling them in '39.'

'That misses the whole point,' she almost screamed. 'The people you mentioned are internationalists. Lester stood up to the Nazis. He gave his whole life to internationalism.'

Gerig showed extreme discomfort. 'I'll get the American delegation to take it up with the Russians—believe me, we have nothing but goodwill to the League people. I must go in now. But, Edith, I'm afraid that it might be one of those things where if I interfere they will do the opposite.'

He looked about and then said conspiratorially, 'Don't place too much trust in Hiss.' He moved away but stopped again, turned and called, 'Oh, where are you all staying?'

Edith told him the California Hotel.

'I'll call when I have some news.'

She stood there glowering, trying to think of a manoeuvre, but her indignation began to congeal, like cooling wax, into cold hard defeat.

Manley looked at her helplessly like a child.

'I don't understand,' she said, bitterly. 'How did we become the enemy?'

'I have to go,' he said simply, and walked off as if in a drugged state, going out of the building and down the steps into the street.

She wanted to go after him and help him but she felt she should somehow still do something to save the situation.

The foyer of the building was beginning to clear. The first conference of the United Nations was about to begin.

From inside the auditorium she heard a booming voice give the familiar preliminary announcements of the conference housekeeping arrangements. The sort of announcements she herself had made at many, many conferences, in many halls, in many countries.

She was now an outsider.

Bells were ringing.

If you want an audience, start a fight, she thought.

She looked around for someone to fight with.

And then Edith realised that she had no fight left.

Close to tears, she put her papers away in her handbag and found her way to the entrance to the top gallery where Loveday was.

As Loveday must have, she climbed the two sets of bare grey concrete stairs with iron-pipe railings.

At the top she was allowed as far as the door to the gallery but the Marine would not permit her to go inside.

She looked for Loveday.

He was seated in the second back row. He was seated as far from the rostrum down on the floor of the conference room as any seating could be.

He sat alone and crushed.

He had some conference proceedings paper in his hand.

She pulled back from the door, not wanting to catch Loveday's eye.

All those years. All the sweat and tears.

This lone figure represented all the thousands and thousands who had worked for the League, those people who'd come across the world from every nation to lend a hand in Geneva.

All this now diminished to a lone representative of the League at the back of the hall.

Thunderous applause broke out as the conference was declared open.

All those present stood and clapped except Loveday who remained seated.

Edith had never felt so cold. She had never felt such true and deep bitterness.

In the strange disembodied voice of the public address system, she heard someone say, 'We are plaiting a rope for a ladder to a ledge of a cliff on a mountain in a range of mountains.'

The words made her feel ill, she was close to vomiting.

She walked down the concrete steps, hearing the clapping from the conference hall recede behind her.

Back at the foyer of the California Hotel, which itself seemed a reproach and a continuation of the humiliation, she wondered what she could say to Lester.

From the lobby telephone, she tried again to call Sweetser but knew that it was a hopeless time to call.

She took the elevator to Lester's room.

She knocked on the door.

She heard Lester call out, 'Yes! Who is it?' in a rather expectant voice, a voice hoping for good news, for the bungle to have evaporated.

'It's me, Edith,' she said, trying to forewarn him of what she had to tell by her tone of voice.

He opened the door. He was straightening his tie, putting on his jacket.

'All sorted out?' he asked, smiling at her.

She gave a small hopeless smile back. 'Ambrose not with you?'

'Sent him away.'

'Alex is seated. Gerig is looking into it. I couldn't get any sense out of the military clerks at the Opera House.'

'We still have no seating, then?'

She felt tempted to lie to him. 'I'm afraid not.'

He looked into her eyes with disbelief.

They went into his room. There was an unopened bottle of Irish whiskey on the table, a bucket of ice, a soda siphon, and glasses.

She decided to report accurately as a good officer should. She was not a nursemaid, she was not a wife. She could not shield him from the world.

She told him precisely what had happened.

'Oh,' he said.

He stood there with his back to her and then sat.

He looked up. 'Thank you for everything, Edith. Thank you.'

'Would you like me to stay with you?'

'I would like to be alone.'

⟫———⟪

Back in their room, she lay on the cool sheets of the bed, naked, with the lights off. Ambrose sat in the armchair still in his new suit, drinking.

The room was very warm, the air-conditioning seemed not to be working.

'What will become of us?' she asked.

They sat for a moment in silence and then she answered herself. 'Remember when the League moved from the Palais Wilson to the new Palais des Nations?'

'Yes, I remember it—the move was massive.'

'I told you that back then we invented a new administrative ploy—a new category for official documents.'

'I don't remember.'

'Whenever some document couldn't be found, or we didn't want to find it, we said it was "lost in the move".'

'Yes, I remember now. You said that everyone began using it. Until you finally forbad it.'

'You and I, dear Ambrose, have been lost in the move.'

She watched his profile as he sat there in the half-light and she saw him nod.

'I've never thought of myself as tragic,' she said, 'but I do now.' She reached for her drink on the bedside table.

'God, it's hot in here,' he said.

He began to take off his tie and then his suit. He hung it carefully in her wardrobe.

He then went to the bathroom and returned carrying a clean towel.

He placed the towel on the time-worn armchair seat and then sat down again, nude, legs crossed.

He looked across at her. 'Not impressed with this American air-conditioning.'

'Did we waste our lives at the League? All those words we wrote and spoke?'

'There is no one to tell us whether we did or did not.'

'I've worked nearly all my life for something which *utterly* failed. And moreover, we no longer *exist* in the eyes of the world.'

'Edith, you have lived *fully*—that's not affected by considerations of success or failure.'

'Maybe I didn't live fully,' she said, trying somehow to pass her mind's eye over her years at the League, catching odd cameos of meetings, speeches and arguments.

'Oh yes, Edith—you lived *fully*,' he said without hesitation. 'You did.'

In a quiet voice he then mentioned to her Haydn's *Farewell Symphony* where the members of the orchestra leave, one by one, until there are no instruments left. 'Remember? It goes like this.'

He hummed the final bars to her, as he came over to her bed. He lay down beside her, naked, still humming, conducting with a finger.

In the dimness she could see his wry smile.

'Oh God,' she said, putting her head on his chest.

They folded desperately into each other's arms.

'What do we do tomorrow?' she whispered.

'Tomorrow?' He lay there in her arms, staring at the ceiling. 'Tomorrow, we find ourselves a place in this new world.'

'Is there a place for the likes of us?'

'We will find a place.'

She took a deep breath. 'No. We will *make* ourselves a place.'

Postscript

The Dinner for Lester

Sean Lester, the last Secretary-General of the League of Nations, waited at the California Hotel in San Francisco for a month but was never asked to speak to the newly formed United Nations.

Alexander Loveday, Director of the League's Financial, Economic, and Transit Section, with twenty-five years experience, was asked to speak only once—on committee structure.

Seymour Jacklin, Treasurer of the League of Nations, and an Under Secretary-General, with twenty-five years experience, was permitted to speak to the conference for fifteen minutes.

Arthur Sweetser organised, and paid for, the only dinner given in San Francisco to honour the League delegation. It was attended by thirty-seven friends and former associates.

At the San Francisco Conference, fifty nations ratified the charter of the United Nations on 26 June, 1945.

In 1946, a final Assembly meeting of the League in Geneva formally dissolved the League of Nations and the Permanent Court of International Justice, and its property, including the Palais des Nations, in Geneva, was handed over to the United Nations.

The League of Nations ceased to exist formally on 18 April, 1946.

The Fate of the League Pavilion at the World's Fair

February 10, 1946

Dear Sweetser,

I have a somewhat faint recollection that during the early days of my coming to Princeton when you were a permanent resident here, you once mentioned that some League property was stored in the farm buildings near the Institute. I believe you mentioned a copper plate or something of the kind.

Unless I am dreaming would you be good enough to let me know exactly what the article is . . .

Signed, P.G. Watterson, Institute for Advanced Study, Princeton, New Jersey

April 4, 1946
Dear Watterson,
The copper plate was from the League of Nations Pavilion at the World's Fair in 1939.
It measured two metres across and its circular lettering read: 'Peace on earth—Good-will to men'.

Signed: Arthur Sweetser

Historical Notes

Languages

The official languages of the League of Nations were French and English and officers of the League were expected to be fluent in both.

Under Secretaries-General

In practice, the Under Secretaries-General of the League reflected the nationalities of the permanent members of the Council, consequently there was never a Swiss Under Secretary-General.

After 1932, one of the two Deputy Secretaries-General was drawn from outside the permanent members of Council.

Rationalism

Edith and her mentor, John Latham, were both members of the Rationalists' Association of Australia, which grew out of the parent organisation in the UK formed at the end of the nineteenth century.

In Melbourne, a Rationalist Association was formed in 1906, in Brisbane 1909, Sydney 1912, and Perth and Adelaide in 1918. Rationalists stated their position as the adoption of 'those mental attitudes which unreservedly accept the supremacy of reason' and aimed at establishing 'a system of philosophy and ethics verifiable by experience and independent of all arbitrary assumptions or authority'. The Rationalist Association had no doctrinal tests for membership and included as members Julian Huxley, Somerset Maugham, Bertrand Russell, Arnold Bennett, Georges Clemenceau, Clarence Darrow, Sigmund Freud, J.B.S. Haldane, H.G. Wells, Aldous Huxley, Albert Einstein, Professor L. Susan Stebbing, Havelock Ellis and Professor V. Gordon Childe. They saw religion as their main opponent. The movement declined after World War 2.

The British Rationalists were responsible for the creation of The Thinker's Library.

Alger Hiss and the United Nations

Alger Hiss, a high ranking officer of the US State Department, played a role in all three of the wartime conferences which worked towards the formation of the United Nations charter (Dumbarton Oaks, Yalta and San Francisco). At San Francisco in 1945, Hiss acted as temporary Secretary-General of the UN.

After this, Hiss became the Director of the US Office of Special Political Affairs.

On 3 August, 1948 allegations were made by Whittaker Chambers, a senior editor of *Time* and a former member of an espionage group spying for the Soviet Union in Washington DC, that Hiss was a member of this same espionage group. Chambers claimed that Hiss had given Chambers classified State Department documents to be handed over to the Soviet Union.

These allegations were made before the House Committee on Un-American Activities.

Chambers allegedly hid some filmstrips of the documents in question in a pumpkin on his farm, and the case was tagged the 'Pumpkin Papers'.

At his first trial in 1949, Hiss pleaded not guilty. In 1950, he was convicted of lying to a Federal Grand Jury by claiming that he had no knowledge of the documents.

Richard Nixon played a central role in the conviction of Hiss.

The Hiss trial was said to have fuelled McCarthyism in the US.

In its day, the case symbolised the left–right political clash—left-wing intellectuals against the right-wing McCarthyites—and was one of those issues which, in the words of Theodore Draper, 'separated friends and divided families'.

At the time this book was being written, the most recent comprehensive account of the case was *Perjury: The Hiss-Chambers Case*, (updated from the original published in 1978) by Allan Weinstein, Random House, 1997. In this updated book, Weinstein, having looked at the records of the NKVD and other material from Russia and Hungary, has changed from supporting Hiss to being convinced of his guilt.

This is also the conclusion of John Earl Haynes and Harvey Klehr in their book *Venona: decoding Soviet espionage in America*, Yale University Press, 1999.

The Debacle of the League and the United States

The failure of the United States to join the League of Nations was a democratic debacle.

It came about by a tangled, confused and dismaying vote in the Senate in 1919 where, despite overwhelming support for US membership of the League among the senators, political tactics produced a majority vote which fell just short of the two-thirds required (49 for, 35 against), and US entry was frustrated.

The best minds of the Republican Party—Taft, Hughes, Root, Hoover and Kellogg—supported US entry, as did the Democratic Party led by President Wilson, one of the architects of the League, and as did the media, the business community and the trades unions.

The Bill for US entry was drafted by the Foreign Relations Committee of the Senate and, while supporting entry, contained reservations about membership which were to be passed on to the League Assembly for consideration after the US had joined. President Wilson thought that the reservations undermined the concept of the League and advised his supporters to vote against it. So paradoxically, the small minority who opposed the League combined with some of the outright supporters of the League to defeat the Bill.

From then on, despite public opinion surveys in favour of the US joining the League, and constant lobbying at all levels of government, the US never joined the League. It did, however, participate in many of the world conferences including the Disarmament Conference, and in many of the League technical and social programs.

American foundations, such as the Carnegie Foundation and the Rockefeller Foundation, and individuals contributed large sums of money to the League.

Winston Churchill, in his book *The Second World War* (Volume One), said, 'Nor can the United States escape the censure of history . . . they simply gaped at the vast changes which were taking place in Europe . . . If the influence of the United States had been exerted, it might have galvanised the French and British . . . The League of Nations, battered though it had been, was still an august instrument which would have invested any challenge to the new Hitler war-menace with the sanction of International Law . . . Americans merely shrugged their shoulders, so that in a few years they had to pour out the blood and treasure of the New World to save themselves from mortal danger.'

Intellectual Cooperation Section

Edith's friend, Jeanne, belonged to the the Intellectual Cooperation Section. The head office of this Section was in Paris but some officers were in Geneva and Rome. It coordinated the Educational Cinematographic Institute in Rome, and the International Institute for the Unification of Private Law, the Permanent Committee of Arts and Letters, the Advisory Committee on the Teaching of the Principles and Facts of Intellectual Cooperation, the Sub-Committee of Experts for the Instruction of Youth.

It planned to rewrite history books for schools and, by so doing, remove national bias.

It had 23 expert committees, and many of the world's leading scholars and artists served on these. With the setting of the United Nations this section evolved into UNESCO.

Kelen and Derso: Cartoonists of the League— Hard Times

Emery Kelen and his collaborator Derso were internationally renowned caricaturists in the days of the League of Nations.

In 1954 Derso wrote a letter to Arthur Sweetser: 'I got your address from Albin Johnson; he told you about the drawing I want to sell and my hope that you might be interested. It is the most elaborate cartoon of the past Geneva scene and the finest watercolour to frame. By offering it for a modest fee, $150, I would like to see it in the hands of somebody who really could enjoy and appreciate it ... (t'was a puzzle for myself to remember and recognise the 150 people we drew in that single cartoon) ... I would appreciate very much if you'd be willing to pay this fee. I am now in bad shape and badly need some support of my old friends ...'

Sweetser replied: '... The great difficulty, which I am sure you will appreciate, is the financial one. For almost two years now since my UN job came to its end, I have been without salary ... in addition we have had several sicknesses in the family which have necessitated heavy expenditures ... to be of what little help I can in your present difficulties, I am enclosing a check for the $150 ...'

Joseph Avenol

The events and interpretations surrounding the departure of the French Secretary-General of the League, Joseph Avenol, in 1940 will probably never be precisely clear.

In the chapters describing Joseph Avenol and the League, some compression has occurred but the course of events is fairly much as depicted.

The sources for the dramatisation of Avenol's last months as Secretary-General are as follows: James Barros, *Betrayal from Within*, Yale University Press, 1969; Sean Lester, typewritten diary, 1939–45, League of Nations Archive, Geneva; Thanassis Aghnides, 'The Reminiscences of Thanassis Aghnides', typewritten manuscript in Oral History Collection, Columbia University, Butler Library (researched for me by Joanna Murray-Smith) and in a second copy at League of Nations Archive, Geneva; Quai d'Orsay archives (researched by Xavier Hennekinne); Raymond B. Fosdick, *The League and the United Nations after Fifty Years*, self-published, 1972, Connecticut; Arthur Sweetser, personal papers, Library of Congress, Washington DC; and internal circulars and memoranda of the League Secretariat.

The Persecution of Homosexuals and Lesbians by the Nazis

The scholarly estimate of the number of homosexual men severely persecuted by the Nazis is around 50,000. The estimates for those who ended up in concentration camps vary between 20,000–30,000. More than half died there, according to Rudiger Lautmann's account in 'The Pink Triangle: the Persecution of Homosexual Males in the Concentration Camps in Nazi Germany', in Salvatore Licata and Robert Petersen (eds), *Historical Perspectives on Homosexuality* (New York, Haworth Press, 1981).

There were no special concentration camps for gays, but they were sent to camps such as Dachau, Buchenwald and Berlin-Sachsenhausen where they were beaten, starved or worked to death. Many also died in penal battalions of the German army.

There is no evidence that the Nazi regime set out to exterminate the homosexuals as they did the Jews. There were various attempts by the Nazis at 'reeducating' and reorienting homosexuals and towards this end some suffered medical experimentation including castration.

Their concentration camp mortality was higher than any other of the 'anti-socials' in the camps (excluding the Jews)— nearly twice as high, say, than that of Jehovah's Witnesses (Rudiger Lautmann, *Gesellschaft und Homosexuality*, Frankfurt, Suhrkamp, 1977).

Homosexuals also suffered discrimination and violence from other concentration camp inmates, which reflected the anti-homosexual prejudices in national communities at large.

Of all the concentration camp prisoners, the effeminate homosexuals appeared to have suffered disproportionate ill-treatment.

After liberation of the camps in 1945, the homosexuals both from the West and the East were still liable to criminal prosecution under the new laws of the two parts of Germany. These laws were not reformed until 1969 and 1967 respectively.

There are also reports of lesbians being ill-treated and confined in concentration camps.

I am indebted to the late Peter Blazey and to Tim Herbert for early research advice on this subject and to Gerard Koskovich for his valuable annotated bibliography, 'The Nazi Persecution of Homosexuals' (http://members.aol.com/dalembert/lgbt_history/nazi_biblio.html).

The News About the Extermination of the Jews

Walter Laqueur, in his book *The Terrible Secret* (Weidenfeld and Nicolson, London, 1980), says, 'It will be asked whether it really would have mattered if the world had accepted the facts of the mass murder earlier than it did. No one knows. Quite likely it would not have made much difference. The Jews inside Europe could not have escaped their fate . . . Militarily, Germany was still very strong . . . There were, however, ways and means to rescue some even then. They might or might not have succeeded, but they were not even tried. It was a double failure, first of comprehension and later of seizing the opportunities which still existed . . .'

Précis-Writers

The task of a précis-writer was to summarise accounts of meetings. They made notes during the debates and then dictated their summaries. This demanded a good deal of judgement. They had to reduce individual speeches to a fraction of their size and to discriminate between short but often important speeches and long but sometimes irrelevant speeches.

The vanity of delegates caused problems, as did the wish for some delegates to have their speeches recorded in full for use back home.

The League précis-writers over the years evolved a unique skill and after a while complaints were surprisingly rare.

James Joyce and the Secretary-General

James Joyce, when he was living in Zurich during the war, approached Sean Lester, Acting Secretary-General of the League of Nations, and asked for assistance in getting his daughter Lucia out of a hospital in France and into neutral Switzerland.

Lester went to see Joyce and tried to help but Joyce died before any arrangements could be made and Lucia remained in France until the end of the war.

Permanent Delegates

As the League went on, a number of member states established Permanent Delegates in Geneva, some with ambassadorial rank and staff with the role of informing their governments of League affairs and participating in committees. At most there were 34 Permanent Delegates.

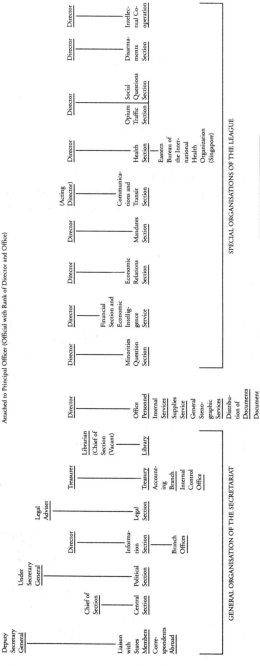

ORGANISATION OF THE SECRETARIAT — 1938

Secretary-General (and Office)
Deputy Secretary-General (and Office)
Under Secretaries-General (and Office)
Attached to Principal Officer (Official with Rank of Director and Office)

GENERAL ORGANISATION OF THE SECRETARIAT

Deputy Secretary General	Under Secretary General		Legal Adviser	Treasurer	Librarian (Chief of Section (Vacant))	Director	Director	Director	Director	(Acting Director)	Director	Director	Director	Director
	Chief of Section	Director												
Liaison with States Members Correspondents Abroad	Central Section	Political Section	Information Section	Legal Section	Treasury Accounting Branch Internal Control Office	Library	Office Personnel Internal Services Supplies Service General Stenographic Services	Minorities Question Section	Financial Section and Economic Intelligence Service	Economic Relations Section	Mandates Section	Communications and Transit Section	Health Section	Opium Traffic Section / Social Questions Section	Disarmaments Section	Intellectual Co-operation
		Branch Offices											Eastern Bureau of the International Health Organization (Singapore)			

Distribution of Documents
Document Services
Publication, Printing and Reproduction of Documents Service
Registry and Indexing of Publications Service

INTERNAL ADMINISTRATIVE
SERVICES OF THE SECRETARIAT

SPECIAL ORGANISATIONS OF THE LEAGUE

Secretariat of Central Opium Board

Secretariat of the Administrative Board of the Staff Pensions Fund

Who is Who in the Book

*denotes actual person

Aghnides*, Thanassis, Greek, Under Secretary-General, Director of Disarmament Section, Secretary to the Disarmament Conference.

Alva, friend of Edith from undergraduate days in the Faculty of Science at Sydney University.

Ambrose, see Westwood.

Andrade*, Will, a professional conjurer and well-known Australian Rationalist.

Angell*, Sir Norman, British intellectual populist, one-time leading pacifist, author of bestselling book on pacifism, *The Great Illusion*, among many others. For a time in the early part of the century there were Norman Angell societies in Europe and the US.

Arnold*, Dot, officer of the Peace and Disarmament Committee of the Women's International Organisation.

Avenol*, Joseph, French, Deputy Secretary-General (1920–1933), Secretary-General (1933–1940).

Bage*, Freda (1883–1970), lecturer in biology at University of Queensland and then Principal of Women's College, Australian delegate to League of Nations Assembly 1926, 1938.

Bartou, Auguste, Swiss, Under Secretary-General.

Berry, Edith Alison Campbell, Australian, member of Section, League of Nations Secretariat, attached to Under Secretary-General Bartou.

Briand*, Aristide, Prime Minister and Foreign Minister of France, great supporter of the League of Nations, received the Nobel Prize for Peace in 1926, died in 1932.

Brittain*, Vera (1893–1970), English writer of novels, biography, poetry and journalism, pacifist, feminist, and supporter of the League of Nations, and part of the literary and intellectual elite of the 1930s and 1940s.

Bruce*, Stanley Melbourne, former Australian Prime Minister, then High Commissioner in London, supporter of the League and President of

Council. Chaired the last committee on reform of the League in 1939 which produced what was known as the Bruce Report. Many of its proposals were taken up by the newly formed United Nations.

Cecil*, Lord Robert, member of House of Commons, sometime member of Cabinet, a dedicated British proponent of the idea of a League of Nations, frequent member of British delegation, helped draft the Covenant.

Charron*, Rene, French, member of the Economic, Financial, and Transit Section, confidant of Avenol.

Comert*, Pierre, French, Director of Information Section.

Crowdy*, Dame Rachel (1884–1964), English, Head, Social Questions Section from 1919 to 1931 (this section changed its name a few times over the years). Dame Rachel was one of the first professional social workers and had a distinguished record during WW1 behind the front lines as Commandant of the Volunteer Aid Detachment (VAD) for which she was made a Dame of the British Empire. She was never officially made director of the section but she was the only woman who headed a section during the history of the League, although for a time Florence Wilson was in charge of the library and Nancy Williams was in charge of Personnel.

Dame Rachel*, see Crowdy.

Derso*, world renowned cartoonist, companion of Emery Kelen (see Historical Notes).

Dingman* Mary, leading American feminist and peace activist.

Dole, Robert, English, journalist, not to be confused with Robert Dell*, doyen of the international press corps in Geneva, representative of *Manchester Guardian*.

Drummond*, Sir Eric, English, the first League Secretary-General (1919–1932). Born in 1876, a member of a prominent Catholic family, educated at Eton, entered the Foreign Office. Was successively private secretary to Asquith as Prime Minister, and to Lords Grey and Balfour as Foreign Secretaries. He was Lord Grey's Secretary at the Peace Conference in Paris in 1920. After retiring from the League he became British Ambassador to Italy.

Eden*, Sir Anthony (1897–1977) British, Minister for the League of Nations and Foreign Secretary, champion of collective security and the League of Nations, Prime Minister 1955–1956. During World War 1 (1914–1918), he fought in France and was awarded the Military Cross for distinguished service. He graduated from Oxford University in 1922. Eden entered Parliament in 1923. He became

Britain's Foreign Secretary in 1935, but resigned in 1938 because he disagreed with the way in which Prime Minister Neville Chamberlain yielded to the demands of dictators Adolf Hitler of Germany and Benito Mussolini of Italy. Became Foreign Secretary under Chuchill during the war.

Eric*, Sir, see Drummond.

Field*, Noel, US, former US State Department officer, joined Disarmament Section of the League in 1937, during war worked for Unitarian Relief organisation in Europe, spied for Soviet Union during 1930s and 1940s, defected to Czechoslovakia 1946. He and his wife and adopted daughter were separately gaoled by the communist government for five years for being American spies. After their release Field and his wife continued to live in Prague.

Florence (Travers, surname not mentioned), Canadian, bookkeeper, Finance.

Follett, Bernard, Swiss, owner-manager of the Molly Club, Geneva, patron of the arts, friend of Ambrose and Edith, part of organisation smuggling Jews from Germany, supplied intelligence to the Dutch until Holland fell to the Germans. Delegate for the International Red Cross.

Gerig*, Benjamin, US, Information and Mandates Sections of the League, Commissioner-General of the League of Nations Pavilion at the 1939 World's Fair, then Department of State and Deputy Secretary-General of the United States delegation at the San Francisco Conference of the United Nations.

Gerty, Dutch, Edith's personal assistant.

Gilbert*, Prentiss, US Consul-General, Geneva, later at the US Berlin Embassy. Was outspoken against the Nazis and met with the German underground.

Gray*, Potato, colourful English journalist of the period.

Haile Selassie* (1892–1975), became Emperor of Ethiopia in 1930 and worked for economic and social reforms, such as making slavery illegal. He gave Ethiopia its first written constitution in 1931. Ethiopia was attacked by Fascist Italy in 1935, and Haile Selassie lived in exile in England until 1941. During WW2 (1939–1945), British forces assisted in the liberation of Ethiopia and restored him to the throne. He belonged to a dynasty that claimed to be descended from King Solomon and the Queen of Sheba. His reign ended in 1974, when military leaders overthrew him.

Hall*, H. Duncan, Australian, a graduate of Sydney University, he worked for the League's Opium Section, 1927–1939, the second Australian to join the Secretariat, Jocelyn Horn being the other (see below). In 1940 he went to Yale as a visiting professor and subsequently held a number of positions in international affairs. He was an authority on the British Commonwealth. He died in 1976.

Harada*, Japanese Under Secretary-General until Japan withdrew from the League in 1933.

Henderson*, Arthur (1863–1935), British, President, World Disarmament Conference 1932–35, pioneer of the establishment of British Labour Party, Labour member of Parliament, Foreign Secretary, Nobel Prize for Peace 1934. Believed in strengthening coercive powers of the League, financial, economic, and military.

Hirschfeld*, Magnus, German, physician and early pioneer of the study of human sexuality, campaigned to reform laws against homosexuality. He established the Hirschfeld Institute for the study of sexuality in 1919. He coined the word 'transvestite'. The Nazis destroyed the Institute in 1933.

Horn*, Jocelyn, Australian, Head of Administrative Department of the Pool of Shorthand-Typists, first Australian to be employed by the League of Nations in 1921, former resident of Adelaide, dismissed for unacceptable conduct including 'dancing too much' at one of the early League conferences in Barcelona.

Howard*, Miss J. 'Tiger', English, private secretary to Sir Eric Drummond.

Hutchinson*, Leslie, black American singer and pianist, thought to be the man involved in the scandal with Edwina Mountbatten.

Hudson*, Manley, US, Judge Permanent Court of International Justice.

Huneeus, a Deputy President in the Azerbaidjhan government-in-exile.

Ingersoll*, Colonel Robert Green (1833–1899), lawyer, Attorney-General Illinois, friend of Mark Twain and Walt Whitman, campaigner against religion and for liberal causes. He entered politics as a Democrat, but he became a prominent Republican after the Civil War. He was a centre of controversy for almost 30 years because he attacked orthodox Christian beliefs. He wrote *The Gods, and Other Lectures* (1876), *Some Mistakes of Moses* (1879), and *Great Speeches* (1887). His writings and beliefs influenced Edith's mother and father.

Jacklin*, S., South African, Financial, Treasurer of the League, appointed an Under Secretary-General. One of the League delegation to the 1945 UN foundation conference in San Francisco.

Jerome Curry, US, horn player with Eddie South's Alabamians.

John* (Latham), see Latham.

Kelen*, Emery, Hungarian, caricaturist world famous in the 1920s and 30s for his cartoons of the League (see Historical Notes).

Latham*, John (1877–1964), Australian, a conservative politician, one-time Deputy Prime Minister, Minister for External Affairs, Federal Attorney-General, several times delegate to League of Nations Assembly. Became Chief Justice of the High Court in 1935, and was briefly the first Australian Minister to Japan (1940–41). First President of the League of Nations Union in Australia. An atheist and rationalist throughout his life.

Laval*, Pierre (1883–1945), French Prime Minister before and during WW2. Became leader again in the Vichy government and under the German occupation almost until the end of the war. After Germany surrendered in 1945, Laval was handed over to the new French government and convicted of treason. He swallowed poison in a suicide attempt on the day of his execution, but the attempt failed and he was shot by a firing squad. In 1935, as Prime Minister, he and Hoare, British co-Foreign Secretary with Eden, decided on the Hoare-Laval Agreement, proposing a peace between Italy and Ethiopia which gave way to Italian demands. This was done without the agreement of the British Cabinet or of Eden and was repudiated, but finally scuppered the attempts to rein in Italy.

Léger*, Alexis Saint-Léger, French, officer in the French Department of Foreign Affairs, Secretary-General of the Department 1933–1940, poet who wrote under the name St-John Perse and won the Nobel Prize for Literature.

Lester*, Sean (1888–1959), Irish journalist, Irish representative to the League of Nations, High Commissioner to Danzig, third and last Secretary-General of the League 1940–46.

Lichtheim*, Richard, German-Jewish, former editor of *Die Welt*, ran the office of the World Jewish Congress in Geneva during WW2, along with Gerhardt Riegner.

Liverright, Howard, Austrian, translator with bohemian tastes and habits.

Loveday*, Alexander, English, Director of Economics, Finance, to which was added Transit Section when the League was reduced and these Sections moved to Princeton University in 1940. Loveday was one of the frustrated League delegation to the UN San Francisco foundation conference in 1945.

Lux*, Stephan, Jew of Czech nationality, film director and writer. Shot himself in the League of Nations Assembly on 3 July, 1936, in protest at anti-Semitic policies of German Nazi government.

Madariaga*, Salvador de, Spanish diplomat and delegate to the League, responsible for the animal peace analogy, 'The lion looking sideways at the eagle said, "Wings must be abolished ..."'

McDougall*, Frank Lidgett, economic adviser to Australian government in many different capacities during the 1930s and 1940s, especially to Stanley Bruce when he was High Commissioner in London (see above). He was born in London, educated at Darmstadt University and in 1909 migrated to Australia and became a fruit grower in Renmark in South Australia. He served in WW1. Among many other international contributions, he was very significant in the planning of the Food and Agriculture Organisation of the UN.

McDowell, George, Australian, businessman, childhood friend of Edith (features in the book *The Electrical Experience*, 1974).

McGeachy*, Mary (1901?–1991), Canadian, Information Section, became first woman appointed to British diplomatic service, served with UNRRA, following WW2, and then executive officer of International Council of Women.

Mountbatten*, Edwina Cynthia Annette (1901–1960), Countess, wife of Lord Louis Mountbatten, socialite in the 1920s and early 1930s, featured in a celebrated court case about a scandal involving a black American musician, for a time a socialist, then Superintendent-in-chief of St John Ambulance Brigade and Vicereine of India (1947).

Motta*, Giuseppe, Swiss delegate to League Assembly 1920–39, first President of the Assembly, Federal Councillor of the Swiss Confederation in charge of Swiss Foreign Affairs 1920–40.

Murphy*, Peter, homosexual, close friend of the Mountbattens.

Nicolson*, Harold, British diplomat and writer, attended Paris Peace Conference, participated in early days of the League, was considered for post of first Secretary-General of the League. He led a homosexual life while married to writer and lesbian, Vita Sackville-West.

Pearson*, Karl (1857–1936), mathematician, first Galton Professor of National Eugenics (1911) at the University of London and at University College. In his book *The Grammar of Science* he attempted to apply scientific training to social questions. Considered 'the father of statistics'.

Pétain*, Phillipe (1856–1951), French, World War 1 general and hero of the great WW1 battle of Verdun which stopped the German advance, later Commander-in-Chief and Inspector General of the Army, Minister of War 1934. He was a symbolic embodiment of the national spirit for many French people. After the German defeat of

France in 1940, Pétain became chief of state in the French government when it moved to Vichy after an agreement with the Germans that some of France should remain unoccupied and, to a degree, self-governing. He collaborated with the Germans in what he saw was an inescapable necessity if any of France was to survive. He also saw it as an opportunity to reshape France along authoritarian lines with grand policies of national and spiritual 'renewal'. However, his government also agreed to repressive legislation against Jews and sent French workers to Germany. The Germans occupied all of France in 1942 and Pétain continued to maintain a false appearance of French sovereignty. He was convicted of treason by the French after the war and died in prison at the age of 95.

Riegner*, Gerhardt, German-Jewish, ran office of World Jewish Congress, in Geneva during WW2.

Rischbieth*, Australian delegate to the Assembly.

Robert, see Dole.

Robeson*, Paul (1898–1976), was a black American, sportsman, singer, actor, and political activist and, in the 1920s and 1930s, part of the expatriate social life in the UK. He had significant influence in the battle against racism in the United States.

Stimson*, Henry L., US Secretary of State (1929–33), accused at the time by his opponents in Congress of involving the US too closely with the League of Nations and Europe. Invented the idea of 'Non-recognition' in diplomatic relations.

Stresemann*, Gustav, German Minister for Foreign Affairs, and Chancellor. Negotiated the entry of Germany into the League of Nations. He shared the Nobel Peace Prize in 1926 with Briand. He died 1930.

Sugimura*, Yotaro, Japanese, Under Secretary, Director of Political Section, League of Nations.

Sweetser*, Arthur (1888–1968), US, journalist, war correspondent and then Captain in the US Signal Corps during WW1 and a journalist at the Peace Conference in Paris in 1920. Joined the League Information Section (1919–40), responsible for League relations with the United States. Because of his personal influence and his wife's private income, he was able, through personality and social life, to bring to bear much influence in the diplomatic world of Geneva. He was made a League officer with the rank of Director in 1940. During the war he returned to the US and was appointed Deputy Director of the Office of War Information. After the war he was for a time special adviser to the first Secretary-General of the UN, Trygve Lie. He was

Director of the Washington Information Office of the UN. He remained active in international affairs until his death.

Toptchibacheff*, A.U., Azerbaidjhan, President of the Peace Delegation to the League.

Tuckerman*, Arthur, student at Sydney University in Edith's time.

Victoria (surname not mentioned), New Zealander, worked in the Registry and during the war with the International Red Cross.

Vigier*, Henri, French, highly respected international civil servant both with the League and the United Nations, was secretary to Eden during the Ethiopian crisis, known as a draftsman of resolutions and other political documents.

Vittoz*, Swiss, psychiatrist who treated the poet T.S. Eliot.

Walters*, F.P., English, former Deputy Secretary-General, former private secretary to English Prime Minister Arthur Balfour and Robert Cecil, author of the official history of the League.

Weber-Bauler*, Leon, French, consulting doctor to the League Secretariat and the International Red Cross during the time of this novel.

Welles*, Sumner, former US Ambassador and Under Secretary of State, forced to resign from the government service in 1943 after revelations of his homosexuality.

Wells*, H.G. (1866–1946), English, a prolific and, during the thirties, influential author of novels and social theories.

Wenz*, Paul (1869–1939), French author who lived in Australia and worked as farmer. His work was brought to public attention again by French writer and scholar, Jean-Paul Delamotte.

Westwood, Ambrose, English, personal staff of Sir Eric Drummond, later in Internal Services. Trained as medical doctor and served in Medical Corps during World War 1. On staff of Lord Curzon and then in Foreign Office. After suffering a breakdown in the late 1920s he went home to England but returned in 1935 to Geneva to work in a non-governmental body called the Federation of International Societies. He also worked for British Naval Intelligence for a time in the 1920s.

Williams*, Miss Nancy, English, head of Personnel de facto, as she was never formally appointed Head of Section.

Acknowledgements

Although the companion volumes *Grand Days* and *Dark Palace* stand alone as novels, the research for both books overlapped and I refer readers to the acknowledgements in *Grand Days* for a full account of my indebtedness.

The private and official papers of Mary McGeachy and Arthur Sweetser, both long-serving officers of the League of Nations, and the wartime diary of Sean Lester were 'rain which fell on my crops'. I intend that this book should honour them.

When Noel Field is recorded as saying, 'To fight and to renounce fighting, to say the truth and not to say the truth, to be helpful and unhelpful, to keep a promise and break a promise, to go into danger and to avoid danger, to be known and to be unknown. He who fights for communism has, of all the virtues, only one: that he fights for communism ...' he is quoting Bertolt Brecht.

The Australia Council's Creative Fellowship Scheme and the National Library's Sir Harold White Fellowship permitted me to do some of the original research which flowed on from *Grand Days* to this volume.

I want to record my appreciation of the staff at the Library of Congress, Washington, especially those in the manuscript department.

The writing of the book was significantly assisted by the following institutions and individuals: the Fulbright Fellowship Scheme; the Woodrow Wilson Center in Washington which invited me as Guest Scholar to permit me to write and research *Dark Palace*, in particular, the Arthur Sweetser papers in the Library of Congress, perhaps the most complete set of personal papers concerning the League's history which exist. I was alerted to the existence of these papers by Professor Martin David Dubin of the Department of Political Science, Northern Illinois University, who shared his scholarship with me in Geneva.

King's College invited me to be writer-in-residence during 1999 and I completed the book in the supportive surroundings and atmosphere of the college, where I was extended especially considerate support by the Vice-Provost John Barber and by Professor Ian Donaldson; Griffith

University's School of Arts on the Gold Coast appointed me writer-in-residence in 1998; the Department of History, University of Sydney made me the Colonel Johnson Scholar in 1995, and I wish to thank especially Professors Stephen Garton and Ian Jack, and St Andrew's College who provided me with accommodation.

I thank Rosemary Creswell, Annette Hughes, Jane Cameron, Sadie Chrestman and Richard Harper of Cameron Creswell Associates who all worked to see that such a large-scale project could reach completion. Rosemary and Annette looked after my affairs while I was overseas and gave critical advice and moral support beyond the call of duty. I am deeply in their debt.

Peter Straus of Picador (UK) and Jane Palfreyman of Random House (Australia), publishers of this volume, and my UK agent Derek Johns all sensitively supported and patiently waited for the completion of the volume. Jane edited *Grand Days* and *Dark Palace* with outstanding professional insight and talent. I wish to thank Heather Jamieson for her special and astute professional guidance in the last stages of the book.

Jean-Paul and Monique Delamotte and the Association Culturelle Franco-Australienne, provided accommodation and advice on matters French and on life in general, and JPD for his translation of *Grand Days* into French for Belfond (French title, *Tout un Monde d'Espoir*).

I wish to acknowledge the following very important support: The Moorhouse Estate left by my father and mother, Frank Osborne and Purthanry Thames Moorhouse and administered by Arthur Moorhouse; Fryer Library for purchase of archival material which was in turn used to fund this project; Errol Sullivan of Southern Star Films; Christopher Pearson of the *Adelaide Review*, David and Kim Parker for working accommodation in Normandy; David Catterns Q.C., for legal advice and for use of his mountain retreat; the late Sven Wellander, archivist until 1993 of the League of Nations Archive, Geneva; Dr Carol Baker, formerly of the United Nations Research Section, Geneva; Professor Gertrude Himmelfarb; Elizabeth Watson, my researcher at the Woodrow Wilson Center; Dr Mary Kinneare, Department of History, University of Winnipeg, for further research work on Mary McGeachy and the League; Dr Lenore Coltheart, National Archives of Australia, for the fascinating information on Jocelyn Horn (see Who is Who in the Book) and other matters; Michele Field, London facilitation and intriguing newspaper clippings; Carolyn Pettigrew; Gillian Trigg; Tony Bilson, on gastronomic matters; the family of H. Duncan Hall; Michael Easson; Barry Jones; Nicholas Hasluck; Linda Funnell, for a critical reading of the first section of the book; for support and information, Brian and Suzanne Kiernan; Richard Hall, whose background in politics and whose fine memory enriched the book; Christine Allsopp for assistance with both books; Tim and Julie Baker, for running the Paris office; Angela Bowne and Don Grieve Q.C., who gave me pro-bono legal support when *Grand Days* was rejected from the Miles Franklin literary award; Noel Deschamps, both personally and through his oral history transcript on early days of the Department of External Affairs; Donald and Myfanwy Horne, for oral and written memories of early days of the Department of External Affairs and Canberra, and for wisdom and insightful conversation; Peter Bartu and Penny Edwards, who shared their first-hand experience with UN affairs with me over the years; Owen Harries, for conversations on international relations over the years; Susie Carleton for all sorts of special help; John Doxat, an eye-witness of the Saar plebiscite who shared his recollections with me; Francesca Beddie, formerly of the Australian Department of Foreign Affairs and Trade, who gave me good advice; Guibourg Delamotte for advice on swearing in French; Professor Chris Simpson of the American University, Washington for opening doors for me; thanks to Amanda Walsh, Margaret Walsh, the Berry Historical Society and Robyn Florance for historical research on Jasper's Brush, even though in the book it has become a wonderful fictional place.

My thanks to Duke and Helen Minks for generous assistance in Sydney, London and Cannes while I was working on this book.

I especially want to thank Sarah Ducker who helped me through a time of darkness and confusion when writing this book.

I wish to thank the late Murray Sime and Meredith Sime, for friendship and support in various forms.

I wish to thank especially Nick and Carol Dettmann, as always, for all sorts of special personal assistance and advice, including the use of Minnamurra House to work on the book in the heartlands of Edith's upbringing and to recover myself. I am deeply appreciative of their very significant and timely gestures.

The following people generously did the tricky job of reading the manuscript as critical readers and I thank them—Dr Don Anderson, (who also informed me on the correct behaviour of Princes), Sandra Levy, Judy Rymer, Suzanne Walsh, Michelle de Kretzer, and Marion McDonald.